The Second Born

-The story borrows from true life, realistically drawing of a young Ohioan family in a gripping, thought- provoking way.
-The prose is easy to consume; at moments, it's even comical. Rich, atmospheric imagery brings scenes to life. Slang, witty dialog, and humorous repartee make the characters relatable...

– Clarion Review –

-Robinson is a natural storyteller, skilled at capturing the detail, color and dialect of the "hillbilly" culture.
-The storytelling and description is skillfully rendered.

– Blueink Review –

-In his well-structured novel, Robinson masterfully depicts countrified poverty in the 1960s especially in the paradoxical mixture of shame and pride James and Arnold Ray seem to take in their hillbilly status.
-A beautiful composed story about the pain of poverty and familial resentment.

– Kirkus Review –

The Second Born

The Gant House

Book Three

Arnold Robinson

Library of Congress Control Number:		2017901919
ISBN:	Hardcover	978-1-5245-8203-6
	Softcover	978-1-5245-8202-9
	eBook	978-1-5245-8204-3

Front Cover Photography by Rye Sluiter www.ryesluiterphotography.zenfolio.com Used with permission.

Photo location courtesy of
Gypsy Rose Revival, Eagar, Az

Print information available on the last page.

Rev. date: 04/11/2018

To order additional copies of this book, contact:
Xlibris
1-888-795-4274
www.Xlibris.com
Orders@Xlibris.com
750973

CONTENTS

CHAPTER 1

Harry's Concerns

"Well now, you must be Arnold Ray." Somewhat stunned on hearing my name I turned quickly from where I'd been talking with Harry. A lady was setting in the bus's driver's seat; flipping its dash and dome lights off and on. The way she was all scrunched up showed that she wasn't very tall, with a full face and chubby body, it looked.

Hesitant at first I opened the gate, before walking on to the bus's door. "And who are you?" I asked while slightly lifting my chin.

"I'm Mable Braggs and very pleased to meet you. I sold this beautiful bus to your dad and was wondering if everything was working out okay." She left the dome light on but still had a readied finger on the switch. *Maybe a nervous reaction*, I thought. Without looking, she reached up and turned a small fan on as if she'd done it many times before, then she tilted the rearview mirror for a better look at herself. It all started to add up now, the deck of worn-out cards and how perfectly the place had been kept up.

Still reeling from how he'd slapped me in the woods that day any mention of him being my dad set me off with the threat that I'd kill him if he ever did it again.

"Well first of all, that asshole ain't my Dad," I said hatefully. Harry cleared his throat as if what he'd heard from where he sat in his swing was none of his business.

"Oh! I'm sorry; I thought you were Arnold Ray." She shot back with a frown.

"I am, but like I said, I don't claim him as my Dad. A dad wouldn't act like he does!" Clumsy in her effort, she pulled a cigarette from a fancy silver holder; but before lighting it up, she slid open a small side window. "And how'd you meet the old man?"

I demanded while putting my foot up on the first step. She fumbled with her fancy holder as if there was no place to lay it down, almost dropping it to

---

1

the floor. My thoughts ran wild. *Is this one of the whores the old man's been running? And the nerve of her to come around us.*

"I met . . . him and Harry at the Bainbridge fish fry a few months ago. He was playin' music and talking about finding a place for you boys to stay in while you were cutting timber up here. I had this camper I'd fixed up for my dad when he'd come visit me." She took a long drag on the cigarette, exhaling most through the small window. "But he died of cancer and never got to stay in it a single night! So I sold it to . . . Jim."

"Well, I'm sorry about your dad," I said, looking down towards the ground. "I know that it must be strange you hearin' me talk about my old man the way I do. You called your father Dad just a minute ago, I can't stand the thought that I ever call mine that again. He's screwed that up a long time ago as far as I'm concerned. And a matter of fact I wish he was out of our family's life all together to tell the truth of it. We'd be way better off if he were to...just disappear, and never be heard from again."

Mable become more nervous of what I'd unloaded on her when she fumbled to open up the ash tray built snuggle into the dash, then with a final jerk the tray opened with a squealing sound of metal to metal.

"I mean gone for good is what I'm after." I sneered while gritting my teeth. Mable looked shocked with her slightly gaping mouth. I wondered how much the old man had told her about James and me. Obviously, she knew our names and who was the older of us.

Overhearing our conversation from where he stood at her 1957 Chevy James lifted his finger from where he'd been tracing the chrome along its back fender. He left the car and went to sit beside Harry in the swing, where they mumbled words that I couldn't make out.

Mable strained somewhat in her effort to get up from the seat. After a quick tug to straighten her dress, she yelled out the door that it was time to eat. I had more questions and was ready to turn the meal down when Harry gently pushed me to the side.

"Now by God boys, let's eat." He declared. James followed him through the door, and with a quick stab of an elbow signaled that I should do the same.

"Now you boys just help yourselves. I'm just not very hungry right now," she declared while putting the food on the table. "Now I'm going to step outside and have a cigarette, so you boys enjoy yourselves." I'd already figured she was a heavy smoker by the way she carried the silvery cigarette holder always close at hand. But I thought it mighty considerate of her to not smoke in the bus while we ate.

Harry didn't turn thanks and wasn't waiting for an invite to be the first to serve himself. He'd not taken the time to place his pipe in its designated hole in his porch swing arm. With the stem pointing upwards and flopping loosely in his shirt pocket he spooned the food onto his plate, hungry it looked.

I thought how his mood was different like than when two women had brought him food one evening. I got the impression that he just wanted them to drop it off and be on their way, telling them he had to take care of some things way before he could even think about eating.

"Why, I'll wash that plate out and have it ready for you the next time you come by." Then he stood up from the swing, leaving them no choice but to leave.

The meal Mable made was a change from our regular one where bologna was usually our meat. Day after day we'd try and change the combos nightly with fried potatoes and onions or with warmed up pork and beans. Mom's homemade vegetable soups were by far the best, but we'd already used them all up.

No matter how we switched things around we simple needed a break from the taste of bologna every night. So, to break up the monotony, and have a little adventure to go along with it, James suggestion that we go to the DQ down at Bainbridge a couple of nights a week. We'd have a couple foot long hot dogs with all the trimmings then followed with an ice cream delight for a fancy dessert. The taste lingered in our mouths for the ten or so miles back to the bus.

The two nights a week quickly turned into three and sometimes four with money in our pockets since the old man had started paying us. On a few occasions, we'd buy extra foot long Coney's for lunch the next day. Like fattening hogs for the slaughter we'd declared, the way we'd devour our food and drink. Money well spent I'd gotten into the habit of saying after every trip.

But what also came with money in my pocket was that I'd founder myself one night on a dare from James that I couldn't eat four-foot longs in one setting. I'd proved him wrong and even had a banana split on top of all that. About three miles out of Bainbridge there was a small road that turned off and ran along Paint Creek for some distance before coming back out on Route 50 once again. It was a staging area for people to drag race late in the night to avoid the law. It was used however for something else the night I'd overdosed on foot long Coney's. James hadn't come to a complete stop when I bailed from the car just in the nick of time.

"What a waste of money Arnold," James laughed when I got back in the car.

Mable had made green beans, corn bread, and a pork roast. But as good as it all sounded, the flavor just didn't seem to be there. Regardless though we ate everything she'd cooked. After we'd finished and walked back to Harry's porch Mable went back inside to clean up after us. We hadn't sat there for a minute or so when Harry excused himself saying he needed to go and get a drink.

He never specified what that drink might be but was happier though upon his return when with a quick wipe to his mouth he came out the door. After loading his pipe, and in a rare occasion, blew a large satisfying grayish plume with his first draw. I guess he'd gotten some needed energy from Mable's meal.

"Now, boys, that was some pretty good food old Mable made us, wasn't it?" he said, while shaking the lit match out. "Now even though . . . old Mable didn't eat anything tonight, you kin tell by just looking at her by God that she ain't shy of doin' so!" Harry teased, slapping the side of his leg with a good whack. I figured he'd not adjusted his hearing aid quite right. I knew Mable must have heard what he'd said. But maybe that was his intent that shortly after she'd finished the dishes, she walked past and bade us a good night. And on the other hand maybe she wanted to avoid any other questions I might have asked.

"So, what's the deal with her, Harry?" James asked. "Is he running around with her?" He had unexpectedly put Harry on the spot with his question. The old fellow started fussing around with his ear as though he hadn't fully understood what James had asked. Harry was the first person I'd ever been around who used a hearing aid. I knew many who held an open hand behind an ear and others where you really had to talk loud for them to understand you.

I could only guess Harry's routine would be like others who used an aid however. After carefully removing his pipe, he opened his mouth just a little. Then with a slightly bent finger he tapped on his cheekbone a couple of times as if his way to fine tune the device, or the damned thang, as he'd nicknamed it. After one final adjustment, he turned to face us.

"Now, boys, the Lord knows that I think the world of ole Jim. But I don't know how a married man can act like he does. And by God, I think he'd run anything that'd have him! But I don't know 'bout Mable..." Harry shifted himself in the swing now setting up a little straighter. After another slow soothing draw, he continued. "It seems anymore no matter where we go out frolickin', old Mable's always there. Now I didn't call her and tell where we were goin'. And just about the time I get feelin' good enough to start showin' my ass a little Jim will load me up and bring me right back here to the house!

"Why my shoes no sooner hit the damned dirt and he's gone again. Now you tell me, by God, what to suspect! And he's always in a God-awful hurry, and for what? Why, he ain't doin' nothin' cept runnin' through a bunch of damned money looks to me like while you boys are up yonder working yer assess off!"

A grim look came to James's face as Harry leaned forward, relaxing one leg over the other. It wasn't a shock by any means what Harry had said. Nothing could really surprise us anymore with the way the old man was acting. He'd only gotten worse since we'd left Pike County. And it was apparent now that it was James and I alone trying to escape the terrible thing we'd done to save our mother from having to move from the farm.

Harry excused himself once again saying he'd worked up a thirst and needed another drink. Upon his return, he seemed more irritated clearing his throat with a spit off the side of the porch. After reloading his pipe and making himself comfortable once again he continued with talk of the old man.

"Now boys, I just think that it's funny how ole Jim can argue and put a person in their place when he gets preachin' about religion, and then a few hours later, he's drunk as a skunk." It was then I caught James's stare. "Hell, I thought he really was a Reverend for the longest time, and wasn't so sure that I wanted to do business with him!" Harry reared back with a laugh.

"Why you know how some of them act. But I do know one thing by-God and that's for sure," Harry winked before continuing on. "I ain't changing my ways for anyone no matter what they declare themselves as bein.' I just ain't one much to foller people. "I've been around for a long time, ninety years the last time I checked…" He laughed toasting his pipe into the air as if to celebrate. Harry's trips for another drink had become more frequent and so were a looser tongued upon every return.

"Now let me tell ye, old Jim ain't the first one that I've seen act like he does. I've dealt with others over the years and they all have one thing in common. They do a lot of fallin' back and forth trying to stay on the right side of that spirit in the sky." Laughing all the while he waved his pipe towards the heavens. "It's like they do everything they can to save everybody else's ass from going to hell but not their own. And, hell they of all people should know better!" He sat back in the swing a little farther.

"Now don't misunderstand me I've come across a few that act like they're supposed to. But it just seems like there's a lot of them who proclaim themselves holier than thou." It struck me funny and I let out a laugh at how old Harry had sounded so Biblical like. There was no need that either James or I say anything while Harry carried on. For us it was simply a re-run of what we'd already seen with the old man but in a different place and time.

"Why, he set right here one night and told me how good your mom sings in church is that, right? Does she sang?" He questioned.

"Why, our mom has the prettiest voice you ever heard in your life, Harry. And when she sings, it makes you feel like your hair's standin' up on your head. And that's without music, if there ain't any around," I boasted.

"Why hell, I'd go to church just to yer' her sang one time, by God." Old Harry's broad smile seemed to entertain the idea for a few seconds longer as he gazed somewhere beyond us. Even though I'd told him a little about the old man's backsliding ways I figured it best I bite my tongue for now. He like so many others would eventually figure out the reverend's way on his own. Then without warning he quickly jerked his pipe aiming it directly towards us while slowly waving it back and forth.

"Never livin' up to what they preach!" he spouted. "I don't know what they call 'em these days but way back when, they were labeled as hypocrites, like somethin' you'd spit on." Then as quick as his outburst had started it abruptly ended. His frown gave way to his normal look, a tight face with a hint of a smile to indicate that he had nothing else to say of the matter.

Even though I'd gladly side with anyone who talked bad about the old man I'd wait for a better time with Harry. Our moment of silence gave into all things that ruled the night. Frogs from up at the pond and crickets hiding in low places would capture the moment for now. A final plume of smoke curled its way from Harry's pipe. He pecked it a couple times on the side of the swing, with spent ambers falling into an empty can on the floor. After gently sliding it into a hole in the arm Harry called it a night, where he'd take his declared frustrations to bed with him.

It was midnight, and I still hadn't gone to sleep yet. No doubt our conversations about the old man had a lot to do with it. And what was the real truth behind Mable Braggs showing up like she had. I'd become half-sick to my stomach thinking there might be a connection between her and the old man. I'd intentionally told her how I felt about him in hopes that she'd pass the word on to him thinking there might be a final confrontation between us.

I couldn't clear my mind of thinking how he'd hit me and that never would have happened had I shot him over in Pike County when I had the chance. Everyone would have been better off. I was truly having a dark time holding back my anger trying not to rouse James as he slept.

I also knew that it was James's words of wit that had stopped me from doing the old man in. I knew all too well that my outbursts had always bothered my big brother. But I'd still confide my thoughts knowing he'd correct me if he thought I was wasting his time as he called it. He had enough troubles of his own with the way things were going right now and the old man making no effort for a better life for our mother. And it was for that reason I stopped telling him of how badly I wanted to do away with the old man.

Old fashion sayings with some from the Bible flashed about in my mind. Fancy ones all decorated up with descriptive words explaining with fine detail how you'd been right all along about something. But even better were the quotes glorifying how easy it was to simply turn the other cheek which I found really hard to do. James was way better than me with his constant reminder, 'it is what it is.' In my case, I'd never overcome my anger quick enough to turn the other cheek.

In the minutes that'd seemed like hours, I lay awake, with my mind scrambling bad thoughts to the point I was ready to explode inside. I'd drug myself once again to the cold depths of a deep well. I sat up quickly gasping for breath as I had when I crawled from that dark hole to feel the suns warm rays sweep across my face once again. I finally fell asleep thinking of a cozy little shelter I'd built for my dog Rebel and me at the very top of a mountain one time to block the wind and snow.

I was awakened the next morning with the sounds of talking just outside the bus's door. Peering out the windshield, I could see James into some heavy talk with the old man, with both using lots of hand gestures. I figured the old man was straightening James out that he'd lied about having a load of wood cut and ready to load. But I wouldn't pry when he came back in the bus, assuring me that everything was all right and there'd be no further problems with the old man.

Whatever James and he had agreed upon seemed to be working as several weeks had passed by without him coming around for which I praised God in James and Calvin's presence.

I was thankful that the old man rehired Calvin again after the falling out they'd had over in Pike County. I'd missed him and Mary both from the time they'd moved back to Camp Creek. Harry's front porch had become our gathering place in the evenings for chat and laughter which there was never a shortage of. On more than one occasion, Harry declared that he'd never laughed so hard in his life with such a mix of bullshit from the five of us. On nights that we all agreed to meet at Harry's, James and I'd drive to Bainbridge for a couple fishtail sandwiches with fries. A great discovery James had proclaimed it when our taste for foot long coney's had faltered somewhat. Most times Calvin and Mary would already be there entertaining Harry. A big contributor to how long we carried on into the night was how many trips old Harry made to his back room for a swig of moonshine.

And so, at some point he'd get a loose tongue and start talking about things that bothered him the most. He sounded upset when he told of the old man's short visits, stopping by just long enough to pick up the checks James would leave on our kitchen table. Things had gotten worse over the last several weeks as he didn't have much good to say about the old man.

But on this night, there was a different kind of shine in Harry's eyes. Calvin knowing his age asked if he'd been born before cars were invented.

Like a little boy's, a sparkle came to his eyes along with a hint of a childish smile. I'd already figured with him being 90 years old that he could tell of things that I could only imagined. I had always been fascinated by all the stories the old timers told. And no matter the hardships they all seemed to have one thing in common, being thankful for what they did have.

I knew the old timers at Turners store would have had to lie to remember back as far in time as Harry would. I drew a laugh from Mary when I chuckled at the thought. Calvin knew by how comfortable Harry was making himself in preparation for his story, that their pipes require a full load of baccer with no interruptions once he got started.

"Well now boys…" Harry said while slowly drawing a wooden match from his shirt pocket. After his pipe trailed a steam of smoke he passed the fire on to Calvin. "Why we lived just across the mountain yonder," he nodded. "at the very end of Whiskey Holler. Hell, I might've been ten or twelve at the time." He paused with a little uncertainty. Harry seemed to have a natural way of captivating people with his fine details and short pauses of things that'd long since passed. Whether he'd ever told the same story to others made no difference to me. I'd place myself in old Harry's shoes as he drew back in time to something so incredible.

"Why, the neighbor boy came running up the road early one mornin' yelling that it was the headlines in the newspaper that the first car ever to go through Greenfield was coming Saturday morning. And don't you know by-hell I'd read about cars in the makin' but didn't put much thought into it. Why it just seemed like something impossible to me."

With us all engrossed in his flashback, old Harry went into how the family had got all cleaned up for such an occasion. Even how his mother checked behind his ears to make sure he'd washed there.

"Oh, hell for big doins like that by God you better look spiffy," he reared back laughing while hanging on to the swings' squeaky chain. He said that all the way to town while riding in their horse drawn buggy he just couldn't figure how a horseless carriage could ever work.

"Now we couldn't hitch up right out in front of the business places like always. They cleared the streets making us take our animals out back behind everything. And by-hell did that end up being a disaster with everybody tryin' to find a place to park their rigs.

"Why boys it was the craziest thing you ever seen. There were people from both upper and lower Twin roads, Buckskin and all the ways from Bainbridge came to see it. We didn't know when it'd git there until a fella come ridin down the road warnin that it had passed through Chillicothe 28 miles away and in just a few hours would be here. He'd been sent ahead to warn everybody and make sure the horses were kept off the damned streets. With everybody gawking down the road the street was full of people and some on the outskirts of town to get the first look. And I'll declare that I'd not believed it had I not seen it myself." Harry quickly removed his pipe looking me squarely in the eyes.

"And all of a sudden you could hear the noise of that damned thang a coming. Loud like I'd never heard before in my lifetime. Why people started clearin' the main street like there was a shootout gettin ready to happen." He leaned back a little further in the swing taking a much-needed breath. "And boys I'd not believed it myself when off in a distance here it came and not a single horse pullin' it. Hell, after they got stopped and shut the noisy son-of-a-bitch off everybody gathered around it actin' like they wanted to touch that thang but about half seemed too scared to.

"The men drivin' it hung around for a couple hours to let it cool down some while they washed their faces and cleaned their glasses then puttered on up the road towards Washington Courthouse. And you know the strangest thing happened a little while after that. Why there was a black man up there in Greenfield who'd been buildin buggies for a long time and decided to start building cars and buses of his own. And they were good cars at that." Harry nodded. "You just wouldn't think that a black man could do something like that." His frown told that he still thought it pretty incredible after so many years.

"I think everybody knew there was a change comin' with more people showin' up to see that car than there was at the county fair that year." It didn't really matter that he remembered the exact year when he and his buddy finally declared there were more cars and trucks than horse drawn buggies on the road.

His facial expressions were easy to follow. With a straight face, he'd talk earnestly of things. But in a split second while tilting his head and along with a slightly jacked jaw he'd swear of it, 'by-God'. Tapping his pipe on the side of the arm he admitted that horses had become a hindrance on the road. Movin' way too slow and leavin' shit everywhere they went. But his smile looked sad I thought as if maybe he missed the days before automobiles came into play. He'd finished his story and relaxed leaning far back into the swing. No one had moved from where they'd sat leaning forward that we not miss anything Harry said. Maybe realizing that he had captivated a listening audience he'd continue with his tale.

"Boy how things have changed even since then." He presented a better picture than what I'd studied in school when he talked of the Wright Brothers flying a plane. It all seemed to go back to a time when everything was simply black and white. The world was changing way too quickly he thought. In his joking ways, he said that if man was meant to fly by-God he'd been born with wings. He talked of how his family had gathered around the radio when there was talk of an atomic bomb which he seemed to think might be the end of man-kind in the end.

"And hell, now they even got space ships, why ole Jim will have a sure way to heaven now." He laughed. "I mean that's with his wings bein' clipped a little too short to fly right now." Our laughter was spontaneous, James and I rolled in the yard while Mary wallowed all over Calvin who'd choked on his pipe over Harry's joke. I thought of James's comparison of smokers sounding like a whooping cough convention with Calvin and Mary hacking away.

It all looked dream-like with the way my eyes were flooded with tears of laughter. I wondered if it looked this way with Harry's first car fading away into the distance. A wavy figurine of the old feller fluttered when he crossed one leg over the other. But Harry was no more than what his stories had reflected, with a passing in time. And would I dare dream that I live as long as him and carry on with stories of an old fellow I once knew?

It was his last yarn of the night of all the incredible things he'd seen throughout his lifetime. Sitting comfortable in his swing and satisfied that he'd leave us with something to ponder on when we'd go our separate ways that evening.

James and I'd talked a few times about making another trip to visit Mom and the family in Pike County, but the timing just never seemed right. We were making five and sometimes ten dollars a day; keeping just enough out to support our DQ addiction and with the old man putting the rest in the bank for us. It was after another one of those great evenings at Harry's porch that James woke me up early the next morning.

"Get your lazy ass out of bed and get those animals in the woods right now!" he demanded while thumping a stiff finger on the table. "I'll have breakfast fried up by the time you get back from the barn. I'm gonna get on the road early this morning, and when I get back from Chillicothe, we're goin' to take the rest of the day off and go to Greenfield and check it out!" His broad smile revealed his excitement.

"What in the hell's gotten into you James? You know that'll piss him off, to where he'll start hanging around and messin' everything up again."

"Well, I really don't care," he sneered, quickly running his comb through his hair. "The way I've got it figured we've worked all summer with not much time off, so I think it's time to have a little fun." He was restless in the way he moved about the bus.

"Hey! Calvin's only goin' to work a few hours today himself. He and Mary are goin' to Camp Creek for the weekend. He reminded the old man about it a couple of weeks back."

"Well, I guess that'll work out perfectly then." James smiled, shoving his comb firmly into his back pocket.

"Well, ya know this'll be the day that prick will show up, 'bout the time we get ready to leave. I mean don't you think it's about time for him to show his ass again?"

"Nope, we are doing exactly what I promised him awhile back. We're getting several loads of pulpwood a week and a couple loads of logs without him being around. He's got nothing to complain about, the way I figure it."

"Yeah, but how many times have we thought that shit before James, and it all goes to hell overnight. Man I'd like to be a fly on a stump when he drives up there and no one's around though!" I laughed. James followed with a short snicker of his own, while giving me the strangest look. "Well, what's so funny?" I asked.

"Arnold, I can envision you up there disguised as a fly but knowing you as I do, you wouldn't be on a stump. You'd be over there where Kate and Bill stand all the time, stirring up shit like you're so good at, you know like the squeaky board in the floor to get your way with something. But, at any rate, I'll leave your sandwich here on the table." After quickly tying his last shoestring, he grabbed the skillet to fry eggs and bacon in. "The sooner I get back, the sooner we can get on up to Greenfield." He advised.

The idea of getting away from the woods for a while was overwhelming, and going to the big city at that. James's comment of the squeaky board in the floor reminded me of how much I missed the old home place and how quickly, gone forever could flood my mind. And even though the fire consumed the squeaky board, nothing would ever erase the sound that lay trapped in my mind.

Kate and Mr. Bill seemed to understand there was something brewing with the way I hastened to put their harnesses on. With this being a short day, I'd forgo the stop at the pond that morning. After swinging by the bus to get my sandwich I headed on up the dirt road. The rumbling of 'Big Bad Red's' uncapped headers was much louder when James exited the woods.

"See you in a little while!" he yelled, while shifting into a higher gear. Calvin had just come out of the woods, tightening his belt up, as Kate and Mr. Bill gave his whereabouts with perked ears.

"Man, that damn junior's sure in a hurry this mornin'!" Calvin huffed. "Hell, I said, 'Good mornin' and he said, 'See ye later."

"Shit, we're goin' to Greenfield after he gets back, Calvin."

"Damnit boy," Calvin whined. "You'uns ain't in' enough trouble already?"

"Hey, if James thinks it's all right, then it's fine with me." I slapped my hands together with a loud pop.

Mary walked from the shack to the laydown yard just like she was supposed to do at eleven o'clock, the time Calvin had decided they'd leave. We'd cut and pulled enough wood for a couple more loads by then.

"Now don't forget to tell ole Jimbo that I barr'ied his saw for the weekend, Arnold Ray." He let out a satisfying grunt while chomping down hard on his pipe. "There ain't no ifs ands or beatin' round the bush, I've gotta get some wood cut fer the winner. Cause like I told you Arnie," he laughed, looking over at Mary, "that's where I'm gonna be when the snow flies! So, look out Camp Creek we's on our way!" After putting the saw in the cars boot he slammed it shut. With a wink, Mary asked if I'd like to go and spend the weekend with her and Calvin at their place.

"Arnie, you'd have so much fun." Mary sounded so sincere. I started laughing when Calvin pointed his pipe towards me, then immediately towards Mary, with his continual joke that there was something going on between us.

"The old lady's got plenty o' friends that you could spend the night with and get you some, Arnold Ray," he said, looking like a little boy who'd just said something very wrong. He quickly flexed his shoulder, preparing for Mary's hard punch, which she did deliver.

He laughed, rubbing the spot; pulling Mary close with a hug, then he pinched her on the ass, netting another hard whack.

"I'll see you come Monday, Arnold Ray!" he shouted as they drove off trailing a cloud of dust. I was so glad that James wasn't there to hear Mary's offer about going with them. Their dust hadn't quite cleared before I headed for the pond with the horses. I didn't want to be late when James got back from Chillicothe.

Perfect timing, I thought, watching from a distance as Calvin opened the gate for James, giving them time to talk for a minute. I wasn't close enough to hear what their outburst was all about but could only imagine when like kids Mary started chasing Calvin around the car as James laughed holding his stomach all the while.

"I'll park the truck at the laydown yard and meet you at the pond!" He shouted while slowly idling past.

The cleansing swim before we'd head for Greenfield wasn't all that added to my excitement. There was a little more to it than that. We were doing something that would surely piss the old man off. And for that reason, I'd enjoy the butterflies that lay in the very pit of my stomach for now.

Mr. Bill and Kate had a little extra kick in their stride as we headed on for the pond. I'd removed their bridles before they started sucking in large gulps of water when James came running up, spooking Mr. Bill a little. I patted his big rump to let him know it was all right.

"Why, you must have run to get here that quick, James!"

"Yeah, I did," he replied while gasping for breath with his hands clasping tightly around his knees taking a moment to collect himself. I stripped down to my underwear and was ready to dive in when it hit me like something falling out of the sky, and standing right in front of me! Why I hadn't thought of it before was beyond me. There were no trees close enough to the pond to dive from, I'd checked that out the first time we swam.

"Hey, James, look at that divin' board!" I pointed towards Mr. Bill's massive ass. "And that's where I'm gonna dive from!" I scurried from my favorite diving spot and, with one motion, grabbed the brass knob on the collar hames as I swung myself up on his back. With my arms held straight out to my sides, like a tight wire walker, I danced from Mr. Bills broad shoulders to where I stood firmly on to his big rump, digging my toes in, to get a better grip.

"James, check this out!" And from that height and distance, I made a spectacular dive, and with plenty of time to flex my back, I split the water like a knife leaving hardly a trace of a splash. My reaction was like that of a baptism when I surfaced, shouting with pure pleasure.

"I've got to do that again!" I shouted as I swam to the edge as fast as I could go. "James! Did you see it?" I asked. There really was no need to ask he'd been clapping his hands from the time I'd surfaced. I stopped long enough to take a bow, just like people on TV do after such a great performance. I shivered with excitement, with an overdose of butterflies of such a great feat, I smiled.

"Man, you've got to try this, James!" I commanded, knowing he'd never jump from Mr. Bill's butt. He'd think it'd be a little cruel to the animal. "Talk about a thrill!" I shouted, taking another bow to the hundreds who'd now gathered in my imagination. "James? Do you remember the Tarzan scene when he was escapin' from the great white hunters and had to jump off that thousand-foot cliff? Well, I think I landed just as good as him! It was a perfect dive! Didn't you think so?"

"It was a good one!" he admitted, nodding his head. Bill had pretty well gotten his fill of water by now and was starting to move around a little. I couldn't hold his attention much longer as I swung up on his back once again. He twitched at the many places where water dripped on him as I walked from his shoulders to his rump.

"Hold still, Bill!" I scolded maybe in too big a hurry to say 'Mr.' "And now attemptin' from one thousand feet off of a horse's ass, the amazin' Arnold will make the dive!" I announced, digging my toes even deeper into Mr. Bill's rump while extending my arms out in front of me. My feet were covered with mud, and when I tried to wipe them off on his butt, he didn't seem to like that at all. But like it or not, he had to be patient as this dive had to be perfect for me to win the gold medal or so at least I'd pretend.

Mr. Bill's mouth was out of the water, ready to go and graze, but then he did just what I needed when he lowered it for one more sip. *Now or never, I've got to go.* I could've just dived off to the side and still cleared the cattails as before. *But I'm gonna need something with a little more difficulty for a better score*, I thought to myself.

This dive simply had to be more spectacular than the last! I'd spring from Mr. Bill's big ass, the full length of his body, and over his head, for the longest dive possible. I was explaining the extreme difficulty to James as Mr. Bill grew more and more restless. Bending my knees and leaning forward, I sprang with everything I had. My arms were extended outward just like Tarzan had done. What a great dive this would be, and I could only wish it was being recorded with a movie camera.

But what I had envisioned was cut short when Mr. Bill spooked somewhat, maybe that I was lollygagging around too long, lifting his massive neck and raised his giant head high into the air, impacting my groin area as I flew past. And his bump would send me even farther out into the pond. But it didn't matter that I was flipping out of control as that was certainly not my worst problem now.

The blow had knocked my breath out worse than any of my attempts at flying. I saw the pond, then the sky, and then the pond again. I had no control of how I was gonna land, with both hands affixed to my groin. For a brief second, I saw the cattails and then James before crashing into the water landing hard, back first.

"Spla...sh!" the water crashed in around me, sending some up my nose. I couldn't move my legs, which were too numb with pain. Trying, to catch my breath, I sucked in water. There was no prioritizing anything as I floated to the top, coughing and spitting up water with the least amount of effort I could afford. I'd almost regained myself when I heard a strange noise as I tried to make sense of it.

It was James applauding with approval. I crawled up on the bank, feeling like I was dragging a lot of stuff behind me. I lay down and rolled over on my back, sipping air a little at a time.

"I've got to say, that's one of the greatest dives I've ever seen in my life, Arnold—I mean a double whammy from a horse's ass and performed by a horse's ass at that! What else could you ask for?" He laughed, looking down on top of me while clapping vigorously like a standing ovation. I still couldn't move. Maybe my hands would be stuck between my legs forever as I rolled to the side feeling even sicklier.

"Today you had two personal bests, Arnold. You flew farther than ever before . . . and made more flips than an Olympic diver ever did! But best was the cartoon look, with you dragging your wet ass out of the pond and your underwear halfway down your ass!" It was all true as I struggled to pull them up a little. The best I could do was claw at the dirt with the other hand, wishing I could get it around his throat right now.

"Oh man! I've got to draw that cartoon while it fresh in my mind!" He snapped a finger and thumb together. I'd regained my breath, but I was hurting so bad that I still couldn't move much, which James knew all too well.

"Mary would have been so proud of that dive, Tarzan." James laughed out of control. No matter how badly I wanted to move, I just couldn't. No matter how badly I wanted to cuss and I really was trying, I couldn't. All I could do was lay there, gasp for air, and eat shit from what used to be my best friend and big brother.

"Speak up, Arnold Ray! I can't hear you!" He squatted beside me to make sure I could hear every damn thing he was throwing at me, which I really didn't need right now. "I sure wish she was here to comfort you. I'll bet you'd jump right up, ready to show off again wouldn't you, Arnold Ray?" he teased. With even such pain, I managed to get out one word that he could fully understand.

"Oh . . . so you think I'm a Ja... Jackass!" He laughed. "Is that what you're sayin', Arnie?" And now he was going for the throat. He'd only use "Arnie" to mimic what Mary had called me so many times before. James had more tears in his eyes now than mine—and happy ones at that. But I knew I'd have done the same to him had the tables been turned however. I finally overcame most of the pain, enough to sit up. Then after a couple of long, slow breaths, I managed to tell him that he was nothing shy of a total jackass!

"What did you say, Aunt Ray . . .?" There was no doubt that momentarily my voice had gained a high pitch. Even though I couldn't laugh, I had to grin at all the things he was throwing at me for now. But still unable to say anything clearly, I tried another word on him.

"Well, that's better than it was five minutes ago, when I was nothing short of a low-rent Jackass."

"I never said that." I made a slow step toward him, holding my stomach and other parts that seemed to have been rearranged. He took a couple of steps and dove into the pond with perfect form, I had to admit. I was not interested in following him, however. I just really wanted to sit back on the bank and feel sick and was doing a fine job of it.

I knew without asking what his laughter was all about every time he came to the surface for air. The feeling that my testicles were halfway up into my stomach was starting to ease somewhat by the time he'd come to join me where I lay on the bank. Now able to talk much better, I also had to laugh at such a terrible dive as I'd made. I thought how bad he'd razzed me after my last attempt to fly, but that fell way short of this. It had become easier to breathe and talk as the numbness was starting to disappear more and more. But a minute later, I was tested once again as James described how I looked like a helicopter crashing into the water whirling out of control—like his laughter, I thought.

"Big splash!" he managed to say, covering his face with both hands. Our early trip to Greenfield would be delayed for some time as I lay back down with my legs sprawled out and certainly not trying to hide anything that felt loose with every moment. James was still having his moment, and not trying to hide the constant outbreak of laughter.

"Did you know that he bought some more timber down by Camp Creek over on Route 753?" Maybe to speed up my recovery, he'd changed the subject.

"No . . . I didn't." I slowly rolled to one side to face him. "How'd you know about that?" I asked.

"Calvin told me all about it down at the gate when I got back from Chillicothe."

I'd managed to get to my knees, but was not straightening up completely.

"It doesn't matter! I could give a shit about more timber right now anyway. I'm ready to go to Greenfield," I said, wobbling for a few steps.

15

"Would you like to race to the bus?" he asked moving a little farther away from me.

"Yeah, if you give me like a hundred-yard head start." I managed a halfhearted laugh.

"Why, it's not even that far down there," he observed.

"Well, that's my point. I'd need one hell of a head start." I said while tempting more laughter. Moving about did seem to help, and I wasn't going to let it stop us from checking out the town of Greenfield. It'd been a long time since we'd peddled blackberries up there as little boys.

After changing into our best set of clothes we loaded up in the Dodge and headed out for our great adventure. James let off the gas for one of the many railroad crossings on Route 41 where overlapping skid marks ran almost all the way to the tracks in some places. Like a green tunnel, trees blocked the view of an approaching train.

"Well, how'd the old man know about that timber over at Camp Creek?" I wondered aloud. "Calvin tell him about it?"

"No, I guess some old woman that Mable Braggs knows owns it . . .," he replied. "Calvin says there are some big trees down there, mostly poplar, but looks like only about a month's worth a work, saying he knows right where the place is at."

"So I guess that means he'll get to stay in his own house and work down there I reckon."

"Well, he says that's the plan," James said, flooring the accelerator after clearing the bumpy tracks. "It looks like we might be going down on weekends and helping out some." He glanced over, snickering. And I knew without a shadow of a doubt what he was getting at.

"What?" I acknowledged, crossing my arms.

"He also told me about Mary inviting you down to Camp Creek for the weekend." The weakness in my stomach suddenly had returned. "Hey it's alright, we both know how Calvin acts, you know Arnie, like it doesn't bother him with you being so close to Mary." He slapped at the steering wheel, knowing I was still too weak for much of a confrontation.

"Ya know James, you can be a real asshole when you want to be, throwin' all this shit at me when I'm ill like this." I pointed to my lower extremities.

"No . . . I'm just kidding about all that going to work down there on weekends since....we've got plenty to do up here!"

"California Girls" came on the radio, which livened me up enough that I could snap my fingers to the rhythm, but only made a weak attempt to sing along. James slowed at the Greenfield City Limits sign then crossed over the Paint Creek Bridge, the town lay in front of us. Now with such excitement, I was feeling much better.

We pulled up behind several cars that'd stopped at a red light when others quickly lined up behind us with radios blaring. They were mostly high school kids; and it looked and sounded now as if we were stuck in a musical traffic jam.

The simple fact was I didn't know how to act trapped in my new surroundings. So nervous in the way I couldn't sit still nor find a place to put my hands that I couldn't feel comfortable.

"James!" I said all excited like. "Check out the Dairy Bar down that road there, we'll have to stop for a banana split!" I quickly pointed to it. James seemed not interested at all giving me a strange look at that. We continued on with the flow as more cars came from the other direction.

"Man! Look at the size of the school." I pointed once again. "It ain't anywhere near as big as Chillicothe, but sure makes you think how small the Willow Springs School is, like a dot in comparison. Now this sure makes ya feel like a real *hillbilly*! Don't it, James?"

"No," he replied. "But you act like one! Pointing at everything you see like you just came out of the woods today." His timing couldn't have been any better when we burst into laughter over such a crazy thought. But not to be outdone I quickly drew my trigger finger to my lips blowing on the tip like a smoking gun barrel before quickly stuffing it in my pants pocket. It had been awhile since we'd carried on like this when eye contact would set us off without so much as a word. In the grand scheme of things however we were no more than all the others in passing who laughed at different things.

"You're plumb full of shit, takin' advantage of me like this James knowin' I'm still hurtin' inside." I rubbed my stomach once again. "But anyways it's gonna be hard gettin' used to so many kids in one school." The school was beautiful, with its mix of big limestone blocks at the foundation, lots of windows, and then red brick the rest of the way up. *Maybe a place where new dreams would really start*, I thought to myself. There were several people painting columns at a bus loading zone. Everything looked brand-new with all the snow-white paint. I wondered why the old man hadn't brought us to this part of town back in the berry-selling days.

Between the two main buildings stood a brick tower with a large clock at the top. I started to point it out but instead hung my arm out the window, saying nothing. Catching my quick reaction, James snickered.

"You almost pointed again, didn't you, *hillbilly*? I saw you!"

"Yeah, yeah I know . . . I've got to stop doin' that shit. But just quit buggin' me about it," I demanded.

"Oh, I don't really care if you point or not. I've just been messing with you, Arnold." He laughed. "Why, these people aren't any different than us. There's just more of them. They're city people—you think they don't point when they come down to our neck of the woods and see things not common to up here?"

"Do you think they're scared when they come down there, James?"

"Wouldn't you be?" He shot a quick thumb in my direction. "They're probably about as scared of being down there as you are up here."

"I'm not scared to be up here, James. But I feel a lot safer in the mountains, with trees and hollers. Don't you?"

"I don't know. I've read about a lot of places and all with different terrain and people. I thought maybe I'd like to go explore them someday. It's a big country out there. But for now, Arnold, this is where it's happening." He stabbed a straight finger into the seat a couple of times. He looked as though he'd already given in to his new surroundings, slumped in the seat somewhat and a lose arm hanging out the cars window.

"I don't know if I could ever live anywhere other than the mountains, James."

"Yeah, I don't think I'd like it much up here at the edge of the corn belt either, too much flat farmland. All the way to Lake Erie, you know."

"Yep, I learned all about 'er in Ohio history," I answered.

"And this is where the great Ice Age came to an end, leveling everythin' from the Great Lakes to the southern part of the state," he drew a steady hand just above the steering wheel.

"You don't need to tell me that shit, James! I just told you that I learned all about it in Ohio history—in fact, my favorite subject. I got a B, remember?"

"Okay, okay." He held a hand up stopping me just short of giving an answer to somethings I knew as well as him. I thought back to how the map's squiggly line showed the giant ice mass stopping at around Greenfield it looked. And there it would stall melting over time while digging out the tributaries forming the Ohio River Valley. From my seat in the back row at school I shot my hand high into the air on a subject I'd studied more than any other. The whole era with the ice age peaked my interest. I read the chapter several times ending with a better understanding of the forest I felt comfortable in down the southern part of the state.

We continued to follow the parade, driving to the end of town to where most turned around at a bowling alley parking lot. Some pulled off to the side where they parked and talked with others. We however stayed in line not knowing a single soul. But that didn't stop James from blowing his horn and waving as all the rest were doing. Suddenly, as though on command, all radios had been tuned to one station, with some turned up very loud.

There were carloads of girls, and I couldn't help but stare and was even tempted to point at them. I felt nervousness with excitement in a way that I never had before, butterflies of a different kind.

We'd never been a part of anything like this, with music from every passing car and even a few trucks. Things livened up even more when a convertible loaded with just girls stopped at the red light opposite us, where several jumped out and danced for the minute or so before the light changed back to green. And it wasn't just confined to a red light as it could happen anywhere down the strip where they'd shut traffic down for a minute or so. They were like something on TV, shaking their hips and showing more than their miniskirts could hide. One girl had buckskin strings hanging from her short dress. I was simply paralyzed at how she could make them dance about her, going round and round so fast that she showed off her under panties. I'd become aroused, quickly crossing my legs that James not catch on to me. She was the best dancer I'd ever seen, and I could have fallen in love right then and there I thought to myself.

I'd never danced other than just messing around to get a laugh at home. But this was different. I wanted to jump out of the car and start dancing like the guy that danced in the rain on TV.

"Do ya think it'd make me popular, right off the bat, if I were to jump out of the car and act like that girl did, James? I mean it'd make me a legend before I even start school up here! I could jump out, with us only goin' this fast with no problem, dance a few licks, and jump back in!" I pushed back in the seat at the thought. He hesitated for a few seconds, rubbing his fingers across his chin with a serious look about him.

"What makes you think starting school would be any easier after doin' something goofy like that?" he questioned.

"Well, I'd be noticed like those girls. Famous already. How can you not remember somebody who acts like that?" I chuckled.

"Well, first of all I know you don't have the balls to do such a thing and I'm sure that your dress will blow up over your head; and by the way do you have your best underwear on by any chance?" He burst into laughter. "But you would probably get a bigger cheer out of the ones with no ass left in them. And there's a more serious problem than all that Arnold Ray."

"Well what in the hell might it be Jimmy?" We joked back and forth.

"See the biggest problem with you jumping out while going this fast is that's exactly how fast we'd be going when I ran over your ass, and you'd be a short-lived legend for sure. So don't even think about it." We'd driven another block or so when James stopped right in the middle of the road and all excited like.

"You know, Arnold, you're right. You should jump out right here and dance all over the place." He smiled. My ass went numb, literally frozen to the seat. My joke had done nothing but open up the door for him. I could never do such a thing knowing that once my feet hit the pavement, they would not move, thinking someone was watching me. I'd end up being a legend all right—that of laughter. And he was right that I'd never have the nerve to do such a thing.

Before I could even come up with whatever my excuse would be, he grinned, quickly speeding up to catch up with the next car. I sat a little lower in my seat as he slapped a beat to the song on the radio.

"Feeling Glad All Over" blasted from every car in passing and looked as if they knew all the words. The parade didn't end there but rocked on with every song. Things had definitely gotten wild. And even though I'd heard the songs many times, they'd never sounded like this before. I didn't know all the words to any of them, but no one knew that other than James as I faked until the chorus; then it was a different story. All songs led to one. I often wondered why there were even other words—why not just sing the chorus over and over? It was the very place where everyone could put their true feeling into it anyway. I thought how church songs were the same when everyone drew a breath to blast the chorus out with everything they had. But there wasn't a single one that put the fire in me like rock and roll did on this day.

I'd seen it on TV, what being cool was all about and the California scene, and now I was right in the middle of the coolest shit I'd ever seen or done in my life. But I couldn't figure out how being so cool could make my heart beat so fast. A girl smiling in passing would put a song in my heart, but then again, they all smiled.

"Where are you guys from?" a girl yelled. James waved, with them both looking about his age, I thought.

"Should I tell them?" he asked.

"Hell, I don't care go ahead!" I said bravely.

"I'm from Ohio, and he's from Kentucky," he shouted loud enough that it wasn't just them who heard the outburst.

"Shut the fu-up, James! What's wrong with you?"

"Well now, you didn't want me to lie, did you?" He laughed. I sunk back into the seat again, momentarily covering my face, embarrassed. There was no reason to get mad with his clowning around even at my expense. But had this been in the woods, we'd more than likely be at each other by now. This simply was a day for pranks with things being out of the ordinary. And I thought we should treat it like we'd never see another like it again. It would be something to think and talk about for the rest of our lives. I thought about the hippie on TV who'd taken LSD and was trying to explain how he felt while on it. He'd gotten started on some sort of explanation, moving wiry fingers all over the place, and then finished with "It's really hard to explain, man." We'd adopted the saying, using it on each other as a joke of course. And it would work for now when trying to explain such a high that I wanted to last forever.

We followed the slow parade to where they turned once more at the Kroger food store parking lot, where again some would stop to talk with one another.

And not knowing anyone made no difference when girls waved and guys nodded in passing.

I could play the game that I wasn't bashful unless put on the spot. I'd find myself looking for one of the less outgoing girls passing by. A true eye contact that we might be one of the same kind with a yearning to capture even more in your next passing.

"This is called 'cruising,' ya know. It's the way young people meet." James sounded more excited than ever, waving at every carload of girls that passed by.

"Why Hell, I know that, James! Ya think I don't watch TV?"

"Well, I just don't want you to come up here to the big city and be lost, Brub!"

"Brub? What the hell's that all about, Doo...dle? I'm no little boy anymore, and when it comes right down to it, you're as *hillbilly* as me! So don't act like you ain't!"

"Yes, I am. But I can fake it, and you can't!" He slapped the steering wheel with a good lick. I knew that it was true, however, that I was backward in ways that he wasn't. He'd have to fake it in order to talk like me. But words weren't the only thing that separated us being labeled as *hillbillies*. I didn't mind the label as long as it wasn't intended to be something of a lower form of life.

I guess it was best expressed at a roadside rest over by Fort Hill, where someone carved ignorant hillbilly on top of a picnic table. While James laughed at the offense, I ramped and raged of the low-down city slicker jackass who'd write such a thing. To insult a person simply because they didn't walk the same straight line as others did was just wrong. Pissed off, I scratched the words off with a sharp rock.

Then there was Calvin from farther back in the sticks. Even though he'd pointed out that we were just one notch above the blacks which was still better than a city slicker.

We were made fun of, but not in a hateful way such as blacks were. Most offensive jokes were about them, whether intended to be funny or otherwise. "The right to" seemed to be on a lot of their signs and riots anymore. It just seemed nobody had paid much attention to them until lately when they wanted equal rights, 'to be a human being'. James had spoken of the cause several times himself. The joke from the old timer's bench was,

"Well, who in the hell would they vote for anyway? There ain't no white person who's gonna push to git that black vote."

The truth was James didn't have to shake his identity of being hillbilly. He was just smart and outgoing in the way he handled himself, never to shy away from anything. I knew from the time he'd started carrying the *Reader's Digest*, he'd planned on something better in life. An artist, actor, writer—not to mention him being smart—would make it easier for him to break free of the label *"hillbilly."* But the way I talked would quickly put me in the southern part of the state or maybe even Kentucky if there was any doubt.

"Man, just think if we had the old man's convertible to cruise in! We'd be like that guy over there with five girls." The guy gave us a pleased nod as he drove past. I couldn't help but stare with envy. Not in my wildest fantasies had I thought of being with more than one girl. And why should I when she'd be the prettiest in the whole wide world anyway?

Suddenly, all music and chatter were drowned out by the loud rumble of uncapped headers. *Blup, bluuup.* The engine gagged for more gas. Everyone threw their hands into the air with hoots and cheers.

James looked on with lustful eyes and for good reason. A guy who completely filled the driver's seat up just pulled into the line of cars in a shiny white Corvette Stingray, and with a pretty girl in the seat beside him. He looked like the lead singer of the Beach Boys, with blond hair covering most of his forehead and along with a square-chin smile.

Occasionally, he'd rev the motor up a few licks like a challenge for a drag race. Then came the cheering from all the guys who mostly didn't have the car of their dreams, it looked. I thought James probably knew as much about the Corvette as the guy who owned it. He had to be one of those rich kids and probably only needed to know when he was short on gas.

We snapped our fingers to slow and fast songs alike in whatever order they came on the radio. Just when it seemed things couldn't get any better, the Rolling Stones came on. "I Can't Get No . . . Satisfaction . . ." Echoes ran up and down the line of cars as guys held their fists to their mouths, singing as loud as they could with Mick Jagger. It was obvious there was a different preference in music between the guys and girls, however. Where the guys needed the music to be loud for them to imitate banging drums and electric guitars and to cover their terrible-sounding voices up, the girls toned it down for the opportunity to sing with the Supremes every time one of their songs came on. It was funny seeing some of the guys with a sour look on their faces with their girlfriends singing so sincerely to them. It wouldn't be that way with me if I had a girlfriend. I'd want to listen to everything she sang.

This was even better than *American Bandstand*—it was live. I acted in ways that I never had before. And at one point I tried to fork my hair down with quick hands, not to get caught by James where I'd never hear the end of it; or better yet, he'd offer me his comb. Could it be the devil-worshiping music the old man had preached about that was making me think and act this way? James proclaimed loudly that it was a high you get only when you're happier than hell such as he was right now.

"Hey, James, we'll see just how damned smart you are at this bigger school!" But then with no hesitation, he shot back.

"Hey, Arnold, we'll see how damned fast you are at this bigger school!" I deflated faster than a balloon that had been popped. But in the end we joked and laughed at how we were going to take the school by storm with our talents.

Words were scrambled into confused sentences as we tried to talk over each other with colliding forearms and elbows. Maybe the old man's convertible wouldn't have been the car to be in with the way we were acting. Then a car with eleven people pulled up beside us, which I promptly pointed at, with them wallowed all over one another.

We'd made several trips back and forth before the traffic started thinning as people darted off on side streets, and in a lot of cases yelling that they'd see them later that night.

"I'd bet things really get rocking then," James said. "I guess this was just an afternoon preview." He continued.

"Well, maybe we should come back later." I expressed hope.

"Na, one more trip up and down main street and we'll head back to the woods," he said while peering into the rearview mirror, not necessarily to look at his hair but to practice his smile with slightly squinted eyes. "There's a couple girls following us, and they've flashed their lights a couple times. I think they want to talk to us, Arnold." He pulled over into Benny's hardware parking lot, where they pulled up beside us.

"Hi! Are you guys new around here? I've never seen your car before," the flirty passenger said.

"Matter a fact, we, we are new," James said, turning the motor off. I felt a cold sweat on my forehead. I simply didn't know how to talk to a girl, especially ones with so much makeup on.

"Well, I hope you're not from Bainbridge or Court House," the driver said.

"No, we're from the little town of Willow Springs south of here," James answered. I'd built enough courage to sit up against the door, where I could see them better. *They look older than James*, I thought.

"You wouldn't have a cigarette, would you?" the passenger asked.

"No, neither of us smoke," James quickly followed. "And we really got to go. Now you girls have a good evening, and maybe we'll see you the next time." James started the Dodge back up, and we drove away, exiting a side street that ran by the High School. "There's not much use of talking when you'd be dealing with a bad habit like that and besides there's plenty of girls out there who don't smoke. And a cigarette is probably all they wanted anyway." He nodded.

"Man that was really cool how you handled that, James. Look!"—I pointed—"Drive up a little farther. Right here, pull over! Pull over right here. I've got to put my feet on the track. It's been almost a year, ya know. And my God, it looks so big!"

There was a different ache in my stomach now as I jogged to the track's edge. I couldn't wait for James to get there it was as if something was pulling me to the lane of my choice. Ever since my last race, I'd yearned to hear the sound that sent legs and arms into motion and hoped to be close or in the lead on the final lap. There still weren't many days that I didn't relive my glorious victories one at a time.

The sound of cinders crunching under my feet was enough to make me want to run as fast as I could right then and there. And at last maybe I'd know the thrill of winning a race on a home track, where the grandstands would be full of people cheering me all the way to the finish line. Or at least I could dream.

"I'll bet there'll be a lot of boys on the track team up here, James, and probably more than just one two-miler." Suddenly, I became nervous thinking how much harder it might be to become a top contender and to get a passing grade at this school. I just knew my life would end if that didn't work out. I knew going to a new school wouldn't have affected James or Judy. They'd already proven themselves with good grades and everything else they tried. Mine one of a lesser talent would be proven when the gun fired for a final lap. The thought alone made my legs feel heavy as we walked around to the other side.

"Hell's big as this school is. I'll bet there'll be fifty people that'll go out for the two-mile run alone!" I looked around to see that no one was there, then quickly took my shoes off, rolling my pant legs up to my knees.

"I'll catch back up with ya, James. I've gotta run a lap round this thang." I knew he wouldn't run with me; that'd put more spring into my step where I'd leave him farther behind. The cinders bit into my toes when I ran the last hundred yards to catch back up to him. He clapped as I sprinted past, while holding my arms into the air as if I were victorious.

"Well! How'd it feel, Arnold? Or need I ask? And was it everything you hoped for?"

"I'll be ready when the time comes," I said fisting my hands tightly. James walked over to a tree that had tall grasses under it the kind he liked to chew on. I hurriedly put my shoes back on without my socks.

"I don't think you need to worry, Arnold. You'll win races on this track." He spat out his prediction along with pieces of the chewed up weed. "You're too much of a sore loser, and for that very reason, you'll win some races." He smiled as if he had no doubt.

"God, I sure hope so, James," I expelled quickly. James was saying everything that I wanted to hear, while giving me the encouragement I needed. "Now wait right there, James. You're tellin' me that you don't mind losing? That you're not a sore loser sometimes yourself?"

"Oh, I wouldn't say that, but I get over it in the end. I guess what I meant is I don't mind it as bad as you do." He laughed, then continued, "The only things I don't like losing at are fighting and wrestling." What he was hinting at was quite clear in his eyes and stance, that of a challenge.

"James, you're shittin' me! You know we ain't in the woods right now! There's people here we don't know and might come drivin' by while we're actin' like fools. Don't you think it might look a little strange, with two grown-up men wallowing all around on the ground? And besides my stomach is."

My last hope of not going to the ground ended abruptly when he plowed into my midsection with his shoulder hitting me harder than I thought he should. We hit the grass, but as we did, I managed to raise a knee just in time flipping him over top me. I could hear him yell "Shit!" just before he landed on his rear end. We were both up in a flash, ready to face each other again.

"James! I don't want to wrestle here. There might be people watchin' us."

"Then run like a little girl. That don't seem to bother you," he razzed.

"I just think it looks strange, and I still don't feel so good—you know, with what Mr. Bill did to me."

"Man, you're just no fun!" He relaxed his stance, turning away to walk to the Dodge. I stopped long enough to look up at the big scoreboard with McClain Tigers painted in purple and gold lettering. It was cool to think once again that other teams would come here to race me at my home field. The lap around the track had made me feel good but somewhat anxious of what lay ahead.

"I think I'd rather be smart than just a fast runner, James. But imagine what both would be like!" I said, sharing my dream.

"You know I really don't think about comparisons of who's smart and who's not. It's more like what do you want out of life and how hard are you willing to work for it." James said. "There's plenty of so called smart people that end up with nothing, you know. I always get a laugh out what Dad calls them kind of people, 'educated fools'. But I'm a lot like you Arnold in ways that I like a little recognition. One example is like my paintings of Kincaid Springs. Now down around Willow Springs and Waverly, I got recognized for those, where you on the other hand got lots of glory by winning race after race.

"But up here, it might be a little harder for the both of us. My point is like I said a minute ago, how hard are we willing to work for what we really want." He nodded in a way that questioned if I got his message. It was kind of my big brother to compare me to himself in any way. I knew all too well that he still had one thing that I didn't. His smarts would get him farther along in life than anything I'd ever do as a runner.

Neither of us made much of an attempt at talking on the way home with our windows rolled down and arms hanging out the sides. With music blaring over the sound of the wind blowing past we could reflect, in our own private ways, on what a great day we'd had. Once again, the phrase the fellow used who was on LSD came to mind. 'It's hard to explain man,' his word echoed when I tried to piece together this day.

The slight panic anytime James would lag too far behind the car in front of us. I wanted to be completely surrounded with music and as loud as it could go and add spark to a way I'd never felt before. Not to be afraid to be daring and part of something such as the song, 'Dancing in the Street', with people clapping their hands which I really wanted to be part of.

And all the pretty girls that smiled whether or not they were intended for me, I could dream of this day. I couldn't read James mind but by the way he'd fancied himself looking in the cars mirror something had truly roused his imagination. We'd gotten a taste of something so different than anything we'd ever had before. But there was one thing for sure we both had enjoyed this day of discovery.

James slowed just before veering off Route 41 and onto Cliff Run Road where a one lane covered bridge crossed a ravine over a steep canyon. Slowly he idled the Dodge into the dark opening while we continued the full span of a hundred feet or so towards the other end. And in that short span of darkness I closed my eyes thinking how reality lay only a couple miles on up the road. My magical day would do nothing to fix the turmoil between me and the old man.

The song couldn't have been any better when we cleared the bridges opening with a trumpeter blowing a slow melody just before Dusty Springfield's sexy voice chimed in. 'Wishing and Hoping' seemed to fit perfectly with what was on my mind with James turning the volume down for a more relaxing sound. We crested a small hill just before Harry's place. At about the same time James tapped the brakes, I asked,

"Ain't that Duck and the boys there along the road?" I pointed. "I can point now, cain't I? Since we're back in the sticks again," I joked.

"Yeah, that's them, all right," he said, slowly bringing the car to a stop.

"And just what the hell are you boys doin' out here, Duck?" They quickly gathered around my door.

"You mean you boys ain't heard we is Dad's spies?" Duck laughed. "He sent us up here to make sure you ain't out lollygaggin' around somewhere and not gettin' any work done!" He joked, after which he spit baccer off into the ditch.

"How long have you been doing that shit, Duck?" James asked, then quickly turned to Larry. "How long has he been chewing, Larry?" Larry stuttered at first.

"Not very long at all," he answered. Things quieted quickly as the boys looked around at each other, not daring to say a word that might get Duck into more trouble.

"Duck! Spit that shit out and get in the car. Right now! And if I ever see you with another chew in your mouth, you'll pay dearly! I promise you that." James was adamant, pointing a finger at Duck. He'd say nothing more of his warning as the boys climbed in the car.

"Did Mom come too, Duck?" James asked, looking through the rearview mirror.

"Yeah, she's up at that old man's house with Dad." He sounded a little hurt I thought while the others continued to be quiet as a mouse. The old man's car was gone, but Judy and Beth where sitting in Harry's swing when we drove up. We were eager to greet them with hugs and smiles.

"Where's Mom and the old man?" I asked Judy.

"They went to that empty house down there in the curve," she replied. Her smile never left her face, but she seemed restless as I glanced over at James.

"Well, what's going on with that?" I questioned further. She wasted no time, a little briggity in her manner I thought. Bursting with excitement she blurted,

"We're going to move up here and before school starts! Dad's going to sell the farm," she said, rolling her eyes up at James and me. She sniffled, her face wrinkling and was about ready to cry it looked. I looked down at little Joe; most of his short life had been at that farm. He looked pitifully up at me, not really understanding any of it though.

Suddenly I became angry thinking how James and I had committed the worst sin of our lives in order to keep our mother from having to ever move again. I felt my lower lip tremble as I looked at all the little lost souls helpless in the face of what was going on.

Judy couldn't hold back any longer whether from joy or otherwise when the first tears rolled down her cheek. She covered her face with both hands to try and hide her deep moans. Forget all the times I'd bragged that I was too old to cry. With eyes closed tightly, I embraced her, pulling her close and pressing my face to hers.

I'd not hugged my little sister many times in my life. I'd simply let things get in the way. Other hands and arms filled empty spaces as everyone joined to hold one another. It wasn't just the single event that we wept for, but all that'd built up that maybe we'd ignored for too long.

I quickly teared up with small hands clinging and tugging for affection as some cried just because we were. At a time like this, I'd not spill my anger and rage that the old man be blamed for all that'd we cried for. Gone forever like the loss of a true friend one you'd never see again, thoughts of the farm completely flooded my mind.

I couldn't help thinking how I'd held his gun in my hands ready to shoot him at one time. I surely didn't need to think of such a terrible thing with everyone needing each other as we did right now. We were the family circle that our mother sang of so many times that our unity not be broken. But there would be one whom I'd never include. I tried to squeeze as many hands as I could, guessing at whose they might be in passing. As our mother had said many times, good can come out of crying for the right things. Several minutes had passed when I felt James's strong hand grip my shoulder. After breaking free, he stood in front of us.

"I feel better now. How about everybody else?" He raked his hair back in a couple places. Judy slowly and carefully wiped her eyes with the end of a sleeve. "Now it's not the end of the world!" he encouraged. It sounded like something Mom would say in such a crisis, I thought. "Now just think—we'll all be together again . . . and see each other every day! That means a lot to me . . . how about you guys?" He looked at each and every one to shake his head with them.

"Yes, and we'll all eat together again," I said, waving my fist high into the air.

"And, Duck, you bein' the only recipient of the Big Biscuit Award will end on day 1 of our first breakfast together. It'll be solely mine from that point on." James announced. My mouth dropped open as I looked at him.

"You might as well look in my direction, James, 'cause what you said ain't gonna happen." Everyone broke into laugher at my challenge.

"And finally, . . ." James started a slow walk around everybody as they all took notice. "DQ every Sunday!" he promised as if it were the greatest thing on earth, which it looked to be, based on the cheering as they all danced about. He'd gotten their attention for sure. "Now there's one other thing that we've got to keep in mind. We all need to show as much happiness as we can. It'll help Mom out." I could hardly wait to see her and was tempted to run down to the house in the curve.

"Where'd you guys go today?" Judy asked. I started to answer, but James spoke up. "We drove up to Greenfield to check the town and school out," he said. Judy's smile perked.

"Oh, I wish I could have gone. What was it like?" Her eyes, although still teary, beamed with excitement. Short of all the details that'd happened, we stressed what a beautiful school it was. Not surprising, Judy said that she could be happy about going to a different school also. Maybe she needed to put things behind her and like James, truly did want to go on to something bigger and better.

I wished Mom, the true center of our family's circle, could have been there in our celebration. I could only imagine the pressure the old man was putting on her to sell out and move away. I knew she missed James and me as we did her also, making it easier for the old man to have leverage to get his way, once again.

"Have you boys been up to the pond yet?" I pointed in its direction. Off in a flash I started running with everyone in hot pursuit except James, who decided to stay up with me for a big part of the run. Pants and shirts flew everywhere as they stripped down to their underwear, with the younger boy's butt naked. It would have been hard to pick out who was the first in the water with splashes coming from everywhere. But one thing for sure no one was waiting on Duck's command.

And just like at the springs, they all tried to dunk Duck under the water; he'd have it no other way. Someone would go flying limply through the air, crashing with a huge splash where he'd thrown them. With so much fun and laughter it wasn't long before they started diving from the banks and having contests on who could jump the farthest.

"Should we get Mr. Bill up here, Arnold? You could show off that famous world-class dive one more time," James suggested with a satisfying look about him. Even though the pain was all gone from my dive I couldn't resist rubbing my stomach at how it felt earlier.

Judy and Beth declared they'd see the pond after they get moved into the new place. I'd noticed they'd left the swing and started walking down to the rent house, to where Mom was at.

"James, can I use the car and give them a ride down to that house?"

"Yeah, go ahead. Just don't be hot-rodding down the road," he said with concern. "Remember, if you tear it up, we won't have any wheels to get around in, if you know what I mean." It did seem we spent a lot of time lately working on the old Dodge. James had pointed out all the places we'd attached wire to hold the muffler and others things in place. They'd walked about halfway there when I stopped to pick them up.

"Would you young ladies like a ride?" I asked, sounding like a sick-minded person. Judy got in the front seat, and Beth got in back. "Do you just jump in anybody's car?" I asked. Judy slapped my arm just before breaking out into laughed.

"It sure is good to see you, Arnold." She smiled.

"Well, it's good seeing you two also." With the thought of seeing Mom, I pushed the gas pedal down a little farther. Beth screamed a couple of times, saying that I was going way too fast and rightfully so as I slid into the driveway, faster than I had really planned, and finally managed to stop right up against the convertible's rear bumper. Among many other things, the Dodge needed new brake shoes, but we couldn't afford to buy them right now. We'd joked for some time how we'd have to give up Dairy Queen for a couple weeks to pay for them. They'll be all right for a while longer, James had proclaimed. They were all still in the rent house and hadn't heard the noise when I ran into the back of the old man's new car. I backed up a few feet, not so obvious as to what I'd done; leaving a small dent in the new car's bumper.

"Do you always show off like this with all your girlfriends?" Judy laughed, wiping her eyes one last time.

"You know I'm gonna tell Dad that you hit his car, and that's after I told you to slow down!" Beth threatened.

"Oh, no you won't either!" I quickly shot back smiling in the rear-view mirror. "I've got so much stuff on you and besides everyone knows how you lie about everything Bertha Mae." She couldn't hide her laughter when she reached from the back seat putting her hands snuggly around my neck, with a slight choke. It was good that we'd grown up from the way we used to act when trying to get the best of each other.

There was never any or at least any good reason why we'd get on each other's nerves like we did. But it wasn't just us, when I'd noticed the same with other large families that the second oldest brother didn't seem to get along too well with the second oldest sister. And whereas James and Judy showed patience with others Bertha and I couldn't.

"I'm gonna tell Mom!" she'd threaten anytime I'd do something that I wasn't supposed to. As I'd tried to explain to James she couldn't understand the difference in a cuss word and a bad word either. With one hand cupped over her mouth off towards the house she'd run eager to tell mom on me. And I knew that I didn't stand a chance with mom either that I slipped and the word came out or I didn't really know that it was a bad word. And never one time did my mother believe me. Her punishment was nothing like our dad who would deal it out in the form of a whipping. She knew how hard it was for someone to set on the davenport and hear everyone else having fun outside.

At a much younger age I could buy Bertha off with a simple horseback ride. But over time it turned into longer rides that seemed to last for hours. As we got a little older the horseback rides gave way to what I hated more than anything. She was fascinated with wearing a crown on her head which she'd picked up on watching the TV show, Queen for the Day. For a long time, she'd cut them out of paper and wear them everywhere she went. With a slight smirk, she'd not tell on me if I called her 'Queen' anytime we passed by each other. I was angrier than ever when I'd slip with a bad word only to add another day of calling her Queen.

"I didn't understand what you said Arnold," she'd smile anytime I'd force the words through gritted teeth. But when the shoe was on the other foot, when she'd done something wrong it would be my turn to hound her.

"Just call me Big Boss." And in the ways of the old man I'd rush my cupped hand to my ear so that she speaks clearly which was never good enough for the first several times. Like a fresh picked flower, she'd start wilting when I'd hound her making sure that everyone was around to hear my command that's until Judy would put an end to it.

Harry was holding the door open for Mom as they were coming out of the house, something I never remember seeing the old man do for her. A perfect gentleman in the way Harry was acting with such politeness, not smoking his pipe while protecting her every step it looked. I thought of the photograph that hung on his living room wall of him holding his violin with his hair parted down the middle so neatly. I knew Harry must have been a classy person in his time. I thought how excited he'd gotten when telling me the story about the picture and all the other musicians that he played with in Cincinnati at a concert hall.

"Well, what's it like in there, Mom?" I asked, wrapping my arms around her. The old man walked right past without saying a word, which was fine with me. It let me know that he still held a grudge also.

After our much-needed and lengthy hug, she answered.

"It's pretty nice in there, Honey, and how have you been doing?" *She was tryin' hard to sound happy*, I thought. The old man had gone straight to the car and looking impatient, backed his ass up to the fender while lighting up a cigarette.

"Well, now like I said earlier, Marie, this ain't a bad place for the money," Harry advised with a slow nod of the head.

I never had time to ask her how all this had transpired and seemingly overnight at that. It should have been expected that the old man would blow his horn and a minute later blew it again.

"What's wrong with Dad?" Beth asked. She was twelve now and was constantly asking Judy about everything. Judy was her go-to person just as James was mine.

"Well I guess I better go, Honey," Mom said with a sad smile.

"Mom, when are you guys goin' to move up here?" I asked.

"Well now, if the Lord's will, it'll be before school starts," she answered. I sensed a little dread in her voice, however. Even with the old man's brief passing, I'd smelled beer, but no reason to complain to Mom she already knew and it'd only make things worse.

"I guess we're going to rent this place while your dad builds us a home on that land up there by a pond somewhere." She didn't seem to put much expression into what she'd said but did sound hopeful, I thought. The horn blew again, and at that point, we all started laughing.

After a kiss and hugs from her and my sisters, they headed back to Harry's place. I'd decided to take a look inside the house. I didn't want to go back up to Harry's with the old man being there. I knew it wouldn't be long before he'd be taking them back to Pike County as it was starting to get dark already. If there was any sort of uplift in the matter of them moving the idea of him building a house for our mother would mean a lot, and I wondered how long it'd take to build one. I knew the old man had done some carpentry work and built the house in Florida, which wasn't anything to brag about. A shack at best. I cringed at the thought of its leaky roof. It was his way to always be in a hurry and do things half-assed. I had my doubts that he builds it anyway.

31

I'd finished looking around and made it back to the Dodge in time to see the red convertible go past, with everyone's hair flying in the wind as they all waved bye to me.

"I love you . . .! See you soon!" Judy blew a kiss.

I drove back up to Harry's, parking under the big tree. I'd noticed Harry had a faraway look in his eyes when I pitched the car keys to James.

"Well, Harry, whatcha think about the rest of the family and did you like Mom and my sister's singin'?"

My question seemed troublesome to him, while slowly shaking his head, and looking disappointed, with the way he held his pipe idle in one hand. Then he finally squared his shoulders and crossed one leg over the other. I'd suspected something wasn't right, James was unsettled and had said nothing to this point.

"Why, Arnold, like I was tellin' Junior there God damn-it. Why I never got the chance to hear your mother or those two girls sing!" His disappointment was obvious now in the way he swirled his pipe about to match such frustration.

"You're kiddin' me, ain't ya, Harry?" Although acting surprised I knew all too well that he spoke the truth.

"Hell no, I ain't a kiddin'!" He quickly uncrossed his legs and leaned forward in the swing. "Why, that damned Jim acted like he couldn't get 'em away from here fast enough!" Harry was frowning, clearly disgusted with every attempt to take a draw on his pipe at this point.

"Well they'll sing for you someday, Harry. It'll happen, just you wait and see," James assured. We visited for a while longer before he finally said good night, still sad when the door shut firmly behind him. I could understand the old fellow's disappointment when long periods of time must pass by before such an opportunity again.

On any other night, we would have gone to bed ourselves but sleep would elude us with all the events that'd happened on this day. We'd not been by ourselves long enough to talk much about any of them. We walked back up to the Dodge where James slid his butt up on the driver's side fender and making himself comfortable positioning his back up against the windshield. I did the same on the other fender as James seemed to be having the hardest time finding the right spot to settle down.

Harry's big maple tree with its massive size had been in many conversations from Harry's porch. It was all James and I could do to reach all the way around it with our fingers barely touching. And there was something else often spoke of at dusk. We sat amongst the lightning bugs, thousands of them it looked as they lit up all around us. It was unique in the way I'd never seen before when they'd umbrella the better part of the giant tree with such an array of flashes. Harry said he didn't know what the attraction was all about other than maybe breeding, he'd joked. He said that over the sixty years he'd lived there, the tree had grown lots bigger—and with it, more and more lightning bugs. He went on to say that some people even called it a phenomenon.

"Man, it's sure been a strange day." James said right out of the blue. Then after a short hesitation, he quickly asked. "What's your take on this day Arnold?"

His question took me somewhat by surprise and had I been able to see any facial expression it might have helped in the manner I'd answer. Stuttering to get started I blurted. "Is there something wrong James?"

"No! I just picked up on some things and started putting them all together and wondered what your thoughts might be. And now I've pretty well come to a conclusion as how I feel about them."

"Well… it definitely had its ups and downs for sure." I stalled for the moment thinking he might interrupt and get right to his point. But there was no movement from where he sat. I arranged myself in a more comfortable way with my back pressed tight against the windshield and arms crossed at the chest. I closed my eyes as we'd done as little boys in the darkness to tell scary stories or whatever came to mind. And best I found it easier to stretch the truth a lot of those times.

"'Cruisin' I mean cruising with the way you say it was one of the best things I've ever done in my life. There's just something about some pretty girls smile whether or not it was intended for you. Have you thought that we might be at that age I mean with girls and all, when things start fallin' into place like they did up at Greenfield today? And just for that little time bein' around mom and the family was so good. It lets you know how much you really miss everybody. But of all the things I never thought I'd do was to cry today. Mom's right as always, if it's for a good reason."

I'd quickly run through the topics of the day hoping one might be what James was wanting to talk about. There still was no reaction or movement that I could detect from his side of the car. Regrettably there was only one thing left to talk about. I'd avoided it up to this point thinking I'd not get James upset by what my reaction would be.

"But what always fucks everything up? The old man couldn't hang around long enough for mom and the girls to sing one damned song for old Harry. They ain't no doubt about it, it'd been a better day had he not been here." The thing I'd saved for last had upset me when I breathed a heavy sigh with flaring nostrils. Had I gotten close to what James was looking for I couldn't say. I'd sit silent in the darkness now and wait for him to fill the void.

"Well I agree with everything you said Arnold it's all true. But I saw a message in what went on here today."

"Yea, there's a message alright and a clear one at that. That assholes selling the farm and there ain't nothing we can do about it. And poor mom it looks like she getting' suckered once again."

33

"Well I don't know Arnold if it's necessarily being suckered as you call it. I think it's more like she's ready to make a supreme sacrifice for something she truly wants. It's in all her songs where nothing is more important than how your heart feels towards something. So, what is the supreme sacrifice that she's willing to give up? I've got some thoughts about today and other matters that I'd like to talk with you about, and see what you think.

"You avoid the old man all the time and I suspect that you'd just as well see him dead, right? But as you already know that's not how mom feels about it. I'm satisfied that we did everything we could to keep her on the farm over there, but when she showed up here today, I knew she had something on her mind. You talked to her! Wouldn't you think that she prayed before ever deciding to come over here? In fact, I don't think he had to coax her at all. It's not that she's worried about herself—it's us, always has and always will be. It's the family circle she's after no matter what she has to give up.

"And there's another thing pretty critical right now—those boys need their big brothers to keep them in line. Mom'll teach them all how to be good, but that's not going to stop Duck from sneaking around and dipping tobacco. And any hopes of our family being together again will include the old man. No matter how much he drags her down she'll never give up on him. How often have you laid awake and hear her pleas that the Lord, look over him? Clearly, he's in bad shape right now and mom knows it. He'll never even look for that holy stump of repentance until she nurses him back to some kind of reality. It's a double whammy for her in the way her prayers could be answered that we all... be together again.

"And that supreme sacrifice I spoke of that she'd be willing to give up of course is our farm. Arnold we can't overlook mom's needs and desires. Clearly, she needs our help with this matter. No matter how wrong it was what we did at the farm we did try to keep our mother a place where she could live forever. And I continue to pray that she never finds out about that."

"Do you really pray for that James?"

"Yes, don't you?" He quickly followed. I was finding it hard to answer him thinking how my desperate pleas had not been answered the day the house burned. For the rest of my life I'd hear the sounds of popping and cracking timbers and with yet another unanswered prayer that they might stop someday. In the silent minutes that followed my mind raged before James finally intervened.

"Now Arnold with that said I have a confession of my own that plays right along with mom's decision. I'll make it as simple as I can. I'm tired of this tug-of-war that we've been dealing with to keep that farm. We go out of our way to not talk about it but as you know it's always there and just a troubling thought away. It's really not been that long ago.

"That damned rope's been slipping through our fingers for a while now, and it's time to admit that we are fighting a losing cause. Somethings got to give. You know what's left over in Pike County!! Memories. Nothing but a bunch of memories and how damned long can we keep hanging on to them? I'll tell you how long. Until we never have a reason to go over there again.

"Now you tell me what you saw the last time we were there. Hold it, I'll answer that one for you after all it's never left your mind yet Arnold." As if it had been planned, in a fleeting moment I opened them where James was looking my way with a leading hand to express himself. And all with the backdrop of the many lightening bugs firing off at one time.

"Where a beautiful forest once stood it looks like a Vietnam war zone at best now, and where our house once stood is a heap of ashes that'll never be cleaned up, or at least not by him. There's only one definition for it. It's downright depressing over there. And grant you all brought on by him one way or the other. So, with what I seen today and to follow my gut feeling, I think we should follow mom's will without resistance that she would have her family all together maybe for one final time."

I was glad James couldn't see me as I wailed up inside thinking of the place I'd fallen so much in love with. The bright flashes had become shinny slivers in my eyes as I closed them once again. Our sudden silence gave way to the creatures of the night with their never-ending croaks that they be heard above all the rest. I swallowed hard not to gag thinking that maybe I'd not prayed loud enough to have been heard above all the rest. But regardless when the farm didn't belong to us any longer the sounds of patting feet running down a well-worn path would follow me for the rest of my life. Uncomfortable with myself I quickly straightened up sitting on the edge of the fender.

"Yeah, you're right, James," I painfully acknowledged. "I know what you're sayin' and truthfully, I've given a second thought to a lot of things myself lately." I cleared my throat with a weak cough. "I think it's more painful for me than you to give the farm up though. I guess in one way it's like that old puzzle that mom had with so many pieces missing. I remember how she still hated to throw it away though. I guess our farm is a lot like that when it's the only one you got."

"I once thought the springs was a giant body of water. I guess it was big enough to fit my needs at that time. If, you don't have much to start with, you are a lot easier to please. You know a time when everything looks bigger and better are the happiest days of your life. But we've been forced to grow up a lot faster over the past two years than most our age has. I fell prey believing the old man would be content and we'd live over there forever."

"Forever!!" James interrupted. "That's only when they put you under the ground, now that's forever." He rattled off in a joking way.

"I know your right about everything you're tellin' me James. You've never misled me in any way, not even one time or at least one I can think of. It'll just take me a little longer than you to get over the loss." I appreciated the time James had allowed me to talk without interruptions as I wiped my eyes while taking a deep breath.

"I don't guess you've been in the house down there in the curve yet. Truthfully, it's way better than anything I'd ever expected him to rent for Mom. It's modern ya know with indoor water and a toilet and has a big mirror. Judy commented on that when we were down there today." I couldn't help but wonder why James had started this whole conversation in the first place. Was he trying to tell me that part of growing up was being able to leave the past behind and simply never reach out to touch it again.

"Your so right James, we ain't little boys no more. Like, remember what Grandma said that time about not looking back on thangs you've done wrong? "Why Honey," you know how she talked James, "the path is in front of you not behind you."

"Well when it comes right down to it Arnold we're about like a worn-out hand pump that can't hold its prime any longer. We just need a new gasket and we'll be good to go." I smiled in the dark then I wondered if James was doing the same with our confessions that we couldn't keep living in the past.

"Mom, Judy, Beth, Don, Ron, Larry, Robert, and little Joe—they'll all leave their stories behind but nothing like ours I'm sure. My point is that we have already missed a whole summer's worth of hearing them go on and on about things they did." His words seemed to echo into the night air. I closed my eyes once again and tried to envision the rope James talked about quickly sliding through my hands and almost to the end.

"Well regardless of what he promised I think Mom should tell him that she'll move over here but won't sell the farm until the house is built. Maybe that'd put a fire under his ass to get it done faster."

"What did you say, build a house, Arnold?" He sounded shocked while sliding off his fender.

"You ain't heard about the new house up there by the pond?" I questioned.

"No, this is the first I've heard of it."

"No shit, you really hadn't heard, have you?"

"Let's go to the bus and talk about this," he suggested. We fixed ourselves late-night bologna sandwiches with fresh 'madders and lettuce that Mom had left with a few other garden things.

"So, when did you hear about this?" he asked, more anxious than ever.

"Oh, I've known about it for some time now." I turned my head, avoiding his watchful eye.

"It couldn't have been that long ago, Arnold. You know I wasn't born yesterday." He chuckled, looking me straight in the eye. I faked a yawn, knowing I had him right where I wanted for now, though.

"I'm pretty tired, James. Maybe we should talk about this tomar." I said and all the while rubbing my eyes.

"Well, that'll be fine. You can keep that little secret while your ass is sleeping on the floor tonight," he pointed.

"Well, to tell the truth, I just found out about it from Judy today. Then Mom was talkin' about it just before the old man started blowin' his damned horn. I'd a liked to have stuck that thang right up his ass about then! That bastard acted like he never wanted me and Mom to even talk to each other. So piss on that frolickin' horn-blowin' prick!" James made a short laugh at what I'd said.

"Well, did he say anything to you at all?"

"Nope, he didn't! And that's good because I don't have anythin' to say to him, period!"

"Have you noticed the old man's eyes lately? He looks weirder than ever. And here's one for ya, James. His Bible was lying in the backseat of the car the other day. Got any wild guesses about what's goin' on there."

"Well, that's pretty easy, Arnold. I'd imagine it was in his plan that Mom see it when he went to pick her up this morning.

"That son of a bitch." I gritted my teeth. "He'll do whatever it takes knowing that Mom would have hope by just seeing that Bible. Think about all those times he preached how he was using his Bible for a road map. Only problem was he got his maps all mixed up with the County Line Liquor Store.

"To me, it looks like he traded it off for a thick billfold and a shiny red car to whore around in. He's put that old Bible on the back burner so he can run with his kind. But someday that map will guide him to some holy-ass-stump up a holler, and he'll get back on the Right road where he left that beer bottle from the last time. You know, James, with the way things go around here, I think of another old sayin' of Granma's. And I can hear her as plain as day. "Honey, laugh when ya can and cry when ya have to." That's about what it amounts to when you're dealing with him.

"Listen. Did you hear that?" I paused while holding my breath. "Thunder and it's getting closer. Rain's on the way, just like old Harry said especially with the tree frogs croaking all around us. He swears they're the best rain predictors there are and Grampa says the same thing." I rambled "Maybe it's the rain a comin' drawin' so many lightening bugs to gather under the big tree tonight. I'll have to run that possibility past Harry."

"Good night, Arnold," James said, climbing into bed.

Strange, I thought, that the old man had not told him his plans for the new house. I figured we would talk more of it after a good night's sleep.

The rumbling had been getting closer by the minute as I lay wondering if that was the way it sounded in Vietnam with bombs blowing up at a short distance. Then suddenly, a bright flash lit up the inside of the bus, followed by a loud crackling, shaking the ground around us. We jumped from the bed at about the same time and closed all the windows against a sudden wind followed by a hard rain. In no time, James was sleeping once again. He could sleep through about anything.

The fast-moving storm had cooled things off and now rumbled in the distance as if a war was coming to an end. I thought James would be in an uproar the next morning demanding everything I knew about the building of the new house. Maybe there were other things on his mind that talk of a house didn't seem to interest him much. All he had to say was, "I'll believe it when I see it."

James made the decision that we should start going to Greenfield for our sandwiches and ice cream after work to the Dairy bar I'd pointed out on our first trip. "Pretty simple logic," he explained his reasoning. "We'll be starting school up there pretty soon so we might as well get to know the town a little better. It's a little farther than Bainbridge but the extra gas will be well worth it I believe."

We'd worked the next couple weeks hitting it pretty hard. There'd been no rain and we'd gotten out nine loads of pulpwood and three in logs. James and I added up our money after every load. Calvin was taking a load of firewood with him every week-end and declared he was ready for the snow. He went on to say how he was stacking it close to the house so the old hag wouldn't have to wade too deep a snow to get a stick or two for the stove.

We came out of the woods one Saturday after working a half day. There was the regular routine of stopping for a swim before our trip to Greenfield for food and cruising. But as we neared the pond James pointed to the old man's car parked in a peculiar way with the front bumper pressed up against the big Maple tree.

"He's got to be drunk." James observed pointing to the rear bumper sticking out into the road a little way.

"Look! Harry's in his swing James but I don't see the old man anywhere. God, I hope he's not passed out in our bus!" We'd hold off on our swim with James saying he needed to get the rear end of the car out of the road. We walked on to where Harry sat in his swing.

"Evening boys," He said offering a place beside him for one of us to set which James obliged. There was no denying he was upset. I'd noticed him talking to himself upon our approach and looking a little angry at that. His normally tight face gave way to wrinkles stretched across his forehead.

"Harry, you going somewhere? I mean it looks like you got your frolicking clothes on." James observed. Harry took a long draw before blowing smoke out the side of his mouth.

"Why Jim and I were supposed to go to a fiddler's contest down at Peach Grove but that's before he showed up like this," Harry said while stabbing his pipe sharply over his shoulder a couple times. It was then I noticed his fiddle case stashed behind the swing. With a wink, I directed James to where it sat. Even though he'd hinted that the old man was in his house I needed to know what shape he was in.

"Well what's he doing in there?" I asked. He had no problem hearing what I'd asked perking up and looking all around as if there were others who should hear his answer also.

"Why that son-of-a-bitch is passed out back there in my little room. Snorin' so damned loud that I can hardly set there long enough for a shot of shine. Hell, he's pissed his self and that may not be all. He's on a good one alright. I don't think I can even get to my cot to sleep tonight. I guess I'll have to sleep upstairs." James's slow steady headshake stopped just before he stood up.

"I'll be right back," he said. And in less than a minute he returned to say the old man would be out for a while.

"Well boys I guess I shouldn't be too mad." Harry reared back sounding a little more relaxed. "Old Jim's had to help me to bed more than just a few times. But boy did I get a hell of a laugh before he went in there and passed out in the middle of the God-damned floor." Harry repeated his previous motion stabbing his pipe over his shoulder in the direction of the door.

"Hell, I was sittin' hear waitin on him when he came driven up lookin' like his breaks weren't working right. Luckily he'd slowed down to about nothin' when he hit that tree up there. I don't think it hurt his car much though. Why I choked on my own damned smoke watching him stagger all along that fence tryin' to find that damned little gate!

"Lost, I'm tellin' ya old Jim didn't have a clue to where in the hell he was at till he spotted me down here in my swing. But that weren't anything once he got on this side of the fence. I'll bet it took him a hundred steps or better to walk that little distance between the gate and porch. And hell, I was a laughin' and fartin' all at the same time thinkin' there was no one here to make a bet with that I'd lost for sure. Why that staggering ass drunk never fell one damned time even stopped twice to take a piss, once over there by the fence where he had something to hang onto and the other right out there in the middle of the yard." Harry laughed and all the while circling his pipe in the general locations where it all had transpired. "And you should have seen him hangin' on to that thang of his and goin' round and around in circles 'bout ready to fall. Shit he looked like he was tryin' to water the whole damned yard." Harry gave us the strangest look before shaking his head. "Why hell it made me dizzy just watchin' um."

It didn't take much imagination to follow Harry's story as we'd seen the very same thing many times. But he did add a flavor to it with his facial expressions a swirling pipe and strange looks that set us all off with spontaneous laughter.

"I'll be right back," James said after wiping his eyes with forefingers." A minute later he came from the house dangling the keys to the red convertible. "Now Harry you didn't get all cleaned up for nothing. Me and Arnold need to run back to the pond for a cleaning up swim and then we're going to take you to that fiddlers contest."

At the pond we agreed that it was better to give up a night of cruising and old Harry not have to endure another lonely night. After changing into clean clothes, we went back to Harry's where James quickly fetched the fiddle case from behind the swing.

"Let's go frolic for a little while!" James chuckled. After we'd all settled down in the convertible James let the top down. "We're going in style." He said. Harry laughed and knowing better asked James if he'd gotten permission to use the old man's car. We joked how we'd all be in jail before the night was over.

Peach Grove was a tad smaller than Willow Springs. The big difference was they had a liquor store there and was set up for beer garden activities. Harry wasted no time in making his way to get a double shot of whiskey. And then another one shortly after that. We'd gotten there a little before the crowd started showing up. The fiddlers would be the first to arrive and pick various places away from everyone to do a final tune-up to their strings with freshly rosined up bows. Guitars, mandolins, banjos and tall shiny basses looked orchestrated as the players adjusted them to satisfy a rhythm that fit the fiddler.

Sadly, Harry sat with other old timers whose crooked fingers and other ailments would render most of them as spectators instead of competitors. Some such as Harry still clung to a dream with their fiddle placed snuggly beside their chairs. I thought how many times they all must have gathered over the years for just such a festive occasion. It took me back to the little smoky store in Kentucky anytime a banjo would lead off with a tune. I thought to myself how rock and roll could set my heart afire with its rhythms and so many changes. But there was something about Bluegrass that lay deep in my heart and would be there when I needed it.

James and I walked to a hot dog stand where some people we knew from down Willow Springs way had gathered including several girls. James, never shy, joked and cut up with them in such a natural way it looked. He was a hard act to follow making it even harder to start any conversations on my own.

Harry continued with his drinking when suddenly he appeared on the stage with one of the groups. In the way they avoided him it looked as if old Harry had done this very same thing before I thought. I felt sorry for him as he fiddled to a different tune than them; barely able to hear his notes. But the crowd pleaser came when old Harry's pants fell all the way to his ankles showing his skinny bean pole legs.

The band immediately stops playing and were beside themselves with laughter. It looked rehearsed with Harry holding his fiddle and bow in one hand while bending over to pull his pants up with the other and his pipe stuck firmly in his mouth. He wasn't embarrassed at all spreading his legs apart to hold the pants in place while he played a little jig all by himself which got the loudest applause of the evening.

By now Harry was in no shape much to walk on his own and had to be helped to the car. He rattled on about how the old timers were way better musicians than what they were today. We helped him upstairs to a bedroom where he insisted that he not sleep in the well-kept bed, but pointed to another room while asking if we could bring him a pee bucket afraid he might fall down the stairs if he had to go. It was well worth our while to see old Harry have such a good time. I wondered with his age and all if he'd make it there next year. I'd have my driver's license by then I figured and we'd go there, he and I.

The old man hadn't moved from where he'd passed out in the middle of the floor. I straddled him thinking how could anyone so helpless be such an asshole.

I eased out of bed early the next morning knowing that James would sleep a while longer, a typical Sunday. I ran to a place up in the woods where I'd found a patch of ginseng earlier that week. I dug it up and put it with all the rest we'd found getting close to a pound of dry, I figured. The old man was gone when I got back from the woods a few hours later. James said he'd talked with him for a minute or two before he left. He went on to say what a sad sight the old man looked unable to hide where he'd pissed himself. But he never had a clue or at least wouldn't say that he knew James stole his car for the night.

This was our day to rest and do not much of anything other than, maybe swim a couple times if the weather cooperated. We'd talk and cut up with old Harry at different times, usually right after his naps. But they'd be far apart on this day with him recuperating from the night before. But there was one thing he wasn't going to miss.

Later in the evening, James would head for the pond with a fishing pole, with Harry and me watching from his swing. And in a matter of minutes, he'd caught enough bass for the Sunday evening fish fry. Harry bragged continually at how good they taste. It seemed to add color to the old fellow's face, while telling how he looked forward to it the next Sunday.

I whistled for Mr. Bill and Kate to come to the barn the next morning. After feeding and putting their harnessed on I stopped to see if James had left yet. He'd already eaten and left a note that read, "Hurry every chance you get, meet you at the pond."

I could see from a distance that he was throwing rocks at something, and upon my arrival, he handed me a handful that he'd gathered up for me.

"That, loose cattail over there, see if you can hit it." He pointed. We'd only made a couple serious attempts at hitting it with little intent that it become a contest however.

"I've been thinking about that new house. Right over there's where we should build it." He pointed to an X he'd made with his boot.

"So, you really think that house bullshit is goin' to happen, James?"

"I know I wasn't too thrilled about it at first. But he did mention it the other morning to me. And let's say if it happens it needs to be right over there. He pointed with a weed he'd pulled from his mouth. Whatcha think about that place?"

"Well I just can't show much interest about any of it. I'm not going to waste my time on anything he says anymore."

"Well, I don't think that it's all bullshit Arnold and I'll tell you why," he said, sitting down close to the very spot he'd marked.

"Look, he's at his wit's end with everything going on like it is. He's going to do this because he needs us in the worst way. I mean what would he do without us? We're his slaves, and that's that. He drives us to the point of leaving and then comes up with something to keep us around, you know, like paying us now. And he's gonna move the family up here to keep everyone happy. He knows that if he keeps Mom happy then there's a better chance that we won't leave anytime soon. So it looks like the trade-off is he's got to sell the place in Pike County in order to build up here. Or at least that's what he's told Mom, I'd bet!"

"Yeah, I thought the same thing last night. But what worries me—and I got good reason, as you already know—is that he sells out and then runs through all the money before a house even gets started." After James had chewed the tender end of his weed off he tossed it to the side.

"You're not telling me anything, Arnold that I've not already thought of over and over again. But if we weigh all the good like we talked about last night regardless if the place is sold or not, it's better for everybody. I think we should play it by ear for now. We can't possibly guess what he'll do next." We lumbered on with the horses to the laydown yard.

"Yep, for the sake of Mom, James. There's a lot of things we can help her with, like me milkin' again—that's if I didn't forget how," I laughed. "And I'm really lookin' forward to startin' school this year, and it ain't that far off, you know. I don't know about you, but I'm ready for a break and get out of the woods to be around people for a change. You don't know what it's like to foller' a horse and mule's ass around in the woods day after day."

"No, I don't," he chuckled. "But you must like it . . . after all, you're still doing it."

"Why in the hell don't you jest kiss my ass, Jimbo Jr.?" I thought calling him that would have warranted a wrestling match for sure.

"There you go thinking about asses again, Arnold!"

"Just never mind." I said. We'd no more than just started loading the truck when we heard a vehicle coming our way, one we'd not heard before. It was Calvin driving an old beat up truck sounding as if this might be its last trip anywhere.

"Arnold Ray!" Calvin yelled after turning the engine off. "If you don't tighten your ass up a little, I'm goin' to have to far-ye...." He grunted, while taking a hard draw on his pipe. There was no way to hold back laughter with his face disappearing behind the smoky windshield. There were several coughs, with him fanning smoke before finally kicking the door open.

"Boys, that first pipe load in the mornin's a real bar's ass!" he said, followed with a throat clearing cough.

"You know, Mr. Williams," I said, looking at my wrist as if there were a watch, "old buddy, if you can't make it to work before noon, I don't think I can use you anymore." Calvin shook his head with one last cough, while pushing the pipe off to the side.

"And where'd you get the new truck Calvin?" James blurted.

"Blowed the car up the other day so thought I'd get me a truck to run around in. And I'll tell ya what... with them heavy duty side racks it'll keep old buffalo ass back there as long as she don't move around much while I'm driving." Calvin raised the hood quickly pulling the oil stick where he wiped it off on the side of his pants. "Why hell," he laughed. "It only used a quart of oil in hundred miles it looks. You don't see many like this anymore Junior, that uses more oil than gas," he laughed while shoving the dip stick back into its hole.

"Man, do we have a story for you, Calvin!" I interrupted.

"Well before we get into that, let's finish getting this truck loaded so I can get on the road! You know, make us a little money today." James spoke up. Calvin shot me a surprised look.

We'd no sooner loaded and cinched it down than James headed out. Calvin walked to the closest log, hiking his pant legs up a little before sitting down to sharpen his chain. I told him about us stealing the old man's car and taking Harry to the fiddler's shindig, which he got the biggest bang out of that. Calvin had not spoken a word that he knew anything about our week-end which led me to believe he'd not seen the old man. Or thought it simply wasn't any of Calvin's business. It might have been better had he known and saved me the hardship of telling him the future of our farm.

Hard-core hillbilly as Calvin was, I never knew anyone that could read a person's thoughts as quickly as he could. Maybe that I hadn't laughed much while telling about our weekend made him suspect that something wasn't quite right. I'd never lied to him 'cause there'd been no reason to. And he would have known had I done so. He just picked up on things and in his own way and could get you to talk of them. He sat up a little straighter, while dragging a heavily callused thumb across the saw's sharpened teeth. After relighting his pipe, he leaned back resting on one elbow.

"Arnold Ray, you got something else to tell me?" My hesitation was short lived.

"Yeah, I guess I do if the old man ain't already."

"Shit, he don't tell me nothin'—least anything that 'mounts to a hill of beans."

I went on to tell him and with fine detail what was happening with the farm over in Pike County and how the old man was supposedly going to build a new home down by the pond. Calvin sat quietly, taking it all in while puffing away on his well-lit pipe.

"Arnold Ray, your old man is still one crazy son of a bitch!" Calvin grunted. "And Marie sure don't need to leave that farm until that house is built! I mean if the Reverend even does it. I just wouldn't trust old Jimbo as far as I could throw him."

"Well, I don't think I'd throw 'em very far 'cause I'd want to be on his ass, beatin' the hell out of him. Did you ever want to just kick someone, Calvin?" I growled.

"Oh, I've done way better than just want to. I really believe I stomped an old boy's guts out one time." He nodded reassuringly.

"Now how in the hell could you tell if you stomped his guts out or not?"

"Do ya know what shit smells like, Arnold Ray?"

"Well, what did he do to deserve that, and did he die?"

"No, he didn't die. But he never came around my place again, tryin' to get some off of the old lady." Whether Calvin was just fooling around with me or not, I was changing the subject and in a hurry at that.

"I . . . I . . . just need to talk to Mom before she signs the papers to sell that place, Calvin," I stammered. "But just so you'll know, James and me thought it might be best if they move over here anyway regardless if he sells it or not. We miss them as much as they miss us, and we also agreed that they need their big brothers. So we think what's best is to just not worry about the part of him building a place right now."

It was the look Calvin gave me, one I'd seen on other occasions when he just wasn't sure about something.

"Well, there's just a lot ta thank about, Arnold Ray. Now you's boys should do what you think is right. And I know it's all about Marie." He grabbed up his saw and after a few cranks to get it started began cutting for the next load. I wanted to ask him why he hadn't said anything to me about the old man's timber buy down at Camp Creek but figured he'd give me a bunch of bullshit and some kind of story about Mary having me a bed to sleep in if we were to come down.

"The yard's almost full!" I yelled over his idling saw. "I'll get the other saw and help you cut the rest of the wood up after I unhook the animals." Calvin nodded his approval.

James was an hour or so late when he backed the truck up to the loading area. There was no acknowledgment of Calvin or me whatsoever when he jumped out and started throwing wood up on the bed like a madman. I gently kicked Calvin on the side of the leg to get his attention. We shut our saws off to watch James from across the yard.

"What's wrong with him, Calvin? Why, look at the way he's actin'."

"I don't know." Calvin studied, pulling his pipe from his shirt pocket without looking. "But don't stop him until he's finished—less work for us, by God! Now old June bug is surenuff in his own world right now, Arnold Ray. Hell, look at 'em! He's like a wild man over there, throwin' that shit all over the place." Calvin started laughing with a couple hard claps with his hands that should've got James's attention.

"Hell, I don't think he even seen us when he drove up, Calvin."

"Shit, I don't believe what I'm seeing, Arnold Ray. Can you pinch my ass to make sure it's not a dream and surely not what I think it is?" He chuckled rolling his eyes up at me.

"Hell no, I ain't goin' to pinch your sorry ass, Calvin." Calvin hastily made his way to the closest log.

"Quick, Arnold Ray, get over here and sit down." I thought the way he'd sneaked over to the log was strange, like a little boy getting ready to pull a prank on someone. He pulled his pant legs up as he sat down with sawdust trickling into his sockless shoes. Scrambling to light his pipe, he quickly fanned the smoke for a clear view of James.

"Look at old Junior, Arnold Ray. Why, who in the hell's he talkin' to? They ain't anybody over there." He laughed. "But whoever it ain't is sure makin' him smile a lot." Our loud outburst should have gotten James's attention for sure. Something was very strange the way he was acting. But it wasn't just James. Calvin's interest was stranger in a way of its own, with the way he'd gotten so excited by James's actions.

"Now, Arnold Ray, you could say something loud and goofy about old Junior right now. But he ain't yurin' a thing." Calvin sounded sure of himself. It wasn't anything new for James to talk to himself; he'd done it as far back as I could remember. It'd always been part of his problem-solving ways.

"Are you two going to help with this load or not?" He finally noticed us.

"Why, Junior you're doin' such a good job that I sure didn't want to get in your way!" Calvin laughed, leaning back on an elbow. He looked uncomfortable I thought.

James rubbed his chin while sizing up the amount of pulp wood he'd put on the truck. With a slight hesitation, he walked to where we sat but wouldn't sit down and seemingly needed to be on the move. Even when he crossed his arms, it was short-lived. It was when he pushed his hands deep into his pockets and pulled nothing out that I knew something crazy was going on.

"Hell now! I reckon at the rate you're going, Junior, you could have that damned thang loaded in about, say, thirty-five minutes or so." After dragging his tongue to wet his lips, he secured the pipe at the corner of his mouth once again.

James clasped his hands together, but not for long, nervous he began fiddling with a piece of bark he'd picked up off the ground.

"Damn, look at you Junior pourin' sweat like a . . . hungover pulpwooder." Calvin laughed. Clearly James was having a hard time finding something to do with his fingers after dropping the piece of bark to the ground.

"Is there something wrong with you, James?" I asked.

"Oh no, no . . . there's nothing wrong at all!" But his answer may have come too quickly. Calvin's long suspicious look, like a private eye and Sherlock Holmes at that was in the way he studied James, with shifty eyes and dragging his pipe from one corner of his mouth to the other. Then as if he'd come to a final conclusion, he slowly removed it.

"You want to load that truck like right now, don't you, Junior?" James nodded sheepishly while looking directly at Calvin. "Then by God, we'll load 'er!" Calvin stood up, brushing the last of the sawdust from his clothes. "That's right after I get this sawdust out of my shoes." We laughed as he dumped a good size mound on top of the log, going on and on about not having socks on. He said that he only had one pair, and it was the old lady's turn to wear them for the day. His feet always smelled pretty bad, and I'd learned to get upwind in a hurry. Halfway through tying the second shoestring, he looked over at me.

"Now tell me the truth, Arnold Ray. Don't you thank the old lady looks sexier with them socks pulled up just past them big ole knee knuckles of hers? She told me the other mornin' the only way I could get 'em back was that I had to take'um offen of her. That's the day I was late getting to work, if you remember. I'd say it all lasted for about an hour or so, with her kickin' and screamin' before I finally got 'em off. Why, hell, I thought she was just in a wrestlin' mood until she explained that I'd missed the whole point. She went on and on why the lamp and transistor radio both was turned down so low. I still hadn't gotten it until she chased me out the door, hollering that I needed to talk to ole Arnie Ray hay about all her wants and needs."

"You're crazy, Calvin," I said in my defense, thinking maybe James wasn't paying that much attention, lost in a different world of his own for sure. I thought how gleefully Calvin acted, thinking he knew why James had gone off the deep end.

"All...righty, let's load that damned truck, boys." Calvin stood up leading the way. For the next couple hours we must have looked like a hill of busy ants carrying stick after stick, throwing them onto the trucks bed. No doubt that keeping up with James, we'd loaded it in record time.

"There's that load fer tomar, Junior." Calvin winked at me as if he knew something I didn't. "Or are you gonna take it on down this evening?" He winked once more before looking down at his watch less wrist. "Now there's just enough time to get there, Junior—that's if you get on the road say, right now," Calvin hinted.

James scrambled up the side of the truck while I secured the hooks at the bottom, then tossed the chains binders on up to him. Securing the load down could well have been a record also.

"See you later!" he said before driving off in a hurry. I realized Calvin was on to something when in a rare occurrence, James grinded the gears between shifts evidently in too much of a hurry.

"Slow down there Junior too many rpm's!" Calvin yelled. "We sure as hell don't want ta load that damn thang again." We walked back to our shaded break area with Calvin having more pep in his step, and with thoughts somewhere else it would appear.

"Hell, Arnold Ray let's take one of them long breaks the kind ole Jimbo wouldn't approve of." Calvin plopped down on the end of the log that he'd claimed as his spot from day one and for that reason we'd not taken it to the mill to be cut into lumber, or at least not for now.

"Thirsty as hell," he'd always say before scooping his gallon water jug up and gulping it down as fast as the small opening would regurgitate air. And seeing that I didn't have much left in mine, he'd try to make me laugh and blow it out of my mouth. He'd try anything from rolling his eyes in circles to pushing his pipe up his nose for a drag. I'd learned to quickly look away any time his swaying pipe got near his nostrils since I'd almost choke to death the first time I'd seen it.

But neither of us had ever asked the other for a drink from their jug. It was common practice that if either ran out before the other, we'd both go for a fill-up at the same time. "Take a break and bullshit in a cool place," Calvin called it. I was glad with what he said over in Pike County, that he didn't like drinking after other people—not even the old lady, after all he laughed, 'I know where her mouths been'. Not only was his remark vile but the grin that came with it I'd never doubt.

I thought of what he said over in Pike County when he'd bring his quart jar with him to the well for a drink of water. He talked about some of the people who stopped by for a drink.

"Now there ain't nothing worse than a mouth full of bloody snags getting hung up on the rim of the dipper. And the ones with no teeth at all are just as bad, gumming the damn thang with their snotty noses shoved all the way to the bottom of the dipper."

Most people knew without saying that chewing and smoking baccer was the biggest contributor to why so many people's teeth were gone. And even though there'd be money for all forms of baccer, there'd never be enough for a toothbrush, let alone toothpaste. Sadly, it was another thing that didn't fall under the bare necessities of life. The old man, like so many, lost his teeth at a young age. And it did seem, however, that those who preached the word of God were the first to get them all pulled out and get dentures for that Reverend looking smile.

I thought back how James and I had remedied the problem with the taste of baccer on Mr. Cox's dipper. No matter how long we scrubbed our hands at the well to drink from them, there'd still be dirt lodged deep in the calluses and fingernails. But we agreed that they were still cleaner than the rim of the dipper and didn't have the taste of baccer on them. But why would I drink from a flowery cup stashed neatly under some touch-me-nots at Kincaid Springs and not even know the person who drank from it? Maybe I didn't think of them as being smokers by taking the time to hide such treasures.

It was commonly known that lots of sicknesses were brought home from school, but it was the passing of the dipper that spread it like a plague throughout our family, and it could go on for weeks on end. For many years, we was simply ignorant to the fact that the dipper was nothing more than a bacteria garden.

We tried to keep a clean one when such visitors would stop by for a drink at the well. Eye contact from family members told that the dipper would need to be washed off after that person left. I'd always longed to have two dippers at our well: one just for the old man and visitors and the other for our family only. James laughed at the thought saying we should separate the two by writing the words baccer users on one of them.

We grabbed up our containers where I poured what was left in mine over my head to wet my hair down; too warm to drink anyway. The springs were just over the hill from the old abandoned house and not far from the laydown yard. I'd throw rocks from the laydown yard and on several occasions heard them land with a thump in the muddy area where it drained. Calvin declared we should take time to soak our feet in the cold water for a while. I'd stumble about until he'd taken his shoes off and seated himself. With Calvin knowing how bad his feet smelt he'd not question when I'd settle upstream from him some little ways off.

"So what do you think's wrong with James?" I blurted. "And how in the world did you know that he wanted to take that load to Chillicothe today?" He didn't answer right off the bat but stood up and straddled the small stream, sloshing his handkerchief back and forth to wet it down. I laughed to myself with all the grunting sounds he was making.

"Well, they ain't no guessin' about 'er, Arnold Ray. It's kindly like this . . ." He carefully washed the sweat from his eyes. I could see a wait coming on before he'd answer when he plopped back down. I'd never seen Calvin put so much care into prepping for a smoke, gently laying his pipe and baccer out across his legs all neat like the way Harry would have done it. And as badly as I wanted to hear his thoughts, it wouldn't be until after he'd taken his first satisfying drag that his 'words of wit', as he'd call them, would come forth.

"Arnold Ray, it's pretty simple: old Junior's got his head up his ass." What followed was the most satisfying plume of smoke I'd ever seen flow from Calvin's mouth clouding the small cove area with no breeze to blow it away.

"Shit, you got to be kidding me!" I blurted, sounding a little disappointed. "I waited all that damn time for you to tell me that shit? Hell, I already knew that about James, Calvin!" I joked with a nervous laugh knowing there was more to it than that. Calvin seeing right through me made himself more comfortable, drawing his bare feet from the water then stomping his heels deep into the moistened bank.

"Now it ain't just a plain ole case of havin' your head up your ass Arnold Ray, like we all get every once in a while. But this is way more serious than any of that. Now there's things at your age, maybe you don't quite understand Arnold Ray." He said while drawing in a full breath of air. I exhaled quickly, realizing I'd followed his lead and had filled my lungs also.

"I thank your brother's found himself a woman Arnold Ray." Calvin smiled with a crazy nod like I'd never seen from him before.

"Oh no, there's no way, Calvin. Why, he'd a told me right off the bat if he found a girlfriend! We've been talking about girls for a while now, but they ain't been nothin' said about findin' one yet."

"Well, I guarantee, he's at least smellin' around on somethin!" I had to turn away from his sudden stare which questioned if I knew the meaning of what smelling around was all about. I knew however it could have been worse had he got right to the point as he'd often do and with no consideration that it might be embarrassing for me. I always liked it better when James was around. I thought back to the time when Calvin told us over in Pike County that he didn't know any fancy words that might make him sound smarter.

"Stuck with what I got," and he sounded proud of it. "If they's don't understand what I'm tryin' to tell 'em, then they can all kiss my big red hairy ass," he boasted that day and more than likely would back it up if needed. Calvin had simply spent most of his life away from those people who might challenge his inelegance and even try and correct him.

He was content with who he was, a man stuck in the woods, for the rest of his life. And in my opinion, there could never be a better person than Calvin with his constant flow of vulgarity in common talk or, the jokes and poetry he told. Even though I'd become much wiser since Pike County I knew I didn't completely understand his meaning of James smelling around on a girl. I knew however that I could talk freely with him about it whenever I got the nerve.

I had no intentions of staying in the woods for the rest of my life as Calvin had done. There was something very bright about the trips James and I'd make to Greenfield. And with the idea there was something possibly better, excited me even more. James said on one of our outings that he thought music had a lot to do with how outgoing one's life might be. But for now, I'd do as I did in Pike County, laugh right along with Calvin as if I knew exactly what he was talking about.

"Arnold Ray, you ain't gonna believe what's fixin' to happen with old Junior. I'm just givin' ya fair warnin'." And like Sherlock Holmes would do, Calvin bit down on the end of his pipe; now the case of why James had his head up his ass had been solved.

"Well, you could be right, Calvin. I think he's old and smart enough, but he hain't got time to look for a girlfriend. Shit, I'm with 'um 'bout all the time, and it just ain't happened."

"I can see right now, Arnold Ray, that you need a lesson about this stuff. Why, it just takes a split second for an old gal to look you in the eyes and it's . . . all over then. You either fall in love or think you are, and then have nightmares for the rest of your life, like I do with that hag a mine!" He laughed.

"And nine out ta ten times, it'd be better to run away and even hide out if you needed to. And if you don't then what happens is you get sucked in, and well, we'll know in a few days how bad a case old Junior's got." Calvin looked stone faced in the way he sat there with such heavy concentration. I thought it better that I change the subject for time being.

"Hey, what's this shit about the old man buying a stand of timber down your ways is that true?"

"Yeah, he did, and it's exactly twelve and a half miles from my front door to that old woman's gate. I'll get to be in my own bed for about a month or so, it looks! Why hell old Jimbo says you boys might even come down and work weekends with me. Now that'd be good I think don't you Arnold Ray."

"Well, it's all new news to me, Calvin, other than what little bit James told me about. But I'd rather be left out in the cold than have to talk to the old man about anything." It surprised me that Calvin hadn't started in with Mary having me a place to stay. "And when's it gonna start, Calvin? Or has he even told you that?"

"Well, let's see . . . If you can believe anythin' your ole man says, it won't be long—more of that quick cash scheme he talks about all the damned time. You know, the funny thing, though, Arnold Ray, is he says he's gonna deliver the logs to the mill himself! Can you believe that one? He probably forgot how to even drive that big red truck?"

"Well, how in the hell's he goin' ta do that and still have time to come up here and go out frolickin?" I questioned.

"That's his business, not mine, Arnold Ray. But I do know that it's gettin' late, and I need to get my draggin' ass on to the house and see what that woman fixed to eat." We filled our jugs up placing them along the edge of the springs where dripping water from sandstone rocks would keep them cool till the next day. After a slow walk back to the laydown yard Calvin bid me farewell, then put the chainsaw in the back of his truck. With a couple good whacks of his pipe on the side of the door, he waved before driving off.

The clock's hands moved slowly, stalling at times, I thought waiting for James with great anticipation that Calvin might be right. There had to be something . . . it was eleven o'clock then shortly after midnight, I heard the truck coming down the road from a distance.

"Man, what happened to you?" I asked with him halfway in the door. "Did you break down somewhere? Do you know what time it is, James?" My pointed questions hadn't put a dent in his smile.

"Shouldn't you be sleeping by now?" he asked, taking one of his shoes off. "You wouldn't believe me if I told you, Arnold. Man oh man!" He shook his head slightly.

"Look, don't start that bullshit this late in the night. Just tell me where in the hell you were at all this time." It didn't sound like I was asking, but more like begging, I thought to myself. "You know I was worried . . . that the truck got broke down or somethin' worse, like you might of got in a wreck and how would I ever have known?"

"Well, first of all, I'm not going to get in a wreck."

"Well, you don't know that! Remember those Kinsley boys that got run off the road and killed last year down on Knockemstiff Holler!"

"No, it wasn't anything like that." He laughed.

"You're just gonna fiddle fart around and not tell me, is that it?" I puffed.

"We'll talk about it in the morning when I'm more rested up from all that heavy kissing going on!"

Heavy kissing, the words seemed to echo throughout the small bus. Kissing as we knew it would be changed in its definition forever with him adding the word heavy I thought. "Did you say 'kiss . . . sing, I mean h...eavy kissing?" Something foreign seemed to have gotten stuck in my throat and no matter how many times I swallowed it still lingered there.

"I'll tell you in the morning," he said, climbing into bed. "It's just too hard to make my lips move much after what we did for hours on end." Sleep, as he'd suggested was the farthest thing on my mind? There was no way as my imagination ran wild with the word he'd used for being so tired. Kissing—had he really gotten a girlfriend and kissed her already? I couldn't imagine anything like that. I'd thought all along that you had to talk to them for at least once. But I had to believe that he'd done it, simply by how he acted and by what Calvin had proclaimed may be love at first sight.

I'd no sooner fallen asleep when awakened with laughter and James talking to himself. None of it made any sense at all—just a long, drawn-out slur of happiness, it sounded.

"James, wake up. You're having a bad dream," I said, shaking him slightly.

He quickly sat up, dazed as to where he was, before lying back down again; then came the sound of what could have been kissing just a minute later.

I snuck out of bed the next morning, leaving him to sleep a little longer. I hadn't gotten much myself because of him—and me trying to make out what he was saying all night long. But I'd no sooner gathered Kate and Mr. Bill up when I heard Big Red start up. He'd headed for the laydown yard in a hurry once again. And worse he'd not made our bacon and egg sandwiches.

I packed our normal lunch—bologna, tomato, and a few apples. I also took the time to make the bacon and egg sandwiches for us.

After watering the animals, we left the pond and hurried on to the laydown yard, where he was already cutting pulpwood up and had thrown quite a little jag on the truck. Calvin straddling his favorite log was sharpened his chain and all the while watching James work like a mad man.

"Well, it looks like ya got your socks back, Calvin!" I pointed. As fast as I'd ever seen, he snatched his pipe away, blowing smoke straight ahead but never taking his eyes off James.

"Yeah, I did, Arnie. But I had to take her ass to the floor again to get 'em off her! I've told 'er a hundred times how they help my sweaty feet, and all she can do is complain how cold hers get through the day. I've covered that whole damned floor up with cardboard and I'm tellin' ya, it don't get that cold. I've been good enough to let 'er use 'em every once in a while. But by God, after what happened this mornin', she can buyer own!" he finished.

"Has he said anythin' to you this morning?" I nodded in James's direction. Calvin leaned back on the log, coughing a time or two before looking my way.

"Yes . . . good morning."

"Ah, good morning . . .," I answered back quickly. "Well, what did he have to say?"

Calvin slowly removed his pipe once again leaving a trail of smoke. "Good morning."

"Good morning! I said 'good morning' already! Calvin, are you just messin' with me?"

"No, that's all, your brother said to me this morning, Arnold Ray . . . and without another word, he started loadin...' the truck.

My mind raced with the thought that James had actually kissed someone. I wanted to give him the sandwich and see if he'd talk about it now, but the way it looked, I didn't think he'd take time to even eat it. I put it on the driver's seat so he'd find it at some point. I took the animals on up into the woods to get our first load, taking my sandwich with me.

"Woo," I said with my best gravelly voice. I had a good view of James through an opening between two trees. After falling a good size Oak tree he shut the saw off gently laying it on the ground. After brushing the sawdust from his hands, he started beating on his chest, followed by possibly the best Tarzan yell he'd ever attempted. And it wasn't just me that'd heard his call of the wild. Calvin whirled momentarily, and after shaking his head, before going on back to work.

"Hey Tarzan," I yelled. "What in the hell has got into you?"

He held an open hand behind his ear, as if an invite to talk with him. I left the horses and ran back down the trail to where he sat with clasped hands nervous in a way I thought.

"Well, are you ready to tell me all about that . . . kiss? Or were you bullshitting me last night?" His pleasurable smile left little doubt that it wasn't the latter. "You kept me awake laughin' in your dreams and now, you're runnin' around here actin' like you could whip half the jungle," I joked.

CHAPTER 2

Scarlett

He leaned back, while comfortably locking his fingers behind his head.

"Do you remember Scarlett Radcliff?" he asked with a questioning smile.

"Yeah, I do our cousin Ezell and Anna Fay's daughter? Man, it's been forever since I've seen her . . . She must be all growed up by now so where'd you run into her at? Wait let me guess . . . she introduced you to a friend, right?" I teased that I'd already figured it all out. But his hesitation seemed lengthy I thought.

"Come on, James, tell me what her name is, damn-it."

"Well, I can tell you it's not Damn-it and that's for sure. And as you know, she's not related to us by blood in any way. She's from Anna Fay's first marriage." Something had become lodged in my throat it felt at what James was trying to tell me. A blow that would momentarily take my breath away.

"Scarlett . . . is your girlfriend?" Her name quickly become poisonous in the way it flooded my mind with thoughts of incest and everything else that made it all wrong.

"James, are you tellin' me that you kissed our cousin last night and on the mouth at that? You got to tell me you're shittin' me and this is all a joke! That's not right, and you know it. You were brought up better than that! It's something the old man might do, but not you, James! This ain't even funny, so tell me it ain't so." I pleaded.

"What started out with kissing turned to love overnight. I'm in love Arnold." My stomach heaved at how quickly he'd gone from just kissing to falling in love.

"So, you're not kidding, are you? You really did kiss our cousin in the mouth?"

54

"Well, of course I did, dumbass! Why else would I be acting like this!" His laugh was spontaneous. "Love is wonderful! It's unbelievable how it feels when you put your lips against hers, and the night just flies by when you're into heavy kissing! Why, some of the kisses last fifteen to twenty minutes . . . You'll understand what I'm saying someday, Arnold."

"James, you just don't get it do ya? You can't be in love with Scarlett 'ca-cause she's our... cousin and it is forbidden by law anyway." There was nothing awkward in the way he laid there rolling his head side to side as to disagree with me. But it was the faraway look that told me his mind was somewhere else. Then as if something went off in his head he jumped to his feet brushing leaves and debris from his clothes.

"You're right. She is our cousin, but as you already know it's not by blood." And just when I thought it couldn't get any worse, he started snapping his fingers to find the right beat before breaking out into an Elvis song. "Well, she's my kissin' cousin, and that'll make it all right, all right . . . all right!" Suddenly, I felt the need to throw up thinking how he and Scarlett must have sung that very song their first time together.

"Look, her last name is Radcliff!" I yelled trying to disrupt the song that I never wanted to hear for the rest of my life, "and so what does that make her? She's related to us. You can't do this, James! Ain't you worried what people will think when they find out?" I slammed my fist against my knee in protest.

"Nope, she's not blood, and that's that. They can talk all they want I don't really care. In the end, they'll just have to get over it."

"Sh..., don't talk so damn loud. Calvin might hear us." I quickly glanced over my shoulder.

"You don't get it either, Arnold. Now listen to me! There's nothing wrong with what we're doing!" His sharp smile seemed to have some kind of justification to it. "And if you only knew what love was like . . . you'd—why, you'd be out there practicing kissing old Kate right now!"

"Do what?" I shouted. Calvin turned quickly to see what all the commotion was about.

"I'm just kidding about Kate . . . but you wait when you kiss that first girl, the world changes right in front of your eyes. I feel like a new person and can't wait to see her again tonight!"

"You mean you're gonna stop over there again?" I continued bitching.

"Oh yeah, and I can't wait to get lip-locked as soon as I can."

"Get . . . what?" I asked.

"Lip-locked is what Scarlett calls it after thirty minutes." He laughed in a naughty way.

"Dammit Junior, you can kiss for thirty minutes?" Calvin roared loudly, walking up on us. "Hell! If I could go for thirty minutes, the old lady might put old Arnie here down the road!" He laughed and in his haste dropped his pipe. "And did I hear you say you got some the first time out?" Calvin's eyes lit up like a new light bulb as he ran a forefinger around the pipes rim to clean the dirt off.

"I think we're talking about two different things, Calvin." James laughed.

"Now I'm tellin' ya right now Junior don't start out the wrong way. If'n you do I'll garintee' you'll regret it."

"And how's that, Calvin?" he asked as we all settled down on the closest logs.

"Don't waste all your time just kissin'! Find out, right off the bat, if she's gonna give you any or not! Why, hell, some of them old gals just want ta' lay around kissin' and never want to screw! You're still a youngin' Junior so go forth and sow them wild oats while ya still can! You can think about all that love shit when you get older. That's all I got to say, I'm just tellin ya to think about it . . . I'm goin' back to work." He stood up slowly, waddling back to where he'd left his saw. I'd held my breath all the while hoping Calvin wouldn't ask her name.

"And me too!" I jumped up, storming off. I hooked Mr. Bill up to a good-size log, sending him over the hill and a minute later, Kate, would follow.

James and I didn't talk much for the rest of the day even though there was plenty I wanted to say. I wondered if the *Reader's Digest* had prepared him for anything like this. But there was no doubt about it, he was happy in the way he was gliding smoothly from one tree to the other. Even the way he sharpened the saw's chain looked orchestrated in the way he pushed and pulled the file between each of the chains teeth.

I thought of what Calvin said about eye contact and the chance of getting hypnotized right off the bat. That surely must be what happened to James. *He didn't stand a chance*, I thought to myself. It must have been quick for him. But what single thing led to them looking each other in the eyes in the first place? I'd figured by knowing they were cousins, they would have looked the other way.

We worked the rest of the week with James going to Scarlett's place every night. I could hardly get his attention through the day no matter what I'd say. And to make it worse, the old man had started questioning Calvin on James's whereabouts and why he was always late getting back from Chillicothe.

"Why, hell! He didn't get out of here till what, a quarter till four was it, Arnold Ray?" he frowned, looking my way. He'd lied to the old man knowing of the adventure James was having. For him to uphold for James was one thing but what would his reaction be if he found out who James was in love with. He'd never let me forget it and I just knew it. I wanted to scream at the very thought.

Present and past love songs flowed from James's mouth for the biggest part of the days that followed. He knew all the words to "You're My Soul and Inspiration" and sang it more than most others. He sang songs that I'd not heard of yet, telling me that he and Scarlett listened to them all the time and of course lip-locked all the while. He went on to say that kissing was a lot like a song and best when you got to the chorus.

He didn't care anytime Calvin or I made fun of the way he acted. He went along with all the teasing we could dish out, laughing right along with us. He'd always liked to sing; but it was nothing like now, putting his heart and soul into every word, it sounded. Constantly trying to interrupt him during such songs didn't work either. He simply wouldn't stop until it was finished and, worse, looked as though he were singing them to me.

I'd laugh anytime one of Calvin's predictions came true with the craziness James was going through. And it didn't bother him anytime we'd refer to him as having his head up his ass. But my reasoning was somewhat different than Calvin's always fearful that James might slip and the truth come out about Scarlett.

"And I guess by now you've heard that stupid laugh of his Calvin?" I asked one day when James was gone to Chillicothe.

"Hell, that ain't nothin', Arnold Ray. Wait till he starts walkin' on his hands and climbing trees after they've already been cut down." Calvin roared with laughter. James had never been much to whistle but chirped like a robin in the springtime now. The Tarzan yells became more and more frequent, but calling me Jane had stopped altogether. I guess he'd found the real Jane in his life as he'd fallen head over heels with Scarlett.

"The weekend's here . . .!" he yelled, snapping the binder shut to secure the load for a Monday morning delivery. He stood at the top of the load and with his hands placed at the corners of his mouth he unleashed one of his best Tarzan yells. The practice had made him much better and to the point that I wouldn't do mine around him. Even Calvin had complimented how good he was at it.

"Bout time for a Kiss!" He yelled to us, quickly removed his shirt flexing his arms like one of those musclemen on the beaches in California. He was clearly defined, stomach and all. I wasn't puny by any means after loading ten tons of wood a day, but James was just stronger and always would be.

It hadn't been but a few days that he celebrated beating Calvin for the first time in arm wrestling. He simply outlasted him, even though Calvin was the stronger of them. Several times, Calvin had almost pinned him, but James gradually worked his arm back up till Calvin finally gave in. But there wasn't much celebration on his part when he announced that the score was at least 30 to 1 in Calvin's favor! But Calvin knew without saying that his winning all the time had come to an end. He'd continually sized James up when he was around and stated that he'd know when ole Junior got him some, as he called it.

"Well, how would you ever know that?" I pried. "I mean look at the way he acts now!" I was sincere with my question but didn't want Calvin to get out of control with his answer.

"Arnold Ray, the only thang I can tell ya is we better get all these trees cut down 'afore old Junior starts climbin' and fallin' out of 'em," he teased with a wilder than ever look in his eyes.

"Well now, I can see there's no reason to invite Junior, but maybe we can all get together sometime this weekend down at old Harry's gatherin' place—and frolic a little on the front porch-bein' we ain't got no money to go frolickin' any other place, like say ole Jimbo does!" A devilish grin came to his face. With a fresh load of baccer stuffed tightly into his pipe, he headed down the holler that led to his shack. He'd gotten to where he didn't drive his old truck much saying it used too much oil.

I tended to the animals, and on the way back to the bus, I saw James heading for the Dodge. He'd washed and cleaned up with his shirtsleeves rolled up to the elbows. I knew there wasn't a hair out of place; he'd been applying Brylcream lately to make sure of that. No doubt he looked handsome where the cream seemed to put a sparkle throughout his hair, just like the commercial on TV.

"Hey, James!" I waved from the distance. "Give me about five minutes, and I'll be ready to go!" I said, hustling toward the bus. "We are goin' cruisin', up at Greenfield ain't we?" I joked.

"Not tonight, old buddy. I've got a . . . date!" He turned back toward the Dodge, making a final adjustment to turn his shirt collar up, something else he did a lot of lately. *Like Elvis*, I thought, *going to see his kissing cousin.*

"Well . . . I guess I'll see you later then." Without much acknowledgment, he waved while getting in his car. Seeing that Harry had been taking it all in from his swing he gave him a salute before driving off. Harry's invite was always open, wanting to hear of everything that went on that day.

"How are you doin', Harry?" I asked after jumping the fence. He nodded his head and smiled.

"Arnold, come on over here, and let's chat for a while . . .," he said, sliding a little closer to his side of the swing. I adjusted to his rhythm, which seemed a little fast tonight, maybe moonshine had something to do with it I thought. I'd noticed the way he held his mouth awkwardly trying to keep his upper dentures in place, was when he'd get a loose talkative tongue. "Now where in the hell . . . is old Junior goin' all spiffed up like that? Why, by hell, he sneaks away 'bout every night, I've noticed."

"Oh, I don't guess you've heard yet, have you, Harry? Why . . . James has got his head up his ass right now!"

Harry quickly pulled his pipe, frowning and looking all puzzled at me. "Why this son-of-a-bitchen thang . . ." He fiddled around with the earpiece.

"Now I thought old Junior sure had an awful big smile on his face when he left here. And, Arnold, he's a handsome feller at that! But. . . what did you say was wrong with his head?" Harry leaned closer, holding his pipe off to the side.

"He's got his head up his ass, Harry!" I spoke loud and clear as though I were the one who'd first passed such judgment on him. "Calvin told me all about it and was right on the money of what James is goin' through." Harry slid all the way back in the swing studying what I'd told him. He tried several times to speak, maybe confused with what to say first.

"Now you're tellin' me, Arnold, that Junior's in love?" He frowned.

I was surprised that Harry came to the same conclusion as Calvin had. It surely must be from an old saying of sort but was all new to me. "Why, I can understand that at his age. But by God, if anybody's got their heads up their ass, it's Jim and Calvin! Now I don't know if you knew it or not, but Jim picks Mary up and takes her all over the damned place while ole Cal's up there workin' his ass off in them woods! And to be truthful, I don't know that Calvin even gives a damn, Arnold Ray."

"Well, I can tell ya, Harry, that it's not whatcha think. It was the same way when Calvin helped us over in Pike County. We suspected the old man and her runnin' 'round, but it wasn't like that at all. We were sure wrong about 'er, and that's why Calvin tolerates it, I think. She's not like the old man. I really don't think Mary would run around on Calvin. She tries to be funny and don't mind flirtin', but I think that's about it."

Harry looking my way slowly shook his head to disagree. And it wasn't just the things with Mary that he seemed so upset about. Lately any time the old man's name came up he was quick to judge and condemn him for just about anything. But I suspected there was something else bothering him hiding behind those dark blue eyes. I'd not nag him for an answer however fearing he'd say something that might upset me also.

On several occasions, he'd brought up the incident of the old man standing him up and not taking him to the Fiddlers contest. It didn't matter that James took him it was the damned principle of it all, he argued. Our gatherings on the front porch had become more frequent with old Harry being left behind more often. There were other incidents he'd talk about such as building the new house. But the one he'd linger on the longest especially after a few shots of moonshine was how he got screwed out of hearing mom and the sisters sing.

"Build a house or to hear them sing' Arnold. Why, do you honestly think either will ever come to pass?" Sounding shitty in the way he'd asked the question. "Hell, if Jim didn't have such a wild hair up his ass all the time I'd have already heard um when they all stood right there." he pointed to a general location with the stem of his pipe." Now frustrated with the matter he started tapping his pipe on the arm, and not in his normal way of letting the embers fall into an empty Prince Albert can that sat next to the swing. But this time he caught them in a cupped hand quickly released them to where the embers slowly flaked to the floor. "Why, Jim wanted to whisk them out of here as fast as he could, so they didn't have time to do anything. And by-God I've been mad ever since! Now you tell me what would've made the difference if they stayed here for just a . . . few more minutes so I could hear 'em sing . . . at least one damned song?"

"Well I'll tell you why, Harry." I stood up to stretch my legs. "He knows the only thing Mom and the girls will sing is Christian songs, and that's the one thing that he doesn't want to hear right now 'cause the devil's having his way with him whipin' his ass!" I felt bad that I wasn't completely honest with Harry about the old man not wanting to hear Christian songs. It wouldn't have mattered what kind of song it would have been with him acting like a complete asshole that day.

I'd discovered over time that whether Harry was finished or not with any complaint he'd always leave an opening at the end of a tirade with a chance that one might quickly change the subject.

"Well, like James said, Harry, after they get moved up here and get settled down, I'm sure you'll get to hear them sing. Why, you'll get tired of hearin' 'um" I joked knowing he'd have something for sure to say about that.

"Oh now, I doubt that, Arnold," he shook his head in an earnest way. The final tell-tale that he was calming down came when the swing slowed considerably. In one motion, he leaned forward crossing one leg over the other and quickly resting an elbow just above the knee cap. From that familiar position, he'd gently hold his pipe ready for a quick draw when he needed.

"Now those little sisters of yours sure are pretty thangs." He winked as his anger subsided.

"You know Judy sings . . . and she also plays the piano." I said. I'd thought maybe the old man would have told Harry of Judy's wonderful talents. But evidently not by the way he quickly withdrew his pipe from a puckered mouth while trailing a short string of saliva.

"Sh... She does?" He stuttered suddenly beaming with excitement! "Why, I've got that piano in there." he said, pointing a thumb over his shoulder. "And by God, she can come play it all she wants. Anytime! All day, I don't give a damn." There was a desperate plea in Harry's offering, that of a lonely old man it sounded. Maybe it was hope that kept Harry around for all these years. Hope that someone ask him to tell a story that might kindle the spark in his eyes once again like seeing his first car.

"Well what do ya do with all those instruments in that room, Harry?" Maybe I'd asked the perfect question as he looked more comfortable now than ever. I watched it all transpire right in front of me with his usual pose and thought what a picture if James would ever take up painting again. He'd showed me a picture one time when he was looking for something to carve, a sculpture called, The Thinker. Harry's pose was equal or at least I thought so, to the famous piece of art with the big difference being the person in the famous sculpture would be many years behind Harry with thought or his pose.

"Why, Arnold, I played in several bands over the years and an orchestra once. He bragged. But most all them old-timers I played with are all dead and gone to hell now!" He laughed, slightly shrugging his shoulders. "Why, we had get-togethers right here in the old days when that room was filled up with pickers and players. And by God sometimes it got so crowded that some had to come out here on the front porch and play. Hell, ole John 'Big Fergie' Ferguson even wrote a song about it called 'Knockin' and a Bangin' on the Front Porch Door.'"

In Harry's broad smile and a slightly tilted chin Big Fergie's front porch song was captured momentarily and reflected in the old feller's gaze. It didn't take much imagination to put myself on this front porch with Harry and his friends as his foot softly tapped to the song which I'd never hear the words to.

"But you know, Arnold, when I go with Jim, I get to play a little. I cain't keep up like I used to, and sometimes I get a little too drunk!" He laughed, closing both eyes for an instant. "I guess I'm just gettin' too old to hang with 'um anymore."

I'd seen the look before when Harry had a sad moment, gazing off toward Whiskey Holler, the place of his roots. And in that moment, I could study the face of a person born just ten years after the Civil War had ended. I wondered what secrets made him live so long. Whatever, maybe even the moonshine had something to do with him making it ninety years. Ever since he'd told of the time he'd seen his first car pass through Greenfield as a young boy, I yearned for more. I wanted to hear all I could in fear that, at his age, he might not be around much longer.

Being around moonshine or any other drink wasn't anything new to us. We'd seen the old man drunk on all of them at one time or the other. And it did seem that shine could tend to put a mean streak in people, thinking old Harry was teetering toward that right now. In hopes of calming him back down with something a little funnier, I told the story about Barbra and the old man the time Mom threw the bucket of cold water in her face, hitting her right between the eyes and so putting an end to her passing out in the old man's arms. As the detailed images grew, so did the expressions on old Harry's face, laughing as hard as I'd ever seen him. But the image of her eyes bugged out was Harry's favorite, with him wanting me to tell it once again.

"By hell, Arnold, I'd give a new dime to've seen that." He reared back, slapping himself on the leg. "And by God, I'll bet that puckered old Jim's asshole up a little too!"

"Yeah, Mom sure performed a miracle that day, no doubt about it." I laughed with Harry as he declared the same as with so many other stories that being the funniest dammed thing he'd ever heard in his lifetime. It did seem though that he'd been drinking more lately, maybe because of the way the old man had left him high and dry, not part of his frolicking scene much anymore.

Maybe just the right amount of shine set the old fellow off like it had. Another way that he'd prep himself for a night of drinking was when he'd lay a navy blue handkerchief across his lap to wipe his eyes and blow his nose when needed.

"By God, Arnold, now that was a sobering laugh," he said, spitting out into the yard. The swing sat silent as he removed his pipe from the cut hole once again all the while shaking his head with a satisfied grin. After a good long drag, he was ready to complain in a more civil way.

"Arnold, there's some things I can't figure, though. Now your mother seems like a good woman," he said, shifting somewhat in the swing to face me. "And you tell me why, when he's got a woman like that, would he want to act like he does? It's awful, when he gets out drinkin'... Hell, I'm embarrassed when he brings one of those . . . whatever they are . . . and introduces them to me. Hell, I've been to them places a many a time and watched some of the ugliest women turn into beauty queens right in front of my own eyes, but that's of course with a head full of alcohol. But he'll drink and carry on with anything that's got two legs, and they probably wouldn't even need them, if the truth be told," he said matter-of-factly.

"Harry, I could talk forever about the shit he's done, but it just ain't worth me getting all riled up right now. And I can also tell ya it ain't the end of his asshole ways, as you're gradually findin' out." His frown deepened.

"Well, you know, Arnold, over the years, there's been times that people's taken advantage of my goodwill just like Jim. I mean I've always treated people the way I'd wanted them to treat me, you might say. But sometimes I thank— and that's even my best friends—folks ain't no better than a bunch of vultures waiting to pick your bones clean. Hell, do I look that close to death?" He reared back a little wobbly, giving me a solemn look as he rubbing his thin leg.

"Now ole Jim told me he was married when I met 'um the first time, and I thought he was genuine. Hell, it didn't take but a few days we'd become good friends and shortly after started goin' out Honky-Tonkin'. I'm tellin' ya I was havin' the time of my life." After a little thought, he continued, "But it seems I always tend to find things out the hard way. I get so lonely out here by myself all the time that maybe I jump too quick at the opportunity to make a friend.

And it ain't just been Jim. There's been plenty others by God." Harry began comparing some of the others to the old man when he told of a couple of men who used to stop by every now and again, drank a little shine, and played some music with him.

"Hell, a couple times, they borrowed a little money for gas. Right then and there, damn it, I should've put their asses down the road. It just seems like the best friends are those who don't ask for money. And wouldn't you know it, Arnold, the two son-za-bitches stopped comin around as soon as they found somebody else to screw out of money. And do ya think I got mine back? I don't know about Jim, but it's startin' to look like he's gonna be like all . . . the rest."

It was sad the way Harry sounded as if he'd used that very line before. He talked of others, such as the two ladies who cleaned his house for him once a week. He'd said he had no living relatives, but both still called him Uncle Harry all the time. He'd figured that all they wanted was for him to leave his place to them so their lazy-ass no-account daughters would have a place of their own. I don't say anything to 'em, by hell. They can clean all they want, but I ain't a signin' a dammed thing over to any of 'em!" He laughed.

"Listen!" I held a steady hand out in front of us. "Harry . . . it sounds like you're gonna have more company here in the minute . . ."

"What about a minute?" he asked hastily adjusting his hearing aid. His frown got me snickering when it became obvious he'd picked up on the sound of Calvin's truck coming up the road. His mouth gaped open, now feverishly trying to turn the aid back down as Calvin turned the motor off, coasting to a stop under the big tree.

"By God, Arnold, I think that truck's on far!" He pointed. Calvin's truck wasn't just a clunker; he'd called it every other name in the book. Harry had worked up a good-size puff in preparation for them. "Why, 'ell Arno! I cain't nell if 'ats Calvin's pipe or his truck 'mokin' now 'at I get lookin' at 'er!"

His tongue had gotten too relaxed from the shine, making it hard to hold his upper dentures in place. There was a fix however and looked pretty natural, I'd guessed, he'd done many times. By rolling his fingers like a cheerleader would a baton, he'd situate his pipe between the second and third fingers. Like something well practiced, he brought both thumbs up and, in a split second, shoved his plate back in its place. I snickered, thinking how quickly the old man would hunker down behind the pulpit for such an adjustment.

I thought that someday I might mention to Harry about Poligrip. I couldn't imagine that he'd not heard of it though. There were many times the old man bragged of it, saying if it could hold a Southern Baptist minister's teeth in through a whole sermon of hellfire and brimstone, then it met the challenge.

"And you just try 'er out on a hot fried chicken leg! Then you'll know exactly what I'm sayin'!" But then I had a private laugh picturing Harry drunk on shine and trying to pry his teeth out of his mouth late in the night.

All us kids watched the first time the old man tried Poligrip out. He didn't read the instructions, applying way too much; and while the whole mess was still in his mouth, he took a finger, rubbing along the edges of his gum and plate to scrape the excess away. My stomach could deal with cow shit between my toes better than the string of saliva that trailed the white goo-covered finger when he withdrew it from his mouth.

"Now, boys!" Calvin roared, pushing Mary through the small gate as if she was too big to get through it on her own. "You're goin' to have to stop makin' fun of the old lady like at!" Mary drew back with a hard slap to his shoulder.

"Now you mind your mouth, mister," she said as they neared the porch. It sounded as if they'd been quarreling, I thought. I moved to the porch's edge, giving Mary my place in the swing beside Harry. The swing was positioned directly in front of Calvin, who had the perfect view while sagged up against the porch's corner post, making himself comfortable. I sat several feet away, enough to distance myself from the smoke as Calvin started loading his pipe. It looked funny, seeing old skinny Harry sitting there with big-boned Mary jostling to straighten her dress somewhat. Harry looked thin and cramped while grasping tightly on to the chain, showing his white knuckles.

"Has anybody seen that old man of yers today?" Calvin's eyes surveyed as he blew smoke into the air.

"No, but then again, I'm not really looking for him either." My smart-ass answer brought a coughing laugh from Mary. "Why, was he supposed to be here?" I asked, thinking I'd stopped Calvin a little short.

"Well now, you tell me, Arnold Ray. I mean if *I* and this old heifer here are supposed to eat next week, I think he needs to pay me the money he owes me." It was funny hearing Calvin say "I" instead of "me." Harry had gotten us all hooked on it, which we'd turned into a joke, with Calvin of course getting the most out of it.

I wouldn't dare tell him that James and I were getting paid at the end of every week and the rest being put in the bank for us. I glanced at him, remembering what he'd told me about the old man being so far in debt that he couldn't pay his bills on time. But we'd taken many loads out since then, with James figuring he should be ahead with all bills by now.

"And where's ole Junior, or need I ask?" Calvin looked around, grunting wildly and scratching his face through his beard.

"I'll give you two guesses, Calvin," I blurted.

"Hell, I don't need two, Arnold Ray. Why, he's out gettin' some, and that's way better than I'm doing!" It was that split second in time that nothing was said when Mary's mouth dropped open with a look that even Calvin should've dreaded, I thought.

Suddenly, as if a hard wind had come up, Mary backed the swing up as far as it would go and, with a shove, sailed forward, making a stab at kicking Calvin. Time and time again, she repeated it, backing up farther every time while he fended her off with his hands. She made no effort to keep her dress pulled down, which was halfway up her thighs, showing her big legs.

There was no funning around on her part; she wanted to kick Calvin in the face, and no doubt about it, as he weaved his head back and forth like a prize fighter. Tears streamed down my face as I had to look away to catch my breath and not so much for the way they acted, but the way old Harry was being flung all over the place in his swing. It was as if she'd forgotten that the old fellow was even there, more violent with every attempt. Just when old Harry'd stabilize his end of the swing, Mary'd take off again, sending him either flying way out in front of her or almost slamming the wall behind him. He grasped the chain with both hands now, and with his pipe clamped tightly in his mouth hung on for dear life it looked.

Mary seemed to have the energy of a little girl trying to see how high she could fly with old Harry trailing behind like the streaming tail of a kite. She whipped him directly in front of me, with his legs pointing straight out to where I could see the bottoms of his slippers. But that wasn't all I saw in that fleeting moment. Harry's face reflected the very story I'd told him about the time mom threw the bucket of cold water in the old man and Barbra's face. Seeing his eyes bugged out and as big as fifty cent pieces I fell apart right there in the yard. But looking away so I wouldn't have to see Harry in flight any longer, did no good when the squeaky chains got my attention sounding as if they were stretching to their limits.

It was then that Mary saw me laughing and took notice of old Harry, who looked a little dizzy. As suddenly as it'd all started, she brought the swing to a stop, surprising Harry, when he firmly planted his shoes back on the floor with a smooth slide.

"Not everyone thinks the same way you do, mister!" she yelled at Calvin, sounding hoarser than ever.

"No, but ole Junior does!" Calvin said, holding his pipe firmly and bracing himself for another onslaught. But this time, she left the swing and pounded on his shoulder for all she was worth, having no effect on him whatsoever. I knew that if Calvin wanted, he could stop it in a hurry. I thought how lucky we all were that he was such a good guy.

He was as strong as an ox, but over the years, he'd worn himself down working in the woods. I'm sure he'd picked many a heavy log up and put it on the back of someone else's truck. He'd probably never had an easy job in his life, I reckoned.

He'd told us in Pike County on occasion that loading wood was meant for the young fellows to show off their hard-ons. He'd gone on to say that he was fine using the saw all day. But in my opinion, it was just as hard. There was truth to what he'd said, that we'd be just like him if we kept doing this kind of work. Mary had finally calmed down or worn herself out when she sat beside Calvin, where he'd swung his arm around her neck.

"Well, you tell that old man of yours when he ya see 'um to come down to our little shack and pay me some mo…ney."

"I'll do that, Calvin," I said, knowing that I'd just pass the word to James havin' no desire to talk with the old man. They were not out of hearing distance when Harry popped off.

"Damit Arnold! I thought I was headin' for the front yard more than just once! And by hell, there was a couple times I might have made it all the way to that tree up yonder!" He pointed with a shaky finger. We laughed for quite some time as Harry added more flavor to what he called the ride of his life.

"Why you tell me why in the hell didn't Jim and her do the damned shoppin' when they were out runnin' around yesterday?" Harry's mood had suddenly changed again. James an I'd noticed how he'd become more irritable shortly after the paperwork had officially been signed for the land. And the invites to go out frolicking with the old man had tapered of significantly also.

I was sure Harry had pretty well got the message on the day of the fiddlers contest. The old man had entertained for Harry many nights on the porch playing his guitar and singing which Harry always loved. And that didn't seem to happen much anymore either. The ex-Reverend had put on his, fake mask on to sell himself to old Harry.

It appeared that we'd run out of things to talk about when Harry slowed the swing, stood up, and announced that he was calling it a night. I cringed to think and hope Harry's problem wasn't the same as Calvin's and that he wasn't being paid either.

James didn't come home that night, and the old man didn't show up to pay Calvin the next day either. Overnight, it seemed James had become someone else. *What's happened to Doodle, my best friend?* I thought sadly throughout the day. Always in a time of need, Doodle was a more fitting name than James. It went back to when we were little boys and only called each other by our slang names. He'd never been gone all night before. The only time we'd ever been apart was when I'd go help Aunt Ray whenever my uncle was going through one of his bad coughing spells.

I didn't do much that Saturday as time slowly drug on and on. I talked to Harry when he'd come out and have a smoke or wanted to chat for a while. I visited the old house in the woods and hunted sang on the other side of the mountain. I'd walked down to visit Calvin, but they were having a nap. Reality hit hard again late Saturday night when I realized that James wasn't coming home again. I fell asleep sometime Sunday morning.

I went into the small woods over a hill behind Harry's house the next morning and found a pretty good jag of sang, but the thrill just wasn't there as I dug it. Harry had told me that at one time there was a house that lay in the small valley, but people stopped living in it when he was just a little boy. I only found several big flat sandstone foundation rocks—all that was left of the place. Kate and Mr. Bill seeing me from the barn came over the hill to have their necks scratched. There was something shiny beside Kates hoof. I dug up a perfect fork with a silvery shine to it. How it hadn't rusted away was pretty incredible I thought. The answer was stamped on the back. Excited as I scurried up the bank that I'd found a silver fork which I couldn't wait to show James. I stopped at the hand pump to wash it off thinking how it really wasn't anything much, and the talk about it would be short lived as his new find was something way more spectacular than mine. I was so used to having him around all the time that I found myself talking out loud as if he were still there.

I took a fishing pole up to the pond, where I caught two largemouth bass, and without James being there I'd win the argument that they were bigger than any that he'd caught. After cleaning them for mine and Harry's supper I decided to climb up on the barn's roof, where off in the distance, I could see Kate and Mr. Bill grazing side by side with tails swishing just enough to keep the flies away. Kate and Mr. Bill had been together for some time now and I wondered how one would feel if the other were gone.

Reminiscing seemed to come much easier when dealing with loneliness. And why I drew back to when we were little boys seemed to fit better than now as young men. Maybe we were easier to please using our imaginations and not knowing how things worked. What was really on the inside of clouds and if they were full of water how did they still float. I thought how James and I'd lay in a grassy field pointing out things in the clouds that the other couldn't ever seem to make out. And always with laughter while desperately pointing to any dark spot or swirl that might indicate to the other what you were seeing. But there'd be no one on this day to point out dragons and human face's swirling just before they'd quickly disappear into something else to stretch one's imagination even farther.

I thought about taking the horses to the woods and log for a while, but it was their day off also, not to be canceled because of my loneliness.

I dove into the pond, my second trip that day. The large crowd of spectators wasn't there. Only James could draw them to watch my heroics as I'd thought them to be.

It was Sunday evening. And after Harry and I had eaten I listen to some music when I heard a car slow at the big maple but couldn't place the sound as being the car of anyone I knew. It had a nice soft rumble to the muffler. Peeping out the bus's windshield, James was getting out of a different car other than the Dodge.

The three oval holes in the fenders made it a Buick, a 1956 Special, with a blue and white paint job. I was out the door like a sprinter clearing the steps, jumping the fence and running to where he was installing a new wiper blade on the passenger side.

"Where the hell did you get this, James?" I asked, climbing in and sliding under the steering wheel.

"It's my new car." He said while backing off for a full view.

"Well, where'd you get it?" I asked, turning the radio on. "Hey, it works!" I held a fist into the air. "Is it really yours?"

"Yep, I traded the Dodge off for it." He said while slowly climbed into the passenger seat, and rearing back making himself comfortable in the big bench seat.

"Well, how much difference did you have to pay?"

"Nothing," he smiled, "it was an even trade."

"This sure looks like a better car than the Dodge! What kind of an idiot would make a trade like that?"

"I traded with Ezell. He told me that he wanted his daughter in a safe car and so gave me the family plan—an even swap!" He laughed again as if there was a joke hidden somewhere in all that.

"God, that's unreal," I said, bouncing my ass up and down in the seat. "The mufflers sure sound good, so I guess that means the motor is too?"

"Purr's like a kitten." He smiled, while looking over at me. "Are you all right, Arnold?"

"Oh yeah, it's just been a long weekend with nobody around to talk much to."

"Do you mean nobody as in me?" He bobbed his head already knowing the truth of it. I was glad the conversation hadn't started out with what love was all about or how good roses smelled or sunshine and rainbows that'd get him talking with that childish voice.

But with no more than I knew about love, I'd seen enough movies to know they'd all started out with love and happiness, just like James and Scarlett for now. Would it be followed by suspicion? And then the saddest part of it all, a broken heart in the end. For now, I figured it was simply comparing eyes to skies as so many songs were all about.

"Oh, by the way, I know someone who'd like to see you," he blurted. The thought sent a confusing chill throughout me. I'd been put on the spot. Sweat rushed to my brow as I fumbled to find the right words and not sound stupid.

"Let me guess Scarlett has a friend?" Is she fat? Is she taller than me? I couldn't keep up with the craziness playing in my mind. I'd gotten weak legs all of a sudden and nervous that James would notice my shirt starting to show sweat. No matter, I didn't know if I was ready for such a thing as love, let alone being with a girl all by myself. There were so many things he hadn't told me yet about it. Some I was too bashful to ask about, and I thought Calvin's ideas sounded too simple and a quick way to get the hell knocked out of you I thought.

"Alright who, is it?" I strained to ask.

"It's Carolyn."

"Shit no, I'm not going out with her, James. She *is* my cousin!"

"Well I don't mean to fall in love with her or anything like that. I just thought we could all go out riding around sometime."

"Well, why can't just you and me go cruisin,' James? You got to admit it sure was a lot of fun. I mean do you have to be with Scarlett all the damn time?"

"Look, I'm sorry the way this all happened—so fast I mean, with Scarlett coming into my life. I can't explain and wouldn't even know where to start. But I've found someone who makes all my troubles go away when I'm with her. Scarlett just thought it'd be a good match, the way you both like to talk."

"No way! You can call it dumb or whatever you want, but I am not ridin' around with my cousin, James."

"All righty then, suit yourself Arnold. We'll come up with a day that just you can ride around with us, okay?" Obviously James had missed my whole point that I just wanted he and I to run around together. I felt sadness as never before. I had to face the fact that Scarlett was the most important thing in James's life for now. I'd been weaned in a way that I'd never have him totally to myself again.

It was well after midnight as I sat in Harry's swing, thinking of James's proposition that I ride around with he and Scarlett. He'd long since gone to bed ignoring my pleas once again how it couldn't be explained away when the question came up of their relationship. To joke of it as him 'having his head up his as ass' was exactly that. A joke, all meant to refer to how a person acted by being in love. Harry knew right off the bat it meant James was in love. But there were other things about it I'd need to deal with.

"They're not blood relatives." Should I shout that out anytime we'd be around people who knew of them. And we'd be labeled as lowlifes in no time. "I can't even go out for track." I said out loud the thing that really had bothered me the most. I adjusted the swing's speed to where its squeaky chains followed along with the frog concerto coming from the pond.

James sang "Cherish" by the Association as he exited the bus the next morning. I guessed Scarlett probably liked that song also. I went to fetch the horses while humming the tune "Monday-Monday", hoping it'd rescue me from my weekend blues.

James with the roar of Big Red quickly disappeared into a thick bank of fog that had swept in and consumed everything momentarily. Thin rays were starting to push their way through and strangely enough almost at the exact place where the old man had hit me awhile back. I thought it was something special when the yellowish rays shined right down on us. I wondered if James could paint such a thing as this, the blend of grayish shadows with the horses snorting and blowing swirls of yellowish fog into a thin mist. Then only seconds later, it was all swept away with a gust of wind. We pressed on when I saw the flicker of a match where I could hear James and Calvin talking while sharpening their chains.

"Boys, this damned fog is about as thick as the old lady's coffee was this mornin'." Calvin laughed, while rearranging himself on the log when the most god-awful fart blasted from where he sat. I had plenty of time to turn and hurry away before it or his fake cough had ended.

"My god!" James jumped a little too late. "What in the world did you eat last night, Calvin?" Pinching his nose, he turned quickly to pick up the file that he'd dropped on his escape.

"Not to worry about this fog stayin' around very long boys! It'll burn it off in no time!" he boasted. "Hell, if it works the way it should, you can call it a miracle if ye 'ont to." He grunted. Calvin seemed to be in rare form, it would appear. "And, boys, you wouldn't believe how much better that makes me feel!" He said sounding sincere. We'd no sooner got back to where he sat when he suddenly grabbed his chest and with a strained look on his face.

"I think the old lady's tryin' to kill me, Arnold Ra . . . ha . . ." He said while grasping at his throat.

"Now why in the world would she do that for?" I asked. A quick smile spread across Calvin's face. I knew I'd been had and there was no way out of it. Feeling much better now he adjusted his collar from where a minute earlier he was practically choking himself to death. We'd stay put until Calvin got his pipe relight.

"Why, she's a wantin' to get rid of me so she can have you all to herself. She's tryin' to poison me ta death, that's what it is! And hell, you seen 'er tryin' to kill me on old Harry's porch the other night Arnie!" James laughed, caught up in the moment, I figured. I stood motionless, hands at my side, sure that I didn't want to push Calvin any further. He leaned sideways once more with a grunt. James backed up a couple more steps as I did also.

"Now hold on, boys! I'm just messin' around! Hell, I can't imagine what another one of them would do to my ass! Hell, ya can't see anythin' anyway, so come on back over here and set down fer a while. And besides, I've got somethin' to ask old Junior." He smacked his lips together a couple times.

"I want to know if you got any yet, Junior?" His question was blunt. I knew Calvin well enough that all he wanted to do was to aggravate James. He wasn't serious about his question as he continued to file on his chain. And besides, he'd already said he'd know when that time came. But I doubted James would brag about it.

I'd seen it down at Willow Springs when some guy would brag of what he'd done to some girl, but it was simply a lie when she got wind of it. I didn't think there was really any way of knowing that people were doing it. Then came the day the word got out that Jane Mosely was pregnant. Her dad was a preacher; she was one of the plain, quiet girls in school who wore a ponytail and long dresses every day, and she was not allowed to date. Her boyfriend finally confessed to being the daddy, which no one would have believed, only that they went to the same church. I wondered if it wasn't all part of the hypnosis that made people carry on like that.

"You'll be the second person I'd tell, Calvin," James said, looking over at me.

"Well, by hell, you keep fartin' around. And old Arnold Ray will beat you to the draw!" He winked. "I mean what would you think, Junior, if your old lady was to invite someone over fer supper . . . and don't even ask you if it's all right? Hell, maybe I ain't even invited myself." He pouted, rubbing his lower lip with the end of his pipe. Calvin could fun around all he wanted, but he knew I was in the dark when it came to the things they talked about. James had never said much about anything that'd happened to him with girls at any age until now. All my experiences at a younger age had turned out bad. I knew that talking with a girl or any fascination with one could sure speed my heart up, though.

I thought back to a note that had been slid onto my desk when I was in the fifth grade. I thought it was meant for me, simply asking, "Do you like me yes or no?" with a place assigned to put an X. She was so pretty when I spotted her, but strange in the way she shook her head darting to one side. So eager to get it back, I signed it "yes," marking the place several times so there'd be no mistake. She covered her forehead after she'd read it, with some of her friends laughing out loud. It was a hard lesson that it wasn't me that the note was intended for.

"It'll just happen, Arnold." James nodded. *Can he be reading my mind, or do I look that desperate?* I wondered.

"Boys, I've got to go piss," I said with a little panic to my voice. I jumped to my feet, walking away before Calvin could say anything else that might embarrass me even more. I let out a long sigh of relief once I reached the woods where they couldn't see me. Now I could breathe better, with a forest to hide my frustrations. I waited till after they'd started their saws back up and began cutting before I returned, gathering the animals' reins and sneaking past them. After the fog cleared a little more, James headed out for Chillicothe.

Throughout the days that followed, James would get home later and later messing and up my sleep. Once, it was two o'clock in the morning. I complained that he'd woken me up. "Sorry" was about all he'd say and not too sincere at that, I thought.

Calvin was right that he'd come home goofy as hell some nights. But no matter, James was happy with his newly found love, and I thought about how he hadn't mentioned Pike County since meeting Scarlett. His favorite songs changed daily. "When a Man Loves a Woman" was the song he sang when he drove off that evening.

Almost every evening, I'd sit and talk with Harry. Calvin and Mary's visits had become more frequent, adding to the night's festivities. But it just wasn't the same without the person I'd shared my whole life with. *Had it not been for him, I might even be in jail right now*, the thought came to mind.

I wanted our parties on Harry's porch to go on for as long as they could. Never would I be the first to leave and even after they'd all gone to bed I'd hold off as long as possible before going on to the bus. Loneliness never sleeps I thought when I'd walk down to the house in the curve in total darkness. If the moon were out my walks would take me far away from the bus even into the woods with a full moon. How we used to sing along and snap our fingers to all the cool songs, was non-existent now. Sounds I'd never paid much attention to flooded my brain disrupting any hope that I fall asleep soon. I'd started leaving the radio on turned up just enough to override all sounds of the night.

Harry was so grateful for having anyone to talk to, especially when he'd be getting juiced up as he was right now. We'd joked privately that it wasn't water Harry went after to quench his thirst. Seldom did he get drunk until he was about ready to go to bed. I'm sure it'd taken many years, the way he could drink moonshine and his tongue not get too twisted and give him away. But he was no different than anyone else when at some point, he couldn't fool anyone and by then was pretty well plastered. But he did have a way to throttle the shine for a long term and well-kept buzz. I thought how the old man had been over the years even to think he was hiding it from God. Calvin, in a joking way one time said, Harry was a tightwad, when it came down to sharing his moonshine or even his baccer. But Calvin came prepared this time, breaking out a small bottle of whiskey of his own.

"Why, just one or two drinks ain't goin' to hurt anybody. And, besides we need to celebrate old Jimbo's paying us, now don't we Honey!" he asked as if he really needed Mary's consent.

"Yeah, I know, mister, how that one or two drinks goes with you . . ." Mary gave him a warning it would appear. There was some meanness on Calvin's part when he blew a large puff of smoke at her. It was one of the main attractions, watching Mary fly all over him like a flogging rooster clearing off the top of his head. Calvin didn't drink but every once in a while, but when he'd did he'd tell stories of how it always got him in trouble.

After seeing that Calvin had his own bottle, Harry confessed that he had a jug of Fletcher Adkin's best 100 plus proof moonshine. Feeling good with the company he had, Harry left for a minute, coming back with a mason jar half full of shine handing it over to Calvin. Obvious by the way Mary rolling her eyes up she was upset but, said nothing.

"Now by God, Calvin, you kin go on with your storytellin' after you down that in one big swoller." Harry reared far back in the swing of his challenge. "And let me remind you by God that shit works in two ways: either like a truth serum or you're the lie-nest son of a bitch in the whole crowd." Harry laughed slapping his hands together which led me to believe that he'd been both ways before. I'd over heard the old timers at Turners store express that if it was any good, it'd make you speak in tongues before the night was over.

"Well, I hope this shit don't make me act like I did down at Portsmouth that time when an old boy accused me of cheatin' in a pool game." Calvin got our attention in a hurry that he had something to confess. He turned the jar up and in a couple of seconds downed the contents right to the last drop. Mary offered to take the glass when Calvin jerked it away saying he'd get a few more drops after the jar sweated a little more. Harry knowing exactly what Calvin was talking about snickered while blowing a thin stream of smoke off to the side.

"He was a loudmouth," Calvin continued, "and whether my hand accidently did bump that ball into a side pocket wasn't any reason fer him to call me what he did! And it just so happened that it was that very pocket that I was tryin' to stuff his ass into, right up 'til the time the law showed up. Hell, I was feelin' my oats and thought I'd just go ahead and whip them six officers' asses while I was at it. And I did. Hell, I's so drunk it turned out those six cops ended up only bein' two though. I was about as cross-eyed as I could be by then!" Calvin huffed. "But the next six that showed up was exactly how many they were. I barely remember wondering why they were draggin' me off into the woods fer. When I came to, three days later and of course, in jail, I was countin' all the knots all atop of my head. And by God, I wasn't kidding that I didn't think the woods was that much of a shortcut to the jailhouse. Why, I think they bumped my head on every tree in there and at least twice." He laughed as if the shine was affecting him already.

I could've counted on one hand the times I'd seen Calvin drinking but never had seen him drunk. 'Ain't goin' to do dat no mo.' He'd simple refer back to the bad times he'd had while drunk on the shine and maybe that was one of them.

Harry's words were getting pretty muffled by now intertwined with smoke sounding as if he were speaking through his nose. The true sigh that the gap between his dentures and the roof of his mouth had widened. Relaxed words such as "oddam" he'd left the 'G' off and several others that kept us on the edge with laughter, anticipating there'd be more to follow. And now with Calvin teetering somewhat, the show was on.

"Harry!" Calvin said, resting his own half-empty bottle high upon his chest. "I want to know when's the last time you got any?" He shot a quick wink over at me. Harry immediately clammed up, slowly shoving his pipe into his mouth like Calvin had hit a sore spot or something. Mary quickly dug an elbow into Calvin's ribs. We'd all gone quiet as Harry straightened himself up in the swing. But we'd been around the old fellow long enough to know that a sudden confused look only meant that he was phrasing his comeback.

"Well, let's see!" He said rubbed his thin squared chin. "Hell, I cain't think back to the last time now that you mentioned it, Cal." Suddenly he looked puzzled somewhat doubtful. "You know I can't . . . Hell! . . . I can't remember the last time I even had a hard-on!" Sitting in a straight up position he craned his neck as if there was a large audience to play to. He'd lived too many years and been through many a bullshit session not to have an answer of some sort.

We all had our ways of telling stories that we wanted to end with a great punch line. Ones that were right out lies were the best or at least I thought so. Timing was everything and Harry was the best in the way he intentionally stuttered right up to the time he'd throw the punch line on you. In his joking way, he'd said that one should never lie about the same story more than twice however. "Now you don't want to lose the flavor cause there's always some smart ass out there who remembered it differently from the first time," he went on to say. We'd seen it before, the sudden sparkle in old Harry's eyes and with a slightly twisted jaw he'd deliver the punch line in his offbeat way.

"But by God, if the Lord above," he pointed a shaky finger towards the heavens, "ever lets me get another hard on why I'll..." His stall was perfect I thought in the way he'd put God in control of such things. I quickly scrambled my thoughts to anything that he might come up with for his grand finale. Acting all calm-like he made a slow draw on his pipe.

"Why I'm gonna freeze that damned thang like a popsicle and then write the date out across it so I won't ever forget it again!" Harry reared back with a solid swat across both legs. Like a fast-spreading epidemic, the words seemed to reach everyone's ears at the exact same time. The outburst was sudden and loud, with Calvin grunting and Mary's gasping cough between laughs. I could hear it all from where I rolled in the yard, clutching at my stomach.

"Why Harry you sure you got enough room to write down the whole date on that thang?" Calvin's follow up joke adding fodder to our laughter. I started to wipe my eyes as it was pretty hard to make things out right now. Then came a roar from Calvin and Mary louder than ever and for a good reason. Harry, sat calmly in the swing, rigid that nothing moves with his hands spread apart as to measure something that would span a foot or better.

I'd seen it with the old timers down at Turners store trading punch lines back and forth until one would declare something so outrageous that no one would dare follow up on it. And like that Harry had answered Calvin's question and in a big way without saying a single word. Nothing else could be said that might make it any funnier than it was already. It took several minutes for everyone to collect themselves with Harry and Calvin carrying on as they had. I thought it something like a checker match with the way old Harry had planned his last move with what to say.

"Now boys, Harry spoke up again, "we had a sayin' when I was comin' up with us thinkin' we were all studs. 'Get up with the Chickens and go to roost with um, before the sun goes down.' That's how we referred to it anytime there was talk of sowin' your wild oats. And by-God did we ever and never thinking that we'd get too old to roost with them young hens. But it seemed like overnight things start goin' downhill. And that's everything, by-God if you know what I mean." He set us off to laughter once more when he quickly glanced down at his crotch.

"Hell, when I hit eighty years old, it was then I realized I couldn't get up on them damned roostin' poles like I used to."

"Eighty!!" Calvin barked. I'm sure he had something vile to add, and surely would have, had it not been that the squeaky chains came to an abrupt stop. And so silenced the small circle where the dim porch light shone down on us.

Maybe it was in Harry's plan with so many frogs croaking loudly from the pond. I'd have to say that in my wildest dreams I could never picture Harry acting like something right out of the TV series The Twilight Zone. It just didn't look real with the way he stared straight ahead and never to blink that I could see. He square his shoulders, up and with a slight arch to his back he looked like a thin toy soldier I imagined.

With his pipe clamped tightly in his thin jaw and pushed off to one side, freeing both hands where they rested directly on top of his legs, one palm up and the other facing down. Mary let out a faint cough which didn't draw Harry's attention at all.

Then such as a windup toy he started out with a slow slap, twisting and turning his hands as they danced back and forth on one leg, then the other and at times on the same leg. There was a rhythm to it all with different sounds jumping from leg to leg. Then the pace picked up as he leaned forward with legs bouncing up and down on the tips of his toes. Now faster than ever, he added the arm of the swing, tapping two and sometimes three thumps where his wedding ring would connect at times when he wanted.

His concentration was furious now, with slapping going on everywhere. It hardly looked real the way he slowly turned his head to the side. But like a toy that was getting worn out he paused for a second or two before rotating his head all the way in the other direction. I doubted I had the coordination that Harry did with fast moving hands and legs and all the while never bobbing his slow-moving head at all. The timing was perfect as everything came to an abrupt end. Straight-faced like a puppet, he hiccupped smoke rings through the bowl of his pipe, where they quickly drifted away into the night air.

Then he was right back to his routine again, adding something new we'd not seen yet. Along with all the slapping and puffing rings of smoke, he now danced a jig all the while sitting in the swing. It all came together and was impossible to keep up with as his hands, legs, and arms all moved about to an unknown rhythm. Too sudden, I thought when it all stopped. A single clap of his hands sounded as if a balloon had just popped; And with it ended old Harry's wordless masterpiece.

We clapped and cheered as if we were a large audience, with Calvin standing up in appreciation of Harry's performance. We cheered more and more thinking an encore would follow. But his encore was when he pecked his pipe a couple good licks on the swing's arm before sliding it into its designated hole. He slowly stood up, taking a gentleman's bow; then without a word, he tipped an imaginary hat and went on into his house for the night.

"I can't believe what I just seen." Mary spoke quietly in disbelief, her fingers pressed against her lower lip.

"Well, I can tell ya one damned thing," Calvin said, clearing his throat. "That ole fart didn't learn how to do that shit overnight! My guess it all came with the many years of roostin' with the chickens and—"

"You can stop right there, mister . . ." Mary sounded a warning.

"I've never seen anything like it either!" I shook my head, shocked somewhat. "I was flat hypnotized! Hell, he should be on TV." I rattled on an on. We talked a while longer till Calvin pointed out that the frogs told him it was time to get on down the road. Yawning, he told Mary to get her big, wide buffalo ass loaded up.

His bottle was empty; and lucky for him, I thought, as Mary didn't appreciate his joke at all. There'd be no forgiveness for him tonight, I thought, judging by the way she looked at him. It would be a long one for Calvin, depending on how long Mary would hold it against him. The first words she said in the truck and with no hoarseness in her voice were very plain:

"So, you think I've got a big buffalo ass, do you?" And even as loud as the muffler was Mary's voice could be heard above it as she repeated the words once again.

James brought the news to the laydown yard one morning, informing Calvin and I that we'd be moving Mom into the rent house in week or so. Not that I didn't believe him but right after he left for Scarlett's that evening I used Harry's phone to call mom and verify what was told to me. She didn't sound too enthused about the matter but said she thought it was best to go ahead and rent the place until the new house was built. I knew without saying and no matter the cost or the sacrifice she'd put the burden on herself to get the family together again. And of course, the chance to help get the old man back on the righteous path. She went on to say that the old man had already paid the rent with the first not far off.

"Now Arnold I think that's the best thing ole Jim has done since I've known him." A calm stream of smoke spiraled from Harry's pipe. There was a new hope in his eyes now that he'd finally get to hear Mom and the girls sing for him. It was hard to believe how he could show so much happiness for such a simple thing as that.

I'd been counting the days off with less than a week till the first of the month. I left the horses at the pond one morning before walking down to Harry's big Maple tree. The rent house was a half mile or so clearly visible from where I stood in the middle of the road. A warm feeling ran throughout me excited that I'd have Mom and the family to talk with. But deep inside I knew nothing could take the place of my big brother and best friend.

It was the very next Saturday when James and I headed for Pike County in Big Red to move the family. We'd reworked the racks, making an enclosure to haul as much as possible. We figured it would take two loads to get everything we possessed.

"You know, James, one good thing about this move is that Mom doesn't have to sell or give away all her belongings this time."

"Yeah, you're right," he replied. Even though he wasn't talking much these days other than about his love affair, I figured this might be a good time to talk about some of my concerns as I cleared my throat.

"James, do you know what's happened to you?" I asked earnestly.

"What do you mean by that?" He sounded surprised.

"Well, half the time I speak to you, I never get an answer. The only thing you ever talk about is Scarlett, Scarlett, and more Scarlett. It seems that Scarlett is all you've got on your mind anymore. Are you gonna be like this forever?"

"Look, I know I've been different lately. But I've got this feelin' right in the pit of my stomach that I can't explain, and I'm not sure that I even want to try. It's just something you want to last forever. You really don't see much going on around you. Wait till you get the smell of a woman, Arnold." He seemed to go off into la-la land there for a second but then continued, "It takes over, and there's nothing—I mean nothing—you can do about it except play along." His gaze pretty well summed it all up with a smile that never left his face anymore.

"I still can't believe how fast it happened, though," he continued. "It's like there's been something trapped in me all my life, and now I've found the key to let it out! But the best part, Arnold, is you never get it all out. It's like every time you see the person, you get reenergized no matter how tired you are. It's like starting all over again . . ." I tried to better understand his happiness, but parts got to be a little too poetic at times, I thought.

"But I guess if I had to explain what love smells like, it would be the cleanest smell in the world. A fragrance of a flower that'd never been smelled before." His thoughts seemed way beyond Big Red's windshield. Song after song came on the radio as if he'd ordered them to his heart's desire, turning the volume up when Johnny Cash came on singing "Ring of Fire," which James had no doubt, fallen into that burning ring of fire.

After "Ring of Fire" had finished, I turned the radio off, to which he complained. And even though I loved all the songs myself, there was something in them that I was missing, but James wasn't.

"Has she ever farted in front of you yet?" I laughed. "Now don't that sound Calvin-like?" I quickly followed thinking how my question must have sounded pretty stupid.

"I wouldn't know if she did or not Arnold with everything always smelling the same." He laughed, reaching over and tapping me on the shoulder. "Oh, and one other thing you might want to know is their skin is the softest thing on the face of the earth." He quickly looked over at me to see my expression.

"You mean even softer than store-bought toilet paper?" I joked nervously. Suddenly, he pulled a small silky handkerchief from his shirt pocket, offering me a smell as proof of his testimony.

"Get that damned thang away from me!" I protested as he laughed, pressing it to his nose.

"How sweet the smell," he sang as if it might have been part of a song. But whatever was on the handkerchief sent him into orbit as he'd inhale and hold his breath for as long as he could. I did get a faint smell as he waved it about. And the truth of the matter was I did want to smell its fragrance.

"James!" I interrupted, but to no avail. He just wasn't hearing me right now.

"When I touch Scarlett's legs," he rolled his eyes at me, "it makes my heart beat faster, and I can hardly breathe at times."

"James!" I yelled. "You need to take a breath and get a hold of the steerin' wheel a little better before you put us in a nice soft ditch somewhere." He sighed, looking at me while stashing the cloth back into his pocket.

"But most of all, it's when you kiss them, Arnold. Now I know what they mean in that song those black ladies sing. 'It's in their Kiss.' They sure hit it on the nail head."

I knew there was no reason to interrupt him and the truth was I wanted him to talk more about how you kiss and what might lead up to feeling a girl's leg. "And when she wants to kiss as much as you do, it's all good." He looked at me, smiling as if he'd answered all my questions. All I could do for the rest of the trip was listen to how wonderful things were between Scarlett and him.

We arrived at the house, where everyone was stacking boxes to be loaded. James backed the truck up at the very place we'd used to load the animals and tractor. He grabbed my arm just before we climbed out of the truck.

"And all day long, you think about 'em, and it's hard to concentrate on what you're doing. Everything they say is funny even if you don't understand it. You know, Arnie, how it is, like when you're layin' there all night long thinkin' about Mary?" My mouth gaped open, not believing what he'd just said. All that time, I had been trying to get his attention, and then he came up with this shit!

I drove my shoulder into his midsection so fast that he never had time to brace himself. And then I had his hands pulled up behind him and wasn't gonna let go. He wasn't putting up much of a fight; he just lay there, laughing.

"What the hell is so funny?" I asked. Duck and some of the others had gathered around to see what all the commotion was about. I thought it was good that they could see me getting the best of him as I tightened my grip. It'd look even better if he'd put up a little more resistance, I thought.

"Boys, keep carrying' those boxes!" James told them. I guess he didn't want them to see how I had him all tied up to where he couldn't get out of my hold. "Well now, when I let Scarlett get to this point, she usually rolls me over and gives me a big kiss." He puckered his lips the best he could. I let go immediately, jumping to my feet and laughing at how goofy he was acting.

"What is so funny?" he managed after brushing himself off.

"Why, nothing, James. I can't believe you even heard my laugh with your head stuck up your ass so far." He whirled around to face me, suddenly looking angry.

"I think people should worry about their own problems instead of mine all the time!" he hissed.

"Well, Calvin's the one who came up with that sayin', and Harry knew exactly what it meant too!"

"Well, what exactly does it mean, Arnold?"

"I . . . I guess it means you're in love. Otherwise, you'd be actin' like you always do. Now don't think that you're the only one who gets talked about, though. You and Calvin both hammer me all the time about Mary, remember?

I don't know much about girls or sex, so it makes it hard to come back with something good with you two pickin' on me." James paused, with heavy concentrating.

"Tell him next time how Mary was good in bed and see what he says about that!" He laughed.

"Not in your wildest dreams, James. Shit like that don't faze him at all. If anything, it encourages him. You know there's no way you could ever embarrass Calvin. No damned way!" I looked up quickly, checking that Mom hadn't heard me. She, Judy, and Beth had gathered at the well for a drink of water. She looked tired even from the distance, wiping sweat from her face with her dampened apron.

"Junior Honey! You and Ray come give Mom a big hug, and then you boys go up there and have some breakfast." She sounded exhausted, I thought. "It's in the oven, and when you're finished, Mom'll wash the last of the dishes and pack them up."

We talked with them for a while, then raced on to the house, elbowing each other as we ran past the charred remains trying to ignore the old home place. The bumping and shoving hadn't ended there but continued from the stove to the table. She'd made biscuits and gravy with bacon and eggs.

"Boy, that was a long time ago the last time we had breakfast over here," I said, licking gravy from my thumb.

"Well, I've got to confess," James said after the first bite, "that I've been luckier than you 'cause every time I spend the night at Scarlett's place, Anna Fay makes this same meal, and it's really good also."

"Yeah . . . but I'll bet it's nowhere as good as Mom's," I bragged with a smile, knowing he'd agree with that.

"I'd say it's pretty close!" he compared.

"What, I can't believe you could even think anyone could cook as good as Mom. In fact, it pisses me off that you'd say such a thing!"

"Well, when you get away from the farm one of these days, Arnold, you'll see things differently also," he puffed. His mind just wasn't working right, and I had to tell him so before he'd get back to the same old thing: Scarlett. *La-la-la- la who gives a shit?* I thought to myself.

"Have you boys eaten everything up?" Calvin yelled standing outside looking through the screen door. "Your momma said if I hurried, I might get a biscuit or two." He quickly came into the kitchen with the screen door slamming behind him.

"No problem, Calvin. Take James's plate"—I pointed—"since he don't like Mom's cookin' anymore." James growled, holding his fork out in defense. Calvin stood at the stove, sopping the last biscuit in the last of the gravy.

"Hell, they ain't no reason ta wash that skillet. I believe that I've sopped it clean." He pointed after running his thumb around the edge to get any that'd spilled over. "Now if you boys don't mind, I'd like to get old Red loaded up and get on back to Cliff Run Road."

Calvin stepped outside to light up his pipe but turned quickly and stepped back in, saying there wasn't any reason to stay outside when the house was goin' to be vacated in just a little while. "The old lady and I"—he stabbed a thumb in his chest—"are goin' down to Camp Creek for the rest of the weekend. Old Jimbo's gonna fill my gas tank up for carryin' Red over to her new stompin' grounds," he puffed.

Duck and his brigade started to come through the kitchen door for another load to carry to the truck when Calvin blew a gagging-size cloud of smoke to slow them. He laughed as they fanned in every direction with a couple faking a cough.

"Boys, if Ida known you were comin', I'd have saved the big biscuit for you to fight over like dogs!" Duck laughed.

"Well, you can bet your ass 'bout one thing, Duck—and that is your big biscuit–eating days are about over!" I smiled. "We, or maybe I should say *I* . . . I will get it every day after we get moved to the new place, being how James here may not be around for breakfasts, and sayin' Anna Fay can cook as good as Mom!"

"No way, Piggy Wiggy!" Duck sounded off. Calvin was the first to laugh at Duck's teasing.

"What did you just call me, Duck?" I asked.

"You know . . . Arnold, the pig on Green Acres and his owner, Mr. Ziffel. I figure that'd be a good nickname for you. Don't you boys thank so?" They all agreed with him of course. He quickly removed a weed from his mouth as though he might want to challenge me.

"Oh yeah, I still like that show." I smiled. "Look, Duck, we're thankful for everything you did since we've been gone. And the fact is Mom said she didn't know what she'd have done without you. And as you know, I don't mind joking around about things. To nickname me Piggy Wiggy is okay I don't care. I mean after all you've been called Donald Duck, forever? But I'm going to tell you something, Duck, here in front of everyone. You're not going to stand there and put on in front of these boys that you can whip me. Now I think it best that you get your ass busy loadin' the truck again!" I pointed to the door, which Calvin opened for them. I felt somewhat bad in the way I'd talked to my younger brother. But he needed a reality check in the way that James had said they needed their big brothers to be around them more.

"Now, Ziffel, you better be careful. Old Duck's gettin' to be a pretty good-size boy," Calvin huffed. *That's all I needed—for Calvin to get started on the Ziffel shit*, I thought to myself.

"Maybe it's time for old Duck to come and work in the woods for a little while, boys." Calvin surveyed his physique from the screen door. "And ya know what? It'd be good to have that little fart around, somebody new to pick on." He turned to face us with a broad smile. "Seems he's got too much energy makin him act like an ass. And I've seen a lot fall by the wayside. I don't hafta tell ya, one day, in that damn woods will put your ass to sittin' down like you ain't used to." He winked.

"You're right, Calvin. We'll let him help with a load and see how that goes," James remarked. "And he'd enjoy helping us any way. He's wanted to for a long time now."

"It's probably about time for him to get away from the boys anyway," I added.

"Him get away from them?" Calvin laughed, holding his pipe at bay. "I'd say them boys are the ones that need the break with the way he makes them snap to attention all the time. My guess is that Donald Duck will fall right in with us once he gets the hang of it." Calvin finished. We'd need to convince Mom that we'd watch over him, knowing how she worried. But in the end, the old man would have the final say-so on the matter. If he could see a way to get more wood out, it wouldn't be a problem working Duck at all.

Calvin scooped up one of the drinking glasses off the table and headed for the well for a drink of water. He and James stopped to talk with Mom and the sisters on their way back to the house to finish the dishes and pack them in boxes. I walked on the well to get the milk bucket.

"The Lord will not put on me more than I can stand," I overheard Mom telling them and loud enough for all to hear. He'd informed her that she could still call the whole thing off if she wanted to.

Calvin tagged along with me to go milk Red. In a matter of minutes, milk splashed over the sides of the bucket. I just knew by all the smoke he'd blown throughout the place that he'd waste no time in bragging to others how fast I was. But was I ever wrong when he started laughing!

"Arnold Ray, I'd give anything if I could milk the old lady like that." His laugh was nothing short of vile, I thought.

Mom tried to find something to put the milk in, but only after my convincing her it just wasn't worth it, she finally gave in. I dumped the milk in an old wooden trough, where the cats could have at it. Five cats would be left behind after Judy and Beth picked their favorite one to take. The old man had someone take the hog to have it slaughtered and packaged. Someone would have to come and pick it up in a week or so. Duck and the boys had gathered up all the chickens. They'd counted fifty-one and loaded them into the cages they'd built that could be stacked on top of one another. They'd be piled in Calvin's truck after we'd load Red. Everyone went into the house so Red wouldn't be spooked as I led her up into the truck's bed.

"I'll see y'all later." Calvin waved, driving away. It was a scene to remember—with chicken clucking and feathers flying everywhere, Red mooing a couple of times while bracing herself for the ride, and Calvin blowing smoke like a tar kettle from the truck's cab. It was especially good to see Mom laugh at such a sight.

"Has anyone seen Rebel?" I asked. A couple of the boys took off to see if they could locate him. They'd whistled and yelled for some time but he never came.

It didn't take long with everyone helping to load the truck. Things were stacked all the way to the top of the side rails. We'd just started tying the load down when the old man came driving up and quickly got out of his car walking to where we stood.

"Boys, let's get this on over to Cliff Run and get 'er unloaded so we can get back and get the rest of these belongings." Like he was in charge now with a quick glance at his watch. He hadn't helped load one damned thing and now showed up ordering us to hurry! I said nothing, avoiding his stare; and as long as he didn't say anything hateful to me, I'd hold my tongue. There was no doubt whatsoever that I'd whip him in a fight now, but that wouldn't help in any way. *I need to be the better man,* I thought to myself, glancing at James for assurance.

We'd planned for a final dipper of water before heading out when the old man followed us to the well. James hurriedly drank the first dipperful with spillage from the corners of his mouth.

"I've made plans for tonight with Scarlett!" he confirmed, wiping his mouth with the back of his hand. The old man made the gesture for the dipper when James bypassed him, shoving it in my direction. "Arnold and me can . . . uh . . . come back over here and get the rest of it first thing tomorrow morning." I quickly agreed with a headshake. The old man took a few steps from where we stood before spinning around, and pointing a lit cigarette at James.

"Old buddy, you'd better get your head out of your ass and stop actin' like a fool all the time. That goddamn girl is drivin' you crazy!" It was no more than a way to show his ass the way he threw the half-smoked cigarette to the ground I thought. With his arms crossed, James gave the old man a slow nod.

"Hold it right there! You don't need to say a thing about Scarlett and especially her name in vain. I'm not going to put up with it!" The old man started pacing back and forth, dragging his heals in the dirt. I felt sorry for James, having to defend Scarlett like he was doing. "We're going to the drive-in tonight and Arnold's going too. We don't have time to get the other load. By the time we get cleaned up and go pick Scarlett up we'll just have enough time to get there before the opening show."

"Well, you boys just don't get it, do you? This move has already put me way behind by a few days. We've got to start working seven days a week to get caught back up. And I need you boys to work tomorrow. I know you've got one load ready for Monday morning but we've got to get two of them if there's any hope of paying the bills on time."

"I've told you what our plans are for the night." James wasted no time in repeating what he'd said just a minute ago. You should have told us a few days earlier your intentions and that way we could have made plans." James didn't waver from his original plan.

It was comical anymore when the old man would throw his open hand up behind his ear before rattling off some long line of bullshit. We'd made fun of it so many times that it just didn't have much of an effect on us anymore. I almost laughed out loud thinking of the time in Pike County when Calvin and I was up on the mountain watching James and the old man talking down at the mill. He was giving James a rash of shit over something when the hand went up behind the ear. 'At ease asshole,' Calvin had said sounding like a military commander. And what famous statement would flow from his mouth that might change our minds now.

"Well if we lose it all, then so be it." Things were getting right down shitty with the way he wanted to lay fault on us for the way things were. We'd more than done our part to keep afloat. I'd avoided talking to him for some time now as I looked around at the place he'd destroyed. Somewhere in the heap of junk and ashes lay an arrowhead that had meant so much to me. And I'd never see it again. But flipping out over it or anything else wasn't the thing I needed to do right now. I needed to be as calm as James.

"Hey!" I interrupted. "School's startin' pretty soon, so we're gonna need you to get our money out of the bank so we can buy our clothes. And if I've got this figured right, you owe us 162 dollars up to this point." My smile was not meant to piss him off.

He looked stunned. "You'll get what damned money I owe you Monday," he snapped, turning toward his car, where everyone had loaded up except Duck, who asked if he could ride in Big Red with us.

"And you don't need to get all pissed off about me getting in your business 'cause I'm not. The money you owe us is our business. You promised it." I reminded him. If looks could kill, the old man would have done it right then and there on the spot with the black look he gave me. He hesitated for a second, maybe to get the last word in before walking on to his car.

"Boy! Dad's sure flipped out lately," Duck said, looking back over his shoulder.

"Yeah, he's like that all the time anymore, Duck." James followed.

"Piss, he used to come over about once a week and take Mom to the store. But there were a couple weeks he didn't make it, so Mom had to call Uncle Piggy Wiggy to come take her, you know, Uncle Arnold Piggy." Duck laughed at his joke maybe just to razz me a little.

"But lately, it's been every day buggin' Mom about selling this place. He's always drunk and gets pissed off when she tells him she's still thanking about it. Then he gets cussin' and flippin' out that if we don't sell it, then the bank will take it back. And he always gets her cryin' just before he leaves."

"Has he ever threatened to hit her, Duck?" James piped in.

"Oh no, me and Larry's made a plan if that were ever to happen."

"Well, that makes me feel way better, Duck," James said.

"So, what's your plan then?" I questioned.

"We've got a place in the barn where we'd tie him up over by the baccer press and leave his ass there till he'd sober up." Duck laughed at what he'd envisioned.

"Well, first of all, Duck, take his gun out of the car before you do all that. I think he's crazy enough to use it when he's drunk."

"Heck, it's all he can do to just stand up when he's drunk, let alone shoot something. I think little Joe could whip his ass when he's like that." Duck finished.

"Well, I'm glad you guys had a plan. But like Piggy Wiggy said, hide his gun before everything else." James smiled while looking over at me.

"And that's about enough of the Piggy Wiggy bullshit." I pointed a warning finger, which didn't slow the humor of my new slang name.

"Well, James? Are you still goin' out tonight, or are we comin' back for the other load?" I asked.

"Nope, I'm going out tonight!" He said while tapped a hard beat on the steering wheel. "He can kiss my ass if that doesn't work for him!" He shifted into a higher gear. "And besides, it's the weekend anyway! And being low of money hasn't slowed his honky-tonking down any, I'd bet? He wants to talk about where the money goes! It ain't moving furniture, I can tell you that."

"I guess Rebel's out smellin' around on another dog, you think James?" He didn't get my joke.

"We'll I guess we'll get him tomorrow," James suggested. We turned off Route 41 and headed west on Route 50.

"Were you jokin' about me goin' with you to the drive-in?" I leaned forward to see his reaction.

"Hell no! If you want, you can go. But just so you know, Carolyn's going with us."

"Well then, I'll go some other time!" I said.

"Well, suit yourself!" He sounded disappointed, settling back down in the seat. There was a sigh of relief on our part that the old man wasn't at the new place when we arrived. Mom said he didn't even get out of the car but dropped them off, saying he was going to look at some timber up by Good Hope and it had to be done today.

"I thought the timber was down on Cave Creek . . .," I informed her.

"Well, I don't know, Honey. Mom can't keep up with everything that's going on right now. I just wish he'd find somethin' else to do." She sounded worn-out, I thought.

We hastily unloaded the truck, putting most of it in the living room. Shortly after, James headed for the bus to get cleaned up. With the boys and me, it didn't take long to put things in their place to make room for the last load.

Duck and I went outside with all the boys following. He'd challenge me to a wrestling match in front of everyone. There was no doubt about it he'd become much stronger over the last year, but all the wrestling I'd done with James over many years gave me a huge advantage for a takedown.

"Mom, I pointed, see that little opening across the road where that path leads between those two trees? That's an old growed-up road. Calvin and Mary's shack is just a little way back in there. If you stay on the path, it eventually goes over the mountain and ties into Slate Mill Road at Granma's house. And it's only about a mile or so over there!" Everyone jumped with joy at the thought they could see our grandparents on a regular basis.

Judy was beside herself that Granma had a piano she'd played a few times when she and Mom sang songs on visits, but that was when the old man was acting Christian like.

"Why, Honey, you'll have to show Mom how to get over there sometime after we get settled in." She was tickled at the idea and giggled like a little girl. "Mom will write a letter and tell Granma when she kin' expect us." It was the truest smile I'd seen on her face that day.

Mom located the boxes that had the pots and pans in them. I knew it wouldn't take long for her to get things in order—once started she wouldn't stop until it was all done.

The refrigerator had been the last thing we loaded so it could be taken off first. Even though it wasn't that old, I felt a great relief when I plugged it in and it started humming away. She heated some chicken and dumplings she'd made the day before just for this occasion. She smiled at the idea of having an electric stove to cook on. Not having to build a fire she counted the years since the last time she'd had the electric luxury.

I'd gotten everyone's attention as we sat around the table, telling of James's adventure and mine since we'd been up here. But I felt saddened when they talked about things at the farm. It didn't take much to send me back to a better time when Duck talked about how the new growth of trees was already as tall as he was. Would this be the last gathering that we'd share of the place we'd loved so dearly? The rope James had referred to in our tug-of-war was simply at its end, with nothing left to hang on to.

Judy sounded so excited about going to a new school. It wasn't that I wanted to discourage her when I talked of how big the school was and that there'd be lots more students than at Willow Springs. She seemed to welcome it. I knew that her outstanding smile and grades would seek out those who were like her. And then there was James—all he had to do was be James.

I'd have to explain once again the reason Judy and I were in the same grade. In lots of ways, it'd been better for me to have stayed at Willow Springs, where I was a track star and had proved myself worthy of something.

I'd work harder than either of them for a grade so that I could go out for track. An 'A' in any subject was plumb out of the question, but if I could win just one race, it would make me feel worthy of something once again.

But there were other things going on in my mind lately. In the past several months, I'd gone through changes that meant I'd become more manlike instead of just a boy. I couldn't help that I stared at the girls at the Dairy Bar long enough that I'd get caught at times. Now that James was dating and telling me how great a kiss was, it simply pushed my imagination even further. Lastly, what was sex all about? I wanted to talk to girls but didn't know how I'd handle it if I was turned down.

I thought of a girl at Willow Springs who seemed stuck-up when James said he was going to get her attention. I watched as he showed the portrait he'd drawn of her. There was no way she could turn him down when his drawing added so much to her looks, I thought. I only wished that I could draw like him. I laughed to myself, thinking it might have helped with the time I gave the love letter to the girl in Florida. Maybe if it had been a drawing, she might not have wadded it up and thrown it in the trash or broke my heart when she stuck her tongue out at me. There was something else that went along with my families personalities. Many times, I'd picked out those I knew who were like James and Judy. They'd never be satisfied with sitting in the back rows. I'd need something more than new shoes and clothes to move me closer to the front, I thought to myself. There was just something scary about it all, or maybe I really wasn't ready to take on such things.

After they'd put their belongings away, I decided I'd run the boys through the woods and show them how to get to Granma's house. Robert and little Joe were too small to make the trip.

"Follow me!" I challenged while jumping over streams and fallen trees, where a couple of them just couldn't jump that far. "Your legs too short?" I'd yell, looking over my shoulder.

We'd not ran and played so hard in a long time, wildly jumping off banks without seeing what lay at the bottom of the small gorges. To run recklessly, to fall and roll, then jump back up with sweat and laughter, heaving with every breath. I'd hide behind trees, grabbing some of the smaller ones as they playfully screamed with such delight. I certainly hadn't had this much fun on my first visit to my grandparents' house.

It had been many years since my grandparents moved from New Petersburg. They loved the idea of being at the end of the road with the closest neighbor a couple of miles away. It was shortly after they shut down the pad factory where Granma worked for many years that she took what money she'd saved and they built their place. By no means was there anything fancy about it, simply put together with what money they could afford. All their sons who'd moved away came at various times to help built the small three-room house in a matter of a couple of weeks. One bedroom, a kitchen, and a small living room was its basic design. They'd sit on the small back porch nightly in the hot summer months as to allow the house to cool down a little. The tinned roof was practically flat. There wasn't enough money for any modern conveniences, and besides, they'd have it no other way than having a well with a nice hand pump along with an outside toilet. Granma bragged that they'd be fine with the small retirement check she received. There was no need for a heating stove no bigger than the house was; a standard wood burning cookstove would be more than enough to heat and cook with. It was nothing like any of the places they'd rented over the years; big farmhouses with lots of bedrooms, where we'd stayed with them a few times ourselves.

At the top of the hill, I held my arms out, stopping the boys from going any farther. Our grandparents' place looked so old-fashioned there at the edge of the woods with the single cow grazing in the small pasture right next to their house. Whether they had money or not, there always was the big garden they'd live off of during the summer, and there was no telling the amount of food they'd put up and stored under their bed and anywhere it was cool and dark.

Coffee, sugar, salt, and flour along with a couple squares of plug tobacco were the bare necessities for them. Grampa would walk the five miles one way to Fruitdale to pick them up when needed. I was there one time when Granma laid a shopping list on the table along with the right amounts of money and taxes included for him when he'd decide to make the trip. He'd hardly say a word after placing the list along with the money on the countertop and wait for the clerk to fill the order.

There's another thing that would never change, I thought, looking down to where our grandfather sat and usually by himself throughout the day. He'd not wanted anyone to help build the small shed he used for his workshop. There weren't many tools to talk of; just a few hammers and wood chisels and files were about all he needed to work with. I'd told him from the first time I'd seen him use the tools that I'd like to have them when it got to where he couldn't use them any longer. All I got was a nod that he'd acknowledged my request.

Stashed in a corner was where he'd hang the years' worth of chewing baccer we'd give him every Christmas. All the money he had to spend on anything was kept on his side, secured tightly in his money belt. He was a man of his word but wouldn't promise anything in fear that he might die before fulfilling them.

Two razor-sharp Case knives were his pride and joy; they were kept sharp all the time, even using the smallest one to shave with at times. I knew James had taken after him with the fine detail of anything he'd carve also. And it was at Grampa Sherman's whittling spot that I spent most of my time when I'd come to visit.

We ran the short distance to their house, barging in without knocking to greet Granma.

"Looord, child!" She turned, showing off the smile that only a grandmother could possess. "Why Honey, did you children come to visit. . . Granny?" She laughed, hugging us all as a group. "Let Granma get rid of this dishwater, and we'll all get us a piece of hardtack candy." With her foot, she pushed the back-door open, throwing the dishwater off the porch where chickens, geese, and, the worst birds with wings ever, guinea hens flocked to the area. It was just like old times when she carefully handed us each a piece of the flowery candy. We talked with her about the family moving and asked if she thought it was a good thing.

"Why Ho...ney, your mom wrote me a letter a while back, tellin' me that you all were movin' over here. And your Granma is so . . . happy about it! I'll be able to see everybody more often, but Looord, I don't think she should sell that place in Pike County yet." She vigorously shook her head no.

"Why, Jim does the wrong things all the time. It doesn't sound like he ever does much right anymore. You'd think he'd grow up after a while! Sometimes I think he's possessed by the devil!" She thrust her chin up, as if what she'd said was written in stone. I didn't say it aloud but agreed with her about all of it. The thought of losing the place in Pike County suddenly made me feel sick once again. 'It is what it is' came to mind, James saying that I could use to detour my thoughts away from things that continually bothered me.

The hardtack had dissolved, evident when all the boys stuck their stained tongues out at one another, getting a laugh from Granma. She made their day offering another piece, of their own choosing this time. I figured they'd be busy for a while, so I went out to visit Grampa.

He was bending over selecting his next piece of wood that he'd turn into one of the many handles he'd carve day after day. It was then that I got my best shot to see his money belt, one that I'd been fascinated with since I was real small. It looked like all the compartments were full, but I didn't know if it was all money or not. Grampa never trusted banks in any way. He could count a little but couldn't read or write a lick, but he knew what a dollar was worth.

At a much younger age, I'd been with him lots of times on long walks to the New Petersburg general store. Grampa hardly trusted anyone. Mom said one time that she thought it was because of his not being able to read or write. For a person to earn his trust, it was exactly that "earn" as he never let his guard down. He wasn't hard of hearing at all but would ask the clerk for the amount of the bill more than once to make sure it matched Granma's original sum. They knew of Grampa's uneducated ways as there were many others around who were the same.

They never intended to embarrass him while going into fine detail when recounting his change to him. He never took his eyes off the person while slowly unsnapping the right slots on his money belt to drop the change into. Other than change, mostly one-dollar bills were all he carried. But only when the small grommets snapped back in place would he feel his money was secure. Grampa said on occasion he'd die with his dignity before he'd hand his belt over to a thief.

My grandfather never spoke much, so when he did, he got right to the point with few words. It almost sounded insulting when with his grumbling voice he'd question you about something. On one of our trips, he stopped at a long lane that led to a house back between two large cornfields. I couldn't make out what all his grumbling was about, but it all ended abruptly when we set our sacks down beside the mailbox; then he motioned me to follow him. Grampa's hands were worn hard with big knuckles and fingernails as sharp as a knife, it looked. His hard knock on the front door was intended to get someone there in a hurry. There was some scurrying going on when I heard a woman say, "Robert, it's Sherman!" I had a good reason to be scared standing behind my Grampa as he tightened his fists.

"Well, Sherman Kent, what brings you all the way to the end of our lane?" Robert laughed.

"Pay me what you owe me right here and now, or I'm gonna take it out on yer hide." Without a word, the man turned and came back quickly, handing Grampa some money and even thanked him for his help. Grampa said nothing as he turned to walk away, knowing the fellow wouldn't double-cross him by shortchanging him. We stopped at the mailbox to gather our things back up.

After securing the money in his belt, we headed on for the house, and all the while I struggled to keep up with him. I'd always thought that he gave me way too much to carry on the way back home.

I thought back how the old man and Mr. Cox compared honesty to "as the day was long." Grampa never went to school or took it upon himself to learn much; but when it came to fairness, honesty, and dignity, there was no one better than him.

"Hey, Grampa, how are you doing?" I called out upon my approach. He didn't like being 'sneaked up on', as he called it. Seldom was it that he hugged a man, but always offered a firm handshake, and with his hard grip smarted at times.

"Let's go round here, Arnold Ray," he grumbled. "Now wait right here. I'll be back." He walked a short distance before disappearing behind a maple tree to pee.

Grampa's simple life was spread out on the ground all around his shop. Splinters and small pieces of broken wood of every length had turned the area carpet-like from the many things he carved on. A chair that he'd made from hickory wood was leaning up against the east wall, where he'd carve in the evening to avoid the sun. He'd switch locations in the morning, putting the chair back in the same spot, all judged by where he spat his baccer. Along the walls were finished handles of all sorts. Hammers, shovels, pickaxes—anything that needed a wooden handle, he'd made them all. Our grandfather was different in lots of ways as to compare with others. He didn't like riding in a vehicle much, so it was nothing to see him walking along the road with a rope pulled tightly over his shoulder, carrying several of the small hickory chairs and as many handles as he could. He'd take them to the little general store at Fruitdale, where they'd sell them for him.

Granma told the story of a lady seeing his well-built chairs that were solely made for little girls it would appear; she offered him three dollars each and would take every one he could make. But again, he was just different in ways that he didn't want to feel obligated to her in any way so he'd only sell what he had with him. He only spoke of two paying jobs he'd ever had: one when he was in the War and the other carrying mail by horseback in Kentucky from one town to another. All his income was referred to as 'pocket change', he'd say.

We talked about a few things, but I never asked his feelings about our moving. A simple "haw . . ." he'd grumble was about all you'd get out of him as a closing response. He never showed much emotion about things that didn't pertain to his simple ways of life.

The boys came from the house, escorting Granma with lots of laughter as she'd given them all even another piece of hardtack for the way home, cautioning them not to be running with it in their mouths.

"Lord, child, you might suck it down your windpipe," she warned sounding as if it were a warning from the Bible. There was always the smell of her homemade lye soap when she pulled you close to her for a kiss on the cheek and a goodbye squeeze—that and Juicy Fruit gum as she slipped a piece into my hand. After the boys all had a handshake with Grampa, we walked to the edge of the forest under Granma's watchful eye that no one run with candy in his mouth. Dead End, a small sign was nailed to a post, and could hardly be made out, overtaken by poison ivy. It was there that most people would have assumed that the road ended. Over the many years of not being kept up, the woods had reclaimed it. Gullies had washed the old road away in many places, making it impossible for a vehicle to go.

I'd not found the road on my own as I'd led everyone to believe. Harry told me about it and how it'd forked halfway down the hill, with one leading to where we'd moved to and the other going past the old house by the laydown yard.

"Why, that was the road that my mom and dad used to move us from Whiskey Holler to over here," he'd declared. And that was with horses and a big bedded wagon."

"Okay, boys, I'll see you at the house!" The bickering over who'd got the hardest handshake from Grampa quickly ended as we all took off in an all-out sprint. They'd run the distance back over the mountain with most falling far behind. In a couple of minutes, I glanced to see Duck, Ronald, and Larry a long way behind me now.

I ran past Calvin and Mary's shack, and as soon as I cleared the woods, I could smell Mom's cooking.

"How long before supper's ready, Mom?" Could it have been in her smile that it sounded just like old times?

"In about fifteen minutes or so, Honey." She laughed, asking how my visit went.

"There's just enough time to do the milking. Duck, ya want to go along?" We hurried up the road to where Calvin had put Red in the small field surrounding the bus, separate from the horses. After several attempts to coax her in the barn, I finally gave up, feeding out of the bucket while I milked her outside. Harry had showed me another feed barrel upon the news of a cow coming. James brought back a hundred pounds of feed on one of his trips from Chillicothe. She didn't put out a whole lot of milk that evening. I knew she was nervous of the new place. Don and I agreed how good it was to all be together once more and how Mom seemed more chipper. I turned Red out into the big pasture with Kate and Mr. Bill, where they had a sniffing reunion. We got back to the house just as Mom had placed everything on the table. I was going to have a home-cooked meal every day from here on out I thought while licking my lips.

Mom turned thanks praising the Lord for the opportunity to have the family all together again. There were two missing that she'd wished could have been there, though. I chorused "Amen" along with everyone else; it'd been awhile since I'd heard it last. Nobody enjoyed their supper more than I did that evening. After we ate, Judy suggested I take her and Beth up to see the pond. The boys all protested, saying they wanted to swim no matter how late it was getting.

"No, this party is just for us three," I said, pointing to Beth and Judy. Duck got the point and quieted the others. I couldn't get a word in edgewise as we walked up the road. I was really content hearing my sisters' soft girlish voices, something I'd missed for a big part of the summer. Judy excitedly talked about what she planned for her sophomore year.

"I can't wait!" she said, sitting down beside me and Beth on the pond's edge. "I've already decided I'll join choir. I may not be able to play the piano up here, but there'll be a place for me to sing," she declared. Beth agreed, smiling and looking up at her hero.

Beth, like me, seemed to doubt her own ability; after all, it was us who'd gotten the whipping for failing a year at school. Judy talked sadly about the way the old man was acting, wishing it was like old times.

"Are we gonna get a whippin' if we fail?" Beth joked.

"We shouldn't have gotten the first one! After all, it was his fault!" I spoke angrily. "And furthermore, he ain't goin' to ever whip me again!" I clasped a single fists tightly. "It'll cost him his . . ."

"It's okay, Arnold," Judy said, rubbing my back. Darkness came quicker than we wanted. It seemed we'd just gotten started trying to catch up on everything. The frogs sounded their first notice and from this moment on they'd own the night. We made it back to the house a little after the sun had set. Mom had left the porch light on for us; worn out, she'd gone to bed.

Still excited, we sat under one of the many apple trees and talked until the bugs got so bad we decided to call it a night ourselves. Clouds were overtaking the moon, leaving not much light to see by. Walking on the piled-up gravel along the side of the road, I found my way to the barbed fence, then sensed my way along it toward the bus.

I lay in bed with a tingling in my stomach, dreaming of the pile of school clothes I'd soon be buying. Money just wouldn't be a problem. I smiled in the dark, finally falling asleep.

"Boys, it's time to rise and shine!" the old man said, banging on the bus door early the next morning. Shortly after I heard the car start; then he drove away.

"My God! It's mornin' already!" James said, sitting up in bed.

"Well! That's the way it is when you lay out all night and don't get any sleep," I tried to scold him in a playful way.

"Do you have to talk so loud?" He cupped a hand over his eyes.

"Only when you don't like it!" I said even louder. I jumped from the bed, quickly putting my clothes on. But that was as far as I got.

He grabbed me and slammed me back to the bed, where we wrestled and finally landed on the floor, where his attempts to pin me did not work. I was getting better, proved by the fact that he couldn't hold both my shoulders down for a three count anymore.

"You're lucky that we've got to go and have breakfast, or we'd be here a lot longer!" I said, straightening my shirt out.

"You can have the big biscuit today, and I'll have it tomorrow." He said while reaching to give me a hand up from the floor.

"What do you mean I can have it today? If I remember right, it's my . . . turn today!" I said, thumbing my chest. "But no! You have it, James. There'll be plenty of weekends you'll be gone, so when your turn comes, I'll just be forced to have yours too." I laughed, vigorously rubbing my hands together.

"You're not even going to consider Duck anymore, are you?" He smiled.

"Duck's just got a little too big for his britches, and besides, he should be foundered on it by now anyway. I'll get the milkin' done, and we'll go get that biscuit and gravy. I'll bet you'll agree to that one." I laughed.

"Agreed," he said. "I'll even go along with you to milk." Red still was in no hurry to go into the barn, slowly stretching her neck and sniffing herself past the entrance. Finally, satisfied that there was no danger of any kind, she walked to where I'd poured her grain.

I had not filled the bottom of the bucket when James came over, leaning up against a pole. "Ya know, I've been thinkin' you're going to need to get your driver's license soon because you never know when you'll fall in love, Arnold." He looked at me all serious-like. "In fact, you should get it way before that happens." He sounded as if he was getting at something. "Anyway, I was wondering if maybe this next Sunday, you'd like to go ride around with me and Scarlett some."

"Well, I'll think about it and let you know." I teased. The truth was I wanted to jump up and down at the invitation. "Man . . . that might be a good day to shop for school clothes also. I mean that's if you can get your head out of your ass long enough—again, the reason you were late getting home last night. Lip-locked, right?" He chuckled, rubbing his eyes with a long, drawn-out yawn.

"Did you know that I took your screwdriver with me last night? You know, the one that's dug more sang than any other person in the ...whole ...wide world?"

"Well, I can tell ya that it's dug way more than yours lately, but whatcha . . . getting at James?"

"Well, it was the only thing long enough to pry my tongue out of Scarlett's throat." He followed with sucking sounds, that of a fat hog going after slop in a trough, it sounded. "And that's exactly what it sounds like when you get enough air between your lips to break that suction." He reenacted it again as if he had the screwdriver in his hand right now. And how glorious to hear him cut up and act a fool with me like the James of old I thought. I'd no sooner caught my breath and started to say something than I realized his lips were covered with spit, and long slobbers dripped at the corners. "I'm not lip-locked anymore! I'm not lip-locked anymore!" he said. I couldn't hold the milk bucket very steady; some had splashed over the sides. His long slurps and other mushy sounds kept me laughing and hardly able to keep my eyes open. He'd gone plumb crazy I thought.

He'd brought kissing to a whole new level than what had been on TV, where all kisses were planned out but never made sounds such as he had. It was easy to see it all coming when the music was right and a sparkle came in the girl's eye. But it was the desperate look they'd have just before she glanced at his lips the part I'd patiently waited on with my heart pounding away. It was a struggle, dealing with things that I didn't understand but really wanted to know more about. *I should just blurt out what's on my mind*, I thought to myself.

"But I can't," I thought out loud.

"Can't what?" he asked.

"Oh, it ain't nothin'. I's . . . just talkin' to myself."

"I don't have to be a mind reader, Arnold, to know there's something you want to know about, especially since I've been with Scarlett and talking about kissing and all that other stuff. Well, ask about anything that you want to know." He reared back as if he knew all the answers that I had questions to. After a moment, he confessed.

"But I'm telling you that I don't know everything, and the fact is I'm still learning. I got a late start myself when you think about it." He frowned, sounding disappointed. Things were about as comfortable as they were ever going to be that I might say what was on my mind.

"Do you act this crazy around Scarlett?"

"Yes . . . and she acts the same around me." Good that his answer was quick with an assuring smile. But he surely must've know I was stalling to have asked such a dumb question.

"So . . . I guess my screwdriver must have done the trick for you guys last night?" From the corner of my eye, I could see him looking over at me and guessed he'd gotten the hint from my nervous laugh that I was still having a hard time.

"Well, what exactly is it that you want to know about, Arnold?" He cleared his throat. There'd be no better time than now to ask my questions, and I knew it. I knew he'd be frank and kid around to save me embarrassment. I took a deep needed breath.

"Well, how long after you start kissin' do you wait to put your tongue against theirs?"

"Why, you do that the first time you kiss!" he answered quickly with not much concern. "Shit, that's when you find out that a tongue can override the 'no' word in a hurry. It's like a new world of exploration opens up, and you want to explore it all in one night. But there's no way, so that's why you keep going back for more." He laughed. Relieved now that he'd not made a big deal of my ignorance, but before I could ask more he went on.

"Look, you don't need to get all hung up on asking me the right questions. There's none that are too far-fetched when you're talking about love. I'll just tell you everything in no particular order." Suddenly, I'd become uncomfortable with no place to put my hands. "And it's okay, Arnold, you don't need to jump out the window!" His short laugh eased my mind even more.

"It starts out when you make eye contact. You almost look away because you just don't know what to do with the shock. Then it's like there's magnets that draw you both back for another look. Then you start talking at the same time, stumbling over words, which quickly leads up to laughter. I can only tell you this because it's how it happened with Scarlett and me, as you've probably figured out by now. And I can't imagine that it starts any other way.

"There not much that happens the first time other than stares and laughter and a feeling in the pit of your stomach that you never knew existed. It's like a stomachache that you really enjoy though. But it's when you lay awake at night, trying to remember every detail, every word of what was said and thinking how she said that she couldn't wait to see you again. That's when the night starts flying by when minutes turn to hours and suddenly it's after midnight. Scarlett knew as well as I did after our first eye contact that we'd get together again. Now did I dream of kissing her all throughout that night? You told me I did." He snickered.

"And talk about love at first sight—it didn't take but the first night that we realized how much we had in common. The next night, we had our first kiss, only lasting for few seconds when we both backed away, to get our breath. I'll never forget the desperate look in Scarlett's eyes, which I'm sure I had also. That was when the kissing led to a lip-lock that went on forever. You'd never get in trouble if all you did was look into each other's eyes. But now here's the good part, Arnold!" Maybe his look was to see if I was ready for the grand finale. I tightened my jaw, thinking my teeth might start chattering. He took a deep breath as I did also.

"Lip honey! That's what you're making when your tongues collide, and it's easy to figure why you need it when you kiss for so long. Remember when we were little boys and used to go on about honey being the sweetest thing there could ever be? Well, I'm telling you right now there's something sweeter." James paused for a while.

"Now there's another thing that happens when you're all tongue-tied for long periods of time . . . and the reality is it happens to everybody. It's what makes the world go around. Remember that dreaded 'no' word I talked about earlier?"

"Yeah yeah-yeah," I answered quickly, not to lose the moment.

"Well, that 'no' word is there for one reason, and that's to fend off the 'yes' word. A thirty-minute lip-lock makes for a thirty-minute 'hard-on,' if you know what I mean." He reached across the seat, giving me a slight shove to ease my tension. "Now is there anything else you'd like to know about, Arnold?" I sighed with relief that he'd opened up with me and not made me feel dumb.

"Shit, it ain't anything for me to get a hard-on, James. And that's without a girl."

"Yep, we all go through that. But when you get that girlfriend, that's when you'll find out what a real hard-on is all about—I mean trying to say no when yes is all you really want to hear."

"Have you got some . . . yet?" I joked in a bashful way, thinking I was no better than Calvin to ask such a thing. He seemed to be sizing me up for the answer when he pulled into the driveway, shutting the motor off. Maybe I'd gone too far with my curiosity now.

"No, I've not, Arnold. But I've run my hand up and down her legs. And I've felt her breasts. Warm and smooth and hot all the time, like you could never even imagine. But too much of that and you can get into some serious trouble in no time. It's about then you try to think about accountability, and you better be doing something about it really quick." I tried to hide how I was squirming from all that he'd said, crossing my leg to not be so obvious.

"Remember 'it takes two, baby,' as the song goes. Don't—I mean *don't* depend on your girlfriend to be the one to stop your desires. You'll go as far as she lets you, but over time, it becomes more and more to where it's hard for either one of you to stop," he warned.

I couldn't just come right out and thank James for all he'd told me, but I did appreciate that he'd shared his love affair with me and gave a warning as what I should expect when my time came. I was a year and a half behind him in such explorations. I thought how much harder it would be as the oldest to pass things such as this down to a younger brother.

He'd certainly aroused my imagination with talk of hot breasts and legs to the point I looked far beyond a planned kiss now. By the way he'd talked, it sounded as if Scarlett knew no more than him when it came right down to it. No matter who'd made the first move, she'd definitely brought a different kind of happiness into his life. And lately, more and more, he'd termed his love affair with Scarlett as "forever." I could only imagine to fall in love and kiss forever. I thought back to the revival in Kentucky and how Karen's eyes had held me captive that I wanted to stay with her forever.

Calvin, in his vulgar way, had described things that boys do in their spare time that made me explore myself for the first time at the cold springs. I suspected James did the same, which we never talked about.

"Now I got a question for you, Arnold, and I want you to tell me the truth. Do I really act any different than I ever did?" He smiled. Normally, I'd been all over that one, but the truth was he was still the same brother who'd helped me through every stage of growing up in my life. He'd simply moved well beyond me. I'd always been one step behind him and would always be. But I knew, however, that I'd learn from my big brother for the rest of my life.

"Nah, you ain't changed, James. You'll always be Doodle to me!" I laughed. About then, Duck stepped out the back door, holding the big biscuit in a plate and acting as if he was going to take a bite out of it. Then he quickly ran back inside as I exited the car.

As always, it would take two trips to the stove for more gravy and scrambled eggs for a final topping of the much sought-after biscuit. I thought better of razzing James when his second trip netted two more biscuits for a grand total of five that morning for himself. Maybe this morning, he'd come back to his senses that there was no better cook than Mom. For her, it made no difference who was the better cook. The blessing that we all were together shone brightly in her tired eyes.

"Mom, your smile looks great this morning," James boasted.

"Are you boys about ready?" Duck asked with a salute, excited that he was going with us for the final load of our belongings. What seemed a far distance the day before was much shorter as James pushed the accelerator in places, racking the headers off to their fullest sounds.

We hurried with the loading, only stopping a few times to have a drink at the well. Several passersby's stopped to wish us good luck on our move and were sorry that they'd missed out on seeing our mother before she left. I could only hope that the new owners would still allow the tradition that any and all that stopped by could get a cold drink from the well. I couldn't imagine that I'd never again be able to cup my hands together and drink to my heart's desire.

Only the people who'd dug the well and I had seen the dark holes where it all flowed from. The wasted amount that splashed on the concrete slab was no more than a way to work up one's thirst before the cold water finally reached your fingertips. So, with my hands cupped together and Duck at the pump I had one last drink. I glanced over at James as I stood up leaving my arms limp at my sides with the last drops falling from my fingers tips.

James had his back to us while looking up towards the heap of ashes and where the old cook stove sat along with all its rusty pipes sprawled all around it. And with any kind of acknowledgement such as James was suggesting right now, it was easy to draw the smell of blackened ashes solely meant to play with one's thoughts. And even though everything else would eventually be given back to the earth it would only be in my passing that the smell would finally cease.

There was no doubt what the old man said about Scarlett had upset him yesterday. But he wouldn't talk about it or at least not for now. I'd been with my big brother for so long I could practically read what was on his mind. Most times it was in his gaze which I thought I'd truly mastered. Without a hint of a smile he turned to face us and I knew he wasn't thinking about hugs and kisses from Scarlett.

But instead looked as if he were at the crossroad's he'd spoken of at times when he wasn't quite able to make his mind up about something. I thought and it wasn't a rarity when he'd gotten close to finishing a book; and with just a few pages left he'd lay it off to the side, upset maybe that he'd figured out the ending way too early. Even his mood at times could be detected by how it all turned out and sometimes not be what he'd expected. On other occasions however he'd come right out and declare, 'Man, what a shitty ending!' But since he'd met Scarlett, the reading had stopped altogether, even with the *Digest*. Jokingly, I pointed it out to him, where he laughed it off, saying that he was working on a book of his own—a love story, he laughed, and one with the perfect ending.

James and Duck carried the last boxes out of the house and onto the truck. I slowly pulled the door shut behind me with a final squeak, sliding the outside dead bolt in place. There'd never been a lock on the door. I guess this house was built in a time that you didn't need one, or whoever lived there didn't have anything worth taking or maybe couldn't afford to buy a keyed lock.

"James, I'm goin' for a run. I pointed to the very top of our mountain.

"Hang on Arnold, we'll run up there with you." He jumped to his feet with Duck at his side. I couldn't tell them 'no' and that I wanted to be alone for the possibility it might be my final farewell to the farm, but more importantly and if I were to do so they not hear or see me cry.

I'd put a lot of thought into James's theory of the tug-of-war and how we needed to let go as we were fighting a losing cause now. "Gone forever" clouded my eyes as I turned and headed up the steepest part just behind the house. It wouldn't take long before I'd be far ahead them.

With all the trails I'd followed the horses for what seemed a million miles quickly formed a familiar map that would be the fastest way to the top of the mountain. Like pictures trapped forever past in my mind, and the events unfolding one after the other. Stump after stump, places where James, me and Calvin had sat and talked. Then just up a way was a bare place where I'd hung the three trees up and pissed James off that I'd walk under them, showing off my ignorance, as he'd proclaimed.

I saw the very place Sam had broken free from me on that dreaded day. With a quick glace over the barren hill to where the sawmill once stood, I painfully reenacted the mule's brutal beating. I realized that if I'd shot the old man and Bill that day, I'd never have this chance to look out over the place I'd loved with all my heart. Sweat ran into my eyes and mixed with sadness I wiped them away with a quick thumb.

I could hear James and Ducks voice's just over the hill away. And like the last lap of a two-mile run I'd push onwards with everything I had; burning legs and gasping for breath the top of the mountain grew near. Standing with my hands pressed tightly on my knees, I made no attempt to wipe the string of saliva that hung from my mouth. It was here at the highest point on our farm that everything unfolded in the valley far below me.

A place where the two fields came together lined with sycamore trees sent a chill throughout me thinking of the cold water at the springs that lay just beyond the forks. I didn't linger for very long on the mountain just across the way where I'd spent the day before the house burned. But lastly, just a few feet away lay the torn-down hutch I'd built to run away to avoid being around the old man a few years back. James had never just came out and told me how he'd managed not to fall a tree on it. He'd seen my desperation that day when he'd came to recue me. I looked at my shaking hands thinking once again of the tug-of-war James spoke of. He'd told me how he felt about it and that it was time to move on. Was I the only person left hanging on to the impossible dream.

From out of the blue, a Bobwhite whistled off in the distance. As much as I wanted to answer its call, I couldn't pucker my lip enough. Finally, I'd done what had been on my mind for so long. To stand on the top of our mountain one final time and face the reality of it all with James's words of wisdom, that 'it is what it is'.

I headed back over the hill to meet James and Duck. They sat on a hickory stump, with James pointing at something when I walked upon them.

"I remember like it was only yesterday cutting this very tree down, and I can show you exactly where it landed!" He pointed to the other side of a ravine. But there was no excitement in his voice in the way the tree crashed to the ground.

I was there that day also when he cut our favorite two trees down that straddled the ravine. Maybe he was setting his mind free of something that he wasn't fond of keeping. The vines we'd used so many times to swing out over the small holler whipped themselves high into the air when the trees came crashing to the ground. And finally come to rest, sprawled amongst the many broken limbs.

"It would have been good in some ways to see all these new trees grow up," James said breaking our silence. The way of an artist I thought with his gaze looking out over the landscape, with squinting eyes and his head slowly weaved back and forth. Maybe he like me should consider that we let go of the vines just part of the tug-of-war going on in his heads.

"Well, they're already as tall as me," Duck pointed to some new growth.

"The baccer sure looks good from up here, Duck," James interrupted possibly wanting to get off the subject of trees for now.

"That da-gone stuff better be lookin' good after all the work I done on it all prickin' summer!" he bragged.

"What did you just say?" James laughed.

"Well, you know that I don't cuss like Piggy Wiggy, but I do say a few bad words."

James and I broke out with spontaneous laughter at the same time with Duck looking at us all confused like.

"Now don't fool yourself, Duck! You're starting out just like Arnold did . . . with a little bad word here and again. But after he carved the F-word into that board, and I don't think he was even ten, man . . . the sky was the limit and in no time was his favored four-letter word."

"Now that's bullshit, and you know it, James!" I protested.

"Arnold, I've never heard so many masterpieces come from one mouth in my life." He laughed.

I held my tongue in defense of myself. I didn't want to mess up the point that James was trying to get across to Duck—that it was an easy habit to start but almost impossible to stop. He got some understanding of it; looking down at the ground, Duck shook his head, maybe to confess he'd said more than just bad words.

"Well, the truth is it wasn't just me that did all the work in the 'baccer." Duck also wanted to get off of the subject at hand. "The boys did help some as long as I could keep 'em away from the springs." He said while looking over at us with a short giggle.

"Well, I remember, and it wasn't that long ago when this guy named Duck used to do the same thing when we were the tenders." I gave him a slight shove as he nodded to the truth of it.

"But it really does look good, Duck." James spoke up once again.

"Listen!" I cupped my hand to my ear, hearing an old familiar sound. Duck pointed toward the springs, where Rebel had barked and was now running our way as fast as he could go. "Look at the old guy. He sure don't run like he used to, does he?" Over the hill, we stampeded to join him. It would have been hard to pick who was the happiest with our reunion, the dog or us.

"You should've had your ass here yesterday instead of out lollygaggin' around Rebel!" I roughed his fur. "This is twice we've about had to leave your ass behind!" I looked out across the field towards the springs, where we'd gathered so many times to play with him. I could almost feel the cold water escaping from under the bottoms of my feet from clear black holes in the deepest part. I knew we couldn't leave today without a final plunge in fear that maybe it would truly be the last.

"Let's go!" James said, shoving me to the side as if he'd read my mind. I remembered how deep the spring had looked the first time we saw them. Maybe I'd outgrown the body of water, but it would always be the memories I'd cherish. I can't say that the swim made it any easier to say goodbye as the three of us were having such a great time splashing about. Then we were four, as Rebel plowed in from the bank to join in the fun. We sat in our old familiar spots on the bank after we'd gotten our clothes back on. It was hard for anyone to make the first move to leave, with the sound of water cascading over the rocks. For a second, in a world of my own, I stared into the water with thoughts of an arrowhead and the meaning I thought it had in getting this very farm. I could only hope that it really had those magic powers, as I'd sacrificed it wherever it now lay in the heap of ashes. Maybe someone would find it when they cleaned the place, never to know the story that came with it. Even though we'd agreed that it was better that we get over the old place and start new, it just didn't seem possible when it lay spread out in front of me. The fact was the memories, not the place, would be forever embedded in my soul.

We walked back up the well-worn path that came out at the mailbox. A snap of my pointing finger sent Rebel scampering to the top of the loaded truck. James never took it out of second gear as we idled along, hardly stirring any dust at all. I didn't stop Rebel as he barked all the way to the bridge. I'm sure he'd sensed something strange was going on. Maybe it was his way to say good-bye. As we crossed Kincaid Creek, a Beatles song came to mind. "Yesterday . . . all my troubles seemed so far away . . ." I hummed along, masked by the noisy exhaust. It did seem that it was no more than yesterday that I sat under the bridge we just past over with James scratching a picture on its concrete wall. Now I could only hope that we'd leave yesterday's troubles behind. We'd still have to come back over and tend the baccer, but this was the day to bid farewell. I guess it just played out that way.

James was the first to point out the old man pacing back and forth as seen through the front room window. Mom sat at the end of the couch, biting her fingernails the whole while. James slowly backed the truck to the front door, where everyone waited to unload it with the exception of the old man, which was expected.

He was going on what a great buy he'd made at both Good Hope and Camp Creek. It was good that he talked solely to James and not me, especially the part about "quick cash." That just meant he could spend it quicker than we could make it, I'd told James.

"Why, I might even have to hire more help!" he said, while expelling a large plume of smoke and mostly from his nose. "And I think it'd be best if we shut our operation down here for a while and make that quick cash at the other place's and then we'll come back here," taking a hard draw on his cigarette.

I thought if there was anything good about the whole deal, it was they were both close enough that we could drive home every night. Excitement ran through me, noticing the two stacks of money on the kitchen windowsill. I nodded to James, which he acknowledged.

Mom's timing for a noon lunch was close with everything unloaded and put in place. We all seated ourselves, with the old man at the end of the table. I had to think back a long ways to remember the last time we'd all eaten together.

"Now you boys ain't gonna be able to go shoppin' for school clothes for a couple more weeks. I need you both to work straight through! No time off until school starts."

"Are you saying we're gonna have to miss our first day of . . . school to go shopping?" He surely must have known what our reaction would be. More smoke bellowing from his nose and mouth that I challenged him.

"There'll be time, Arnold Ray!" His temper suddenly flared, quieting everyone's movement except for James's.

I'd seen it other times when James would shake a small amount of salt in the very center of his empty plate. Then with a relaxed forefinger, he'd start in the middle, pushing a circle till it spiraled to the outer edges. I'd thought it was something to do till Mom put the food on the table or maybe his artistic mind at work. But this was different—nothing smooth about his circular pattern and now with a stiff finger it all ground to a sudden stop resting at the top of his plate. He slowly pushed his chair back from the table. After standing up he placed both hands on it while looking in the old man's eyes.

"I've got a date with Scarlett next Sunday, and I plan on being there." He slowly sat back in his chair, anticipating there'd be a rebuttal.

"Well . . . Mr. Junior, the only thang I can tell ye is that you need to call Scarlett up and tell her the date is off till further notice!" I thought how well the old man accepted Scarlett as James's girlfriend saying nothing of them being related by blood such as I had done. James looked around the kitchen as if to survey the barren walls.

"I don't see a phone. And furthermore, if there were one, I wouldn't make that call." He craned his neck, not taking his eyes off the old man. He'd not intimidated James at all with his demands.

"Well . . . I don't think you get the picture . . . old buddy. So I'll put it to you like this." Just the thought of him explaining anything to James and in such a downgrading way was enough to turn my stomach. "If we don't get us some quick cash, they ain't gonna be enough money to buy school clothes for anybody! Let alone all the other bills that keep stacking up!" James shook his head all the while wanting to say something.

"Now I'll say it one more time: if we cain't get some quick cash for a couple weeks, there ain't gonna be enough money for much of anything!" I glanced over at Judy, with her head bowed, staring into her plate and unwilling to look at anyone.

I thought of the excitement she'd expressed of going to a new school, and explaining what her new dress would look like on her very first day. With yellows, blues and greens she talked of the many combinations she'd mix and match throughout the days that would follow. It had been that way ever since she'd caught me in the fourth grade when I wanted her to have new clothes every year. And especially now as a sophomore and in a new school she needed something to show off her ever-present smile.

Mom had noticed her also but knew it'd do no good to say anything right now. She never argued with the old man much when the family was around. She looked tired and with good reason, I thought. And like always, I knew when everyone had gone to sleep, she'd pray and cry her heart out to the Lord that he might send a guiding light to help her one more time.

I would never understand the old man's conniving ways; maybe all in his plan that with Granma living so close, she and Mom could make everyone clothes if they needed to. *But there is no way Judy is going to school, her sophomore year, and not have a few store-bought clothes,* I almost said out loud. I glanced at the heaps of money once again. *I'll give her half of it,* I thought and feeling more satisfied now.

"Now like I said, it's a little while before school starts, and I need you boys to bust your asses right up till then!" James quickly pushed his chair back from the table for a better view of the old man.

"What did all the money go for that we've already busted our asses for?" He'd asked the perfect question, putting the old man sorely on the spot and in front of everyone.

"I explained to you before about all the expenses we've got!" he said loudly. "There's no more to say about it!" He stood up, coughing a couple of times, and walked to the living room while rattling loose change in his pants pocket.

"Well . . . I promised Scarlett that we'd go out riding around, and that's what we're going to do!" James said with an ever stiffening jaw. "And you're telling all of us that you don't have money to buy school clothes with! Is that what you're saying?" It was unusual for James the way he raised his voice, asking for a simple answer. The old man whirled with an angry look, only to be met by James holding a hand up to stop him.

"Now that the whole family is here, why don't you tell everybody what you did with all that money? I bring you a check from Chillicothe about every day, and sometimes two, that's always more than fifty dollars—and that's still not enough?" I'd held my tongue for as long as I could afraid of what I'd do if the old man were to point a threatening finger at me.

"Ask him how much his drinking and cigarette bill is a week," I lashed out. James ignored my outburst.

"I'm not bad at math, and I can tell you that just a couple checks would be more than enough to cover school clothes for everyone including me and Arnold."

"Hold your horses right there, old buddy." The old man placed his hand up behind his ear. "I've told you it takes a lot to support a family this big with food, payments on two farms, gas—they ain't no end to what has to come out of my pocket every day. So you go right ahead with your plan . . . Me, Arnold Ray, and Calvin will go and do the best we can until you pull your head out of your ass!" he snapped.

Even though the comment was directed at James, it hit me as hard of a punch to the stomach as I'd ever felt. I almost choked with just the thought of having to work with him in any shape, form, or fashion. That'd be like not having anyone there at all! James never said another word but started walking for the kitchen door, then turned just before exiting.

"You know, Dad, that comment about me having my head up my ass? Well . . . if you'd pulled yours out and kept it that way, this family would be lots better off, and I'd guess we'd still be over in Pike County living happily ever after!"

"There's you boys' money for your damned school clothes." He swept a quick finger toward the windowsill. I picked the two piles up, following James out the back door.

We hadn't gotten far up the road when in a joking way I asked James which handful he wanted, saying that maybe the old man had overpaid one of the piles. It was enough to give us a much-needed laugh as James grasped the closest one to him, folding it into his shirt pocket. My laughter slowed after I turned the first twenty-dollar bill over with all others being one-dollar bills. Quickly flipping them over, I was thinking there must be a hundred-dollar bill on the bottom. But there wasn't as a slow panic came over me. I counted it for the second time, knowing I couldn't be off that much.

"What's wrong?" James asked while slowing the Buick down.

"There's only sixty-five dollars here James!"

"What?" He frowned, looking at the money spread out over the seat.

"Let me count yours." My voice cracked with panic. Any hope that the old man had mistakenly put the two hundreds in one pile quickly faded when suddenly I was finding it hard to breathe.

"You've only got sixty-five also, James!" He slammed on the brakes, sliding sideways and coming to a stop in the middle of the road. Gripping the steering wheel with both hands, he gently pressed his forehead against it, looking out into the field.

"Why can't things ever turn out right?" he exploded, pounding the seat with a fist. "Why can't that bastard just do one thing that he promised!" He angrily slouched back into his seat folding his arm at the chest.

"You know, James, I've been thinkin' about this all summer. And now . . . boy, do I wish I'd made that . . . fucker pay me cash after every load."

"It was all that bullshit 'that you boys need a bank account'! That was just him planning a way to screw us out of the money he owes us." James revved the motor up and turned a donut in the middle of the road, slinging gravel as we headed back toward the house.

"Where in the hell is the rest of our money?" James screamed, barging through the back door. I'd never seen him so furious over anything in my life.

"That's all the money you've got comin', old buddy," he said, putting his pen back into his pocket and dropping a crumbled piece of paper into his standing ashtray.

"Bullshit!" I intervened.

"You shut your damn mouth, Arnold Ray!" He pointed the warning finger that I'd been waiting on. I lurched at him when James fended me off from grabbing and breaking his finger in half. Now more angered than ever, I reached in my back pocket and pulled out the paper I'd been keeping a tally on for all summer, carefully unfolding it not to tear one of the many worn places.

"Right here! Right here you low rent asshole. I shouted. Right here is how many loads of pulpwood and logs that we've loaded and taken out of here!" I scribbled a shaky finger back and forth a couple of times, stabbing at the final count. "You still owe us a hundred more dollars, and here's the proof." I fanned it in front of him.

He never looked at the paper, not even a glance. "I don't owe you boys a goddamn thing the way I see it!"

"Jim, you don't need to talk like that to them boys," Mom pleaded.

"You stay out of this, Marie. It's none of your Goddamned business anyway!"

"Oh, I think it is her business when you're saying there's no money for school clothes." James now stood within striking distance. "And tell me with school right around the corner, why did you wait till now to bring this shit up?"

"Well, it's not a problem, James." I sneered. "Why they can all afford to miss a year like I did 'cause of this very reason. Then what? Bust their asses for failing? And what happened to that bank account that you told us we should start? You know a safe place to keep our money, right?"

"Whoa . . .! You can stop right there, boys. I hain't charged you a red penny for room and board up here!" he shook a warning finger at us. Getting to her feet, Mom motioned for the rest of the family to follow her outside.

"RENT! That's bullshit that you'd even think such a thing when we've been nothing but a couple of slaves for you!" James sounded hurt. "When we agreed to do this, you told me and Arnold that you weren't going to charge us for room and board. So what happened to that?"

"I never said any such a thang." He shook his head slightly as if to try and remember back. "No . . . I don't believe I said that at all, Junior."

"You know, Dad, you're nothing short of a lying asshole—something that I should have admitted to a long time ago. You told me and Arnold to do a terrible thing for you over in Pike County so you could buy this place over here. Now I'd give anything to have that split second of time back to reconsider. I doubt that we'd be here today! I'll tell you what, and so help me God you better do it or I'll . . . You take the money that you . . . fucked me and Arnold out of and buy your children school clothes or so help me..!"

The insult and threat hung heavy in the air. With that said, James turned and headed for the kitchen door once again.

Judy, who'd left Mom and the others out by the driveway, greeted us with a hug at the backdoor, where she'd been listening to what the old man had said. She gathered enough strength to tell us that everything would be all right. But neither James nor I could find comfort that things would ever be all right in any way. James walked away in his frustration, leaving us by ourselves.

After she'd said something to James, Mom walked past us, asking that we join the others at the Buick. With all the windows open, every word could be heard.

"Jim, tell me, what exactly happened over in Pike County?" Mom's question sounded as if she were ready to cry.

"You don't worry about it, Marie. Like I told you before, it's none of your business!" he shouted at her.

"Well, I hope it's not what I've suspected Jim 'cause a Christian just wouldn't—"

"A Christian!" I mocked as loud as I could that he heard me. James told everyone with the exception of me and Judy to get in his car and stay there. "James, I'm going in there and drag his ass out here and whip the hell out of him. I've had enough."

"No, you're not, Arnold. I'm the eldest," he said while rolling his shirtsleeves up to the elbows. He'd gotten about halfway there when the old man exited the back door. Seeing James approach, he went straight to his car, wasting no time in his getaway.

We stayed awhile longer to calm Mom down somewhat. She hadn't and never would ask James or me about her suspicions of what went on at the Pike County house. It would be another one of the things she'd hide from everyone only to pray that all be forgiven. But for now and possible forever I hoped we never talk of that tragic day again.

Judy knew what the fix needed to be as she started singing the words. Not a song like that of an altar call, but one with an upbeat rhythm to it. All the rewards of heaven if you'd lived a righteous life here on earth. All your troubles were over now. "I'll fly away, sweet Jesus," I belted the chorus with them, bringing a smile to my mother's face. It worked in the way it always had, with her having a good cry in the end.

There was only one thing said in the half mile to the bus. James with determination in his voice said he'd do the old man in if he ever laid a finger on our mother again. He wasn't the type to have a cussing match before doing what he'd promised. I, on the other hand, would want all the anger I could fester before getting out of control. Where James would stop after he'd done the deed, I wouldn't; and for that very reason, I'd want to be the first to get at the old man.

To hear my big brother cry was out of the ordinary. It just didn't fit his disposition, thinking back to how happy he was when telling me that he was going to buy Scarlett a really great present with some of his money. I thought about how he'd opened my eyes as what to expect when falling in love just an hour or so ago. How could things have turned so sour in such a short time? I looked out the car's window, watching everything fly past us. Everything seemed to be going way too fast and totally out of control I thought. It could strike fear into one's soul to wonder what lay ahead and how to deal with it. And it wasn't good for me to be left alone if there was a run in with the old man.

I thought to the time fighting our principal Mr. Boyd over something I knew was right and he was wrong. I'd gone so far as to plan an accident that would finish the old man off. And there wasn't just the one I'd thought of. Just for the sake of knowing, I occasionally checked to see if he still kept the 38 under his car seat. Each and every time I'd need to escape my terrible visions I'd turn to one thing. Praying absolutely did no good other than lead me to my mother's true guidance. I snapped to when James shut the car door behind him. I jumped out following him into the bus, where he went straight to the small closet, removing what few clothes he had hanging up.

"What are you do-doing?" I stuttered.

"I'm packing my stuff and getting the hell out of here!" he said. I stopped in my tracks floored as what to say.

"Well . . . where are you going to stay at, James?" I stuttered even more.

"I don't know yet. It's a toss-up between Scarlett's, Granma's, or even Uncle Arnold's place, where I could finish school at Willow Springs. You know none of them would mind if I stayed with them. And I don't need that bastard's permission either."

"Well, it sounds like an easy choice to me. Scarlett's, right?" I tried to sound excited for his sake.

"Well, that one might be a problem." He sat down on the edge of the bed. "Ezell and Anna Fay have wanted me to move in with them for some time now, and it seems like it'd be so easy to do. I think they'd do anything for Scarlett, and maybe that's why it might just be too easy." He paused and leaned forward, resting his elbows on his legs.

"I love being with her, but all the time might be another thing. I need to think more about this with school getting ready to start." He stalled before putting a tee shirt into the large flour sack. After laying it off to the side, he stared at the floor with his hands clasped together. "She'd head for Bainbridge on a school bus, and I'd head for Greenfield in my car. We've already talked how this is going to make things real complicated." He nodded.

"Well, look at it like this, James. You're a senior, so maybe it'd be best to just stay right here and finish your last year. I mean look at the shit I've been through, and I'm still here. But of course, it's all because of you talkin' me out of leavin' ever damned time. I really think you can hold out just a little longer, can't you? And what about Mom?" Had I not distracted him with so many reasons that he should stay he might've noticed that it was for me, the biggest plea of all.

"School hasn't even started yet, but I know it'll fly by like everything else has lately. I know you're right about Mom also. I don't need to put further burden on her. She's got plenty already, and more to come, you can bet on that! The fact of the matter is I don't see her as much as I should," he confessed. A minute passed, with him into heavy thought.

"I'll never forget the desperate look in her eyes when the house burned down over by Carmel. And how she counted us time and again to make sure we all were there and okay. She'd look me in the eye, starting with the oldest, and count 1, then turn to you and say 2 and so on until we were all accounted for. But never sure that one wasn't still missing. She's always been afraid of losing one of us, and I can't imagine what her life would be like if that was to ever happen. There could be no greater love than what she has for us, Arnold. I feel so sad for her when she throws her arms up and says that it might be best if the Lord was just to come and take her home. I can't think how bad it would be if we didn't have Mom, Arnold. But it's not us that she's having a hard time with.

"So what I'm going to do is just go away for a while to get my head together." His frown had lightened up as he'd come to grips with himself.

"So how long ya gonna take off for, James?" I inquired.

"I don't know. I might change my mind and be back here tomorrow morning. I'll make that call when the time comes." Satisfied with the decision, he threw a couple pairs of socks back into his drawer. Turning to face me, he asked, "Oh! And you need to tell me right now so we can make a plan. Do you want to go riding around with me and Scarlett next weekend?"

"Hell yes, by God, I'll go! I sure as hell don't want to be stuck in the woods with just him! I mean what if Calvin's gone too?"

"Good, I know you'll enjoy it, Arnold," he said.

"Oh, there's one other thing, though. I really don't want Carolyn to go with us. So please don't ambush me, okay?"

James hesitated for a few seconds before putting the rest of his clothes back into the small dresser drawers. "Well, you know it's mostly Anna Fay that insists that Carolyn go with us everywhere we go to make sure we don't screw up, as she calls it. It was pretty bad for a while till Scarlett told her to turn her ass around in the front seat and look out the windshield or take a walk but just stop watching us."

"You mean she watches you guys kiss?"

"Oh yeah and turned the dome light on once while I was feeling Scarlett's leg, and saying she was going to tell on us."

"Well, how much trouble did you get into?" I laughed.

"None. Scarlett threatened her with something that I sure wouldn't want to be on the receiving end of." He smiled. "Once during one of them really long kisses, I opened my eyes to see Carolyn hanging halfway over the front seat, watching us very closely. I think she's just at that age, if you know what I mean, Arnold." His suggestion embarrassed me that Carolyn was as curious about things as I.

"But since then, Ezell has got more involved, saying that we could go do some things on our own, but that was after he had a long talk with me about the birds and the bees and other responsibilities that I needed to consider."

"So, I guess you'll want me to look out the windshield and take walks also?" I joked.

"No, it's nothing like that. You've seen people kiss before." He was giving me the benefit of the doubt. "It's like Anna Fay gave her a list of all things that we shouldn't be doing. I'll just bet you'll know when it comes time to take a walk if you need to, right?" He grinned. "But don't worry. We're not going to have sex or anything like that." He burst into laughter.

"We're still trying to find how far we can carry on with those words of wit, such as, 'yes I want to' and 'No, we shouldn't,'" and now it's how much longer can we put it off.

"You're talking about havin' sex, right." I'd turned my head slightly so he couldn't see my curious look.

All laughs have a certain meaning to them. To do so just because it was expected always sounded the lamest of all I thought. To fake it, when no one got the punch line after a long drawn out joke was pretty bad also. But the ones where all communication shuts down when you literally gagged for the slightest breath of air were my favorite.

James laugh was strained I thought sounding as if he and Scarlett were running out of options to not go all the way and have sex.

He put an extra pair of pants and a clean shirt in the Buick, then left for Scarlett's house shortly after.

I felt good that he'd reconsidered and not move away. With everything in better order now, he'd go see the one person that could heal his needs. I could only hope that soon I could fulfill my dream of a kiss from a beautiful girl. But the reality was that my heart was breaking. My brother and best friend might still leave me to fend for myself. The nightmare would continue that I would be stuck at the bottom of a deep dark well, smothering to see the light of day once again.

But on a brighter side, I'd spend the rest of the afternoon with Mom and the family. She thought a picnic up at the pond would be a good way to round off the day. We carried several chairs from Harry's place, which he insisted after we'd invited him to eat and enjoy the afternoon with us.

"Why, I'll say one thing, Marie," he giggled, "that's the most people I've seen in that pond at one time." Judy and Beth changed into cutoffs and a blouse in the bus before they came up. All dares were that I come in so they could baptize me as Duck yelled. But I simply wanted to sit with Mom and Harry to talk for a while.

There was no planning to what happened next when Mom started singing a song. No doubt it was to celebrate our gathering. Even though the song spoke of such unity I thought there were better ones to celebrate with. But it was the one that was in her heart at the time with everyone at the pond. 'May the Circle be Unbroken.'

Slow with a soft bluegrass beat, she'd no more than sang a few words when Judy and Beth chimed in from where they stood in the pond waist-deep by a cluster of cattails. Maybe that we were close to the pond's edge their voices soared with such delight. Harry made no effort to wipe his tears away. And even though no words came from his mouth his lips moved in the way I thought he must know every word to the song. Regardless of the times he talked about going to hell he'd been to church before pointing out a picture hanging on his wall of him and his wife dressed to the hilt. And his very words he said they had their 'Sunday go to meeting clothes' on.

It was close to dark when Mom left Harry standing in the road. She and everyone started walking down the road with exception of Duck and Larry who'd go with me to milk and then carry it on to the house. After straining it they'd bring the bucket back to me. I sat with Harry as he went on and on that this was the best day he'd had in a long while. He'd got his wish and was truly happy that they'd sang several songs just for him.

I stood in the doorway of the bus the next morning, dreading the heavy gray fog, where wavy imaginary figures slowly glided past. It was the place in your worst nightmare where something unknown would grab you, sending a frenzy throughout, such as in the painting *The Scream*. "Fright with outlined definitions" was how James said Mrs. Thacker had explained it to the class. The scariest movies all had fog lifting in just the right places, with the villain's silhouette in the dark background. I thought about how the old man was like that in many ways and might appear right in front of my face at any time.

"Little too much TV," I laughed out loud, stepping off the last step. Inching my way through the field, I could finally see them all standing at the barn, waiting for their grain. For now, I'd feed Kate and Mr. Bill on the outside so their stomping hooves wouldn't make Red so nervous.

Even though the fog hadn't come into the barn, it's heaviness was still there. But no matter the weather, the barn would always keep its look and smell of its age. No barn could ever rid itself completely of decades of old manure and mildew. Large spider webs straddled dirt-stained windows hanging heavy with gray dust. Long stringy cobwebs swept slowly from high places in the rafters their catches long gone with the ages.

Hidden back in shaded corners, wooden barrels held shovels and rakes that hadn't been touched by human hands in many a year, I'd guessed. A dark opening from above could tempt one into climbing the old wooden ladder nailed to the loft beam, where rungs disappeared up into a dark hole. Any noise sent the occupants of the barn into a frenzy. They hardly ever had company after all. Up in the mound lay hay from many years back, which would sift through cracks as rats and mice scampered to their hiding places.

I sat down to milk and was nearly finished when out of nowhere,

"Arnold Ray!" a loud voice blurted from the darkened hallway. I quickly jumped from my stool, sweeping the bucket out from under Red before she kicked. I couldn't imagine how she or I hadn't heard him sneak upon us. Had his pipe been lit, it'd been a different story. "Boy, ole Jimbo's in rare form this mornin' ain't he?" Calvin grunted. "Why, that damned prick came beatin' on the door this mornin' like I was his damned slave or somethin'."

There was no pleasure, with the way he blasted the first puff of baccer smoke into the barn with two more quickly to follow. A different kind of fog now mixed throughout the area. I didn't tell him that I thought the baccer smell seemed to fit right in with the barn's other smells. He slid the pipe far back in his mouth, chomping down on it.

"Now, Arnold Ray, if ole Jimbo don't thank I won't pack up the shack and leave, then he's got another thang comin'." Calvin could barely be seen standing in darkness of the stall next to me. A match lit the area up for a brief second when he had to relight his pipe where swirly smoke quickly exited the cracks in the wall.

"Did you get your muffler fixed? I never heard you drive up," I said, patting Red to calm her somewhat.

"Why, hell no, that old man of yours don't never pay me a full week— when he does pay me! I walked all the way up 'yer this mornin', hauling that hemorrhoid-makin' sons of a bitchin' saw. And I'll not be doin' much of that shit, I can tell ya that right now! And it ain't the muffler that's the real problem. It's that little gauge that's sittin' on empty right now," he said, finally stepping out from the darkness.

"What happened? You forget to get gas?" Maybe it wasn't such a good thing to kid about, I thought.

"Hell no, I didn't forget it. I didn't have enough damned money to get any. By that time, we already bought food and a little drank! Why, I think old Jimbo better be gettin' his act together real soon, Arnie," Calvin warned. "And I'll be damned if I'm workin' for free, and I sure don't like anybody owin' me money. It always gets confusin' in the end on how much they said they already paid ya."

Suddenly, a faint draft swept through the area, leaving a smell that I was all too familiar with. Camel cigarettes. The old man came walking in through the same dark doorway that Calvin had.

I whirled around, thinking maybe I'd have to confront him, accidentally kicking the bucket of milk over, which spooked Red into running out of the barn. He walked to the dirty old window, shadowing his wagging finger somewhat.

"I'm gonna tell the both of ya somethin' right now!" he threatened. "If you . . . don't like workin' here, then hit the Goddamned road!" He pointed.

Showing no sign of disappointment that the man had shown up at such an inopportune time, Calvin quickly jerked his pipe trailing smoke from his straight arm, while aiming it directly towards the old man.

"Well now, Jim, like I told ya, me and the old lady was gonna be leavin' in about two weeks . . . anyway," he said calmly. But I knew Calvin all too well, that he was leading up to something as he drew wind. "I mean that's unless you piss me off before that!" He barked a laugh. "And by God, don't think for a minute I won't leave right fuckin' now! These nut-bustin' jobs are a dime a dozen!" His mouth flared faintly, showing many teeth. "Now by God, they ain't no date set in concrete fer me goin', as you already know that, Jim." The old man had no more than turned to walk away.

"Now there is one other thing, Jim," Calvin interrupted, knocking his pipe against a wooden beam, deadening all sound for an instant. "Whenever I leave on my own or you decide to put my ass down the road, you better have ever' damned dime that you owe me! I mean ready to put in my hand! Because if you don't, 'old buddy,' we're gonna have some serious problems. And most of 'um will be yours!" He sounded a lot like the time with Bill McCoy, I thought.

The old man had gone quiet. Not even a whistle. The barn had temporarily returned to its normal dusty silence once again. I'd been angry about him cheating James and I out of our hard-earned money and figured I'd say what I wanted now, with Calvin there.

"Oh! And when I graduate, you can bet your ass that I'll be leavin' also!"

"Well, ole buddy!" He turned quickly to face me. "Why don't you pack your shit and leave right now? I'm sure not holdin' you back!" He coughed a couple of times, spitting off into a dark corner.

"Mom is my main reason, but there's plenty others that'll keep me here awhile longer. First of all, the law is on my side—that you'll support me till I'm eighteen. And furthermore, the law don't agree with you about room and board either! Way it sounds to me like I don't have to hit a lick and you still have to provide for me." He'd been shaken his head all the while, eager to interrupt.

"Well, ole buddy, that's not the way I interpret the law." He snapped his head back, running fingers through his hair. "Why, it clearly says that—"

"Wait, just hold it right there!" I interrupted. "This ain't no old Bible sayin' that you can throw at me!" I held a stiff arm out. "What you're goin' to try to tell me is nothin' but bullshit. You ain't got a damned clue about the law 'cause if it agreed with the way you interpret it, I'd already be gone! So you can quit talkin' that shit!" I hadn't stuttered a single word as I slowly unclenched my fists.

"I couldn't start the first grade of school because you were in jail, and we didn't have any money. Do you know how it feels to have started a year later than most just because I didn't have shoes or descent clothes to wear on my first day of school? Hum, and now clothes have come into play once again. I was really young, but I knew that you were no better than a fuckin' drunk way back then!"

The old man turned quickly, trying to walk away once again.

"I'm not finished yet!" I leaned over to pick the empty milk bucket up. "I failed the fourth grade because of your bullshit too! I missed sixty-six days of school while you hauled us all over hell and gone!"

"I don't have ta stand here and listen to this from somebody like you!" he yelled.

"You'll hear me out even if I got to follow you out the barn! And what did I get from you when I failed that year? I got to go and cut two switches, one for me and one for my baby sister, who was too small to cut her own and also too small to be whipped! The one thing that has stayed with me all these years is why you really whipped us. Do you remember the reason?" I shouted. "You hated to break a promise! You threatened to whip anyone who failed that year. What a lame-ass, hateful reason to whip someone for! Especially when you alone were the reason we failed!! ...Florida!!!" I breathed my contempt. The old man held his hand behind his ear, looking pitifully weak I thought. After a single cough, he stepped back into the dark place in the hallway, then left.

How could anger toward someone become so bad that I considered maybe even the barn might be a good place to hide him? There still were places in the barn that I'd not investigated fully. These were thoughts that I couldn't ponder on for very long as they were draining my soul. "Eternal hatred," he'd preached, where for those who couldn't seek the Kingdom of God for that very reason.

"Do you know how embarrassing it is, Calvin, knowin' that I'll be nineteen when I graduate high school?" It could have been a baited question as fast as Calvin pulled his pipe.

"Why, hell, Arnie! If it makes ya feel any better, look at me, I still hain't grage-ated." The barn echoed with laughter. But best of all was the way I stood up to the old man. James would have been proud of me, I thought, when Calvin extended his hand for a shake.

"Now I can't say in all honesty that I wouldn't wanted to see a good ole-fashin' ass whippin'. But, Arnold Ray, you did good." His grip was hard as usual. I gritted my teeth as I squeezed with all that I had. He'd had to break my hand before I'd give up, and that might have been the reason he eased up a little. But most important of all it was a manly handshake at that.

"So, whatcha think, Calvin, did I shorten my time to stay around here? I mean did I wear my welcome out this time?" He hesitated for a quick answer; taking the time to study my stance.

"Well, I don't know what you're gonna do, Arnold Ray. But I know that I'm goin' to get serious about gettin' the hell out of here before I have to knock the hell out of ole Jimbo . . ." I thought for an instant about the sixty-five dollars in my pocket and wondered how much Calvin would take to beat the shit out of the old man before he left. It really wasn't worth the thought though, thinking I'd rather do it myself for free.

Red began grazing a little way from the barn. I'd milked enough that she'd be okay till evening.

"Well, while I'm here I'll help you get them harnesses on these beasts!" He grunted with a smack on Mr. Bill's big ass, like a wake-up call.

"Now where in the hell's Junior when all this excitement's going on, Arnold Ray?"

"Oh, he already had his knock-down, drag-out of sorts with the old man yesterday so decided to act like him and take a day or so off. And he's been ready to calf ever since James told him off. And man, you should have seen the look on his face when James told him that he was the one who had his head up his ass! I don't think the old man took that too good, but it is the truth, ye know!"

Calvin started clapping his hands with big loud pops like the older men would do at church. "Well now, I think it's good that ole Junior said something like that." Calvin blew a plume straight up. "Hell, when I thank about it, ole Jimbo's had his head up there bout ever since I've known him, Arnold Ray."

"Well, I just don't know what's gonna happen next, Calvin."

"Well like we told you before, if it gets too bad you know you can come and stay with me and that old lady, by God, down on Camp Creek."

I knew Calvin had the best intentions, but I wasn't gonna stay with him and Mary. I could hear James now doing his best Mary imitation. 'Arnie this and Arnie that.' He'd never let me live it down, especially since he'd become a little more vulgar about things, himself anymore.

Mr. Bill and Kate stood at attention, it looked, with their harnesses adjusted to a good fit. They'd eaten their grain and were ready to go.

"Well, I guess it's good in one way that I spilt the milk, Calvin. Now I won't have to carry it all the way to the house since James ain't here ta give me a ride, and besides, Mom's got plenty from last night's milkin'."

"I know! She's already givin' us more than we need!" Calvin growled. "No matter how much the old lady dranks we can't keep up with it." Suddenly, his eyes lit up. "Arnold Ray, have you seen the size of that heifer lately? Why, she's so big now I can hardly roll her over in the bed anymore." He smiled, lifting his brow slightly.

After Calvin hung his saw over one of Mr. Bills collar hames we walked on to the pond, where he started the truck up, and headed for the laydown yard. I wouldn't be far behind him.

CHAPTER 3

Bob and Mickel

We worked hard, taking advantage of the morning coolness, and had no sooner sat down than the old man's car could be heard coming toward the yard.

"Now I guess ole Jimbo thanks we're quittin' too early to eat and is comin' up here to get on our ass, Arnold Ray, you thank?" Calvin laughed, then proceeded to take an animal-size bite from his sandwich and all with a satisfying grunt.

"Well, I'm glad it took um' till noon to get up 'ere, but best would be if he never came at all!" I toasted to what he'd said with my Frosty held high into the air.

"Why, who in the hell are those people with him Arnie?" Calvin pointed over my shoulder. He laid the rest of his sandwich down on the log and quickly grabbed his pipe like he was late for his smoke. After a pinch, he packed it firmly with a wide thumb. A few flakes fell to the ground, rare on Calvin's part. His attention was definitely elsewhere. I never made any attempt to look over my shoulder where the old man had parked. Calvin lit his pipe, shaking the match quickly to put it out.

"Arnold Ray, I thank our replacements are finally here! By . . . God, that old sucker in the backseat's old 'nough to be Harry's daddy, looks to me like!" Calvin spoke loud with no regard that he might be heard. I started laughing as I spun around to see what Calvin's rambunctiousness was all about.

"Calvin! You might be talkin' too loud!" I said with a high-pitched whisper.

"Yeah, you're probably right, Arnold Ray. I've tried to talk over that noisy-ass chainsaw for so many years that I b'leeve it's deafened my yurin. Or least that's what the old lady says anytime I don't jump when she's raisin' hell about something. She already told me that I need a yurin aid like old Harry's got, but I'll never make enough money for one of them damned thangs." He laughed.

117

Two men gathered with the old man at the car's hood, where he pointed out various things before leading them off into the woods without so much as looking in our direction.

"Arnold Ray... them two are gonna start workin' here!" Calvin laughed once again. "I don't see how Jim's gonna get much out of that one old fart there." He pointed his pipe. "Why, hell, he can barely walk, looks like. And anyone who rubs his gut like that has got somethin' wrong insid'um," he observed.

Calvin seemed too interested in the two fellows to finish eating his sandwich as flies had gathered all around its edges. "Get off there! You nasty sons of bitches!" He swished them away, putting the rest in his lunch box, then snapping the binders shut.

"That's why I never put my sandwich down till I'm finished with it, Calvin."

"Well, that's one reason I lit this pipe up sometimes, smokin' at the same time just to keep them off'n me and my eaten! Hell, when I go to shit, I blow smoke all over the place and even in the hole. If there's anything I can't stand is damned flies runnin' up and down the crack of my ass when it's takin longer than usual in there! Yeah . . . this smoke works on keepin' them away for a while, but there's one thang it don't affect much, Arnold Ray." I knew better than to ask, so I sat there, knowing he'd tell me anyway. "Do you know what it is?" he asked.

"No, I don't, Calvin," I said, shrugging my shoulders.

"When I get ready to do that thang to the old lady, they—"

"Hold it right there, Calvin. I don't think I need to hear about that stuff!" His laugh that followed sounded raunchy.

I dreaded when the old man came back out of the woods, but instead of bringing the two fellows to where we sat, he pointed an effortless finger in our direction. After a handshake with them, he took off.

Calvin was quiet in the way he studied their every step as they approached us. His effort was weak at best to blow his smoke very far. I noticed the younger of the two had lots of scratches on his hands and arms when he extended one of them for a handshake.

"I'm Bob, and this here is Mickel!" he introduced them both in a lively way.

"I'm Arnold, and this here is Calvin," I joked that I'd copied Bob's introduction which he picked up on. Mickel didn't put much effort into his handshake looking as if he were in pain vigorously rubbing his stomach. With pinpoint accuracy, Calvin's smoke blanketed Mickel as he shook his hand pretty hard and aggressively, hanging on to it longer than necessary for the smoke's full effect.

It was obvious that Bob was the more outgoing of the two as he dug out a pouch of chewing baccer from his rear pocket. His face was full and with some excitement, it looked, whereas Mickel's was drawn in at the mouth—more of a sad or painful look, I thought. When Bob opened his mouth to shove the large wad into it, it showed dark teeth almost worn to the gum. Calvin drew slowly on his pipe while Bob, with every chew, compacted the baccer tightly in his mouth. I glanced at Mickel, who'd never stopped rubbing his stomach from when we'd first seen him. In a minute or so, a dark-stained juice appeared at both corners of Bob's mouth who became seemingly more comfortable after his first spit well off to the side of us. To finish his routine, he removed a rag from a back pocket, wiping his mouth clean of all spillage. It was Mickel who spoke up first when pointing a stumpy finger at Calvin's lunch box.

"Do you boys have anythin' left to eat?" he asked, dragging every word like they were painful to say. Calvin opened the lid up, never taking his eyes off Mickel, and revealed the half-eaten sandwich as a single fly escaped, gone in a second.

"Hain't you gonna eat the rest of it?" he asked.

"No, you want it. Go ahead and have'er. And there's a ripe madder there too if you ont' it." Mickel went after it like a starving man, taking a bite of sandwich, then gnawing on the tomato. His teeth were all gone, reminding me of Mr. Miller the way he had to chew for such a long time. Everyone sat about on different logs except Calvin and me.

"Well, what are you fellers gonna be doin' up here with me and old Arnold Ray?" Calvin leaned forward, shooting a quick wink in my direction.

"Well, Mr. Richardson"—Bob spoke up—"is gonna have us do anythin' and everythin' is what he told us." Calvin and I started laughing before Bob finished tellin of what their duties would be and now looked at him dumbfounded.

"Mr. who?" Calvin quickly cleared his throat spitting off to the side like he couldn't get it out fast enough. "You mean Mr. Asshole!" He followed up.

"Boy, I hope he's not an ass . . . hole . . .," Mickel whined while wiping tomato seeds from the edges of his mouth and nose. "We've been workin' this shit all our lives . . . and they ain't nothin' that we ain't done! And we surenuff worked for some . . . assholes in our time. Hain't we, Bob?" Bob nodded as to agree but seemed anxious to get off the subject, checking his new surroundings out.

I looked over at Calvin, who was tipping his water jug up for a drink. He spat the first mouthful off to the side, wiping his mouth with his open hand. After several gulps, he sat the jug back down on the ground in the shady side of the log. He was fed and watered now and ready for a fresh bowl of tobacco. I'd noticed Mickel looking at Calvin's water jug more than just once. Calvin had noticed also when he slowly removed his pipe. "Didn't you boys bring any food or drank with ya?"

"No, we didn't bring anything, but it looks like you've got plenty." Mickel pointed to Calvin's half full jug. Odd I thought how it wasn't that long ago when Calvin went on how he didn't like drinking after other people. Bad teeth, no teeth, and now a person who continually rubbed his stomach all fell into the same category I figured. I kinda knew what to expect when Calvin quickly expelled a large cloud of smoke.

"That's my water. You'll have to git yer own, and that means yer dinner too."

"Hey, ole buddy, you don't need to get all worked up about it. We just need enough to make the day," Mickel shot back.

"Didn't Jimbo show you where that spring's at? Over the hill yonder?" Calvin nodded its direction.

Bob quickly interrupted, saying, "Yes, sir! Mr. Richardson showed us right where it's at."

"And another thing . . . I'm sure not your old buddy, ye old fucker. I want to make that plain and clear right off the bat." He said with a hard stare at Mickel.

"We get ours from that spring and it's good water. It's a deep spring." I spoke up, trying to ease the tension Calvin was creating. "It's been all cleaned out really good. I spent a lot of time putting those flat rocks back to where they originally used to be. But now before we go any further, I need to tell you that you don't need to call him Mr. Richardson 'cause—"

"Hold it right there, Arnold Ray!" Calvin sat up straight, interrupting me. "You boys'll call him every name in the world other than that one when it's all over with." He laughed, sounding ornerier than ever.

"Well then, let me ask you this." Bob moved over to a log closer to Calvin and me. "How long have you fellers been working for him?"

"Ha! I've worked for him my whole life! He's my old man. I just can't stand to call him Dad anymore. He's a no fatherin' son of a bitch in my opinion."

"Well, that's not very respectful to say somethin' like that about you own father." Mickel frowned.

"Well, you don't know him like I do and if you did, you'd understand my point of view better," I said in a kind way. "Calvin here's worked for him off and on for what . . . about three years or so?" I could tell the conversation wasn't what they wanted to hear. Mickel glanced over at Bob, looking as if there was more than just pain in his stomach now.

"At any rate, I do the loggin', and Calvin cuts everythin' up. Then me and my brother James load the truck. James isn't here today."

"Well . . . where is he? Is he tryin' to get out of workin'?" It was starting to sound as if Mickel was nosy about things.

"Oh no . . . James is one of the hardest-workin' people you'll ever meet. It's just that he's havin' a hard time seein' right now," I said.

Calvin burst out coughing, forcing smoke out his nose which set him off with a couple good sneezes.

"I guess that's a private joke," Bob observed but joined in the laughter anyway. Mickel never moved from the log, not even cracking a smile. I thought he'd looked sickly, just making his way out of the old man's car.

"Well, let me ask you another thang . . .," Mickel continued. "How many hours do you boys work a day?"

"From before daylight till after dark," Calvin blurted, I guess seeing what the old guy was leading up to. Calvin practically jumped from the log, while shoving his pipe into a back pocket. "And we're burnin' daylight the longer we stand 'round here bullshittin' with all these questions you got. Why, hell, we could about had us another load cut if you hadn't held us up with so many damned questions!" I knew Calvin was trying to give old Mickel a hard time when he winked at me in passing.

"Now, boys, I'm seventy years old. And they's no way I'm gonna keep up with you young fellers," Mickel warned. Bob laughed, shaking his head like he'd heard this all before. He and Mickel glanced at each other, with Bob still shaking his head. I thought they must have a private joke between them also. Old Mickel had just given us fair warning that he wasn't gonna be much help. Calvin took a couple of steps to where Mickel sat and offered a hand up, not like Calvin at all, I thought, as Mickel accepted.

"Well, thankyeeeeeee . . .!" he screamed loudly when Calvin jerked him up like a feather. It startled Mickel, who grabbed his chest like he was having a heart attack. Bob laughed all the while. It seemed funnier to him than me or Calvin. Mickel walked around for a minute or so, still clutching his chest, with Bob laughing out of control now. Calvin truly could be evil when he wanted. I was thinking how quickly Mickel had exited the log and now had properly been introduced to Calvin.

"It looks like that hit yer funny bone?" I asked Bob after he'd collected himself somewhat. He wiped tears and finally blew his nose.

"I've known Mickel for about all his life, but I . . . I never seen him move as fast as he did just then. He looked like one of them rocket sleds on television, takin' off!" Bob continued to laugh, which Mickel shared no pleasure in.

It was good to know that Bob had some humor about him, whereas Mickel didn't seem to have much. Then like a loaded question, Mickel asked if any of us smoked cigarettes. And was Calvin all over that one.

"The only thin' I smoke is this here freight train." He held the pipe up for all to observe. "And I sure as hell ain't gonna share it with you!" After lighting it up, he blew several puffs toward Mickel, who waved a hand to clear the air.

"I don't smoke anythin'," I said. "But if I did, it'd more than likely be a pipe for sure."

"Well, I don't know how much longer I kin go without a cigarette!" Mickel wheezed.

"Why, Mickel, that's the reason you're in the shape you're in right now . . .," Bob said, still snickering a little. His laugh was loony "he . . . he . . . he" in rapid fire, which was enough to get me laughing also.

"Now, Bob"—Mickel waved a finger—"I done told you this before! You need to keep out of my business."

"Yeah yeah-yeah, it's the same old shit. Nobody can tell you anything anymore." Bob then turned to walk away.

"Well now, I don't even know your sorry ass, but I can tell right off the bat you ain't gonna be much help around here the way you drag your sagging ass around." Mickel stood there giving Calvin the longest stare. "And by the way, how damned old are you . . . Mr. Bob?" Calvin posed the question.

"I'm seventy-two," Bob said, rubbing his hands together while glancing back and forth between the two of us. Calvin's pipe fell from his mouth, bouncing from the log before hitting the ground where he scooped it up immediately and started blowing the dirt off the mouthpiece.

"You're shittin' us, ain't cha?" I asked.

"No! He is older than me!" Mickel sounded reluctant like he'd had to admit to it before. Calvin spit on the end of the pipe, then rubbed it clean with his shirt, grumbling all the while that he'd dropped it in the first place.

"You sure don't look your age, Bob," I said, knowing no matter how I phrased it, I'd probably hurt Mickel's feelings one way or the other. It was hard to grasp that the man in front of us was that old. I'd thought Bob looked to be in pretty good shape from the first time I saw him and guessed him to be about fifty-something years old. He had a trim waist along with muscular arms and legs. But it was obvious that he didn't want to talk about their ages when he asked,

"Now what do you boys need for me and Mickel to do?" Mickel, who seemed in no hurry to get started, slowly circled a log before sitting down.

"Listen!" Mickel said, jumping back up and spooking Calvin at that. "Do you hear a car coming?" he turned his ear towards the road.

"All I hear are them goddamn birds a chirpin', and that tells me that I need to go cut more of their houses down!" Calvin lunged to pick his saw up. Mickel gave him a strange look.

"Damn, ole buddy! You cuss about as bad as I do!" he said, sounding short of breath.

"Now I done told you ten times since we've met, I'm not your old buddy, and if you keep callin' me that, I'm gonna have to show you why I'm not!" Calvin pointed a steady pipe at Mickel's face.

"Mickel, there's somethin' I need to tell you about my brother James. See . . . he's not big on cussin'."

"Hell no, he ain't big on it! He'll whip your old wore-out ass if you cuss too much around him!" Calvin chuckled lifting both eye brows. "You just ask old Arnold Ray here . . .," he huffed.

"Well it ain't quite like that. But it does bug him a lot, though." I'd cut Calvin short, but that didn't last long.

"But the good thing for you, Mickel, is James is hard of hearin' right now. And at times, he cain't hear nothin' at all!" Calvin roared.

"Well . . . was he born that way?" Mickel questioned, now curious, it sounded.

"No, it just happened overnight," Calvin went on. "Why he could hear perfectly good one day and then the next was deaf as that stump over there. It was pretty sad how it all happened." Calvin set his saw back on the ground. I knew what was up his sleeve.

"Well, I sure hate to hear that!" Mickel said. It was all I could do to not laugh, watching how Calvin was playing old Mickel like a fiddle. And he had him right where he wanted him.

All the while, Bob had been paying close attention to Calvin. He'd been around enough to know something wasn't just right. He cleared his throat with a couple coughs.

"Well, let me ask you something. How old is your brother?"

"He'll be eighteen next February," I said. He nodded his head slowly, drawing small circles in the dirt with our measuring stick he'd picked up. Unlike Mickel, Bob seemed to think things out before saying much of anything. A good listener, as James had called certain people. He'd told me one time after I'd made a wrong assumption about a person that you had to take time to feel them out. And that meant you needed to listen to them for a while before pinning an assumption on them too early. And he was right—I was always too anxious to tell my thoughts of someone. 'Wait your turn,' he'd said. 'If someone's going to hang themselves with lies or whatever, they'll do it pretty quick—most times that is if you don't interrupt them, however.' I was absolutely sure that, through no fault of mine, a lot of my cutting into conversations was because of our large family. We were always trying to talk over one another, where nothing was accomplished other than loud confusion.

Bob hadn't said much of anything but instead waited. He studied Calvin's every move. I'd watched Bob right up to the time he turned to look at me.

"Well now, boys, it sounds to me like your brothers got his head up his ass—maybe in love, is that it?" Bob declared, wiping a dark drip from a corner of his mouth. He laid the measuring stick down on a log, rapidly rubbed his hands together with some sort of pattern to it, and then quickly leaned back to a relaxed position.

Calvin looked over at me, raising his eyebrows once again. I guess one benefit of being old was that they'd seen and heard it all before. I was a quick learner but definitely a beginner with these guys, I thought to myself. I was pushing sixteen, which couldn't even be compared to the ages of Harry, Bob, and Mickel, where they had me by two hundred years in age.

Bob had noted the same as everyone else, relative to the whereabouts of James's head. I hoped they didn't look at me as if I were future prey. But I didn't need to waste my time talking about it because I knew it'd never happen to me. Nobody'd ever get the chance to say such things behind my back.

"Mickel! That's Jim. He's back with your damn cigarettes." Bob pointed toward the opening in the trees. *What a bastard*, I thought. *No money for school clothes or to pay James and I what was owned to us.* To watch a request for hardtack candy be scratched from a list that it not be a necessity. We'd done without things that we shouldn't have because of his alcohol and cigarette habits. And now, he's delivering cigarettes to someone we hardly knew!

I just couldn't stand to look at him. I wondered if it were quick cash that funded the cigarettes. I just wish he were dead. The terrible thought came to mind once again and more often lately. Calvin had been watching the expression on my face all the while and could probably guess that I was pissed. He'd seen my angry explosions and how badly I talked about the old man. I'd told him one time where many would consider it murder, I called it a solution.

"Arnie, you, all right?" Calvin got my attention, winking when I looked his way.

Mickel had a little more pep in his step as he walked toward the car and avoided rubbing his stomach altogether.

"Now boys that old fart moves pretty fast when he needs a stinkin'-ass cigarette, don't he?" Calvin pointed out. Bob slowly nodded his head looking our way agreeing with Calvin.

Mickel and the old man both lit one up at the same time, sharing the flame from the old man's lighter. After a short conversation, the old man left again without saying a word to any of us. Mickel drew hard on the cigarette, sucking his cheeks in.

"Stupid bastard . . .," Bob muttered. "You, stupid bastard!" he repeated. I didn't know if he intended for it to be funny or not. I wondered how long it'd been since Mickel's last cigarette. He'd smoked about half of it by the time he reached us. And just as I'd suspected there were the yellow fingers.

Instead of rushing off to cut down more birdhouses, as Calvin had suggested, we stood around listening to Mickel talk while finishing his cigarette. The very first cough was loud, followed by another and then another. Mickel stumbled around the yard, trying to find something to hang on to.

"Stupid bastard," Bob repeated himself once again but this time was much louder. Mickel's face had become beet red, coughing out of control. He staggered to a small sassafras tree at the edge of the yard, which he clung to hold himself up. I thought for sure he was going to cough himself to death right there on the spot with his tongue hanging out.

"Can we do anything to help him?" I asked Bob, thinking Mickel really was choking to death.

"No, soon as he upchucks, he'll be okay." A disgusted look came over Calvin as he quickly withdrew his pipe, and making a terrible face.

"Arnold Ray! Let's go load some wood! God almighty, I can't stand to look at that stuff!" Calvin shivered at the thought. Turning away from where old Mickel looked to be getting sicker by the minute Calvin headed for the truck with me and Bob quickly catching up with him.

"No, it's not a pretty sight. I keep telling him he can't keep smokin' like he does, and he always tells me the same thing, and that's to go screw myself!" Bob nodding. But no matter how fast we wanted to get out of hearing range we were too late. Calvin whirled around, pointing a threatening finger.

"Now, you old son of a bitch, you better not throw up where I eat!" he shouted. Mickel couldn't have heard anything; he was making too much noise of his own by now.

We'd gotten a pretty good jag of wood on the truck before Mickel came back from where he'd gone to the springs to get a drink. I knew Calvin would have something smart to say as he'd had plenty of time to come up with it.

"It's about time you made it back, old man. Oh, I'm sorry! I guess I cain't call you that bein' Bob is older than you." Mickel wiped his mouth with the sleeve of his shirt, looking weak with dark circles under his eyes.

"I don't know what you had in that sandwich, old buddy. But whatever it was, it made me sick as a dog." I couldn't believe what I'd just heard with a sudden ringing in my ears.

"Now, you, stupid bastard . . .," Bob blurted loudly, spitting his whole wad of baccer off to the side, then made a half ass effort to wipe the corners of his mouth. Calvin dropped the piece of wood he'd been carrying to the truck. I was still trying to absorb what Mickel had said. Birds stopped chirping, flies flew for cover, and of all things a sudden chill was in the air. I held my breath as Calvin rose up, flexing his massive body.

"Listen here," Calvin hissed, jaw clamped firmly down on the pipe as he spat the words. "You old dumb fucker! It wasn't that sandwich that made you sick. It was that stinkin'-ass cigarette you sucked down."

"Well . . . you got a lot of room to talk . . . a man who smokes a stinkin'-ass pipe!" Mickel sassed right back. I couldn't believe this broken-down old man was arguing with Calvin and, worse, standing so close to him. I calculated that Calvin's big ass weighed as much as Mickel's whole body did. "Stupid bastard" was starting to make sense now.

Calvin let out a laugh and shook his head, dumbfounded as what to say next I supposed. Had it been anyone other than a feeble old geezer, I'm sure

Calvin would have been all over him by now. But I also knew, feeble or not, that he wouldn't let old Mickel have the last word.

"Well, I'll tell you one thing right now, you old sorry asshole! You better never ask me for a damn thing again, and that includes the time of day!" He held his finger close to Mickel's nose "But I will tell you this—it's time for you to get your old rack of bones to work! But if you need, you better carry your ass back over there and clean up where you puked all over the damn place. I can't stand seein' that shit, and there better not be a spot anywhere! Now I hope I made myself perfectly clear?"

"Stupid bastard," Bob uttered loudly as Mickel turned to glare at him. Then like all confrontations, there was that moment of silence before any reaction. Mickel had created the whole affair by letting his mouth override his ass and should never have blamed Calvin's sandwich for making him ill.

I'd heard Calvin make the argument many times that smoking a pipe was nowhere near as bad as a nasty ass cigarette. And there was one other thing that Mickel should have considered when Calvin pointed out that the same sandwich had not made him sick.

"Stupid bastard" was the mild epithet as Mickel stood there. The whole thing looked so funny, I thought, with Mickel's face at about Calvin's chest, looking up at him all tough-like. Here was a scene I'd never forget for as long as I lived, them standing a foot apart and Calvin towering down on old Mickel.

I always knew I had a good imagination even though James said I was definitely out there at times. And maybe I was this time when I pictured Calvin sweeping Mickel up off his feet and literally slapping the piss out of him. The thought alone was enough for a stifled whimper when I cupped a hand over my mouth. They all turned looking my way as I faked a yawn. Quickly I'd become the center of attraction.

Think about something else, anything, I told myself as I looked away from them. But it was when I dared to look back that set me off to one of the best laughs I'd ever had in my lifetime, period.

I could surely lay some of the blame on James who at a young age could turn about anyone or anything into a cartoon character. He elbowed me one time in church showing me his sketch of the old man up behind the pulpit with his false teeth being blown from his mouth while preaching hell far and brimstone. And even though I couldn't draw them with any quality such as he did my envisionment was spectacular.

His dark leaded pencil moved quickly about the paper; scratching dots and smiley dashes to form his opinion. Never to put much time in one place he moved to another where he'd do the same. It was like dotting the end of a sentence with his final lift of the pencil when it all came together to set you off with such hilariousness. In most cases he wouldn't have had to add a title to any of them. And like the old saying; every picture tells a story, the small caption simple added a flavor of its own. Where I would have saved them all, James wouldn't keep for very long. He'd throw them away not wanting anyone to see how he thought of them in his most unfavorable way.

By now there was not much of a chance that I pull out of my fit of laughter with loud sucking sounds from between my cupped hands held tightly over my mouth. Like a crazy dream a cartoon staring Calvin came to life. And so picturesque, with him holding Mickel on the ground while blowing smoke in his face. Tears flooded my eyes, with no spare hand to wipe them away. And why would a screwdriver come to mind that I break the seal such as a lip-lock to my hands? It didn't matter that they thought I might be crazy when I knelt down on a knee, still unable to control myself.

"Arnold Ray, what in the hell are you laughin' at?" Calvin yelled. No way could I have answered him, thinking about the hippie's words as I seemed to do a lot of lately. 'It's really hard to explain, man'. It was then and there that I thought I was going to be the first person ever to laugh himself to death."

I finally managed a tilt of my head and maybe too soon as the three watery images were now looking down on top of me. 'And this bunch is the backbone to the old man's logging business?' Why did I have to think of such a thing that sent me back into a worse tizzy?

I peeped for an instance as they walked away, with Calvin in the middle like the ringleader that he'd always been. My mind would have no rest that I pictured him as the grand marshal of the Big Top Circus—top hat, black jacket split in the back, and high black boots, running in circles and kicking Mickel in the ass with dust flying everywhere. I couldn't call time-out from the craziness spinning through my head. I'd simply have to play it out and laugh it off. *I've got to breathe! I've got to stop this shit right now*, I forced the thought on myself.

There would be no explanation for what had set me off to one of the craziest fits I'd ever had in my life. I'd shared many with James, but never anything off the wall such as this. He'd declared once after one of our laughs that they seemed to come after something bad had happened—the best way for one's mind to relieve itself of stress. I had one final thought that did seem to sober me some. *It's hard to explain, man*. I shook my head, thinking the old hippie had been right all along.

I stood for an instant, then hurried over behind a big piss elm tree to take a leak. I'd gather myself somewhat before I'd go to face them. I stepped out into the open with hopes that it'd be a normal-looking world once again.

I walked back to the yard, where I saw Bob and Mickel busy rolling wood toward the truck. But then I had to steady myself when I saw Calvin stretched out on a big oak log, looking all comfortable with one hand propped up under his head and the other vigorously scratching his big hairy belly. Enough to set me off again if I wasn't careful. His pipe hung limply in his mouth, ready to fall out at any time, it looked.

"Arnold Ray, I figured if you were goin' to laugh all day, I'd just lay right up here on my nut sack and let thangs digest a little more." He grinned. "I got those two old pecker heads doing something that might even get ya ta laughing again. But now you gotta tell me. What in the hell was so funny?"

"Honest to God, I thought I was gonna be the first person on earth to die from laughin' myself to death, Calvin." I still hurt in the stomach. "I swear, laughin' like that was as hard as runnin' any two-mile race I was ever in."

"Well, what in the hell was you tryin' to tell us before you went off into lulu-land again?"

"I don't even want to try and explain what my imagination put me through, Calvin. Shit, I don't think I could handle it again! But I will tell you this—that lulu-land turned out to be a circus." I cleared my throat with a couple of quick swallows.

"Well, by God, you don't have to tell me 'cause, I finally got them circus acts a doin' something other than bein' a couple of goofy clowns. But then again, maybe they ain't clownin' around at all, Arnold Ray. Maybe that's just the way they act all the time."

I was tempted to laugh but thought better of it, telling Calvin how I'd envisioned him as the grand marshal over it all.

There was some serious huffing going on from Bob and Mickel's direction as they were struggling to hoist a large piece of wood up on the truck. It was obvious that Mickel wasn't gonna get his end up high enough. They jumped clear when Mickel let go, almost not getting out of the way in time. With his head tilted forward, and hands clutching to the trucks bed he wheezed loudly sounding out of breath.

"Mickel, why don't you take the measurin' stick and mark off the rest of the trees that's not been done yet so Calvin can start cuttin' them up. Me and Bob will work on getting this truck loaded. Is that all right with everybody?" I asked, looking around at each of them.

"It's all right with me." Bob spoke up. I laughed as Calvin wallowed all over the log, before finally sitting up. Without any further ado, he started his saw up then quickly began throwing chips and dust our way—surely in his plan, I figured.

"Now don't let me catch up to ya, old man!" he shouted over the buzz of the idling saw. Mickel said something back but spoke too low to be heard.

Quitting time finally came around with the truck loaded for Chillicothe the next morning. Calvin made a hiding place where we put the saws as if anyone would ever steal them anyway. Bob was to drive it down to the end of the dirt road just in case it rained that night and the road got muddy. Calvin and

Mickel were gonna ride along with Bob, but Calvin had a change of heart at the last second, informing them he'd walk with me and the horses on to the pond.

"I'll see you fellers come tomar!" Calvin yelled over his shoulder. "And don't forget to bind that damned load down again 'afore you leave here! I'd hate to see you two have to load it all again tonight!" We walked a short way before Calvin observed, "Now you tell me, Arnold Ray, that that's not a winnin' pair back 'ere." He gestured with a head nod.

"You know, I really like ole Bob. I think he'll be ok." Calvin said while coming to a complete stop. "But that old fart Mickel, he ain't worth the powder and lead to kill 'um, to tell the truth. Hell, I caught up with him two, three times today. And all he was doin' was markin' lengths and spending too much time rubbing that stinkin' gut of his! Where in the hell did Jimbo find those two, Arnold Ray?" He rolled his eyes making me laugh.

"I don't know where he got 'um, Calvin. But let's get out of the road cause here they come now."

"Mickel, you get some rest tonight so you'll be a little spryer come tommar. Do you hear me?" Calvin hollered, then quickly looked at me. "What in the hell did he say?" he asked as the truck crept slowly past us.

"You know what he said, Calvin," I answered.

"Well, that old son of a bitch!" He coughed. "All he wants to do all day's stand around and rub his gut, and now he's got to say something like that to me." Calvin coughed again, sounding like one of Mary's wild episodes. After parking the truck and checking the booms, they got into an old car and drove off.

"Yeah, you're right about Mickel, Calvin. And it sure seems he wants to argue about everything? And you know, I still think of him as bein' older than Bob and I mean by a lot, it looks."

"Boy now old Junior will be in for a real surprise when he gets back, won't he?" Calvin said, taking his shoes off at the edge of the pond. After laying his pipe on a flat rock, he slid his feet into the cool water. "Ah . . ." He sank them up to his knees, sounding nothing short of pure pleasure. We talked mostly of the old man's new recruits and couldn't help but laugh of how the day's events had turned out.

"Well, the damn frogs are startin' to croak awful loud, Arnold Ray. So I guess I better get my ass on down the road before it gets too dark to see." He put his boots back on with no socks. Leaving them untied, he headed on down the road, dragging his heels with the boot strings trailing behind.

Mom was making fried chicken with all the trimmings for supper that night. The biscuits would be golden brown, where she'd lightly patted chicken grease on their tops with the backside of her favorite spoon. I closed my eyes as I bit into a hot, greasy leg; but as much as I wanted to savor every bite, I ate quickly, knowing that the old man might show up at any time. I wanted to avoid him altogether and would go out of my way to do so. The timing had been right, eating in peace, and spending time with the family before he came driving up to the backdoor. I made sure I was leaving at about the same time he made it to the back door.

"I'm going to have Bob drive that truck startin' tommar mornin'," he blurted, holding a hand up behind his ear. "That way, Mr. Junior can do more than just barrel ass up and down the road and cut a few trees down when he feels like it."

Why was he saying such shitty things about James in front of me? Talking to me at all was useless at best. I'd told him time and again that I hated everything he stood for and that he was no father of mine. The temptation was great to slap him with his hand all propped up behind his ear and telling me that James had become worthless.

Sure, it was taking him a little longer than normal to make the trip to Chillicothe and back. And so what if he was stopping by Scarlett's for a little while? With just hearing him talk of kisses, I'd be doing the same thing. I'd not waste my breath defending James to such a lazy, useless asshole as was standing right in front of me. Ever since James had set him straight over shorting us our money and putting Scarlett ahead of the old man's desires he'd been finding ways to get back at him. I continued to be silent on the outside but raged on the inside while looking him in the eye.

Mom had no sooner come to the door than he blurted,

"Me and ole Harry's goin' to play some cards tonight." He seemed to want to help everyone other than us. I thought how he'd made a special trip to buy old Mickel a pack of cigarettes. I'd bet he wouldn't go and buy me a pack of bubble gum or a *PAYDAY* candy bar if I'd asked.

"Well, since you're leaving, I think I'll stay around for a while longer." I stepped back into the house, letting the door slam behind me. He left without so much as a goodbye. I couldn't hope that something tragic happen to him on this night with old Harry in the car and besides it was good that he take him somewhere.

I'd heard many sermons preached over the years that a Christian shouldn't play with cards—just another one of the devil's tolls. All forms of alcohol would be close behind leading to even greater sins. The old man himself preached about it in his holiest years. It was another one of those things to blame on the devil if you were too weak to fend off such temptations.

We heard the testimony of a woman who told of her uncle playing cards one night and even laughed telling everyone he was sinning. It was called an accident in the paper that he smashed a finger off while he was changing a tire the very next day. But she and others knew better and would declare what the truth was all about.

I thought back to when we were much smaller how the old man would have a few people come over to our house to play cards and drink beer. Mom's protests were always in vain; when she'd send us to another room or outside to play. She was throwing his beer away once before anyone got there but was stopped with a terrible threat. James and I'd played cards for years over in Pike County before Mom found our deck pushed up under our mattresses. James explained how we played for points and no money was ever involved. Then he argued further that you didn't need a deck of cards to make a bet. It was one of those things that should never be questioned, for in the Bible, it is so written under temptation.

Our mother knew that we wouldn't gamble, but everything she'd seen that came out of playing cards had always been evil. We witnessed one of those very sins once when James and I were playing marbles in Granma's backyard. We suddenly heard her shout,

"...Lord ...child!" As if the world was coming to an end. We ran around to the back porch where she'd caught her youngest son Floyd playing solitaire. "Lord, child!" she said again while forcing a bar of her homemade lye soap into Floyd's mouth. "Honey, now the devil made them with his own hands." She pointed. "And you see now what trouble they lead to, Floyd Honey?"

The sight of a bar of soap sticking out of his mouth was reason enough to make both James and I to start spitting all over the place. I told James that I never wanted to play cards because lye soap burned my eyes, so I sure didn't want it in my mouth. He told me later that the cards weren't the reason Floyd had to bite down on the soap. It was because he said some cuss words after Granma stopped him from playing. But the soap was nothing next to the whipping Grampa put on him later.

Judy, Beth, and I played some crazy eights after they'd helped Mom with the dishes that evening. The boys were all gathered up watching television and complaining how bad the reception was. The old man had told everyone that when he sold our baccer crop this year, he was gonna buy a brand spanking new color TV and a new antenna especially made for it. It'd become our new best joke, sure that he'd lie to all in the end.

But TV wasn't the most important thing for me on this evening; it was hearing all their voices clamoring throughout the house. Questions about something the boys were watching was quickly answered by Duck, whose joking ways about everything got them all laughing. We caught Beth trying to cheat a couple of times in cards, fessing up that it was the old man who showed her how to do it. There was no doubt that the old man would cheat with about anything he got into, I figured. It was getting late; time to head for the bus. I said good night to everyone and thinking what a great day it had been. I could hear Rebel barking off in the distance probably checking out his new hunting grounds I figured.

I stood in the middle of the graveled road where a full moon had just crested the ridge overlooking Whiskey Holler. Tall trees lining the fence rows casting shadows far out into the fields. There was something very fresh in the air on this particular night. The deep breath I drew in suddenly lit a fire in my heart. Streaks of moonlight and shade from the trees lay across the road like a strange maze ahead of me. If I were an artist I'd surely paint it I thought to myself. Then came a familiar twitch in the tips of my fingers as I lifted a nervous foot into the air. I had the need to run and with spring in my legs I took off. There was no one to race against other than myself and I'd surely win, after all I could run the distance wide open.

Like rapid blinking of the eyes the mix of light and shade swept across my face as I picked up the pace. And if I fall then so be it. Now with Harry's big Maple tree in sight I'd run for all I was worth. I cleared the edge of the maze and now nothing but bright moonlight shining brightly. I never slowed up while sprinting on past the bus. Farther and farther with my legs burning and along with heavy breathing I finally came to a slow stop where an old run-down house sat just off the road.

After I caught my breath and regained the strength in my legs I walked over and sat down along a fence row for the best view of the old house. It didn't take much of an imagination to change the moons silvery light into a snowy landscape. I could only guess as to how close I sat to where James had pulled me from under the snow and saved me from freezing to death, long ago.

Other thoughts of this place quickly flooded my mind. It ended up that Cliff Run Road wasn't exactly the stranger to us as we'd once thought before our move from Pike County. It hadn't been that many years when we gathered canning jars in an old dump below a small cliff and just a few miles down the road from here.

James and I had reminisced many times of this very place over the years but never had a clue of its whereabouts until now. But even so we swore that it was the worst place we'd ever lived, and Mom had plenty to say about it herself. The year of the Blizzard she'd relate to it as the coldest house she'd ever lived in, in her life, she said out loud.

"We've traveled a full circle Arnold, remember this place?" James pointed it out when we were going to the town of Fruitdale to pick up some milk and cereal for Harry one week-end. James had seen it earlier with his very first load of pulpwood on the way to Chillicothe. I was thinking how we'd even seen old Harry when we'd lived here.

It was a bitter winter day when the old man sent us to a neighbor who lived down the road a way, asking to borrow cigarette money. We didn't know it was Harry's door we knocked on. There was no answer. With our fingers feeling like they were freezing and too cold to knock any longer we went around to the back of the house, where James got a small stick to peck on his window with. All we could see was the back of an old man's head where he sat in a chair reading a paper but never heard our knocks.

I was glad after all these years to have met old Harry. Funny how things turn out sometimes. I sat with him in his swing one evening and told him the whole story of how we had to walk all the way to our uncle Jesse's house to borrow the money so the old man could have cigarettes. I thought what a gypsy circle we'd lived from the time we'd left here almost ten years ago. Now with thoughts of the farm I wondered if we were in any better shape. A dry swallow tempted me with anger that Mom was living in a rent house once more only a mile or so away from where I sat.

I ran the two miles to a covered bridge, touching it before running back. "I'm goin' to smoke some ass this year when track starts Rebel just you mark my word."

Mr. Bill and Kate were standing along the fence with their ears perked, nickering loudly as I approached. I'd heard a car coming up the road for some time, watching its headlights reappear after every curve. It was coming from the wrong direction to be James, and it was way too early for him to come home anyhow. I continued scratching the animals' heads when Mable Braggs pulled up under Harry's maple tree in her '57 Chevy.

"Arnold!" She waved to get my attention. "Could you please come over here, please..." She motioned. "What are you doing tonight?" she asked as I got closer. Her question took me by surprise.

"Well, I I'm not doin' anythin' right now," I answered curiously, "but I was about to go to bed." The truth was I could never have fallen to sleep with so much running through my mind right now.

"See, I've got a problem." Clearly, there was panic in her voice.

"Is there something wrong with your car?" I asked.

"No, nothing like that," she said, turning the motor off.

"Did the old man wreck and get—"

"No." She stopped me short, shaking her head. "I heard Wilma is real sick, and I've got to go check on her, and my problem is I cain't open that darned gate at her driveway. I was wonderin' if you might go along and help me with it." She held crossed fingers up to where I could see them. I'd not seen Mable since our first encounter at the bus. And Harry hadn't said anything about her for some time now.

"Who's Wilma?" I asked, trying to buy time.

"Wilma Reed, the person Jim is buyin' the timber from down at Camp Creek. Don't he tell you anything?" She laughed as if she already knew. "It's about a forty-minute drive down there," she said. "I'll even pay you if you'll help me."

"No, you don't have to pay me anything." I shook my head, looking off to the side a little.

Mable didn't seem like a bad person the first time I'd talked with her. But with suspicion and knowing the old man's ways I'd not wanted anything to do with her. But I certainly couldn't prove there was ever anything between them, other than rumors. If I'd know so it would be easy to simple turn and walk away. I wondered if the old man wasn't just using her to buy the timber at Camp Creek. Maybe she just happened to be another one of the people he needed just long enough to get something out of them, I could only guess. I almost said no, but I saw how truly panicked she was and if there was something going on with the old man he would have surely been with her instead of going to play cards somewhere with Harry. And that was strange in the way he'd not taken Harry anywhere for quite some time now.

"Well, I'm not doin' anythin' right now," I said. I got in the car, and we headed for Camp Creek. We hadn't gotten far when she asked if I had ever been down there before.

"No, I don't guess I ever have, but we bought a tractor close to there," I answered.

"You don't smoke, do you?"

"No, I don't," I said bluntly.

"Do you care if I do? I'll roll my window all the way down."

"Go ahead," I said. She was polite enough to ask, not like the old man, who didn't give a damn if you liked it or not.

"My mother stays on my butt all the time about smokin'," she said, blowing the first drag out into the moonlit night. The smell, though, seemed to have gone over the top of the car and right into my window.

"I tell her over and over again that someday I'll quit."

"Well, are you really going to?" I questioned.

"Someday," she answered with a not-so-sure laugh. There were long periods when we had nothing to say. I really didn't know what to speak of anyway, wondering if the old man had "gotten some" off her, a terrible thought as I gazed out the window as the night sped past.

"Where is your dad?" she finally asked. I'd already figured she didn't know; otherwise, he'd probably be with her.

"He and Harry went out to play some cards somewhere." I leaned a little her way so she could hear me better with the wind coming through the windows.

"Cards? Cards," she repeated herself, giving me a questionable look.

"Hey, that's what the bastard told me."

Mable was into heavy thought while frantically smoked her cigarette to the end. She fumbled around in the seat, finding the fancy case that contained her pack and a lighter. Ironic, I thought, when she pulled one from the pack of

Camels, same brand as the old man's. It looked as if this one would be smoked pretty quickly also when she left it dangling in her mouth for the time being. I thought it pretty cool how I was riding in one of James's favorites cars a 57 model Chevy. And even better he'd never ridden in one yet.

She asked questions about our logging business and shortly after enlightened me about both Good Hope and Camp Creek. In some way, it pissed me off that she knew more about it than I did. I wanted to ask her what her dealings with the old man were other than the bus but knew I'd be lied to and that she'd possible be hiding something. I'd glanced at the radio several times before she'd finally noticed.

"Would you like to listen to some music, Arnold? What do you like to hear?"

"I like rock and roll," I said with some peep in my voice.

"Well, I like some rock and roll myself," she said. We listened to music for the rest of the trip to Wilma's. There was songs I would have turned the volume up had she not been there. We pulled up in front of an old wooden gate, where along with the headlights Mable shined a spotlight pivoting close to her side mirror. James said it would be the first thing to go if it was his car. The moonlight would have been plenty good enough to see the chain wrapped loosely around the post. Mable was right that it would have been hard for her to open as one of the hinges was broken off.

It was obvious that the road hadn't been traveled much with tall chicory lining both sides and even taller in the middle as it dragged the car's undercarriage, making a continuous ringing sound. The road started climbing and winding around a tall hill until we finally arrived at the top, coming out into a treed area, where an old house sat attached to the side of a barn.

"How do you know Wilma?" I asked after she'd shut the engine off.

"Oh, she's a distant aunt and's had trouble takin' care of herself for some time now. I'm the one who's been tryin' to convince her to sell out." Smoke trailed from Mable's nose and mouth. "But I've not seen her myself for some time now. I came up here and cleaned her place this spring. I talked to her son on the phone occasionally, you know as to how she's doing. He's nothing but a joke at best, hardly ever stops by to see if she needs anything. But a couple weeks back, he called me, saying he was ready to sell the timber and put her in a nursing home, where she could be taken care of. I guess Wilma was adamant that by no means would she leave her home here on top of the mountain. But I could tell the last time I talked to her that she was slipping pretty badly. And that's why I'm here. So he come by this morning to check on her, then called me asking if I could swing by." She threw her cigarette butt out the window like she'd done with the four others that I'd counted on our trip.

The house was dark with no lights even on the inside. The yard was completely grown up with weeds almost as tall as me. I just couldn't believe that anyone really lived there. But it looked like it'd been a fine place at one time, though.

"Wilma, Wilma . . .!" Mable yelled as she opened the front door slightly. A gagging smell of something dead blew past us.

"My God, what's that awful smell?" I backed up a way for fresh air.

"Oh . . .! That's . . . terrible," Mable said, backing into me. After digging around in her purse, she dug out two handkerchiefs that had a good-smelling fragrance about them. "Here, hold this over your mouth and nose" she advised.

I opened the door just enough to find the light switch. *Click*, nothing happened. Once again, I flipped the switch.

"I think the electricity's been shut off, Mable. There's not a light on anywhere in the house."

Mable seemed more cautious now as she shines her flashlight through the crack again. Whatever perfume she'd put on the hankies wasn't enough to overpower the dead smell that was trapped in the kitchen however.

"Are you sure she's not dead and that's her smelling like that, Mable?" She seemed fearful and nervous of what we might find as the flashlight's beam shook, bouncing from one thing to another.

"Here!" she said, passing it to me. "I'm too nervous to hold it steady." I slowly opened the squeaky door a little more to a pitch-black kitchen it appeared. The smell rose from dead cats lying everywhere, decomposed to only flat hairy spots wherever they'd died. There was no way to count them with the way they were stacked on top of one another. Some lay on the dinner table with others in the windowsills. A horror movie couldn't have showed it this bad, with many more stacked in all the corners. I thought they'd all starved to death or never had water.

"Wilma!" Mable yelled once more with panic in her voice now. Mable was no sooner headed to Wilma's bedroom than noises came from behind the door. It was hard to make out exactly what they were. A whining sound maybe like a little girl might make and desperately trying to answer us. If I had been alone and had heard the whine, I would have been halfway down the hill by then and would never look back.

"Listen, I think I hear her . . ." Mable clung to my arm tighter as we avoided stepping on the cats. We stopped just shy of the door, both hesitant to open it. The whining voice sounded once again, immediately followed by what I thought sounded like sheets flapping in a stiff wind, but only for a few seconds.

"What is that?" I whispered.

"I don't have a clue, and I'm not sure that I even want to know." She squeezed my arm tighter than ever. I stepped toward the door, pulling Mable along my side. There came a sound I'd heard many times, but how could it be?

"Those are chickens! But how can they be in the house?" I wondered out loud. I opened the door slowly just as the flashlight dimmed. *Just like something right oughta Chiller Theatre*, I thought. I hit it with the palm of my hand, knocking some life back into it. It revealed something worse than *Chiller Theatre*, when we both backed up a step. The smell was worse than the dead cats when it swept past us and on into the kitchen to mix with the rest.

The flashlight danced around the dark room with a quick survey. Suddenly, clucking sounded from above us as I shined the light into a black void. White feathered wings fluttered above us in the most confused way. Some fell into the light's rays, looking like snow falling. I quickly shined it away from them and stepped back, once more bumping into Mable pretty hard.

Grabbing my hand, she redirected the light to the bed, where Wilma lay with the covers pulled up tightly and still seemed to be tugging on them. Her long gray hair hung all the way to the floor. The lighted scene moved from one to the other as we tried to take in what lay in front of us.

I banged the flashlight against my hand with a couple of good whacks when a flicker had dimmed it. With the flashlight losing what little power it had, we saw chicken dung mounded up on the bed below where they'd been roosting and forcing Wilma farther to the edge of the bed. Mind-boggling, I tried to calculate how long they'd have had to roost there to build such a heap. I gagged as Mable turned to leave the room.

"Ben . . . is that you?" a groggy voice asked. Mable stopped, turned back quickly, while covered her mouth with her hanky. Without thought she walked to the old woman's bedside. I shined the dim light as fumes made my eyes water. There was a hole in the ceiling about three feet wide with a tree limb sticking through it. That was how the chickens got in and out. I needed to swallow but wouldn't with the terrible smell of rot. I needed to go somewhere and spit for sure or maybe even worse.

"Ben, is that you?" Wilma sounded hopeful, while trying to get out of bed.

"No, Honey. It's Mable."

"Who? Ben, who is that?" she asked again.

"This is Mable, your niece, Honey."

"Oh, Mable, bless your heart! I wondered whatever happened to you. It's been so long since I've seen you. Would you like somethin' to eat or a cup of coffee or tea? It's probably time I get up anyway," the old lady grumbled.

"I don't think she knows who I am," Mable said with concern.

"Is Ben her son?" I whispered.

"No! He was her husband, and my Lord, he died over twenty years ago! That's why she needs to go to a nursing home. She just can't take care of herself anymore, as you can see."

Mable lifted the covers to help Wilma get out of bed. The smell was like no other, with chicken shit a foot deep on top of the bed. The sheets were saturated all the way through and into the mattress, but wasn't only the chickens. Wilma was covered with her own filth too. It wasn't just the smell but also the sight of such a thing that made me gag as I fought to hold it back.

"Wilma, let's get some clothes on you. You're going to go home with me tonight," Mable said softly while helping her to a dresser. It was hard holding the light on them as she stumbled around naked and ghostly white. I thought I could stomach about anything as I gagged once again. There wasn't much shit of any kind I hadn't stepped in one time or the other. And James and I'd cleaned out about every toilet wherever we'd lived, and there wasn't anything good about that either. But I'd never seen anything like this as the light faded slowly, barely able to see them now.

"We've got to go, Mable. The light's goin' dead," I warned.

"Well, here, Honey. Use my cigarette lighter." She found my hand in the darkness.

"Is Ben going with us?" Wilma asked.

"He's already there, Honey," Mable said, pulling a long loose dress over the old woman's head.

We helped her into the car, after which I spit, flushing my mouth, several times at the gate.

I didn't complain of the dozen or so cigarettes that Mable smoked on the drive back. I'd never thought I'd ever want to smell a cigarette, but I welcomed them over the smell of the old woman who rode in the backseat.

It was after midnight when I got home. As soon as Mable had gotten down the road a way, I headed for the pond, ignoring the frogs party.

Rebel jumped a rabbit up in the cattails and was gone in a flash. There was a perfect reflection of a solid white moon as I dove in, grabbing for it with every stroke. Deep under the water, I could see the moon's wavy light dancing on the surface above me. *I wish James could see this. I bet he could paint it,* I thought as I crested the surface. I didn't swim long. I just felt like there was something dirty on me that I needed to wash off.

I thought about poor old Wilma as I walked back toward the bus. She'd talked about her dead husband, Ben, as if she'd seen him recently. I imagined that most the people she talked about had passed away; and with that someone should have known the shape she was in. How sad it must be to outlive all your good friends, leaving no one but a worthless son who wouldn't take care of her in the end. I thought about Mom and how nothing like this would ever happen to her as long as I was alive.

I was almost to the bus when I heard squeaks from Harry's swing. He sat in the darkness for a late-night smoke, which he did often when he couldn't sleep.

"Evening, Harry."

"Why, a good one to you too, Arnold," he shot back, sliding a little to give me more room. It didn't sound as if he'd been drinking much at all with hardly any flavor in his words. And it was easy to figure by the way Mable acted without an invite that they weren't going to play cards at all. Maybe a front that they didn't want her to know their whereabouts I suspected.

"And how'd the card game turn out?" I quizzed.

Harry stopped the swing with both feet sliding to a sudden stop. "Why, Arnold, I don't know anything about a card game. Jim left me at a bar up by Good Hope and was gone for a couple hours or so. And I'm tellin' ya I don't appreciate that kind of shit. Hell, I's afraid to do much drankin' thinkin' he may not come back for me."

I told Harry about the incident we'd had with the old man, the reason James was gone for now. Harry did more head shaking than right out answering. Clearly, he was disgusted as to what the old man had done to him and all the other things I'd talked of. There didn't seem to be much pleasure with the way he handled his pipe either.

"Well, I guess it's that time, Arnold." Without another word Harry went on to bed. I stayed up a while longer, thinking James might come in. There were so many things that'd happened since I'd seen him last. I wanted to tell him about old Bob and Mickel and maybe my trip with Mable. But I'd have to think about that one. He might want to turn it into something other than what it really was.

I thought it was good that the old man had hired a couple more people, with all the new work coming up and school so close to starting. And more folks to talk with made work especially good, like it was today. But like Calvin said, "He could have gotten them a little younger like about fifty years or better."

But no matter how good things were, there was always the thought of the old man lingering in the darkness, like the ambush he'd pulled on Calvin and me in the barn. And now with Scarlett in James's life, the old man realized he was losing his grip on his eldest son. I woke the next morning, and to my surprise, James was there in the bed. I made my normal noise that would have at least made him move a little, but not on this morning.

"James, wake up!" I said, pulling on his leg. "You overslept again. Why, I've already got the milkin' done. So come on, let's go down and have breakfast," I shook him again agitating that he gets moving around some.

"Okay, okay give me a minute. I need to open my eyes." He sounded tired.

"So, what time did you get in last night?" I asked.

"I think it was about two," he replied with a loud yawn.

"I really thought you'd gone for more than just a couple days, so what happened? Was it something other 'n bein' lip-locked all night?" I laughed, prying for information. "Or did you . . . ah . . . di-did you get some?" I stuttered.

"No, it wasn't anything like that." He rolled over onto his back. "But things are kind of fucked up right now."

"What did you say? Did you just cuss James?"

"Me and Scarlett fell asleep on the couch watching TV last night. Anna Fay woke us up, pissed off as hell! They've been letting me sleep on it, but that didn't include Scarlett, of course. She jumped all over Scarlett, telling her to get her ass in her own bed and now. I said that it was my fault, and I shouldn't have stayed another night. Then she told me to get my ass home." He shook his head as if he'd really done something wrong.

"No shit!" I replied.

"Well, I figure I'll stop by on my way back from Chillicothe and try to apologize to Anna Fay one more time. I guess we have gotten a little carried away lately with the way we've been acting. We've been like kids, I guess, thinking we can get away with anything until we get caught."

"Well, that's all cool, James," I said, snapping my fingers and changing the words of "Wake Up Little Susie." He didn't seem to think of the song as being funny, though.

"Well, let me sang it the right way for ya, old buddy!" I said with my best Elvis voice, which wasn't even close. "Now look here." I pointed to my shaking leg and was snapping my fingers to a quick beat. I grabbed the saltshaker like it was a microphone and started singing into it. "Wake up! Little Scarlett! Wake up!" I shook my leg faster. *Elvis would be proud*, I thought. "Wake up, little Scarlett, wake up! Well, what we gonna tell. Anna Fay? What we gonna tell Ezell…? uh la-la…! Wake up, little Scarlett. . ."

James snorted one short laugh before telling me to please shut up.

"Okay, then try this one out for size, James . . . One of them new people that the old man hired yesterday is goin' to be the new truck driver! He's the guy who drove it down to the pond yesterday." James was making a slow attempt to get out of bed but stopped suddenly, frowning.

"What new people are you talking about?" He gave me his best James look—three wrinkles across his forehead, squinty eyes, and a chin like stone.

"The old man hired a couple people yesterday, and one of them is gonna be drivin' the truck." I clasped my hands together, rubbing them fast as I'd seen Bob do.

"You're so full of shit, Arnold!" He laughed. "Good one, though."

"Oh, you think I'm bullshittin' you, James?"

"I know you're bullshitting me!" He smiled. I was dumbfounded that he didn't believe me. I guess I'd messed with him so much over the years that he didn't know what to believe from me anymore.

"You should have been here yesterday, James. I'm tellin' you, I never laughed so hard in my life! I'm not kiddin'. Those two old guys are crazy and then mix

Calvin in with that. It's a circus, just you wait and see. Remember what I said, a circus." I thought of making an attempt to explain how the day had gone, opening my hands for an explanation, but no words came out.

"Okay, enough is enough!" James laughed.

"All right, you'll see. You'll find out." I said.

"If you're lying to me, there's gonna be an ass whipping!" He pointed a warning finger.

"Now why would I lie to you, James?"

"Then swear to God you're not!" I had James thinking as he looked me straight in the eye. He needed to know if I was lying, and what better way than put my soul at risk?

"You know, James, I've not been to church for a long time or prayed with any sincerity much. So I don't know if I should swear right now," I teased. "But there is one way to get the right answer without God. You were born into it, ya know, after all. I mean you bein' the oldest son, why, it's been handed down to you name and all James L Richardson."

His eyes questioned when I extended my wrist straight out with my palm facing upward and my pulse easy to get to. His laugh was spontaneous. "And why would I do that when I've seen you slip past 'his' test without blinking an eye?"

"I'm not lying about what I told you, James. I swear I'm not." He pushed his hair to one side making a heartless effort to grin.

"I believe you, Arnold," he said solemnly. We loaded the milk in the Buick and hadn't gotten too far when we saw the old man's car coming in our direction with his hand waving for us to stop.

"Keep going, James. Don't stop. We'll wave and drive on past 'em. He'll just have some shitty thing to say anyhow." The old man must've read my thoughts as he took up the better part of the road to block us. We slowed as James rolled the window down.

"Boys, it's all about time and money!" He glared at his watch, then drove away.

"Can you believe that shit? I told you he'd have some shitty thing to say. We're hardly ever late, and the one time we are, he acts like a prick."

"Good morning, Honey." Mom said meeting us at the kitchen door with her normal greeting of hugs and kisses. It showed in her eyes how glad she was to see James. I carried the milk to the sink thinking how much easier it was to strain in the sink and wash the pail out with warm running water.

"Duck, what do you think you're doing?" I asked whirling quickly seeing that he'd gotten the big biscuit, covered up with all the trimmings, and had eaten about half of it.

"Hey! If you boys are over five minutes late, it's mine!" He laughed. What was even funnier which he'd added to his clown act was when he tilted an open hand upwards that the boys join him with laughter. I had noticed lately however Larry's unwillingness to jump any time Duck commanded. I thought of what Calvin had said about the boys maybe needing a break, away from Duck.

"Okay, we'll let it go this time, but maybe you should give us more than five minutes!" James said in a stern voice.

"Yeah, we work all day! Not like some people around here . . .," I said while looking all about the kitchen. The boys all started laughing again until Duck gave them a more serious look.

Breakfast was fun like it used to be, with everyone cutting up and acting a fool. We knew that the old man wouldn't be back for a while. Mom and Judy began singing some of their favorite church songs after we'd finished breakfast. It was good being able to hear them on a regular basis. And just like in church or any other time as far as that was, not one time did I remember when Judy didn't hug her mother after they'd finished. Mom went on and on about how pretty Judy's voice had become, declaring it got better every time they sang. Her eyes told of her love for her oldest daughter who never turned down the chance to sing with her.

"Why, she's a young woman now!" Mom proclaimed, pushing Judy's bangs off to the side a little.

"You know, Mom, that I get my voice from you, don't you?" She smiled. I thought how the old man would disagree with that, being how all the talent in the family came from him or at least that's what he'd tell everyone who'd brag about any of us.

Mom was so glad to have everybody there together. She asked that we all pray and thank God for such a blessing. Happiness had filled her soul as she opened her heart to the heavens above. I made a short silent prayer knowing all along there was no way God would answer it with the old man to never come home again.

James was helping me harness the animals when Bob started the log truck up at the gate. He quickly looked over at me, somewhat disappointed, I knew.

"I tried to tell you, James . . ." The wrinkles on his forehead deepened.

"That pisses me off!" he said.

"I tried to tell you, James . . . The old man knows he can get more done by you stayin' here, hooked up to that chainsaw all day . . . Hell, I finally agreed with him bout somethin'!" I joked, deliberately missing his stomach with my elbow.

"What the hell do you mean you agree with him?"

"Well, it's not a great loss if one of those old farts are gone for a couple of hours instead of you. But I think it'd be better if Mickel drove the truck. Even though Bob's the older, he's twice the person as old Mickel. But better than that, it gives me more time to mess with you, big brother." I grinned. James got my drift giving me a slight nudge.

We'd just stepped out the barn when the truck started to leave. Bob gave a quick wave before shifting into second gear. James nodded with every shift when Bob reached the perfect RPM sliding into a higher gear.

"Well now I can tell you one thing. That's not his first trip to Chillicothe with a load of wood." I was wrong thinking James would be mad of the whole affair. The difference in he and I came out once again.

"That's okay, Arnold, he's not going to get the best of me!" His jaw quickly stiffened to the challenge. "One more year and I'm out of here! I don't need that truck to go see Scarlett anyways"—he smiled—"because I've got a Buick, and I won't be stuck under his thumb when I need to go somewhere. And the next time he talks that 'my way or the highway,' I'll remind him that I've got a car."

"Well, so much about that, Arnold." He brushed his hands clean. "I'm ready to go meet those new folks now." Calvin was sawing away while Mickel hacked a notch where the cuts would be.

"Wait till you meet old Mickel, James. That old fart cusses more than me and Calvin put together."

"Well, you just got a pretty good head start right then Arnold."

"You'll see, he'll catch me and pass me in no time. Oh by the way just so you'll know, Calvin's already told 'em that you might whip his ass because you don't like to hear a lot of cussin'!"

Seeing us coming, Calvin shut his saw off, almost dropping it to the ground, and jerked his pipe from his back pocket, all while waiting to greet us.

"Junior, did you get your finger wet over the weekend?" he asked with a hopeful grin. After stuffing a large pinch of baccer into his pipe, he welcomed James with a hard hands shake.

"Well it looks like Mary took the scissors to you beard again Calvin" James laughed. It wasn't the first time we'd seen him with gashes all over his face.

The conversation had come up over in Pike County when he had a similar trim from Mary. Mom suggested that maybe he should just shave it all off and start over again. It was definitely the laugh of the night however when Mary panicked acting as if she were going to run out the door spouting;

"No sir, you don't want to see that." But Calvin would not be outdone on the matter drew a heavy breath.

"Hell, its cause' she knows how attractive I really look and's afraid some old gal might come on to me. I keep tellin' her she should trim it and not use the brail method." he laughed. He'd barely finished with his comeback when Mom said,

"Why Honey, I think Calvin is a handsome man, with or without a beard." Outer appearances didn't mean anything to her; what was more important was what lay deep in one's heart. She'd always followed up that Calvin had a kind heart.

His heart might be one thing but whether it was anger, a dirty joke, or just plain talk all came from the same hairy face. His quick wink suggested a joke; but when an overgrown brow dipped to cover a glaring eye, there would be something vile forthcoming, such as he'd just quizzed James about—a wet finger.

"Now that's old Mickel," Calvin pointed, bringing James up to speed. "And he told me this mornin' that he got some last night, and that means he won't be worth a fart for the rest of the week!" The timing couldn't have been any better than when Mickel let out a Calvin-sized fart as he gently pushed in on his stomach with a fist. I yelped a short laugh, thinking maybe this day might end up being like the day before, and James could go through what I had.

"Damn!" Calvin shouted, stepping away quickly and shaking his pipe as if the taste had gone sour or something maybe even worse. The smell was as bad as anything I'd ever smelled in my life, and that was saying a lot considering Mable's aunt Wilma or even Calvin as far as that went. After we'd distanced ourselves, Calvin stopped in hopes of lighting his pipe once more but had failed in the attempt when Mickel started walking our way, and still rubbing his stomach.

"Hey! Keep your stankin' ass over there! My damn pipe won't even light after what you just done, fillin' the air with all that stank."

"Welcome to the circus, James! I'm glad you get to see this!" I said. Calvin finally got the pipe going after flopping his ass down on the fat end of a log.

"Now let me tell you something, you old fart! You're not gonna stand around and shit on me today!" Calvin sounded more confident after a couple good draws.

"Boys, them beans are really workin' me over this mornin'." Mickel's effort looked weak as he tried to light a cigarette.

"Shit, Mickel, you ain't got the strength to even light that damn stankin'-ass thang up. Now I done and told you I can't stand the smell, so carry your ass right over there next to the woods and get away from me. And another thang . . . I'll expect you to check the way the wind is blowin' from here on out and not be upwind of us." He pointed a warning pipe toward Mickel. "And . . . I don't want your stankin' ass to start throwin' up all over everythin' again!" Calvin winked at James trying to hide his obvious smile.

It looked painful the way old Mickel made a hard drag on the cigarette.

"And I've got a new name for you, Mickel. Now, boys, listen at this." Calvin faked a cough, one solely intended to get our attention. "Stanky." He frowned acting as if there were a foul taste in his mouth followed with a spit off to the side of us. "Now I think that fits you pretty good, Mick! 'Old Stanky', that'll be your name from here on out!" Calvin teased, toasting with a satisfying blow into the air.

I hadn't paid much attention to what James was doing as I was too busy laughing at Calvin. Then there came the twinkle in his eyes that I'd seen before that suggested he was working on a poem. And sure enough a few seconds later he delivered.

"Old Stanky old Stanky who comes to work cranky.
He rubs his gut till it blows from his butt sendin' us all a sailin.'
Some run left and some run right but you ain't gonna out run the smell of old stanky tonight."

We laughed of course as Calvin said he'd come up with more verses as the day went on.

"I see what you mean, Arnold," James laughed and was doing a pretty good job of holding his own stomach. But Calvin was on a roll now, and once he got there, he wasn't gonna stop until he'd worn it out.

"When you, git finished pushin' all that gas out of your rotten gut, you kin start markin' them trees over yonder so's I can cut 'em up. Then I want you to march your ass over there by them stinkin' piss elm trees, and maybe you won't stank the place up here so bad, Stanky." He laughed.

Mickel looked helpless to Calvin's threats, which I knew was no more than his way of funning with Mickel. But I didn't dare look over at Calvin. I knew what the outcome would be. James was having a good laugh over the whole affair, enough so that I wouldn't have to tell him much of what had gone on the day before.

"Come on, James, you can get it out. What did I tell you?" I knew that would make him laugh even harder.

"C-ci-circus!" he choked the word out. Now he fully understood what I'd been trying to tell him. "It is like a circus here." He stood up and walked a couple of steps away. He wiped his eyes clean, saying, "Anybody that can make me laugh like that is okay!" He walked over to old Mickel, giving him a firm handshake.

"Junior, you better make sure you didn't get anything on your hand from old Stanky ass there!" Calvin hollered with a loud goofy laugh.

"You'll meet my partner, Bob, when he gets back from Chillicothe." Mickel dragged the words.

"Yeah, he's the olden of the bunch." Calvin spoke slowly, trying to imitate Mickel's Southern Ohio drawl and doing a terrible job at it.

"Yeah, he is older than me. I know I'll never hear the end of it as long as that loudmouth asshole needs somethin' to laugh at!" Mickel nodded, to where Calvin sat.

"I'm sorry, Mickel . . ." Calvin made a quick draw on his pipe. Knowing Calvin as we did, the quick draw only meant one thing. I'd hoped Mickel didn't have his hopes up about a real apology. "I'm sorry that you wasted so much of our time, havin' to let that stank clear the air! Now get your stankin' ass busy while I finish smokin' this load in my pipe."

"Has he been up here this morning?" James asked. I knew he'd avoid calling the old man Dad after what he'd put him through lately.

"Yes, he has!" Mickel spoke, placing his hands on his hips.

"He told Bob to take off for Chillicothe and told me and that fat prick to git busy." Mickel managed a rare laugh of his own. Calvin grinned at Mickel's description of him. I felt sorry for Mickel, however, all broken down like he was and figured he was in pain most of the time for sure. I figured that's why he didn't laugh much either. Mickel threw the short butt to the ground and made a half-ass effort to crush it out. Even that showed a weakness.

"Well I guess you're the one's gonna go up and cut the trees down?" He cocked his head toward James. "And Arnold's gonna drag them down to the yard with the animals. And Calvin is gonna cut them up into logs and pulpwood . . .," he said slowly.

"And now that we know what the hell we're doin', what the hell are you gonna be doing besides standin' around and shittin' your pants all day?" Calvin grunted. Mickel wouldn't answer but instead continued talking to James.

"I guess your dad gave your job away to Bob, didn't he?"

"Yeah, it looks like it," James said as he grabbed the other chainsaw and started to sharpen it. "But you know!" He flashed the file at Mickel. "He can give all my jobs away that he wants to. After I graduate, I won't care anymore." James sounded gleeful. Mickel got the point that James didn't want to talk too much longer. Shortly after the sharpening, he hurriedly headed for the woods.

"Now he sounds like there might be somethin else botherin him, is there?" Mickel asked. Calvin true to form jerked his pipe, orchestrating it directly to where James was walking. After several stabbing motions, he advised.

"Why in the hell don't you march your old bony ass up there and ask um? You might come back down that there hill faster than you went up, though!" Calvin huffed.

"Look! All I did was asked a question . . . I didn't mean to piss nobody off." He slowly waved a hand in his plea for no trouble. Calvin understood it completely, but all Mickel did was open more things up for Calvin's orneriness.

"Why, you pissed me off the first thing this mornin'!" He shot me a wink as Mickel looked away.

"And how did I do that?" Mickel had to ask.

"When I saw you, right off the bat, it pissed me off just thinkin' that I'd have to be around your old sorry bony fartin' ass all day. Now get that markin' stick and start puttin a notch big enough that I can see it. I need something better than just a scratch. You need to draw back on that hatchet a little farther."

I took the animals up into the woods, deciding to work an area that wasn't so close to James. I could tell he probably wanted to be by himself for a while to think about all that'd transpired.

Bob got back from Chillicothe, and James wasted no time walking over the hill to meet him. There was a handshake, and they began talking, but I couldn't hear anything they were saying. They laughed loud at times. I thought Bob seemed to be an all right person, and I knew James would see it also, and everything would be all right between them.

Mickel started walking toward them while digging a cigarette from his pack. From my vantage point, I could see what Calvin had observed was true. Old Mickel was as slow as the seven-year itch. He'd carried on that old Mick was so slow that his itch would go away before he got around to scratching it. It was then when no one was paying attention that Mickel made a desperate painful looking attempt to pull at the back of his pants. For whatever the reason it plagued him for the better part of the walk. Calvin shut his saw off and, in a loud voice that I could hear clearly from the distance, shouted,

"Get your old sorry ass back over here and keep workin'! Don't make me cut a dammed saplin' and wear it out on your ass since you ain't got much left anyhow!" What a view, I thought, to watch everything going on at the yard. It was a circus without the animals or had they all finally arrived?

James raised the hood up on Big Bad Red, and he and Bob were making an adjustment on the carburetor as Mickel and Calvin approached the front of the truck. After a minute or so, James shut the motor off with an agreeable nod from Bob that the adjustment was right. Seeing them chatting away did my heart good. And Mickel by now should know that Calvin would never give him a minute's peace after their rocky start. Calvin just wanted to have fun with whomever he picked on but could make it hard if you didn't adhere somewhat to his ways.

As all the distractions were unfolding in front of me, the evilness of the old man could quickly steal them away. I slowly shook my head, tight jawed with hatred that he'd cheated James and me out of what he'd promised and never paid Calvin on time either. I considered Bob and Mickel, who more than likely needed every penny they could get and on time at that.

We'd pretty well figured that the new house was nothing more than a ploy for the old man to get Mom to give everything up and hope on a new dream. "The Lord will not put on me more than I can handle" echoed through my mind the many times she was having a hard time. It was always brought on by him. I guess God really did give her strength in some ways to push on, but never the miracle that I wanted to see. I'd lost my faith a long time ago when none of my prayers on her behalf had been answered. I wondered how God could let my mother endure so much and never come to her rescue. It scared me the few times she said it might be better if the Lord were to just take her on home to be with him. The very thoughts of her flying off toward the heavens saddened me. I didn't want her to ever leave me.

I lay back on a patch of soft green moss beside two trails. The sun felt good as I worked my shoulders deeper into the fine greenery.

I knew there was no hope of keeping the place in Pike County; it was simply doomed. Maybe the sooner he sold it, the faster I could start getting it out of my mind. But tucked back somewhere when I'd need it would always be the memory of a warm house on a cold wintery night. *What would the devil bestow upon us next?* I thought to myself.

I dozed off for a short while, waking up with a sudden jerk to James's loud laughter above all the rest just before they all joined in on what was probably a good joke. Reality was back again. It sounded like a good bullshit opportunity, something that I should be part of. I hustled to hook the animals up to a couple of logs.

Secretly, I liked what the old man had done by having Bob drive the truck. It was just good to have more time with my big brother and talk about growing pains. I thought it also good, but couldn't say so, his having to leave Scarlett's at nine o'clock for a whole week—punishment for falling asleep on the davenport together. He didn't complain, though, saying he'd gotten off lightly. The week flew past and way too quickly. Saturday morning came with James proclaiming that the weekend was here. Shortly after he was on his way to Scarlett's. It was the difference in night and day when he got back from her house that evening. He joked and cut up like old times and was truly ready for me to run around with them come Sunday morning.

I'd almost finished with the milking the next morning when I heard the Buick start up. "Summer in the City" by the Loving Spoonful played, with James turning the volume knob up. The words echoed throughout the barn as I sang along. Red gave me the strangest look when I tried to imitate the jackhammer sound in the song. She lifted her leg slightly, maybe indicating that I was irritating her.

I hadn't gotten much sleep, wondering how this day would turn out—riding around with them, that is. I really didn't know if I was ready for it or not. I thought I knew more than Carolyn must have, or did I? Scarlett must have told her all the same things James told me, I figured.

"Are you about ready?" he asked when I brought the bucket of milk to Harry's hand pump.

"Almost, I'm gonna strain it here this morning and leave some for Harry. He told me last night that he was almost out." I held the bucket steady in the floorboard as we drove on down to the house.

"Da-gone, you're here just in time to beat me out of the big biscuit again!" Duck complained, laughing when we walked through the door.

"I think it's my turn," James stated while looking at me.

"Now you boys ain't gonna fight over mom's biscuit, are you?" She laughed.

"Not unless Arnold thinks it's his turn." James smirked.

"Well, what happened? Did Anna Fay stop cookin' fer ya, James?" I joked around.

"Where's he at this mornin'?" James asked while parading his plate of food over the top of my head. Two scrambled eggs and sausage gravy he more than covered the big biscuit.

"You really know how to hurt a guy, James." I sniffed as he walked past.

"Your dad said he was goin' back up to Good Hope to look at that timber again." Mom shook her head looking a little disgusted. "I don't know why he doesn't just stay right here and work in these woods!" James paused before looking up at me.

"Well, Mom, he says there's some quick money to be made up there," he answered. "And I've got to say, this is the best biscuits and gravy I think you've ever made." James looked at me as if he were inviting a scuffle.

"Just shut up and eat. Enough is enough!" I laughed. James had always been a fast eater, but since Scarlett came along, he hurried more than ever. It didn't seem he savored the taste like he used to. I was doing all right keeping up, even as nervous as I was.

I didn't know if I'd think of anything to say while we were riding around. *I can see it now*, I thought to myself. They'll be lip-locked, and I'll be tongue-tied. I knew that we couldn't talk like we normally did, with Scarlett being there.

"Honey, why don't you bring Scarlett over here with you sometime?" Mom asked. James had his mouth stuffed and couldn't talk, so I spoke up for him.

"Anna Fay's 'fraid they might do somethin' they're not supposed to do at their age," I blurted out. Mom shook her head and laughed. James never said anything; he just kept on eating.

"Okay!" James stood up. "Let's head for Pfizer's Ridge." Almost all of Big John and Mallie Radcliff's children had lived up on the ridge one time or the other. As they'd gotten older a couple of the boys decided to stay in Florida and call it their home.

But John, just like the old man, always wanted to be back in Ohio in time to get a garden out. I didn't think much about Florida anymore ever since Mom made the statement after the last trip, that it would be her last. And for the sake of argument told him if he wanted to go, he could and without her.

We hadn't even got out of the driveway before James started talking about Scarlett. I wanted to talk more about Bob and Mickel and maybe be courageous enough to tell him about Mable. It would be a long fifteen miles I thought to Scarlett's house.

"James, time-out!" I said loudly. "Can we talk about somethin' other than just Scarlett? Maybe turn the music up a little more?" I suggested.

"Halfway," James said, looking over at me.

"Halfway what?"

"This is exactly the halfway mark to Scarlett's." He roared with laughter while slapping the stirring wheel.

"You've got to be shittin' me James." I laughed.

He wheeled the Buick into the driveway as Scarlett came running off the front porch. Anna Fay, at a much slower pace, walked behind her. I hadn't seen Scarlett for quite some time and was struck by how pretty she'd gotten. She bounced with every step, before jumped into James's arms, straddling his waist.

They'd have had to practice such a stunt, I thought, as James had barely made it out of the car. There she was with her legs gripping tightly around him and flexing. Her dress was pushed all the way up her leg as they kissed. James slid his hand down on her ass. I swallowed with some difficulty when he gave it a squeeze. I just couldn't believe what I was seeing.

Suddenly the car door was being jerked open by Anna Fay. She grabbed my shirt by the collar, dragging me out. It was then and there that I got my first kiss, just missing my lips. I started spitting all over the place, wiping my mouth furiously as Ezell and Carolyn walked upon us. Anna Fay had never been shy of anything and always ready for a dare. Scarlett slid from James's waist, running around the car to give me a hug. She smelled really good, I thought.

"Your face sure is red!" Carolyn said, twisting at the waist with hands on her hips. We shared a bashful hug of our own. It was the right thing to do, though. She smelled faintly like roses, maybe a cheap perfume I thought.

"Now, Arnold Ray, you tell me that my little angel ain't the prettiest thing you ever seen in your life?" Anna Fay pulled Carolyn close, holding her hair off to the side. Carolyn twirled around slowly posing for my response. She was very pretty with a smile that fit her rounded face well. There was no doubt that if she hadn't been my cousin, I'd have wanted her to jump into my arms, just as Scarlett had done with James. But then what would I have done? I'd never been in that predicament before. Ezell had always been the quiet one of the family for as far back as I could remember slowly extended his hand for a shake.

"Yeah, she's really pretty." I said and really meant for it to sound sincere. Charlotte smiled at my complement, pulling my face close to hers and giving me a kiss on the cheek. It felt foreign when Carolyn forced her hand into mine. I never squeezed back, simply letting my hand go limp as I backed up a couple of steps. It was obvious that she was way more outgoing than I was. I knew she'd dressed for this occasion with hope she might tag along with us. Maybe I should give in I thought then at least I'd have someone to talk with. Her hopeful smile quickly faded however when I didn't invite her at just when the moment was right.

"Well, Arnold Ray, I guess you're my date for the day." Anna Fay joked while getting a mean look from Charlotte. "And look at you . . .," she said. "My, my, you're all grown up. And what a good-looking young man you are!" I was speechless. I glanced over at James for help, but he and Scarlett were already kissing again. "Come on, old man!" She pushed Ezell towards the house. "We've got to get that garden hoed today."

We were just ready to get into the car when she turned, shaking a finger, and said in a meaningful voice,

"Arnold Ray, you keep an eye on these two today! I don't want any hanky-panky goin' on! They're too young, and I'm too old for them to be getting in trouble!" Her laugh was strained, meaning she meant what she'd said. Strange that I was supposed to be responsible for two people older than me, I thought. "Now you'uns have fun!" She waved bye over her shoulder.

"Get in the car, Arnold . . . hurry and let's get out of here!" Scarlett motioned, pulling on James's hand. Carolyn looked like a little yellow-dressed statue with her hands clasped behind her back.

"Are you sure Arnold we can't take her? Look how cute she is!" Scarlett pointed. I felt bad that I couldn't just say okay and have her come along. We were about the same age and would probably have had plenty to talk about. I was ready to learn about love and all that stuff, but it wasn't gonna be it in a car with my cousin while my brother made out with her half-sister in the backseat. James lived up to his side of the deal by not pressing that Carolyn should go with us. But now Scarlett had put me on the spot.

I slowly turned to Carolyn, gathering my words while thinking about what James had told me. I knew exactly how she felt being all alone and guessed she'd lost her best friend also when James and Scarlett fell in love.

"I'm really sorry, Carolyn, but I might not even be with them all day myself. I mean I don't think anybody's got a plan for sure."

"Oh, that's ok," she smiled. I stumbled for a minute and I had to look away as her smile left her face. She brushed a tear from her cheek; and unable to say anything.

"Oh yeah, we've got a plan, all right!" Scarlett remarked to my lousy excuse while looking quickly over at James. A second or two passed before they both broke out into childish laughter.

"But you know what? Maybe we can go ridin' around with 'em some other time, okay?" Now with all hope gone, she turned and walked off toward the house without another word. Scarlett said no more about her little sister but turned all her attention to James. I'd no more than got one foot in the backseat before he started backing up.

"Damnit James, give me time to get in!" With Scarlett's goofy laugh and James's surprised look made me realized it was she who had a foot on the accelerator for the quick getaway. Scarlett pulled herself tightly up against James, who now controlled the accelerator pushing it down a little further. There was nothing awkward to the way they fit so snugly together with Scarlett's arm around his neck. This wasn't anything new; I figured they'd had practice. He leaned to the side where he could get his arm around her neck also, pulling her in even more tightly than ever.

Scarlett's fingers worked like lightning, turning the radio knob to find a favorite song. She turned the volume up, snapping her fingers, clapping her hands, and shrugging her shoulders back and forth all at the same time. In some ways, she reminded me of the girls at Greenfield when we'd go cruising up there. If a song came on that wasn't cool, as Scarlett called it, she'd find a different AM station in a flash. It didn't matter if she hit on a song that was half over as long as there'd be one last chorus for that dedicated kiss. I figured she'd heard the top 40 songs numerous times, and it didn't take long to see which was her favorites. "Good Lovin'" by the Rascals came on. She backed away from James like it was the most unbelievable song she'd ever heard. "Oh, my god, I love this song!" she said just before covering her mouth with open hands.

I liked the song myself but figured they knew the meaning way better than I did. I could only daydream about good lovin'. I'd already seen more kissing up to this point other than on TV than I had in my entire lifetime. It looked easy, but I couldn't understand all the goofy shit that went along with it, especially the stupid baby talk that I'd been tired of hearing for quite some time. James stopped at the stop sign and, with no hesitation, headed in the direction of Bainbridge.

"So where are we going?" I spoke up. Scarlett turned in the seat to face me.

"Me and your brother are gonna go and make out somewhere. What are you gonna do?" She snickered while quickly glancing over at James. "Aren't we, sweetheart? Aren't we?" She repeatedly rammed her elbow into his ribs, which didn't last long when he grabbed her and pulled her tightly up next to him once again.

I thought how dumb it must've looked with no one in the backseat with me. Maybe it would have been better to have Carolyn and someone to at least to talk with. *I should never have come with them*, I thought to myself. James began slowing down and pulled off to the side of the road at Buckskin Creek, which followed Route 41 and emptied into Paint Creek down by Bainbridge.

We'd come here to wash the Dodge before he traded it off for the Buick. It was the way he and Scarlett started laughing that led me to believe that they too had been here before but it wasn't to wash the Buick. James no sooner parked the car than he and Scarlett were doing some serious kissing throughout the whole chorus of a song.

So this is what James called a lip-lock. I observed for a second before looking away. I thought how concerned Anna Fay was about them, but what could I do? Other than just be in the car with them. Maybe that was her point. I was feeling embarrassed about the whole thing, though. I could hear heavy breathing above the radio, which Scarlett must've known when she felt about the dash, turning the volume up without even looking.

"Hey ah, I'm not gonna just sit back here and watch you guys kiss all day long! You sound like a couple fat hogs sloppin' in a trough!" I meant it as a joke, trying for some conversation. They looked at each other before bursting out with laughter. *They're goofy!* I thought to myself. Then like something went off in their heads at the same time, they scrambled over the front seat and got into the back with me.

"What the hell?" I said as they wallered all over me.

"Arnold, how about you drive and me and Scarlett will ride in the back here?" James said, not taking his eyes off hers.

"Now you know that I don't have a driver's license, James," I pointed out.

"We won't get pulled over if you drive right." He chuckled.

"Hey! I'm over here, James! Not stuck in Scarlett's eyes somewhere." I waved a hand.

I climbed over Scarlett into the front seat, and as I did, she punched me in the rib cage. *Why would they laugh at such a dumbass thing as that?* I wondered.

Even though I'd never driven on a paved road, I drove plenty on gravel whenever James would allow me. I knew that the practice would be good when it came time to get my license. I drove into curves a little too fast at first, which made the tires squeal.

"Arnold, turn the radio up louder. I love this song! I love it, I love it, I—"

I glanced in the rearview mirror as James cut her short when he forcibly pressed his lips against hers, but that didn't slow her snapping fingers to the beat.

"I'm sorry, Scarlett, but I can't do that." I slid my fingers from the volume knob. "It's not a Beatles song. James told me that you're all hung up on them right now." She looked at him all hurt-like, gently slapping him on the chest. I couldn't believe how he reacted from such a small hit, taking her hand and placing it over his heart.

I'd gotten comfortable with the fact that they thrived on acting goofy or anything else that would lead up to kissing, which I witnessed in the mirror.

Like a movie, they'd rub against and hug all over each other workin' their way to that aggressive lip-lick of love. Maybe it was there that Anna Fay had her concerns.

"Last Train to Clarksville" played as we drove through Bainbridge, where I stopped at a red light.

"Oh shit, James. The law's right behind me. What the hell now?" There was panic in my voice for sure. All laughter ended as the cop eased closer and closer to my bumper. "The light's stuck on red," I said, gripping the steering wheel tighter.

"No, it's not stuck. You're just panicking! When it turns green, hang a right and pull into the Dairy Queen," he advised. The policeman drove on past, a great relief when I could start breathing again; quickly wiping sweat from my forehead. We all had banana splits where their game was to tickle each other while they had a mouthful of ice cream. I was trying to learn all the tricks of the trade, but some just seemed really dumb I thought. But on the other hand, I wasn't in love either. Seeing my reaction, Scarlett ran around the bench to tickle me. I'd have no part of it, fending off every attempt she made. But no matter if I learned anything on this day, it really was fun just to watch how they acted.

Maybe it wasn't so bad to have your head up your ass and not really care what people thought of you. And evidentially it wasn't anything new with Harry and the likes of others knowing all about it.

I'd avoided their playfulness long enough; after all it wasn't like they'd not tempted me all day. I had plenty of laughs they weren't even aware of when they were really being goofy. Scarlett tried to make it as easy as possible when she said that I should sing along with them and then to even dare me. You wonder what little thing it takes to set you off and to act out of norm. To overcome bashfulness for that minute in time. I thought what Calvin said when you were on the teetertotter edge of a decision and had to go one way or the other. 'Balls Arnie, sometimes you got ta pick 'em back up and admit ya flat fucked up.' He laughed telling how some of his decisions were from a knee jerk reaction. I could relate to what he'd said If there'd been one more tingle on the end of my finger no doubt I'd killed Bill McCoy and the old man a couple years back.?

Scarlett's dare that I sing with them seemed to linger in the Buick when I blurted the first words to a song that'd just come on.

I'd heard Scarlett sing all day and not one time mess a single word up. I figured more than likely with so much hand clapping and body movements might be a distraction that her voice wasn't that good. But the point was she made the attempt to express her true feelings. I couldn't count the times that I feel way short of even trying something. James was better when they sang a duet together but didn't put the heart and soul into it like Scarlett did. But I'd not tolerate Scarlett's dare any longer when the next song came on. And I wouldn't just sing along to be drowned out by the two of them. I just knew that neither could belt the song such as I. From the time, my voice had gone through the change I'd sang it with such a high pitch to it. Any place if I were alone either a high point on a ridge a valley where it would echo back to me. 'In the jungle, the mighty jungle the lion sleeps tonight,' I belted even louder than the radio. Scarlett's voice faded quickly possible shocked that I even sang and let alone I could reach the high notes. After the song was finished they over reacted I thought to how well I sang it.

We rode around the better part of the day. James called it burning gas for a damn good reason. "For a damn good reason" seemed to be their catchphrase for about anything that had no logic to it I thought to myself. But I got caught up in their happiness with a better understanding of how love could make you act and feel. If the world would have come to an end, I really believe they'd miss out on it; with their happily ever after attitudes.

"Hey! Ah . . . it's . . . ah . . . five o'clock, James. I need to get home and milk the cow." What Scarlett found so funny in that was way beyond me. "What the hell is so funny about milkin' a cow?" I played along peering through the rearview mirror. Neither one could come up with a good answer, so they did the next best thing and fall apart all over each other. I had a laugh of my own, thinking about how it wasn't just James who had his head up his ass. Calvin and others were right as to such a meaning, which I'd truly witnessed on this day. Scarlett asked what I was laughing so hard about and if I'd like to share it.

"No." I shook my head looking at them in the mirror. I'd driven 118 miles that day when I pulled up under Harry's shade tree. There was no time wasted on their part. As soon as I'd got out of the car James climbed into the driver's seat while Scarlett dove over the seat to win their bet as to who could get there the fastest. "Now you two better get your asses on over to Pfizer's Ridge 'cause I'm not going to lie to Anna Fay about what time you left here." I laughed. There simply was no letting up with them as they drove off and laughing all the way.

I turned towards Harry's porch where it took exactly twelve steps from the small gate to where he sat in his swing. I'd stopped counting how many dotted lines there were in the road between towns or whatever I'd determine as a final destination. James was the only person I'd boast to of my final tally. Could it be part of my jealousy that I'd have one more thing I could beat my big brother at. He was short with his answer however saying I was off in the head and then as always said it seemed like a waste of time to him. I had a private laugh thinking of all the other things going around in my head that I'd not even consider telling him about.

Even though I'd never counted how many steps it took for one lap around the track I found myself counting how many it took to pass someone. But it wasn't just me with other determined faces possible counting also till that final sprint to the finish line. I did mention to James that I thought it helped me with such a long distance and no one to talk to. James joked as what would happen if I counted as far as I could but the finish line was still away off. I had to laugh along with his envisionment of me sprawled out all over the track and not for the lack of energy but that I couldn't count far enough to finish the race.

Needless to say, a wrestling match pursued James's plan all along. It was like there was something always needed to be counted. A field with baled hay I'd count how many bales lay in a particular area. Seldom that I didn't know how many logs were in the laydown yard. But almost any time when I'd be walking somewhere, right out of the blue a number came to mind and then the next one. I could just about gauge from where something had set me off to start counting. It didn't bother me in any way. But the big question was why did I do it?

It hadn't taken the whole twelve steps to figure something was bothering old Harry slouched forward, and looking uncomfortable, I thought. He wasn't his normal cheery self, where he'd toast his pipe into the air, whether lit or not, and always proceeded by his handsome smile. And regardless, whether he was blue or happy, he always offered a hand shake before patting the place beside him for you to sit down.

"Here, pull up a seat, Arnold Ray! By God, let's chat for a little while." His welcoming words were usually the same every time. He leaned back, looking a little more at home after I'd positioned myself in the swing. "Now, Arnold, ...by god I'd like to know where in all the hell you've been all day." He asked followed by what sounded like a planned cough.

"Harry, I've been chauffeuring love birds around all day." I said followed with whistling sigh.

"Why . . . did you learn anything from it?" He reared back, slapping his leg.

"Yep, I did." I shook my head. With Harry's anticipation, the swing began to move a little faster. "I learned that I just wasn't cut out to be one." I looked Harry straight in the eye like I'd finished a joke. But he looked a little disappointed that I didn't have something juicier maybe to talk about.

"Well, Arnold I don't think I'd be much of one either!" He slowly nodded. There was hardly any expression in his words as he pushed a fresh load of baccer into his pipe. I really wasn't much surprised though when he blurted, "Have you seen Jim today?" His to the point question played right into the way he was acting.

"No, I ain't, Harry . . . why? Were you guys supposed to go and do something tonight?"

He slowly crossed one leg over the other while holding his pipe a smart was off to his side. "Why, he was supposed to take me to the bank Friday and make a payment on that place across the road over there."

"Let me guess he's late on a payment, right?" I tried to joke but probably sounded sarcastic about something I really didn't want to hear. Harry gave me a suspicious look from the corners of his eyes. After a long draw, he tilted his chin upwards releasing a steady stream of blue smoke into the air.

"Why, Arnold! Harry's sudden stall was as if he wasn't sure he wanted to even finish what he'd started to tell me. Followed by a short fake cough he turned to face me.

"He's never paid me a damn dime to what he owes me! Period! I haven't heard nothin' but promises from Jim since the first time we talked about that timber across the road there. Why the agreement was that he'd pay me two thousand dollars down right off the bat and then we'd work up a reasonable payment after that. And then your house burned and I know it put you all in a bind for sure." I recalled how serious Harry's complaint had been when the old man bought the new convertible, saying that it would've paid down a lot on his debt. It was easy now to figure where the down payment on the land went to.

Maybe it was a mistake when I told Jim that I wasn't hurting for money right then but by god it's got to where he seems to have forgot about it all together. Harry snapped to attention with his eyes wider than normal. And I hope ole Jim don't think I'm a dumbass. I see that truck parked up there at the pond about every evening and see other loads taken out during the day also. His pipes smoky stem followed his frustrations in the way he whipped it back and forth with every load that was heading down the road.

"Now I'll tell you the truth about it Arnold Ray. Why I simply let it ride because Jim was showin' me a good ole time and I got to go play my fiddle. He winked. And don't get me wrong by God I, I enjoy the drinkin' part of it also. Harry's laugh was short and faint. But all I do anymore is rosin up my bow and set right here on my ass night after night. He stabbed a stiff finger on the swing's arm.

I was speechless, suddenly paralyzed with what Harry had just told me. But even worse and like always, I was helpless that I could do nothing about it. I thought of the many times before when I'd cried over such disappointments. But the crying had long since turned to hate and anger of the old man. To hear he'd not paid a fucking dime on the land shouldn't have been such a big shock to me. To hear him ramble, and through no fault of his own, there'd be no money for school clothes shouldn't have been such a shock either.

Even that he never paid James and I the money he owed us should have been expected. And to think how over the years we couldn't afford nine pieces of Goddamned hard tack candy for me and my siblings. He'd scratch it from Moms short list of bare necessities and always followed by a sharp whistle; satisfied that he'd taken care of that problem. I hated it anytime he'd toss an extra pack of cigarettes upon the dashboard. James did the math one time figuring how just one pack alone could buy enough hard tack that everyone in the family could have five pieces a day for two weeks and with one single piece left over. There was no reason to ask him who got the last piece with such a sparkle in his eyes.

By now I could hardly sit still with so much frustration clawing at my insides. I'd be fooling myself to think that I could hold my angry any longer. I'd stopped breathing just before letting out a long and deep sigh which momentarily got Harry's attention.

"I want to kill that no account bastard." I grumbled not wanting Harry to really hear me. But maybe he did with his sudden cough and followed with a spit off the porch. "Harry that low down bastard is running through money like there's no end or lack of it." I raged as I'd never done before in front of Harry.

"Why, Arnold I don't know where it all goes but I can tell you there's nobody goes thirsty when old Jim's at the bar. By God, I seen him throw down a hundred-dollar bill and tell everybody, 'The drinks are on me,' till it's all gone." Harry hadn't blown all the smoke from his mouth as he continued "Why, in my day, they called that a big spender, someone who really had money. But I know Jim ain't got any to piss away like that!" Harry finalized.

I thought how little Harry truly knew about the old man. I'd bit my tongue many times to avoid telling him the truth. But one thing for sure was I didn't want him to know the real reason our house had to be burned down. So, why say something that would aggravate and keep him awake at nights.

Harry slowed the swing considerable to where I could hear a sudden puff, throttled by his thumb, and now primed for a better drag. He'd not stumbled much and not on the moonshine which led me to believe his concerns were well thought out. I wondered how long he'd wanted to talk about this to me. He'd calmed down more relaxed than just a few minutes ago when the swing's chains seemed bound by Harry's outburst of anger. But he'd continue to vent but in a less belligerent way.

"And he keeps comin' up with some lame-ass excuse why he can't pay me anythin', and I keep tellin' him it's okay." Sad, I thought with the way Harry tilting his head while looking off to one side maybe realizing he'd been taken. "Now I know Jim wants to build a house up there by that pond . . ." Harry pointed a steady finger. "And by God, wouldn't you know, why I'm the one who suggested it! And that's okay, but he needs to pay me some money before he starts all that! But the thing that saddens me more than anything Arnold is how he can drag a woman like your mother around with just a damned promise of something."

"Well it's always been like that Harry. Think about a promise that began just up the road here some years back. Hard to believe that was 1957. And now right back where we started from, following yet another one of his allusive promise." Harry sat idle with deep thought. With his head cocked off to one side his unstable nod slowed to practically nothing. "Mom's still got one thing that I don't Harry and that's hope for the old man. I gave up on that shit a long time ago. My only hope that the asshole dies somewhere just ain't going to happen, don't look like. Of course, Mom would never see it that way. It's her Christian way ya know with any chance the old man might be saved once again. She'll simply not give up. But I can't handle disappoint like that anymore and that's why she's a stronger person than me and by a lot.

"Why, by hell Arnold I just can't imagine old Jim livin' a Christian life with what I know about him. But I do know one thing for sure he's got a gab about him that you could easily be suckered in to something."

"Well and that actually worked pretty good when he was preachin' Harry. And I'd have to admit that there were some golden years when he could be satisfied with preachin' the gospel and a fried chicken dinner every Sunday. But the only problem was he should have been preachin' sermons to himself before others. Now you saw how our mother was at the pond. All she ever wanted and needed was a little happiness in her life but hope seems to be about as close as she'll ever get to that. When we were little boys Harry, and heard stories in the Bible how all the saints struggled throughout their lives we'd practically brag that our mothers was worse. And lastly she'll never stop as long as she lives with that same hope the old man will find his way back to the lord in time." Harry had been paying close attention all the while to every word I said and at times, followed my lip movement a trait I'd suspected from his hearing ailment.

I thought back to how fond Harry was with all that happened at the pond that day. The picnic alone seemed to put a warm place in his heart that maybe took him back to a different one many years ago. The songs Mom and the girls sang with one after the other had totally captivated the old fellow.

"Why, Arnold to sound that good with no music I'm tellin' ya that's special in its own way," he'd declared more than just once on that day. Then as a child showing off its newest toy everyone followed him around as he pointed to all the place's that had interested him throughout the many years he'd lived there. Maybe James had showed him but it certainly wasn't me when Harry guided everyone to the X James had proclaimed as the spot for the new house. And it was right then and there when he expressed so much excitement in how he could walk up to the new house every night for such songfests. And I knew he was serious about that. Clearly, he'd enjoyed the attention from everyone as he drug the day out for as long as possible. The old man's name never come up and I was glad of it. Harry had done nothing but praised Mom in every way possible and with the way he acted I wondered if he'd give the land away if she'd just stay there and sing for him on occasion.

"And at one time Arnold, I thought ole Jim was a good person, when I first met him. But now by God, I just don't know!" Harry turned looking sharply at me before continuing. "And by god I really started having my doubts that day he showed his ass up there in the woods, when he slapped you, telling me ahead of time that he needed to straighten you up a little, kinda like a stubborn mule." His all intentional stall would leave me the opening that I needed. I stopped my side of the swing pushing my foot hard against the floor.

"You know Harry I've been prayin' ever since that day to kick that bastard's ass and it is goin' to happen at some point and time. James promised me he'd not interfere the next time. But that don't really matter now. I really don't suspect him being around to witness it. Have you ever thought about killing someone Harry?" My anger had gotten the best of me but Harry didn't seem surprised of my question.

"No, I think it's crossed everybody's mind one time or the other Arnold Ray. But, but smart people like you and I would never carry through with it in the end."

Other than an occasional quick glance to set a joke off Harry and I'd never looked in each other eyes in the way we did right now. I guessed he was intent that I take heed to his many years of wisdom when he said.

"Don't forget Arnold Ray smart people like us." He wouldn't have had to repeat himself, I got his long stare. I was however the first to look away hoping Harry couldn't read my mind that maybe I wasn't that smart person he spoke of.

"I'll fix his ass someday!" I managed to squeeze the words through tight lips, which Harry chose to ignore. I'd said enough that any more might really set me off to craziness. I figured Harry needed to hear something more uplifting. "You know I'd almost bet he plans on paying you some when he sells the place over in Pike County Harry." I wasn't shy at this point to beg Harry that he might be patient with the old man and we start yet another dream of a place to live forever. "Well I can tell you one thing Harry and that is how much we all appreciate that you sold us this land. It could be a dream come true for our mother. I'd leave him with that simple thought as things had gone quiet between us as the swing slowed to stop. "Well, Harry, I've got to get the milkin' done. So I'll talk to you later . . . Do you need any?" I stood up slowly, stretching my arms over my head.

"No, I've got plenty enough to last through tomorrow, Arnold. But thanks anyway." He tipped his pipe and smiled as I left his porch.

Everything Harry and I'd talked about flooded my mind as I milked. I thought of the first time I'd met him and how honest he seemed. Maybe the old man had seen the same thing but was quick to take advantage of the old fellow's loneliness. Over at Pike County, Mr. Cox talked about a person "bein' as honest as a day was long." Even with the old man being all Christian-like at the time, Mr. Cox saw right through him and wasn't going to take any chances on a handshake.

It took a while to carry the full pail of milk the half mile or so to Mom's house down in the curve. The distance did however give me more time to consider all that Harry and I'd talked about. I doubted Mom knew there'd never been a payment made to Harry and I wouldn't say anything about it and add to her already mountain of problems? There was a problem no matter which way I turned anymore, and all because of a sorry ass of a father I had. How much of this could I escape if I were to be like James and parked somewhere and making out. I too wanted to kiss a girl and fall in love, a fantasy that I yearned for day and night anymore.

Mom and I talked a little about building a house but we got carried away with laughter reminiscing of the "mansion" he'd built in Florida. I was careful not to slip and say something of what Harry and I'd talked about earlier.

With no higher power to turn to once again she would leave everything in the hands of the Lord, saying if it was in his will then so be it. I wouldn't argue that it was more like the old man's will than the Lord's however. Even though she'd think differently of it I thought the Lord should have been more generous to our mother who'd put all of her faith in him.

It was my first trip the next morning when I stopped Mr. Bill halfway over the hill, asking James if he'd like to ride along with me on down to the laydown yard.

"Arnold nothing has changed since Pike County I don't want to ride on the top of a log. It's crazy to do such a thing with all those hazards."

"But it's not like that in these woods James shoot this is smooth sailing compared to those steep ass mountains over in Pike County."

"Yea and you probably still think it's going to be an Olympic event someday right!" He laughed.

"James, now you know I was just kidding about all that shit."

"Wait, he quickly interrupted. I've got it Arnold," he said snapping his fingers of his new idea. "You should start a hillbilly's Olympics. Log surfing, cow milking, jumping hollers, climbing trees you know all the things that you can beat me at. Now, for the hundredth time or maybe even more I don't want any part of riding on a log," he scolded.

Even my simple rules weren't enough to attract him. The idea was to ride from one point to another without losing you balance. Every time your foot left the log and touched the ground, you'd get charged five points and if both were to touch, ten was deducted. And it was seldom I ever walked to the laydown yard anymore. But I did learn a lesson over in Pike County that smooth barked logs on rainy days could present a problem with how slick they could get. I never told James how I'd fallen in between two good size Beach tree logs and had to scramble before they closed back up again and with the chance they could have crushed me.

"Things to never do" he'd proclaimed, and with log surfing being close to the very top. And he was right about all the ways you could get hurt. They'd continually bounce from one stumps or tree to the other while guided by roots that'd been exposed in the trail. Any of them could stop a horse in its track, and if you weren't paying close attention, you'd be thrown off and land where you hadn't prepared. The simple fact and always was that I was just out for the competition.

I called it talent when the logs would separate two or three feet apart, making you widen your stance before they'd slam back together. The chance of just losing your foot alone should have been a deterrent which James had suggested over and over again. 'It'll never happen to me!' I smiled with my quick answer. And of course James would counter, 'Complete ignorance!' referring to his first condemnation at the farm. Angry at me one time with my continual antics, he'd called me a "dumbass fucker" when I went sailing after the log hit a stump. I hadn't time to make much of a jump and landed poorly up against a different stump where I rolled away just in the nick of time as the log slammed into it, tearing off a big chunk of its bark.

James was always relieved that I didn't get hurt but showed me no encouragement, telling me that I was an absolute idiot to do such things. And his loudest threat was to beat the shit out of me if he ever saw me surfing again with my eyes closed. It was also the time that my name wasn't necessarily plain old Arnold Ray. With increasing anxiety, each new name would be worse than the last one and followed by yet another new threat. I was truly amazed at such name callings with so few cuss words with all the scolding's he'd bestow upon me. With him constantly trying to discourage me he finally admitted that I was out of control. Then once again he reminded me that if I do stupid things long enough they'd eventually catch up with me.

"I will resist the challenge of ignorance," I announced as Mr. Bill dragged me and the log past James. I'd gone out of my way to do everything he'd warned against: riding the log and facing backwards, while never seeing what was in front of me. Now that he could easily see me, I held my hand over my heart, proclaiming myself Napoleon of the Woods with stiff-knees and all the while gazing into the future like that of a statue. He yelled that I looked nothing like Napoleon, but more like a dumb ass pulpwooder who'd probably never make his way out of the woods period. He finished by saying that it had a double meaning but doubted I had enough sense to figure it out. He shook his head before going on about his business as I glided on down the hill.

I could better understand James concerns in Pike County but the woods here were practically level compared to over there. There weren't many places where a log could roll off and into a holler. It all seemed so easy to me when I challenged him again just to give it a try. Surprisingly he agreed on terms that if he did so, I'd stop bugging him and never ask again. "Now that means you've got to ride it all the way to the laydown yard without getting off." He shook his head to agree.

The plan was put in place, and as Kate passed by, he jumped up on the logs, one foot on each one. But I couldn't leave well enough alone. There was nothing said that I couldn't mess with him. He simply wouldn't look at me as I ran beside him, cutting up and trying to get him to screw up and have to jump off. I hadn't told him of my intentions as he was into total concentration, bracing himself ahead for everything that lay in front of him.

"Cool, James! You look like one of those surfers on TV with a fake ocean behind you." I laughed. He looked rigid with arms straight out to balance himself and, in no time, could have rung the sweat from his shirt. "Should I speed Kate up a little grandpa?" I bugged him even more. But no matter how I tried he'd not response with his face chiseled with determination. "James! Grab your comb there's a hair out of place," I pointed running along the side of him.

All of my attempts had failed to this point. He'd gone about halfway and was out of the hardest part when I jumped upon the logs with him, stopping just inches where we stood face to face. I knew he'd make no effort to throw me off. And even though I stood right in front of him his concentration would not falter.

He wasn't afraid much of anything, but always used commonsense with those things he did not understand.

I knew all too well whether he managed to stay on the logs or not that it would be his first and last trip. He just never had the dare or ignorance as he'd put it to be part of my challenges. It along with so many others feel under the category of a, waste of time to him. He'd endured my constant hounding all the way there and for one reason. Kate came to a complete stop when he stepped off the logs. He slowly straightened his back to its fullest while wiping sweat from his eyes with a shirt sleeve. It took a while for him to gather himself.

"Now I just done something that you haven't Arnold." He smiled while pulling his shirt off and shaking it to air it out.

"And how do you figure that when I've ridden hundreds of logs down to the here." I pointed.

"Well, I made it all the way without falling off so how many times have you done that? And don't lie to me you think I don't see you doing crazy shit." He left me standing pondering to what he'd said. And he was right that it wasn't much fun to me if I didn't tempt fate and push myself; rare that I not make a full ride without a foot touching the ground and worse at times.

"Arnold, he yelled from a distance. My log surfing days are over." He laughed before heading on up into the woods. His way of measuring success was somewhat different than mine. He'd walk away happy with what he'd done where as I would never settle for good enough.

I figured I'd better not tell him of my latest challenge of ignorance where I'd run and jump from a stump, and land on logs trailing Mr. Bill. James just wouldn't understand such a challenge. There could be no mistakes, not even with a blink of the eye. My jumps had gotten farther and farther to the point that I thought they may be getting a little too far myself. But I had jumped eighteen feet, and three inches just messing around at a track meet one time.

I'd need to time it just right that when Mr. Bill made the turn where the trail dropped a little, I'd make my leap from a stump about fifteen feet away. And this would be my final jump I told myself once again as I had so many times before. I thought back to the horrible crash it took for me to stop trying to fly while praying that I catch my breath before I die. I knew this was by far worse with a chance I could break something. But the fact was whether I got hurt or not I needed to know if something was beyond my capability. I would never admit or at least to James that his smartness had a whole lot to do with not being all skinned up most the time like me. Even though it was him that I wanted to impress most of the time. He was never shy, especially when I lay there with my breath knocked out to tell me that; it looked like a waste of time to him.

I'd need to go high into the air to make the distance and land on the log in an upright position. I could hear James's saw laboring and at a distance where he couldn't see me. Mr. Bill pulled the two logs I'd picked just for this occasion. *Now's the time*, I thought as I headed for the very stump I'd picked to make my leap. I'd rehears several times how many steps I needed before my jump. With the right count and speed I planted my foot firmly in the center of the stump and with a heave, soared high into the air.

James's warning came to mind as I started my downward plunge that things would eventually catch up with me. The thought unfolded quickly when Mr. Bill stopped to take a piss at about the spot where I'd planned the logs would be at about right now. There was the split second before I slammed chest first into Mr. Bills big ass. And my hands were of little help when I did a face plant right across his tail strap spooking him, to where he took off in a hurry. Luckily, I'd bounced several feet, while holding my stomach to try and regain my breath. I watched as the logs rolled past thinking how lucky I was to not be underneath them.

I couldn't blame the horse it was no fault of his even though he'd been involved in both of my world class crashes. But I did think it was strange how both times were all about perfect timing; with mine being off and his being perfect and right on time.

As insistent as James was later in the day to know how I got such a mark across my forehead, I told him a small tree snapped back up from a log running over it. I didn't understand fully what Calvin said that the mark looked like I'd been trying to kiss a horse's ass until I looked into the pond's calm waters to see what the print looked like. A leather strap for sure. In my own way, I'd confess a few days later that I'd pushed my luck as far as I should and that it would be my last leap from a stump. I'd not stop surfing however but was content with just riding them to the laydown yard.

"Whoa . . .!" I growled with a pitch of authority stopping them a short distance from where the old man had parked his car. He, along with two gangly women climbed out of the front seat pulling it forward to let kids out of the back. Two small boys hustled to be the first ones out. They looked to be about the same age I thought seven or eight years old. Others scrambled to follow as one at a time they emerged to stand in line leaning up against the car. A girl maybe a year or so younger than me came out last and was pretty at that, I thought.

There they all were in some sort of pecking order, Bob's and Mickel's families. The kids all stood silent while the adults talked. Suddenly, one of the women snapped her fingers while pointing to someone still in the backseat motioning for them to get out. It was like a miracle happening right in front of me. My eyes widened when a shapely leg appeared with a dress hiked a good way up her thigh, as she exited the back seat.

Maybe it was intentional that she took her time in pulling her dress all the way back down. She made her way to the side of the car to stand with the others. The two older girls stood side by side with an uncomfortable looking slouch about them, with no place to put their hands it looked. Then the younger one followed suit as the older girl clasped hers together just below the pit of her stomach. They seemed nervous in a way that maybe they didn't really want to be there. Maybe our ages being about the same or simply my stare had tempted the girl to glance my way more than once. But there was no smile to greet mine. She looked really pretty from this distance, and best of all I'd have a good reason to get closer as Calvin sat just beyond them.

I couldn't take my eyes off her and didn't care that she saw me taking in all her features. I stumbled trying to slow my pace aroused even more the closer I got. A chill ran up my back and down my arms then to the very tips of my fingers. Like one I'd never felt before with blood churning and pounding in my chest; along with a strange dizziness now. Her chest swelled slightly; followed by a long sigh when she rolled her eyes up to meet my stare. Calvin hadn't been full of bullshit after all, maybe I was even hypnotized when I walked on past her sharing the moment. I walked to where Calvin was sharpening his chain.

"Arnold Ray, which bunch belongs to who?" Calvin questioned upon my approach. Most everyone at the car—with the exception of the old man, Bob, and Mickel—turned to us, at hearing Calvin's remark. But my interest had grown to the point that I stared brazenly with the sun shining through her hair when she shook it to straighten it out. Then she leaned back on the car, locking her hands behind her neck, and all the while gazing up into the woods. *I wonder what her name is*, I thought to myself.

"Calvin, you're talkin' way too loud and you know they can all hear you," I said in a low voice.

"Well, why are you whisperin' fer, Arnold Ray? Hell, I can barely hear you even if they ain't no commotion goin' on." He was loud enough this time to embarrass me. "Hell, I think all these years of runnin' this noisy son-of-a-bitchin' saw has made me deaf!" His follow up which I'd seen on other occasions was to start digging sawdust out of his ear with his little finger.

Every stolen glance at her lit something new up inside of me. The song 'a ring of fire' came to mind when my chest heaved with the thought I would get the chance to talk with her some time. She surely must be thinking the same by the way she keeps looking back at me. I felt like I needed to turn away and catch my breath; breathing had suddenly become more difficult than ever. And now we couldn't take our eyes off each other. I wanted to go stand beside her. I wanted to hold her hand. I wanted to kiss her and hadn't said a single word to her yet. *What the hell am I thinking?* My daydream came to a sudden end when Calvin's big hand waved right in front of my face while giving me one of those 'caught you' smiles.

"Calvin, ah . . . ah . . . l ah let me show you somethin' on that log I just dragged in," I stuttered with a burning need to walk past her again.

"By God, it better not be somethin' that old Mickel left on it!" he yelled, trying to razz Mickel. I needed to get Calvin far enough away that they couldn't hear him talk. And it was in my plan with a jog of only a few feet I could get even closer to her and possibly see the color of her eyes.

There was no looking away for either of us and clearly now I saw a pretty girl with a faraway look in her eyes, like something trapped with no way out. Maybe we had a lot in common, I thought. We hadn't gone far enough when Calvin turned back toward them.

"Why, Arnold Ray, if you were to throw some good clothes on them two little gals, they wouldn't be too bad to look at, now would they?" My look of humiliation at Calvin's crude remark was met by her embarrassment when she crossed her arms at her chest, turned and looked in a different direction.

Calvin was right, saying how poor they looked with the clothes they had on. Her dress was homemade and not put together very well, with the front being a couple of inches shorter than the back, which I thought was cool. But she fit into it perfectly with her thin body and pretty legs. I didn't care anymore if she caught my burning stare. I wasn't sure now that I could even look away had I tried. Her shoes were worn-out with a small toe visible on the side. She tried to hide it by crossing her legs with one shoe on top of the other. I felt sorry for her. She turned back toward us, slowly twirling a long strand of yellow hair and pinning it behind an ear. She was everything I could imagine which would play out to its entirety in my dreams. I yearned for something that I didn't completely understand as my heart raced on.

I'd not answered Calvin about their clothes and had no intention to until we were far enough away that they couldn't hear us.

"I think she's real pretty, Calvin." I spoke with no bashfulness in my voice. I jumped up on a log and looked back once more.

"Ya, she is a pertty' little thang alright, and Arnold Ray, about your size." Calvin drew hard on the pipe. I turned to say something but was met by a puzzled look on his face. "You hain't even checked her teeth yet, have ya, Arnold Ray?" The question was so cruel that it seemed to freeze my brain for a second. "Do what?" I asked, jumping back down off the log.

"You should've checked out the teeth. Like you do a horse to see if they're worn out or not . . . you notice they ain't any ovum smiled, not once since they got here. Maybe they ain't got no teeth!" He laughed loudly. The younger of the two girls elbowed her friend as they made a halfhearted attempt to smile to show their teeth. We still hadn't gone far enough away for Calvin's loud roar.

Thinking about her smile was the furthest thing from my mind as I watched her leg slowly dance up and down to maybe a song in her mind. I thought of many songs that would easily match her rhythm. I wished she could have been with me on the weekend, cruising with James and Scarlett. *I wouldn't have been the one driving.* I smiled at the mere thought. *What am I thinkin'?* I shook my head trying to clear my thoughts.

"Now which one of them old farts do you think that old tall skinny thang yonder belongs to Arnold Ray?" Calvin grunted, pointing his pipe at one of the two women. The old man said something funny that got them all laughing and coughing up a storm they sounded.

"Well, the one leanin' against the hood looks to be younger, so she must belong to old Mickel." But it wasn't her that I wanted to look at.

Sure enough, Calvin's pairings were just as he'd guessed. She started talking and shared a cigarette with Mickel.

"Look, Calvin, the old man's hand is goin' up behind the ear. So here comes the punch line." I'd made Calvin laugh, which drew almost everyone attention in our direction. But when Calvin choked and started coughing, it set them all off to laughing at him. He coughed just like old Mickel said, like a dry-throated mule. The small boys started jumping on logs, one to the other. It looked as if they had done it many times before, being the children of loggers, for a kinder word than children of pulpwooders.

The old man gathered them all up and walked over the hill towards the old Gant house. She and the younger girl lagged behind in no hurry it looked. She broke off a wild flower stopping just long enough to push it into her friend's hair. She said something to her that made them both laugh and look in our direction.

"I guess they're gonna live there, it looks like, Calvin. Ya know Harry told me that it used to be where the stagecoach stopped, and people could stay the night in its heyday. He even said that General Grant and Sherman stayed there at times!"

"Who in the hell is Grant and Sherman?" Calvin asked with a look that got me laughing.

"They were Union generals in the Civil War and surely you know Grant was one of the presidents, don't you?

"Well, they sound like one of them damn law firms to me!" Calvin said, while poking his pipe back into his mouth. The familiar sound of a saw cranked up as blue smoke rose from up in the woods.

"Well, it sounds like ole Junior thinks it's time to get back to work," Calvin said, taking one last draw on his pipe before tapping it a couple of times against his hard-callused hand with small burnt flakes trickling to the ground.

"Calvin, I'm gonna pull these logs all into one area so you don't have to move all over the place to cut 'em up," I pointed. You couldn't fool Calvin about much of anything. He smiled, knowing why I wanted to hang around in the yard a while longer. His nod continued for some time as he studied me, head to toe.

To my disappointment, the old man came back from the house with just Bob and Mickel. I wanted so badly to see her again. I couldn't get her out of my mind, and my stomach was sure havin' a bout with something. I couldn't hear what the old man was saying to them, but it was brief. Then he got in the car and left.

Calvin never missed much of anything that went on around him. If he hadn't already figured something out he wouldn't hesitate to be nosy. Suddenly, he started walking to where the two of them were standing by Big Red. Seeing him walking way faster than normal I caught up quickly to walk beside him.

"Now you boys need to get your asses back here as quick as you can," Calvin cautioned. He seen what was transpiring.

"My God, I'd say so! Did you hear what he said?" Bob asked with a laugh. "It sounds like Jim wanted us to work all week and just sleep on the floor in that old house," Bob said, picking at a dirty fingernail.

"Well, I ain't layin' on no hard-ass son-of-a-bitchen floor at my age!" Mickel managed without taking an extra breath.

"Why don't you stop your bitchin', Mick! Arnold Ray just told me that two famous Civil War generals stayed there a few times, and they probably didn't bitch, glad to have a roof over their heads. And hell, I'm livin' in their outhouse that slid over the hill a hundred years ago, and I ain't a whining."

"Well, I really don't give a rat's ass how you feel about it, Calvin. We've got families to shelter." Mickel sounded humble with his effort.

"Damn, you don't think that ole heifer of mine is a family? She's a family all in one. Why you seen her, and I'll guarantee she eats more than that bony bunch you're throwing feed at. I can't think what the bill would be like if old Arnold Ray didn't bring milk by every day. Yeah, he's the milkman alright!" Calvin laughed, rolling his eyes over at me.

Mickel could have gone on with the comparisons but maybe had figured it best not to mess with Calvin any further.

"Well if you got any extree left over Arnold Ray we'll sure take it off your hands," Bob said with a smile. "But if we're gonna get back here before tomorrow mornin' and still get a load of wood on the truck, like Jim wants, we best get on our way." Bob opened the door, climbing up into the driver's seat. Mickel was making an effort but strained at getting in on his side.

Calvin seeing his strained effort jerked his pipe with lightning speed, a sure sign words of wit would come forth.

"Mickel, do you need Arnold Ray to push your ass up in that truck, ya old feeble fart? Now ya know I'd hep ya, but you probably got shit on you somewhere!" Calvin laughed. Mickel never said a word but flipped Calvin the bird behind his back as he struggled on into the seat. Calvin laughed as if the smoke he'd blown all over Mickel might have helped the cause. We watched them until the truck got out of sight. Still with an evil grin on his face, Calvin said,

"Arnold Ray, it don't sound like Junior's slowed down any, does it? Listen at 'em. I guess we better get hepin' some before he pulls his head oughta his ass and sees we're goofin' off." I took the animals back up into the woods for another load and thinking of the condition the old house was in.

No one had lived in the old Gant house for a long time. Some of the windows was broken out and boards were missing in the floor, where groundhogs lived up and underneath of it. It wouldn't have taken much to make it livable, though. James and I'd talked about it a few times, making it our place to stay, but there was and never had been electricity. This was the sixties, and to be without music was unheard of, especially when you were in love like James.

The old outhouse had fallen to the ground, and they'd have to use the woods until another one could be thrown up. The spring was just over the hill, and had plenty of water where I'd cleaned it out. But as bad as the condition of the house was, I still wanted them to live there, and I knew why.

After making sure Calvin couldn't in any way in the world see me, I made my way back through the woods to get a view of what they were doing at the Gant house. The kids were all outside, exploring with some playing tag. One of the women had just finished rolling a cigarette and, after lighting it, passed it to the other woman to share. They didn't seem too sad about the place, laughing continually. There just didn't seem to be much desperation with them as maybe they'd left some place far worse than this. But I couldn't see the person that I was looking for. For a better viewing place I climbed up in a small tree where she appeared from over the hill, readjusting her dress as she walked from behind a bush.

Maybe I'd been shaking the tree a little too much when she turned, gazing at the hillside. Maybe she sensed that I was up here. But I didn't want to get caught and be put in a bad situation, knowing that if Calvin found out, I'd never hear the end of it.

Dropping to the ground, I started running back through the woods as fast as I could go. I hooked the animals up to a light load and went back down to the yard, where Calvin studied my arrival.

"Arnold Ray, are you gonna work all night? Git your head oughta your ass, and let's leave a little work for tomar!" Calvin grinned always funning with the 'head up your ass', the way he looked at me now, I wasn't so sure he didn't really mean it.

"I guess James has already left for Scarlett's." I'd interrupted Calvin from going any further with his joke.

"Yep, the way that Buick sounded, by God, I think he straightened that curve out down there by the pond. Come on, Arnold Ray. I'll walk to the pond with you so we can talk a little more." He gathered Kate's reins up in one hand. I'd thought he'd have had plenty to say about his observations but instead quietly enjoyed his pipe all the way to the pond. We sat on the edge, where Calvin soaked his "aching ass feet," which he'd started doing on a regular basis.

"Oh . . . that feels good!" he grunted with satisfaction. "The onliest thing better than that is . . ." He took his first draw of the pipe, blowing smoke throughout the clump of cattails next to us. Our laugh was spontaneous as flies and all other insects that lived there evacuated them in a hurry. It was no surprise that he blew the wasted smoke into other clumps, laughing all the while. And best he'd forgotten about the "onliest" thing better than soaking his feet.

"Now by God, that sure is one sorry lot up there, ain't it Arnold Ray! You talk about not havin' a pot to piss in! That up there's a prime example!" He leaned back on an elbow to get more comfortable. "Now's me and the old lady don't have much, but that little twenty-five acres down at Camp Creek with a shack is all paid fer. So when I've had enough sweat runnin' down the crack of my ass, I'll just go down there and live out the rest of my life. Hunt a little sang and maybe get some hep' from the govamint, and we'll be ok." There was a second of hesitation as he looked out across the cattails, smacking his lips together a couple of times, satisfied with his dream, it sounded. "And by God, if I don't quit this woods workin' bullshit, pretty soon, my life might be over quickern I want it to be." He grunted loudly, picking one leg up all the way out of the water.

"Ya know . . . I don't think them people up there's even got a damned light to see by tonight." The hint was in his stare when he quickly looked my way. "Why, hell, they can't even see to go take a piss." I waited as he slowly slipped his shoes back on, stuffing his socks into his pants pocket. "Yeah, you could be somebody's favorite person, Arnold Ray, if you were ta show up with a big bright light tonight. Just don't let that light get in your eyes and end up like ole June bug, though." He laughed after vigorously brushing the dirt off his butt, then bade me good night. He hadn't gone but a couple of steps before turning back to me however. "I guess you've got a lantern, don't you?" He knew exactly what I was thinking.

I guess he'd seen my desperation and maybe had even read my mind. After all, he was the first to notice when James fell in love. *Fell in love! What the hell am I a thinkin'?* I quickly jumped to my feet.

"Am I fallin' in love?" I asked myself while nervously pacing back and forth and pulling at my fingers to make them pop. Even though the whole affair hadn't lasted but a few minutes it seemed we both desired one another. How could I think such stupid shit when I don't even, know her name? Names just didn't seem to matter right now however. I imagined myself passing the lantern to her with my well-lit smile. The thought made me giggle, thinking that something as simple as that would have set James and Scarlett off for sure. I couldn't stand still or hold any kind of thought for any period of time. She'd simply filled me with something warm it felt. And God how I wanted to talk to her.

I quickly tended to the animals. My stay at the house after toting the milk to Moms was short lived. I ate quickly and was running up the road, thinking of all the things the Gant house needed for someone to live there. The springs could use a few more, flat rocks around the edges to make it easier for her to get water. I went on to the bus and immediately started pacing the floor, listing all of their needs. The truth was I wanted to see her, and having a good excuse was all I needed. Maybe I worried too much that I'd look stupid by taking the lantern up to them. I slid our emergency lantern out from under the bed placing it on the table just in case I'd get brave enough to deliver it.

My God, what's wrong with me? I thought, slapping my forehead a little too hard. I'd overheard Bob tell Calvin there was no way they could make it back before dawn. I pictured them all huddled up in a dark corner away from the holes in the floor. Calvin was right—that they hadn't brought anything with them and more than likely not even a candle, as nothing had seemed planned on their part.

There was no reason for me to be pacing the floor like I was. The hour hand finally hit nine o'clock, the time I'd set to make my final decision to take the lamp up to them or chicken out. *It's the darkest night I've ever seen in my life,* I tried to convince myself, looking out the bus's windshield. I took a deep breath, scooping the lantern off the bus step the last place I'd laid it down. My bravery had completely given out by the time I reached the pond. The lantern seemed heavy when I set it down on the highest point of the levee, where its light reflected out over the calm waters. A love story grew thinking that I could meet her here some night and swim when the moon was bright. But any thought of such things was no more than stalling for time, and I knew it.

I thought of Scarlett the day when I rode around with them, pulling individual petals from a flower she'd yanked up at Dairy Queen, laughing how the last one would decide if her and James were going to get married or not. How simple, I thought; and as the end grew near, she'd simply pull two at one time to make it work out for her. I can flip a coin. I scurried around in my pocket. But I knew that neither flipping coins nor pulling petals would get me anywhere on this night. Why take the chance or even have to cheat when you know exactly what you wanted to do? To waste time on any of them would only prolong the burning desire running through me as the minutes flew past.

What if they do make it back early with their belongings? I just couldn't blow the chance of seeing her tonight no matter. *No turnin' back now, hell or high water,* I bravely told myself. Jumping up from the bank, I blew the flame out in hopes they'd have enough fuel for the whole night. The small light I'd left on in the bus faded quickly when I turned and headed up the winding road. The frogs' croaking gave way to the squeaking sound of the lantern's wire handle as I swung it back and forth to match a tune in my head. "It's fer her, it's fer her," I interpreted the squeaks to be what I wanted to hear. I picked up the pace swinging the lantern farther out in front of me. It didn't matter that my reason for going was solely to see her—they all needed the light and it was a good excuse if I were questioned.

I struck a match, raised the mantle, and lit the wick at the edge of the forest. A cast of many shadows sprang throughout the woods, and changing with the passing of every tree I walked past. Down steep hollers and beyond the lantern painted a spooky scene that raised goose bumps up my backbone and feeling as if my hair was standing up. The thick smell of horse manure and urine hung in the air at the laydown yard. The Gant house was just around one more curve and down a slight hill. I stopped for a minute, listening for any kind of sound coming from the old house. Suddenly I thought, *What if they have a gun and shoot me in the dark?* But there was no sound, only dead quiet.

"Hello! Hello . . .!" I yelled a short distance from the porch. Suddenly, there was scrambling going on, with some of the younger kids starting to cry. I suppose I'd scared them.

"Who's out there?" a commanding voice asked. I thought she sounded way scarier than me rousing goose bump on my arms.

"Hey, it's me, Arnold. I've got a lantern for y'all."

"Shhhh, it'll be all right. He's got us a lantern," someone hushed trying to calm the kids. And even though I'd never heard a word from her mouth, I just knew in my heart that it was her voice that settled them down.

"Where do you want it?" I called out. I could hear low voices but couldn't make out much of what was being said behind the walls. The lantern cast a pretty good light on the front porch as the door slowly opened, when the taller of the two women came out alone.

"Now tell me again who you say you are." She faced me with her hands on her hips, with a challenging look about her.

"I work in the woods up here for my old man," I answered. She then hurriedly stepped off the porch to get a closer look at me. With the light shining on her skinny pale face, I thought she'd fit right in with *Chiller Theatre.*

The rest of the family scampered out to stand on the porch, crossing their arms and standing close to one another as if there was a chill in the air. Clearly, they were frightened. I lifted the lantern higher into the air to see the girl that'd drawn me here. Two young children, more than likely her siblings, clung to her side, where she held them close. I raised the lantern even higher for a better view. The whole scene from the porch was black and white other than her long yellow hair falling down past her thin waist.

She held a hand out to block the light. There was no doubt in my mind that she was trying to see me when a faint smile came across her face. She moved off to the side of the two kids, giving me a better look at her. It looked intentional when she nervously bent at the knees, then straightened to her tallest before crossing her arms just below her breasts.

I felt sad for her as I handed the lantern to the lady, who, without a word of thanks, turned and walked back into the house as they all followed the light. Tall ghostly shadows danced along the bare walls as they made their way to the one room that didn't have broken windows. Maybe she knew that I stood in the darkness, hoping for a final look at her when she turned and, with a smile, waved into the darkness. My heart was suddenly on fire with desire, elated that her smile was meant just for me, and certain now that there would be more. Their shadows crossed the doorway before closing it behind them, followed by laughter and small hands clapping. For the moment, I could pretend that what I'd done for them made me a hero as my chest swelled even bigger.

Lightning bugs dotted the darkness, making it near impossible to find any kind of direction. Closing my eyes, I stretched my arms out and started walking slowly back up the narrow road. Touching leafy limbs that grew on both sides, I made it to the laydown yard. I bumped a log, which told me exactly where I was. My old habit of counting how many steps it was from one object to the other would pay off from this point on. After passing the two trees at the edge of the field, I opened my eyes to see the light shining in the bus that would guide me for now.

Dreams I thought were simply a way to satisfy an overwhelming need that you couldn't have what you wanted. I lay for hours it seemed, drifting in and out, thinking of her, and wondering if it was one of my fabrications or the real thing. I could be Tarzan, and she could be Jane swinging through the jungle. Or trappers trapped in a snowstorm with just enough time to build us a shelter and fire before we got snowed in. I watched her wade into the cool pond with every step, pulling her dress tightly around her. The phrase 'what dreams are made of' surely pertained to mine when she motioned for me to follow her. She turned to face me with the moon haloing around her. Silvery waves rolled outward from her silhouette. She slowly put her arms around me as I joined her under the water to embrace her thin waist.

But dreams also have a clause of uncertainty as to how they end. In my conscience, I knew my most excellent dream was coming to an end when I thought I'd heard the truck returning with Bob and Mickel.

"No, no, don't go . . .," I begged. My hopes of a watery kiss drained away with something loud, flooding my ears.

"But I'll not stop until . . ." *What the hell*, The, pond like a lifting fog disappeared in front of me. Where was all the noise coming from? I opened my eyes to a different reality. It was James beating on the bus door.

"Oh, my God," I whispered, quickly letting go of the pillow I'd been squeezing so tightly. I felt embarrassed even with no one around. I unlocked and swung the door open, where James rushed in.

"What are you doing here so early?" I must have sounded, startled.

"I don't know . . .," he said, "I just feel good today. I woke early and thought I'd get here, and we'd get down to Mom's so Duck won't get the big biscuit." He laughed.

"Okay, I'll get the milkin' done, and we'll go." I glanced up at the pond, wishing this was just an odd part of an unfinished dream.

"Well, I'll go with ya. We can talk for a while."

Red hadn't made it to the barn but wasn't far away, when she came running as soon as she'd heard us talking.

"Good morning, Red," I said, pouring her grain with a scratch on the top of her head.

"How do you see in here?" James surveyed.

"Well, usually, it's a little lighter than this. Think about it. And besides, all I've got to do is get the grain and then find her tits and get going." I didn't want to tell him about taking the lantern up to the Gant house for right now. He'd want to know, as if he hadn't guessed already, why I'd do such a thing. I couldn't just come out and tell him that I thought I was falling in love with the girl when I never even knew her name. I imagined the laugh that would bring on. The sound of milk hitting the bottom of the pail took me back to wishing for the watery kiss that I never got.

I breathed a sigh of relief when James pulled into the driveway and seeing the old man wasn't at the house. Mom as always was happy to see us and, after a kiss, James said he had a surprise for everyone.

"Well Honey tell Mom what it is," she said while slowly stirring the gravy.

"Mom, I've asked Scarlett to marry me."

"You've got to be shittin' me!" I blurted in front of everyone.

Judy jumped up and down, hugging and congratulating him; she truly was happy about the news. Mom had a little different view, however.

"Honey, Mom hopes the best for you two, but I think you're a little too young to think about marryin' right now . . . And do you and Scarlett have God in your hearts yet?"

I'm sure she'd been more agreeable had James and Scarlett been churchgoers. But if they had been, they wouldn't be carrying on like they had in the backseat of the car a while back. I wondered if my mother wasn't thinking about herself while she was advising James. She'd said a few times how she loved all her children but was too young to get married and might have done it differently had she to do it over. The old man was sixteen years older than her, and I knew he'd taken advantage of her young age. I was older now than she was when she got married.

"Where's Dad? I want to tell him the news also." James sounded excited enough that he'd called the old man Dad. I was completely blown away that he'd not told me of his plans for marriage before anyone else. Scarlett's plucking flower petals had certainly seemed like a joke, or at least that's what I took it for. The whole thing set me to wondering if the decision hadn't been made overnight. I thought back to what Calvin had said that you should test-drive 'em before you get hitched. But that could sure turn into something that'd mess your world up. When a girl didn't show up for school on the first day, rumors flew that she'd gotten pregnant. Then scorn poured in from all directions, especially if religion was involved.

A good Christian girl wouldn't act like that and be pointed out shamefully to her family. Pregnancy was referred to as "knocked up" if it was out of wedlock, which made the whole thing sound even more disgraceful and dirty. James told me that only an asshole referred to it as "knocked up," including the old man who'd heaped blame that it was always the woman's fault.

You'd have thought it was the greatest sin of all times when a girl from church going parents did come up pregnant. The earlier they found out, the better. They could whisk the two off to North Carolina or Kentucky to be married. The plan was of course to hide it from everyone, which hardly ever worked. Most played along, but there'd be plenty of gossip behind their backs till the baby was born.

I thought about the time Calvin asked James if he'd gotten any. I was all ears anytime the conversation came up. And was it temptation, I wondered, that'd brought on the talk of marriage with him and Scarlett? I thought about the day I rode around with them. With all the noises coming from the backseat, obviously, they were thinking way beyond just being lip-locked. But for the life of me and even with all the goo-goo talk and head up his ass, as so many had proclaimed, I just couldn't picture James as one of those that'd get their girlfriends pregnant before marriage. And funny that it hadn't been but a couple of weeks back that he'd joked with Calvin, asking him if he had any rubbers. The joke surprised Calvin so that he wheezed and coughed for quite some time, declaring he'd about choked to death when he sucked the whole load of baccer smoke, fire and all, into his lungs. We'd talked a little about protecting yourself when he'd point out that there was no reason for a girl to get pregnant at all.

Even mouthy boys would go silent; a ghostly look about 'em, with the news they'd gotten a girl pregnant. Some would go on like they'd done something special only to be corrected by others with "Man, you fucked up" or "You didn't pull it out in time." Most times, the girl who'd gotten pregnant was happy about it, spreading the word quickly to celebrate with her friends.

Judy and Beth went to set on the davenport with James to talk more of a wedding. I wouldn't say anything for now about Scarlett being our half cousin, but marriage would only make it harder on me to explain.

It was time to eat as we all were waiting for Mom to turn thanks when she asked that we all hold hands. She thanked the Lord for everything as usual, putting her heart into the fact that we were all there and together for another meal. Never closing my eyes, I noticed Judy peeping at me while squeezing my hand tightly. A sad look, I thought, when she nodded in Mom's direction.

"Amen," Mom finished, somewhat short of her normal prayer. There were things she'd left out. I glanced at Judy where her nod once again was trying to tell me something.

"Mom, are you, all right?" James asked. He too noticed her feeble ending.

There was a short hesitation just before she looked at me and then at James where she'd not let go of his hand yet.

"Well now, Honey, Mom might as well tell the truth. Your dad didn't come home again last night."

"Well, it's not like he stays here much anyway, Mom," I said.

"So, now what's he up to?" James chimed in.

"Go ahead, Mom, tell them what happened." Judy spouted, crossing her arms.

"He didn't hit you, did he?" I stood up from the table.

"No, Honey, he knows that he can't do that again," she said, looking at James and me again. "I told him the other day that I was going to go with him and Harry to wherever they go frolicking at. The Lord knows I wouldn't drink or anything like that, but I could sit there and see how they all act. I could drink water . . ." I felt sadness for her and the loneliness she'd been through for a big part of her life.

"Now, Mom, you being a Christian, you don't want to see what goes on in those places!" James warned.

"Well, let Mom tell you what happened when I tried to go. Your dad tried every way in the world to stop me, but I told him that I was goin' and that was that."

Listening to my mother even talk of such a thing made it hard to set still thinking what measure's she'd go to, to get him right with the Lord again. But her going to the bar wouldn't change him a bit and would have only hurt her more. She suddenly paused as if she didn't want to finish the story after all.

"It's okay, Mom." James said. "If you don't want to tell us, it's all right." After using her apron to wipe sweat from her face she'd continue.

"Well, he finally told me to suit myself after we'd been arguing over it for a couple days. He finally said that after one trip it should fix me right up to where I would never go back again. I don't think he really thought I'd go through with it. But we got all cleaned up and went up to Harry's to pick him up, but when he came out to the car and seen me, he refused to go. He told your dad that it just wasn't right for a good Christian woman like me to go to such places, and no matter the cause. And he turned right around and walked back to his house carrying that fiddle case with him. And he looked so sad I thought. Jim brought me back down here, tellin' me to get out of his car, and threatening to hit me if I didn't. He was as mad as I've ever seen him in my life and couldn't get away from here fast enough."

177

'Victory in Jesus', we'd all heard our mother sing the praises over the smallest of things. She never received anything that the first words from her mouth were, 'thank you Jesus'. I could understand how glorifying and thankful it would be for her if the old man were to come back to the fold. A reward she could truly sing about and not like she hadn't done it before. Then she'd pray that the old man never turns his eyes away from the Lord ever again. I thought how his departures from Christianity to livin' like the devil had gotten farther apart. He'd had money in his pocket for a while now and didn't need God in his life. Our mother never had many victories in her life other than with her God. Her short laugh over her and the old man's incident could be taken as a victory I thought. She'd followed her heart once again to try and help him.

"So, I guess that's why he never came home last night." I could see her eyes tearing up, and I could feel my heart breaking for her.

"You know, Mom . . . if he never comes home again, it'd be all right with me! And that's the way everybody should feel about it now," I said trying to hold my anger back but doubted I could for very long.

"Honey, now don't feel like that. He's still you father, you know."

"I hate him, Mom. And I mean that with all my heart! I hate him!" I put a fist on the table.

Everyone hushed at what I'd said. The oldest ones knew of the old man's deeds, and not a one of them had many kind thoughts toward him anymore. But none yet had said they hated him. Mom had tried her best to encourage us to not use that word towards anyone. And as a good example she'd never once said it about anyone.

"Oh well, it's all said and done," she declared knowing the more we talked of it the more I'd get upset. "He'll be in sometime," She said. I looked at James; his excitement of getting married had faded to nothing.

"Duck, are you ready to go to work this morning?" I changed the subject so that we not pressure our mother anymore.

"Well, Piggy Wiggy, you know I am. So don't threaten, me," he joked and throwing the last part in for the boy's sake. Mom didn't say anything about Duck, but her worried look said it all.

"Well, Mom, what do you think—can Duck go work with us today? He'll stay in the laydown yard and measure for Calvin, if it's all right with you?" I tried to make her decision easier. But there still was hesitation on her part. Maybe it just wasn't a good day for Duck to start.

"If you boys promise to watch over him and make sure he doesn't get hurt?" He expelled a heavy breath.

"Why, you know we will, Mom," James said, accepting the responsibility. The boys cheered for him or maybe for themselves. They'd get a break from Duck, who controlled their every move. Then Mom and Judy sang a song they were practicing to sing for grandma upon their next visit which she said would be soon.

Judy walked with us to the car, telling us how Mom had dressed up like she was going to church the night she was going out with the old man and Harry.

James and I talked how out of place Mom would have looked on our way back to the bus. "I know how Harry misses going out and frolickin but I'm glad he stood up to the old man knowing that Mom wouldn't have good time at all. I said. And it really breaks my heart that she's got so desperate to think that would even do any good."

I threw rocks out in to the pond while the horses drank, thinking of the dream I'd had. As I neared the laydown yard, I saw Big Red pulling away from the Gant house with James, Duck, and Calvin riding on the bed and Bob and Mickel in the cab. I was disappointed that I'd not made it in time to help unload the remainder of their belongings. And I'd missed the chance to show my muscles off to a certain person.

Mickel stressed how they hadn't gotten any rest coming home so late in the morning. Bob piped up that he'd rest on the way to Chillicothe and back as soon as the truck was loaded. With everyone helping, it was loaded in no time and Bob was on his way.

Had there not been the urgency to get Bob on down the road, we'd have had our normal morning start, gathering up to bullshit while James and Calvin sharpened their saws. It was never a contest to see who could finish first. James usually did and would be on his way. But Calvin would drag it out a little longer needing a few more minutes to finish his freshly over filled pipe. Whether it be to sharpen his saw for a while longer or to finish with a bullshit story, he'd puff away then as always bang the pipe on the side of the log and declare it was time to go to work.

But instead of heading for the woods, James took Duck over to the log pile, where he handed him the hatchet along with the measuring stick, showing him how to mark the pulpwood.

"And don't cut your finger off on your first day, Duck," he joked and surely thinking of mom. Calvin had the biggest laugh when Duck shot back asking what he could do after all the wood was marked. Mickel made his way to where they stood.

"Well, I guess blood's thickern' water . . . jist what am I supposed to do now?" Calvin sighed, shaking his head at what Mickel said. Bob's words of "stupid bastard' rushed to my brain. Mickel had said the wrong thing when Calvin pointed his file directly at him while getting ready to scold him.

"I'll tell you what to do, you old complainin' ass fart! Now if I were you, I'd go over 'ar and take my stick back away from that young buck an send his ass back to the house with his tail tucked between his legs and a cryin'."

Calvin got over excited, inhaling smoke that set him off to a good coughing spell. "Damn you old son of a bitch! Look what you made me do," Calvin blamed Mickel.

Mickel knew better than to challenge Calvin and instead turned to Duck once again.

"Hey! Donald Duck! Just how dammed old are you?"

"I'm old enough to work in the woods now," Duck declared. After one final cough, Calvin pushed his pipe back into his mouth and commenced to agitating old Mickel a little more.

"Now, Mick, I don't think you should complain that ole Duck's doin' the measuring . . ."

"Well, I think he should start out at the bottom by rollin' wood down to the loadin' area and work his way up like I had to." Mickel talked so slow that even his hand gesturing barely moved.

"Shit, Mick, you didn't get moved up no damned ladder. They just ain't nothing else you can do on your own without shittin' yourself. Old Donald Duck will smoke your ass in no time, and you know the better man always gets the best job. Hell you can't make it up the ladder any farther. Now they's only one way left for your old feeble ass to go, and that's back down to the bottom and start over again. The onliest thing left that's lower than that is the damned graveyard." Calvin laughed, stabbing his pipe towards the ground.

Mickel looked around, surveying all the places Duck had notched the logs as if he were trying to find just one place he'd missed. Noticing what he was doing agitated Calvin even more.

"Mick, they ain't nothin' left to mark. Not like you, ole Donald Duck didn't miss a damned thang. Why, hell, ole Donald Duck here's done more in just a few minutes than you get done all day!" If it was true what the old man said that only a fool laughs at his own joke. Calvin could have been the greatest fool of all times with the way he carried on right now.

There just wasn't much energy left in old Mickel. His pants were way too big around at the waist, held up by a tightly cinched belt well above his hips, and too long by a lot with at least three rolls of the pant legs. Calvin had accused him of wanting to look like the cowboy Roy Rogers but said, "Ole Roy didn't go around dragging his feet all the time, he had other ways of filling his cuffs up with dust and dirt."

It wasn't just Calvin who noticed Mickel's constant dragging his feet everywhere he went. He had other ailments also. Most times, his arms hung lifeless at his sides. Several times throughout the day he coughed to the point of getting sick. And lately, just rubbing sore places on his stomach took a pretty good effort. He looked like a slouch about all the time.

Regardless though of Mickel's condition Calvin wouldn't show much mercy; relentless in his pestering to keep him moving right along. Calvin wasn't just sitting there idle bumping the stem of his pipe against his front teeth. He'd been surveying the two of them for some time.

"Well now, here's how we kin solve this right here and now." He winked, kneeling down by one of the biggest logs in the yard. "Whoever wins at arm wrestlin' gits the measuring job. How 'bout that?" He grinned at Mickel. "Right here, boys! And right now!" He slapped his open hand on top of the log, raising sawdust and clearing a spot for them to place their elbows.

"Why, he's just a kid! That wouldn't be far!" Mickel protested.

"I got a dollar, says he kin beat your old sorry ass, Mick." Calvin dug furiously into a deep pocket, dragging a single bill out.

"Now by God, Calvin"—Mickel nodded—"I'll take that dollar, you . . . asshole!" Mickel slowly knelt down on one knee. I laughed, thinking how slow he'd be getting to an altar and could die before he got saved at his pace.

"Hey, I'm sorry, Duck, for cussin' in front of you like that." Mickel humbled himself as Duck reached for his hand.

"Da-gone, don't worry about cussin' in front of me . . ." He pointed. "Arnold's my brother! I reckon he's got the world's record for cussin'! Don't ya, Piggy Wiggy?" Duck's snappy answer got everyone laughing.

"Now that's something to be proud of, isn't it, Arnold?" James added. Calvin was jumping back and forth between the two of them like a referee until their arms were in the right position.

"All right, boys, this is it!" Calvin let go, and before he could get out of the way, Mickel complained. "Hey, I wasn't quite ready yet!"

"I agree you might not have been ready, Mick, 'cause they ain't no way a person could get beat that fast! Hell, that was quickern lightning!" Calvin beamed with satisfaction.

Mickel got back up to his feet while slowly rubbing his shoulder. I felt sorry for him that he hadn't held his own, not even for a second and now had a new ache to rub.

"Pay up, asshole!" Calvin held an open hand out. Mickel reached into his pocket and pulled out what looked to be the only dollar he had, shoving it in Calvin's hand. Calvin squeezed it tightly and thanked him.

"Now do you want to make it two out of three or twenty-six out of fifty and maybe win that dollar back?" Calvin raged, pushing the bill into his watch pocket. Mickel turned to walk away when James, who hadn't said much to this point, stood up and stretched his arms high over his head before speaking up.

"I think Mickel's right. Duck should start out by rolling wood to the loading area." Mickel nodded at James as his way of thanking him. And I thought the same, I mean as helpless as Mickel was what else could he do that could be productive. Even though Calvin respected James's decision, he wasn't gonna leave well enough alone when it came down to dealing with Mickel

"After Arnold gets some more logs pulled down here, I'm gonna give you a five-minute head start . . ." Calvin stuck his pipe firmly back into his mouth. "And then I'm gonna cut everythin' that's marked up, and if I catch up with you, I'm gonna run that buzzin' saw right up between the crack of your ass!"

Mickel never turned back; but as he walked away, he flipped Calvin off. He'd finally smartened up enough to know that any confrontation with Calvin was a losing cause. And I knew even though Calvin carried on like he did with Mickel that he wouldn't have wanted him to get hurt. I think that he secretly enjoyed it when Mickel didn't back off from his teasing. I thought it funny to see a big mean, ugly son of a bitch like Calvin putting up with an old broken-down slouch such as Mickel. But we were all lucky including Mickel to have Calvin as our friend, I thought.

Duck enjoyed his new job way better, rolling pulp wood to the loading area. He could burn a lot of his youthful energy challenged by the bigger pieces which I knew he'd not back down from. Now that things had settled down James disappeared into the woods, carrying his saw. With Duck busy rolling wood and Mickel chopping places to be cut into logs Calvin would take a few more minutes to finish sharpening his chain. I joined him for a minute before going after another load. I'd no sooner than got comfortable when he peered around me like there was someone sneaking up behind me. *Like I'm really going to fall for that old trick again*, I thought to myself.

"Would you like a drink of cold spring water?" a soft girly voice asked. At first, I thought Calvin was trying to do one of his ventriloquist acts of sounding like a little girl, but there he sat sheepish grin and all right in front of me. He winked, giving his head a sideways nod. She thought it funny the way I whirled and stumbled, and stirring up dust.

Kate hadn't warned me of her and the younger girls approach. They still laughed at my awkwardness. She hardly looked like the same girl from the day before. And my dreams hadn't done her justice as she stood a couple feet away, pinning her windblown hair behind an ear. She looked brand-new, I thought, with her hair combed back, rolling off her shoulders and down below her waist. I felt awkward with her holding the dipper out for me to take.

"Oh yes! I-I'll have a drink. Thank you so much!" She giggled at how I fumbled with my words. I could hear Calvin's half-ass grunt followed by a sudden blast of smoke that blew past my head. She fanned it away the best she could. I must have sounded like the horses drinking at the pond as I quickly drank it all, with some running down my chin and onto my chest. She laughed, quickly covering her mouth. And best of all, this wasn't just another made-up dream of mine; and like love stories on TV, there could be a happy ending.

"Why, you don't have to drink it so fast, Arnold. There's a whole bunch of water just pouring out of that spring down there, ya know. Was it you that stacked the rocks so neat and easy to get to the water?" She turned her head, gesturing with her chin in the springs direction. I'd never seen such a pretty girl in my life as I gingerly passed the empty dipper back to her. I'd never heard my name spoken so softly from flowing lips that I'd almost kissed in my dreams. Then came the gaze solely intended for me as she slowly looked up at me.

"I told Momma this mornin' that the first thing I wanted to do was ah . . . to . . . well, thank you for bringin' the lantern up to us last night. It was awful scary in there in the dark, with those strange noises coming from those holes in the floor." Her eyes widened with expression. She spoke the most perfect words I'd ever heard in my life! Then looking off to one side, she continued, "I don't have anything to give you, but I thought I'd offer a cold drink of water . . ." She turned to face me once again, this time with a full smile. She'd have had to rehearse such a beautiful sentence, I thought. I pretended a quiet cough, nervously looking away for just a second myself. I could hardly look at her with so many desires and attractions to see.

"Oh, it's okay. Heck, I knew it was gonna get plenty dark up there in that old house," I said, while crossing my arms over my ever-expanding chest. I could hardly stand still with a sudden weakness in my legs, arms, fingers, and toes . . . but through it all, I managed to sound brave, as was my intention.

Calvin was carrying on behind me, seemingly to disrupt with fake coughs and quick grunts. But she'd made it easy for me to talk to her, and I'd do so even if it meant drinking the full bucket of water by myself to quench a thirst. I ignored Calvin the best I could since I could talk to him anytime. For now, I'd feast on something that I'd never tasted before.

"Why, there wasn't even a moon shinin'—shining, last night." I corrected my word before continuing on with my heroics. "I mean it was dark like you . . . wouldn't believe." I rambled on, waving my hands in front of her. "And no way could you make the road out comin' up here! Why, I almost fell three or four times on the . . . ah . . . way back." I was starting to stutter by adding spice that really didn't happen. But she stood there, taking it all in and seemed excited following my words. Having her attention, I could have gone on forever, but what was all my babble leading up to in the end? I wondered.

"I'd have been scared to death with no light to see with," she interrupted, slowly rolling her eyes up to meet mine. The place where all good dreams originate from, just as James had said. I couldn't and didn't want to look away as my normal bashfulness would have led me to do.

A strange quietness rushed to my ears as I was drawn deep into her eyes and to a place I couldn't even imagine existed. Reflective scenery in perfect rings of blues and greens and other colors that lay as deep as space itself, I thought. Both silent, we dug deeper into each other's endless stare with neither wanting to look away.

It was as if she shared my fantasy that we be at Kincaid Springs with me drinking from her overflowing cupped hands. I wanted to swim in the pond with her and finish my dream with all its realities.

"And I knew there wasn't a man up here to protect you, so I brought the lantern for you to see with." Hard to believe that in one sentence, I'd declared myself a man and told her she was the reason I'd brought it anyway. It was as if her eyes begged me to run away with her and I just knew it.

"Well, wo-would you like another dipper?" she said, pushing every teasing word it sounded. But she didn't need words—her eyes spoke of everything I wanted to see and hear.

"Sure." I slowed my tone quickly, wiping my lips with a sweaty hand. A sudden blush beamed on her face when our eyes engaged once again. She wanted me to kiss her, I just knew it. I wasn't wrong about this. James had explained it to the tee how all this would transpire, and he was right. Sweat poured down my face and onto my bare chest. I had no way to wipe it off other than an already-wet hand. The thought of a first kiss brought on more sweat, now dripping from my nose and chin. Her quick glance at my heaving chest set my heart on fire.

A gust of wind swept loose hair into her face once again. She gently pushed it back, holding a full ponytail with her other hand. Like a magnet our eyes were drawn to each other again. This was my first case of real lust, something I only thought I'd had before now. I wanted her badly as I stepped forward.

The time was at hand, no doubt about it; the want in her eyes reflected mine. I couldn't put it off any longer; after all, it was my duty to make the first move, not hers. I attempted one last breath before I'd kiss her. But it wouldn't be now. She gently set the bucket on the ground, quickly pushing the dipper under bringing it back up full to the brim. Holding it with both hands, she slowly started raising it toward my mouth, determined to not spill a drop it looked.

Stupid questions with stupid answers clogged my mind all of a sudden. The timing had been right just before she'd set the bucket down. I *should've kissed her right then*, I thought regretfully. It could have been in a movie, the way I pictured her holding the dipper and my hands on her waist as violins played. A scene where the last minute would be us kissing as the sun went down over our shoulders. But I wanted to still be kissing long after "The End" faded away into oblivion on the TV screen.

My head swirled to a newfound dizziness that I never wanted to end. I just couldn't think right now and wasn't sure if I was reaching for the dipper or, as James had suggested, put my hands on the side of her face and see what reality had in store for me. I froze at the thought as she pushed the dipper to my waiting hands.

My fingers clumsily searched for hers. There was a warmth as I'd never felt before when they finally touched. How could something so foreign feel so warm. But that would only last a second before we'd reconfigure them again, then finally locked them tightly, intertwined with each other we squeezed them.

There was no doubt about it. *I may never get this chance to kiss again*, I thought to myself. She continued bringing the dipper toward my mouth as I showed no resistance. I definitely needed help from above now. I was supposed to breathe, drink, and stand up all at the same time with her now pressed up against me, while tilting the dipper to my mouth.

With her finger softly touching my lower lip, a tingle ran throughout me. I just knew my head was going to explode. I drank until there was no more left, but she continued to hold the empty dipper to my mouth. I felt her need with her pushed up against me so tightly. She reached to wipe a drip from my chin as I leaned in toward her when she softly closed her eyes. I closed mine as I puckered my lips the best I knew how.

"It'll . . . never happen to me . . . by God! Not old Arnold Ray!" Calvin whined with laughter. I'd momentarily forgotten about him with all that was going on. But there he was, as loud as ever.

She opened her eyes with a startled look. I stepped backwards, turning quickly to Calvin. Everything had gone silent for that brief period of time. I'd been inches away from kissing her. How could something so wonderful end up like this? It sure wasn't the way I'd have scripted it. This was not a dream. Words would be hard to come up with right then. Calvin had ruined the moment. I couldn't think of anything to say that would have taken us back to the place we'd just left.

"Oh, thanks for the water," I said. "I guess I better get back to work." What a dumbass I must have sounded like! I let go of her arm, which I couldn't remember even taking hold of, and hurried away. "Get up there . . .," I said in a low groan to Kate. *Why am I leaving for?* I asked myself. The dizziness still ran through me as I held on to Kate's reins.

Maybe if I hadn't been thinking about kissing so much, I would've thought of something smart to say there at the end. God, I sure wanted to kiss her. My stomach ached for the taste of something I didn't know much about.

"Woo...," I growled stopped the animals in their tracks. "Christ! I didn't even ask her name!" I said out loud, turning quickly to see her still looking at me. Maybe I should just start running toward her and let history tell what happened at the end.

She waved, then started passing water out to everyone else. I hid in a clump of trees to watch her for a while longer, lusting after her every move. I should have known that Calvin's limp arms hanging to his side meant he wanted the same treatment as I'd got. After teasing her long enough to get a laugh from everyone, he finally took the dipper from her hand.

What just happened to me? I still lusted for the kiss that I was inches away from. With trembling hands, I exhaled quickly, squeezing them together. I frantically jumped up from the small trees, leaping high into the air. This would finally be the day that I'd fly. I ran through the woods with no particular place in mind. Faster and faster, I ran dodging low-hanging limbs, and jumped across gorges I'd not attempted until now. Nothing could hurt me as I jumped into unexplored places. I challenged limbs where I'd soar high in the air and to ride them to the ground. Hurt could come later with my stumbles, hard landings and sudden stops as I pushed on with a love driven energy.

Can I let this happen to me? "Yes, yes, I can," I repeated several times, thinking how we'd both looked deep into lustful eyes. Songs were a dime a dozen as they spun throughout my brain when I found one that I could dwell on. "It's in her eyes." I sang a few words. James's explanation rang true that it all evolved from there. I jumped over a fallen tree thinking, *If I hurry back, maybe she'll still be there, and I can have another cold drink just like the last one.* But it wasn't water I thirsted for now. I ran back to where I'd left the horses; hastily gathering their reins. I hammered the metal dogs into the first two logs that I came to, then told Mr. Bill to 'get up.' He made a lunge forward but stopped abruptly. In a panic move, he started swinging his big head back and forth.

"What's wrong with you Bill! Go just go!" I said in an urgent way that got him even more confused it looked. He pranced back and forth for a few seconds before leaning into the load and then headed down the hill. I hastily hooked Kate up to a single log and slapped her on the butt. Then I cut down through the woods ahead of them to get there before they did. But I'd gotten there too late the girl was nowhere to be seen. I was disappointed thinking when would be the next time I'd see her. The problem was I wanted it to be now.

I blamed my own stupidity that I'd not asked her what her name was and even more that I didn't follow through with the kiss when she wanted it as badly as I did. But what kind of bragging rights would there be to kiss a girl without even knowin' her name? Regardless I'd yearn for the day when my lips would meet hers, and sooner the better. I felt run-down and weak, and there was not a dry place on me from sweating so much.

"Arnie, there's somethin wrong with that picture, over there ain't they?" Calvin yelled pointed to where Kate and Mr. Bill stood. It did look funny with

Kate hooked up to a large log and Mr. Bill with the smaller ones behind him. So that's why Mr. Bill acted like he had, trying to tell me, that I wasn't thinking clearly. I felt like a fly hung up on a sticky strip and couldn't get away from Calvin as he took a more than satisfying drag on his pipe. I could only shake my head at how I'd gotten their loads so crossed up.

Now dreading to see him so pleased thinking maybe I should disconnect them in case I needed a quick get-a-way. It was the worst thing ever that Calvin had witnessed and I knew that he'd hound the hell out of me. It would have been easy to blame him for ruining my chance of a first kiss. But then again maybe I really wasn't ready, or I would have gone through with it. I thought how he teased the girl before taking a drink from the dipper. He had to do so in order to flirt a little with her which I saw from a distance. But I'd not say anything to him about drinking from the same dipper as me and everyone else had. I'd wait till the right moment to let him know that he'd shared it also with old Mickel.

I watched Calvin from the corner of my eye, situating his ass to a more comfortable position on his favorite log. His loud fake cough got everyone's attention, including mine, of course.

"Mick, how about bringin' your old sorry broken-down ass over here?" I quickly turned planning my escape when he focused on me. "And, Arnold Ray, you bring your ass right over here too!"

"All right, what the hell did I do wrong this time?" Mickel made the effort to shout.

"Why, hell, everything you do is wrong, Mick," Calvin shot back. In no hurry to get there, Mickel lit a cigarette up and waited on James, who'd come down out of the woods to get more chain oil. I thought it good that James had not seen my performance with the girl. I just wished I'd known as much as he did. I would've surely gotten lip-locked, and it wouldn't matter if anyone was watching us.

"Now, Arnold Ray, you can see good enough to get over 'ere, cain't gee?" Calvin roared, with a devilish blast of smoke straight up into the air. I knew without answering what he was leading up to, and there was no way I could stop him so best to say nothing for now, I figured. "And you need to wipe that sweaty ring from around your neck!" He pointed. His joke roused Mickel to laugh momentarily before the coughing set in. I could already feel my ears ringing inside.

"You had your head up your ass a little earlier, didn't ye Arnold Ray?" Calvin said, while patting a place on the log for me to sit beside him. It was the same thing James had gone through with Calvin and others though. And I was no better in my harassment thinking back to one of my condemnations of James, and pointing out that no one would ever be able to accuse me of such a thing. I couldn't understand at the time why he'd simply play along with everyone. But thinking of how deeply I'd penetrated her eyes I saw that world that James had told me of. And Calvin's remark of how one could get hypnotized rang true more than ever now.

"Oh . . . yeah . . .", Mickel suddenly came to life. "What in the hell were you doin' sneakin' around up here in the dark last night, and knowin' me and Bob were gone? Are you tryin' to run our wives or somethin'?" I was speechless to what he'd asked. But Calvin wasn't; his eyes lit up like a Christmas tree focusing them directly on me.

"Now you best look out, Mick! I think ole Arnold Ray here's got a hard-on for that purdy little daughter of yours."

"You're crazy, Calvin!" I tried to defend myself as they all laughed with the exception of Mickel. James smiled I guess hearing all that he needed to know. Evidently, he had other things on his mind; grabbed the oil and headed back up into the woods. I could only wish to blend into the greenery and disappear as he had.

"Why, hell, Mick! You should see the way Arnold Ray and my old lady act when they get around each other. Calvin whined. Why, she asked him the other day if he'd like to move in with us and worse, asked me where in the hell I was goin' to sleep! I think there might be a woodpecker in the hen house somewhere." I laughed right along with Calvin to stall him as long as possible. There was nothing funny with the way Mickel looked at me however. Surely, he wasn't serious with his remark about me and their wives.

"Now, Arnold Ray, you make sure'en wash behind your ears tonight when you go for that swim. It looks like a little may be caked on the back there." Calvin was on one of his better rolls, and it wasn't James or Mickel he was picking on right now. He'd witnessed my ordeal, and now knowing what I'd done last night was all he needed to get carried away with out-of-control teasing. I simply had to leave in a hurry—too late though, with Calvin grabbing my arm, forcing me back on the log.

"Hell, I enjoyed that little love nest you's abuilding a while ago with that little gal. It was like bein' in the front row at a picture show. Why, I had to lay my pipe down several times, thinking the smoke was what brought tears to my eyes. But all the while, it was you, Arnold Ray, actin' like a regular Romeo." He burst into laughed. Mickel didn't see the humor when he spat off to the side.

"You better not be lookin' at my daughter", he said with a very serious look and all the while waving a finger at me. "She's gonna marry a rich man, and they're goin' to support me in my old age. And besides, she's too good for pulpwood trash anyway!" It was bad enough being called a pulpwooder, but "trash" to go along with it pissed me off. My ears burned to what he said when I turned quickly to confront him, good and ready to say my piece, when Calvin spoke up.

"Mickel, you old goofy son of a bitch." Calvin leaned forward, letting go of my arm. "It's too late to worry 'bout you getting old ain't it. So you don't need to fret 'bout who she marries. Hell, the way you sound right now, tonight might be the big-in, and I won't have to hear all that damned coughing and throwing your guts up every damned minute of . . . the . . . day!" Calvin sounded pissed off, while getting a little winded himself.

"Well, I gotta go back to work," I said, walking to the horses in a hurry. I ignored the shouts and laughter best I could. I'd waited all the while hoping that Mickel might mention his daughter's name, but he hadn't and even with all the talk of her supporting him. I spotted James a way off, sitting on a stump and sharpening his chain.

"What's the ruckus all about down there?" he asked, dragging his thumb along the saw's sharp teeth.

"It's just Calvin bein' the nut that he always is . . ." Even though he hadn't said anything down at the yard I wondered if he'd seen my failed attempt at a first kiss.

"What was he talking about? Something about Mary and a woodpecker?" James looked up at me with an ear-to-ear grin. I made a dive for him as he dropped the file just in time before we hit the ground.

"Why you . . . sorry....," I said, pounding on his shoulder; with him laughing all the while. I jumped back up from where he lay with him showing no resistance to my onslaught.

"You just don't stand much of a chance with Calvin's constant teasing about things, and especially when it's about you and Mary." He nodded. I extended my hand to help him back up. We fumbled around on the ground till we found his file. Regardless if he'd seen my attempt at a kiss or not he had heard Mickel's rant about my late-night visit to drop off the lantern. But now more than ever I needed his help. He'd been right all along by telling me of the craziness I'd be going through. I wanted to tell him about her eyes and how they'd blinded me of everything and driving me mad with desire. And finally, how I couldn't get her out of my mind.

"Hey, did you know that the old man's going to hire a friend of Calvin's from down on Camp Creek and also is going to hire Baby John Radcliff for a little while."

"You gotta be shittin' me!" I gasped.

"Nope, I wouldn't shit you, Arnold. You're my favorite turd." His smile widened. "Where'd you pick up on that at?" I laughed.

"I read it in the *Reader's Digest*. Not really," he joked. The heat of the day was on us which made for a good time to extend a break and continue our talks. I sat back down on a mossy spot while slightly turning my back to him.

"Hey, I wonder if Baby John still sucks his thumb."

"God, I don't know," James chuckled. "It's been a pretty long time since we've seen him last. I think he was about eleven the last time we were around him. Les and Venus moved around 'bout as much as we did back then, if you remember. But heck, they've lived up on Pfizer's Ridge for some time now." But it wasn't Baby John nor Calvin's friend that I wanted to talk about right now.

I thought how quickly James had gone from such happiness this morning telling Mom of his future plan that he and Scarlett were getting married, to now, how the joy of it all seemed lost somewhere.

"Are you really gonna get married, James?" I asked.

"Well, I don't know," he answered. "Anna Fay says we're too young, and after a while, we'll get tired of each other and go on our different ways. You know how she is with that saying 'Mark my words, mister.' She must have said it a dozen times to get her point across with us."

"Well, what about Ezell? He's the man of the house, and that's who you're supposed to ask anyway isn't it."

He stabbed the file in the ground beside his shoe before clasping his hands together. "I think you know Ezell better than that, Arnold . . . with Scarlett being his stepdaughter, he stays out of it. But on the other hand, in private, he told me it was all right with him. He's just a good guy you know."

"Well, I think Mom was tryin' to tell you the same thing as Anna Fay, and she . . . of all people should know something about that!"

"But it was a different situation with Mom," he said and relaxing a little more. "She told me that Granma wanted to get her and Aunt Betha married off and out of the house as soon as she could. You know they had a houseful also, and evidently their ages didn't matter much or if they finished school when it came right down to it." He pulled a weed to chew on while gazing down at the laydown yard where Calvin and Mickel were still carrying on with each other.

"Scarlett cried on my shoulder last night, talking about all the rights and wrongs and 'should we or 'should we not.' She picked a wild flower the other day and pulled the petals off, sayin' we do, we don't. And the last petal said we do. That was enough for her. Then she jumped on top of me and—"

"And what?" I interrupted, all excited-like.

"Oh, nothing . . . but we know we're in love, regardless if we know what we're doing right now or not . . . Oh, and by the way . . . I think that daughter of Mickel's is a really good-looker, and if I wasn't goin' with Scarlett, I'd probably ask her out!"

"Well, you know you . . . can't do that because you . . . are going with Scarlett and maybe even getting married!" I stammered.

"Well to tell the truth, I thought from the first time I saw her, she was prettier than Scarlett. And I've been thinking lately what you told me about

Scarlett being our cousin and maybe it would be better if I started dating someone else, after all."

"You just told me that you're madly in love with her James. And besides, she ain't really our blood cousin, you know." All of a sudden, I worried about James taking the girl of my dreams away. Seeing my reaction he burst into laughter, with a good whack to my shoulder.

"It won't be long, Brub." He teased, grabbing his saw, and headed for the next tree he'd cut down. I realized what he'd said of Mickel's daughter was to see what my reaction would be. I felt pretty dumb and decided to not question him any further. I hooked the animals up to a good load, trying to get enough nerve to go back down to the laydown yard and take what they had to dish out to me.

I knew Mickel was still talking about me with a pointing finger as I jumped off my surfing log stopping Mr. Bill at the yard. I was lucky in one way that the old man just drove up. I watched as he and two others climbed out of the car. After walking to where he'd parked Calvin said something, which got a laugh from them all. I drove the log dogs out of Kate's log and was ready to do the same with Mr. Bill's when Calvin and a new guy walked up on me.

"Arnold, now this here's Freddy. Make sure you ask him how he likes his chickens." Calvin hunkered down like a little boy in trouble when Freddy pointed a stiff finger at him.

"Now non't git narded on me, mitch! Gis shut yer mouf." It was hard to understand some of his words, and being pissed off to the point of huffing probably didn't help much either. But he had a hard grip in his handshake leading me to think that he was a hard worker. He was clearly upset however with Calvin's chicken joke whatever that was all about.

Calvin, drew heavily on his pipe, pulling deep from within. I didn't know what to expect next. Calvin was supposed to be a friend of Freddy's but sure wasn't acting much like one. But that was the way of Calvin, friend or foe. He pulled his pipe, aiming it toward Freddy like a pistol.

"Now you tell ole Arnold Ray 'bout them twenty-five chickens." He turned to walk away but stopped after a couple of steps. "Why, I don't know if I want ol' Freddy stayin' with me and the old lady or not . . ."

"You shunt'ov axe me da come up'ere," Freddy fired back, but to no avail. Calvin laughed, then continued on to where he'd left his saw.

"Freddy, what is it that you do in the woods?" I questioned seeing that he was really upset with a reddened face over whatever Calvin was trying to imply. But I knew when the time was right Calvin wouldn't hold back on the chicken story.

"Oh, I d-new a wittle of evyfing," he said. "Whatevy comes up."

"Do you work with the horses?" I asked talking slowly so he'd understand me. His eyes beamed at the question.

"Oh yeah." He took his loose billed cap off to wipe his sweaty forehead. Freddy had other problems than just speech. He didn't have one hair on his head and never had it looked. There were a few long hairs, where it looked as if he was trying to grow a mustache. I'd seen others that had the same afflictions as Freddy. I'd heard everything from it being hereditary to inbreeding. I'd often thought of the suspicious look the people had who referred to it as inbreeding, when they themselves seemed really dumb about the whole thing. But whatever the reason, you wouldn't just come out and talk about it right out of the blue. And his face was tight like the top of his head. With the few long hairs above his lip and the tightness of his face, I thought he resembled a Chinaman. He looked younger than Calvin, but no one had seen Calvin's face for over fifteen years, so who could say?

"Er . . . nose da amnals?" He pointed.

"Are those the animals?" I questioned and not meaning to embarrass him to make sure I got it right. Freddy nodded with a smile.

"Yeah, that's Mr. Bill and Kate, the mule," I said.

"Man, nat's a mig horse! I'll met he can pu... a howse!" I had the urge to laugh at how some of Freddy's words sounded but thought better of it. I didn't need to get off to a bad start even if I were kidding. It had gotten easier but not fully to understand him after I'd figured out why his words sounded as they did. The letters *P and B* was his biggest struggle sounding as if they were being forced from his nostrils. And maybe that was the reason his tongue didn't flex much while forced it to the roof of his mouth. Words that had *T*'s in them came from the corners of his mouth, which sounded awkward enough. Others were strained at times when he'd pooch his lips out to make the *S* sounds. In places where he'd get a little excited and difficult to get his point across; hand motions would come into play to calm himself somewhat it looked. His words became much easier to understand as long as I was patient with him.

"He can pull a lot," I bragged of the mighty Mr. Bill. Freddy seemed to be a good person and I'd only hope that when Calvin decided to tell all about him, it wouldn't be in Freddy's presence. But I knew better of Calvin. He would embarrass you worse if there was an audience, and the more the merrier for him.

"Why, the other day, right after a big rain, Bob got the truck stuck coming up that hill," I pointed, "and that's with a load on it. I hooked Mr. Bill up to the front bumper, and he helped pull it out. Hard to think that one horsepower could do so much". My laugh tapered quickly. "The only problem was he messed his harness up in three places, and it took a while to fix it."

Paying close attention to all the details, Freddy slowly reached into his pocket and of all things removed a pipe.

"Oh, you've got to be shittin me you smoke a pipe also." I said slapping my forehead and rolling my eyes straight up. Freddy quickly stuffed it back into his pocket.

"No, no. I, I didn't mean anythin' like that. I'm only kiddin'. I mean Calvin smokes one, and old man Harry does too."

"Yeah, mut I know nat moke boders some meople, zo I won't moke wound 'em."

"Man, it doesn't bother me at all except when it's indoors." I thought for a second and, on a hunch, said, "But I hate the smell of Prince Albert." Freddy's face turned redder than a beet, it looked. "All three of you smoke that brand, don't you?" He nodded his head, somewhat confused. "Really, I'm just kiddin' again, Freddy."

"You som ma mitch," he laughed.

"And I'm sure, as you already know, my old man smokes anywhere he wants and don't give a shit who it bothers."

"Ell I'm not wike 'at," Freddy quickly answered.

"Go ahead and light it up," I said. "The truth is I kinda like the smell of pipe smoke, but I flat hate smellin' stinkin'-ass cigarettes."

We led the animals to their resting area by the two big piss elm trees. They took a liking to Freddy right off the bat as he scratched their manes and rubbed places on their noses. It made me believe that he'd be kind and not overwork them.

"New know nat Yon Wadciff fella nat came up wiff us?" Freddy chuckled, looking off to the side and trying to light his pipe all the while.

"Yeah, he's our cousin on the old man's side of the family. Why?" Freddy's face quickly flushed when he looked over at me and in a quiet tone, said,

"At guy nucks his numb!"

"Do what?" I asked, not fully understanding him. He drew in a breath and looked around that nobody hears him. Leaning forwards a little and holding an open hand beside his mouth he whispered.

"E . . . nucks . . . his . . . numb!" I'd had plenty of opportunities to laugh at how some of Freddy's words sounded but I couldn't hold back when I finally got his meaning that John sucked his thumb. It was then I knew Freddy had some humor about him when he joined in with laughter.

"Oh yeah! He's done that all his life," I answered quickly that Freddy not think I was laughing solely at him.

"New mind if I go up en fetch a woad of wogs wiff em amnals?" he asked.

"Yea, go ahead. Heck come on, I'll show you where I left off and where James is cuttin' right now."

James had just landed a tree, and after a minute, I managed to get his attention. Right after their introduction, I left them to themselves, then headed over the hill to see Baby John, but somewhat reluctantly, though.

As I got a little closer, I could see that he had his hands in his pockets, with thumbs sticking straight up and ready. They stuck out like a sore thumb bright white and clean most all the time. But it was inevitable that he get spit on my hand as we shook them. A sick feeling as I rubbed it off on my pant leg, with him laughing and pointing as if it were his intended joke. He'd mastered thumb sucking and wasn't ashamed of it at all. I thought back to the times when everyone would get on to him to quit doing it. With great anticipation he'd patiently wait for you to get finished. Then with a slurping grin, he'd tell you and all others to simply kiss his ass.

"How the hell are you doin', John?" I asked. His thumb went straight to his mouth with a few hard sucks followed by a gurgling sound like small bubbles escaping from his lungs. John hadn't changed much from the last time I'd seen him. His hair was still snow white and thick. I could only imagine how hard it must be to run a comb through. And being of light complexion, he couldn't go without a shirt for any period of time where the sun would turn him red in minutes. James thought he might even be an albino.

"I tole Uncle Jim the other night at his party that I jist needed ta work for a couple a week to pay for the work I'm gettin' done on my race car."

I didn't know if it were a slip of the tongue when he mentioned the old man's party but the thumb sucking was minor as I became angry. Harry's story came to mind of the old man throwing a hundred dollar bill down, and calling for free drinks for all. And then to think that he had no money for school clothes. And no money to pay Harry while swindling James and me out of half of ours. I couldn't help that the three always came to mind when money came his way.

"Sorriest person on the face of the earth," I mumbled.

"What'd you say, Arnold Ray?" John quickly removed his thumb, showing his broad smile.

"Oh, nothin', John. I was just thinkin' out loud." I wasn't going to put him on the spot with any inquiry about the old man's party. Whether it was supposed be secret or not, Baby John wouldn't have known any better to not talk of it.

"Well, what all's wrong with your car, John?" I asked more or less for something to talk about.

"I'm havin' it hopped up a little." He grinned. "I'm havin' six cams put in it to race this old boy's Vette, title for title. The guy that's puttin' the cams in said there won't even be a race to it." John laughed sure of himself.

"Oh, really . . .," I said. "Well, that oughta make it run like a scalded dog, John!" He thought a scalded dog must be really fast; choking on his saliva while bent over and gagging he never removed his lifelong dependency from his mouth.

"Now that was funny, Arnold Ray. I don't recon that I ever heard that one 'afore. But I've got to remember it, and maybe that's what I'll name my car, the Scalded Dog." It was then he cut lose for several seconds sucking as if he were running out of time it looked. But he was a good guy by all means and would give you his last nickel if you were to ask.

Behind John, with the laydown yard in the background it looked as if Duck was doing jumping jacks, maybe bored that he'd got caught up with everything marked up. But I knew better of Calvin, who wasn't jumping but flinging his arms wildly into the air trying to get my attention.

It was too late to look away, with Calvin swaying back and forth acting dizzy with both thumbs aimed toward his mouth which was already occupied by his pipe of course. Duck's pose was that of a cowboy ready to draw his pistols, with hands in his pockets and thumbs sticking straight up. And if that wasn't enough John stood directly in front of me sucking his thumb. I couldn't control myself any longer thinking how the circus had grown with old and new clowns alike.

"What's so funny?" John asked, while kneeling beside me where I'd gone down on one knee. I covered my face blocking the commotion at the laydown yard but I couldn't get away from the sucking sounds just inches from my ear. Then to make things worse came the sound of the small bubbles once again, cracking and rising from within his lungs. I was tempted to glance over at Calvin and Duck but knew that'd be a worse mistake. What I needed was a time-out of sorts. I stood back up, feeling embarrassed. I really needed to get away from all these people for a while.

The old man had been talking with Bob ever since his return from Chillicothe. Mickel was like a magnet anytime the old man came around. After a short gathering, they all came over to where Baby John and I were standing.

"Arnold Ray, I need you to run up there and get Junior down here. I need to talk with both you boys about somethin'," He said with no hesitation.

"Okay!" I answered, short and simple. I tried to think back to the last time we'd spoken to each other and was about to leave when Baby John blurted,

"Hey, Arnold Ray! Have you heard that new song on the radio that sounds kindly like this, 'my baby's got the hanky-panky,'" he attempted to sing a verse while wallowing his thumb all through his mouth.

"That's not the way it goes, John. It's 'my baby *does* the hanky-panky.'" John slowly removed his thumb showing a broad smile.

"My baby's got the hanky-panky because . . . she hum, hum . . . de hum, hum." It was pretty easy to see that he knew hardly any of the words. Calvin winked as I walked past him. He must be at the height of his glory I thought with such a smorgasbord of characters to have his way with. I hadn't got far up the trail when I stepped off to the side when Kate came past me pulling a log. She looked surprised with her long ears flopping in my direction. I'd been the only person for some time now that'd ever worked her. But the gees and haws that she'd got so accustomed to would come from a stranger who'd command with a whole different voice. I took a second to wipe my eyes clean after my visit with John. Then Mr. Bill came lumbering down the trail with his load and Freddy following right behind. Freddy never said a word as he passed by, happily content; he winked and saluted with his pipe in hand. Mr. Bill didn't have as big a load as I'd have him hooked up to, but that was okay. I figured Freddy was just testing him at first till he got to know him and Kate better. A little way on up the hill I threw a small stick at James, which hit him on the leg to get his attention.

"Now! what do you want?" he demanded, setting the saw off to the side.

"Well, the old man told me to come and get you. It's time for me and you to hit the road, bein' he's got our replacements down there." I pointed over the hill, looking as serious as I could and never cracking a smile. But I knew I wasn't fooling him when he shot back.

"Well, by cracky! That's all right with me, but he better be paying the rest of the money that he owes us." He chuckled, while wiping the sweat from his face. "Let's just sit down over here for a while and watch him go, round and around in circles." He grinned then looked over at me. "Have you been crying?" he frowned.

"Yeah, from laughin' so hard. You sure miss a lot of shit when you're up here alone all the time, ya know. I'm tellin' you, my damn jaw hurts from laughin' so much. Oh!! And wait till you hear Baby John sing 'my baby's got the hanky-panky.'"

"Well, that's not the way it goes," he corrected me.

"Jesus I know that, but it's the way he sings it; that his baby's got the hanky-panky by doin' the hanky-panky with somebody else. That's what it sounds like to me."

James grinned. "Well, I wonder if he knows that it sounds like his babys got a venereal disease or something like that?" he joked. "And I cain't even guess what his girlfriend must look like. Hell, maybe she's a thumb-sucker also. Imagine how those kissing sessions would work out. I'll bet ole Baby John can really get into some French-kissing." James envisioned. "And can you imagine going from lip-locked to thumb-locked as fast as he is with that thumb? Heck they probably get all out of control and suck each other's thumb Arnold!"

"Jesus, James, that's sick and sounds like something Calvin would come up with, not you." I scooped up a handful of sawdust that lay on top of the stump and letting it sift through my fingers.

"Are you alright Arnold?"

"Sure, why wouldn't I be?"

"Well you sound as if you're having trouble breathing, and you're awful antsy about something."

"I'm alright James," I sighed. "I guess I ran up here a little too fast, carrying the latest breakin' news that the old man's finally puttin us down the road".

"Yeah, breaking news all right!" James sounded sarcastic. He stood up and walked over the hill a little way and returned with a double fisted size knot he'd cut off the side of a oak tree. Quick with his knife he started trimming the heavy bark away revealing its burled texture. He'd given one to Scarlett a while back with his and her names carved on its face and looked real pretty I thought. Only someone truly in love could have carved it with such fine details I thought. I'd compared its meaning to the two coffee cups at Kincaid Springs. They'd been placed upon a thin slate mantle and shoved back in amongst small flowers and wet drippy vines and lastly surrounded by touch-me-nots.

Damn-it, if I can see the meaning behind all those things than I surely must be ready for a girlfriend, I thought to myself.

"And who's that one for?" I pointed.

"This! Oh, this one's for Judy!"

"What!?" I hastily asked. "Why does she want one for, she's got a long way to go before she's old enough for a boyfriend. There's just not much use for it if you don't have a name to put along with yours." I was being hypercritical that she didn't deserve one. My list of reason would go on and on why I was more deserving than her. But most of all I should be the one because it wouldn't be long now before I'd find out the name of my girlfriend.

"Oh, I think she's old enough to date right now, don't you Arnold? And I'd bet you that it wouldn't take her anytime to find a boyfriend". His sudden and flashy smile prompts me for an answer. Suddenly I felt dizzy thinking how Judy had caught up with me in the fourth grade and now with the thought that she could possibly get a plaque before me was more than I could bear. I drew in a deep breath thinking this will all be solved when I find out her name; then I'll ask James to carve one for me.

"Why yes I think she's old enough for a boyfriend. But there's a, a lot of things she just don't understand yet James." I nodded as if I were way beyond my sister on the matter. But the fact was I really wasn't. My slight stutter was enough to get his attention and I was fooling him by no means when he gave a slow nod and along with a halfcocked smile. I had to face the fact that I didn't have a name to give him to carve on the knot and how I might express my feelings towards her. The thought that I blew the chance for a kiss was bad enough, but it angered me more that I never asked her name. I needed to talk about something else for the time being.

"James, is it's just me, you seem way happier since you've stopped drivin' the truck?" With hardly any thought to my observation he seemed more than ready to answer.

"Well . . . to tell the truth, it's good to not be in such a hurry all the time. Drive like hell to Chillicothe and back . . . get another load and head out again." He nodded. "It's good to just slow down with only one thing on your mind." And plain to see in his smile was all he needed to show that Scarlett was on his mind.

"Did you ever tell the old man about you and Scarlett getting married yet?"

"Nope, there's no need," he followed. He sounded rather sad of the whole affair I thought. We made ourselves more comfortable on the tree he'd just cut down where it straddled a small ravine and we could dangle our feet from it. And from there we also could see the old man pacing back and forth with his hands pushed deep in his pockets, and all the while staring at the ground. We watched his patience growing thin when he picked up Ducks measuring stick and began tapping it on the top of a log, then suddenly whacked it several hard times in a fit of fury it looked.

"Ouch, that one really hurt daddy...!" I whinnied in a playful way while grabbing at a place in the middle of my back that I couldn't quit reach. James didn't seem too interest in my joke but payed more attention to the old man as he stormed around in the laydown yard. And as always impatient about everything he was constantly checking the time on his watch. That of all things looked to be bothering James the most with muscles flexing the full length of his jaw. The sudden change in his attitude led me to believe that my question of he and Scarlett's future plans had upset him with the old man in some way.

"Well you know why he's pissed off don't you James? It's cause it's taking us way too long to get down there. Don't ya think?"

"Yep, it sure looks that way." He slowly responded.

"Well no problem, we'll just tell him that we stopped on the way to eat a few berries, ya think that'll work?" I kidded while pushing my elbow into his side.

"Yea, that'll work about like it did that time when we lived over off Route 50. It's hard to believe that he whipped us for taking too long to walk to the damned house. He was looking at his damned watch that day also same as he's doing right now. And we were just little boys way back then." James hardly ever talked of the whippings we'd gotten over the years. But he was right it was a hum damn dinger on that day and for no cause at all.

I thought back to how hard I cried seeing the size of the switch when we started up the final hill. I prayed' and I mean with every step that all we'd get would be just a threat. But that didn't happen when he grabbed James by the arm and started in on him. I knew the damned thing wasn't goin to break and with my turn a comin' it would be broken in just right. It was one of the worst whipping we'd ever gotten and from a switch cut by him to his own liking.

James had finished peeling all the bark off the knot and obviously had lost interest when he placed it on the stump alongside his knife.

"Lollygaggin around too long to get to the house that evening; a piss poor reason when you really think about it. And are you ready for another one like that Arnold?" He reared back while giving me a stern shove.

"You know I don't think about him hitting me anymore James. I've told him what I'll do and he better believe it. Hell, I'm way beyond that part. I've already picked out places to lay his sorry ass to rest for the last time." He had nothing to say; he'd heard it all before. But there was a question in his look as his eyes swept past mine.

"Yep just like you said James getting' whippin's for lame ass reasons! Now since we don't get whippin's anymore maybe you can explain why he whipped me harder than you or anyone else. It's a fact that there were more switches broken on me than anyone. I gave him a solemn look knowing that he wouldn't agree with me on this one.

"You know better than that." He quickly shot back. "Just hold it right there," he said while holding his open hands towards me. "Let me ask you this. If you were a total stranger and didn't know either one of us wouldn't it be pretty easy to figure out which of us you'd want to bust their ass the hardest Brub? I'd say you," he laughed while stabbing a stiff finger in my direction.

Not funny, I thought to myself and was ready to lunge forward and take him down when he suddenly pointed to the old man who couldn't see us from our vantage point. He'd already scanned past us several times. He checked his watch once again, shaking his head angrier than ever. He said something to Baby John, sweeping a stiff finger to the area he thought we'd be in.

"Shit, James, he's sendin' the thumb-sucker up after us now." I pointed, sliding farther into the clump of brush. I knew that with Baby John on his way, I couldn't fiddle around for very long. I simply had to tell James of my failed attempt at my first kiss. I'd come so close I felt like anywhere would be a good starting point. And besides, he'd already told me that there was no question too stupid when it came right down to love anyhow. I drew in a deep breath to calm myself.

"Well I believe I blew a good chance of getting my first kiss today, James." I said while looking him straight in the eye and with no shyness.

"Yep, it sure looked that way from up here." He said with a shy looking grin.

"So, you seen what went on down there, right?" I was excited and somewhat relieved that I wouldn't have to explain with fine detail what had gone wrong.

"I saw it, the short hug and all." He nodded.

"Well… then you saw how Calvin messed everything up for me." Suddenly I'd become nervous with him saying my whole affair hadn't lasted long at all. And worse I tried to lay my misfortune on Calvin which James quickly shrugged off.

"Well first of all you can't blame Calvin for you not kissing her. I mean you were only a couple inches away from her soft... lips," he snickered while dragging the words. "I could see her desire also and I can tell you Arnold she was not going to stop you. My, my Arnold Ray look what you've gotten yourself into". He said while giving me the slightest shove.

"All the times you he-hawed around and asked me about how to act with a girl then all of a sudden and without warning she's standing right in front you. It's one of those life changing events when you think you're going plumb crazy. And there's no way out now since you've had a taste of the most wonderful thing in the world. And best that's without even a kiss. So, tell me how deep in her eyes did you look, Arnold?" He smiled. How could he tell where my thoughts were at that very moment. But it hadn't been that long ago that he'd gone through the very same thing as I was now. I faked a coughed to hold his attention.

"I need to know everything James, even though I don't know her name damn it. I'm so stupid, and everybody down there is making fun of me, I just know it. I can almost hear 'em now ... laughin' and cuttin' up with how I've got my head's up my ass all of a sudden. And heck maybe there's something to it after all!" I was disgusted with myself and even more that James said I should have ignored Calvin and followed on through with it.

"Well, don't worry so much. Heck, when you get that first one, you won't give a damn what anybody says or thinks after that." He quickly spat the sassafras leaves out that he'd been chewing on.

"Now don't tell me James that it didn't bother you when everybody, includin' me," I stabbed a thumb to my chest, "was talkin' about you havin' your head up your ass all the time? And all the while you just showed that shit-eatin' grin like you didn't give a damn. And even with me bitchin' about you goin' out with Scarlett you just seemed to overlook it all like you didn't hear me."

"Well to tell the truth I didn't hear much. There's something strange and happens right after your lips touch hers for the first time. Remember what you said a minute ago how I ignore things. People can call you names and tell you how ignorant you are but it won't faze you, and do you know why that is Arnold?" I was beside myself with what he might say at this point but hoped it wasn't some kind of craziness that might embarrass me.

"Well I guess it's when you're thinkin' about someone all the time and don't pay attention when people are talkin' to you. So, I guess you get hard of hearin." And now that I think of it everything had gone quiet when I gazed into her eyes. Damn-it if Calvin hadn't butted in; it's all his fault and...and he ruined everything. My thought had overwhelmed me when I heard James snapping his finger and close to my ear at that.

"Hello, over here Arnold." His laugh brought me back from where I'd drifted off momentarily.

"OK, I give the hell up James! What is it?" I paused thinking maybe he'd give me a quick and honest answer of the quietness that he spoke of.

"Well it's not like you get hard of hearing or anything like that Arnold. The fact is you can hear everything people say but it's all muffled up in a strange way. So you get used to that and just agree with everything and keep smiling all the while. And believe me that ole first kiss can put your mind in strange places for sure." But even stranger I thought was the way he turned his head to the side as if he were trying to hide something. Suddenly I'd become suspicious that he was fooling around with me.

"Well I never heard of such a thing, James. You're messing with me, right?" It wasn't in his eyes but in his questioning grin that he had me stumped about what the muffled sounds were all about. He could toy with me knowing that I didn't have much patience for anything. "Wait!" I said before grabbing him by the arm. "Just hold it right there James. So your tellin' me that with everything that was going on with you all you could hear was some kind of a shittin' muffled sound all that time?"

His effort to hide his snickering suddenly turned to spontaneous laughter and then a coughing spell that went on for some time.

"OK, spit it out." I gingerly poked at his ribs before he leaned back against the stump a little harder. His effort to say something just wasn't happening for now. "Now what the hell are you tryin' to tell me?" I poked at his side once again forcing him to set up straight. After several long drawn out sighs his laughter finely trailing off somewhat as he wiped his eyes clean with his shirt sleeve. "Man o man." He finally managed to say something without laughing.

"Arnold that muffled noise I was trying to explain to you was leading up to a good joke of course and then you added the icing to it." He looked to be on the verge of losing it again when he quickly collected himself while sitting up to his fullest.

"You know from the first time I heard that expression 'head up your ass' I thought it was pretty lame to tell the truth. So I took it for what it was worth and imagined what it must sound like if a person was in that predicament. And that goofy smile that you accused me of having anytime people laughed and made fun of me. Well that was true when you put your mind to gut growling sounds, then you come along and added a flavor to it when you called it a 'shittin' muffled sound.'"

His timing was perfect when we both started laughing and rolling all over the ground. It was good for James to loosen up to whatever had been bothering him. And from this time on when anyone talked of where my head must be I'd smile and think of the place that my big brother talked of.

"My God James you're crazier than me," I said while getting back up off the ground. He seemed back to his normal self now. There was no doubt in my mind however that it was brought on when he'd decided to not tell the old man of his proposal to Scarlett. We dug all around where we'd wrestled until we found the file he'd dropped; after which he continued to sharpen the saw.

"Now I want you to tell me the truth James. Did I look like a dumbass when she was passing the dipper to me?" I meant to sound earnest with my question.

"Nope, not really. But you sure were having a hard time letting go of it there at the end." He laughed. What he'd said took me back to the very place in time as I felt the cold water run down the sides of my mouth. James saw me when I quickly licked my lips.

"The first time's not so easy with your heart ready to fly out of your chest. And if you'd have kissed her that's what we'd be talking about right now. You'd be telling me that she had the softest lips in the world and a smell like no other. And ready to just float away. Am I right?"

"Yes, I'd say you're right on the money James," I laughed while slightly rubbing my stomach which he took notice of also. And what if it wasn't everything that you expected.

"Look you know it's just a matter of time before you do it. But how do you know you're not just in heat like Calvin would label it."

"Yes matter of fact I have thought about that and believe me I was in heat today for sure." We cut up and carried on with what I'd gone through that day while relaxing us both in one way or the other.

"Well I'm glad I waited till the time was right for me and Scarlett because this is a whole different kind of pain to deal with, Arnold." He was right even though I never considered it as pain I found myself rubbing my stomach that I yearned for her constantly.

"It's okay, Mickel." He laughed as I quickly removed my hand from my stomach.

"So, I guess your first attempt was about like mine?"

"Oh yeah, you wouldn't believe what I went through." He laughed, leaning back against the stump once again.

"So, you just met by chance and not a kiss the first time?" I pried.

"Yep, that's about the size of it Arnold. Well…, it looks like Baby John has spotted us he's just over the hill from you. There's not enough time right now to tell you about me and Scarlett's first encounter. But after we got over that hump it was on and I can make it as spicy and drag it out for as long as you want to hear it." He stood up, pushing the file into his back pocket. I knew at this point he'd tell me everything including if he'd made love yet.

"So stop rubbing your stomach. You won't go crazy or anything like that. Hey, Baby John, how you doing?" James reached for a handshake and left-handed at that, seeing John's right hand was preoccupied.

"I'm doin' good other than car problems," John answered. Maybe it was because of Johns snow white hair and a sun burn just waiting to happen; he was the whitest person I'd ever seen in my life which for some strange reason made his lips look moist and bright red about all the time.

"And how're you doin', cousin Junior?"

"Well I'm doing great, John. So… what, brings you up here?"

"Well uncle Jim wants you guys down at the yard and like right now!" He'd pulled his thumb for the special announcement. "And I think he's mad at you cousin Arnold."

"Hell I don't give a shit John, he's pissed off at me about all the time anyway."

John had a short laugh before turning back to James.

"And how's my cousin Scarlett doin' Junior? We never get to see her anymore since you come around." He grinned. "And when I do get to see her, all she talks about is you!" His grin widened. *Shit!* I thought to myself. The news must have traveled like wildfire throughout the Radcliff clan and would surely be waiting on me the first day of school.

"Well, let's go see what he wants," James said, heading over the hill as Baby John and I tagged along.

CHAPTER 4

Good Hope

"Now you boys get on in the car!" The old man pointed before he climbed into the driver's seat. It was the first car we'd owned with air-conditioning and felt good where I sat in the backseat. But air-conditioning or not, I had no desire to be around him and even less as he dug in his shirt pocket; fumbling for his pack of cigarettes.

"Now, boys, I've decided to split the crews up for a little while. You two are goin' over to Good Hope and get ta cuttin' that big old growth timber. I'm gonna send Calvin and Freddy down to Camp Creek and get that timber ready for you boys to help load on the weekends. Bob, Mickel, John and Duck will stay right here and carry on. What . . . with three crews workin', I'd think we can make some good quick cash if we play our cards right. I'd like to put some more towards school clothes." The same old babble I thought to myself. I quickly lost all interest in what he was saying when he blew the first stream of smoke all over the dashboard.

I peered out the window, to survey all that was going on in the laydown yard. Calvin was busy with the chainsaw while Freddy made adjustments on Mr. Bill's harness. Bob and Duck were rolling pieces of wood toward the truck while Baby John sucked his thumb, and Mickel walking beside them, while rubbing his stomach. I had my doubts that much would be done without James or me being there to help them along. Bob would be the worst off, stuck with the two deadbeats who was supposed to help him. I knew that Calvin could've put all of them to work, but lately, his interest seemed to be heading south with Camp Creek on his mind. And I knew for sure he'd not take another tongue-lashing like the old man had done to us in the barn that day. It was like he was waiting for any excuse to hit the road.

"Did ya hear what I jist said, Arnold Ray?" the old man asked; maybe his second try at getting my attention.

"No! The air-conditioning's too damn loud to hear anythin' back here. And do you think you could . . . roll your winder . . . down a little? I can hardly breathe with all that damned smoke everywhere, and I gotta piss anyway." I must have sounded aggravated when he quickly got out of the car and folded the seat forward so I could get out. He scowled.

"You don't need to know anything anyway! I'll explain it all to Junior, and he can tell ya later." He was pissed at me, with smoke boiling from his mouth and nose, and slamming the door behind him.

I walked over to Freddy, who'd just finished adjusting both harnesses to his liking. And like Bob, Freddy was quick with handshake and throughout the day in passing, they'd shake again. James and I thought first thing in the morning was a plenty, with James saying he'd tell them so eventually. And one handshake a day from Baby John was more than enough. Calvin was the complete hold out and had no problem telling John he wasn't going to shake hands with a thumb sucker.

John didn't tell Calvin as he had everyone that they could kiss his ass. But he kept his distance and never did offer a handshake with Calvin even though they shared plenty of laughs together.

"Well, Freddy it sounds like me and James are gonna go to work up at Good Hope tomorrow,

"You mean nu nell me yer nads got new yobs goin' on?" The talk of more work really seemed to excite him. He rubbed his stiff chin, while into heavy thought. "Are you gonna nake any da amnals wiffou?" He sounded worried.

"I don't know. I couldn't hear over the air conditioner what his smoking mumblin' ass was sayin'." Freddy laughed at what I'd said.

"You wily non't wike yer nad new you?" His face quickly turned red with anticipation.

"No, I hate him and lied to get out of the car, sayin' I had to piss. I can tell ya, Freddy, that I wouldn't cry at that bastard's funeral that's how much I love him."

Maybe because of his speech impediment, Freddy was never quick to answer, which made him a good listener, I thought. I noticed when Calvin mentioned chickens how red Freddy's face had gotten before he snapped back at him however. Maybe in some ways, he was like the stuttering fiddle player in Kentucky who'd stop and start over. Freddy like him would wait till he calmed before making an attempt to talk at all.

I looked on past Freddy, where James had rolled his window all the way down and was shaking his head at something the old man had said.

"James'll tell us all about what's going on later, Freddy," I assured him.

To my surprise James didn't have much to say that evening when I'd returned from milking; he was anxiously rushing around to get ready and head for Scarlett's.

"I suspect that you want to know what he said Arnold but I'm really in a big hurry. I'll tell you either tonight when I get home or first thing tomorrow morning." He waved bye from the big maple and was gone in a flash.

"Well, Arnold, are you 'fishened' for the day?" I jumped back a step as Harry'd spooked me when I rounded the corner of his house. I set the milk on the edge of the porch and joined him where he sat idle in the swing. "Why . . . Arnold, it looks like you missed your ride with ole Junior there." Harry laughed, leaning all the way back in the swing. It was then I smelled a trace of moonshine on his breath with a whiff of pipe smoke. It wasn't overbearing such as beer and cigarettes on someone's breath; that being the worst smell in the world. I guess smelling it on the old man from the time I was a child had made that conclusion easy for me.

But the smell of moonshine was different from all the rest. It smelled powerful, and whereas drinking nights were long with beer, shine could put you down early if you were to misgauge its potential.

It was pretty obvious, his glassy eyes along with a chipper smile was enough to show he'd already hit the jug a few times. James and I'd seen a plenty over the years how funny people could be when trying to hide their drunkenness. It was one of our favorite games as children when the old man would leave us in the car and go into a bar somewhere.

By the time we pretended to have outrun the police and wrecked a few hundred cars, some people had started leaving the bar. We'd scramble over the front seat for a clear view out the back window, and from there we'd play our guessing game of "drunk, or not, drunk," judging everyone that left the bar.

Some were easy; they'd stand at the door, looking all around to make sure the law wasn't waiting. "Drunk," we'd proclaim. Nervously putting your hands in both pockets and pulling them back out quickly could be classified as "drunk" also. But our favorites and the ones that made us laugh the most were those who'd stop and pee on someone tires. And there were others that you couldn't really tell at all.

Once, we'd declared a person not drunk when he came out and walked a perfectly straight line—only to stagger and collapse right in the middle of the parking lot. There were many ways and means to try and hide drunkenness. But no matter how hard they tried, the first telltale was what came out of their mouths. When Harry'd asked if I was "fishened" for the day, I knew right off the bat he'd been drinking. Now how much, I couldn't say, as he had ways of hiding it also. Holding his upper partial in place with his tongue wasn't working very well, sounding as if it was too fat to fit into his mouth.

Whether drinking or not, Harry was usually a good listener most times and would show concern about one's problems. He was at the stage of just being ornery for right now, but I knew his mood could change after multiple trips to his back room.

"Arnold, I gotta get a drink. Would you like some water while I'm up?" he'd usually asked.

"No, I'm good, Harry. Thanks anyway." I chuckled, thinking how you could hardly see the difference in a plain ole glass of water compared with white lightning, only that the clearness looked to be thick, and strangely magnified.

I thought about the two women who'd come over to clean his house one time. He'd dreaded their arrival simply because he was drinking that day. He even came right out and told them they needed to come back some other time. One asked 'why' even though she must have smelled the shine when she'd intentionally got close enough to smell his breath. But they gathered their things up in a hurry and were gone in a flash when old Harry announced that he was getting ready to piss right off this front porch 'by God!' making the move to unzip his pants.

It was a sight that few people get to see in a lifetime, and I wished everyone could have been there to see it. Harry had his red long johns shirt on, which he wore at times when he drank the shine. It was wrinkled but stuffed neatly into his pants, and were held up by a set of dark gray suspenders. He'd told me on other occasions his reason for wearing them when drinking at home was that he'd be dressed for bed no matter where he went down, always with a laugh.

Harry was usually pretty happy when he drank, and no matter how riled up he'd get when ranting over something, he'd lace it with humor for a good laugh in the end. Hardly did he ever wear a hat, but tonight he wore a "gentleman's hat" as he called it.

Determined, with his sagging pipe stuck in the far corner of his mouth and smoke blinding one eye, he feverishly pulled at his zipper. I'd never in my life seen such a struggle to take a leak as he'd pick one leg up, then the other. Long drawn-out cuss words that couldn't even be spelled poured from old Harry's mouth. What I did see for as long as I could before practically falling out of the swing was his working at the long end of his red shirt, which was sticking out several inches from his zipper. He simply couldn't find hide nor hair of what he was looking for. But he finally got straightened out with a long sigh of relief peed off the porch just as he'd threatened. I could barely see by now, crying from laughter. His words matched his wobble as he made his way back to the swing. He held a hand up behind his ear while asking me to repeat everything I'd say, which I did, louder than the last.

"What'd you do, Harry, forget to put your hearing aid in?" I shouted. After making out what I'd said, he withdrew to his side of the swing.

"Oh, I don't wear that damned thang much anymore when I'm drankin the shine by-God." He smiled. After a quick swipe of his mouth with his handkerchief he let out a short laugh. He was ready to tell me why I figured, but it would have to wait until the lighting of his pipe. I'd never seen him fumble so long trying to get it lit. The match seemed frozen in place a couple of inches from the bowl. He puffed and puffed, but to no avail, till I guided his fingers to where the fire flickered over the bowl. He winked, his way of thanking me while shaking the match out.

"Why, Arnold, if I can remember to take them damned things out before I get too drunk, I'm way better off." He rolled his eyes, looking over at me. "Yeah, now that was a night out on the town all right!" And now the connection between his hearing aids and moonshine would come out.

"Why, don't ya know I went to a bar one night and had them thangs tuned in like a fancy fiddle to all that good-sounding music? I'm tellin' ya now they had some musicians at that place!" He said and all the while stabbing a stiff finger on the arm of the swing. "They hain't no doubt about it I was one of the happiest people there until everybody started laughin', cussin', and talkin' too damned loud! You know how a bunch a drunks act when they get together." He laughed, forcing a small whiff of smoke back up through the pipes bowl. "Why, don't you know, Arnold, the musicians had to turn their music up louder and louder to get above all them noisy ass people? Hell, that didn't work either!

"Shit, they all just got louder and louder, screaming back and forth. And after that, you couldn't understand any of it. I fiddled with that damned hurin' aid for the longest time, tryin' to get it to where I could just hear the music. And by hell, I finally got so drunk I couldn't remember which way was up or down on them little damned knobs. I should've known something was wrong when I took a leak at my truck, and it sounded like a cow pissin' on a hot rock. Why, I couldn't believe how loud it was, Arnold!" He roared with laughter and a solid whack to his leg. "And hell, wouldn't you know that I thought I lost my muffler on the way home till I realized I still had those thangs in my yers, and still turned up all the way. Why, I's so . . . drunk I couldn't take my hands off the steerin' wheel and a good thang at that." He said while shrugging his shoulders and pointing his pipe to the shed he kept his truck parked in.

"And, right over there, stuck halfway in that doorway, was where I spent the rest of the night, too drunk to get any farther than that." His frown tempted me to laugh. "And shit, Ida been content with sleeping there if it hadn't been for them damned frogs being so loud. But they weren't really any louder than normal. I still hadn't turned them damned hearin' aids off yet." It sounded as if old Harry had just the right buzz with the way he teasingly laid his story out to me with more to follow it sounded.

"Arnold, now laying all jokes aside, I's too drunk to find my own yers to turn them damned things off." To picture such a thing set me off with laughter, which had been Harry's intent all along. Possibly the drunkest time in his life he proclaimed. Slowly, he blew a thin line of smoke into the evening air, allowing me time to catch my breath. "But you know what I did find, Arnold?" he questioned while giving me the strangest look. "Hell, I found my nose, and I'll be damned if I didn't start pickin' the thang. And even that was loud and squishy sounding." Harry had me right where he wanted as I laughed out of control with the vivid picture of how it must have looked that night. Then without another word he got up from the swing and staggered into his house for even another shot of shine. I couldn't make out exactly what he was saying as he'd talked all the way there and back.

"So, you never did take 'em out that night, Harry?" I asked, wiping my face of sweat and tears. "It sure sounds like that was a night to remember though." I sighed.

He slowly pulled his pipe, trailing smoke from his mouth.

"Why, hell, Arnold, that wasn't the end of it! Shit, I'd been plenty happy to wake up with a week's worth a hangover, which I did. But worse than that was the sound of them crockin' frogs going off in my head, day and night. Couldn't get rid of that noise." He sniffled a couple of times, pinching his nose with a finger and thumb and wiping it on the lower part of his pant leg.

"Why . . . why, I'll bet my yers rang for a week with all that loud frog-ass snoring, Arnold." He laughed, shrugging his shoulders again like a little boy. "Now I'll bet you can guess what the hell I did first thing when I came to the next day," he reared back in the swing with a surprised look on his face. I could only imagine how quickly he must have removed the earpieces. "It ain't what you're a thanking either," he said before I could answer.

"Hell, I don't know if from bein' so drunk that I thought my nose was a shortcut to shut them damn thangs off, but I still had a finger stuffed in there when I come to. Now I can tell ya that that was as rough a week as I'd ever had, what with being hungover, frogs in my head, and hurtin' my nose from digging around, trying to find them damned hurin' aids."

I'd had lots of laughs with old Harry, but nothing like the drunkest night he'd ever been through. Our laughter lasted for quite some time when I finally dried up enough to talk. The foam in the milk bucket had settled to a solid white liquid now. It was time to get it on down to the house.

"Harry, I'm gonna run this milk down and eat. Then I'll be back up to chat a little more, if you'd like, okay?"

"Okay, Arnold. Why, do ya know what you're gonna have to eat tonight?" His curious smile told that it was more than just a question.

"I think we're havin' fried chicken, Harry." I knew what the old guy was getting at. If it wasn't too late in the evening, I'd sometimes bring him a plate of food that Mom would fix for him. And he'd already agreed that her fried chicken was the best he'd ever had.

It was almost dark by the time I made it back to his place. The crickets had started in with their relentless chirps at about the same time the lightning bugs were beginning to flare up. The smaller frogs at the pond were sounding off and would be joined later in the night by the big bulls to add bass to their harmony. It didn't look as if Harry'd moved a muscle from the time I'd been gone. One leg still crossed over the other, with his elbow resting on it, and holding his pipe at bay. But he hadn't taken his eyes off the plate of food from the time I'd stepped through his small gate.

"Mom said to enjoy it, Harry." I passed it to him as I sat down. Sometimes, he'd sit in his swing and pick away at his food; but on special occasions, such as tonight, when there was gravy, he'd eat at the table. The only thing ever in his fridge, it looked, was the milk we'd given him and a little lunch meat. He ate more cereal than anything. The women who cleaned his house once a week would bring him a meal that'd last a couple of days or so also. It didn't have to be much of anything to light up old Harry's face with anticipation.

He went straight to his fridge with his meal tonight. He'd never eat till late on nights he drank the shine, and other times depending on the severity of his condition, he wouldn't eat at all. He'd barely sat back down and with no attempt to swing.

"By God, Arnold, what you think we take that damn old truck up to the Gant house and visit with Bob and Mickel for a little while?" A rush came over me with the chance that I'd get to see her again.

It appeared that Harry was at the bottom of the jug when he came from the house upset, pulling the front door shut firmly behind him. I'd overheard him telling the old man a while back that it was about time to make a run over the mountain to Flick Jones's place. People who drank shine bragged on Flick for making the best in southern Ohio.

Love songs came quickly to mind as we walked to the old leaning garage that housed his truck. Harry owned a 1937 Chevrolet pickup that James and I'd drooled over from the first time we saw it. It took a whole weekend for us to sand and hand-paint it fire-engine red. Harry'd insisted that he be there to watch us work our magic, as he called it. He loved the new red shine and offered us a dollar apiece for the work we'd done on it.

"Why, that wasn't easy doin' all that work," he argued when we refused to take his money. James did get Harry's promise, though, that if he ever decided to sell it, he'd have first dibs on it. James, laughing and cutting up that day, stated he'd rob a bank if he had to, to pay for it. He thought that a high horsepower 327 engine would fit nicely in place of the old original one but later confessed that the truck be best left as it was.

Harry'd already declared that he thought the truck was worth at least a hundred dollars or so. He never offered to pay for any gas, reminding James to check the tank when we ran errands for him. He said he didn't know if the gas gauge worked right anymore and he couldn't remember the last time he'd put gas in the damn thing. And that was obvious when we'd tried to start it the first time. We drained what looked to be gas and joked that Harry's moonshine smelled way stronger.

I'd not once driven Harry's truck. James just wouldn't part with the steering wheel when we'd drive down to the general store at Fruitdale to pick something up for Harry, such as baccer, bread, and cereal. The old truck was a great ride whether you were the driver or the passenger. Two giant headlights perched like large lazy eyeballs at the end of long sweeping fenders. The only tricky thing about it was that the clutch didn't engage until the pedal was all the way to the floor and then some, James had added.

"Now, Arnold, you're the chauffer tonight." Harry laughed, climbing in on the passenger side. I slowly backed out of the narrow garage with only a couple of jerks. Shifting into first gear, we were on our way. "Hurry every chance you get, Arnold it might be your last!" He slapped his leg, aiming his pipe up toward the Gant house. "By God, you got 'er now!" I shifted the long rod into second gear, grinding the transmission. James had said the clutch would be the first adjustment he'd make after Harry sold it to him.

The ruts in the road I hit didn't look that deep but gave me a better understanding of how older leaf springs worked. Or, maybe I was in too much of a hurry to get to the Gant house when we both landed back into our seats. I was lucky to have the steering wheel to hang on to as poor ole Harry's arms flailed everywhere, lit pipe and all. *God, I'm drivin' like I've got my head up my ass,* I thought but quickly shrugged it off. I thought that the ride through the air would've scared the hell out of Harry, maybe even hurt him; but there he was, laughing his ass off.

"Now, Arnold, that was better than any carnival rides I've been on in a long time! But ya know that was way back in the thirties and at about the time I bought this here truck." Harry laughed and was tickled about something. "And if'n I 'member right Arnol', I think I was a drankin' that night!" He toasted his pipe towards the dash and laughed once again. Now there was no doubt about it—old Harry was lit. "Shit, Arnol' let's press on." He motioned after a loud burp, while glaring out the trucks dusty windshield.

I slightly held my head out the side window till Harry's moonshine burp had cleared out. I shook my head thinking how Harry'd gone after several drinks that evening and tipping the jug till it was empty. I'm sure the last gulp was to finish it off and was probably a doozy at that. And now it was catching up to him in a fast way. We rounded the curve at the laydown yard, where I had to slow up between the trees with one having the 'G' sign nailed to it. Once we'd cleared them, the Gant House lay at the bottom of a small hill.

"Arnol' . . ., I thought them damn headlights must a come loose back there in the field, with the way they were bouncin' all over the place. Shit! Did jou see 'em damn trees? Why they's dancin' too." He slowly pointed a thumb over his shoulder. "Did jou see 'em?" But even as big as the headlights were, they cast a short dim path. But I knew it wasn't the headlights, it was more like the white lightning was slushing around in old Harry's head. "By God this" and "by God that," he'd chattered throughout the whole ride. I could barely make his face out with the dim lights of the dashboard where he stared straight ahead.

I hadn't seen any of the things he had. If it wasn't the fact that I wanted to see her so badly, I'd more than likely have turned around and taken him back to his house at this point.

"Wake the hell up in there!" he yelled, while leaning over and tooted the horn a couple of long blasts. I slowed to a stop just a little way from the front porch. "Now by God that ought to wake 'em up!" Harry laughed, falling against the dashboard. By the time I helped him get back upright in the seat, a single lamp shed light on their gathering on the porch. Harry looked surprised or maybe confused for a second, like he'd forgot where he was even at.

"Damnit, Arnol, where'n the hell'd that bunch come from?" He pointed. Barely regaining himself, he opened his door with a bump of the shoulder and a weak grunt at best. I smiled that beyond the pear tree, they'd built an outhouse from the wood I'd gotten out of Harry's barn just for that purpose.

It only took a second before I spotted her while blocking the glare of the headlights with her hand. I wanted to leave Harry there with them and take her for a ride, a fantasy I'd been dwelling on from the time we'd left Harry's place. There were so many songs that would've been perfect for a ride with her, I thought. I wanted to touch her warm fingers again, and knowing that wouldn't have been all. With the motor idling, no one could hear my low hum. "And when I touch you, I feel happy inside . . . it's such a feelin' that, my love, I can't hide . . . I can't hide . . . You got that something . . ." I moved my lips, wishing she could read them.

Reality rushed back quickly as Harry was out of the truck and, having let go of the fender, was weaving his way to the porch. I stayed in the cab with the headlights on to shine the way for him. He staggered several steps one way, then the other before stopping just a few feet from the porch, but nowhere close to the step itself. Stopped but still wobbling, he aimed his pipe as if shooting at a target with it, saying "by God" about something or the other. He pointed it again before taking too long a step, lurched, and suddenly stumbled, falling hard onto the porch floor. He hadn't noticed or had forgotten that there was a step. He told me it'd been many a year since he'd been up to the old house. In a second, Bob and Mickel were helping him up as the womenfolk brushed the dirt off him.

Harry was fumbling around, looking for his pipe even in his pockets that he'd dropped when he'd fallen. One of the younger boys quickly retrieved it, where Harry immediately stuck it back in his mouth unlit, blowing smokeless air it looked.

It wasn't just another disappointing dream that I'd wake to when she stepped off to the side, waving for me to come in also. She stood by herself now as everyone else staggered with Harry and on into the house. With shaky fingers, I shut the headlights off and killed the engine at the same time. Out of the truck and onto the porch, I leaped, wishing it could've been higher—something more impressive for her to witness. Not that I couldn't have stopped sooner as I gently bumped into her with her hands pressed against my chest. Awkward in the way I slid my arms around her thin waist and in that brief second, I pulled her tightly to me. I wanted it to last forever with my hands tangled in her long hair. She moaned as I pulled away when I intentionally brushed her cheek against mine. There was no exaggeration that it was the softest touch I'd ever felt. There was no attempt at a kiss with my jaw locked so tightly. I thought what James had said of the reward for something you really had to work for. She giggled, sending a chill throughout me that I had made her do so. I wanted to grab her by the hand and run away to calm my every need. But it was she who gathered up the lamp in one hand before stepping on into the house that no one suspect us.

I reached to pull the door shut, finding her hand already on the doorknob as I gently placed mine over hers. Our fingers locked together, and for a short moment, we squeezed them tightly. The song "I Want to Hold Your Hand" wasn't something that I'd dream of anymore. We didn't hold hands for very long but in that brief time clasped them tightly as if to share our very souls with each other. A numbness ran through me that it wasn't just my jaw that had tightened. Maybe it was a sin the way I burned inside while looking deep into her eyes before stepping on into the living room.

There were several lamps burning throughout the kitchen and other rooms. The old familiar smell of lamp oil lingered. It was then I noticed the lantern I'd brought up to them was sitting on a piece of wood with a white cloth spread underneath it. It had to be a love memorial as I quickly looked her way, met with a smile and an assuring nod. I'd never have thought my heart could beat any faster thinking what surprises lay ahead.

The lamps were placed to shed light on a particular area or object. The scene took me back to those hard times when we had to use them. One placed at the front door with a low burning wick was to go and use the toilet or the bucket that was set out on the front porch at nights.

But with all lamps burning at one time, dark places still pooled in some places, but especially in the corners. As a child, I remembered how most unidentified noises came from such dark places. I watched the little boys thinking of myself, how they also stayed close to the lamps, it looked.

With a sudden panic, as if there may be no tomorrow, I turned slightly to face her once again. With everyone fussing to make Harry comfortable on the davenport, I'd simply do as James said—just plant one on her. I'd do it fast, and no matter if we got caught or not, the whole family would clap and cheer in the end with celebration. *What the hell am I thinkin'?*

She slowly turned towards the kitchen. *Now,* I said to myself that I only had a split second to reach out and stop her. But I was a second too late when out of the darkness, a disruptive shadow swept past as her younger sister now stood at her side while putting an arm around her waist. There could be no words in my vocabulary to explain such a disappointment. The whole scene could have been scripted right from a movie as once again we'd be denied our first kiss. I thought to what James told that it would happen in due time. But best of all was I'd not worry that she catch my stare when she glanced back over her shoulder.

She placed the brightest lamp directly in the middle of the table. And from its light we cast our eyes on each other and to all places that we might have dared before. I just knew I could kiss her at any time and she wouldn't resist me.

I sat down on the davenport opposite side of where they'd helped Harry to. The old davenport looked as if it should've been thrown away long ago, but judging by the blankets, it was also someone's bed. Bob told me how they'd covered the broken windows with boards and covered the holes in the floor, making more room for everyone. The dining room and kitchen were all in one. There was enough light that I could see beds lined along the walls in two of the bedrooms. A man with many talents it looked, Bob had built sleeping quarters for everyone. There was nothing fancy about them, but they looked cozy, I thought. The davenport faced the kitchen about fifteen feet away from the table.

"Where'n the hell's Arnol' at . . .?" Harry's words were muffled and worse he was looking right at me.

"I'm right here, Harry." I waved slowly.

"Why, how in the hell did ya get over 'ere, Arnol?" Clearly, Harry was momentarily lost about where he was at.

"Would you boys like to have some beans and corn bread with us?" Bob asked politely while surveying the pot that had been placed in the middle of the table by my girlfriend.

"No thanks," I answered. "We just ate before we come up here." Harry clumsily removed a pinch of baccer from the small pouch, forcing it into his pipe. After several tries to strike a match on his leg, and almost toppling over each time, he managed to finally get it lit. His first puff sent smoke all throughout the room and directly toward the kitchen table. He'd not asked if it was all right to smoke as the house already reeked of stale cigarette smoke anyhow. Had Harry been his sober self though, he'd have asked before lighting up and that I knew.

He was as drunk as I'd ever seen him and without his hearing aid, was in a world of his own. I raised a finger to my lips to hush him, pointing to the table where someone was going to turn thanks. The three younger kids stood at the very end, with no chairs for them to sit. And I'd not dare bow my head nor closed my eyes with her staring at me.

With sincerity that nothing be left out in her prayer the younger girl thanked God for the house they lived in and right down to the beans and corn bread they were about to partake in.

"Amen," Bob responded after she'd finished but didn't unclasp his hands for a few seconds longer looking as if he had a special request of his own. One of the young boys, and in a playful way reached for the cup that was used to dip soup beans with. Mickel slapped his hand driving it hard against the table and was quick to remind him that the people who work would be the first to get fed.

"Linda! Give me that damn cup!" Mickel barked. *Linda!* My heart throbbed as I tasted her name in my mind and on my lips. Mickel's wife quickly slid her chair back and began doling out equal portions to everyone with exception of Mickel being the first and having a full bowl to start with. It wasn't so obvious to the others when Bob slightly shook his head, more than likely to disagree with what Mickel had done.

There was no way Harry could have heard Mickel's slap and let alone the warning that followed without his hearing aid in. But he had witnessed it when he looked over at me shrugging his shoulders. The normal brightness in old Harry's face had changed. He looked rough now and was having a hard time focusing in on things including me.

"Wha, Arnol', I wonner how they'd all act if a person was to bring a big ole bag of 'tater chips up here and strew 'em out all over the floor!" He, weaved back and forth a couple times before a sloppy effort to slap his leg to justify his joke. He leaned a little too far and I got ready to grab him if he started for the floor. They'd all heard what he said with their spoons becoming quiet for the minute. I couldn't look at Linda for the time being embarrassed over what Harry had said.

The mean side of moonshine had finally caught up with old Harry. He'd never intended that anyone other than me hear his snotty remark. But he was at a disadvantage by not having his hearing aid in, to gauge how loud he was really talking.

I saw Linda look into her bowl, where she'd placed a piece of cornbread. But with the cup digging deeper and deeper into the bottom of the pot there wouldn't be much left by the time it got to her, the last to be served. I felt so sad for her that I wanted to grab her hand and make a run for the door. I wanted to take her to the Dairy Queen and buy her everything that she wanted to eat. And cap it all off with an ice cream delight of her own choosing.

I leaned back into the davenport a little farther knowing that what I really wanted was to just be alone and kiss her in the darkness. Harry looked to be getting worse by the minute however.

"Well, Harry . . ., I think it's time for us to go, I've got to get up early tomorrow." I glanced at Linda to see her reaction when she brushed her hair off to one side revealing a puckered lower lip as if asking me not to leave; what reassured me was a slight shake of her head.

"Why, hell, Arnol', we just got here, seems like?" Harry looked curiously over at me.

"Harry, I I've still got to milk." My lie put him to thinking, however.

"Now don't forget Arnold," Bob interrupted just at the right time, "we'll take you up on that offer about giving us some milk. We've got a cooler and all I've got to do is stop at Fruitdale and pick up some more ice to keep things good and cold," he smiled.

"Don't worry I'll get you some milk up here in the next couple of days." I directed my comment solely at Linda however. Harry was to the point that it looked as if he was having some difficulty with holding his head up.

"Why, hell, Arnol', I'll bet that old cow's bout ready to bust, ain't she?" He'd forgotten that I'd walked right past him with the milk earlier. But I knew he'd embarrassed everyone with his joke about the potato chips so figured I better get him away from there before he'd say something else crazy like that.

"Well, we're gonna go I guess I'll see you guys tomorrow," I said, giving Harry a hand up from the davenport where he seemed ready.

"Here, I'll open the door for you . . ." Linda rushed from the table, which got a glare from Mickel as he crumbled more cornbread up in his beans. Harry slung a clumsy arm over my shoulder as he could barely walk by now.

"I'll see you later Linda," I said in a low whisper as she walked past me to open the door.

"I'll see you later Arnold," she said close to my ear when she grabbed my hand, squeezing it tightly with all of us crammed together in the doorway. Harry was so limp that I could hold him in place and squeeze her hand for a while longer.

She quickly let go when Mickel told her to get her ass back to the table and eat, and right now he barked. Now I really wanted to say something especially with Bob giving him a mean look of his own. I looked across the way to where he sat with the pale lamp showing the deep wrinkles in his face. Linda quickly made it back to the table where in passing the lamp cast a dark wavy shadow of old Mickel on the wall.

Harry passed out before we got all the way to his house. It was just as well with my mind running wild that I'd deliver milk to her, and every day at that. I mean to 'them' I corrected myself with a devilish grin. I'd borrow Harry's truck every evening I thought as the butterflies churned in my stomach. And oh how I yearned to be her milk man, I howled out the trucks window.

I woke Harry up making him more confused than ever of his whereabouts now for sure. With some difficulty I got him to the small cot which he slept on in a back room. I picked his legs up and straightened them out then laid a thin blanket over him. And just as I'd suspected, pushed up beside his rocking chair sat the empty gallon jug. He was back to snoring before I ever left the room.

"If Bob and Mickel weren't there, I'd go back right now!" I said out loud, while sitting on the bus' step. I thought again of the look old Mickel gave me when Linda held the door open and wondered if maybe he'd seen her grab my hand. I'll go back up and wait in the trees for her to come out, she surely must be thinking the same as me. But what about Mickel's watchful eye? All of a sudden I didn't want her to get in trouble.

I smelled my hands where she'd squeezed in hopes there might still be a hint of her on them. Quickly, I jumped to my feet, thinking I should go back up and ask Mickel if her and I could take a short walk together.

"God, I'm dumb!" I said, slapping my hand down on the floor. "What in the heck's happenin' to me?" I asked myself. With my hands locked around one knee I rocking back and forth to a restless rhythm. Hours passed before I finally went to sleep. I'd wake up at times thinking she was beside me. I reminisced about the nights James had talked in his sleep and now wondered if I were doing the same.

I didn't know what time James came in but it must have been very late. I'd just finished milking, and was waiting at the Buick excited to tell him about my evening. But he'd no more than made it to his car when the old man come flying up the road with his convertible top down.

"Now your mother's got breakfast waitin', so hurry up and get on down there! We've got to get on up to Good Hope!" He commanded and all the while checking his watch. But neither of us could see the need for panic as he did.

We hurried through breakfast, with hardly any time to talk to Mom. We went back up to the barn and put the racks on the log truck, then loaded Mr. Bill. He and Kate knew something was going on as they nickered back and forth to each other. I finally had to put Kate in Red's milking stall for the time being, when she'd started circling the truck. They'd been together since we'd started logging, and not one time had they been apart. I thought about the loneliness that I'd gone through with James since he'd fallen in love and was gone all the time. I could feel for Kate, being she'd have to work and graze alone for a while when I opened the stall to let her out.

Bob walked down from the Gant house to drive the truck up to Good Hope and, after delivering Mr. Bill, he'd come back and continued working. The old man met Calvin and Freddy under the big maple tree where he gave them gas money for the trip to Camp Creek to cut the logs down there.

I expected the whistling to be intense, which it was, along with the gagging cigarette smoke; which I had every intention of demanding that he roll his window down the second he lit up. But to my surprise, he rolled it halfway and left it there.

The trip took less than an hour when he slowed and turned off at a fancy-looking gate. The terrain was practically flat compared with where we lived and sure would be considered so by Pike County standards. We'd only logged in hilly areas before, which made this all look unusual with not one valley to look down into. I didn't necessarily like being out in the open. James and I'd talked about it before, feeling exposed where people could easily see me. I held the gate open till Bob got through it then he drove to an actual cattle loading chute. Shortly after we unloaded Mr. Bill along with his harness so Bob could get back on the road again.

"Boys there's twenty-eight of these big boys to cut . . .," the old man said, pushing his hair back. James gazed while sweeping a counting finger towards the trees. "And for God's sake, don't land a tree on this farmer's cattle! Make sure that you shoo em away, Arnold Ray!" He hurriedly walked us through the large stand of black and white oaks, all giants, which he'd not lied about that. He pointed out a handful of trees that were spread about the pasture, which the owner wanted left standing to shade his cows.

"Now, boys, there's another stand of wood on down the road here apiece," he pointed. "I've got to hurry and go look at it before that bunch from Bainbridge gets over there." We unloaded the saw and gas from his car; then shortly after, he drove away.

"My God, look at these trees, James . . . I'll bet they've been here like forever! You really think your saw's even big enough to cut through 'em?" James surveyed the area once more while softly biting his lower lip.

"Truthfully Arnold I think we're in over our heads."

"Well I can tell you one thing! Even if your saw is big enough to cut through one of 'em, Mr. Bill ain't goin' to pull a twenty footer for very far, if at all. We need a team of horses to pull these. But you heard the old man, giver her a try' anyway." I did my best at mocking him. "All the years he supposedly logged you'd think he'd know better."

"I think your right about that one Arnold those are going to be real heavy for sure."

"Oh yea, for sure. Now remember when I told you James that he shouldn't sell that Farmall tractor? Well guess what? We could use it about right now, ya think"

"Sure but then what, after that? Park it in the barn again? No I think he was right that all it was doing was collecting dirt and rust. And we knew that it wouldn't be going back to Pike County ever again. Now what the money went for is another story." James slowly nodded to that fact.

"You know the only ones that would come close to these were the two that I cut over in Pike County. You remember them and all the times I kicked your ass loose from the vine sending you to the ground and on down the gully. And you sure had a well-worn path to get back up the hill if I remember right."

"You best be getting' that damned weed out of your mouth James and I mean right now cause if anybody had a path back up to the top it was you and Duck! You know that I was actin' like Spider Man on them vines. And the truth is I let go on purpose sometimes just to remember what it was like to fall."

"Give me a break, you're still full of shit Arnold." James quickly spat the weed out just in time before we both started laughing over the fact that we'd all trudged up the hill and many times at that. "That sure seems like a long time ago doesn't Arnold?" I shared with James a silent memory how we'd push off from the bank with our legs dangling to soar high over the ravine and back.

"You can let go of the vine now Arnold." James laughed, and picked his saw up, holding it up beside one of the trees. "It's going to take a while to cut one down with the size notch I'll have to take out in order for the blade to cut all the way through." He gazed up at its limbs to check the trees balance and which way it would fall. "These are all perfectly crowned trees, and none are leaning so I can land them about anywhere I want. And to think that all of Ohio used to be covered with trees like this at one time. Can you picture what it'd have been like clearing a place to farm and using a crosscut saw?"

James pulled his file from a back pocket twirling it into the air and then catching it by the handle ready to sharpen the chain.

"I gotta put a super sharpening on this cause I'm gonna need it!"

"You know, James, this is kinda like what those long-haired hippies are raisin' hell about out there in California—them giant redwoods being cut down. It's all over the news, right along with Vietnam. But their always raising hell about something anyway. Hell they're even marchin' with the blacks now!"

"Well, there's a lot to be said about all the things they march for Arnold. Some things are just wrong, and the truth is we'd never know about a lot of them if it wasn't for those hippies protesting," he pointed out.

"Hey, when you go to college, are you gonna grow your hair long and bitch about everything also?" I laughed, and meant to joke.

"I don't think I'd look right with long hair, and besides, that has nothing to do with the way you think. I mean, after all, look at how many don't have long hair but still march in protests. There's people of all ages fighting for some cause. I'd say it's a bad time for this country and way overdue for a revolution. There's things that need fixed for sure, like ending that war," He nodded.

"Well, I think it'd be easy for me to grow mine long if it wasn't a sin that is." I smiled while giving him a quizzical look.

"Why, the way you cuss, Arnold, long hair should be the least of your worries!" "And why do you think it's a sin?" He frowned.

"I guess you never paid attention to some of the old man's sermons, did you? Not just him, but most preachers. I just can't figure how you can stand up there behind the pulpit and preach against something like long hair when a picture of Jesus is hanging on the wall right behind you. His hair is hanging down past his shoulders!" A slight grin came to his face at my observation. "And worse is when he himself continually pushes his hair back when he's preaching all that hellfire and brimstone. To me some of those preachers sound like hypocrites, sayin', 'Don't let your hair send you to hell.' Don't you think it's funny how a comb run over your head a few times can wash that long-haired sin away, James? I actually thought one time how it'd be to walk into that church at Cedar Chapel with long hair and see how they'd all react. I'd bet those old women would flip out, maybe even pass out!" I laughed.

"Man, you sure look at things in a strange way, Arnold. Long hair don't make you any different than anyone else. You've got to look beyond prejudice and not condemn someone just because of their hair," he sounded as if it shouldn't even be questioned. "It's just another way to protest against the establishment and those that want everything their way and never to be questioned. Hippies are like everybody else there's good and bad in all," he finished.

"Well, I don't think Christians should condemn people with long hair. Why, some ain't any better than the very ones they're condemning! I used to get the biggest bang out of those people when they'd all gather after church to smoke cigarettes and talk about all the wickedness in the world. I'm telling you, James, you should've . . . laid that *Reader's Digest* down and listened to some of the craziness they talk about." I slammed my open hand to the ground with a heavy thump such as a preacher would on a pulpit to get my point across. "But my favorite was when old man Turner ranted about a black guy he was working with up at Hillsboro, and telling him that God was black. And can you imagine that picture of Jesus hanging up behind the pulpit being black?" I laughed. "A black Jesus with an afro as big as a washtub! You ever think, James, that maybe there's a God for every color of people in the world? It'd sure make it a lot easier for everybody, don't you think?"

"Nope, I'm sure not going to waste my time worrying about something crazy as that. It's all too complicated." I knew he'd given the subject thought however, by the way he shook his head in a confused looking way.

"Shit it's always the same old answer when the old man talks about it—that blacks have got souls but I don't think there's any doubt in his mind to the color of God," I finished.

"Well, if everybody reads the Bible like they say, then they'd know that Jesus was a Jew. And some people believe that only their race will go to heaven? You'd be wasting your time on religion if you thought that. Imagine telling Mom that she's been wasting her time all the while Arnold."

"Man, it all confuses me since I ain't read the Bible any more than I have the Reader's Digest, James. I guess I've been one of those followers all along and too dumb to know the difference in about any of it." He hesitated for a second before giving me a sharp look.

"Did you ever finish learning the Ten Commandments Arnold?"

"Almost." I shot back which set us off to laughing at about the same time. "But anything I don't understand and may need a little guidance, why I just ask daddy, I joked. But now think about this, if you're livin' right James why would you even need to know the Commandments anyway?"

"You wouldn't, he quickly answered. Look Christians are like everybody else there's good and bad with all also." James proclaimed of his own observation.

But facts didn't seem to matter much with those who were followers and satisfied with how they'd been told to live. I only wanted one miracle and mostly for my mother's sake that the old man would be saved and never backslide again. The many disappointments I'd been through with him and my endless prayers never being answered lead me to believe I'd prayed in vain all along. And I could only pray that I have the patience of my mother who would never give up on anyone or thing even to take it to the grave with her.

But you had to be careful with your complaints and not be judged as a "nonbeliever," to be cast into eternal darkness, with nothing worse than that. These threats were instilled in one's brain at a young age. I thought of the many preachers I'd heard over time who each had his way of describing the tortures of hell, with such sayings as 'never-ending hellfire and brimstone' and 'lost in darkness for eternity'! The list of threats was never-ending and had kept me scared as a young person that I might do something wrong without understanding.

"You know, I always thought Toby Wilson said it best, when he talked about color that it didn't matter in the eyes of the Lord and best not for anyone living here on earth either," James recalled.

"Yeah, I really liked ole Toby . . . I never heard him say a bad thing about anybody. And if I was around him much, I'd probably still be a Christian myself, James." A smile along with a questionable look told that James might have some doubt of what I said.

"But you know Arnold and to tell the truth, I'm going through some changes in my life right now also." He confessed. "I don't know why, but more than likely, it's my age that all of a sudden I look at things differently than I did say just two years ago. You know, just because things are established doesn't mean they're right all the time. Whether government, religion, or whatever, you should have the right to disagree. Now you tell me why a man and woman can't just live together and not be married?" I was startled thinking maybe something had gone wrong with he and Scarlett's wedding plans.

"Ha! Cause it's a sin, James, says so right in the Bible." I smiled.

"And if you don't believe in war, is it a sin to move to Canada?" he asked.

"Yeah . . . it's wrong. You'd be a draft dodger, and everyone knows that we've got to wipe Communism off the face of the earth."

"Well, at one time, Arnold, I believed that way also. But now more than ever, I side with the protesters about lots of things."

"You're shitting me, ain't ya? Why, were fightin' for freedom!" I argued.

"Hey, I agree that communism is bad, but that war isn't changing a thing. You see the score every night, a hundred or so of ours killed in one battle—and for what, when it comes right down to it? We're not winning, Arnold. It's not like all those hippies are trashy either. Some are really smart, like lawyers and doctors, and they talk about things that we don't normally hear about. We used to think that everything the old man said was true, but know we now better, right. And that's why there's starting to be more and more protests about things. You tell me why they need to cut the redwoods down? They've been there for thousands of years and the earth as we know it may not last long enough for others stand to get that old. And lately I'm kinda in to that mindset of live and let live."

"Well, believe whatever you want James but I'm going to war as soon as I get old enough' cause it's my way to get the hell oughta here!"

"Ya, well, I know we've talked about all this before. And like I told you, there are other things to do, Arnold."

"And again, like what?" I asked all impatient like. "It's a simple fact James you're smart enough to go to college. I'm not." Realizing our conversation had become fruitless and was going nowhere, James cranked the saw up then motioned for me to shoo the cows away. It looked as if they'd all gathered and were curious to what we were doing in their pasture.

I started counting backward from twenty-eight as tree after tree crashed to the ground. But not one time did James let out one of his patented Tarzan yells. He said it just didn't seem right to celebrate the end of something that had stood fast for so long. I'd never heard such thunderous crashes when massive limbs shattered, and snapping like toothpicks up under the tree's weight. Soon, he'd cut the broken limbs off.

He'd fallen a dozen or so when I asked him to cut the first log, a twenty-footer as most were before their first limb. I had to try out Mr. Bill for the old man's sake, and as luck would have it, he drove up as I was repairing the harness along with a cracked single tree that I'd laid up on the stump.

He observed the log, shaking his head in disbelief at the short distance Mr. Bill had pulled it before everything had gone haywire. He cussed a few oaths but now was satisfied that it was too much for the horse or equipment. He stayed around for the next hour or so till we'd finished for the day. He thought it'd be best if we brought two saws the next day to get the logs cut up quicker. We left Mr. Bill in the pasture with the cows that night. Bob would come up sometime in the afternoon the next day and take Mr. Bill back to our place.

The old man didn't hang around very long the next morning telling us we should be finished before noon and that he'd be there to pick us up. James cut the remainder of the trees down, where together we trimmed and cut them up into logs.

When the old man returned, he said he'd cut a deal with the sawmill that they come out and pick them up with a high-powered loading machine in a day or so. So much for the quick cash he'd planned on, I thought to myself. Not for our family's sake could I say that I enjoyed it when things went wrong for him. He was disappointed that we couldn't deliver them ourselves. The quick cash just wasn't goin' to happen.

Bob arrived shortly after three in the afternoon. The old man had been complaining all the while that he should've been there way before that. Without laying blame on any certain person, Bob explained that it'd taken longer than normal to load the truck, further explaining that from Chillicothe to Good Hope was quite a bit farther than just back to our place.

"Look, James, the old man's about ready to shit a brick." I nodded to where he and Bob stood by the truck. Bob didn't seem too happy that he had to defend his whereabouts when he spat baccer more aggressively. I was sure some of his aggravation stemmed from John and Mickel not helping out much. I'd wager that Duck mostly helped him with the loading. Putting the racks back on the truck, we loaded Mr. Bill up and with no resistance on his part. After securing the saws, we walked to the old man's car and was about to climb in when he stopped us short.

"Don't you boys want to ride back with Bob?" His question sounded more like a protest, I thought.

"No," James said quickly. "The sooner we get back the sooner I'll get to Scarlett's.

The old man's shrieking whistle came to a sudden stop with the tires squealing when they hit the pavement. From where I sat in the backseat I watched as the speedometer hit seventy miles an hour before he let off the accelerator while taking notice of a house that set off the road just a little ways. He sure seemed interested I thought and I wasn't the only one when James asked.

"Do you know who lives there?"

"No, do you?" His answer was blunt and nothing shy of a smart-ass, I thought. He pushed his hair back and looking into the mirror, where we made eye contact. There was something sinful about his quick glance in the house's direction once again. I knew he wouldn't tell us what his interest in it was— simply none of our business, as always before.

I had other things to think of as I lay down in the backseat. White clouds slowly drifting past the rear window could have been the beginning of a lover's poem, I thought. I smiled at the fact that I knew her name and had a burning desire to see her again as soon as possible.

From the time Mickel said her name I started putting poems and paintings together. I wanted to paint a field of yellow flowers with her sitting amongst them. No other girls name came to mind with Linda being the prettiest of all and echoing throughout my brain continually. I sat up quickly when the car started swerving back and forth like the old man was trying to miss something in the road. There were two boys riding their bikes straight toward us, looking as if to challenge for the right of way.

"Dad!" James sounded a warning. "Do you see those boys?" He made an attempt to grab the steering wheel as the old man slowed, while rolling his window down, and finally coasting to a stop right beside them. I figured he was gonna get on their asses good for riding so far out in the road.

But what I saw when they peered through the window left me speechless and it was impossible to swallow. I felt as if I'd been hit squarely in the stomach seeing how the two boys had lots of the old man's features. It was hard to look at them for very long after we'd made eye contact the first time. In an eerie way they resembled us. Suddenly my mind ran wild to face what I was seeing unfold in front of me.

"And where are you boys going so fast?" The old man kindly asked while climbing out of the car. And with no hesitation, he hugged them and they hugged him back. James shot me a puzzled look as a deep frown slowly chiseled across his forehead.

"So, what's that mother of your up to?" He asked the oldest, who looked to be about my age.

"She's home, cookin' up somethin' to eat," the youngest stuttered. I looked quickly towards the house that he'd pointed to, where a woman stood at a clothesline with a young girl at her side. About Bertha's age I thought.

"What in the..." I couldn't finish what I'd started to say. And James being as shocked as me made no attempt either but slowly shook his head in disbelief.

The old man motioned for the boys to follow him a ways from the car, I guess so James and I couldn't hear them talk.

"James, I don't know what to say. I, I can't believe what I'm seeing! Who the hell are those boys?" I asked, leaning half way over the seat.

"I don't know..., but I've got a pretty good idea." He frowned with deep penetrating eyes. The old man turned his hip slightly to the side trying to hide it when he reached for his wallet. I saw one of them glance our way before shoving something into his pants pocket. It was as if the old man had stabbed me in the back with what I'd just witness. With pain that only he could inflict, I had never imagined that I could hate him any more than I did already.

Not enough money for school clothes. Not enough money for my brothers and sister to have a single piece of hard tack candy. Always just the bare necessities so that my mother never have anything pretty. And lastly cheating James and me out of what he owed us. I quickly narrowed my search for place's that I wanted to bury him.

"I hate him and I wish he... were dead!" I screamed from the backseat. The three looked our way; then suddenly, the oldest started walking in our direction, mad with fists clenched. James was out the door, walking fast toward him. I guess the old man knew what the outcome would be if James got a hold of the boy. He grabbed his arm, and pulled him back a couple of steps.

I snatched the .38 pistol out from under his seat and hid it in the back floorboard. I knew how quickly he could get to it if he wanted it. I hurried to where James stood, facing the three of them. The boys looked confused and scared. Even though they were close to us in age they looked weak in their physical ability, nowhere near ours. There'd simply be no fight to it if one was to ensue. They stood behind the old man without saying a word, but there were many questions in their confused looks at one another. I wanted to hate them but I couldn't. They like us, were dumbfounded over what had transpired.

"You two get your asses back in the car and right now!" He pointed a snappy finger at us.

"You low down asshole!" James pointed a finger back at him advancing close enough that he could reach any of them, including the old man. Rarely had he ever talked to the old man like this. Seeing the bad situation at hand and without being told, the boys jumped on their bikes and took off.

"Who the fuck are those bastards?" I shouted loudly.

"Those are your half-brothers. And by God, you don't need to call 'em bastards. They're good boys!" He declared while watching them peddle towards their house.

"You sure got the bastard part right, Arnold." James glared with flaring nostrils.

"Hallelujah, Brother James!" I praised while flipping the old man the bird when he took a step in my direction. "Come on, you son of a…!" I drew my fist tight and positioned myself for the fight. "There's nothing I'd more like to do than knock your ass to the ground, you worthless asshole. You worthless son-of-a-b…!" I repeated wanting him to take a swing at me. But he made no effort and it was then and there that I knew he'd never fight me. He fully knew that I'd do what I'd promised him.

"Back to bastards . . .," James interrupted, "If they're not your real family, then I guess that makes them bas…tards! Maybe they are good bastards, but that's still what they are." James's face hardened once again. "Look up what a 'bastard' is in the dictionary, and then you tell me what those boys are, and you know the bad thing about it? Is it's not their fault that you brought them into this world while being married to our mother! And you best stop shaking you finger at me right now, or I'll break if off!" James threatened, gritting his teeth tightly. The old man now really upset took one step forward before thinking better of it, that he'd get the worst whipping of his life had he pressed on.

"Yeah, but you've got to be able to spell it to read what it means," I interrupted. "And that don't mean to just act like you know how!" I sneered. The old man backed away, unclenching his fists.

He'd always been frail with his coughing anytime he'd get worked up, and a fight just wouldn't last very long. I thought about the last time he slapped me. James was right to have held me back, something that wouldn't happen again, though, as he'd promised.

"Arnold Ray, if I ever . . . ever hear you call me a son of a bitch again . . . I'll kill you, so help me . . . ! I'll promise you that!" he threatened with a stabbing finger towards me.

"No, let me correct you about something right now. If you ever lay a hand on me again . . . I'll kill you. And if you ever hit Mom again, I'll kill you. And you can bet on that! You sorry SON OF A BITCH!" I screamed loud enough that the woman at the house scurried her kids inside. I'd invited him to back his words up as I readied myself for the fight once again.

James stepped in between us, asking a pointed question.

"How many other half brothers and sisters have we got out there, Da…d? You must have been running that whore at about the same time me and Arnold was bein' born!" he ranted. "There's really no reason to go on with this. You are what you are . . . and that in no way is a real father or at least not to this family!"

Bob downshifted the truck, stopping right behind the old man's car. Maybe it was meant to be this way before someone, other than James and me, was gonna get seriously hurt. I'd already made my mind up that I would head him off if he made any attempt to get to his gun.

"Is everythin' all right?" Bob asked, spitting out the window quickly and wiping his mouth with a red rag. "And don't tell me that new Che...vy's broke down already!" he joked.

He'd not seen the commotion going on, but his interruption came at a good time as everyone backed off from the inevitable. James, having the hardest time to back away, finally turned to where Bob sat calmly in the truck. Then he turned back to face the old man one more time.

"I think we'll take that ride with you after all, Bob, so he can go spend more time with the abominations he's made." While pointing a stiff finger toward the house, he continued, "I can't remember the last time you hugged any of us, your real family, like you did those two boys. So don't you ever waste my time again!" James hissed.

Bob could see now that there was serious troubles and started fussing with something on the dash.

"Now I told you to stop callin' them boys names, and by God, I mean it!" he shouted back in their defense.

"You're just a sorry asshole, and that's all you'll ever be!" James declared. "And Arnold's right about what'll happen if you ever hit Mom again! And you better hope that it's me who'd find out first with the threats I've heard Arnold talk about doing!" He glared for a moment before turning to climb into the truck next to me.

The old man was still standing in the middle of the road, making a half-assed effort to comb his hair as we drove around him.

"Boys, did I say the wrong thing back there?" Bob asked, shifting to a higher gear.

"Nah . . . it had nothing to do with you, Bob. The truth is you probably saved the old man from getting the hell beat out of him or even worse," James said, holding his hand out the window.

"Yeah, I could kill the bastard and not regret it at all. I just don't think I could stop beating on him once I got started. We just found out back there that we've got two half-brothers and maybe even a sister, Bob!" I sneered. Bob spit out the window, and it was then I saw in his side mirror the old man feverishly hunting for something under his seat. I wished I were there to help him find it. Self-defense I thought to myself.

Maybe seeing our loss of words for the time being Bob turned the radio on, adjusting the volume to override the loud rumbling mufflers. Favorite songs meant nothing for now as I wondered how the old man had kept his secret for so many years. Faces with no first names and was their last names Richardson. I wondered if James had thought the same yet. There wasn't much said for the rest of the trip. With all the noise inside the cab it was easy for an occasional sigh of relief. But to just collect myself for now was way better than the release of cuss words that hung on the tip of my tongue.

Kate came rushing to the fence as Bob backed the truck into the ditch to unload Mr. Bill. They were truly happy to be together again and shortly would be grazing side by side in the pasture.

"Well, I guess I'll see you boys in the morning," Bob said, as he climbed back into the truck.

"Have a good night, Bob." James waved. We watched from the barn as he drove on up toward the Gant house where the truck along with its trail of dust disappeared into the trees.

"I'm gonna go to the bus and get the milk bucket James and by the time I get finished it should be about suppertime."

"Hang on, I'll go with you, James said grabbing my arm. We've got a lot to talk about before we go down to Mom's." I gave Red her grain, and in no time, long strings of milk hit the bottom of the pal with its old familiar ring. James pulled his knife and made himself comfortable on a bale of hay situated next to a stall and with a board at eye level. I knew his carving would be something to do with Scarlett. But he didn't go after it in his normal way when it looked as if the knife needed no guidance. He looked clumsy in his effort, I thought.

In a holler where we'd cut and removed most of the trees there stood a good size Beech tree. It's smooth bark made it easy to carve on it. He'd designated it to he and Scarlett and from his first encounter with her started carving hearts with arrows and their names everywhere and plain to see. He told me that someday he'd take her there and show her his memorial of love.

"How old you think those boys looked to be, Arnold?" Red picked her leg up to remind me that I'd squeezed too hard with James's question.

"I don't know. I'd guess they're pretty damned close to our age, wouldn't you think?"

"Yeah, that's about what I figured also." I rotated the milking stool to face him.

"I guess that means he'd been runnin' around on Mom through all her pregnancies or at least three that we know of. That girl looked to be a little younger than Judy, I'd guess, from that distance. Maybe closer to Beth. I'm telling ya when that guy looked in the backseat at me, I was blown away. This is just another bad dream that there'll be no wakin' up from, James."

"No, this is not a dream it's another nightmare, Arnold. One right after another with the house burning and now this." More hurt than angry I thought when he stabbed his knife deep into the board. "I've got a hunch we'll be dealing with nightmares for the rest of our lives. Those boys up there at Good Hope have the same bloodline as us. And you'da thought he'd taken another way home and avoided us seeing them, wouldn't you?" James's anger suddenly flared. "Had they not been in the middle of the road, he'da driven right on past them. I guess the odds just wasn't in his favor this time. When I got out of that car, I had every intention of knocking that oldest one on his ass. But when we faced off, I actually felt sorry for him. The truth is they both looked pretty puny, and he didn't even hold his fists right."

"I know I thought the same thing James."

"I doubt either one's been in a fight before by the way they acted. And truthfully Ida felt bad had I hit either one of them," he confessed. "And besides, it wasn't them that I wanted to hit anyway," he said while placing a tight fist up under his chin.

"No, you're right. I thought they looked pretty wormy myself. I know that I could've whipped the both of them at one time. And I'd say by the way they took off, they knew better than to take us on."

"Well, I'm glad they left when they did, leaving that sorry asshole by himself," James concluded.

"Well, I can tell ya that when everybody was about to start swinging, I'd already made my mind up that it was the old man that I was goin' after. I'm telling you, James, it wouldn't take much right now for me to kill him." A silence fell about the barn as I continued, "And I know plenty of places where I could hide him, and he'd never be found."

"All right, hold it right there, Arnold." He waved a hand while shaking his head. "We've talked about this how many times before? There's more to consider than just him. What if you didn't get away with it? I can tell ya right now, Mom would rather put up with all her miseries than you be executed for murder or put in prison for the rest of your life! Now can you imagine the burden that would put on her Arnold?"

"I know that, James. That's why I said no one would find him."

"Okay, now think about this. Do you think he's happy right now?"

"He, as in that prick you talkin' about, James? Hell no! He's pissed off all the time. But I'll bet it's not like that up at Good Hope . . . with his other family," I puffed.

"I'll bet it's not so perfect up there either. Now think about this." James made himself more comfortable on the bale of hay. "You know that saying about you've made your bed, so sleep in it? Well, he's never made that bed up from the first time he slept in it. Must be one of the reasons he drinks, with all the torment he goes through all the time? Two families? Maybe more who knows? I know how you always wanted him to go to a real altar to get saved, and can you imagine how long that confession would last? And what Mom might hear? He's an alcoholic, so when things catch up to him, he turns to the bottle heavier than ever. Then after another long episode, he turns Christian again, until something sets him off. So it's like he's stuck in between the two and no way out. Ones as temporary as the other when it comes right down to it Arnold. There will never be happy ever after in his world and unfortunately he drug two family's down with him one way or the other.

"I'll just hate the day when mom starts bringing his ass back to life and then as always gets hurt in the end. I interrupted.

"I'd bet things up at Good Hope are pretty sour about right now also. He's sure made a mess of things. James slowly nodded. But when you talk about killing him, think that maybe he deserves what he's got to go through with. The fact is that Mom does have God on her side, and whether she ever sees relief from any of this, she has something to turn to as she's made her bed and can sleep without thoughts of wrongdoings Arnold." His long stare seemed to beg that I consider what he'd just told me, and I would as always. From the time we were little boys I'd thought James was wise when he didn't let things bother him like I did. But he really hadn't told me anything that I didn't already know. But with what I'd seen up at Good Hope would only add to the hatred that I had for the old man. But even before Good Hope my anger had festered to the point that I'd thought of places among the dead giants of Copper's Mountain for his final resting place. And there were many others but always the same with no way for me to get him there.

"Are you going to Scarlett's tonight?" I asked.

"No . . . I'm not going anywhere tonight after what we've been through today. And I'm 'bout half-sick to my stomach, to tell the truth."

"And what about Mom? We've got to tell her!" I said. James quickly sighed, choking some at the thought.

"No, we can't say a word of it, Arnold. She's brokenhearted enough with the way everything is right now anyway. I just don't know if she could handle anymore. Think of all the years he's kept this hid. I'm blown away by it. Honestly, what could be any worse than what we found out today?" James worked his knife loose from the board where he folded it shut and slid it into his pocket.

"You know exactly what Mom would do, James. She'd pray to find that place in her heart to forgive all. There's no way in hell that I could do that James. And I think as long as she keeps doing so, he'll continue to take advantage of her forever. James, there's only one way to fix this, and you know it." I'd become angry and put myself in a dark place once again. Suddenly, James's face was inches from mine when he sneered,

"Don't talk like that anymore, Arnold. From here on out, you keep those thoughts all to yourself. Do I make myself clear?" His eyes had teared up while making his point.

"Okay, I'm sorry, James. I'll not say anything more to you about it."

To our surprise, Mom seemed in high spirits when turning thanks that evening. I avoided eye contact throughout supper, thinking maybe she would see that I was hiding something. We talked for a little while after we'd eaten, but it was too hard to stay, knowing what we did.

"Well, we'll see you tomorrow, Mom." James stood up from his chair with me going to get the empty milk bucket. Mom gave us a reassuring look that she loved us, and after a kiss on the cheek and a hug, we left.

Harry sat patiently, swinging on his porch as we drove up. He waved his pipe in the air to get our attention. He hardly ever slouched, sitting upright all the time, except when on the shine of course. He looked comfortable tonight, relaxed with one leg over the top of the other.

"Boys, come on over here, and we'll have us a sit-down and chat for a while." He sounded tickled with his wording and was wasting no time in reloading his pipe. We sat on the edge of the porch, where he could see both of us at the same time.

"Well, by God, what you boys do with ole Jim? Land a tree on 'em?" He laughed, giving his leg a couple of good whacks. I thought it strange Harry saying the very thing I'd pictured in my mind more than once.

"No, Harry. If we'd a landed a tree on him, we'd be drivin' that new shiny car around!" I joked, looking over at James. Harry gave us a suspicious look as he blew a thin line of smoke into the air.

"Harry, can I use your phone to call Scarlett?" James asked while making the effort to stand up. "I'll . . . I'll just be on it for a minute or so."

"Why, you go right ahead, Junior. Use that damned thang fer as long as you need to!" He winked, stabbing his pipe toward the door.

"And you know Arnold, that damned Jim still owes me for a phone bill, by God." He reared back a little. "And hell, the damn thing is a month and a half old." Clearly, Harry was upset but still managed to joke of it.

"I know, Harry! All I can say is he's just a no-account at best." He drew his pipe to the side with a questioning look as if he'd misunderstood me.

"Now is Junior all right? He's lookin' a little pale around the gills," Harry said, casting a suspicious look at me also.

"Nope, he's not doing very good at all, Harry. Shit we found out today that the old man has got a whole other family up by Good Hope! We met them in a bad way today."

Harry drew back in his swing, clutching his chest like he'd been shot. His mouth gaped open, swinging his head back and forth with a panicked look on his face. He started scratching the back of his head, which probably didn't itch but looked more like a nervous reaction, I thought.

"Arnold, I don't know what to say other than I'm sorry and that your Mom and you've all got to go through shit like this. Your poor Mom, more grief for her to deal with." Harry's anger slipped.

"Well, we've decided we're not gonna tell her, Harry. She just don't need to know about that."

James stepped out the door, pulling it shut behind him. "Okay . . .," he said, walking to the edge of the porch, where he sat down once again.

"Did you tell her why you weren't comin' over, James?" I peered from around a support pole of the porch.

"Yeah, and she's pissed off and blown away also."

Harry had leaned forward to hear our exchange. "Did you say she got blown up?" he asked hastily, while adjusting his hearing aid.

"No, I said she's blown away from what I said." James said louder with a short laugh.

"Oh, I see." Harry leaned back into the swing. I knew he didn't understand what James meant by her being blown away. James took his knife out and started whittling on the piece of wood he'd left there a few days prior.

"Listen! Is that what I think it is?" I asked. Harry tilted his head as we all listened to the loud noise coming up the road.

"Now, I don't need this yearin' aid to know what the hell that is!" he said, stretching his neck to look around.

"There's only one truck as loud as that. It's Calvin, and he's headin' this way." I laughed."

"Oh... shit Arnold! Git up here and set with me on the swing before they gitchere. That damned Mary swings too damned fast for me! Why, sometimes I think she's gonna throw my ass all the way out into the yard somewhere!" He flinched at the thought.

Calvin shut the motor off several feet away and coasted to a stop under the big maple. As usual, Mary was slapping away on him about some rotten thing he'd said to her, we'd suspected. The door wouldn't open on Calvin's side and hadn't since he'd owned the truck. He'd told us at the laydown yard once that the door wasn't a problem unless you had to wait for a certain passenger to get out first.

"Get out, woman, so I can get the hell out of here." He started pushing on Mary, who didn't seem to be in a hurry at all. She knew that we were watching of course and was putting on a show. We all laughed, along with Harry's wheezing through his pipe as the truck rocked back and forth with the two of them waging a tug-of-war.

"Hell, this is better than the picture show." Harry applauded. It was funny, with Mary looking like she had the upper hand with Calvin at first, but she finally gave in when he got a little too physical with her. Now he meant business, and the shit was on.

"Hell, woman, it's like tryin' to move a damned big kicking-ass buffalo to get your ass out the truck!" he fumed. It was almost the same words that'd gotten him in so much trouble the last time. "I'm gonna make ya start ridin' in the back if you cain't get to movin' your ass when I need you to. Why, your ass's got about too big for the front seat anyway!" By no means was Calvin holding back to what he wanted to say. His bearded face could no longer hide his anger.

"Shit, Arnold!" Harry panicked, looking down at where I sat. I hadn't gotten to the swing in time when Mary plopped down beside Harry, making me think of the first ride she'd put him through. And once again just like before, he clung to the chain like he was going on a thrill ride. He'd uncrossed his legs and planted his feet firmly on the floor when they were swept out from under him. Mary, still angry with Calvin, had dropped the full load of her ass on the swing without slowing down. I had to laugh even after I'd looked away at how Harry's house slippers sounded like sandpaper anytime they touched the floor in passing. And once again, his long skinny fingers showing white knuckles clamped tightly to the chain, holding on for dear life.

"Harry, can you front me a pinch of smoke? Hell, I runned out a couple hours back." Mary saw the difficulty she'd made when old Harry made no effort to reach for the Prince Albert can. It was then she got the hint and slowed to a complete stop. After a long sigh of relief Harry handed Calvin the can, then immediately grasp onto the chain once again just in case it looked.

"Why, by hell, what brings you two up this way?" Harry asked as he laid his pipe on the arm of the swing with no effort for a reload. Mary with shifty eyes looked around at us realizing what she'd done, gave in so that Harry controlled the swing's speed. Calvin stuffed as much baccer into his pipe as he could, even with Harry's watchful eye.

"Why, hell! This is the big day, boys! I guess you boys being up at Good Hope all day didn't see all those banners flyin' overhead, now did gee?" He grunted, while striking a match off of his kneecap.

"What's that? That you're having a baby?" James acted all excited like; which set us all to laughing at the same time.

"Hell, they better not be a baby, Arnold Ray," Calvin threatened. I laughed right along with everybody, but there was no way I'd comment on such a thing. "No, layin' all jokes aside, boys, this is the day that old Jimbo can kiss my big hairy red ass Good By!"

Harry must have had his hearing aid set perfectly, declaring what Calvin said as being one of the funniest things he'd ever heard before, with a wink and a head shake to verify it.

"Now me and old Freddy-Heady went down to Camp Creek to start loggin' down there, day afore yesterday the same day you boys headed for Good Hope. And don't think old Freddy cain't work when he wants to, especially when I've pissed him off! We cut a lot of logs that first day. But along in the afternoon old Jimbo showed up and complainin' that we needed to tighten up and get a little more done, that was the end for me! So the old lady and *I*," Calvin said, flashing his eyes over at Mary, are headin' for Camp Creek." It was a satisfying plume of smoke that exit Calvin's mouth and quickly disappear up behind the rain gutters.

"Now you remember, Arnold Ray, when he came sneakin' up on us a while back and told us if we didn't like the way he ran things, what could we do? Well, guess what?" It sounded as if he'd bumped every tooth in his head when he shoved the pipe deep into his mouth, and grunting all the way.

"Oh, now that ain't it, Calvin!" Mary laughed. She'd been pouting over the way Calvin had acted in the truck with her. Calvin waved a finger at her with a serious look about him. I knew he'd been homesick ever since he'd talked with me about everything being paid off and that he'd saved a little money.

"Yeah, I'd like to leave too and more than ever now," I said as James shot a warning look at me. "I'd just like to get the hell away from here myself and none too soon at that."

"Well, like I said before, Arnold . . . Ray, if you want, you can come and stay with us. Can't he, Calvin?" Mary said in her usual hoarse voice. Calvin agreed with a couple hard grunts. James coughed a couple times that only I take notice with his constant hounding me over Mary.

"I appreciate it, but I think I better stay her to help Mom for as long as I can—you know, with James gone all the time and his head up his, well." I thought I'd better cool it before Calvin got started in on me.

"I'm not gone all the time," James snapped. "I do show up occasionally—to eat, you know." His comeback was perfect. We all laughed, sending Calvin into a coughing spell.

"Well, suit yourself, but you're both welcome anytime." Calvin said as he had before when he cleared his throat and spit out into the yard. "And on that note, fellers, we gotta go." He motioned for Mary to follow him, who looked as if she were ready to cry. "Why, my damned headlights quit workin' the other night, and I don't need to get pulled over by the law." He winked. Mary hugged everyone, including Harry, and I could have sworn I heard his backbone crack.

Calvin shook hands without another word. It looked as if he were holding back tears also. Maybe from the anger that'd festered in me, I couldn't show emotion but knew I'd miss both of them one way or the other.

"Calvin." Harry held the Prince Albert can out. "Now you take the rest of this can with you for the way home!" He shook what was left in the can before handing it to Calvin. Then as he had in Pike County, Calvin showed an emotional side, which was rare, when he turned and grabbed James and me at the same time, pulling us close to him.

We stood silent as they drove off, with Calvin's big hand waving goodbye. After spending day after day in the woods with hardly anyone to talk to, I knew I'd miss him more than all the others. I'd miss the way he'd go on about something and then deliver the message with some vulgarity to it. We were losing one of our best friends ever—a lonely thought that we'd ever see him again.

"Now, boys, I sure like ole Calvin . . .," Harry said. "And Mary ain't a bad sort, but I'd sure hate to wrestle with her for any amount of time, would you, boys?" he asked, slapping the side of his leg with a good whack. "Why, you know that hug she gave me seemed to help my back out some," he said, all serious-like, which got us laughing.

We talked on into the night, having several long laughs about things Calvin had done over the years. I bragged how he'd stood beside us in Pike County when the old man was siding with Bill McCoy. James and I'd continue telling our best stories about Calvin as Harry listened. About every couple days or so old Harry'd clean his pipe and had done it so long it looked like a ritual I thought. He reached down under his swing to retrieved a flat tin that he kept his pipe cleaning tools in. And in the most professional way he lined them all out on the swings arm in the order he'd use next. From scraping the bowls inside walls to taking it apart and running felt cleaners it was all done in an orderly manner. After it'd all been put back together he'd gently slid it in its hole in the swing's arm. He's do it only in the evenings and after his last smoke. He looked forward to the fresh taste of tobacco after a couple cups of coffee in the morning. After storing everything back in the tin box he stood up brushing the debris off his pants and swing.

"I'll see you boys tomorrow." He waved. Then halfway through the door, turned to thank us for taking the time to chat with him. There must have been many lonely nights when he sat in his old swing and longed for someone to talk to. I thought it a little scary, the idea of being old and all alone.

Sleep was the farthest thing on either of our minds after a day like we'd been through. On several occasions James had caught my stare when he'd been pondering for too long on certain events.

After we'd gotten ourselves an ice cold Frosty root beer he turned the radio on and broke out the deck of cards.

"So, whatcha thinkin' James?" I asked while dealing them out.

"Well to tell the truth I've come up with way more dead ends than fixes by far." He concluded. "The simple fact is there are things that are out of our control Arnold. Those boys are our half-brothers and is something we'll have to live with for the rest of our lives. Like it or not they share the same blood line as our father."

"Well you could have said all of that shit without calling him father." I protested but I knew that for the sake of argument he'd not have a comeback of any kind. And I couldn't make a joke of it with the serious look on his face.

"What would you think Arnold if I told you that I am convinced that Mom knows about the family up at Good Hope?"

"Oh, I'd say you're probably right James. I thought the same thing and not just about that incident. I've had my suspicions all along about her knowin' what really happened to the house over in Pike County. But you know how she is when it comes to talking about things like that. She'll put it in the hands of the Lord like she always does when it's too much for her to bear." I said, while pointing a single card at him.

He slowly shuffled through his cards while moving them to different places in his hand. Obviously he was in no hurry to react to what I'd said when he slid them all together and laid them on the edge of the table.

"You do know that those are the same boys who got our paddle cars many years ago, don't you?" He was sincere with his question. Suddenly I found it hard to swallow. "And that was just before Christmas." He continued. "And there was another time when I was really little I heard Mom crying and asking him where the three Teddy Bears went that Granma had sent us for presents. And that too was just before a Christmas. So I can tell you Arnold that Mom has known about them for a long, long time now.

"Man, I gotta go take a leak James! I'll be right back." I quickly dropped my cards on the table and exited the bus where I ran a ways out into the dark field before falling to me knees. Looking up into the starry night I wanted to scream as loud as I could that I wake the whole universe. James had brought back memories that had tormented me in such a way I'd blocked them from my mind and forever I'd hoped. I thought back how it was like an old friend that day when I put my hands on the paddle cars stirring wheel and just knew it was the same one I'd raced round and round our house so many times. And I couldn't have been wrong or could I. There was no dent in the one that I knew Duck had wrecked and the new paint jobs were so fresh that I could almost smell their colors. And James's look that day assured me that I was right. But beyond two young boys imagination we couldn't understand why the cars were here and not still at our house anymore.

None of it made any sense but I'd enjoy my ride all the way down the hallway where strange noises came from a bedroom. I peeped through the crack in the open door to see my father jumping up and down in a bed with a woman who wasn't my mother. Seeing what I did touched me in the strangest way so evil and wrong that I'd shut my mind off to that day. And to help me get over it I told myself they were not the same paddle cars as we'd had. These would remain in a dark place forever I'd hoped.

But now once again I'd be forced to face a cruel reality the same as my big brother. With one last look at the heavens I unclenched my fists and headed back for the bus.

Upon my return James had already flipped his cards up, showing he had absolutely nothing only a Jack high. With my shaky laugh I pointing to all his mismatches. He slowly placed his elbows up on the table with his fists doubled up under his chain while looking up at me. I stood there flipping my cards up one at a time, revealing that I didn't have much either. We joked how a queen high would've taken all the money had we bet any. My stance more than likely showed of my sudden anger. "I don't want to ever see them people again James. I want it to go back like it was before today."

"Maybe I was too young to understand back then, and maybe now I'm too old to want to." Once again anger overcame my attempt to be calm. "I really wish Ida shot him when I could've done it legally."

"It wouldn't have been legal, Arnold, to shoot him over a mule. Look, he's been covering his shit for a long time now, and we only find things out when we step in it. It's just that simple. And just when you think all the great shocks may be over, another one comes along. He simply has no shame," James finished, while pulling the curtain shut at the table. "Look we'll never see them boys again Arnold so let's stop driving ourselves crazy over it, OK?"

"So we're going to Chillicothe tomorrow," he quickly changed the subject, "to do our school shopping. And I think it best if we don't talk about any of this. After all, It'll only bring back bad memories."

"Yep, you're right, James. I'm with you on that one. But what he'd said was short-lived when the nameless boy's faces sprang to mind once more. If I never thought of them again it would be a lot easier not to drum up hatred towards them. They also were dealing with things that no one had prepared them for either, I figured. How would the old man tell them that we were their half-brothers? And would he brag on us to them saying that we were good boys also.

Thinking but not talking about them seemed best as we lay in bed with long periods of silence, broken by an occasional sigh from one of us. But try as I did to think of better things, such as holding hands with Linda, I failed. Sometime late in the night I fell asleep.

I was glad that the old man wasn't at the house the next morning. I didn't want to see him, afraid of what I might do if there was a challenge of any kind or that I might make one happen myself.

Mom told us during breakfast that she and the family were gonna walk over the mountain and visit Granma, 'on such a pretty day' she said. They'd have to be back before noon as the old man was taking them shopping for school clothes. James offered to take her but said it couldn't be today. From the first time I'd showed her the small path leading into the woods, she said that it would do her good to walk over to Granma's.

"Why, Honey, Mom might even find a piece of sang on the way." She giggled. "And I don't want you to worry about how we'll get the school shoppin' done. Jim's got the money, and I know we'll argue on how much I need for everybody. He always forgets that everyone needs shoes, and that does take a lot of money. And, Mom appreciates your offer anyway. God bless your heart." She hugged him.

She'd written Granma a letter, telling her they'd be coming over for a visit. I'd have been more than glad to run across the mountain and deliver the news myself. But she enjoyed writing letters, saying that you could put your true feelings into words that way. To Aunt Ray, Aunt Betha, and Granma, she'd write telling of her love for them. She'd never talk of hard times but instead would write about a good blessing that'd been bestowed upon her. Throughout the week, she and Judy had been singing songs that they planned to sing for our grandparents.

We watched as she and her seven other children disappeared into the forest, trailing little Joe, just five years old.

"You know, James, it's hard to believe I'm gonna shop for my own school clothes! I'd probably buy more than I needed had that jackass not cheated me out of half my money, though." I snarled, "I'm tellin' you, I'd like to kill that son of a—"

"Stop right there!" He raised a hand in front of me. "Remember, we weren't going to ruin our day by talking about him," he said, tapping softly on the steering wheel.

"Yeah, you're right, and I'm sorry . . . James. But now I've got to tell you that we better stay close together for a while. We don't know what he's thinkin' right now."

"I know, I've thought the same thing," he answered back.

"You know it'd be worth seein' the smile on Granma's face with Mom and everyone trickling out of the woods over there. I know she's always got a big one when they sing for her. And you know what the last song will be, don't you, James?"

"Sure, 'The Old Rugged Cross,' Granma's favorite." He smiled back.

"God, these are such better things to talk about, James. And do you remember what page the song was on?"

"Twenty-eight, if I remember right," he answered quickly.

"Why are we goin' this way to Chillicothe? Wouldn't it been closer to take Route 50 all the way? Just why are you takin' the long route for, James?" I teased. Without comment, he reached under the seat and pulled out a notepad that he'd sketched on and tossed it to me. On the first page was a well-drawn picture of him bent over in the most awkward looking way with his head up his ass. I laughed as he explained that anytime somebody had a problem understanding him, all he had to do was whip out the drawing and they'd understand then.

Scarlett was standing out along the road when we drove up. I had suspected it all had been planned on the phone the night before. I would have rather had the day with just James, being we never ran around much since Scarlett had come into his life. I looked at the sketch one more time and laughed before Scarlett climbed over me to get beside James.

We all sat in the front seat on the way there. I thought there was probably enough room for another person or two, being Scarlett was almost sitting on James's lap. She talked most the way there, which was all right with me. Blue denim was the thing; some of the singers on TV were wearing them, and they really looked cool, I thought. I bought a shirt that pulled over my head and laced up in front with a real deerskin cord. I never had such nice clothes in my life.

James told Scarlett to hang out with me for a few minutes so he could go to the restroom; but all the while, he was in the women's section, buying Scarlett a new dress.

"Here, Honey, this is for you." He handed her the pretty wrapped box. "But now you can't open it till we get home so Anna Fay can see it too." They kissed in the store right in front of everybody. I backed away a couple of steps to make it look like I wasn't with them. But their long kiss sent me back to the day that I should have kissed Linda and not worried about anything else, such as they weren't.

James's eyes told of his love for Scarlett and the first time I'd heard him call her Honey.

His biggest thrill was a pair of black boots that zipped up on the side with a square-cut toe. But he was right as to how soft and comfortable the boots were.

"I bought new underwear, wonderin' how a tight fit would feel, and enough outfits for four days." I joked on the way home about my tight-fitting underwear, which got Scarlett laughing; and in no time, she broke out into a song.

"Well, I've got . . . new underwear . . . and enough pants for a spare . . ." She fell apart with laughter, which was quite often, with me thinking she was plumb goofy at times. But I could understand why James loved her, though! She made it easy to be around her. There was never a dull moment, and that surely could help ease your mind when needed.

James hadn't bought as much clothes as I had. I figured the price of the dress would have been enough for another pair of pants and a shirt.

"Honey, I can't wait to see you in your new . . ." She'd been plucking at the tie strings and all the while rolling her eyes up at him. And of course, this was followed by a long kiss till I warned of a sharp curve coming up in the road.

"Can I jump in the backseat and put it on now?" She practically begged.

"No," James said as she tempted tickling his ribs.

"That's about enough!" I warned. "Scarlett, you need to get your head out of your ass so we can make it home without wreckin'."

There was a few seconds of silence before they started laughing; then she attempted to tickle me as I dove over the front seat to get to the back. It was obvious she didn't have the problems that James and I had going on in her life.

"James, you know it's only noon right now. And if we get home too early, the old man's gonna tell us that there's enough time left in the day to go and do some work."

"No problem," James answered. "Scarlett's got to model her new dress for Ezell and Anna Fay," he said while quickly rolling his eyes to meet hers. For a minute, Scarlett twisted in the seat with different postures, and showing off her modeling skills.

We'd made it to Bainbridge when Scarlett screamed, "Turn here, turn here!" She grabbed at the steering wheel as James fended her off. We stopped in front of a house, where Scarlett blew the horn until James broke her free of it.

Then like a well-planned dream, the door swung open, and a girl younger than Scarlett with long brown hair swinging at her waist came running out. She wore a short miniskirt, showing a lot of her thigh. She looked like one of the girls on *Shindig!* as she danced all the way to the car, snapping her fingers out to the sides. Scarlett no sooner opened the door than she jumped in. Maybe at my age, I thought all girls had something pretty about them; but no doubt about it, this girl was beautiful and had smiled at me.

"Who's your friend, Scarlett?" she asked, winking at me. Before I could say my own name, Scarlett blurted, "This is Arnold with the t...ight-fitting underwear!" She laughed, falling back into James's waiting arms. Her friend smiled before covering her mouth to laugh also. A slight headshake sent her long hair sliding over her shoulders to cover most of her face before she flipped it back.

"This is Jeanie, my bestest girlfriend, Arnold." I reached for a handshake when she came all the way over the seat, landing on me with hugs and a kiss on my cheek. I didn't know what to do as she moved freely on my lap. Something inside forced me to put my arm around her waist and squeeze back.

"I'm glad to meet you. I've heard so much and . . . all good." She glanced at Scarlett, and why it was so funny for them was beyond me.

"Got to go," James said. "Scarlett's got to model her new . . ." Jeanie's mouth gaped open. She was beside herself, wanting to see the present herself. "Oh, come on," she begged with a pouting lower lip, which would have been plenty good enough reason for me to let her see the gift. She slowly slid off my lap to open the car door. I couldn't look away as she adjusted her dress after it'd slid up to her panties as she got out.

"Shake your butt for 'em one time, girl!" Scarlett yelled as we drove off. It was as close a thing as I'd ever seen to *Shindig!* the way she twisted and flung her hair to the sides. I couldn't look away until she was out of sight.

"My God!" I said out loud while they laughed at me.

"We'll see if I ever introduce you to another one of my friends, mister." Scarlett sounded just like Anna Fay scolding. "You shouldn't be acting like that with her. I mean, after all, she's going steady!" Scarlett wagged her head, with hair waving everywhere.

"I didn't do anything. It was her jumping on me." I waved my hands in protest.

"Well, what do you think about her?" Scarlett turned fully in the seat to face me.

"I think she's cool," I said, looking away.

"What else?" she demanded.

"Well, she's pretty. I mean she's beautiful."

"What else?" Scarlett followed.

"Well, I never smelt anything like her in my life."

"Wind Song, it stays on your mind, just like the commercial on TV!" Scarlett teased. "What else?" She smiled.

"Well . . ."

"Well what? Just come out and say she's got a pretty set of legs on her too, and I'm jealous!" She laughed and looked at James, waiting for his remark.

"Okay! She got a pretty set of legs, she's beautiful, she can really dance, and I'm in love and even got a hard-on!" I blurted. "Now did I miss anything, Scarlett?" I was stunned at myself for saying such a thing as a "hard-on"; maybe I'd gotten too comfortable with the situation she'd put me in.

"No, you didn't miss any of it, and that's the same way her big bad-ass boyfriend feels about her too." What she'd said made James snicker as if he knew something of the matter.

"She's n-o-t available," Scarlett spelled it out. *She's beyond goofy*, I thought as James pulled her closer to him once again.

"So what else are we goin' to do to kill the rest of the day, James?" I ventured to ask. Scarlett popped up, waving a finger.

"You want to go back to Jeanie's, don't you?" she said with an all-out sexy voice.

"Yeah, let's go!" I sat up straight, eagerly rubbing my hands together. But had we gone back, maybe I'd not been as brave as I let on. And how would I act if she made a move to kiss me? Stupid thinking on my part when it should be me making any kind of move as it was well-known that it was the guy's job to do such things. Scarlett was right that I couldn't get the smell of Wind Song off my mind. While they were kissing, I smelled my shirt quickly, which could have put me into a Wind Song moment of my own making had I been alone.

Things quieted when a song came on the radio, one that I didn't listen much to, solely intended for those who had a real lover, I figured. It must have been really special to them when James swung out of the road along a little creek while he and Scarlett made out to the song. My mind drifted with violins playing, thinking how Scarlett and Jeanie were so outgoing and happy. I relived with fine detail how she'd moved around on my lap, situating herself on my uncontrollable desire. Strangers in the night . . . exchanging kisses at first sight. I ached with how badly I wished Jeanie would have done as the song said, but again, it was me who should've made the first move.

I savored how I'd intentionally laid my hand across her leg as she climbed out of the car. My heart raced as her sheepish smile forgave me. I could take this and turn it into dreams to suit as I sniffed my shirt once again.

James pulled back onto the road after the song was over. I thought of Jeanie's eyes and how pretty they were, but spoken for by someone else. *Or were they?* I wanted to question it but thought better. "Poor Side of Town" came on the radio next, sending my thoughts to the Gant house, where Linda sat in her poor, unfortunate world. She had no fancy smell about her, just the smell of soap. I thought for a second that I should buy her a dress. That would be the icing on the cake I thought to myself.

Scarlett jumped out of the car before James had completely stopped and was on her way to the house, showing Anna Fay and Carolyn her pretty wrapped box as she ran past them. Anna Fay had us all sit on the front porch to wait on Scarlett to model her new dress. The look on Scarlett's face was glowing when she finally came out and, after a twirl, ran on out into the yard as they all followed her.

"Honey, you are gorgeous!" Anna Fay exclaimed as she clapped her hands. Scarlett twirled a couple more times before falling into James's arms. I thought they'd have had to practice, the way it all fell into place and being so romantic-like. I remember James telling me how two people think the same way when they're in love. It seemed like they knew every move the other one was going to make. I thought they were acting awfully childish and then remembered how it was for me when I was looking in Linda's eyes or, even worse, knew Jeanie could have done anything with me that she wanted.

I thought about James's picture in the notebook and imagined the both of them whirling and turning with their heads in the wrong places. Anna Fay looked at me, asking, "What's so funny, mister?" I talked with Ezell, Anna Fay, and Carolyn while James and Scarlett went back into the house. After no more than a minute or so however, Anna Fay announced, "It's time to go in." Ezell frowned, rolling his eyes up at her.

"You worry too much, woman! We need to leave them kids be." Ezell stood up and headed to the house, with Anna Fay leading him by the arm. I didn't resist Carolyn's hand when she took mine. She was my young cousin, and just needing to be part of something also. We followed them to the porch, where Ezell turned to advise me.

"Don't you ever get married, Arnold Ray." And hearing what he said Anna Fay smacked him on the arm, which made a pretty loud sound. Ezell laughed, shooting me a wink.

Ezell and Anna Fay watched TV while I played cards with Carolyn. And did she have a mouth, babbling on and on about anything just for the sake of talking. Her constant chatter reminded me of Scarlett. But no matter what we talked about, her young smile never left her chubby face.

"Ah . . . um . . ." I cleared my throat. "I think it's about time to go . . . home, James." It was clear to see now the reason he came home so late. "Somebody's got to milk, and I know it ain't gonna be you!" I didn't mean for it to be funny, but they literally rolled on the floor with laughter. After I'd repeated myself, he agreed it was time to go; but even then, they dragged their kissing out longer till I wondered when they'd break it off. He and Scarlett stood on the outside of the car and went on and on with the giggling, tickling, and kissing. I was starting to get a little pissed off by now.

I reached over and tooted the horn one good blast, which scared them both with elbows and knees driving into the side of the car. It was the best laugh I'd had all day, with them trying to get at me through locked doors. And before any door would be unlocked, I made James swear to God that he wouldn't let Scarlett get at me with the threats of what she was going to do to me. Another forever kiss, then we were on our way.

"How in the hell do you and her just stand in one place with your lips mashed up against each other for so long?"

"Do you know what French-kissin' is, Arnold?" he asked.

"Of course I know what French-kissing is," I answered back. He gave me a not-so-sure look. He knew better, after all, I'd just asked him about knowing when it's the right time to kiss a girl, not that long ago.

"Are you . . . sure you know, Arnold?" He grinned.

"No, I ain't 'cause I ain't never done it," I quickly replied.

"Well, let me tell you. It's when you touch your tongue against hers." He sighed, looking over at me. "It gives you this good feeling and makes your pecker get really hard." It was as frank as he'd ever been with me. At times, he'd used a roundabout way to answer my questions. I was speechless from ignorance and lucky that a good song came on the radio as he turned the volume up. I gazed out the window, thinking about how badly I'd wanted to kiss Linda. Maybe it was hard because she'd never done it before either.

Everyone was showing off their new clothes when James and I arrived at the house. Judy told us how the old man had hurried Mom to get the shopping finished, saying that he had some pressing "business matters" to take care of.

"Did he say where it was at?" James poked a finger in my back as a warning to not get out of control.

"He said he had to check the lumbermill's measurements to make sure they were the same as his with that timber up at Good Hope," Mom answered.

Judy and Bertha showed us their new clothing, sashaying from their bedroom to the kitchen and back with every combination of skirt and blouse they could come up with. Judy asked to see our new clothes and seemed more excited than us when she went through everything we'd bought. And she loved my blue denim shirt that laced up in the front. Her face reddened, and she laughed when the new underwear fell out of the sack as she quickly put them back in. I felt sorry for her when she complained that she wished she had more money to spend on clothes, herself.

"Honey, you've got enough for a while." Mom spoke up. It was funny seeing all the boys parading around with their pant cuffs rolled up. We laughed when Larry pointed how extra-long Duck's pants were, which needed two rolls to get them off the floor. It was a big disadvantage for Larry to get his hand-me-downs from Duck, who was short-legged and stocky, while Larry was tall and thin. There was the smell of new clothes every time someone walked past.

Judy got her dresses a couple of inches above her knees. She told us how the old man went on and on about it, saying that she wasn't going to start dressing like a whore in his house. She said that he was too drunk to argue about it for long before he left, and all the while with Mom shaking her head.

"I don't think her dresses are too short," Mom remarked. "And another thing, I'm not going anywhere with him again when he's drinking, and I'd just as soon he not come around here if he's going to talk to these children like he did today."

James looked disgusted, shaking his head. It'd gotten harder to talk to Mom with so many secrets that we couldn't tell her. But like James and I'd agreed, she probably knew about most of them anyway. It did no good to keep hounding her to leave the old man. I'd tried in vain so many times to the point that I must have sounded evil in testing her faith that God would take care of her.

She changed the subject, telling of what a wonderful time they'd had at Granma's. Over the years, she'd talked of Granma's pretty smile and said how good it was to just see her for that reason. In all the pictures that hang on the walls with Grampa, in not a single one was he smiling. They looked odd in a way that regardless of how dark and faded they were, Granma was always smiling in them.

"Honey, the walk over there done Mom a lot of good. That's a pretty little path, and I might start going over there and be with them instead of trying to find a way to church every Sunday. Now that's as long as it's not lightnin' and thunderin'. Mom needs to see them while they're still here on earth as much as she can."

"Well, I'll see you all later," James said as he headed for the door.

"You're kiddin me. You're not goin' back over to Scarlett's tonight, are you?" He smiled as the screen door shut softly behind him.

I talked with Mom and Judy for a while before declaring it was time to milk and also remembered that Harry wanted to talk about something. But even better I now had to deliver some milk to the Gant house as I'd promised Bob. I told her how Bob asked that if we have any extra they'd take it.

"Why Honey we got plenty and can spare a couple quarts I'd say about every other evening. And this would be one of those evenings I thought to myself. Hastily I grabbed the bucket sitting by the back door where Mom had washed it out and put two quart jars with lids to put Bob's milk in.

"I'll walk with you to the end of the driveway, Arnold." Judy's words sounded like a sad song, in the way they faded out towards the end.

"What are you laughing for?" she asked.

"Oh nothing, I was just thinkin' about a song that Scarlett was singing today."

"Well, it sure must have been funny . . .," she teased me for a real answer.

"You'd had ta been there to understand how stupid them two act!" It was when she looked up at me that I noticed her puckered mouth like she was ready to cry. "Is there something wrong, Judy?" She pulled at a loose thread on her dress and, after a hopeless sniffle, started crying. I laid the bucket next to the mailbox, then put my arms around her, pulling her tightly to me. It was all I could do not to break down in front of her, and not even knowing what she was crying about. But this was my little sister who had really been a big one to me over the years. And now I could feel her warm tears on my neck.

"Dad was real drunk today and even had his gun on," she sobbed loudly. "Mom and him got into an argument, and he threatened to shoot her if she didn't shut the eff up. . ." She cried louder.

"Did he hit her?" My question was explosive. There was a hesitation before she answered.

"No, but I thought he was going to," she said, while taking a long needed breath. "I don't like telling you this stuff because I know how mad you get . . . and I'm afraid you'll do something bad to him someday. But I've got to tell someone. It's like he's left Mom all alone again for her to take care of everything. She pinches money to no end. And for him to treat her like that and threaten to kill her, I just can't stand it Arnold!" Tearfully, she looked down at the ground. I gently placed my fingers under her chin lifting upwards so I could see her eyes.

"I bet Granma had a good time today, didn't she?" I sighed loudly, wanting her to stop crying.

"Oh, you should have seen her, Arnold. She cried through lots of the songs, which at times me and Mom did also. We all had a good blessing, and Grampa even cried." She wiped her eyes with the tip of her collar. "I guess you don't want to talk about Dad anymore. Is that it?"

"No, I don't, Judy. And I . . . I've got to go now. So I'll see you when I bring the milk back down." I took only a couple of steps before I heard her mournful cries once again. I walked back to hug my little sister, where I quickly brushed a tear away. Maybe my way of showing my manhood was that I'd never wanted her to see me cry. She, like me, though, needed someone to turn to in a time of need; and even I would have to admit that I always felt better after a good cry. And it was better with someone else instead of by myself, as I usually was.

The picture came to mind once again of the old man hugging the two boys. I thought of what James said that you couldn't hate the boys for what they were. But I never wanted him to hug me, never again. My jaw tightened as I held Judy close.

"I'm sorry, Judy, that everythin' is so messed up. But I've really got to go now." My voice quivered.

"You really smell... good, Arnold. Have you been with a girl?" She tempted a laugh.

"Matter of fact, I have. It's a long story, but nothing became of it."

"Gosh, I wish I had the money to buy some Wind Song."

"You know about that stuff, Judy?" I sounded surprised.

"About all girls know what that perfume is. After all, it doesn't just stay on your clothes it stays on your mind. I didn't have money to buy any, but I did smell it." She giggled.

"Bye" was all I could manage, turning quickly to hide the strain on my face. I'd run a ways before turning to see her walking slowly back toward the house, using her blouse to wipe her face with. *I'll get James to buy her some when I get paid again*, I planned. *The surprise on her face will be well worth the money.* Judy was going through changes in her life like everyone else our age.

I thought how it would've been better had we never found out about the things the old man had done nor witnessed some ourselves. And James was probably right when he said there'd be more surprises to come the older we get.

Harry was waiting like always in his swing when I cleared the corner of the rickety garage. He knew I'd be there close to the same time every night and as always waved his hand like there was a chance that I wouldn't see him.

"I'll talk with you as soon as I milk, Harry!" I called out, where he nodded, blowing a thin stream of smoke into the air. I thought he looked pale and not his happy self. Many things ran through my mind as the bucket filled with warm milk. I set the full bucket down on the other side of the fence as Harry took notice of me backing up the five steps I'd need to jump it. He'd watch with excitement every time, then toast to my feat, raising his pipe high into the air.

"Well now come on over here and have a sit-down, and let's chat a while, Arnold." He patted the place where I was supposed to sit. "You know, Arnold, that shine sure kicked my ass the other night!" He sounded shocked as if it'd never happened before. "Why, I woke up feelin' bad and did all damned day long! Why, you'd think at ninety years old, you'd have enough sense to stop doin' that shit now, wouldn't you?" He reared back, laughing. But the fresh smell of recent shine told me that he'd been hitting the bottle and probably in between naps all day. He looked around like there were others to entertain, and not just me.

"Why I ain't shaved for a couple days now, as you can see . . . Now I've got to get that done real soon," he said, while looking over at me and dragging stiff fingers across his chin. "You just never know when a good-lookin' woman might come along askin' for directions how to get somewhere!" He covered his mouth to burp.

A skinny, frail hand lined with blue veins shook slightly as he removed his pipe from his toothless mouth. He'd go a couple of days before putting his teeth in after a good drinking spell. I'd seen him go through dry heaves before, and at a time like that, the last thing he needed was his false teeth in. Usually, old Harry'd drink for a couple of days or until someone would listen to his reason for doing so.

"Well, Harry, school starts tomorrow. And man, I'm ready to get out of the woods for a while," I said, thinking that a different conversation might pry into what was on his mind.

"Why, Arnold, I don't know how in the hell Jim's going to get anythin' done with that bunch he's got up there workin' right now! And, don't you know I think that ole Baby John's thumb must be dryin' up on him a little!" Harry looked all concerned.

"And why is that, Harry?" I had to laugh knowing that whether he was drinking or not something witty would come from his mouth.

"Why hell Arnold, he never gets filled up sucking on that thang all day long. Now I've never seen anyone, especially a grown man, go after a thumb like that! Why, Arnold, I think there's somethin' real wrong with him and in the head I mean." He slowly stabbed his pipe towards his forehead.

"Harry, you don't know the half of it." I said.

"And that old Mickel is about as worthless as tits on a boar hog, if someone were to ask me. Why, I think *I* could outwork him, Arnold, even after I've laid out with a good-lookin' woman all night!" He laughed while raising a leg into the air.

"Why, Jim took me up there with him the other day, and all I saw that Mickel do was stand around and rub his gut and fart like a fat mule." Harry turned, quickly while hanging onto the swing's chain. "I don't know how in the hell a body could get so much gas in it." He frowned. "Why, I never heard the likes! And for someone that don't even have an ass to speak of!" It sounded as if the moonshine had started to kick in.

"But on the other hand, Arnold them two little ole gals up there ain't that bad-lookin' now, are they?" Harry relaxed himself somewhat. But I didn't think he remembered the night he wanted to throw potato chips on their floor to watch them all fight over them.

The swing slowed to a point that I thought old Harry was going to call it a night. But when he hacked and spit off the side of the porch, I knew that he had more to say. Turning to face me once again and with the most serious look, he'd suddenly become upset.

"Why, don't you know that, that damned Jim told me he had to watch you and Junior to make sure you don't get all knotted up with them gals? Why, Arnold, he said all they'd wanted to do was get knocked up so's to have him support 'em for the rest of their lives!"

"That low-rent son of a…!" I interrupted, jumping from the swing. *So this is what Harry really wanted to talk about,* I fumed.

"Harry, did he really say that?" I demanded. Harry pointed his pipe toward the sky for a split second.

"So help me God, Arnold, that's what the man said. Sittin right here beside me!" I bit my tongue a little too hard, angry with what I'd heard.

"Why, you should've seen the way he acted when that pretty little girl asked him if he wanted a cold drink of water! Why, she's just a youngin!"

"What an asshole!" I whirled. Harry ducked his head as if someone had thrown something at him. "It'd be a cold day in hell before he'd ever support me and my wife, and he don't really support me now. And I sure don't need him makin' plans about who I'm going to marry either! He's the luckiest person in the world to have someone like Mom who's put up with him all this time."

"And that's another thing, Arnold, why he's sure is a fine one to talk! Why, you'd think havin' a person like your mom he'd be satisfied, but hell no! Jim runs with the sleaziest people he can find. Hell, I can spot trash a mile away and know to stay shy of 'em, but he goes for 'em like a damned vulture goin' after a dead animal." Harry's frown thickened. "Why you know how trash attracts trash." He nodded in a knowingly way.

Harry was rightfully upset. I knew he thought the world of Mom, and I'm sure it pissed him off every time the old man headed out with some of the trashy people he had spoken of. It was a conflict for ole Harry, who loved music and to frolic throughout the night but had no other way to get there and knowing all too well what to expect of the old man.

"Well, Harry, I guess I better get this milk on down to Mom's." Harry noticed the two quarts jars that I'd laid off to the side but said nothing of them up to this point.

"Arnol are those for baby John to stick his thumbs in when he's runnin' a little low?" Harry reared with laughter knowing that I'd have to answer him. My plan was to ask Harry if I could borrow his truck long enough to run the milk up to the Gant house. But what if he wanted to go along for the ride and it end up like the last time?

Simply put I wanted to go by myself. I wanted each fleeting moment to be mine and hers alone with no disruptions this time. Maybe I should wait until he goes to bed and then drive up. He told me many times that I could use it and didn't matter that I had no driver's licenses cause he didn't either.

"Bob asked that if we had any extra milk he'd be more than glad to take it." I said while pacing back and forth on the porch. Maybe Harry could see that I wanted to be alone to deliver the milk when he stood up and still a little wobbly said. "By God, Arnold, you take that damned truck and run that milk up to that little gal before it gets too late! And you have a good day tomorrow ya hear me now?"

He made an attempt to pull his pants up a little as he went to turn the porch light on. I gathered the bucket of milk along with the two quarts and put them in Harry's truck.

Then I stopped at the corner of the garage to take a leak. He couldn't see me in the darkness as I watched him make his way back to the swing once again. He'd smoke one more bowl in the dim porch light before going to bed. I stood a while longer, tempted to join him once again, thinking of his loneliness. I knew the day would come that his swing would blow in the wind without him.

At ninety years young, as he'd said his age was, his stories were unlimited and kept me fascinated, glued to a different time in life. Somewhat older than the old-timers at Willow Springs, he also told of better times; the good old days they'd talk of in their tall tales. But at some point, their private stories would be lost forever unless people such as I had the opportunity to pass them on. Would the farm in Pike County be the good old days I'd talk of when I sat on a bench somewhere hoping that some young person would be fascinated enough to capture my faraway look?

Whiskey Holler, where Harry was born, lay just beyond the hilly range that could be seen from his front porch. I thought it might be a good picture for James to paint of old Harry sitting calmly in his swing, pipe in mouth, and shadowed by the small dim light.

I hopped in the old Chevy and while sliding my foot along the floorboard I pushed the starter knob. There was excitement as I'd never felt before when

I slowly backed out from the leaning garage. I'd take milk to Mom's first and then on to the Gant house with some for them. Everyone with the exception of Mom came running out of the house to see me in Harry's truck. They all wanted to go for a ride but I told them it would have to be on some other day.

Judy's smiled and understood my hurry to leave. After Duck got the milk out from the passenger's side I quickly put the truck in reverse and backed from the driveway. And as if I weren't nervous enough every bump in the road seemed to unsettle my stomach to the point I had to pull over at the edge of the field to take a final pee.

After rounding the curve at the laydown yard I pushed the clutch to the floor; coasting to a stop just a little ways from the house. There was no one in sight other than Bob and Mickel sitting on the porch's edge with their feet planted firmly on the ground.

It looked as if they were feuding over something with several feet separating them. Neither had their shirts on and where Bob showed muscles in his arms and chest old Mickel was flabby with loose skin hanging everywhere. It was easy to see that something wasn't right with no one else around and the quietness inside the house.

I closed my door behind me but before I got the milk out from the other side Bob came to greet me. With his always earnest hand shake and a friendly smile he ask me to walk to the back of the truck with him. I was dumbfounded as to what was going on. I glanced at Mickel with a cigarette hanging from his mouth making no attempt to clear the smoke; clouding one eye. He looked rough I thought and it was then I saw the half empty bottle of whiskey pulled up next to him.

"Arnold there's some crazy things goin' on and I don't feel at liberty to talk much about um right now." Bob said in a low tone.

I could see over his shoulder that Mickel was heading our way with his bottle in hand. He staggered to where we stood.

"Did Bob tell ya old buddy?

"Tell me what Mick?" I shot back thinking whatever was going on must be between Mickel and me.

"That you ain't got no reason to come up here anymore. That laydown yard is as far as you need to go." His answer was snotty while aiming his whiskey bottle towards the laydown yard. "And we don't need milk delivery I'll pick it up at Harry's place myself!"

"You stupid bastard," Bob raged when he quickly grabbed Mickel's arm spinning him to where they faced each other.

"What the hell'd you call me?" Mickel said while holding the bottle in a cocked position. Bob quickly released his grip from Mickel's arm then he took a step towards the truck removing the plug of baccer from his mouth; placing it on the rear fender. After wiping his mouth clean with the palm of his hand he turned to face Mickel once again.

"Now Mick I'm tellin' you this one time and one time only. You turn around and head your ass towards the house and don't stop walkin' till you're on the other side of that damned door down there." He pointed a commanding finger and with his eyebrows pushed upwards. "And if you say a word between here and there I'll do what I promised before Arnold ever got here. And you better not start any commotion in there either!!"

I saw a side of Bob that I wouldn't want to be on the receiving end of. Stern in the way he was braced, not to protect himself from Mickel but to deliver a blow it looked. Large veins had swollen in his forearms from tight held fists, and there was a wild look in Bob's eyes a feature that I'd not seen before either.

At first I thought Mickel was going to use the bottle on Bob but instead turned it up with a gulping swig and a little running out the side of his mouth. Bob held back on what he was going to tell me until Mickel had gone into the house.

"Damn Bob what in the hell is goin' on? Has old Mick finally lost it?" I snickered; lost to what the problem was really all about.

"Well Arnold let's just say that I've had about enough of him. He's smokin' and drinkin' himself to death and everybody is tired of bein' around it. And think about this. He's jealous of you when it comes to Linda. That's what this whole problem is about. You wouldn't believe how he's been acting towards her lately! He's sick! And I'm goin' ta fix it one way or the other.

"I'll take what you got for milk right now buddy. But I'd like to hold up on it for a while until I get this mess straightened out; then we'll talk about it some more. It's just not worth the trouble right now. But by-God things are goin' to change around here one way or the other!" He walked back to the fender to retrieve his wad of baccer and after a few hard chews spit a couple times. He didn't seem nervous about the ordeal but I figured he needed a minute to regain himself.

"Why hell Arnold, I know how you and Linda feel about each other. It was obvious from the first day, what with that faraway look you both had. But now comes the problem. Mickel is a sick person and I'm not just talking about his physical condition, as if that ain't enough. And it's been going on for a while now but something's come loose up there in that head of his!"

"Well thanks Bob for tellin' me about all this but you know I can take care of Mickel on my own." Bob put an open hand on my should while giving it a slight squeeze.

"I know you can Arnold Ray but that wouldn't fix what's going on around here." Suddenly there was commotion coming from in the house and Bob turned quick to walk away. "I'll see you later Arnold Ray."

I'd no sooner pulled the truck back into the rickety garage and closed the door when I heard the Buick coming down the road. I hadn't expected James back this early. I waved in the darkness till his headlights captured me when he flashed his low beams.

"I guess you wanted a little extra sleep tonight before school tomorrow?" I asked after I'd opened his door for him.

"Nope. Anna Fay seemed to think that Scarlett needs to get to bed early, and that she needed to get her beauty sleep for the first day of school." He was clearly disappointed.

Mom agreed with Anna Fay when we sat down to eat, saying that it was time to think about other things now. Judy smiled from across the table. She'd told me at the backdoor that the cry she'd shared with me relieved a lot of the frustrations that'd built up in her and for some time at that.

In a moment of hate I stared at the old man's vacant place at the table thinking how he might be seated at a different one and with a different family. James had looked my way more than once and more than likely read my mind.

Mom asked me to turn thanks, which I hadn't done for a long time and was certainly out of practice. But the words came, like a repeat of prayers that I'd said many times before. I tried to shuffle words in ways that didn't sound like the old man would have. It was hard to thank God for anything when my mother was being treated the way she was. The fact was, I wanted to blame it all on God. *He should have fixed it by now*, I thought. Mom had given the Lord her soul, and what did she get in return? *The sorriest person on the face of the earth*, I concluded.

"Amen," I finished.

"Amen," Mom repeated.

We stayed a while longer after we'd finished supper as Mom helped the boys lay their clothes out for the first day of school, something Judy and Bertha had done long before.

CHAPTER 5

The New School

My plan of a good night's sleep just wasn't happening, hopeless with so much craziness going through my mind and what lay ahead in just a few hours from now. Making the track team was just one of many things that plagued my thoughts and had set me to worrying. I certainly couldn't depend on good grades to show what I'd call a real talent.

More panic set in that I'd be assigned to a front-row seat, where everyone could see the back of my head! I just couldn't handle that. And would I be able to talk to girls any easier now that I'd had short encounters with Linda, Jeanie, and Scarlett?

James had long since fallen asleep, comfortable in the way he breathed as though he hadn't a worry in the world. He had all the things that I needed to do likewise, a soft hand to hold, eyes to look deep into, and a pretty smile to kiss when needed. And lastly to be smart enough that he didn't have to depend on a sport for any kind of notoriety.

I needed a destination with a halfway mark to point out as how much farther it was to my lover's house. I could only imagine James's dream of Scarlett when she glided out the front door, wearing the pretty blue dress he'd bought for her. And which kiss of so many had he lingered on before falling asleep.

God, if I only had such distraction, I could be sleeping like him right now, I thought to myself. And now I could understand much better his reasoning to see Scarlett all the time. Only she could help funnel his problems away with a plan of a future.

And how could things have gotten so messed up and spiraled out of control and so quickly I thought? *It didn't seem that long ago that all I needed was a patch of tall grasses to lie in and nap my troubles away.* The smell of Jeanie's perfume suddenly came rushing to my mind, and oh . . . how her timed moves had numbed me as I'd never felt before. It was intentional when I brushed her leg with my hand followed by a deep desire that I wanted more. *I . . . . want!*

Why, that low-down....! My thought suddenly shattered, flashing on what the old man had told Harry that he wasn't going to support James or me if we knocked a girl up. No way in hell would either of us ever ask him for a dime's worth of support anyway. And he couldn't even call it by its real name; he had to make it sound dirty and disgusting referring to it as "knocked up." My eyes were wide open now as I fumed at the thought. I quietly climbed out of bed but careful not to wake James. It was all I could do not to cuss out loud, wondering which way he'd referred to it with that woman up at Good Hope.

"He knocked her up, three times!" I whispered, gritting my teeth with the thought.

Maybe Rebel could sense I was awake when he came scratching on the bus's door. Most times, he'd come up from the house whenever a storm was brewing at nights and lay in the bus's floor until morning. But there was no storm tonight other than what was brewing in my head. Shirtless and in a pair of cutoff blue jeans, I tied the last shoestring on the new tennis shoes I'd bought.

It wouldn't be a run in the dark, with the way the bright moon cast its silvery shine on everything. At two o'clock in the morning, it hung directly overhead like a giant lightbulb in the sky. Rebel led the way as we galloped down the road, where several times he roused a rabbit, chasing it but only to return for a pat on the head.

"Rebel, stop!" I commanded. We stood at the top of the hill looking down into the valley where the covered bridge straddled a narrow gorge. It looked as if clouds had fallen from above and flowed into the confines of the gorge itself. It was brilliant with the way the moonlight shone on it like a long white snakes winding all throughout the valleys and its tributaries.

I'd never seen anything like it before. James's description of something such as this "picturesque" fit the scene perfectly, I thought. I'd ran to the old covered bridge and back plenty of times, but never this late in the night, never seeing it like this. The flow of its thick cool mist lay just beneath the bridge and halfway up the sycamore trees that lined both sides of the bank all captured in the ghostly looking fog.

"This would be a great place for a horror movie, Rebel," I said. "Maybe a vampire would live up there in the rafters and sweep down on people crossing the bridge in the fog." A slight chill ran up my backbone as I tried to coax Rebel to go in first. But he never had nor ever would cross a bridge—period, even in the daytime. His wagging tail was the last thing to disappear as he went over the bank and into the mist. But in a couple of minutes, he stood at the entrance on the other side, shaking water from his coat.

A scary movie couldn't have portrayed it any better as long streaks of moonlight shinned through the many gaps in the bridges wall. And so with each they flashed across my eyes blinding me for a split second. Had anything touched me I would have shit my pants for sure. I counted twenty eight such places before I stopped and sat down right in the middle of the bridge.

Maybe something spiritual would descend on me like when all those hippies sat in a "circle" holding hands and chanting. But they'd "got their minds right," as they called it. The old man said they were out of their minds and on 'mariwoney' as he called it. But not one time did I ever see them act in any way other than happy after smoking it which also showed in their eyes, I thought.

James said many times how the old man was wrong in his judgment against all hippies or anything else as far as that went. I crossed my legs and thought how this would be the perfect place to chant with no one around. So I did, like a foreign language that seemed to mean nothing.

I thought about how one of the older hippies said you had to be "connected" in order to get the right meaning, however. I thought too how it sounded at church with everyone praying so loud that you couldn't make hide nor hair of what any were saying. A different kind of a spiritual blessing, I'd assume.

It all led me to believe that if the old man would make it to heaven, it shouldn't be a problem for me compared to all his wrongdoings. I laughed out loud at the thought as Rebel looked curiously into the dark tunnel.

Fog started rising up through the floor as I stood back up, brushing off my butt. But anything spiritual I might have found inside the dark bridge quickly faded when I thought of the exchange of money between the old man and the two boys. All the bad things he'd done suddenly flooded my mind quickly overwhelming me with anger. And there was another lingering thought to add to them. How would I deal with old Mickel? I just couldn't go for very long without seeing Linda. I was pissed off now to the point of rage. *Why not?* I thought. *There's no one around.*

I let go a terrible oath where my screams sounded as if trapped in the confines of the bridge. They'd go no farther than the walls and quickly to disappear up into the bridges heavy oak rafters. It wasn't the first time my outburst of anger had deafened me for a short period of time. But as always my hearing would return once again with the sound of rushing water just below me.

The hoot from an owl started back up again, and a dog barked a ways off. My bad thoughts would continue however. "Many young prayers," I continued to unload, "could have been answered with just one piece of hardtack candy!" I refused to let a tear run down my face quickly wiping it off my cheek.

"And poor Judy Ann doesn't have near enough clothes to make the whole year." I stormed, while pacing back and forth the full length of the bridge. And just when I thought I'd considered everything I froze in my tracks. Which family did the old man consider as bastard? I felt weak in my legs as to what the answer might be. I took a deep breath of the night's misty air knowing that I couldn't keep carrying on like this. I just had to calm down.

"Okay, stop right here." I held my hands out into the darkness as though James was standing right in front of me. "Shit!" I shouted when suddenly the dog's barking had gotten closer. My shouts of anger had escaped the confines of the bridge after all when Rebel's ears perked when he turned quickly where a flashlight beamed from down the road away. I'd aroused more than just a dog.

"Come on. Let's go, boy!" I slapped the side of my leg before taking off into a full sprint running for all I was worth and splashing gravel with every steep. I fought back tears the best I could feeling as if I'd not accomplished anything at the bridge. "I won't cry it'll do no damned good anyway," I kept telling myself with every driven step of the way. Maybe it was in her plan that at times like this her words would flood my tired mind, 'Honey, it's okay to cry.' And as plain as day the words rushed to mind as I slowed my pace before I collapsed up along a fencerow where I'd cry my heart out with no reason to fight it any longer.

Rebel came from where he'd crossed the creek a ways up the road, wagging his tail and giving a gentle lick to my hand before we pressed on. I felt peaceful and calm at last. I sat on the Buick's fender, wiping my eyes once more before going back into the bus, where shortly after I fell asleep.

I'd no sooner started with the milking the next morning when Red slowly lifted her leg as a warning that I stop thinking about last night's events. I'd told James how I couldn't sleep and had made the trip and how I'd expelled my anger just a little ways down the road.

"Well, it's all under the bridge for now!" he joked. I thought again about having someone or something to turn to in times of need. He said I looked kinda tired and suggested that I leave all my problems behind so they not interfere with my first day of school.

"Now I think we should get to school a little early so we'll have time to find where all our classes are at," I suggested. I didn't want to tell him that I was afraid I wouldn't get there in time for a back row seat.

"Don't worry about that there'll be plenty of time, Arnold. So don't get yourself all worked up!" He laughed at how nervous I'd suddenly become.

I poured some water in the wash pan and, with a soapy facecloth, washed my face and underarms. I put on my best outfit, the one I'd picked especially for this day—the blue lace-up denim shirt, which seemed to look even better than the day before, I thought. James sat in the bus's driver's seat combing his hair. From the small mirror at the bottom of the windshield he surveyed with fine detail that every hair be in its proper place.

"Hey, James, you'll comb it a few more times before we get to school. So don't worry about it right now!" He never acknowledged me as he turned his head to the side for a different view. My patience had worn thin by now. I mopped my hair down with my open hand and gave a quick glance in the mirror. I could've stood there all day combing it, but it'd still look the same when the sun would go down.

"Well, I'm gonna run down to the house, so I'll see you when you get there."

"Okay, okay . . .," he replied. "I'll be there shortly." He answered.

I'd covered about half the distance when I heard the Buick start up. He took off slowly to not spill the bucket of milk I'd placed in the floorboard. But now the race was on as I started running as fast as I could, thinking the big biscuit might be at stake, if he were to beat me there. I jumped a fence that ran along the road when the Buick rumbled past. I knew that if I was gonna beat him, I'd have to take a shortcut through the edge of the cornfield.

I saw him turn at the driveway from out of the corner of my eye. I couldn't slow down any now, even if it meant falling to the ground, best shirt and all. It'd be close. He slid to a stop blocking my pathway to the kitchen. But he still had to get out of the car, and that gave me just enough time to slide over the hood and beat him to the back door. I was out of breath, needing a minute, before I could say that I'd smoked his and the Buick's ass also. I got what was left of the milk a lot having splashed into the floor.

Everyone was all smiles, wearing their favorite outfit. Duck and the boys were walking back and forth from the kitchen to the far bedroom, showing off their new shoes and seeing who could make the most noise, it sounded.

"Now that's a sound you don't get to hear very often around here, new shoes hitting the floor," Duck said while the other boys stepped aside for him to pass.

"Six pairs of new shoes clicking on a hardwood floor!" James laughed. Duck stopped just long enough to do a little tap dance of his own, which got a favorable clap from all of us.

"Time to eat," Mom said after she'd removed the last pan of biscuits from the oven. She prayed, thanking the Lord for everything he'd bestowed upon us and especially that everyone had clothes to start school with. Even with murky clouds outside, she declared it a beautiful day.

"Now get busy. The bus'll be here in a few minutes," she warned once again.

Judy looked so pretty wearing what she'd picked for her first day, a blue short-sleeved dress that was a little more than two inches above her knee and a thin white blouse with flowers around the collar that she'd sewn on herself. I thought she looked perfect with her shiny gold hair brushed down and turned up on the ends with lots of bounce. All this along with a perfect smile, assured her of a great day, I thought.

The showing off of clothes and joking around ended quickly when Bertha shouted from the window that the bus was coming down the road. And with her leading the way and holding little Joe's hand, as she'd promised, they poured out the front door, making their way to the end of the driveway. Mom mentioned that for the first time, she wouldn't have anyone at home with her now that little Joe was starting school.

She got the best tickle that they'd be going to Buckskin School, the very place she'd gone as a young girl herself. She said it was a long ride from where they lived over on Lower Twin Road and just a few miles up from Bourneville. But then with a gleam in her eye and a smile that matched she told how she and Aunt Betha would bounce up and down in their seats all the way to school. Her giggle sounded like that of a little girl I thought when she recounted that the least little bump would send them high into the air.

"Honey, that's where Mom lived when your Dad came by one day, ridin' on a big white horse," she said, looking out the window as the bus drove away. "Your Mom was in the eighth grade that year," she said, shaking her head, a little regretful, I thought.

"You'd probably had a better life if he'd a just kept on ridin', Mom," I said matter-of-factly. She turned slowly to face the three of us.

"Why, Honey, if I hadn't married your Dad, I wouldn't have any of you'uns!" There was no doubt that she was sincere with what she said. I wasn't going to upset her with talk of the old man as she still had high hopes of God's will.

Judy told us that she'd like to ride with us for the first day if it was okay. She said she'd probably ride the bus most of the time, but with us on occasion. James didn't blink an eye, assuring her that she could ride with us anytime she wanted. But just to mess with her I said that every day that she rode with us she'd have to give us her lunch money.

I reminded James again that I wanted to get there a little early to find my homeroom.

"Honey, you're not scared, are you?" Mom asked.

"I'm not afraid of anythin'." I swelled my chest. Mom was the first to laugh, then Judy and finally James. She reassured us that she'd done the paperwork to let the school know that we'd be going there this year.

"Okay, let's go . . . !" James finally said. I quickly wiped a bead of sweat from my chin, which he might have noticed.

We'd no more than made it to Harry's place when Bob flagged us over; standing at the gate with Big Red.

"Well I got them kids on the bus so now I'm heading for Chillicothe with that load there," he pointed. I supposed that Linda rode the bus also and then would go onto Greenfield from there. The idea hit me that she could ride with us, and Mickel need to know nothing of it. "But the real reason I wanted to stop you was to tell you that Baby John quit; bragging that he had a score to settle; babbling on and on about a drag race. I've often wondered about that boy." Bob smiled. I guess by the way we all sat there and with other things on our minds no one spoke on Baby John's behalf pretty well showed that it wasn't a great loss.

"I don't even know if Jim knows about it or not," Bob went on to say.

"Well, Bob," James sighed, "it is what it is."

Once again, he turned the radio on as we headed for McClain High School in Greenfield. From the moment we'd left Bob standing along the road, we sang along with every tune with rhythm and good vibrations. Not one time did he have to turn the channel to find a better AM station!

We'd never sung in the car with Judy, with her voice ringing out loud and clear. "You Can't Hurry Love" by the Supremes played in its entirety as we snapped our fingers and danced with our shoulders as we barreled on down the road. I thought about the weekend James and I had gone cruising at Greenfield, where everyone was listening to their radios turned up as loud as they could go.

I was as high as a kite when we flew past the Greenfield City Limit sign, when the song "Time Won't let Me" lit up the radio. I was doing a fine job of outdoing both of them on that particular song when James, without me noticing, turned it down quickly, leaving me singing to everyone walking down the sidewalks.

"Asshole!" I hissed, sliding down into my seat a little. He and Judy laughed, agreeing that I sounded better with loud music to drown me out some.

We gathered at a door, where many others stood waiting for it to be unlocked from inside. I'd never been among so many people at one place, nothing like the comforts of being in the woods. I was feeling uncomfortable with no room to move as more squeezed in behind us.

"I'll meet you at the board!" several people yelled back and forth.

"That board'll tell us where our classes are at," James managed to say before the loud commotion got worse as the doors finally sprang open. And whether we wanted to or not, we were being swept through the narrow opening and on into a wide hallway.

"This is a madhouse!" James shouted as other doors flew open with more and more students pouring in quickly, scattering in all directions. And if the confusion wasn't bad enough, yells, screams, and incredible loud whistles came from everywhere in hopes of locating someone. It mustn't have looked any better than a mob scene with everyone acting crazy, inching forward a little at a time. Even with no idea of where we'd end up, I was starting to enjoy the craziness of such chaos, and experiencing a taste of something new.

Sweet perfumes trailed girls as they squeezed past. I never knew there were so many wonderful smells. Wind Song put a smile on my face in passing, thinking of Jeanie's short skirt and all. And best of all, I didn't need to shy away when it came to looking at girls' legs with such pandemonium going on everywhere. And I wasn't alone by any means, as boys whistled and some being out right vulgar with their comments about certain girls. I had no need to do either. I just wanted to take in as much as I could.

There were lots of miniskirts as short as Jeanie's, and if there'd been such a thing as a leg gauge to register my sinful thoughts, I'd a been hell bound for sure with so many flocking around me.

I'd come face-to-face with a girl somewhat taller than me. No matter which way she or I sidestepped, we couldn't get past each other.

"Crazy," she said of our weird dance that'd gotten us nowhere. She put her arms around my shoulders, making a slight spin that put us on our separate ways. I had the split second to notice her leather skirt riding high above her knees. But the waltz would continue throughout the hallways, which I'd taken advantage of in my not-so-shy ways for now.

Like movies I'd seen on TV, some girls were slapping their boyfriends for looking where they shouldn't. And like Willow Springs, it looked as if most pretty girls were already taken, and you certainly didn't want to get caught looking at them by their boyfriends.

Pushed up against the wall and moving slower than the mainstream were the plain Jane girls, too scared to get in the mix of things, it looked. They dressed in ways that they'd never get whistled at, other than a joke, with their hair done up in old-fashioned ways so as not to be sexy or attractive. They just looked too Christian with everything going on all around me. Feeling bad that I'd labeled them as such, I glanced back at Judy, who was all smiles. She was about as Christian as anyone could be but still wanted to look attractive.

I'd been more or less following James with Judy struggling a few steps behind me.

"You're telling me all this confusion is to find your name on that bulletin board?" I pointed. "Look, Judy, there's our names right down there together with our assigned classrooms." The quick survey however showed that we'd only have one class together.

Several teachers had started mulling through the crowds when I overheard one tell a girl, who had a lot of boys gathered around her, that her dress didn't 'meet the code'. There was a loud roar, however, from the guys, showing their disapproval of what she'd said.

"I'm blown away by all the art and sculptures in this place," James surveyed. "It's unbelievable." He took time to study a few pieces that we could get close enough to.

I pointed a finger to a marble stairway, where two large sculptures of Roman soldiers guarded it with spears in hand. A sign sat at the entryway stating Seniors Only. It was a privileged shortcut to the second floor, it looked. We waited with envy until James came back down from his trip.

"Cool stairway," he said with a final rub of the polished handrail. "Okay, I'm going to go find my homeroom right now," he said, pushing himself into the crowd once again.

There was cheering and celebration when boyfriends found out that they'd be sharing classes with their girlfriends. I thought about James and Scarlett as people kissed, hanging all over each other right in front of everybody. The same teacher that'd complained about the girl with the short dress broke up several serious kisses taking place.

"Now this . . . is not the time nor the place!" She waved a finger in front of their faces. She repeated herself when the guy acted like he couldn't hear her, by placing his hands up over both ears. The gesture alone made me laugh.

Math was the only class that Judy and I would be in together. It would be different not having her when I needed help. She and James were right that I could do it if I'd apply myself more. It was simple. If I wanted to go out for track and show my real talent, I'd have to get the grades on my own.

I knew there'd come the time when I'd have to confess that I'd failed a grade and Judy had caught up with me. I couldn't use Judy's original idea that we were twins as I clearly looked older than her now. I couldn't use the excuse that I'd missed so many days that year because of the old man when James and Judy had passed. I could only hate the person who'd caused my misfortunes or at least put the blame on them. There was simply too much going on to allow dread to enter my thoughts right now.

"I'm sure glad Mom sent those papers enrolling us. Can you imagine how crazy this would be if she hadn't done that?" Judy laughed.

"I can't imagine it," I answered. "Well, Judy, I guess it's about time for us to go on our separate ways. Look at where the hands are on that big clock over there. We're about out of time." I pointed. She puckered her lips and rolled her eyes up at me as if saying it'll be alright. I watched as she disappeared into the maze of people, same as James had done.

I thought the place had been pretty chaotic until a loud bell rang throughout the hallways, silencing everything for an instant. It seemed to shake my insides, and now I was part of the mad scramble to get to a homeroom. Through all the pushing and shoving, I felt someone grab my arm for a second, turning just in time to see Judy pointing across the hallway to where my homeroom was located.

"I know where it's at, Judy," I said before she vanished once again. I'd already been heading that way, but I guess she still worried about me.

People started disappearing in all directions and with last-minute kisses and hands that just couldn't seem to let go. I stood at the entryway of room 208, turning for one last look, hoping that Judy made it to her room in time.

Other than a lot fewer people, the classroom wasn't much better than what I'd left in the halls, with noise and such carrying on. A plain piece of paper with your name lay on top of the teachers desk, and showing where your assigned seat was located.

"Oh . . . man!" A guy frowned with a big mouth and lips to match, disgusted and complained of his seat assignment. "I don't want to have to sit across from your ass all year!" he threatened a guy before letting the paper glide back down on the desk.

"Well then, see if you can switch out with someone, bitch," the person advised. "I'm really not crazy about being around you either when you fall asleep and start snoring like a fat hog!" I thought there was gonna be a fight right off the bat as the guy stood up, sizing himself to the big-lipped guy.

"Hey, I'll put my money on big lips!" someone shouted from across the room.

"I'll take care of you as soon as I finish off this future dropout!" He pointed a threatening finger at the other guy. Then out of the blue, they started faking punches like they were fighting in slow motion; and after a few seconds, they sat down and started talking of other things. They were friends, just full of shit, I figured. There were only a few seats left as I worked my way toward the back of the class. As if my prayer had been answered, a desk in the back row would be my place for the year.

"Okay! Okay! Let's all quiet down now! You've had all summer to scream and act crazy," the teacher warned with a smile. "It's time for science to start!" After the threat, he walked to his desk as the noise continued. "Now!" he suddenly thundered, which hushed everyone up immediately.

I'd noticed there were two other students who had not been talking to anyone before the teacher had come into the room. I figured that they also must be new at this school. The fellow sitting in front of me immediately raised his hand and was waving it like mad in the air. The teacher took notice of him several times while he was talking to the class but seemed to ignored him.

"I think all of you know me, except for the new students." He'd already spotted us off the bat with his coal dark eyes. "My name is Mr. Toll." Several of the kids and including the guy in front of me, stood up clapping their hands and cheered. I'd never seen anything quite like this as they shouted loudly.

"Coach! Coach! Coach!" they cheered. No one would ever dare do anything like this at Willow Springs. It appeared that none of these guys were bashful at all. After they all sat back down, the guy in front of me started waving his hand into the air more vigorously than ever. Mr. Toll sat on the corner of his desk, something he'd done often, it looked, while making himself more comfortable. He'd looked at me and the other new students several times.

"I'd like everyone to introduce yourselves to our new pupils." Then the same ones who'd done all the clapping for Mr. Toll stood up at the same time and started telling their names, trying to talk over one another, which got the whole class roaring with laughter.

"Okay . . .," Mr. Toll said, waving both hands in the air and smiling as if he should have expected this from them. "You boys are going to be kids all your life, aren't you? Now sit down, and let's start in the front row with Lana." She must be pretty popular, I thought, by the way they all hooted and hollered when she stood up.

"I think everyone already knows me except for the new students." All the guys cheered once more, making her blush. "You guys don't know me that well." She smiled. "Anyway, I'm Lana Petty, and welcome to our school. And if I can help you in any way, please let me know." She waved at each us before taking a bow, then sat back down.

Her speech was perfect, I thought, and could only wish that mine would be half that good. I took another long breath, waiting my turn as everyone clapped for her. *I can't stutter about who I am*, I thought while trying to relax. I simply couldn't be lazy with my accent, thinking these people might never let me live it down.

I'd be the first of the new students to introduce myself as my turn grew ever so near. People who were pretty well-known simply stated their names and sat back down. It was good to see an occasional shy person fiddling with their hands or tugging on their clothes. Mr. Toll had to stop one of the vo-ag boys who started reciting who he was and how he'd gotten there from the day he was born.

It would appear that they were all in a contest to see who could get the most attention. But knowing them all too well, Mr. Toll pointed them out by name and said they could introduce themselves better in the hallway after class, which got a laugh from everyone. Then after a lot of commotion on their part, he let them go on with their introductions, but this time with a finger shake and a threat.

I'd not expected so much pressure on my first day, but how hard could it be to just introduce myself? Oh my God, I thought, these boys who razzed everyone wore the same jackets: Future Farmers of America. I immediately broke out into a sweat, thinking what they'd do with a name like Arnold. Farmers and pigs ran hand in hand, and they'd all know me as Arnold the pig. The laughter would surely bring the ceiling down on everyone. The room went dead quiet, not even a shuffle of feet as I stood up.

"My name is Arnold Richardson, and I just moved up here over the summer from Willow Springs." I'd done well to not show my nervousness even though my legs felt weak when one of the boys asked if Willow Springs was in America. "Hillbilly" came from a far corner of the room, which I ignored the best I could. But most knew the whereabouts of Willow Springs, with Mr. Toll knowing the coach, and named off several basketball players from there.

"Richardson . . .," he repeated a couple of times before I sat back down. I said nothing of Mr. Boyd, thinking he might have heard about my run-in with him. I was happy in the way I'd not messed up and become the laughingstock of the whole class' other than being red-faced, I'd not stuttered throughout the ordeal. Mr. Toll sighed loudly after the last introduction.

"Yes, Steve, what do you want, or should I guess?" He sounded impatient.

"Mr. Toll, I've really got to use the bathroom in the worst way, and my arm is about worn-out trying to get your attention," he said. I found myself laughing with everyone else, including the teacher who'd turned his head to the side to hide his all-out grin.

"Steve, I'll give you a break since it's the first day of school. But you know not to try this again tomorrow, right?" He'd made his point clear.

"Oh yes, sir," he answered, moving quickly on his way out the door.

"Now I'd like to know what everyone did with their time off this summer," Mr. Toll said, settling himself on the corner of his desk once again. He pointed his finger randomly and asked each person to stand up and give an accounting of their summer. *How could I ever survive this?* I thought to myself.

There was a girl who'd spent the summer in France. I could tell by her clothes that her parents must have money, wearing a long dress that only showed her ankles. A couple of the boys went into coughing spells as she went on about going to the top of the Eiffel Tower and seeing all of Paris, which she pronounced in French as 'Paree'. Mr. Toll gave them a stern look when one guy interrupted her.

"I climbed a real tall tree the other day and could see all of Washington Court House!" Everyone, including the teacher, had to laugh at his, joke however. But the girl, whose name was Vicki, didn't allow any of the harassment to bother her. She continued on to the other places she'd visited that summer. I'd pretty well figured my turn was at hand when his dark sweeping eyes settled in on me.

"And . . . what about you, Mr. Richardson?" He dabbed a finger in my direction. "Did you just lay around all summer and do nothing like these boys?" He pointed a circling finger that took in the rowdy bunch. There was plenty of protesting from them, however.

I froze the second I stood up, with my jaw tightening to what I would say. It would be embarrassing to tell them that I was a mule skinner and that my whole summer consisted of following a mule's and horse's ass around in the woods all day. I thought about lying for a second, rubbing my callused hands on my pant legs before grinding to a stop.

"We own a farm down on Cliff Run Road," I said, giving in somewhat to my hillbilly accent. A guy wearing real thick glasses who'd introduced himself as Gene laughed and blurted out,

"I didn't think there was a place flat enough to farm down there." He challenged, and looking around at all his rowdy friends. "And what grows down 'ere in them'er hills?" Gene went on to ask. I stood motionless, slowly drawing a deep breath. He'd already sized me up as being a hillbilly, I figured.

"Well, I spent a lot of time working on our potato patch." Now everyone, including the vo-ag boys, was looking at me with interest. "We plant 'em around the side of the hill so that when harvest time comes, all ya gotta do is dig a hole at the bottom of the hill, and they all run out and fall right into your buckets!" At that, everyone started laughing, with the vo-ag guys clapping their hands with loud approval.

I felt a calmness come over me with my witty joke. I guess no one had read about the hillbilly farmer in the *Reader's Digest*, which I wouldn't have if James hadn't read it to me one time at the springs. I'd told the tale without stuttering, saving myself from embarrassment.

"Very good, Mr. Richardson." Mr. Toll applauded. I'd overcome fear, an achievement of my own, with no help from anyone. Over the years, James and Judy had prepped me for this very day, it would appear. It had taken a long time for them to get their message across—that all I had to do was apply myself. I pictured them introducing themselves in their classes, with all the confidence in the world. They had the smarts and the talk to back it up. I knew that James could simply say that he was a hillbilly and work from that and have all their attention in no time.

I was excited to meet up with Judy in our math class and tell her all about my newly felt confidence. We talked right up till the teacher quieted everyone down. She'd made several friends, introducing them to me after class. Even the fear of being asked why we were in the same grade was less now.

And there was no reason to try and explain things in such fine detail. People weren't dumb, and I knew that without question they could figure me out.

I didn't need to blame the old man for my misfortune. It just wasn't necessary anymore. And now I could laugh about it and joke if needed at how much better "retained" sounded than "failure." Judy told me one time that "retained" didn't mean "forever" whereas "failure" might. I had moved on after being "temporarily retained" and wanted to succeed on my own more than ever. I didn't need to run to the hills and hide when I was pressured about something such as pointing at someone or calling a bust a 'head of some famous Roman'.

The girl who corrected me laughed along with her friends but said it was cool the way I'd said it.

I had several of the vo-ag guys in each of my classes throughout the day. But there were too many to remember all their names yet. It was the last two periods of the day, when I'd be with all of them at one time. Gene had told me that our teacher wouldn't be there the first day. The substitute didn't have much to say other than for us to find something to do out in the shop and no roughhousing. I met many others that I didn't share classes with and listened as they talked, mostly about how their crops had faired that year.

I avoided any talk that might lead up to the acreage we were growing, which was nothing. But if cornered, I'd have to fall back on our Baccer crop in Pike County. It sounded like whoever farmed the most corn had the best bragging rights. But regardless how small the farm, neither Cliff Run nor Pike County could come close to the hundreds of acres these guys farmed.

Where I could stand on top of the mountain in Pike County and see our whole 120 acres, there were fields up around here that would dwarf it. Even to add the two places together netted three hundred acres, still way shy of farms around here it sounded. Three hundred acres of corn and that much more in soybeans wasn't uncommon in their eyes.

They told about driving new International Harvesters that would pick twice as much corn as their old ones. My mind drifted around the sudden fact that we weren't farmers at all with our big garden and a two-acre baccer crop. I knew at some point, I'd have to admit to what we really did for a living. We were nothing more than pulpwooders after all.

They'd never understand what log surfing was all about. The difference between the two cultures was huge, separated only by a few miles. Folks were poorer and for sure less educated not too far the south of here. It was where the hill country began separating the flat farms of the north from the steep hardwood forests running all the way south to the Ohio River. But regardless of our divisions, I'd make whatever adjustments I'd need to become part of this new environment. I thought of the girl and the sparkle in her eyes knowing that no one had seen Paris other than her.

It'd been a good day and enlightened me about a lot of things that I'd dreaded before. The last bell of the day sounded, with everyone scrambling around the same as they had that morning. James had given fair warning that we didn't have time to bullshit with anyone after school. He'd give us a ride to the house but complained that it would put him behind a little to go visit Scarlett.

It would have been hard to tell who talked the most on the way home that evening, Judy or I. James said it'd been a great day for him, but clearly, his thoughts were elsewhere.

"Hurry up, James! You're wasting time," I said when he dropped us off at the driveway. "And to think that someday we'll be acting just like that, Judy." I laughed, waving bye as he sped off.

"I don't think so." She laughed, shaking her head slightly.

From Buckskin, it would take the bus over an hour to get to our place, putting us home before the rest. Mom sounded like a schoolgirl herself as she asked how our day had gone and was visibly tickled waiting for the others. After the short visit, I grabbed the milk bucket and had no sooner gotten out the back door when Judy asked if she could go along with me. There was plenty to talk about as I pressed her to stay up with me.

Harry sat quietly in his swing at his usual spot. I'd not ambushed him many times that he'd not seen me as soon as I cleared the old rickety garage. He pulled his pipe, looking concerned, and then laid it down on the arm of his swing.

"Why, Arnold Ray, where in the world did you find such a pretty thang as that?" He stood up and swept an open hand, offering Judy his seat.

"Hi, Harry." She waved and smiled.

"Now don't tell me you're gonna start doin' the milkin' since old Arnold's fallin' in love with that gal up at the Gant house?" he teased, sitting down after Judy had taken her place. Judy quickly looked over at me as a slow smile spread across her face.

"No, I just thought I'd come along. We've been talking about our first day of school, Harry."

"Why, you know, I don't think ole Junior retained much of anything the way he flew past here a few minutes ago. Why, I never seen such a cloud of dust! It pertineer run me back into the house. I think he's still got his head . . ." Harry stopped short with a couple of hard coughs.

"Up his ass . . . I'll finish it for ya, Harry," I said.

"Yeah." He coughed once more. I thought it cool how old Harry could talk, drink, and bullshit with the best but would become the perfect gentlemen when he needed to. Even the way he held his pipe at bay from Judy showed his respect toward a female.

"Well, Harry, we're goin' to get the milkin' done. And we'll stop by on the way back." I nodded.

"Why, that won't take long. I never seen the likes of the way he milks," Harry said, nodding at Judy. "Have you ever watched 'em, Judy Ann?" He laughed, slowly crossing one leg over the other, surely pleased that we'd stop by again before pressing on to the house.

Judy got a big bang out of watching Red running toward the barn; slinging milk from her tits. She said it reminded her of the first time we ever got a cow and my first attempt at milking, which made her laugh even harder.

"See? Milking ain't so hard, Judy. Why, all one's gotta do is get the bucket under her and just let it drain out. Would you like to give it a whirl?" I joked, knowing that she wouldn't. The three big fat cats that'd started living in the barn since I'd started milking there swarmed around Judy's feet, rubbing up against her legs. I squirted a stream close to her shoes, with perfect accuracy so as not to get any on her. The cats rushed to the spot, licking the warm milk from the board.

"Watch this, Judy." I shot milk to several other places, which kept the cats running back and forth, trying to keep up.

"Poor old cats," she sympathized.

"Oh, I don't do that very often, Judy." Then I hit one squarely between the eyes with a good shot. On seeing that I certainly did take aim she shook a warning finger at me. *If she only knew the half of it*, I thought.

"Well, it sure sounds like you had a good first day at school, Arnold. I mean neither James nor I could get a word in edgewise on the way home," she stated matter-of-factly, and putting her hands on her hips.

"That's crazy Judy. I couldn't get a word in edgewise with the way you carried on." I laughed as she made a couple of steps my way, waving a finger of protest. I'd churned the milk into foam, where it ran down the side of the bucket. I'd need a minute to let it settle before finishing. I walked to the small dust-covered window carrying a small tin pan filled with milk for the cats.

"Can you believe I had everyone laughin' in homeroom this mornin'? Imagine that!" I said, rearranging the stool under my butt. "I really didn't expect to say a word to anyone. I thought I'd just be deaf and dumb, but instead, I think I talked all day . . . to different people." I glanced at her with a quick smile. "And I got to say, this might be the best day at school I ever had in my life. Hell, I even had shoes to wear!" I joked as we broke into laughter.

"I know!" She giggled. "You're repeating yourself. Remember I did ride home with you guys."

"OK, enough about me. Tell me more about *your* day." I said and started milking once again.

"Well, I had a good day too and think I might've found a boyfriend already!"

I whirled around quickly just as she'd expected, of course. She'd crossed her arms and was patting a foot on the ground with anticipation.

"You did what?" I snickered.

"It's no big deal, Arnold. I had boys talking to me all day. Some were good guys, and others were just stupid, if you know what I mean." I motioned for her to stop talking.

"Hold it right there," I said in a calm voice. "You're too young to start actin' like James, Judy."

"Well, you're just a little over a year older than me, Arnold!" she said, putting her hands back on her hips, this time in protest. I thought she looked and acted more like a little girl than her age right now, though.

"I'll bet you've never even kissed a boy yet. You're just too young to know about things like that." I squeezed the last of the milk from Red.

"Well, sure I've kissed a boy!" she said. Red's quick reminder made me let go of her tit. "Have you kissed anyone yet like, uh, like the girl at the . . . Gant house?" She pointed in the direction.

"Well, God, of course I've kissed!" I said, sliding the bucket from under Red. It was easy to have lied to her, I figured. She'd never know the difference. All I had to do was put words to the fantasies I'd had over and over again with Linda. But if she and James would ever talk, she'd know better. "No, I haven't kissed a girl before," I blurted. "But I've come real close." There was silence for a minute. I'd become angry and embarrassed. Without looking at her, I asked whom she'd kissed.

"Well, let's see. I kissed Bill Whiley . . ." I whirled quickly to face her once again.

"You've got to be shittin' me! I beat the hell out of him that one time because of what he was saying he wanted to do to you . . . and what do you do? You end up kissing him? Damnit!" I said loudly, which sent Red heading for the doorway. "La . . . Look! Now you've got Red all riled up, Judy."

"Well, I'm not the one cussing and raising hell," she said, stomping a foot on the ground.

"I cain't believe you just said 'hell,' Judy."

"Well, I'm used to hearing you say it daylight till dark, so why shouldn't I?"

"That's really a poor excuse and a piss-poor one at that, Judy. So try somethin' a little more real! You can't blame your filthy mouth on me," I said, shaking my finger at her as a thin smile came to her face.

"You know, Arnold, you probably wouldn't cuss like you do had you not been around Dad's filthy mouth all the time." Her smile widened.

"All right." I swallowed hard. "I get the picture, so you don't need to say anymore."

"Arnold! You just need to ca...lm down a little," she expelled. "I said I kissed him once, and that was all!" she said in a stern voice. "It was my first kiss, if that's what you'd called it. It lasted a split second with our lips barely touching. I can't really say it amounted to much, to tell the truth. I've never kissed anyone since, so I don't guess I'm an expert at it myself." She laughed.

"Well, at least you did kiss someone!" I hurriedly grabbed the milk pail up and walked out the door, and leaving her in the darkness. "But damn it, someday I . . . will!"

269

"Oh, I know you will," she said, running to catch up with me. "I was pointing you out to my new girlfriend today, and she thought you were really cute."

"She thought I was cute?" I said in a sarcastic way.

"Well, what's wrong with that?" she asked.

"'Handsome' is what a man wants to hear, not 'cute! I can't even imagine what a cute mule skinner would look like. They don't make such a thang, Judy."

"Oh . . . ! So now you think you're a man?" She giggled, stopping me in my tracks.

"Look! You don't need to turn into a jackass like James." I turned to face her.

She gave me a hurtful look making me feel stupid for what I'd said. It wasn't her that was acting like a jackass as I'd accused. It was me, and it was nothing shy of jealousy on my part to think my younger sister had been kissed and I hadn't yet. Waiting for each other to say something, our stare dissolved into spontaneous laughter.

"It's like James tells me, Judy, when I get all concerned that I ain't had a kiss yet. If he's told me once, he's told me a hundred times that it's not the end of the world. And a minute later, what's he talk about? Lip-locks lasting for hours."

Before I could finish, she quickly hugged me. "I love you, Arnold, and someday we'll talk about this very time and have a good laugh about how dumb we were back then. Our day will come, just you wait and see." She smiled all eager-like.

We sat with Harry, and with admiration in his eyes, it was obvious that he was eager to chat with Judy. I was simply old news, it would appear, but that was okay with me just watching them laugh and cut up as Judy seemed to be having a good time of it.

"Now, Judy," Harry said, sitting up more erect and looking her straight in the eye. "I was wondering what it'd take for you to just play one song for me on my piano, just one," he humbly requested. I'd seen the smile many times at church when she stood up to walk to the piano.

"Why, it won't take anything, Harry. I'd be more than glad to play a song or two for you."

Harry looked like a long-lost sinner making his way to the altar the way he headed for his music room. He'd not taken the time to unload his pipe of spent baccer but instead bumped it a couple times against the side of the house when Judy turned to following him.

"My gosh, this sure is a beautiful piano, Harry!" she said; slowly running her fingers the length of the keyboard. With all the politeness in the world, Harry slid the stool up under her as she sat down. Harry's music room had only one purpose, and that was to play music in with no audience. A few wooden chairs lined the walls with no arms that might get in the way of picking strings. I grabbed a couple for me and Harry; but before I got very far, he intercepted one, dragging and positioning it to sit right beside Judy. But that was understandable as he'd been around plenty at honky-tonks and just wanted to watch her fingers move up and down the keyboard, I'd guess. I positioned myself on the other side of her.

She dropped her fingers to the keys, making the most God-awful sound, I thought. For a minute, I thought old Harry's piano must be out of tune.

"Now by God, that's pretty good, Arnold," Harry declared, while shaking his head in my direction. Judy smiled at me, and along with a wink. I was as shocked as Harry when she pushed eight keys and with all blending together. Harry didn't move as she played and sang song after song and just for him.

I couldn't see old Harry's face all the time, but instead watched his shoe and with its perfect rhythm told me how much he was enjoying himself of the whole affair. Some were little sassy jigs with a lot of pep to them while others tended to show how beautiful her voice really was. I guess it was expected that he'd wipe his eyes a few times throughout her concert. I thought she was finished as her finger slowly ran the full length of the keyboard when suddenly she started banging something out that didn't have a Christian beat to it at all. But Harry seemed to recognize it right off the bat, removing his pipe; and in no time, the old guy at ninety years old danced about the room with perfect steps. I had to laugh thinking he'd start shouting just any minute now.

Harry offered her money for her performance, saying he'd be more than glad to pay her to come up once a week and play for him and more often if she wanted. She'd not take the money but had to promise she'd play again for him at some point and sooner than later. She also took it upon herself to say that she and Mom would come up together and sing for him. Harry was beside himself with such an offer, telling me that I could come up and get the truck to deliver them back and forth. He'd said it before. I guess time had just slipped away, I thought.

We left Harry in his swing with a smile that'd last on into the night. Judy insisted on helping carry the milk home. So with her on one side of the handle and me on the other, we walked on down the road, talking more of experiences that we hadn't had yet.

I lay in bed in the bus that night, thinking how nice it was talking to my little sister, who wasn't that little anymore. I thought it was good that she'd confide in me when she needed to. She was a young lady now, with expected needs like anyone else her age, I figured. I wondered what the girl looked like that thought I was cute. "Cute" just wasn't the way I wanted to think of myself as I fell asleep.

I hadn't heard James come in that night when the alarm went off the next morning, interrupting one of several dreams I'd had throughout the night. I sprang from the bed and landed squarely on the floor and started to sing, "I want to hold your ha...nd . . . I want to hold your ha...nd!"

"God! I sound as good as the Beatles." I laughed, snapping my fingers. He'd barely moved through all the commotion other than telling me to shut the hell up, which I didn't.

I'd finished with the milking and had just cleared the corner of the barn when I noticed James pacing back and forth at the Buick. It looked as if he were acting a part out, pleading with words and hand movements of frustration. I walked on to Harry's hand pump to act as if I was going to strain the milk but instead snuck to a corner at the porch for a better view of him.

Over and over, he repeated the same thing, which I couldn't quite make out. But each time, he seemed more exaggerated than the last in his explanations. It couldn't have been anything about our first day of school; he would've already told me something. It simply wasn't the way James acted, which could only mean one thing—it was something to do with he and Scarlett.

Were they breaking up, and would I finally get my way and not have to explain the family tree at school anytime it came up? I should be jumping up and down with excitement, but I wasn't. I felt weak-kneed seeing my big brother and best friend suffering with something that seemed hard even for him to come to grips with. I slowly backed around the corner to where I could peep and he couldn't see me. I felt sorrow for him and guilt on my part, thinking back to the last time I'd raised holy hell about him and Scarlett being related. But the real truth was that it was me that had a problem with it more than anyone else. Even Mom said that in the eyes of the Lord, there was nothing wrong with them being together.

Maybe I'd been too harsh with my reasoning, playing along with the rest that his head had disappeared somewhere. I almost laughed out loud, thinking of the cartooned drawing he'd showed me on the way to Scarlett's house that day.

I couldn't be mad at Scarlett either; she was so much fun to be around, as James had figured out a long time ago. "Cousin" had become something poisonous in my brain when referring to her however. I picked the bucket up and coughed a couple of times as a warning of my approach. I walked over to where he was leaning up against the Buick.

"Well, I guess I'm ready to roll," I said, placing the milk in the floorboard. "Now we should maybe get on to the house before the milk spoils, James," I joked to get his attention.

He turned to say something, but I guess he thought better of it. He backed from under the big maple tree way too fast as milk sloshed onto the floor and onto my shoes.

"Jesus Christ, slow the hell down!" I scolded, trying to balance the bucket a little better. "What the hell is wrong with you?"

He immediately let off the gas, while softly tapping the brake a couple of times. When the milk sloshed once again. "Is there somethin' we need to talk about?" I asked.

His answer was no more than a slight shake of his head and a stiff chin.

"Well, I guess whatever it is, you don't want to talk about it, right?" I pried. It looked as if he'd positioned himself to hit the steering wheel but didn't. After running the car up to about forty miles an hour, he threw it into neutral so we'd coast on to the house. He took in a deep breath, collecting himself it looked. "No, I really don't want to talk about it, but there's some things going on over at Scarlett's and I don't like it." His jaw flexed at the thought.

As badly as I wanted to hear what it was, now wasn't the time to ask. But I knew he'd eventually tell me. It was obvious enough to Mom that he wasn't acting normal either when she too asked if he was okay. He pepped up a little through breakfast, I thought, and maybe just for Mom's benefit.

Judy decided to ride the bus on our second day, and to quench my suspicion, I watched as a guy stood up to let her sit next to him. I figured he must be the guy she was talking about at the barn.

I thought James would say something on the way to school of what bothered him but he didn't. I started talking about girls and other events I'd encountered on my first day. Not interested at all, he turned the radio up just enough to drown me out and I talk no more. "Cherish," his and Scarlett's favorite song, came on as he sang every word like he was singing it solely to her. It sounded like a plea on his part, I thought. There were a couple of times I wanted to interrupt but guessed he needed to finish every word of the song. "Cherish is the . . . word . . .," he faded, stopping right with the music. What had been such a great song for them to ride around and sing to, now sounded sad as if he'd forgotten to tell her how much he loved her.

"Okay, everybody, listen up now!" Mr. Toll said in his normally quiet way.

"It's time to get this class started." Some mimicked him, knowing how he started every class. I could have guessed without looking who they were.

"Now I gave everyone time yesterday to talk, so today we're going to start learning something . . . Yes, Steve, let me guess what it is you want . . ." Mr. Toll's voice sounded different than the day before and not as kindly.

"Mr. Tool, I really need to use the restroom. I'm not kidding around either."

Without a word, Mr. Toll's dark eyes hinted that Steve should not ask again. We'd started working on a science problem when Mr. Toll left the room, leaving the girl named Vicki in charge. As soon as he shut the door behind himself, almost everyone started talking, with others throwing rolled-up balls of paper at one another. After a minute, Vicki walked back to her seat, joining some other girls who laughed at the guys who acted like kids half their age. I'd never seen anything like it before. I tried to imagine the outcome had Mr. Boyd walked in on a class such as this.

"So, Arnie, do you play football?" Steve asked, after turning in his seat to face me.

"Oh no, I don't think I'm big enough to play football," I said with no hesitation.

"Oh sure you are! See that little scrawny guy up there in the front row?" He pointed, which made me laugh. "He may be scrawny, but he can rip your head off if he gets a hold of you."

The big guy who sat across the aisle from me interrupted. I'd paid notice how huge he was the day before and figured he played football for sure. There was nobody at Willow Springs as big as him except Mr. Bright.

"Hey, I'm Steve Olson." He extended his hand for a shake. He seemed to be a real mild-mannered person and, other than the class introduction the day before, hadn't said much to anyone. I'd made the connection that he was the guy with the Corvette who looked like the singer for the Beach Boys however. "I go by my last name, Olson. There's just too many damned Steve's around here. Hell, when someone says Steve, half the room acts stupid." He laughed.

"Yeah, and my name's Steve Smith," the guy in front of me said, interrupting Olson. "And I just go by Smitty."

"Yea, it's Smitty until he's got to go to the rest room. Then it's little Smitty's got to go to the poo-poo room." Olson laughed, while catching others' attention.

"Who told you to pull your head out of the sand this morning?" Smitty joked; obviously, they were friends also.

"Well, do you play any sports?" Olson asked. I was hesitant to say anything at first. The guy they'd pointed out that could rip your head off wasn't any bigger than me, and he played football. But just like Willow Springs, track wouldn't be the preferred sport here either, I figured. I'd dreamed the whole summer about this very day, when I'd explain that I was a track superstar. But luckily, I came back to my senses in the nick of time.

"I run track," I said, keeping my voice low so that only a few around could hear me. "I ran the two-mile at Willow Springs last year."

By now, thick-glassed Gene Wilford, the only Gene in class, was making his way to the back of the room. He'd been listening in on the conversation with an occasional peep back towards us. He'd slammed me about the land down on Cliff Run Road not being level enough to farm much of anything on, but I'd gotten a laugh from the class with my answer. He strolled back to where we were sitting at our desks.

"If I remember right, Willow Springs doesn't even have a track!" he challenged with a smile as he approached, quickly leaning up against Olson's desk. I thought how cool it was having all these guys talking to me. I just wasn't sure that I wanted Gene to be part of the conversation. I thought that maybe he wanted to catch me in a lie or something.

"You've never even been down there before!" Olson said, shoving his science book into Gene's stomach making him flinch.

"Willow Springs doesn't have a spot flat enough to make a very big circle." Gene grinned, jumping out of the way when Olson grabbed his book again.

"Gene, you wouldn't even be able to walk on ground that wasn't flat! You'd turn your scrawny-ass ankle on a small rock if you stepped on it!" Olson retorted. There were several people who heard and laughed at Olson's comment. "You missed half the season last year with that turned ankle of yours!" Obviously, Olson wasn't going to let up. "Now I can see if you done it in a game . . . but in the Kroger parkin' lot? Give me a break!" The whole class laughed now as Gene's face turned redder than a beet.

Gene suddenly ambushed Olson with a pretty good whack on the shoulder, which didn't appear to shake a hair on his head. At that, a couple more guys came back and got into the conversation. Gene and Olson pinched and poked at each other for a minute, and everything was cool, it seemed. I couldn't help but occasionally stare at the size of him, wondering how he could even get into a Corvette! But one thing was for sure—he'd be great to have on your side in a fight, I thought.

This was better than I could ever have imagined, having all these people to talk with on only my second day of school! I had no sign of lockjaw as it was easy talking with them. It seemed the question of track had faded in the conversation, which was all right with me until Gene frankly asked,

"Well, what was your best time in the two-mile, Arnold?" I thought about coming up with a faster time than I'd really ran but figured it'd be hard enough trying to catch the fastest person at this school anyway. There was silence as they curiously waited.

"I know it's probably no where's close to the best time here, but I ran it in ten minutes and seven seconds." I waited, thinking they'd start laughing; but instead, Smitty jumped out of his seat, while grabbing his chest.

"You're shittin' me!" he said, while slumping over. "My God! I think that's like fifteen minutes faster than anyone here has ever run it!" They all laughed at Smitty before suggesting he go back to the second grade and learn math all over again. It was funny as he tried in vain to explain that he was only joking about the difference in times. But with no letup, they continued to taunt that he really should go back to the second grade for numerous other reasons.

Mr. Toll finally came back into the class and in a most polite way asked everyone to return to their seats.

"Please." He said while looking about the room.

"Hey, Mr. Toll!" Smitty said, making a half-assed effort to raise his hand. "This guy says he can run the two-mile in a little over ten minutes! Isn't that, like, a whole lot faster than Bolson ran it last year?" A smile slowly came to Mr. Toll's face as he slowly wagged a finger.

"When you said your name yesterday, it rang a bell, but I couldn't make the connection." His smile grew. "You're the guy that set the records at Piketon and Waverly!" Then he frowned, asking what had happened to going to state. "Why didn't you go? You'd have gotten at least third, with the time you had."

Suddenly, there was a breeze blowing through the open windows as I floated toward the ceiling. *Why does Steve Olson look smaller now? Why is my seat higher than everyone else's? Why are all the girls whispering to one another? I can't believe that Mr. Toll has even heard of me! And finally, where is all this sweat coming from?*

I'd never seen a newspaper as to what the outcome at State had been or the time that even won it. I couldn't tell them how track practice interfered with my work as a pulpwooder or the fact that my coach said if I did better the next year, then I'd go to State. I just didn't think he had time, what with being the baseball coach also.

I hadn't begrudged anyone that I didn't get to go to state, however. Now the thought that I'd be better suited a year later and certain that I was by far the best at this school made my coming year brim with heady possibilities.

"You're well over a minute faster than the guy we had last year," Mr. Toll assured me.

"That's what I said!" Smitty laughed as everyone joined in razzing him once again.

"Oh, I think I could walk it that fast!" I bragged when a couple of girls smiled from the front row.

"But just remember, Arnold"—Gene waved a taunting finger—"you're only the best when you've beaten the best."

"Oh, for cryin' out loud, Gene, just shut the hell up!" The guy with big jaws and loose lips said.

"Enough!" Mr. Toll said, taking control of the class. "Well, good luck, Arnold. And I'll mention to the track coach that you showed up to run for us. Now let's get back down to business."

It was good to see Judy in math class for the fourth period even though there wasn't much time to talk. Her smiling face was a welcome sight as I bragged of how no one could outrun me at the new school.

Otto Bader's forehead had six perfect wrinkles running across it with the shortest and finest definitions, starting just above his nose. The size of his massive bald head matched his body well, connected by a mass that started just behind his ears and tapered down to his shoulders. And for that reason, he continually adjusted his jacket, which didn't seem to fit right. Like Earl Bright at Willow Springs, Otto Bader was a big man, telling me after my introduction that he knew him very well. I was blown away however when he went on to say he hadn't played football, but instead wrestled in College.

He'd taught vo-ag at Greenfield for many years; and at some time, put in place an initiation where everyone, as I'd been told the day before, would get one hard crack across their ass to become an FBU (Farm Boys United). But the phrase never went anywhere beyond our class. Mr. Bader was no more than the enforcer to the event that no one else in school needed to know about. He explained that he had no favorites and we'd all start with an even playing field. I'd had all night to think about how stupid the whole thing sounded, but as I looked around the room, I thought that it might be pretty cool to belong to something as strange as this.

The atmosphere that Mr. Bader created was to let boys be boys when they needed. Even though he went to church himself, he seemed to think that farming had a different kind of language than almost anything else. He told us with all honesty that sometimes a cow wasn't just a cow and that if a piece of equipment were to break down on a hot day, they could all combine for "a rash of words to clear your system," as he called it. Whereas no cuss words were tolerated, bad words worked as long as you didn't direct them toward someone in a hateful way. Nothing could justify the F-word other than smashing your finger off, but by no means did you ever use God's name in vain.

I had to laugh under my breath, thinking how I'd like to have this bunch as pulpwooders for a day with Calvin directing them as to which "words" to use when needed. Any thought of Calvin made me realize how much I missed him and all his craziness.

Mr. Bader thought of himself as being a fair man and would say so in giving you the choice of which of the three paddles he'd use on you. "None of the above" had never worked and never will he'd explain at the beginning of each year.

Steve Smith and Douglas Cob agreed that there wasn't much difference in which paddle hurt the least as they'd taken more licks than anyone the previous year. And they bragged about who'd get the most this year as they'd tied the year previous. The paddles hung by strings behind Mr. Bader's desk, and all had names written on the handles. Mr. Bader required that you sign your name and date on it afterward.

"Proof of the paddle, so I won't have to do it again," he laughed. Only one guy in the class would take all his cracks from a paddle named Hot Damn. He was the quietest person, never saying much of anything. He had long whitish hair and a wave that seldom needed attending by way of comb. I thought his hair looked solid like the marble statues that lined the hallway in the main building. When he did speak, it was with a red face, one as red as I'd ever seen. He, like

Gene, had thick glasses and continually pushed them up on his nose. I could see he worked hard as shown by his short sleeves that stretched somewhat with muscle. I was told he didn't play any sports but sure looked like he could've.

There was a reason this class could be so much fun and still learn agriculture and many other things. Mr. Bader was the director of how the shop was run. "Boys'll be boys," he'd humor us; but when he'd had enough, it ended then and there without a threat as they all respected him.

We had five minutes between the seventh and eight periods to just sit around and talk with one another, whereas Mr. Bader would make his way to the teachers' lounge and was always a couple of minutes late getting back.

There was clapping and yelling and threats of a crack from Hot Damn because of his late arrival. He played along, taking a bow at the doorway. He'd no sooner collected himself than Smitty and Cobb stood up, taking their wallets out of their back pockets, and faced each other for the challenge.

Cobb joked that he'd be the eventual winner, and backed it up with a smile. Smitty disagreed, and now it was on. I, along with everyone else, broke into laughter when Cobb's big lower lip bounced when Mr. Bader delivered the crack. But it was only the beginning. Cobb ran to the wash sink at the back of the shop, jerking his pants down; and while sitting in it, splashed water on his ass. And I'd never seen anything like it when he turned to show the redness off.

"Hot Damn!" he pointed.

Gene suggested that a guy named David get a crack for trying to castrate a female pig earlier that year. Everyone agreed with lots of laughter that it was for a just cause and voted so by slamming their fists down on their tables at the same time. The class was jury to almost any cause for you to get your crack as it was all in fun anyway. David wasn't even average in size with the smallest FFA jacket but stood and walked to Mr. Bader's desk. The cheering was intense when he selected the paddle named Hot Damn as the two previous had, then leaned over the desk.

I knew by the look on his face that the swat hurt, but it was obvious that he'd do whatever to be part of the scene. Now he was finished for the year unless he did something that would justify anothern'.

"And . . . and . . . all the new people should get their first crack today!" Gene said, while looking at me as did everyone else. I thought he looked Chinese, the way the wrinkles ran up his face toward his magnified eyes.

Mr. Bader turned quickly, looking around the room and even up at the ceiling before directly at me. "I guess you're all the new people, Richardson. So what do you think?"

"Hot Damn!" I said in a daring way. It was those two words that brought me acceptance into this group of guys, acceptance that was different from any norm in the school. Gene said we were elite, the way they all stuck together, whether over cracks in the ground or cracks across your butt. They abbreviated lots of their sayings, such as MTH, meaning "man that hurt." And they'd yell it out after their crack.

And it did smart, but nothing like what I'd endured from the beatings the old man had put on me over the years. There was no blood or anger intended here. There was cheering from everyone as I walked back to my seat. But the laughter and stomping on the floor was cut short when Olson spoke up above all the noise as they quieted.

"Now I think the guy with the big runny mouth needs his today also." Olson grinned. I'm sure the roar that proceeded could be heard in other buildings. Gene's glasses looked thicker and somewhat fogged up, I thought, as he walked past on the way to a waiting Mr. Bader. "What showmanship," Olson laughed as Gene took a bow after his crack, which seemed harder than most, I thought. It ended up that everyone took their crack that day except for the guy named Paul. He pushed his white hair back over his head, declining the crack on this day.

"Paul, you know the rule. Every month you wait, there'll be a crack added," Mr. Bader said, smacking the paddle hard against his own leg.

"Well, I think after all you've been through today, you might need to rest up some before you give me mine." It was all in fun as Mr. Bader nodded to Paul before hanging all three paddle's back up. Smitty and Cobb were already planning on how they'd get ahead of each other at some point for most cracks in a year.

The crack didn't slow Gene with his relentless questioning of me, however, mostly when there were other people around so he could get a rise out of them.

"Do the hogs and cows down on Cliff Run have short legs on one side from walking on the sides of the hills?" His eyes drifted back and forth the full length of his glasses. I couldn't think of a good comeback right off the bat, which I guess Olson caught onto, giving Gene a good solid punch, which moved him a couple of steps backwards.

Olson asked if he lay around and thought things up at night when Gene asked how we killed chickens down there, on Cliff Run Road. I could guess his suspicion. I'd been welcomed to the class in a way that I felt no discomfort in telling him that we "wrang their necks." It turned out that only a handful could attest to doing that. I wondered if someday Gene would take a drive down to see where we lived just to satisfy his curiosity. Then he'd surely have something to say of our half-assed chicken coop the boys had just thrown up for them to roost at nights. Harry'd made the offer to put them at his place where a coop was already in place, but Mom wanted them closer for gathering eggs and had declared that she liked to watch them scratch around on the ground.

It was toward the end of the day that several of the guys talked quietly in the shop as to where they could gather to drink beer on the weekend. Danny had given the okay earlier that his parents would be gone but now informed all that his place would be occupied by the "old farts," as he called them.

It was good to hear of such a thing, where the old farmers could gather and talk of equipment, seed, and how deep they'd tilled the soil. And lastly, how much better times it was way back when. I almost laughed out loud, getting a look from Paul, who I sat beside, thinking how the old-timers at Willow Springs would talk about how deep a hole it would take to cover one of the others' bullshit by the end of the day.

Vo-ag wasn't the only class where I'd hear about words I wasn't saying quite right. I'd always thought and said that English was the biggest waste of my time there could ever be. But now I found that it was a class made especially for me, when I had referred to a book belonging to a girl as hern instead of hers. In health class, I said yer instead of ear and was laughed at even though Mr. Toll said it was rumored that it came over with Irish immigrants. It looked as if Gene was going to challenge Mr. Toll over its origin when he made a half-assed effort to raise his hand. But his turn would come later when he'd hammer me about a cut finger that a guy got while grinding a metal plate in shop.

"It's pronounced finger, Arnold, not fanger," Gene scolded, loud enough that all could hear. By no means was I bad compared with some others I'd known over the years. I wondered if Gene knew that in his correcting me, his lip movement looked the same with both words defined with a square jaw and puckered lips.

To be corrected was all right, but not in a way that might offend someone. I'd often thought that that person should look in a mirror and see how ridiculous they looked with sliding jaws and puckered lips for such easy words. It was referred to as 'lazy speech' by some teachers as if it were a technical term.

I thought of the guy in Kentucky and the many times he must have been stopped for stuttering but found a way to fix it. I thought of Freddy's efforts in his tongue-twisted, jaw-sliding ways to try and make words come out even close.

"Why is that so funny, Arnold?" Gene asked when I'd burst into laughter, thinking how I'd love to have him around with old Harry wiped out on moonshine and with a loose upper dentures.

I'd actually corrected many words with the help of James and Judy and a few others over the years. Maybe it was that I had no desire to correct my lazy speech that I ended words without the *G* on the ends.

Most people didn't have a problem after they got to know your ways though. Even teachers other than English showed some sympathy that it just wasn't that important.

There were many things on my mind other than the way I talked. Maybe this was the opening I'd been waiting on for a long time. To know that no one could outrun me in the two-mile had set my heart on fire.

I'd never had a better week of school in my life with the acceptance of so many friends who made me feel comfortable. It was Friday and with a mad rush everyone evacuated the school in a hurry with me running to where James had parked the Buick for our quick getaway. I'd thought that by now he'd be ready to talk of his problem since the weekend was here. But once again, the radio filled the void when he sang along with all the sad songs.

"Hey, grab your bucket," he said stopping at the back door. "I'll take you up and hang around till you're finished milking." He smiled.

I went on and on about how I really liked the new school and that it was nothing such as I'd expected. He sat and talked with Harry while I milked and after I'd finished he gave me a ride back to the house, then headed for Scarlett's.

We gathered around the TV after supper with the boys grumbling that I watched my favorite shows. The younger boys complained that they wanted to see something else other than girls with short skirts on and shaking their butts fast. Whereas it used to be the old man that wouldn't allow James and me to watch *American Bandstand*, the boys couldn't understand why I wanted to see go-go girls dancing to all the new music. Maybe it was my age and the year 1966 that mixed for such mind-boggling times that I had the desire to see those girls dancing in cages.

Mom didn't approve of it much either but was usually busy with cleaning the kitchen and other things. I didn't necessarily need to hear the music to enjoy what I'd come to watch in the first place.

I'd get my way, but it always seemed the devil would work his way into my pleasure. "Shit!" I'd say under my breath when the screen would become all snowy just before the caged girls came back into view. "No, no, damn it!" I'd hiss. But it was too late—the TV looked worse than a blizzard in a Wild West movie. But supposedly, the problem was going to be fixed with everyone's Christmas present being a new color TV, complete with a state-of-the art antenna. It would stop the practice of having to go outside and turn the antenna every time the picture faded out. The baccer crop was going to pay for it all. Judy joked that we might be the only people left in the world that still had a black-and-white TV.

"I mean it is 1966, after all!" she laughed. It was just before dark when I made my way toward the bus.

"Come on over here, Arnold, and have a sit-down and chat for a while." Excitedly, Harry slid over to give me more room, which as always I didn't need. I adjusting to his slow pace. *No shine on his breath tonight*, I thought.

"Now by God, old Junior was sure in a hurry a few minute ago," Harry said upon his return from putting the plate of food I'd brought him in the refrigerator.

"Yeah, and I don't know why, but I think he and Scarlett might be having some problems, it sounds to me like. But knowing him like I do, I can tell you he ain't going to talk unless it's pretty damned serious."

"Why I thought the same thing Arnold when you went to milk. I don't think he had five words to say. It's easy to tell when somethings botherin' him. We talked about how beautiful the weather had been, mostly clear skies and cool with fall just around the corner. Harry said he dreaded the winter coming on, though. "I'd sure like to block that old man winter off this year," he said. "Why, Arnold, I miss sittin' out here on the porch and smoking my pipe. It's a good place for thought, if nothin' else.

"Why, the problem with winter is the minute you open that damned door, you want to turn and run the other way," he said, dipping his shoulders as though having a chill. "Why, I used to come out here when I was younger and didn't make any difference if a little snow was flying around or not. But now by God, the cold wind cuts right through my ass no matter how much damned clothes I've got on." He pondered for a minute on what he'd said. "I think I'm gettin' too old for about anything anymore, Arnold. Reality, is what's bitin' my ass. You and I both know ninety is old." He let out a spontaneous laugh, assuring that his age wouldn't stop him from carrying on for as long as he could.

I tried to say something to the effect that he still had plenty of life left in him and there was plenty that he could still do. He blew a thin stream of smoke into the air and declared,

"Why, there is one thing that I'd still like to do . . . before I pass away." *Is there something that he wants to tell me?* I wondered. *The conversation could be sad*, I thought. He pulled his pipe with a trace of smoke trailing between his lips and the pipes mouthpiece. He then turned slowly to face me. I swallowed a couple of times to ready myself for what he might have in store for me. And with a serious look at that.

"Arnold, I'd like to get just one more hard-on to remind me of what it felt like. Why, if I could do that, I'd freeze that thang harder than a Popsicle!" His laughter was spontaneous with several good whacks to the leg. He'd come alive again. His end of the swing moved as if Mary had returned, which added to my laughter.

I didn't know if old Harry'd forgotten the time that he'd talked about the same thing when Calvin and Mary had come to visit him. The difference was he was all whiskey'd up on the other occasion. But it still drew a hard laugh that he'd compare it to a frozen Popsicle once again.

We talked of other things, but mostly about Bob and how he was so much different than Mickel and eventually lead up to Mickel's family.

"Why, Arnold, I don't thank many people even know that that bunch up there exists! That old stringy-haired woman of Mickel's, I'll bet, don't say five words a day. But by God, she can sure put a pack or two of cigarettes away in no time, and do you know how many beans that'd buy? And I'd bet if the school knew about them kids, they'd throw old Mickel's ass right in jail!" Harry took a couple of long soothing drags, which seemed to calm him a little, but he wasn't finished just yet. "They aren't no tellin' what goes on up there in the nighttime, Arnold!"

I guessed Harry was pretty well done with his thoughts about old Mickel when he lightly tapped his pipe on the arm of the swing. But by the very way he reached for the Prince Albert for a refill, I knew he had more to say. He'd often hee-hawed around, talking about one thing or another before getting to what was really on his mind—that is, unless he was on the shine, of course.

All I could do was sit and let the old fellow talk of wherever his thoughts led to that day. I waited patiently while he went through his normal routine to have another smoke. His first drag was always the biggest; and after expelling, he'd slowly cross one leg over the other, now ready to talk again.

"What the hell is Jim up to these days, Arnold?" he questioned without looking at me.

"I don't know, Harry. He wasn't home when I left there a few minutes ago, and I didn't want to ask Mom about him. She's got enough to worry about with the kids and all, ya know."

"Arnold, I just don't see why Jim's got to treat your mom like he does!" A moment of silence passed as he drew softly on his pipe. "Why, I think she's the most perfect lady I've ever met in my life and pretty at that! Why, a person like her would make me feel like the luckiest man in the world if I had 'er!" His gaze wondered out into the darkness of the evening. It was the time Harry would do so himself or ask me to pull the short string to turn the outside light on.

"Why Arnold it seems like we turn that thang on a little earlier every night now. The days are getting' shorter and the night a little longer." I let Harry do most the talking on this night I mean after all he had all day to let things bother him. But like the changing of the seasons Harry's evenings were shortened also by the chill and early darkness.

I think I'm goin' to call it a day and get to that plate of food in there." He winked. "I don't see much use leavin' the light on that's unless you want to stay longer."

"No, I'm all right, Harry. I'll see you tomorrow." There just wasn't much change through the day in Harry's confined world without the old man coming around much anymore. His stories had become more of repeats with nothing new to talk about. It was starting to sound as if he'd given up hope of having anything to do with the old man anymore. And their relationship had been faltering for some time now.

CHAPTER 6

Conditions for Stripping

The old man left a note lying on the bus seat saying that the baccer needed to be cut this weekend and went on to threaten that if we didn't, we'd have to miss school to do it. The only part which I liked and read twice was that he wouldn't be there to help, and I didn't care that he'd left no reason why.

The note wasn't that much of a shock; we'd already anticipated a week earlier that the time was close at hand, about the same as last year. The growing season had come to an end as things were starting to die back. Lots of plants had already started dropping their seeds.

The thought of the first frost sent a chill up my backbone when a gust of wind rocked the bus a little. I laid the note back in the seat so James would see it when he got home later. But I'd no sooner shut the light off than he pulled up under the big tree. I acted as if I were asleep when he turned a small light on just above the table. With my eyes squinted I watched him quickly read the note before releasing it to fall wherever it might. He looked tired and hurt, I thought; and by coming home so early, I figured that something surely had happened with Scarlett.

"Is that you, James?" I sat up after he'd turned the light off.

"I'd say you better hope it's me," he yawned. He said nothing that there might be a problem but agreed that an early start the next morning would be good as the alarm was set for an early wake-up.

"That's Uncle Glenn's car," James pointed out when we arrived at Moms. We hadn't seen him since he and the old man had their falling-out over church. It was so good to see him and bring back so many fond memories.

"Now I guess ole Uncle Jim is still mad at me, boys." His gargling laugh hadn't changed a bit. "But I'll catch up to that rascal at some point because you know ole Uncle Glenny ain't one to give up easy. I told Aunt Ree I'm a takin'

Donald Duck and the boys fishing down on Paint Creek for a little while, and maybe he'll be back by then."

It was the way our uncle tilted his head, cocking his jaw slightly, that would always remind me of the first time he talked of hitting someone right between the eyes.

I told Mom to not worry about making breakfast and that we'd stop and buy some sweets and a couple carton of milk for the ride to Pike County. Glenn intervened, saying that he also wanted an early morning departure. But Mom had put her foot down that everyone was going to eat breakfast before they left, pointing out that all she had left to do was stir a little more flour in the gravy and open up another jar of blackberry jam.

Uncle Glenn didn't need the invitation to turn thanks; there was a lot that he wanted to share with us. Mom followed with an "Amen" that the old man be guided back to the fold.

James cut the big biscuit in half, a little heavy on his side, I thought. He and I'd share it alone but as we'd seen before, our uncle could put a few biscuits away himself. The visit was uplifting for James and me but now it was time to go. We'd no sooner made it to the Buick than we heard Mom and Glenn praying from the living room.

James slowed as we turned off Lapperell Road and onto Butler Holler. There'd not been much talk on the way over, although I'd commented about our uncle and how he'd fattened up somewhat, it looked. Another sign that James's had his mind on something else when he twisted the radio's knob back and forth, looking for that perfect song that might fit his mood.

He crept forward and for the next half mile we surveyed how overgrown everything had become. Fence rows that at one time were kept clean were now overgrown with vines, tall weeds, and lots of poison ivy.

"I guess this is what a place looks like when you let it go to hell, James. You'da thought that he would have got somebody to at least mow along the damned road!"

There was barely a nod when he stopped in the middle of the small bridge, shutting the motor off. All was quiet other than the sound of water being funneled around rocks that we'd stacked to make a place deep enough to dip our buckets in at baccer planting time.

He knew there was not much likelihood that someone would need to get around us. I knew it wasn't just the sound of running water that sparked his interest as he climbed out of the car with an invitation for me to follow. By the time I got to the other side he'd stomped a path of tall weeds down to get up under the bridge.

And this looked to be exactly what he needed for now when his eyes dancing about the concrete wall as a slow smile came to his face. Though the colors had faded somewhat the arrowhead that I'd asked him to put on the wall still had a sharp color to its tip. Maybe that of an old habit I pushed my hand deep into my pocket thinking of my supreme sacrifice that lay somewhere under the houses heap of blackened ashes. And even though many of the objects; ones that had been exposed to the springs floods were washed away the detailed scratch marks were still there but without color.

"Those were the good old days weren't they Brub?" He smiled before turning back towards the car. I wanted to mock and call him Doddle his slang name that we used in those good old days. Maybe he just wanted to see something that he'd made in those good old days that we'd shared together.

And from the little bridge had been my favorite viewpoint of our house with the farm all spread out right in front of us. I'd often thought of it as my gateway to the most wonderful thing I could ever see when I'd open my eyes at this very spot. Maybe it was the reason James wanted to go under the bridge and see the only piece of art left that he'd done.

Not that I wanted to ponder on it for very long that his paintings of Kincaid Springs all went up in flames on that terrible day. And I'd never forget how he'd lined his tubes of paint up in the window sill with his three brushes placed neatly between them. It looked as if he placed them in a ceremonial way and that it be his last connection with them.

The baccer crop stood out as a field of gold with its "meller-yeller" color. It was the only well-kept thing on the farm, it looked. We'd not been back here since we'd moved the family to Cliff Run. The old man brought the boys over several times to sucker the plants, chop the weeds from the crop, and scythe around the edges of the field.

James's good times at the bridge didn't last long when he gassed the car in the middle of the curve to get onto the barn. I didn't think he even looked at the baccer crop. But now it was time for the inevitable - that I'd have to look at where the old house once stood. Always the same, I'd start at the top of the chimney, tracing it down to where a rusty stove still stood upright. Would it have been any better had it all been cleaned up? I doubted so when every time I'd close my eyes to the horrible sight that I could never clear my mind of it.

There were thick, tall horseweeds that'd completely surrounded the barn and all the other buildings. Tall weeds had overtaken the garden, where some had been pushed to the side when Granma had brought Mom over for a final picking of green beans, carrots, and cucumbers a while back while everyone was in school. She'd told us what a great time they'd had and possibly it was them also who'd parted the weeds back in front of the old stove. I'd loved to have been a fly on the dash of Grandma's 1953 Chevy. James had said her car looked all hippy like with the way she'd lined everything and including the rear view mirror with artificial flowers.

"Man, I hope you don't need to shit, James." I pointed to the toilet, laughing at how hard it would be to get the door open with such weeds blocking it.

We stomped a path to get into the barn and gather our first bundle of baccer sticks. It took a good hour with so many trips to the barn to spread them throughout the rows of baccer. The last trip would be to retrieve the spears and hatchets from the stripping house.

Suddenly, as if James had gotten a reprieve or something, out of the blue he loudly commanded,

"Go!" Then like clockwork, we each pushed a stick into the ground; and after fitting the spear on top, the old familiar race between Doddle and Brub was on once again just like old times.

There was no talking as we cut and speared stalk after stalk onto the sticks. I was much taller now, thinking back to the first time when I had to stand on my tiptoes to reach the top of the spear. It wasn't long before I peeled my shirt off; saturated with sweat and tossed it to the ground.

"Copycat," I scolded as James had done the same thing. It would take an all-out effort to get as much as we could in order to finish it the next day. We hadn't stopped for four solid hours and now thirst set in.

"Listen . . . Do you hear that, James?" I held an open hand up behind my ear while directing it towards the well. It was never questioned by either of us when it was time for a drink of water. The faint call was still there anytime the dipper banged up against the side of the pump with the slightest breeze. The same old rusty wire that'd held it for many years was wearing thin now. It didn't appear, however, that the weeds had stopped people from still getting a drink at our well. Tracks in the mud showed big and small shoe prints and some bare feet all around the pump's slab. The water tasted slightly different from what I'd remembered. But our break was short-lived, knowing we still had a lot to do. A few more hours passed with no slacking up and now could easily see that we'd cut way more than half the crop.

"Well, cold water or not, I'm headin to the springs, James. We've done a hell of a lot today and should be able to finish it tomar with no problem," I said, tossing my hatchet to where I'd cut my next stalk. What had once been a well-worn path from bare feet running continuously throughout the day, weeds and the like had completely taken over now. There was a short reckoning as we stood on the bank, sizing each other up from head to toe.

"Is it just me, James? Or does this hole of water seem smaller from the last time we were here?"

"Nah, it's the same size as it's always been, Arnold. We just outgrew it and back then didn't have to swim so far to forget our worries. I'm really glad we've got a bigger place to swim now because it takes a lot longer to rid myself of everything, with so much happening anymore. I've always thought that the day the house burned down was the day we outgrew this spring . . .," James finished.

I dove in, quickly coming back up in the shallows on the other side with James right behind me. But it was still what we needed as we thrashed all about the place as the spring still seemed to possess its healing powers that we not have a worry in the world it might appear. It had always been the oasis that we thought we'd never get tired of.

We decided to stop at Bainbridge and get a milkshake to celebrate the most baccer we'd ever cut in a single day. It was almost dark when we turned into the driveway, where Mom and Duck had started walking up the road to milk Red. James told me to take the Buick, but not be hot-rodding. He'd stay around and talk with everyone till I got back.

Harry wasn't on his porch that evening. The light in his room was off, and I figured he'd given up on me being back in time for a chat. James had eaten his supper and shortly after my return headed for Scarlett's place. I stayed only a short while after I'd eaten before heading back to the bus. Tomorrow would be another early start for James and I. And he promised he'd be home early from Scarlett's. I'd no sooner gone to bed than he showed up. But he seemed sorrowful about something I thought.

Mom had breakfast waiting for us the next morning. Duck said he'd like to go with us instead of going to church, but Mom would have no part of it. Uncle Glenn was going to take her to the new church he'd started pastoring up by New Martinsville.

In a way of celebration, James and I cut the last two stalks of baccer down at the very same time while yelling and holding our hatchets high into the air. Unless for some unexpected change, it would be the last we'd ever cut at this place. The times that we'd need to be there were coming to a quick end.

We'd leave the crop lying in the field for a few more days before coming back over to hang it in the barn. Two days to strip it and a few hours to load it for the trip to Maysville and sell it. And with the last day, I'd declare that I'd no longer be haunted by the old cook stove that still watched my every move. I wondered if my lucky arrowhead had managed to fall close to it as I'd hoped for. I'd never attempt to recover it from its blackened grave however.

I'd gone with a friend at school the next day to wait on his girlfriend to get out of class. As we waited, I overheard the teacher announcing some of the students who had the top grades in class so far, James and a guy named Harold were part of those who were named. He combed his hair the same as James, straight back with a rolling wave on the top. The only difference was Harold had blond hair, and it looked like it needed attending to more often.

I'd never put much effort ever into having manageable hair. Even now in high school, where girls seemed more attracted to slicked-back hair, I still wouldn't make the effort. There were others like me who let their hair go and not be tamed. I notice that the ones who never put much into fighting for a spot at the restrooms' mirrors were more likely to hang out together, it looked.

James joked once, telling me that it definitely made you look smarter, if nothing else. And maybe he was right to say that it was laziness on my part. Maybe like the hippies it was my way of protesting that I didn't have to be like others.

"Yeah, I can see it now, James. If you spell the word fast and it just happens to be wrong, why, you shouldn't worry. The teacher will let you slide simply because your hair looks so perfect! Come on, that sounds like somethin' right out of the old man's playbook of holy bullshit, doesn't it?" I couldn't tell if he'd heard a word I'd said; he was too busy gathering a comb full of hair to wash that perfect wave all the way to the back of his head.

I thought about all the hippies in college with some not looking too smart, but they sure didn't have any problem saying what was on their minds. I wondered how it'd come about when one would decide to let their hair grow long. They'd have to be people more like me, I thought, or was it that I was becoming more like them? I didn't have the perfect wave to give up like James and some others would. In fact, I thought it might be cool to have long hair. I'd seen some of those guys walk past the mirror with a simple glance and make no adjustments other than a shake of the head, where their hair trickled back into place. *I know that some girls thought it was cool too, and if Jesus had long hair, then it must really be okay*, I thought. So why did preachers condemn it so badly? Some things were just best left alone, I figured.

It was on the way home that evening when I told James that I was going to grow my hair down to my collar, the acceptable length for school. All I really wanted was to get a rise out of him and did when he shot me a stern look along with a thoughtful headshake.

"You know, almost all the draft dodgers have long hair, and they're the ones who burn their draft cards also," he warned.

"Well, I'm not a draft dodger! I'd join the army right now if I was old enough!" I snapped back.

"Hey, I don't care if you grow it long, Arnold," he answered quickly with a smile. "I'm just saying that people look at you differently. I mean how many times have you heard anyone say 'There's a good Christian,' for example? You don't hear that if he's got long hair, whether he's Christian or not. It's sad to say, but some Christians won't accept you for what you are—either you'll be like them, or you're shit out of luck!" he concluded. "And think about the times we've seen a recent drunk, like you know who, be welcomed back to the fold with open arms? More than likely, a longhair would have to get it cut to be accepted by all," he laughed.

"You're right! Remember when those old women over at Cedar Chapel cast a final judgment on old man Horton, sayin' he'd never be anything other than a drunk? I thought it was good when he found out what they'd said. Boy, did he have a lot to say that evening before telling them all, including the old man, what hypocrites they all were.

But best was when he turned at the back door, tellin' old Janice Hoop, 'Once a defilin' lard ass, always a defilin lard ass.' I'm tellin' ya, I never laughed so hard in my life seeing those rolls of fat bounce, with her huffin' and puffin' jaw and with no comeback what so ever. Hell, she couldn't even fan her face for more than a minute before running out of breath. I guess it was good for her to find a place to worship and still be so fat she could hardly walk without a cane. I mean if you're a Christian, is there any difference in the way you defile your body? I wanted to clap my hands for old man Horton cause what he said was the truth!" I looked over at James, expecting a comment.

"Yeah, no doubt about it. There's a lot of hypocritical people who need to take a look at their own selves before they condemn others. I think there's more than just saying you're a Christian and only picking out parts of the Bible that you want to live by," he concluded.

"Well, I heard Mom tell the old man that she didn't think long hair looked good on a man, but also said that it had nothing to with that person's soul. I never got so tired of hearing him goin' on and on 'why this' and 'why that' and never coming up with a good answer other than his own condemnation.

That's when I reminded him that all pictures of Jesus I've ever seen has long hair, a beard, and a mustache! And you know what? He stood right there with that stupid moron-looking smile and told me that that's just a way an artist painted him up to be. Remember that time in church when he was preachin' how bad long hair looked on men, and I told you I'd seen a miracle? How Jesus was rolling his eyes up in that picture behind the old man?" I laughed.

"Yeah, how in the hell could I ever forget something like that? I didn't quite make it to the back door before laughing out loud. Boy, did I get some looks. And why was it always when he was preaching that you'd do shit like that?"

"Well, first of all, if you remember, it was a contest. But I was just better at comin' up with good stuff. I just thought it funny how he continually pushes his hair back every time it falls in his face. I guess he thinks long hair is okay as long as it's back over your head!

"I'm telling you, James, it's just hard for me to understand how anybody can preach against long hair when Jesus looks like a hippie. Hell, look at *The Last Supper.* If they weren't bald, most had long hair. And have you noticed lots of things are okay for a man, but not for a woman? She's disgraced and hell bound for sure if she cuts her hair short, and you tell me why it's okay for a man to go without a shirt, but woe be upon a woman who would do so."

"Well, that one's easy," he shot back. "Would you want your girlfriend walking around with her breasts hanging out for everyone to see?" he snickered. "And I know you wouldn't covet another man's possession now, would you Arnold?" He laughed at how he'd put me on the spot. "So don't tell me 'no' because I know way better." We joked and laughed while he put the finishing touches to his hair.

There'd been several boys called to the office because they didn't meet the hair code. Pictures were posted as to what was acceptable for boys' examples on all bulletin boards, including one that was right outside the principal's office. Many had been torn down and thrown on the floor. One guy in particular would say "f--you" with every sign he'd tear down.

It didn't take long to see which boys disagreed with the rules and insisted that they should be able to grow their hair as long as they wanted. Either way, they all came out of Mr. Terry S. Conner's office pissed off, with some threatening to go to court over it.

I knew that the old man would have a problem if I decided to grow mine long. I felt a tingle thinking how it would be to go over the edge and let it grow in protest of everything he stood for. My protest in not wanting to call him Dad but instead "the old man" had worked out just right and without long hair.

I'd gotten used to the fact that Judy would be walking around with boys and holding hands between classes. It looked like she'd be with a different one every few days, content with a short term because she wasn't allowed to date. But there were plenty who took it for what it was worth and still enjoyed spending time with her and her girlfriends. I figured it was all in preparation for when she would be allowed to date.

There was also the fact that her being a Christian turned some of them off also. The word got around as she and others were bypassed when guys were looking for a treat. I felt bad knowing that I was one of them who didn't want a Christian girl right off the bat. I could only dream of a kiss but had to confess that I'd wondered what sex was all about also. I mean it was the age of free love after all, as the hippies would say on TV.

I was glad Judy was able to separate the bad guys from the good with no help from me. I thought they all were bad when it came down to my little sister and wouldn't have a problem straightening any of them out if I had to. But I knew in my heart that she'd pick the right person when the time came.

We had such great times riding home when she was with us. She started riding in the front seat, complaining that it was always cold in the back and she couldn't hear very well from back there either. She'd always been a pretty good talker; but now with boys asking her out on dates, it had overwhelmed her, which was the real reason she wanted to be up front with us.

She'd grown up a lot that summer, witty and quick with answers—something she and James had in common. They'd both asked one time or the other why I hadn't asked a girl out yet. With no real explanation, I said I needed to concentrate until track season was over and joked that after that, girls would be asking me out. Overwhelmed with so many girls to feast my eyes on, only occasionally I thought of Linda. It angered me that after a girl would smile, I couldn't get the nerve up to at least say hi to her. I could only picture myself trying to talk, shaking all over, jaw locked up so tight that I couldn't squeeze a word between my teeth. James had enlightened me that talking would be easy once I got started.

Maybe my goals were beyond my reach, that I looked at pretty girls only. After all, none would want to date a pulpwooder. It simply came down to one thing: the fear of being turned down. But James was right, that I should get my driver's license just in case I fell in love overnight.

Judy and I ran our mouths most all the way home, and at times, James had to call a time-out when we'd get too carried away with our goofiness. I had to study harder, and there was always the distraction of the old man. But all in all, I was having the time of my life, and the best was still to come when track season would roll around. People would know me better than just someone who didn't say all his words right when I'd lift my arms into the air after winning my first race.

"James, watch where you're going!" I grabbed at the dash when he'd swerved off the side of the road a little. "You don't need to be looking in the mirror and combing your damn hair while you're drivin!" I shouted.

Judy laughed, poking her elbow in my side. "We didn't go that far out of the road, Arnold," she said, leaning heavily against me.

"Someday you're gonna wreck us over one damn hair!" I said, leaning back in my seat once again. Then without warning, he swerved onto a gravel road, where we spun all the way around before finally coming to a stop. Dust settled around the car, filling the inside as Judy with a puckered face tried to fan it away. While quickly rolling his window up, James snatched his comb, pushing his face close to the mirror.

"And so where is that runaway hair you spotted, Arnold?"

It would have been a strange sight with us sitting crossways in the road, laughing at the way James was acting.

We let Judy off at the house, where I grabbed the milk bucket. James dropped me off at the bus before he headed for Scarlett's.

Donald was at his prime and had a dirty joke to tell me about every evening when I'd come in from milking. From a distance, I could see him and the boys standing under an apple tree, far enough that Mom couldn't hear him. There weren't many days that he didn't have a new one and told them in a way that he wouldn't say some of the real bad words. Instead, he'd say, 'you know what I mean' or 'what I'm talking about', leaving you to picture or guess as to which bad word he intended. Larry joked that it sure wasn't the way he told it when it was only them around, however.

I told Mom that I thought it was about time Duck started doing the milking; after all, there'd be plenty of them to help carry it to the house. She'd always avoided the suggestion, thinking he was still a little too young. But I thought that after she'd given it some thought, she'd be okay with it as I'd told her he did fine in the woods with helping us there.

Judy and I took a walk down the road that evening, when she'd informed me that some girls were asking if James was dating anyone. I stopped before clutching my stomach like I'd just had my breath knocked out. The fact was I'd rather have it knocked out than what I'd just heard.

"Are you all right?" She grabbed my arm. I was suddenly feeling sick to my stomach.

"Damnit Judy! I knew that this day would come . . . Why in the hell does he insist on goin' with our cousin? Damnit! Do you know how much trouble it's goin' to be for you and me at school now? You can't even imagine what the boys in vo-ag will do with this one! I'm tellin' ya, those guys'll have us related to inbreeders like you wouldn't believe. They're not a bit bashful," I went on. She slowly patted my shoulder, showing her concern.

"I've got a feeling that it'll be all right in the end, Arnold."

"Yeah, that's what James says also," I said more stubborn than ever. "But it ain't gonna be all right in the end, Judy. The dumbass needs to leave her and find someone else! That's all there is to it!" I said, unclenching my fists.

"Well, just so you know, I've already told them what James's girlfriend's name is." She giggles.

"Oh Sh…it!" I let out a yell.

"And hers is Scarlett Portman." Judy swung her hand elegantly such as Ed Sullivan would have done with an introduction. I'd have laughed had it been anyone other than Scarlett. "That is her real name, you know. And nobody will suspect anything even if they investigate it, but why would they?" She frowned. We sat down at a culvert that channeled a small creek underneath the road. Judy remarked how nice it was to let the cool current tug at our feet.

"I think that you let this bother you way too much, Arnold," she continued. "Scarlett is a good girl and is no relation by blood; none whatsoever! And she is Scarlett Portman regardless of who she lives with." She repeated the name several more times in her effort to separate it from Radcliff. It all sounded so simple for her. But I knew it'd be awfully hard for me to explain, especially if it were Gene doing the interrogation.

Judy said she'd ride with us to school the next morning but would take the bus back home, giving us three guesses as to why. I figured her intent that morning was to keep the peace and for me not to flip out over Scarlett.

I had to admit that saying Scarlett Portman made me worry less than Scarlett Radcliff. But as the day went on and I kept seeing one of the girls who'd asked Judy about James, I grew more wary about the predicament James had put me in. Scarlett Portman or Scarlett Radcliff really didn't make any difference to me. As far as I was concerned, the problem could be fixed overnight. All James had to do was pay attention to what I had to say. I had a lot at stake and was plenty willing to give it another shot that evening on the way home when there'd just be the two of us.

"Hey, did Judy tell you about all the girls asking about you at school, James?"

"No, she didn't say anything to me." He looked over at me and all concerned.

"Well, one's in your class . . . I think her name is Janet. You know, the one with the short black hair and has got really pretty legs."

"Yeah, I love her short dresses." He glanced once again. "The other day, she intentionally dropped her pencil on the floor and kicked it in my direction, with a sheepish look and one of those tempting smiles. And when I leaned over to pick it up, guess what I saw?"

"I don't know. What'd you see?" I asked quickly.

"I saw her panties! They were as white as a cloud! Why, can you imagine what must be just on the other side of them, Arnold." He smiled broadly, taking notice of my squirming around in my seat.

I looked out my window, thinking of Mrs. Thacker in the mirror that time and wondered if James had seen Scarlett like that before. Suddenly, there was a slight tightness in my jaw. I knew I needed to say something, but when I looked back at him, he was quietly trying to not be noticed that he'd been leading me on.

"You asshole!" I said of his trickery to get my attention. "But Judy did tell you about those girls, didn't she?"

"Those girls, including Janet, have all asked me to take them to the drive-in a bunch of times already," he acknowledged. "and they sure know how to flirt."

"Then why in the hell didn't you go with one of them?" I demanded. "James, she's our cousin!" I said loudly.

"She's our cousin, but not by blood!" he repeated the very words that I simply didn't want to hear.

"I'm sick of hearin' she's not blood. Other people don't see it that way, ya know. She's our c-o-u-s-i-n!" I spelled it out loud. "Do you know how bad it'll be if someone finds out that you're goin' with your cousin?" I shouted.

He rolled his window up a tad as to be heard better and assured me that he wasn't going to leave Scarlett and that I might as well stop pestering him. Here was a chance to get himself out of the situation and save me from all the embarrassment I might have to go through. I knew that eventually someone would find out—I just knew it. Gene came to mind again, with his interrogating thick glasses. He'd have me sweating in no time, and I could only imagine what he'd do then. I guess I was lucky that Scarlett went to school at Bainbridge instead of here, though.

"James, some of those girls are real nice lookin', and they ain't none of 'em any relation to us!" I'd seen him talking to a couple of them, looking as if he was flirting himself.

"Look, Arnold, I love Scarlett. But best of all, she loves me too."

I silently mocked him as I'd heard the same shit with every conversation we had. My questions and threats were all in vain however. I'd just have to prepare myself for the worst. *Scarlett Portman, Scarlett Portman.* I shook my head. I knew there was no need to carry on any longer; he'd said his piece, and that was that. I needed to think about something else.

"Well, what do ya think about the old man never bein' around, James? My guess? His ass is up at Good Hope with that bunch! What do you think?"

"I think it's bad, of course, but then sometimes I think it's better for Mom that he stays away." He slowly nodded. "I don't think she cries as much anymore when he doesn't come home. Judy told me the other day that it's sure better hearing Mom pray when she's alone than hearing her cry when he's there!" He turned the radio down, slowly sinking back into his seat. His look was a little different this time.

"There is something else you might want to know about him, Arnold." He paused. "I wasn't going to tell you because I know how you can get when you're pissed off." He frowned.

"Now you ain't gonna feed me a line of bullshit, are ya, James?"

"No, but it is bullshit all right with what Scarlett and I saw the other night. We'd gone into Bainbridge to get Anna Fay some bacon, and of course, you know she puts a timer on us every time we go anywhere alone anymore. I have to drive faster than normal so we'd have a little time to go parkin'."

"Yeah, yeah, you can just skip all that bout making out. I know what goes on when you're out together."

He slightly tapped the brake. "Do you want to hear this or not?" He asked sounding a little upset now. "I know what I'm fixing to tell you will piss you off, so do you want to hear it or not, now you tell me? It's no problem to keep it a secret." I wanted to know but stewed for a minute longer. I'd been forewarned of the consequence, but I just had to know.

"Yeah," I said humbly, "I do want to know."

"Okay, Arnold, you know how the store is right across from Number 3 beer garden in Bainbridge? Well, we saw Dad come out of their drunk, and staggering all over the place; almost falling down had he not had help."

"I don't know how he can show his face in public anymore!" I quickly interrupted. "But people already know all about that son-of-a-bitch and besides he ain't tryin' to hide anything anymore. And…!"

"Okay, okay…, hold it right there Arnold." James said while franticly shaking a hand at me! "You can't stay cocked and ready to fly apart over everything you hear about him. You just can't think straight when you get that way and besides I haven't got to the worst of it yet. So save it! At least think about what you're going to say before flipping out. I've been blinded by anger myself at times but nothing like you.

"You'll go crazy waiting for the next time he does something wrong. It's been like this forever Arnold. If you're not careful you'll do something that you'll regret for the rest of your life and all because of anger. Arnold I'll say it again. It is what it is and there's nothing we can do about it. Dad was staggering all over the place with the help of a woman who looked to be in about as bad a shape as he was!"

"Don't you ever call that son of a bitch Dad in front of me again James, I hate him!" I screamed. It felt as if my outburst had shaken the car.

"Look!" He interrupted. "I got just as pissed off as you are, but I didn't blow up and start cussing all over the place. And my referring to him as Dad doesn't have anything to do with how much I dislike the way he acts. He is and always will be our Dad. Like it or not."

"Well, then tell me what the hell you did do! I guess you and Scarlett just laughed it off and drove away and made out for a while," I sneered loudly. "James, you should've gone over and knocked the hell out of him! I sure would have!"

"Do you know how many times you've said that same thing over and over, Arnold? You sound like a worn-out record with the same old shit over and over again. I know how bad you hate and want to kill him and that's the very reason I hesitate to tell you anything when it comes to him. Sure I could've walked across the street and knocked the hell out of him. But even if he would've remembered who it was it wouldn't stop him from doing it again. He's got a terrible addiction, he's an alcoholic. And like always you're first reaction is to blow up without thinking!" James shouted, now angry himself.

"Now take a . . . damned breath!" he ordered. "I try not to stay angry about things for very long. It just doesn't do a person any good! Its way better to find a way to deal with it 'stead of wasting other people's time and energy! Some things are not going to change, no matter how much you want it; pray or beg it makes no difference. Like calling him Dad or the 'old man,' as you want it—it makes no difference what he's called! If he cared any about his family at all, he wouldn't be acting like he does. We already know that. Anger doesn't solve a Goddamned thing, but hope does. The only thing we can do is have hope like Mom that he'll straighten his ass up a…nd"

"And what? Become a temporary Reverend again!" I cut him short. "Why, in no time, he'll be singing that old song again, 'I'm Using My Bible for a Road Map.' The only problem is his interpretation is a lot different than most when it comes down to that biblical map to heaven that he sings about! I went into Mom's bedroom the other morning with every intention of taking his Bible and burning the damn thing on the first stump I come across," I raged.

"Mom had it laid out all nice and neat-like and turned to a page I guess she wanted him to read. I'm tellin' ya, James, I don't have any reason to forgive him whatsoever! I gave up after Toby talked him into givin' the Christian life another whirl. I was so sure that would be the last time he'd backslide." I said boldly looked at him. "Well, I can tell ya, that *hope* surely went to hell long since then, James! But I do 'hope' that we never get ambushed with more of his bastard children out there somewhere! I 'hoped' we could keep those pedal cars . . . Hmmm, wonder where they went off to . . ." I sounded sarcastic. "Should I hope that he'll never hit Mom again, even after we've threatened him? I'm not crossing my fingers on that one at all.

"James, there's not a day goes past that I don't want to kill the asshole, especially when I'm mad as hell like this. Crossing fingers, prayin', or hoping ain't goin' to fix that! But you just keep hoping because I know the kind of person that you are. Yep, hope and wait just like Mom, eighteen years—and it ain't got her anywhere either, James. I guess the best thing for me is to come up with new cuss words since I can't help my hate for him. And another thing! I'm not goin' to that asshole's funeral unless it's to celebrate, and that ain't goin' to happen when I'm in jail."

Suddenly, without warning he choked, spraying root beer everywhere, including the windshield. He came to a slow stop and quickly opened his door, coughing and to the point of throwing up, it sounded. Maybe my threat of killing the old man had set him off again. While leaning out the door, he held an open hand up to insinuate that I shouldn't say anything else while he recovered. After several hard coughs, he sat back up in the seat, wiping his eyes.

"I guess you swallered the wrong way, huh?"

"Can't talk right now!" He wheezed the words. I waited patiently, conjuring up that I had more to say.

I knew that everything he'd said about me was true, about how quickly I could explode over the old man. I'd driven myself to the point that all my anger was concentrated solely on him.

"What's so funny?" I demanded as he leaned back in the seat, slightly rolling his head to where he could see me. His attempt to point a finger fell way shy. Laughing out of control, he slowly pushed his forehead against the top of the steering wheel. To go from such blaspheming rage to laughter was in itself a shock of sorts that I joined him without knowing what he was even laughing about.

"Okay, now tell me what we're laughing at, James," I managed, which got him really carried away. He simply couldn't talk right now. I left him to his misery, getting out of the car to take a leak.

It was somewhat hard to take when he finally told me that his laughter was all about new cuss words that I'd said. He said that he couldn't imagine what a new one would sound like since I'd added the word "double" to about all of them already. He was right that a common son of a bitch anymore was a double common SOB or any other words that I couldn't think of as a worse way to use them.

"Well, even if he does straighten up, I'm not forgivin' him for all the things he's done to us, James. He's put us through this shit too many times before! Remember livin' with the constant fear that he'd drag us off to Florida again, without a pot to piss in? You know, like every time we went down there? Then was the agonizing fear of losin' the farm no sooner than we'd got it! So guess what? Granma's saying about walking on pins and needles is the way it's been all our lives with him. I'm tellin' you it's the way he is, and it ain't going to end until something's done about him."

"Well, tell me this, Arnold. What stopped you from burning his Bible?"

"What always stops me, James?" I shot back. "Mom! There was a folded up letter lying right beside it." My short hesitation tempted James to ask.

"So... what did it say?"

"I never read it!!. I knew it was just another humble plea-and a waste of my fuckin' time." I pushed myself back into the seat feeling somewhat uneasy at his question. "I was afraid that if I did read it, I'd get even more pissed off at him. James, I ain't hopin' for nothing on his part anymore, but there is a way to fix this and get him out of everyone's life once and for all."

"Arnold, you're talking like an idiot again!" James snarled. "I'll say it again that I don't want to hear of another threat about killing him. How can I get it through that thick skull of yours that it wouldn't fix a damned thing? I just hope you take the time to think of Mom before you do something crazy like that." All in one motion, I was out of the car and gone in a flash, making no attempt to close the door behind me. Ignoring James's beckoning yells I jumped the fence, and quickly disappeared into the woods. I raged on, daring small trees and thick brush to stand in my way until I was finally out of earshot of the Buick's horn. Tripping at times and crashing to the ground I quickly sprang back up to my feet and running more wildly than ever. Adrenaline grew with every injury to the point that there wasn't any pain where I bled from my arms, hands and along with a burning scratch running down the side of my face and dripping onto my shirt. I'd fled the car a good ways from our bus and would have several small fields and woods to cross to get there. Finally worn down from frustration I staggered to a stop, dropping to my knees at a small stream where I washed the blood and sweat away.

Sadly, from the calm reflective pool a lonely boy starred back at me when a single tear fell from my nose, sending small ripples throughout the still waters. I was beaten down in so many ways that I couldn't fully understand them all. But it was however the true picture of myself with so many disappointments lately. I'd have to face the fact that there could be no hope of a miracle to fix the way I felt about our father. But worst of all I couldn't keep lying to James to what my true intentions were all about. I took my shirt off and after washing my face and arms I scrubbed the blood from it.

I sat in the tall weeds along a fencerow, seeing the Buick parked under Harry's big maple. It'd be hard to face James with my renewed vision of what I wanted to do to the old man as there seemed to be no way out.

I made my way on to the barn, throwing anything I could get my hands on once inside. I'd turned with every intention to throw the feed scoop through the small window when a voice interrupted.

"Here's your milk bucket, Arnold." I wheeled around to the dark corner where others had ambushed when James walked out. I must have looked pretty whipped when he came over and put a hand on my shoulder. The kindness of my brother's touch settled me somewhat as my nostrils flared with a sudden need to cry. I'd not wanted him to see me like this with my jaw trembling so badly. I drew a long sigh, wiping my face quickly.

"I'm glad you made it back." He said earnestly. "I was just getting ready to milk, and you know how good I am at that! Like not at all." He squeezed a short sympathetic laugh. Red, was hesitant at first to come into the barn but did so after I poured the grain in her trough. I quickly gathered the stool, never saying a word, and sat down quietly to milk.

"Now I'm going to finish what I was trying to say earlier, Arnold. As you know, I'm not much to carry on about things when I've made my mind up to do them. I twisted my ankle that time when you were ready to shoot Bill and the old man over Sam. I was desperately trying to get there before you done something crazy. I know Arnold, with all my heart that you'd shoot him under the right circumstances. And for that reason, I'm asking you to promise me one thing as my brother."

I pulled my head from Red's side, looking up at him.

"Me and you both agree—and that's on our word, Arnold!—that if it does come to the point where he hits Mom and for no other reason than that, we'll talk about it before either one of us reacts." He walked the couple of steps to where I sat and held out a hand to help me up. He rolled his wrist slightly, showing the small scar on its side. "Remember when we became blood brothers,

Arnold?" He smiled. "Now talk about too much TV when Geronimo and that army captain became blood brothers to stop fighting with each other."

I slightly turned my wrist, revealing the same small scar that'd hardly drawn blood that day. But as little boys, it meant that we couldn't lie about anything and to finalize everything that we swore to it. Without questioning, we flexed our arms and pulled our wrists tightly to each other.

"James, I wish I could see things like you do. I wouldn't look like this and all tore up." I held my arms out, turning the side of my face to show my big scratch. "And the worst part about it is the old man doesn't ever get hurt over the shit he causes! I've wished a million times that I could be just like you! But I'm not! And I never will be. We're just different in some ways James."

"Well, don't think for a minute that all this doesn't bother me as much as it does you, Arnold. It's almost too much to comprehend that you just get over the last terrible thing he does, and then you're looking in the eyes of other kids that have some of the same features that you do. Again, I just don't let it bother me like it does you." He held an open hand toward me as not to be interrupted. "Just put it somewhere in the back of your mind. Think of something else. That's all you can do. But most of all don't dwell on it."

"Well, you got a girlfriend to talk to about everythin', and that has to be better than what I've got." I didn't want his pity by no means; but since Scarlett had come into his life, my true source of help when I needed it had practically come to an end.

"Yes, it does help, but I don't tell her about all the things that go on here either," he said.

My eyes started to water once again. I didn't see how there could be anything left after my flight through the woods. I softly dragged my callused fingers across the scratch on my face. It'd be an easy lie when Gene would ask what happened; that a locust branch had scratched me while cutting fence posts. Careful that a tear not fall into the milk I slightly turned my head while pushing my forehead deeper into Red's side. Taking notice, James turned toward the door, saying he'd meet me at the car.

I thought of how over the years I'd prayed and thought things out while milking.

After finishing I turned Red loose in the pasture, where she walked immediately to the stream for a drink. James would not blow his horn to hurry me while I paced through the dark barn to collect myself a little better. With a couple of deep breaths and one final swipe of my face, I gathered the milk up and headed for Harry's pump to strain it.

James left it up to me to speak first, which I needed to show that I was all right. There was plenty to talk about, but it all seemed so sad for now.

"Are you goin' to eat with us tonight, James?" I asked as we pulled into the driveway.

"Oh, I don't need anythin' to eat . . . I'm living off of kisses and hugs right now." He laughed and, with a wave, drove away. I started feeling lonely all over again as I watched the rear end of the Buick disappear over the hill at Harry's place. Maybe it was my age that so much aggravation and so many questions about life made it seem like the whole world was falling in on me. I could understand why James was so eager to get away from all this as fast as he could. He was right about the fact that the sooner you got your mind on something else, the better off you'd be. I thought kissing and hugging would surely be the way to go. I wondered how often I'd see him after he and Scarlett would get married and move away.

"Honey, you'll barely be able to see it by tomorrow," Mom assured me after tended to my scratches with some Blair salve. But I knew however that I wasn't fooling her nor Judy when one of the boys asked what had happened to me. Duck laughing all the while and saying that maybe I should pick a better place to jump the fence where there weren't so many berry briers.

After we'd eaten I hung around and watched some TV with everyone for a while. The big news of the day which I encouraged to draw less attention to my face was how Duck had gotten in a fight and whipped two boys at once. Duck hadn't talked much but just sat there with an occasional nod to make sure Larry got the fine details of the fight right and most of all to not leave out a single punch.

"Piggy Wiggy, that one guy's face looked almost as bad as yours does right now," he joked while the boys laughed along with him. "I kept tellin' 'em, I'd knock 'em back down ever' time he got back up. But I finally quit when I realized he must a been hard a hearin'." He laughed once again.

"Well, what happened to the other guy?" I asked. Larry started cracking up as Duck looked around as though he was looking for something.

"He ran off like a little girl after he got back up his last time. Didn't he, Larry?"

"Yeah! He ran off like a little girl straight to the teacher!" Larry said, moving himself away from Duck a little farther. "I could hear that paddle all the way at the end of the hall!" Larry bragged of Duck.

"Did it hurt?" I snickered.

"Da-gone! I didn't thank that old skinny principal could even hold a paddle up, let alone swing it like that. He told me that I better not be a fighting anymore, and I'm tellin' ya . . . I think I'll be the one runnin' like a little girl the next time!" Duck's punch line was perfect. I needed a good laugh but knew all the while it would still be Duck who'd lead the boys with most paddling's for the year.

"Hey! I'll see you boys tomorrow . . .," I said. "There's somethin' I need to talk to Harry about before he goes to bed."

I sat in the swing, adjusting to Harry's pace after his usual warm welcome. But then he wasted no time; saying what was on his mind.

"Arnold, now what the hell is botherin' you? Why, you look like you just lost your best friend . . . and what in the hell got a hold of your face?" He inspected closely. "Now by-God you ain't been with one of those scratchers, have ya?" He laughed. I didn't understand what scratchers was all about, but it must be something as old Harry paused to dwell on it for the moment.

"Oh, that little scratch"—I pointed—"ain't shit, Harry! A low limb grabbed me when I was runnin' in the woods." Harry was convinced with what I'd said while making an attempt to strike a match when it flickered and went out just as it neared the pipe. I laughed as he expelled air with no smoke.

"Why, these are the sorriest bunch of damned matches I've ever had in my life!" He reared in protest, focusing on the match's blackened end. The second attempt was good however; when he expelled smoke into the air. After shaking the match out with a couple flicks of the wrist he turned to face me. With a frown and a slight wobble of his head he quickly withdrew his pipe.

"Arnold, do you ever get pissed off, and I mean at the least little thing? Why, you and I both know they's no reason to have cussed that damned match like that, now was there?" Ignoring Harry's question I went straight to what I wanted to ask.

"Harry, I've got to ask you somethin'," I said in a curious way and to disrupt him. He slowly acknowledged with a tilted chin. He wasn't drinking, so I figured there'd be more of a thoughtful answer. He cleared his throat while crossing a leg, and then gently laid his pipe down.

"I'll bet this has got somethin' to do with ole Jim now, ain't it?" He said while nodding sounding sure of himself.

"Harry, do you know the whore he's runnin' with?" I spoke loud and clear that there be no reason to repeat myself. But he still fiddled around with the hearing aid, the one closest to me; maybe a stall of sorts to conjure up the right answer.

"Why, Arnold, like I told you before; Jim will run with any woman that'd have him." After a quick spit off the side of the porch, he stopped the swing; clinching the chain looking uncomfortable with what he had to say.

"Why, hell, he's runnin' that damned ole Mable Braggs right now!" He quickly rattled off. "I used to like old Mable, but now I don't know if I want her around me anymore." I didn't need to coax Harry; as he was ready to tell all.

A sick feeling groped my stomach, regretting that I'd ever helped her that night with Wilma . . . But then again, what would have happened to the old lady had I not? James's words that I couldn't do anything about these situations was true but that still wouldn't stop my anger. *I cain't do a thing about this even if I was to confront the old man,* I thought. *I'm not goin' to flip out! I'm not gonna go off somewhere and cuss with every word I know.* James must have known it was Mable; with her stumpy figure and all.

I thought how he'd told me earlier that he didn't like telling me things that'd get me all worked up. There was a lot to be said about taking that deep breath before reacting to things. The talk of Mable and the old man had pretty well taken up all of our chat time with not much good to talk about.

"Harry, I think I'm going to call it a day. I need an early bed tonight, so I'll see you tomorrow sometime." I stood up as Harry reluctantly brought the swing to a stop; rare that I call it a night before him. A simple fact that there were lots of days I'd be his only visitor.

"Thanks for telling me everything, Harry. I appreciate your honesty." Harry wasn't one much for a handshake after he'd met you for the first time. I held my hand out for a handshake. Cold to the touch and along with his skinny finger I shook the hand of an honest man; one that I could bank on if I needed.

"Anytime, Arnold." He assured. "Why, you know my door's always open. And you have a good night for what's left of it." He retrieved his pipe, tipping it high into the air to end the night.

I pulled a curtain to the side, peering out the window, as Harry lit his last bowl for the evening. My loneliness could never match the countless years he'd sat there, waiting on the chance that someone would stop by and talk a while. There was never a car that passed that he didn't wave at or tip his pipe whether he knew them or not. I thought it good that he had the hearing aid to at least hear his own surroundings. But I also knew that sounds alone could never fill the void of one's loneliness.

How many tunes had he eked out from the swing's squeaky chains to that of a fiddle that might conjure a song up in his mind? I couldn't even imagine the thoughts of so many years that'd run through the old fellow's mind. But there he sat with his usual look. One leg lapped over the other; resting an elbow with his pipe in hand. It was hard to imagine the years it had taken to wear the chain so smoothly where he held on to them.

And through that very chain, he'd gauge the swing's speed as to its tightness and steady squeak. It was from their he'd watched the maple tree grow for the past sixty years of his life. It all looked so picturesque from where I viewed him silhouetted by the small dim lightbulb, casting a pale halo over him.

The sadness was hard to take knowing the way the old man had practically stopped visiting him, let alone take him anywhere anymore. He'd gotten what he wanted from the old fellow and now didn't want to mess with him much anymore, it appeared. But only on occasion did Harry say much about it. I let the small curtain drift back into place after Harry pulled the string to his porch light to go to bed. I sat in the bus seat, staring into the darkness as I'd got so accustomed to lately.

My promise to James—that I'd tell him before I'd have a final confrontation with the old man—stayed on my mind till late that night. I thought how my big brother would always let me go first with about anything that he thought was a waste of his time. And he knew all along that I wanted to outdo him. But it certainly was not this case when I'd shown my anger for the better part of the day and at one point James proclaimed that I was the angriest person he knew of and he was right—even his comment had upset me. But all along, I knew that I'd not say anything to him—blood brothers or not—when the time might come to take care of the old man.

I shook my head in an attempt to clear such thoughts. At one time, I'd considered that my mother was probably right that the Lord could help me as he did her, whereas she had way more problems than I. I thought of the countless times I'd told myself to not even consider the thought, but something always seemed to get in the way.

It hadn't been that many days since Harry had predicted that I should mark his words of an early frost; any day now.

"Why, I feel it in my bones," he said while rubbing his legs with a stiff hands; something I'd witness so many other old timers do. The Almanac couldn't have predicted it any closer when I woke to the year's first frost the next morning.

It was a beautiful Saturday with the sun just coming up over Whiskey Holler. The year's first frost was exciting and could sure enough put some zest into your step. The old barn crusted with frost looked like a painting that maybe James should try to copy, I thought. But I had to wonder with everything going on in his life if he'd ever paint again. Maybe as I had with my arrowhead, he'd also left things behind for good.

But before I milked I'd give Kate and Mr. Bill their grain so they'd be ready for Freddy to harness them after his walk up from his shack.

I cupped my hands together, blowing air onto my fingers knowing Red would have no part of me milking her with freezing hands. I laughed thinking of what Calvin had said in comparison when I told him of how she'd kicked me over my cold hands. He said he felt the same way anytime the old lady laid her big cold, clammy-ass paws on his tits but didn't mind if they were good and warm, and preferably hot, he'd winked. It was just one of the many thoughts we'd shared to remind me of how much I missed ole Calvin.

James had scraped the ice from the windshield for the drive to Mom's as I held the milk steady between my shoes. We quickly ate breakfast in hopes of enjoying the frosty wilderness, which wouldn't be there but for a short while. I told James that I was going to run up through the woods to see how beautiful everything was and that I'd meet him at the laydown yard.

Duck decided that he'd ride with James which I'd already hinted. There was a different smell to things as I drew the chilly dampness into my nostrils. The old man's calculation that we got the baccer hung worked out perfectly, as we'd beaten the early frost.

At a distance, I'd spotted Freddy at the pond.

"Get your ass to work!" I yelled when he spun quickly, with his familiar military salute. The phrase, seeing one's breath was clear watching fog pouring from Mr. Bill's and Kate's nostrils as they also were looking in my direction.

Mom would make a birthday cake for me on this day October 1, 1966. And they'd all sing to me after supper. I didn't expect that the old man be there even though he'd suddenly started spending more time at home, but usually through the day when everyone was at school Mom told me. But we couldn't quite figure his reasoning unless he was tired of how he'd been acting; which I had my doubts about that one. Judy told me he acted better toward Mom but was still short-tempered about things. I'd continue to ignore him and not to say a word if I could help it.

But this would be my special day and I wouldn't let anything including old Mickel stand in the way of my plan; one I'd set forth from the time I'd left school on Friday. I hadn't even told James of it. And like Mr. Bill and Kate at the pond, I exhaled long breaths of swirling clouds, disappearing quickly as I ran on toward the laydown yard. It'd been awhile, since I'd seen her last with the baccer cutting going on in Pike County and with school starting.

I'd come to the conclusion that there was no need to look for a girlfriend at school. Everything I needed had been at the Gant house all the while. Besides if I would find a girlfriend at school I didn't have a car let alone gas money to get me to a girlfriends house.

Like James with Scarlett, I needed Linda who could sweep my troubles away, with what was going on around me. With her to talk to every night, things would have to be better, or I could dream. I couldn't wait to see her with my mind made up, where she'd rush to my arms and I'd see the frosty morning in her eyes. It would be then and there I'd kiss her no matter who was around. Mickel could simply go to hell.

A different kind of chill other than the cold morning shot up my backbone or spine, as Gene had corrected me. I had to laugh at such a crazy thought and at a time like this.

I ran faster, thinking of her pushing bright-colored leaves off to the side before sinking her dipper into the cold springs water.

"Oh, if I could only be there to drink from the dipper or even better from her hands," I said loud enough to be heard, which stopped me in my tracks. And even looked around as though someone might hear me. "Goofy ass," I laughed.

I'd made it to the edge of the woods when James pulled up beside me, revving the Buick's engine. I climbed in, rubbing the chill from my hands.

"Da gone, Piggy Wiggy, this is as far as you made it? I thank I could've done better than that," Duck joked.

"Well, when you want to back your words up with money, Ducky, we'll set a time. And I'll even give you a head start."

"I'm only kiddin', Piggy." He smiled.

"Today's the day, James," I blurted while cutting Ducks joke short.

"And the day for what?" James asked.

"It's the day I'm gonna kiss Linda. I nodded. I've got nothin' to lose."

"Bullshit. I've heard this how many times now of your puckering threats?" He laughed. "And, I'll bet you a dollar that you don't do it." I shook his hand with all the confidence in the world.

I'd simply gotten way more sure of myself since school started. I really couldn't imagine why it'd taken so long. Maybe being around a bunch of loose-talking guys in vo-ag had something to do with it. And there was also a lot to be said about TV and how easy they made it look to fall in love and live happily ever after.

I'd rehearsed what I was fixing to do a thousand times just like trying out for the part in a movie. Seeing it all play out on TV or hearing others talk was better than what James could tell me at times. But there was no doubt in my mind whatsoever that this would be the day that when she brought the morning water I'd simply run to greet her.

They were loading the truck when we pulled up and as usual, Mickel complained every time he had to bend over to pick up a piece of wood. He gave me a shitty look and had nothing to say. I thought about what Bob said the night I'd delivered the milk and how jealous Mickel had become of Linda and I. But even before that he seemed to have a watchful eye over her anytime she and I were talking with one another.

"Mickel, just roll them over to the truck, and we'll load 'em," James ordered while pointed his finger to a certain spot.

"I told him not to drink that shit last night!" Bob growled in a low voice. "Why you'uns wouldn't believe how much he's been drinkin' lately and it's got worse Arnold since you delivered the milk that one time. He hardly does anythin' now 'cept complain all damn day! Why, hell, me and Freddy do 'bout all the work anymore . . . But when Jim comes round, you'd think Mickel was the hardest-workin' son of a bitch in the world! And to tell the truth, I'm tired of it." He nodded along with a poor effort to smile.

I glanced down the road with anticipation when Bob intentionally cleared his throat.

"I guess you didn't hear 'bout Linda," he interrupted my gaze. "She ran away night 'afore last Arnold!" My heart skipped a beat with a sudden dryness in my throat. I needed a drink in the worst way. *This can't be,* I thought to myself, looking down the road and thinking he might be pulling my leg. But it was his strained look that told the truth.

"Really, well where did she go?" My question must have sounded panic-like.

"Well, we don't know." Bob said, swishing a fly away from his mouth. "She was gone when we got up that morning. She left a little note sayin' she wanted a better life than this, and I sure don't blame her, Arnold." Bob pulled a small piece of paper from his shirt pocket, handing it to me. "Here, you read it. It's kinda hard to make out."

"Der' Mom, fur give me I'll be alrit' I want somtin' better than this. I Love you, Linda."

James shot me a sorrowful look as sadness had overtaken me. My plans of a first kiss and on my birthday had been swept away. I'd had my chance and blew it for sure. A harsh reality, I thought, in a way I'd not felt before. With a broken heart that she was really gone I walked down to the springs at the Gant house where I could be alone for a minute. I read the note once again, picturing her effort to spell something out. Sadness weakened my knees, wondering at what private place she'd written the note.

The flat rock I'd placed for her to sit on to fill the water buckets looked to have a loneliness about it also. She hadn't given a hint of leaving in the few times we'd talked. *She always seemed happy,* I thought. *Had she been waiting all this time on me to rescue her?* But as badly as I wanted to fall in love the reality was that I was too young to do such a thing. I could barely manage myself, let alone rescue someone else. Bob had waited on my return as everyone else had gone back to work.

"You know she has a crush on you, Arnold. But Linda's different than the rest of that bunch. She has a lot goin' for herself. You kin see how bad her spellin' is, and I think that's one of the reasons why she left. She was always talkin' 'bout how she'd like to read a book and maybe write a story of her own sometime. The poor little girl had nothin', and then Mickel treating her and the rest of those kids, as far as that goes, like shit all the time! Maybe it's because she wasn't his child that made him act like that." Bob looked off towards Mickel, who was having a hard time with a small piece of wood.

I felt anger as I looked at him and how broken-down he was and wanted to go and knock the hell out of him. But I couldn't. I knew I'd hurt him if I did. *It is what it is,* I thought with a loud sigh.

"Well, how old is she? I mean, is she old enough to take care of herself?" My jaw was numbed with worry now. I wanted there to be another letter, one that she wrote to me, but Bob would've already given it had there been one. *But how could there not be a goodbye note?* I thought. *Maybe she couldn't spell well enough to say what she wanted to tell me.* Or maybe she didn't want to burden herself with all the problems I had.

"Well, happy birthday to me", I thought to myself.

"She was fifteen," Bob answered, looking again to make sure Mickel couldn't hear him. "I think she went down Portsmouth way." He spoke quietly. "Now I'm not for sure, but I think ole Mary might've talked her into runnin' away and goin' down to stay with them. I know they felt sorry for her, and Calvin talked with the girl several times before they'd left for Camp Creek, but neither Calvin nor Mary seemed suspicious about anything when they left, though. If they were the ones behind her leaving, they sure kept quiet about it." Bob reckoned. I breathed a sigh of relief, knowing that she would be safe with them. I knew Mary'd treat her like her own, and Calvin wouldn't show his vile ways around her as much. He could be kind when he needed to.

"Now you kin keep that note if you want to, Arnold. They think it got burned up startin' a fire in the cook stove this mornin'."

A flash of excitement ran through me as I folded the note back up, stuffing it in my pocket. I thought that maybe James could take me to see her if she had truly gone to Calvin's. But what would I do if she were there? Maybe it was time to admit that I wasn't ready for anything beyond a kiss. The truth was that we were both way too young to venture beyond that and with any kind of outcome.

"Did you know Arnold that she'd never been to school in her life? And I've heard her tell Mickel and her mom both and I mean every year that she'd wanted to start school and to be like all the other kids. She pleaded with them saying she'd walk with our kids down to where the bus could pick her up in front of Harry's. And ole Mickel drunker than hell the other night laughed about it and got her cryin' when he said she'd be fifteen years old and in the first grade. That's as close as I ever come to hitting him with my hand around his throat like it was. And I sure didn't mean to get Mickel's family upset. Everyone except Linda who I didn't think would have minded if I'd carried out my threat.

"So that day you flagged us over it was only your kids that got on the bus?"

"That's right only mine." He answered back in a matter fact way.

"Why have any of those kids ever been to school, Bob?" I asked while turning to the side that I not have to see Mickel at all.

"Hell no! Why if the law ever finds out about them, old Mickel will be goin' to jail." Bob sounded more disgusted than ever. "They already got on his ass a couple years back for not puttin' them to school, so what did he do? He just moved to another county. And to tell the truth, it's to the point, Arnold, that I'd turn his sorry ass in but then I'd have to take care of that family too.

Me and Betty are gettin' ready to leave, and I don't want Mickel tagging alone' with us anymore. I've carried him with me for a long time 'cause I felt sorry for him, but I don't feel that way anymore especially since he don't show any desire to make himself any better off. But I do feel sorry for those poor kids, they're not bad at all. And every time one of them does something wrong he's always quick to point out that they're nothin' but a bunch of step kids to him anyway. But I cain't afford to be raisin' them at my age. As you can see Betty and me got a late enough start ourselves; a long story that I don't need to get into. And Mickel's too old to have any kind of family. You can see that his health ain't the best in the world. He passes a lot of blood when he goes to the toilet." Bob slowly shook his head; looking discussed.

"I told him he needs to go to the doctor the other day, and he told me to mind my own damn business. So from here on, I'm gonna mind my own business until we leave." Bob spat a mouthful of baccer off to the side.

"So none of those kids are Mickel's?" I questioned.

"No, they ain't! And if the truth be told, I've wondered if that might be another reason why Linda run away. The times Mickel drinks, he starts doin' strange things. He'd get drunk and keep askin' Linda if he can brush her hair, and no matter how many times she shied away, he keeps askin'. He just sets there in his chair all drunk, and continually stares at her. And she couldn't walk near him that he wouldn't slap her on the butt every chance that he got. Hell I had to put an end to that one night with another threat."

"Well what does his wife think about it; don't she ever say anything?" I asked in a curious way. Bob's long strained look could pretty well sum up his thoughts on her with an uplifted brow.

"She's about as useless as him. Hell half of their money goes for liquor and cigarette's anymore. Maybe I'm no better though with a pouch of chew a week.

"Shit Bob that's not even close. That's nowhere near what a pack of cigarettes cost and let alone a fifth of whiskey." Bob pulled a knee up far enough that he held it between his locked fingers while slowly rocking back and forth.

"Try two bottles a week Arnold!" He said with a slow nod.

"You've got to be shittin' me Bob!" I countered.

"Nope. Like I said Arnold Ray I'm at my wit's end with all of it."

I grudgingly looked Mickel's way as he kicked at a piece of wood while massaging his stomach with both hands. What a sorry bastard I thought when suddenly he bent over; clutching at his stomach and crying out in pain. Everyone heard him but made no effort to help as we'd all seen the aftermath plenty of times. It took a while before he could straighten back up then he immediately turned and started walking slowly off toward the Gant house. Bob, quickly stood up from the log.

"And where in the hell do ya think you're goin'?" He put it bluntly.

"I just don't feel up to workin' today," Mickel grumbled, and never looked back.

—

"Well, this is really gettin' old . . ." Bob shook his head. We watched as old Mickel barely managed to lift his feet through the mounds of dirt. Dust surrounded him until he made it to the small road, where he disappeared on over the hill.

Then suddenly, like a good song coming on the radio, there was the old familiar sound of hooves and harnesses clopping and clanging from the other end of the yard.

It was perfect timing when I left the log to pat their rumps and scratch behind their ears. And even better was when they pushed up against me just enough to unbalance me a little. I glanced back, to where James had joined Bob and were talking quietly between themselves. I had a feeling it was about me and more than likely of what my plans had been for that day.

A minute later Freddy walked up, quickly pulling his pipe before his usual salute and then a hard gripping handshake.

"Oh, I snee how it is now. I make dem work aw day, in you show up and nay get wewarded." Freddy laughed as he removed a match from a small box, striking it on the side of Mr. Bill's harness.

"So, what'd you do, Freddy? Take a shortcut to get here? I kept waitin' for you to come up from the pond."

"Well, I'm mullin' wogs from da last holner over, so I yust go from da pond to nere and save da horses a few neps. And where in da hell is nat Mickel at?" Freddy asked, looking all around the yard. "Non't ell' me, he's gone to da howse again?" James and Duck had begun tossing wood on the truck's bed as Bob eased his way to where Freddy and I were standing. "Non't ell me, wet me gess, hez gone to da house again?" Freddy asked Bob and all the while looking disgusted.

"Yeah, you got that right, Freddy."

"Nare still mus me som licqner weft in nat botnal." Freddy winked. I could tell by the way they looked at each other that Mickel had gotten under their skin and was a real problem for both of them. "Moys, now let's see how quick we can get a woad on dat 'ruck. It nooks wike o Junior's in a hurry!" There were still a few words Freddy said that was hard to understand. But by the time he'd finished what he was getting at you could pretty well put his meaning together; nothing like the first times. Freddy's speech impediment didn't stand in the way with anything that he wanted to say. I'd not had to ask him to repeat himself for some time now. 'Sn…arlette', Freddy's joke of why James was in such a hurry set the three of us to laughing as his face redden by the minute. Satisfied that he'd got a good laugh from us; Freddy blew a steady stream of smoke straight up into the air.

He emptied his pipe with one good whack on the side of Kate's log, then walked over to where Mr. Bill stood. Carefully he shoved his pipe in a slot between the collar and the hames which I thought fit the purpose well.

Like a well-oiled machine Duck rolled piece after piece to the back of the truck where James and I threw them upon the bed. It was all Bob and Freddy could do to stay up with the stacking.

"Now boys, I don't think I kin keep up with you young whippersnappers like this for very much longer." Bob said with a quick swipe of his brow. "I'd be like old Mickel, in no time headin' for the house!" He playfully nodded towards the Gant House.

James and I'd talked many times of Bob's stamina whether physical or mental. We never had to take into consideration his age with any task at hand. James's thoughts had always been that Bob could have found a better line of work than pulp wooding. We all laughed at Bob's remark as James handed him the chain binder's as if they were a coveted trophy.

"You're the driver, Bob and we don't get paid till you get back." James said. He figured if we could get a couple loads out on the week-end it would pay for our gas for the next couple of weeks.

"Oh, I wouldn't have it any other way," Bob said with a smile as he quickly climbed up the side of the load and on to the very top. After he'd finished binding the load down, we walked to the break area for a rest. The sun had pretty well erased all the frost by now, but the morning was still on the cool side.

"Have you boys seen Jim lately?" Bob tugged on a stumpy finger until it popped. Suddenly he seemed nervous, I thought. "I stopped by and asked your Momma the other day', but seems nobody knows where he's at right now. I even stopped by and asked old Harry also and he told me that If I did come across Jim to tell him to swing by his place." Bob looked down at the ground with a dreadful look.

"I guess ya know why we need to see him, don't ya?" James shook his head in disbelief. I tried desperately to control my anger by taking a deep breath and expelling it slowly. "Ya know, he's kinda got us in a bad way if'n he don't pay us ever week." Bob seemed to stumble for the right words. "And I can tell ya that I'm not stayin' around here and starve to death especially with winter comin' on." He assured.

"Nu' . . . non't nink he nook Linda down ta Camp Reek, do ya?" Freddy interrupted as the tension become more visible. My blood went cold at the thought, knowing that the old man would be more than happy to take her anywhere had he the chance. And just the thought made my stomach heave. Maybe seeing my stress, Bob spoke up once again.

"Nah, I don't think so. Linda's a sweet gal and smart at that! I've known her since she's a little girl, and she just don't do bad things. She just wants to do somethin' with her life, and that's why she ran away. And I can tell you another thang for sure, is that it wouldn't be . . . with a damned drunk!" His words quieted all movement, with Freddy slowly shaking his head in full agreement. It was rare in itself that Bob ever said much bad about the old man other than an occasional joke.

"There's nothing wrong with telling the truth." James's comeback was quick and to the point. But what Freddy said about him offering Linda a ride whether it was true or not didn't set well with me. I knew him all too well when a sharp whistle suddenly came to mind.

"Freddy, I'd like to hook Kate and Mr. Bill up to a load just for old time's sake you might say." I pointed toward them before standing up and brushing the dirt from my butt.

"'Ell, dur yer nam amnals, so don ass me." We all burst into laughter at the same time with Freddy's most excellent comeback, but leaving him with a red face. Squeaky harnesses with chains dragging dusty singletrees deadened all conversation as I left the yard.

I knew they'd talk of my disappointment as how Linda had left without a trace. I went to the same soft mossy place I'd laid and dreamed of her so many times. The idea of never seeing the heavens roll past in her eyes again put a pain in my heart. She'd not laid back on the spongy softness such as I and dream of endless kisses. Had she stopped at the bus I wondered, without me hearing her knock? I would've given up my dreams of a kiss to have had the chance to say goodbye to her. Why couldn't I have told her the countless times that I'd said "I love you" under my breath? I'd always love her in a way that no one would understand, maybe other than James.

The thought of her gone forever tempted a tear when a sudden breeze blew past scattering leaves and dust in the fall air. I slowly opened my eyes after it had all settled back down. I thought how nothing had changed in the few minutes that I'd laid there. Whipped, would be a better word as to how I felt about everything right now. I hated to hear that Bob and Freddy hadn't been paid. And Harry still waited on the old man's promise. But worst of all was to rob our mother of her youth and treat her as nothing short of a slave had bothered me from the time I was a little boy to witness him hit her for the first time.

How many more half brothers and sisters were still out there and was he giving more to them than his own needy family?" Like James had said awhile back; there were probably things that we'd never know of and hoped we never would. And so it was here, as I laid back on the soft green moss's with fingers laced behind my head, knowing more than ever that I had to face reality.

But before doing so I had to be honest with myself that I'd always been a time bomb and with a short fuse ready to explode in a fit of anger. The best examples of such where the times I ignored my big brothers advise and even turned against him for not siding with me on some matters and especially with the old man. But he'd been right to point out that anything could set me off. Even his advice to take a deep breath was usually taken the wrong way on my part and could infuriate me to the point of getting out of control.

Looking up through the tree tops I drew that much needed breath that James had advised so many times before. First of all I couldn't change things that were in the past that the old man had done to everyone. I just didn't need to linger on them to the point of driving myself insane and knowing all the while what they'd all lead up to. I needed to face the fact that it wasn't just for the family's sake that I wanted to do away with him. Sam the mule getting whipped for no reason. Half brothers and sisters whose faces appeared before me in the dark of night. And there were plenty others that came to mind.

"Stop," I said out loud that I not get completely carried away. Mom! And for her sake all things should be considered that I not do something crazy. The thought alone gave me a sigh of relief, with Mom being my most precious excuse.

I turned my thoughts to Linda. I had to face another reality. The fact that I wouldn't go see her even if she was at Camp Creek with Calvin and Mary. It was mostly in my dreams that I knew her best anyway. "What a day for a daydream," as the song went and my love for her would eventually be no more than a dream itself. It ended as quickly as it'd started when it came right down to it. I simply couldn't dwell on it any longer. I had to get over something that I'd never had in the first place. But blue skies and white fluffy clouds in her eyes would be forever on my mind.

A crazy thought that maybe this is why the old man comes to the woods to confess, it was better that no one was around to condemn or interrupt you. A place where you could truly be frank with yourself. But would I be any better than him and keep my confessed promise to stay calm in times of turmoil. I lay there for another minute or two letting everything soak in before making my way back to where I left the animals standing.

"Why, Kate, you're gettin' a little gray around your ears, it looks like," I said, hugging the side of her head, which she always gave into. I hitched them up to a couple of small logs and, after disconnecting them at the yard, handed them back over to Freddy, who'd been nervously milling about. Things looked to be back to normal; James was busy up and around the hill a ways, cutting for the next load. Duck looked happy measuring and notching where the next cuts would be on the logs. I started up the other saw and began cutting while Freddy continued pulling more logs to the yard. Upon Bob's return the five of us would quickly load the truck again, and he'd be on his way to Chillicothe once more.

We all shook hands over our accomplishment after we'd loaded the truck for the second time. After a check of his watch Bob hastened to be on his way.

After we finished the day James and I climbed into the car and headed for the bus. Duck would do as always, cut down through the woods to get to the house saying there might be a left over biscuit laying around which always got a good laugh from James and I.

"You know, James, it's sad not being up there workin' with those guys all the time. I miss it, don't you? But more than anything, I wished ole Calvin lived a little closer. I sure miss his ways."

James listened to what I had to say but knew all too well that I'd want to talk of Linda just one more time.

"Do you think it'd sound stupid, James, if I told you that I loved her?" I blurted.

"No, not at all. I understand. I mean, how many years have you known her and just now admit that you love her?"

"What in the hell are you talkin' about? Why, you asshole." I pointed a finger at him that he insinuated that I was talking about Mary.

"Oh, I'm sorry. I thought that's what you meant by the Calvin comment." His grin widened. "I know who you meant, Arnie," he razzed further. "Just kidding, I know that you're really missing Linda, and I'm sorry that she left. And I really knew this would be the day that you'd kiss her."

"Well, how'd you know that?" I turned to face him.

"Because I couldn't see your head—it was too far up your ass." He laughed. "No, I'm still kidding. You know, I could see it in your eyes. But it just didn't turn out that way, Arnold. I wished with all my heart that your dream would have come true, especially on your birthday and all. I just thought to joke about it, might ease the hurt a little. And I knew why you went into the woods today. Sometimes it's best to be alone and think things out."

"Yeah, I had great intentions today James. And you can only imagine how disappointing this is to me. Kinda like being ambushed if you know what I mean. And all the times that you've knocked my breath out; and not that I didn't deserve it; never hurt as bad as this blow did. Ya know how it is when you wake up from a dream and I don't mean a bad one. But one of those strange ones that you can't quite understand but feel relieved after you wake up. Well that's about the way it's been with Linda that suddenly I wake up and it's over. And to tell the truth I'm not so sure that I was ready for her. Maybe one kiss is all there ever would have been, I don't know. And as bad as it sounds, I'm relieved in some ways that she's gone. At our age there just couldn't be a happy ending. Kinda like the young couple the old man married over at the farm and lying by sayin' they'd both lost their birth certificate. Remember how they laughed and said they'd live on love but I'd be willin' to bet that they still live with his parents. And that's my point James I don't want to depend on anyone. But at me and Linda's age I'd be stuck in somebody's woods for the rest of my life.

I've got three years of school left and I've got every intent of graduating with my class. But I know that I'll never forget her. Even though I never kissed her I got the chance to gaze into a world such as I'd never dreamed before. It's in their eyes. Right James!" I smiled.

"Arnold that's some of the smartest shit I ever heard come from your mouth. I mean that was like far out man." James laughed while giving the steering wheel a good whack across the top. "I'm glad that you considered everything and came up with the right answers. Take a breath and go on with life brother. And when you're ready for round two there are others out there, you know," he concluded.

"Yeah, there sure is." I shot back. "And does she still have a boyfriend?" I joked in a playful way. James shot me a strange look.

"Boyfriend? What are you talking about?" He laughed. "A boyfriend, they've been married for a long time why you know that."

"I'm talking about Jeanie! Who the hell are you talking about?"

"Ma...ry," he laughed, reaching over to shove me up against the door.

"Asshole, pull this car over right here and now so I can put a decent ass whipping on you!" I shook a fist at him and with no hesitation he slammed on the brakes sliding to a dusty stop.

We met at the hood, where we locked arms, and the tug-of-war was on. It was seldom we'd go to the ground anymore, unless it was over something of a more worthy cause. James by no means had meant for it to be anything other than to help relieve my frustration which I appreciated.

James had gone to Scarlett's but was back in just a couple hours, way short of a normal visit. He let on as if there was nothing wrong but his constant frown led me to believe differently. Throughout Sunday he distanced himself from the laydown yards normal activity with all its craziness. He stayed in the woods most of the day never coming down to join us when we took a break. I'd heard him cut many a tree down and could tell when he was anxious about something especially when his saw stalled for long periods of time. And I on the other hand avoided Mickel by staying clear of him and not so much as even a good morning. But by the end of the day we had the truck loaded and enough wood cut for a couple more loads.

And just as the night before James returned early from his visit to Scarlett's. We sat and bullshitted with Harry for quite some time before returning to the bus to play a few hands of Crazy Eight which neither of us could really get into. It just seemed a way to stall until James decided he was ready to go to bed.

There was a loud banging on the door early Monday morning. We'd been locking it from the inside for quite some time so the old man couldn't just barge in on us.

"Tough titie, big . . . daddy!" James whispered.

"Tough what?" I whispered back.

"Titie, just like it sounds." He snickered.

"Let me guess," I wheezed with excitement. "Readers Digest right?" I'd gone from a whisper to a sudden laugh enough that the old man heard it.

"Open this damned door right now!" he commanded.

"The titie thing is a saying from Scarlett and Jeanie's Digest of craziness when they rattle on about everything." James made it obvious with his normal conversational tone that he was going to finish what he wanted to tell me and whether the old man liked it or not.

"Now I said to open this door and I mean now!" He commanded louder this time and with authority that set off a short coughing spell.

"Or I'll huff and puff and blow... the damn bus down." My cartoon effort of the big bad wolf was better than I'd ever done before. With one hand on his forehead and the other pushing on his stomach he tried to set up in bed. It didn't matter if the old man heard what I'd said and he wouldn't know that it was directed at him. We could hear him mumbling just outside the door and sounding as if he was arguing with someone.

"Junior, open this Goddamned door!!" He swore with one final bang that might have been a kick I thought.

"Hold on, give me a minute," James said, collecting himself somewhat before climbing out of bed.

The old man wasted no time, however, once in the driver's seat.

"Now I need you boys to miss school today, and there ain't no way out of it." With not so much as a good morning, he'd gotten straight to the point. The old familiar smell of his cigarette filled the small bus, which quickly irritated me. "Now there's enough moisture in the air that I'm sure the baccer's in case," he proclaimed.

"Like, do you think you might not smoke in here? I mean this is where we sleep ya know."

"I own this damn bus, and I'll smoke in it any time I want to, Arnold Ray! You can go stand outside if you don't like it," he pointed. Granted that I didn't want to see him in the first place, but I didn't think my request was unreasonable at all. But I wasn't going to humble myself in any way to say "please" as a rush of anger ran throughout me.

"Well, it's not just your stinking-ass cigarettes that's enough to gag a maggot, but I can smell the stink' of beer all the way over here too!" I shot back.

"Well, old buddy, like I told ye . . . if you don't like it, there's the damn door. And you can hit it anytime you please." He nodded as if it were the solution to all his problems.

"Oh, don't worry, that day will come," I followed.

"Well, until it does, there's things got to be done, damnit! So let's get crackin'," he ordered, followed by a quick sharp whistle as he stood up to leave. I considered how long it'd been since I'd seen him remove his hand from behind his ear as he did so now. "Ree got up extree early to git breakfast ready, so you boys need to get rollin'."

The whistling sounded a little less intense as I peeped out the window, watching him make his way to the car.

"Well, I guess we should've gone to school a little early today." James let out a half-ass laugh. He stretched his arms over his head but drew them in quickly when I faked a punch to his stomach. The old man spinning gravel as he took off was pretty common anymore. He just couldn't get to wherever fast enough. *Including hell*, I thought to myself. But instead of heading down the road he went up towards the Gant house with intent to pay them I'd hope.

"I told you, James, that asshole would show up like this, stay gone for days drunk and then come home like nothin' ever happened. Hell, with all the time he's been gone, he could've had a lot stripped by himself!" I suggested. "And have you noticed how it doesn't seem to bother him much anymore when we threaten him back other than tellin' us we can hit the road? It's more like a joke we've heard a thousand times, but it really ain't funny anymore."

"Well, I've got a hunch that it's not just us that's counting the days before we leave by the way Bob sounded the other day.

"But the problem for him is—and he knows it—he can't legally kick us out till we're eighteen." James smiled. "And we'll see how that plays out come February, when I turn eighteen."

"Well, shit, I'll be way beyond that age before I graduate school." I laughed.

"Don't worry, Arnold. I'll be living somewhere else by then, so you can come live with me." There was no reason to tell my big brother how grateful I was; he already knew.

Mom was quiet when we came through the back door. I'd let the screen door slam behind me, bouncing several times before settling to a stop. My intention was solely to irritate the old man when I'd noticed the empty Anacin tin lying beside the sink; obviously, he had a headache.

"Stop slammin' that damn door!" he bellowed. I thought that if I had a dollar for every time I'd heard him get on someone about the door, I'd have enough money to leave right now.

"And how are my boys this morning?" Mom asked as she hugged us. Her eyes looked weary, evident that she'd been crying.

"Now you boys need to hurry up and eat so we can git headin' for Pike County!" the old man continued with his rage. "If that baccer goes out of case, I don't know when we'll git the chance to strip again!" he barked with the stench of cigarette smoke following him into the kitchen. I'd determined by how many butts were in the ashtrays that he'd possibly spent the night here. Mom sighed, looking over at him with limp arms hanging at her side.

"Jim, they just got here, and they need to take enough time to eat their breakfast. I know that a few minutes more ain't goin' to make that much difference," she followed. He took a step toward her, waving a warning finger.

"You don't know what you're talkin' about, Ree, so don't even get started on me!" He kept poking his finger closer to her face.

"You can stop waving your finger at Mom right now!" James said. "So why don't you go on over, and we'll be there after we eat." he suggested.

"All right, but I don't need you boy's pissin' around here fer very long. I need you in Pike County! They ain't no time to be lollygaggin' around!" He'd had the last word as usual with the screen door slamming behind him.

"Quit slamming the door!" Duck ordered after the old man distanced himself from the house. Everyone started laughing, including Mom. You couldn't help but laugh at Duck's imitations of the old man.

I pulled a curtain to the side and watched as he drove away desperate in the way he pushed his hair back over his head. It hadn't been but a few minutes ago that I wanted to break the finger that he'd threatened our mother with. And it wasn't just me anymore with James saying he'd break the old man's neck if he ever hit her again. I looked back into the kitchen, where James was talking with her and reminding me of our renewed promise that we'd confide in each other before any confrontation with the old man. To make a promise to my brother was one thing but to lie was another which he always seemed to know if I were to do so. But seldom did I have a reason to lie to him in the first place.

It hadn't been but a few days back that I'd come to a better understanding of how I thought about certain things. Or at least I thought so at the time. But it wasn't anything new as I'd made such promises before and couldn't keep them. I was no better than the old man with his addiction to Alcohol and with mine being anger. One was no better than the other as how it could lead you astray I thought. I'd come to grips with myself about Linda that day and how it would only be in dreams that I'd ever have an encounter with her again. And I knew James would have taken me to find her if I'd asked him. But as bad as James disliked the way the old man treated our mother, or any other thing, I knew that under no circumstances would he agree with me to get rid of the old man once and for all.

Even though I'd told him of such plans I really doubted he could have imagined the horrible thoughts that had plagued me for many years. But without his help I'd have to abandon my latest place high up in the woods, where a house once stood and flowers still grew overlooking our farm in Pike County. I wanted him buried there on the top of the mountain that maybe in some strange way he could see what he'd done to all of us. James's comeback to quell my anger was always the same. "Arnold, for the sake of your mother what if you were to get caught." James knew exactly what to say. He'd warned on other occasions that there was a good chance, that I would get caught. But it was me and me alone that continually put myself in this position. I should have figured by now that I never thought too clearly anytime I raged about anything. Now mad that I'd put myself into this state of mind where confusion would control my every thought.

I hadn't gone to church in a while, but on several occasions, had asked for forgiveness for my plans. I knew that my prayers that he would die in some mysterious way would never be answered; and it was a sin for me to ask such a thing. I'd never give my mother the slightest hint of such thoughts, knowing she wouldn't sleep at nights, worrying about my soul. I glanced at her still in the kitchen with James and Judy, while thinking about the two boys up at Good Hope and how we and they resembled the old man in some ways.

With a deep sigh I looked around the table at favorable features we all had gotten from our mother. She turned thanks, trying to sound somewhat cheerful. "Amen," she finished. Then there it was, heat rising into the air with a golden-brown crust capping the top. James made no attempt to get it, and neither did I. It just didn't seem that important now; it seemed childish to fight over something that used to be so much fun.

"Duck can have it." James smiled as he scooped gravy on the three biscuits he'd just covered with eggs and bacon.

We quickly finished breakfast, knowing all too well that the old man was right; without moisture in the air the baccer could go out of case in a matter of hours. James turned the music up just enough to drown out all noises as he sifted the Buick through a cold thick fog, the perfect conditions for stripping baccer. Our favorite songs would come and go without much effort to sing on our part. Any conversation would have been a repeat sounding like a broken record at this point.

Black smoke swirled slowly from the stove pipe at the stripping house. We'd all complained one time or the other that he'd get the room way too hot and dry the baccer out quicker. "Strip faster," he'd say which was funny at the time. His excuse for always being cold, was because of poor circulation he'd say. Any follow-up on my part was that it, and every other problem he had, was simple because he smoked. And drinking didn't help either, I'd throw in at times.

"Now boys, the baccer's just right fer stripping," he announced when we walked into the small stripping house. There was almost a kindness to his voice, I thought. "Arnold Ray, now sees if you can get us a couple good armloads so, me, and ole Junior here can get started." He sounded completely different to what he did just an hour or so ago. But I figured like it always had been, that he needed us was all it amounted to; then he'd go back to being the same low-down ass that he always was.

Neither James nor I had spoken a word yet, and besides, what would we say anyhow? I thought how we'd exchanged words of love with Mom before we left the house that morning. And granted boys always seemed to have more affection for their mothers, I couldn't remember a time the old man ever telling me that he loved me. But as far as that goes I'd never told him either.

The thought of him hugging the boys at Good Hope would stick in my mind forever when they acted as if they loved him also. I left the small stripping house somewhat angry, thinking we, not them, were the stepchildren, after all. I thought back to the last time I'd even called him Dad. I climbed up to the first tier and dropped several sticks to the ground. After gathering up as many as I could carry, I headed for the stripping house.

James stood rigid while gazing out of the dirty little window, leaning forward on fisted knuckles planted firmly at his end of the stripping table. I couldn't tell if they'd been talking or not when I threw the large armload in the cradle where the old man waited. I'd never tell him that he was the fastest baccer stripper I'd ever seen. Even Uncle Arnold confessed to that fact. But the real surprise came when he'd go outside to smoke his cigarettes. Even the whistling was less intense. We had a private laugh afterwards when he went to Willow Springs and came back with a loaf of bread and a pound of ham to make sandwiches with.

We got to a stopping point and decided it was getting late and time to go home, being I still had to milk. The old man seemed to think that Mom would take care of it, which I quickly disagreed with and would have no part of that. All in all, it was probably the best day we'd spent with him in a long time. But I wondered how short-lived it would be this time.

"Well, I'll see you boys here bright and early in the morning." He said but sounding more like a question too me.

"You mean you're not going home tonight?" James asked.

"No, I'm going over to Tom Kinsley's and play a little music tonight. By the time we get finished, it'll be late. I'll have this place warmed up and ready to go by the time you boys get here, and as you know the earlier the better," he hinted. We stopped in Bainbridge and got ourselves a strawberry milkshake to wash the baccer taste out of our mouths.

Mom was making fried taters with onions along with fried chicken for supper. It happened to be the old man's favorite as it was mine also. Just the sound of it all frying up could put a salty taste in one's mouth. Her anticipation that he might come home that evening vanished when we all sat down to eat. She'd stalled for as long as she could but finally had to ask,

"Is your Dad comin' home tonight?" It sounded as if she already knew the answer.

James frowned as he looked my way. "No, he's staying at Tom Kinsley's tonight, Mom." She became quiet; hope had eluded her once again. Her mouth puckered as she placed her hands together to turn thanks.

"Oh, heavenly Father," she prayed. I didn't close my eyes but watched her facial plea that the Lord show Jim the path back to the fold. *This is all in vain*, I thought. But I'd not dampen her hopes, that I thought she was wasting her time. "Take care and guide him, O Lord," she went on to say. She sniffled for a few second as did Judy also before continuing on to finish her prayer of hope. Judy's hand trembled as she wiped a tear away. I didn't feel the sadness as I had so many times before with my mother's prayers. They'd never be answered, and I knew it. Prayer should be a time of reasonable requests and thanksgivings, with no place for mine.

"Thank you, Jesus, and amen." She dragged the last words. Maybe it was the same sound that over the years set everyone to laughing when the steamy chicken leg landed in my plate before they'd even opened their eyes. But Mom didn't laugh; she went to the bathroom running water to help drown out her crying.

It was disappointing enough that all my efforts to get her to leave him had failed. She simply couldn't see that we could live happily without him as I'd predicted. She'd trust that the Lord would eventually come through for her once again, she'd pray. I drew my fists tightly under the table, knowing the old man would do as he pleased, and our poor mother would always wait on him. On the way to the bus, James offered that Mom knew of no other way than the way of the Lord.

"Well, I guess I'll see you later, James," I said, climbing out of the car.

"No, I'm not going anywhere tonight," he said, turning the ignition off.

"You're not goin' to Scarlett's tonight?" I grabbed at my chest. He slowly lowered a shaking head, leading me to believe he might be hiding something from me.

His mood hadn't changed overnight as we drove toward Pike County the next morning.

Anything for conversation, I'd bet a nickel that the old man wouldn't be there—still drunk from playing music all night, I figured. But then low and behold, there he was with a fire going and whistling coming from inside the stripping house. Maybe I didn't want to hear it after the night my mother had gone through. I hurried my pace toward the small building without a hint to James that I'd become angry.

I burst into the stripping house quickly walking to where he stood.

"Your whistling hurts my damned yers, and if I'm gonna strip this shit today, you're gonna haft to stop whistling so... damned loud!" I raged. The old man backed off, leaning up against the table and crossing his arms while staring at me.

"And just what the hell's wrong with you this mornin', Arnold Ray?" I took a deep breath making sure that I didn't start out with a stutter.

"I cain't believe you'd ask such a stupid . . . fuckin' question! What the hell is always wrong? You! It's always you! Mom asked about you last night and even made your favorite meal. She prays and cries for you every damned minute of the day that you'll straighten your ass up and maybe she'll have some kind of a life again. That's what the hell's 'botherin' me—the way you've treated her forever! And why don't you come out and tell us just how many more bastards are out there in the world so we won't be ambushed ever again!" Now my anger was running wild. The old man raised a wavering finger to cut me off.

"Oh no!" I shouted, putting myself within arm's reach of him. "That shit ain't gonna work anymore. You're gonna hear me out even if we've got to fight this morning! And I don't ever want to hear that shit again that 'only God knows your heart' 'cause there's two people standing right here that knows it pretty damned good. If I were God, you'd be a dead son of a bitch by now! And I'm given you fair warnin' the day will come that you better be right with your Lord!" I threatened. "Like it says in the Bible, ye don't know when the time is at hand!" I stabbed a hard finger onto the stripping table.

He stood up straighter, looking at me in a strange way, looking somewhat hurt. But I wouldn't cave into that thought for very long.

"We had everything we needed at one time." I started counting on my fingers. "Happiness and the prettiest farm in the valley and a way to pay for it till you fucked it up. Now it's in shambles, all grown up and abandoned—I mean look at it!" Suddenly I found myself pacing back and forth just like he would.

"You're damned drinkin' and carrying on has put us so deep in debt that we'll never get out of it. And worst of all, you don't know and probably don't care anyway the torture and sleepless nights James and I have since we burned that house down." I pointed up the hill toward the rubble.

"And who goes to hell for that one? The list goes on and on! There's nobody to blame other than you for the shape we're in. And why is it that as soon as we get a little ahead, you mess it all up again? You use everybody, including God, to get what you want, then drop 'em all because you don't need any help turning into a low rent drunk again. And you've sure been good at that all your life." I'd finished with what I needed to say and turned to leave when James grabbed my arm.

"Right on! I couldn't have said it any better myself Arnold." He said. "You know, everything Arnold said about you is true in the way you've let this family down and so many times." James spoke calmly in his well-thought-out ways. "And you can treat me like shit all you want, Dad. I've done my best and gone out of my way to help you even when I knew it was wrong. But I can tell you that what Arnold and I did was all for Mom's sake. But of all the people you've messed over, how could you do such things to the person who's stuck with you through thick and thin and always forgave you each and every time?"

"Yeah," I interrupted. "She should a left you're sorry ass a long time ago." James's quick glance told me that I need say no more.

"It's her that suffers more than anybody. And Arnold's right, that we'd be way better off without you with the way you act!"

A dead silence rang throughout the little stripping room except for a crinkly sound of the old man fumbling through his cigarette pack for the last one it looked to be. Angry in the way he shoved it in his mouth, crumbling the empty pack and pitching it to the dirt floor over by the stove. Clearly, he was rattled in his clumsy effort to get it lit with shaking hands. After a hard drag, he blew smoke in our direction, bellowing from his nose and mouth alike.

"Go pack your goddamn shit and find a place to live; the both of you!" He nodded his head frankly that we understand. "I can git' all the help I need to strip this baccer. I don't need anybody comin' in here on my property and jumpin' on my ass this mornin'," he threatened. I thought back to the many times he'd preached how you could fool everyone other than God in his holy wisdom. But still, the way he'd said the "G——d" word was muffled in a way that maybe he thought God couldn't quite understand it. I'd told James one time how cuss words sounded much worse, I thought, when laced with cigarette smoke. My stomach growled as he took another puff.

James slumped with a slight limpness before he straightened back up to his full size and then some, it looked. He hardly ever got loud about much of anything, even during his angriest times with me. But I'd seen this posture before confrontations at school when his mind was made up that there'd be a fight.

"Now as far as your property . . . Arnold and I have worked our asses off to help pay for everything you've got! So don't give me that shit about your property," he said in a calm but angry way. "And as far as me packing up my things and leaving, you're going to provide me a roof over my head until I get out of school, and that's that! But the day after I graduate, I'll get out of your life, Dad. I'll come to visit Mom, but I won't care if I ever see you again as you've made it clear that you want nothing to do with me.

"I've always thought that this day would eventually come, but I guess I just couldn't admit to myself that you could be so cruel. Now you can treat me like shit till I leave, but how in the hell can you keep treating Mom like that is beyond me! She, of all people, has been your guiding light—even more than God himself." James proclaimed in a soft manner. "And what has she got in return?" James slowly waved an open palm around the room to insinuate that we'd lost the place in the end. "I can only wish that I have her patience throughout life. We've watched her be torn down by you so many times, but never did she falter and completely give up on you. Ya know, Dad, you really should be ashamed of yourself!" His words slowly tapered off.

I was disappointed to hear James call him Dad with his condemnation and it sounded as if there could still be some kind of hope mixed in with his words. I wanted to add to the old man's wrongdoings, but I didn't think I could do any more damage than we'd already inflicted on him when suddenly he slung his cigarette to a dark corner of the room.

He broke down crying, covering his face with both hands. It was a heart-stopping shock at first, but I knew him all too well to think a little crying would change him in any way. He'd do whatever it took to get what he wanted. I'd faced the fact that over the years, his Christian life would only be temporary at best. But it did me good to see him humbled and crying the way he was right now.

Neither James nor I made any attempt to be sympathetic with him. I'd hated him for so long now that he looked cold and I never wanted to touch him again. Toby Wilson once convinced him to turn his heart back over to God, which seemed like forever ago. I thought how Mom had praised God when he emerged from the barn that day and would do the same again if he was to go home and cry on her shoulder.

But his wailing would not alter the fact that I'd never trust or forgive him no matter if he got on the right side of the Lord or not. There'd simply been too many failed attempts on his part. And I'd never allow myself to have the faith such as my mother possessed to forgive him even one more time.

He continued to weep with an occasional "O Lord, what have I done?" His words muffled somewhat; choking their way through his fingers pushed tightly up against his face. I thought this was the way it should sound, but with him kneeling at an altar, not at some stump on the side of hill, or pissing on a fence post, asking for forgiveness.

He was right, that you could get saved anywhere, as he'd preached after each and every bout with the Devil. But his sermons about getting saved in the middle of nowhere just wouldn't hold merit with me any longer. I thought of the many prophets he'd preached of in the Bible, along with the hardships that in the end made them all holy. I wondered if maybe he wanted a chapter of his own where the story of Moses and the burning bush wouldn't be shit to his stories of the greatest repentances of all time. The Book of Jimmy would suit him well I thought to myself. I'd have no remorse for my crazy thoughts of how I felt about him. It was an awkward situation with James and I leaning up against the stripping table while the old man continued to sob.

Today's event would only add to the many memories that had come from the little stripping house. We were here the day when President Kennedy was shot and later talked how destructive a nuclear missile would be that even the hills of southern Ohio wouldn't be enough to protect us. As hurried as the old man usually was to get anything done, there'd been times when he'd break out the guitar, where he and Mom would sing a couple of church songs before we'd get started. And at his best he'd pray giving thanks to what the lord had bestowed upon us. It was a joyful sight the time our mother sang "Victory in Jesus," while shouting and waving her hands high into the air. The song was such a blessing of her obedience to the Lord as she reached for the heavens above. Those were the good old days when the old man still prayed.

A small gap in the little stoves door revealed the flame inside which I'd stared at on different occasions. A fixed point; James called it. Simply a place for concentration to let one's mind drift away as I was doing right now.

A guest preacher had come to Cedar Chapel and preached about faith, saying if you didn't get everything that you prayed for, then you weren't praying hard enough. But I knew better when it came down to our mother who never lacked in faith while continually pouring her heart out to God. I thought that it was God himself that'd failed her.

There were many temptations to test one's faith as so many preachers had warned. And worldly thoughts would eventually lead to them, they'd proclaim. But since I'd become old enough to take notice of girls, I didn't think that it should be wrong to think about them, and even to the point of lusting. And poor James; hell bound for sure with all he'd done with Scarlett, I suspected. It was truly a time to test what little faith I had that couldn't keep up with all my desires.

The preacher was wrong about unanswered prayers because of lacking in your faith. I'd witnessed things that you could pray for till you were blue in the face, and they'd not be answered—with mine being the old man himself. But what really struck me odd was when there'd be a gathering of preachers holding a healing service. Some services would be proclaimed as "old-fashioned" in a way that promised to make them even holier. Usually, those were the preachers who'd pronounce that big denominations didn't do the will of the Lord and were out there just to make money and show off their clothes.

I'd known all along of the old man's jealousy of the televised preachers. Once there was a man who had a terrible time struggling down the long aisle of the huge church with two crutches who was pitiful with the way he dragged his legs.

"That poor old thang, why don't they just help him?" Mom talked of the many that nudged him on. I found myself leaning and pulling at my own legs as he got closer to the pulpit. It was proclaimed a miracle when the preacher prayed and touched the man's head when he leaped into the air tossing his crutches off to the side.

I was amazed at how he ran up and down the church's aisles, and shouting of his healing. I was glued to the TV on a regular basis to watch such miracles that repeatedly sent chills up my backbone, scary in the way it numbed the top of my head. But then the day came when the world found out that their "healings" had all been staged. It was truly disappointing that it was all a farce, and no miracle had been performed at all.

Our father was all over the outcome saying that they weren't real preachers or Christians to stage such events. The old man said that you didn't have to be a high-dollar preacher in order for the Lord to heal someone. But I thought he, like all the others, lusted for something that no other had ever achieved. Even though they'd all say "in the name of the Lord," while placing their hands on the afflicted person, the glory and rewards would be all theirs if someone were to actually be healed. I'd wondered who would get the glory if a miracle had been performed when there were so many preachers gathered at an altar to pray. I'd watched many times to see who put the most into their prayers when you couldn't hear anything with such loud praying going on.

There was never a single preacher, including Toby, that hadn't said someday they'd set on the "right-hand side of God," with that being about as holy as one could get. But only a miracle would have assured such a position, I thought. I didn't think any of them, however, tried any harder than the old man himself when he was living right. Days before the services, he'd work himself into a frenzy with determined prayer like never before.

"In the name of the Lord," he'd command with a faithful hand wavering into the air. I'd watch with great anticipation as he lowered the other hand to the afflicted persons head. "Remove this sickness and restore this person back to their full health." He'd command loudly. "Remove Satan's awful hand, O Lord." But in the end the pitiful truth was in the little boy's eye that night at Cedar Chapel.

The old man along with Uncle Glenn and all others had done their best, but that wasn't good enough. My expectations never came to pass that I'd see a real miracle performed. The little boy left as he'd come in, on a stretcher. In my disappointment that there might be a real healing of such an affliction, I told James that I didn't believe in miracles anymore. But most Christians, especially those such as our mother, looked at everything good as being a miracle in itself. And I knew that if the old man were to get saved again, she'd declare it too a miracle.

I'd prayed many times that God do something special for the old man in front of the congregation that would've changed his and our lives forever. *Maybe he should've staged something like they did on TV*, I thought. But I always knew that he expected the real thing, like walking on water or sitting so close to God that he'd be able to smell his holy breath. We'd seen our father fall from grace so many times that it was fairly predictable when the end was close at hand for him. There could be no way to prepare ourselves other than with dread.

Following our mothers ways and at a young age, I prayed and pleaded for him to not backslide again. "Please, please," I'd asked sincerely, but always with doubt that the fault might be with me by not praying hard enough.

But it was only after James and I'd gotten older that we talked of why the old man would backslide in the first place. What single thing would set him off? Whereas his sermons had brought many to the altar to be saved, there was not a single healing by his hand authorized by God. Did he feel betrayed after so many failed efforts I wondered?

We could only speculate as there were so many to choose from. But whatever the reason for his demise the end result was always the same. The devil once again had led him astray.

He wiped his eyes while taking a couple of steps toward us, where he reached out and put his arms around us. For an instant I felt sorry for him, thinking how he had no problem driving all over the place to bring people to church that didn't have a way to get there. He'd joke, saying he worked for the Lord and would get paid in full when he reached the pearly gates of heaven. The thought was short lived however and as I'd suspected he felt cold and foreign to the touch. The smell of baccer and beer was strong on his breath as he continued to cry. And it wasn't what love should have smelled like at all, I thought.

I glanced over at James, who towered over the old man, his face rigid with not much expression. Maybe neither of us showing him any affection in return was why he removed his arms and without another word, he turned and walked the short distance back to his place at the stripping bench.

"Boys, I want you to forgive me for saying this place didn't belong to you too." He removed his handkerchief and blew his nose, while still sniffling. "I know, Junior, you'll be gone soon enough. And I'll hate it when that day comes. I don't want you as my enemy 'cause you are my son. I just can't imagine never seein' you again after you leave home." He choked up a little.

"I know that I've done a lot of wrong in my life, and you're right about Ree. I don't know where I'd be without her," he said, stumbling somewhat. "I'd hid that other family for many years before your mother found out about them." He covered his face, and now crying harder than ever.

"I'll go get some baccer to get started with." I hurried for the door, thinking I didn't need to be in on conversations about our half-brothers. In one way, I was glad that Mom knew of the other family, which we'd suspected all along and had kept it to herself as only she could do. And I knew that with the help of the Lord, she'd forgiven him. But hell would freeze over before I'd consider such a thing. I doubled my fist at the thought.

I hadn't planned on being gone for very long as I climbed up into the rafters, where I'd left off the day before, quickly dropping several sticks to the ground. I thought they needed more time to talk as I climbed on up to the highest rafters.

An old familiar feeling crept throughout me as I leaned back against the barn's center beam. I'd declared this spot as mine when the boys would all gather to talk and tell jokes. But there was no time to reminisce of such great times with the way the old man was acting.

His cries of sincerity sounded true, but I'd only tolerate it for the sake of my mother. After all the letdowns, any forgiveness would be hard now. As I'd thought before, he could never be trustworthy until he went to a real altar, witnessed by me and others. *Why. . . can't he just go to the altar for my sake?* I thought, softly bumping the back of my head against the support pole. *Or will that even do any good to temper the way I hate him?* I sat silent, thinking that maybe there was nothing he could ever do that would satisfy me.

My mother had warned of a hardened heart many times. Maybe I was like that from the day I'd started calling him "the old man" and hardened myself toward him ever since.

"I'm sure as hell not going to blame myself for hating him," I said out loud. His crying by no means convinced me that I'd ever trust him again. "I'll not go through another ordeal like all the other times. He can die right now! That'd be fine with me. In fact, I'd like to be the one . . . who . . ." I rocked back against the support beam again. I knew it was best for me to avoid him as he was the root to most of my problems.

I scampered down the ship's mast as the boys and I had pretended so many times. Luckily, no one had ever fallen. Duck joked that landing on the ground below would be nothing like water.

After removing the baccer from their sticks I gathered up an armload; ten to fifteen stalks then headed for the stripping house. I hesitated to barge in but instead eavesdropped on what the old man was telling James.

"Now as you already know, I promised them youngins that I'd get them a color TV and new antenna for Christmas." He sniffled with an effort to dry up it sounded. "It'll be a good present for everybody," he said.

"Swear to God, you asshole," I muttered before kicked the door open, and with every intention to interrupt him.

"Well, what took ya so long?" James joked. I laid the stalks in the holding cradle where the old man wasted no time spinning the plant, while quickly stripping the bottom leaves.

"If it wasn't for me carryin' that heavy ass load, I'd show you what it's like to be lookin' up at that ceilin'!" I said with a puffy voice. The old man, thought our playful threats were funny, laughed out loud.

"I'll deal with you later!" James mimicked, kicking the dust from my ass as I walked past. It was the longest either of us had talked with the old man in a long time. I'd try and stay out of most conversation while letting James answer all questions. When he did ask me if I thought I'd win a race at Greenfield, I could have said plenty but stopped myself way short of any victory.

I made lots of trips to the press and carried many a load of baccer to be stripped that day. Normally, I would've complained just for the hell of it that James could've helped a little more; but he and the old man had been doing a lot of talking, which, I thought, was good for both of them. There was a time when he confided in James about our logging business, but that all seemed to have fallen apart with Scarlett coming into James's life. The cold fog settled into the valley once more as darkness set in.

"Now we can finish up tomar that's if'n you boys'll miss one more day of school?"

I looked at James as if there was any choice. And without Moms help the process was slowed a lot. She had considered helping but would have worried herself to death with the kids coming home and no one being there to watch over them. We had worked late, and now hunger was setting in.

Missing the days of school wouldn't affect my grades as they had before. But the truth was I didn't want to miss a single day. I was having lots of fun with my newfound friends. I wasn't the bashful person I used to be, thanks to them.

From the very first day at Greenfield, I wanted to become a part of something, with a desire to succeed that I'd not had much in school before. We talked of soil, animals, trees, and everything else, it seemed, in vo-ag. We laughed out loud in history class when our teacher, who was missing the end of one finger, guaranteed that the small guillotine that sat on the corner of his desk worked. And homeroom with Mr. Toll and the rowdies was the best way ever to start off a new day.

I'd thought there was no way I could ever leave the comfort of the hills and trees of southern Ohio, with people more like me. It was a place I could go to and vanish, if I needed. It might have been one reason I never enjoyed Florida much either, as I'd spent most my life in the wooded rural areas.

There was a quote James used when I was in doubt about something. The *Digest* called it "fear in the face of the unknown," which he associated with all new things pertaining to me. He'd been right, as some things I'd been afraid to confront seemed stupid now. I didn't have to hide behind him or Judy anymore as they'd carried me long enough.

The old farm and all the great years I'd spent there would forever be in my thoughts. But I wasn't interested now in a hand-me-down life such as what I'd get in this part of the country. I wanted more than to just settle for whatever I could get.

Less than fifty miles north of here is where I wanted to be for now. Never in my wildest dreams did I think that a challenge could be so much fun. I'd simply worried too much of failure.

The old man seemed nervous but knew we had no way out. We agreed we couldn't wait a week to finish; we'd all meet the next morning at daybreak. Our drive home was slow because of the dense fog once again, but it gave us more time to talk of the day.

Everyone had finished their supper except Mom, who'd waited on us and, I guess, hoped that the old man would have showed up also. We told her about his breakdown and crying. It brought tears, which she wiped away with her apron. It was hard to swallow that him shedding a tear could give her a glimmer of such strong hope. In her eyes and the Lord's, it would signal a weakness in his sinful ways.

We were up early the next morning, and after convincing Red that I was allowed to milk that early, eventually made it on to the house. We were greeted at the back door with the smell of sizzling bacon and eggs being turned in the skillet. Mom had fixed a sandwich for us to carry to the old man. She guessed that he must have spent another night at Tom Kinsley's.

James and I talked that clearing the air with the old man was good but we had to confess that it'd probably be short-lived.

"I'll bet you that he'll have beer on his breath, James," I warned. His slow nod along with a faraway look led me to believe that his mind was on Pfizer's Ridge and Scarlett. In the past few days, he'd hardly said anything about her. It was obvious that there were problems, and he didn't want to talk about them. But I had to indulge my suspicion. I just couldn't wait any longer. He had to say something of it.

"Are you and Scarlett breakin' up?" I got right to the point. He puckered his mouth without answering. "I mean, you ain't said anythin' about her for some time now." He shook his head, looking as if he were ready to talk but instead turned the radio up a little louder. A couple of curves later, the song "You've Lost That Lovin' Feelin'" came on. Normally, he would've put his heart and soul into singing it, but now I could hardly hear his effort. His voice sounded tired. It was obvious there'd still be no talk of Scarlett.

I was lucky James had not taken my wager on the old man having beer on his breath. He sat by the small stove, warming his hands and getting up immediately to hug us. James hugged him back, but I couldn't, holding my arms limp at my sides. I considered Mom's words about a good cry. It looked like some of the frown had left the old man's face from just the day before. We sat around the stove, where he told a joke we'd never heard before, and it was funny enough that we all laughed at the punch line. As he polished his sandwich off, I thought how easy it'd be to drop my guard over his willingness to cut up. But I couldn't let that happen even if there was no beer on his breath. I reminded myself of how much I truly despised him.

I put the last few hands of baccer into the press shortly after noon and pressed the last of our crop. Working late the day before had panned out for an early finish today. All said and done, we thought it looked to be the best crop ever. But there'd be no joyful celebration as it was our last one—never to have another to compare it with.

The old man thanked us and seemed sincere with a handshake before driving away. James didn't seem to be in any big rush to leave as we walked to the old hand pump and stomped down more weeds for a better path. The groans and squeaks from the old pump hadn't changed any from the last time we'd used it. We passed the dipper back and forth several times flushing and gargling to strip the taste of baccer from our throat and mouths. Flashbacks flooded my memory, such as the day I went down into the well itself. The thought alone still sent a chill throughout me.

"You know, James, I wish I had a dollar for every dipper of water I've drank from this well. Hell, I'd have so much money I wouldn't know what to do with all of it! You know what I mean?" I giggled watching James pull on one of the tall weeds till it broke loose rendering its tender end. He made himself comfortable on the corner of the pump slab where he'd bite small pieces of the weed off and spit it to the side.

"Yeah, I could think of a thousand things to do with more money than I need," he said while tossing the stem away. I could see that with his sudden frown Scarlett was on his mind more than the money.

"Well, are you about ready to go home, James?" I asked.

"Yeah, I guess . . ." He slowly got up.

"Hey, I got an idea James! Since we've got plenty of time on our hands, let's go visit Uncle Arnold and Aunt Ray, it's not that far out of the way." I tried to sound excited that it might perk him up a little.

His facial expression changed immediately as he slowly nodded at my request. There were two ways to get to our uncle's house, the shortest being up over Dry Bone Ridge, where at times the gravel road would wash out. And without hearing from others that it'd done so, you wouldn't know until getting almost to the top, where there was no place to turn around. Then you'd have to back down the steep grade for quite a ways, which would put butterflies in anyone's stomach. We had seen where several drunks had been forced to back up and had slid over the side of the hill. There were a couple of cars that still remained from years past and always would. They'd been stripped of everything that was worth much however.

The decision was quick on James's part, saying we'd take the 124 Route, which would put us close enough to Willow Springs that we'd swing by and get ourselves a Root Beer. It'd be a nice little adventure that would also take us past the stone quarry house, which we'd not seen in a long time.

James snapped out of his slump somewhat as the tires squealed around familiar curves when we passed Kincaid Springs. I thought about the two coffee cups hidden away that brought a short-lived desire for Linda. As we came into Willow Springs, I looked down the narrow road that led to the bridge where we'd held up on one horrifying day.

"Look at those old geezers, still sittin' on the bench, James." I pointed. "Hell, I figured they'd all be dead and gone by now." I squinted my eyes. There were only two of the original ones left. Now there were two new old fellows, bringing a fresh batch of lies to the bench, I figured.

It was sad that Don Jr. wasn't behind the counter. I knew he and James would have loved to have seen each other again. But I surely wouldn't complain, and neither did James when we saw Sharon Garman tending the store. She and James hugged like old friends, as I positioned myself to where I could see her legs, which no doubt about it looked better than ever. She didn't catch me staring, but James did.

I was starting to wonder if we were even going to make it to our uncle's house as they laughed and carried on about Korn county and other good times they'd had. I decided to go outside and talk to the old-timers, thinking maybe James and she'd hit it off and that would take care of the problem with Scarlett, especially now when there seemed to be a problem.

"Where in the hell have you been, young man?" the talker of them asked, extending his hand for a shake. They all shook hands with me, but sadly enough, the other original old timers couldn't remember me. He'd snapped his fingers on occasion, pointing, but that was about it.

"Hell, you remember him, Claude. He's that young feller that used to stand here just to look at all the girls' asses when they walked past." He elbowed the old fellow, then as always spit baccer out into the road, where they all followed suit, including the one who'd lost his memory.

Some things would never change, I thought. It struck me funny how the two new guys looked, both with new canes tucked tightly between their legs like someone was going to steal them. I wondered how long they'd waited for their place on the bench to be vacated so they could live out their lives with "first-class bullshit," as one of the departed had called it at one time.

"Let's go!" James hollered on his way to the car. I sadly bade the old-timers goodbye with another handshake, wondering who'd all be there when I'd pass this way again.

"God, it was so nice seeing Sharon again," James said, gripping the steering wheel in a strange way, It looked.

"Yeah, she's as pretty as ever," I said.

"You are talkin' about her legs, right?" he laughed.

"Yeah, them too," I said.

The talk with Sharon had no doubt lifted James's spirits somewhat, and her pretty legs had aroused me, of course.

James pulled up beside the weigh station, where he parked and we got out. Most of the windows had been broken out, and the roof had collapsed around in the back. We walked down to the small creek, pausing at its deepest hole where we'd both learned to swim. Then on down a little farther to the spot where a flood had carried our heavy coins away on a stormy night. I thought, how badly I hated this place at one time; but it like all the others, had good and bad memories also.

"Remember the time James when we floated on that sheet of ice to about right here before jumped off just before it broke apart?"

"Yea, I do! 'Abandon ice!' was the command." He snickered. "And it really wasn't that long ago if you think about it. It's sure a lot easier to get excited about things when you're just little boys." He finished.

James walked over to the bank and pulled a tall weed to chew on. Nothing of a coincidence that he'd pulled one from the same spot some years back. "And we sure had to grow up in a hurry when we left here." He spat. Our flashbacks fizzled out that neither of us had anything else to add. We walked back to the car and in a quarter of a mile we turned on to lower Dry Bone Road.

They looked like a picture, sitting there on their front porch, with Aunt Ray in the swing and our uncle comfortable in his cushioned rocking chair. I always thought a front porch was made just for those people who enjoyed life at its best. It was like a reward of some sort for making it through another hard day. It was simply a viewpoint to witness your day's accomplishments and to plan for the next one. And what better thing to do than wait for the lightning bugs to fire up. Why watch TV when there were so many other things to look at?

I couldn't wait to hear Aunt Rays high-pitched voice when she asked James and I if we wanted a glass of cold ice tea. We drank it quickly as the root beer seemed to have made us thirstier. Then she poured us another one with extra ice cubes, which we'd make last the rest of our stay.

"I guess ole Jim disowns me anymore, bein' he never comes around to visit." Our uncle laughed, sounding as if he really didn't care.

"You wouldn't want to see him anyway, Uncle Arnold, the shape he's in all the time," I answered. We told how he'd cried the day before and seemed to have settled down a little. Throughout our conversation our uncle's whistle was no more than a whisper at best.

Happy as they always were, laughing and carrying on about everything I thought the visit was too short when James stood up and declared that it was time to go.

They made us promise that it wouldn't be so long the next time we passed through. There was another promise we'd have to fulfill—to give Mom a hug for Aunt Ray. "And be sure and tell her that I'm gonna write her soon." Aunt Ray wheezed.

I was along for the ride and wouldn't complain of anywhere that James wanted to go. It was great to ride around with him, just like old times and familiar places. There was still lots of daylight left as I thought about all the different ways we could get back home. The long way was over through Cynthiana, then onto the Seven Caves area to follow along the cliffs above Paint Creek. But to my shock, he turned right at the end of our uncle's driveway. Instead, we'd go back through Willow Springs and more than likely treat ourselves to another Root Beer, or so I hoped. Maybe it was that James wanted to see Sharon again. I was justifying the need to stop at the general store, clowning around and intentionally coughing knowing what the only fix could be.

"This is worse than any of those desert crossin's on TV, James." I wheezed and grasped at my throat with both hands. "Sorry, ole Doodle, I ain't gonna make it to the next root beer hole." My voice hoarsened. "Now, now, I ain't got much, but I want ya ta have both of 'em."

I'd gotten carried away with my clowning around, letting saliva run down the side of my mouth. But when I drew air as if it were my last breath on earth, I accidently inhaled a mouthful of collected saliva. For an instant, James saw how my eyes had bugged out and the look of shock on my face just before I let loose with a horrendous coughing spell—a deep cough, one that could choke out any effort in communicating a single word. I'd taken the hoarse throat a little too far, strangled down almost to a squeaky sound. James laughed at my loud throat-clearing efforts before spitting out the window. I'd had no intention of getting laughed at for choking. I did need something to drink now but would carry on with my last will and testament.

"Take care of ole Katie." I'd regained some voice and didn't need to imitate hoarseness now as it was all natural. "She's been a good ole mule over the years, and now she's gettin' a little gray around the edges." My voice quivered on command. I wouldn't have had to say any more in my Hollywood effort as he slowed for the stop sign, resting his forehead against the steering wheel. Totally carried away that I make him laugh harder I sank into the floorboard, looking up at him, when he chanced to look my way. With desperation on his face, he turned to the steering wheel once again, wiping tears from his eyes.

"And ole Rebel's missin' bout half his teef, so you might have to chew his food up a bit for him, Doodle. Wait, this might be it . . ." I held a trembling hand to where he could clearly see it. "It feels like . . . like everything's stoppin', Doodle . . . I'm a dumb what? What did you call me?" I asked, climbing back out from the floorboard.

We sat at the stop sign, where after several efforts he managed to say "dumbass" between laughs. It was like old times, watching him gently wipe his eyes with a finger and thumb. He'd hardly gotten a word in edgewise as I squirmed around in my seat, waiting for him to calm somewhat, and then I'd start all over again with another act of stupidity. I just couldn't sit still when I had him like this.

"Okay," he finally managed. "We'll stop for another Frosty, dumbass!" He wiped his eyes clear before continuing on, "But you know, I think I'll let the boys take care of the animal kingdom when you're gone." He concluded.

James and Sharon picked right up right where they'd left off, laughing and joking as she sat on a high stool, legs crossed perfectly, I thought. I traced them, from her snow-white tennis shoes to the short green skirt halfway up her legs, which was sliding farther with every laugh. I didn't care if she caught me looking as I had in school, and she didn't seem to care back then. James warned of wasted opportunities in life if you were too bashful to take advantage of them. I knew I'd done that with Linda and had regretted it ever since.

She and James talked about going to college. She'd already picked Ohio University at Athens with her parents' approval. I felt bad as James told of his uncertain plans as to what he'd do after school. It sounded as if she already had the money to go, whereas James and I were trying to scrape together enough to put tires on the Buick. Sadly, I thought that he was so smart but had no money for college, but I knew him all too well; he'd make a way somehow. Sharon said he should apply for aid with his grades the way they were. She was one of the coolest people I'd ever been around. She talked freely about things, like against the Vietnam War.

"Well, we've got to go," James said, sipping the last of his root beer. We'd been leaning over the countertop as we talked with her. James straightened up, standing erect, as I tongued the end of my bottle for the last drop when suddenly I realized Sharon had been laughing at me all the while. I got a final look at even more of her beautiful legs when she slid off the stool to say goodbye. I watched every detail about how the two hugged before I turned to leave. Sharon's crisp and clear voice called my name.

"Oh, Arnold...!" I whirled around to see her motioning me back with a beckoning finger. "Don't you want to give me a goodbye hug?" Her hair bounced with her headshake and a pouty lower lip. I'd seen James turn to butter when Scarlett wanted something. I'd thought it ignorant all along until now as Sharon coaxed me further with a sexy smile. James winked as he walked past.

And where was the song that was supposed to play with all this to make it easier? Why wouldn't my feet move any faster? *Say somethin'!* A scared little voice came from within me.

"Why, yes! I wanna give you a goodbye kiss. I mean . . ." *Oh my god, did I just say what I thought I did?* She started walking my way with slightly open arms. "Shit," I couldn't remember now if James had his arms on the outside, or were they on the . . . ? It mustn't mattered to her that I said "kiss" instead of "hug." But a hug from such a pretty girl would be okay, also something to add to my dreams at nights. I opened my arms and would have my hug if I didn't die within the next few steps, I thought. I'd need to remember every detail for when I'd tell James how much better mine was than his.

All the fine details fell apart when she pulled me close to her. Now I struggled to even stand up with my nose buried in her silky black hair. With a slight move of her head, my lips were suddenly at her neck. I'd gone rigid for an instant as her perfume rushed to my head. *Dare I kiss her neck and joke of it while she slaps the shit out of me?* I thought. My mind raced on.

I felt Sharon's hug slacken as I hung on for every second I could. *I could stay right here for the rest of my life,* I thought. *And how long can I go without food or water, and can I live off of a scent that makes fools of men?* I eased my grip, disappointed, as she backed up a step. But all of James's coaching and all the planning and dreaming in the world wouldn't have prepared me for what was about to happen next.

Maybe it was the desperation in my eyes, or it was in God's plan when I met her halfway for the first kiss of my life. It would have lasted for hours had James not been there, or at least I'd say so. Swallowing was hard enough in this breathless moment when she slowly teased her tongue in my mouth. I hadn't just been kissed—she'd French-kissed me! She pulled away with a slight giggle, leaving my mouth wet from her lips. I swallowed but wanted more—much more. James had never told of such a thing, or maybe I wasn't paying attention like I should've.

It happened so quickly that I could barely remember it with my head swirling the way it was. I needed to do it again, but much slower. I almost panicked with the need to grab her and kiss her just one more time. But anything beyond a single kiss was intended for people falling in love, I thought, as air filled my lungs once more. I knew she had no intentions of falling in love with me. I just wasn't in her class of people. But this would be a day that I'd remember for the rest of my life.

"Have a good day, Arnold." She drew near once again, whispering in my ear that I needed to let go of her hand. I could have ran right through the front door, glass and all with the way I felt right now.

Tarzan was out of the picture as Superman had taken control of me now. I licked my lips in a desperate attempt to find any kind of wetness she'd left there. I swallowed once more as she turned to walk away. I started to thank her but was glad I didn't. That'd been stupid on my part. James saw the whole thing, holding the door open for me as I seemed to float past him.

I heard Sharon's laugh, to which I turned and made a bow. *Was that stupid?* I thought to myself. She curtsied back, while slowly pulling her dress up to show me more than her legs and all intended for just me, I'd brag.

It didn't seem as if my ass was touching the seat while I tried to relive my romantic moment of a short-lived kiss. There was no need for James to try to say anything. He wouldn't have gotten a word in anyway, let alone me hearing it. Now I could thoroughly understand how one could spend hours on end just kissing. I didn't remember us passing through Morgantown or even crossing the bridge at Pike Lake as far as that went. I went on and on about "kisses sweeter than wine" as if I'd known the difference. I didn't need to tell James how I swallowed the wetness from Sharon's tongue as he'd done a million times with Scarlett.

A thought crossed my mind as we crested the top of Copper Mountain that maybe James and Sharon had planned my first kiss all along. I'd not waste time on the thought, nor would I ask him. *She wanted to kiss me, and that's that,* I thought. Besides, I knew that he wouldn't ruin my first time in such a way. I just wouldn't do anything to get him pissed off at me ever again in my life.

We got home a little after dark, and somewhat to our surprise, the old man was there.

"Maybe he's come to his senses, James," I said, making it sound like a pissy joke, to which he never answered back. He hadn't been there too long, I suspected, which was confirmed when I laid my hand on the hood of his car; still pretty warm.

I knew it was what our mother wanted, but I'd have been happier if he'd not been there in some ways. My first intention was to find Judy and tell her about what had happened with Sharon and me. I knew she'd love to hear my news. My racing thoughts of tender lips and a scent that would follow me for the rest of my life faded quickly when we stopped and listened at the back door.

"I'll go anywhere I want and stay out as long as I want!" The old man sounded like he was quoting something right out of his Book of Wrongdoings.

"Jim, you're a married man, and you have a whole house full of children here. Why can't you go back to being the person you used to be?" she pleaded. I peeped through the side window and could see the kids all sitting huddled close to the TV and none were smiling. Judy was silent as she helped Mom set the table.

James pulled the door open and quickly stepped inside, with me following close behind. The screen door slammed shut, getting everyone's attention.

"Boy, something sure smells good!" James said with a long satisfying sniff into the air.

"Oh! And hold it right there, Mom. Don't move . . ." James put his arms around her and gently hugged. "Aunt Ray made us promise to give you a hug just for her."

"Why, did you go see her today, Honey? Bless her heart, I sure miss her." Mom sounded cheery at the thought.

James turned to face the old man, who seemed upset over our interruption. "They also said to say hi to you and that you need to stop by and visit sometime, for old times' sake, Uncle Arnold said." James just wanted to be a peacemaker as our uncle never hinted at such a thing.

"Well now he's got a car, and if'n he wants to see me, he knows where I live." The old man raked his hair back up over his head, revealing a tired looking face when he turned to walk toward the living room. All thoughts of song and goodwill fled as my veins heated, surging with anger. I brushed aside my commitments that I'd declared when I laid on the soft moss just a short while ago. How could I think that I could hold my temper with the old man anyway. James had done his best for any kind of civil conversation, even to have lied to try and make things better. In a few steps, I'd collected the old man's arm, gripping it firmly that he not shake loose.

"Well, have you thought that if he were to come over, where in the hell would he start lookin' for you?" The old man desperately made a couple attempts to jerk his arm loose.

"You let go of my arm right now Arnold Ray or I'll..."

"Or you'll what?" I wanted a confrontation, even in front of the family would be all right now. I fisted my right hand in anticipation. "So which bar should we send him to so he'll have the privilege to see his brother at his best?" I snarled with gritted teeth.

He stood calm, thinking of the challenge I'd presented to him as I still clung tightly to his arm. He knew I could whip him pretty handily and also that I could get to his gun way quicker than him. And what a planned accident that could be, I thought to myself. Duck slowly closed the living room door before turning the TV up a little louder. They didn't need to hear any part of this anyway. Mom stepped between us, putting her hand on my chest and forcing the other to remove my grip. James had made no effort to separate us.

"Honey, there's fried chicken and mashed potatoes and gravy over on the stove." She smiled, hoping to calm the moment. She'd made another one of his favorite meals, hoping that he might show up. Her hand shook when she pointed toward the food. I felt taken in again, thinking how he'd asked us to forgive him long enough to get the baccer stripped. Mom slowly opened the living room door, telling everyone that it was time to eat.

"Honey, shut the television off," she reminded Beth.

"Dad, have you eaten anything yet?" James asked while softly putting his hand on the old man's shoulder. I guess a soft touch and calling him Dad might help to keep him there for a while longer to satisfy Mom.

"No, I hain't!" he shot back. With a slight jerk, he'd dislodged James's hand before walking to his place at the head of the table, where he seemed to drop into his chair. Mom moved quickly to the stove and started fixing him a plate of food as she'd always done before without question. I followed behind her, not concealing what I wanted to say.

"He's not a cripple! He can fix his own." She ignored me as if I wasn't there and placed it in front of him, and along with the salt and pepper shaker. Judy and Bertha Mae set out the remainder of the food as everyone else seated themselves.

"Jim, would you like to turn thanks?" Mom asked hopefully. The question hit me about as hard as it did him, I guess. I'd never even considered him turning thanks. I looked across the table at him, thinking it might be easier to have asked the devil if he was ready to be baptized in the name of the Lord.

"No, you go ahead, Ree." He sounded rebellious and shitty, I thought and began wondering if sometimes he wasn't jealous of my mother. She'd kept her faith through all the hardships while he backslid time and again. I never remembered a time she didn't give thanks for whatever we had. Even for something as simple as an apple, she'd be thankful for it.

There was nothing short in her prayer on this evening, however. She seemed to be dragging it out, as the reason was obvious. I stole a peep toward James, who looked as if he were praying for something altogether different. It looked as if everyone's eyes, except for two, were closed as Mom prayed. With such hatred, I could only see him as the devil himself as he glared back at me.

With neither of us looking away, I looked deeper into his stare when one of a lonely and sorry Da . . . stared back at me. Was there something hidden in them that stirred me to almost call him Dad? I looked away quickly so that I'd not be drawn into being fooled by him ever again. That he'd come here tonight and act as he did put a quick damper to my thought of any kind of peace.

"Amen," Mom finished. I successfully got the piece of chicken I'd spotted. The potatoes made it around the table, to where I'd get the last serving. Seeing this, James, without hesitation, scooped them all into his plate, leaving none for me. Before I could complain, he laughed, scraping half onto my plate. He did so trying to keep things rolling without incident I figured.

"Not funny," I said. There'd be no talking for the next few minutes with sounds of spoons and forks mixing a conglomeration of potatoes and gravy and biscuits all together. Not once did I look at the old man again. All the things that happened at the stripping house with him crying had turned to bullshit, like they always did. But then after a few minutes, he cleared his throat with a cough.

"Now I didn't mean for this night to turn out like this." He calmly laid his fork in his plate. "I'm havin' a bad time, as everyone already knows. I've not been livin' right, and I know it! But I don't need anyone askin' me where I've been! I can't stand the pressure . . ." He leaned forward in his chair. "What I'm tryin' to say is that I need a little more time to straighten myself out. Ree, if'n you wait a little longer, I'll come round in a few more days, I'll promise you that." He got all teary and seemed sincere. I thought, *The perfect time for an altar call!* But we didn't have a single stump in the house.

It was encouraging to Mom, though, for him to admit that he'd been doing wrong and sounding as if he'd had enough and was ready to become a Christian again. There was a new hope when Mom quickly walked around the table and hugged him. They both started crying. He should have felt good that the one person who'd stuck with him through thick and thin still waited for him.

James and I quickly finished our supper. I grabbed the milk bucket on the way out to the car. It was a great relief, we sighed, not for us, but for our mother that she might have some happiness in her life once again. And once again, she'd plan that it'd be forever.

I'd need the lantern to milk by tonight and asked James if he'd like to tag along with me and let me continue on how a single kiss had made me an expert. It did get a laugh from him, but he said he'd just hang out in the bus for the time being and wait on me. I peered through one of the bus' side windows where James sat on the edge of the bed, bent over and resting his arms across his legs, while heavy into thought.

"I'm done milking, James, I warned just before going on in to the bus. Do you want me to just take the Buick to deliver the milk?"

"Nah, I'll run ya down. I'm not doing anything anyhow . . ." He dragged the words.

"Honey, Mom's sorry I didn't do the milkin' this evening. But I've been so busy today."

"Oh, don't worry about that, Mom. It's okay," I said, looking past her where the old man sat on the davenport with Beth on one side and little Joe on the other. The scene looked awkward as he made no attempt to put an arm around either of them. My thoughts, of course, went straight to Good Hope. He looked run-down in a bad way and ready for sleep, I figured.

"Are you ready to get back up to the bus, James?" I hinted.

"Yep," he said, walking quickly to the kitchen door and on out to the car. That he'd not been over to see Scarlett for the last three days had everything to do with his actions. But he could have fixed it all at Willow Springs by asking Sharon out on a date. It was clearly in her eyes that she was open for the invitation. I thought how much more she seemed grown-up than Scarlett. She wasn't so goofy acting. *My kind of girl.* I thought but only for a second.

There was no need to try and say anything to him; even a joke wouldn't have gone over right. I wondered if maybe talking with Sharon only made things worse and that it put him to thinking even more about Scarlett.

"I'm going to take a little walk down the road a ways, Arnold. I'll see you in a few," he said, while slowly getting up from the bus's driver's seat.

"Well, would ya like for me to tag along? You don't have to say anything. I'll do all the talkin'! You know I ain't got done tellin' you how Sharon. . ."

He lowered his head, shaking it slightly before stepping out of the bus—his answer was obvious. With no clouds in the night sky, the full-moon cast brightly.

"Do you want Rebel to go with you, James?" And as I'd expected, there was no answer.

I held the dog back as James walked down the road, eventually disappearing where it dropped down into a steep holler before rising up again on the other side. It was also a place that would never allow moonlight to penetrate its tall thick trees. I'd been through there several times on a run, and regardless if it was day or night, there was something spooky about the area. I thought about a night, in particular, on my way back from a run, the sound of something breaking and not far off the road put me to running as fast as I could go. It wasn't Rebel. He'd jumped a rabbit a ways back and could never make a noise such as that anyway. It had to be something very large, I thought, such as in my dreams as a little boy, where I wasn't looking back to see the monster that chased after me.

I jumped the fence at the bus, never missing a stride and never stopping until I shut the bus door behind me.

But out of curiosity, I went back the next morning to see what it'd been. Low and behold, Harry's feeble old horse had got itself tangled up in a large vine that had lodged between his belly and a rear leg. It looked as if it was helping him stand somehow, his head lowered and his heaving nose stuck against the ground. He'd smashed several saplings in his attempt to escape the vine's grip. He was too old to back up, so all he could do was lean forward. He'd stood there all night and would have probably died had I not come back to see what had scared the hell out of me.

I ran back and told Harry of it; after getting the handsaw, we loaded up in his old truck and cut through the field, which put us closer to the horse. Harry watched from the edge of the woods while I cut the vine, then slowly guided the horse out of the place, pushing on his rump at times to help him along.

Harry was grateful and thanked me as we rocked in the swing that evening. He confided that he'd seen the buzzards gathering that day and had eased on indoors, joking that they'd come for him. It was the laugh of the day when he celebrated with a shot of shine.

I petted Rebel, while sitting on Harry's side of the swing, where we'd wait until James got back. It was different however with no lightning bugs or frogs grouping for nightly entertainment. It was cold now as I stuffed my hands into my pants pockets with Rebel rooting around, wanting to be petted more. The coldness fit right in with the silvery blanket the moon had spread out over everything.

Nervous that a half hour or so had passed and he'd not come back, I started pacing back and forth on the porch. It wasn't just James that was on my mind as I sat down on the swing once again. Without an invite, Rebel pushed his nose up under my hand. I wanted to go wake Harry and tell of my first kiss that'd lasted so... long. The thought put me to rocking faster in the swing, however.

I heard a howling off in the distance that made Rebel a little uneasy. With perked ears, he looked in the direction James had gone. The dog knew of everything that moved about in the night. If he didn't stay in the bus, he'd roam between us and Mom's place continually. There was a place on Harry's porch he'd also curl up and keep watch. Harry liked the idea, saying, 'Why, he'll keep them damned burglars away from here now, won't you, old buddy?' He patted the top of Rebel's head, then quickly looked around like there really might be such a threat, followed shortly by a boisterous laugh.

I think he liked the notion that the dog picked his porch and was looking so natural, lying within arm's reach of Harry's side of his swing. Regardless of where the dog slept, he'd be there almost every morning waiting, except if he was out chasing a rabbit or some other critter. Suddenly, he whined quickly getting to his feet, while still looking down the road.

"It's just another dog, buddy." I held my breath in order to hear better when I realized it wasn't a dog at all. The sounds were coming from the dark dip in the road. It was James, but I couldn't make anything out of what he was saying.

I quickly put Rebel in the bus for the time being. I had to know if James was okay. I eased along the fencerow, shading myself from the moon's light. The words were plain and clear now as I settled beside a clump of sumac trees. Total confusion and hurt, it sounded like.

"Why? Why... God, does it have to be like this?" The words echoed up the holler toward the laydown yard. He was repeating the same thing over and over again until he started crying. I tucked my chin to my chest, swallowing hard at hearing his pitiful plea.

I thought of another time that he'd cried as much, agonizing about burning our house down. And of the times during whippings, where he'd cry out in pain, altogether different from now, crying with such frustration. My heartbeat quickened thinking how hurt he might be if he caught me spying on him at

The Second Born

a time like this? Maybe he'll talk to me later about it, I thought, backing up a ways before running back to the bus.

I'd no sooner opened the bus's door when Rebel bound from the top step and was gone in a flash. He knew something was wrong with James as he bolted full speed down the road before diving over the hill and into the darkness. It'd been easy to claim the dog solely as mine as I'd spent more serious time with him than everyone else. There wasn't much that he wouldn't do if I were to make the challenge. James joked once that I should jump off a cliff and see if he'd follow me. But after which, he joked saying it would be a sad waste of a good dog, however.

But Rebel always with a wagging tail would go to anyone in the family that would welcome him with a pat on the head or even better a heavy scratch to his chest. I thought of the many, many times he'd come to rescue me. No matter if I were angry or blue, his wet nose rooting up under my hand would get my attention and lessen my troubles right off the bat. And he was the very thing that James needed as the wailing suddenly stopped. I stayed up a while longer before sleepiness finally overtook me.

When the alarm went off the next morning, I quickly reached over shutting it off before it could wake James up. I snuck out of bed, putting my clothes on to go milk, thinking how tired I must have been myself for him to not rouse me when he came in.

Upon my return, James was at Harry's pump vigorously shaking water from his hands. "Well I guess where pretty well stuck with this for a while Arnold," he said, holding them out to show the yellowish stain from stripping the baccer; stains that even Granma's homemade lye soap couldn't take off.

"Well for me right now the stain ain't as bad a problem as the calluses are. Red let me know a couple times this morning that I need to take the rough edges off a little better. I don't quite have the touch when they're so callused over like this." I held my open hands out for him to observe.

"Yea, it's that way with Scarlett when I've not sanded mine for a while." It sounded like a slip of the tongue that there wasn't much expression on his part when he pulled his knife out and started scrapping on his heavy callused hands.

"Stay here James I'll go and get the sandstones." The idea had come from our Grandpa who worked with different grits of the light brown stone as he'd put the final touches on the many canes and other wood products that he'd make. He'd place them all in order on his work bench by their various degrees of smoothness. So, by having them in his hands for a good part of the day he kept them smooth of all hard and sharp edges.

I made it back from Harry's porch handing one of the stone's over to James as we started scrapping away the callused yellow stains. But some of the stain we'd not get off on the un-callused parts of our fingers. We also had a good supply up at the laydown yard where we'd tend to them when we'd take breaks throughout the day. Calvin had placed his up in the fork of piss elm tree the day he left advising Mickel that he shouldn't use it on hands that didn't work enough to get calluses.

But the rocks were being used less and less with a generation in passing and along with all the new products coming out for such uses.

I watched the old timer's use them many times but with a light rub as any sign of a callus had been gone for many years. And at this point they were used for no more than a bullshit story at best. I didn't care so much about the boys at school seeing how callused my hands were. There were plenty of them who never seemed to get all the grease and dirt from under their nails, but that didn't seem to stop them from having good-looking girlfriends.

Our talk along with cleaning our hands a little better seemed to have side tracked James somewhat from whatever his problem might be.

"Man, where in the hell did you go last night?" I cautiously asked. There was a long hesitation before he answered me.

"Oh, I didn't go too far, just down the road a ways."

"Well, what time did you get back? I waited up for a long time you know thinking something might have happened to ya."

"I lost all track of time…." He shrugged his shoulder and then heaved a sigh of relief. I knew better than to push him any further. I figured getting back to school would probably be good for the both of us and get our minds back on something other than baccer and the old man.

CHAPTER 7

The Letter

Judy decided to ride with us to school where she went on and on about another boy she'd met. Tom Denison was in my science class and seemed to be a really good guy, but kind of wimpy, I thought, figuring the hardest thing he'd ever done was mow his yard.

I was glad however that she rode with us, it was the perfect opportunity to tell of my encounter with Sharon. But there was no place for me to interrupt with her constant babble of Tom this, and Tom that, which in my case mostly went in one ear and out the other. My patience was starting to wear thin with the sudden taste of Sharon's lips still fresh on my mind. James asked her a couple more questions about Tom which I'd give her the time to answer before I'd tell my story of possibly the greatest kiss of all times.

"Judy Ann! Snap out of it!" I said slowly waving my hand back and forth in front of her face. "You're repeating yourself." I scolded which drew a quick reaction from James.

"Yea, just like someone else I know!" He laughed. But I ignored him while jabbing a stiff thumb against my chest that I get her attention. My disruption had taken her by surprise when she looked at me and then over at James.

"Sorry, I guess I got a little out of control there," she said, twisting her smile to the corner of her mouth.

"You'll never guess what happened to me yesterday Judy."

"Well, I'm waiting what is it, Arnold?" She shot back and maybe a little upset that I'd cut her short. I licked my lips and filled my lungs to their full capacity before blurted,

"I kissed a girl!" Judy studied me for a second as if I were joking.

"You did what? Oh my God!" Her eyes widened. "You really did!" She clapped her hands, grabbing my arm and squeezing it tightly. "And who was

345

it?" She bounced with excitement. "Who..., who was it?" she repeated. "And do I know her?" Her excitement grew.

"Do you know her?" I surely must have sounded all proud of myself.

"Now . . . calm down, Judy," James snickered. "Contrary to what you're going to hear, it's not the greatest feat of all times." James interrupted. But I'd simply ignore him as if he'd said nothing at all.

"Yep, you know her alright," I boasted. "She's a little older than me, but I like my women older to tell the truth. They've got way more experience, you know."

"Jesus!" James said swerving the car to the side of the road, which got Judy's attention even more.

"Well, who is it? Just tell me," she demanded, squeezing my arm even tighter. I drew another breath for such an introduction as this.

"Well," I expelled. "Remember Sharon Garman down at Willow Springs?" I paused, to see her reaction. Her brows lifted as her mouth gaped with surprise.

"You're shitting me! Oh my . . . God!" she yelled above all noise.

James tapped on the brakes, I guess surprised, as she rarely had a slip of the tongue with a dirty word. She quickly covered her mouth which got a good laugh from James and I both.

"And he . . . didn't kiss anybody," James grinned.

"The hell I didn't! So don't start that shit! You were right there and jealous evidently!" I heaved my chest.

"Yeah, you're right, I was there. But what I saw was her kiss you with your mouth wide open like a little bird trying to get a worm from its mama's beak." He laughed, setting Judy off also.

"You're such an asshole, James! Why would you say such a thing? You know we kissed and for a long time before she finally had to quit and a French kiss at that!"

"Well, it really doesn't matter. I think it's great that you kissed a girl and especially such a nice person as . . . Sharon!" Judy winked just before hugging me.

"Then good enough," I said, brushing my hands together and leaning back in my seat. But no matter how badly I wanted to impress my little sister, James was right—that it'd been short-lived, nothing to how I'd continually licked my lips with every imagined detail.

"OK, let's talk about something else." James advised. "Let me ask you this Judy since you're around him way more than me or Arnold anymore. Does it look like he's doing any better, I mean with sobering up?" His question put her into heavy thought and that she be sincere with her answer.

"Well, now I can only hope that he was telling the truth with what he said last night. And he was humble for a change instead of being mad like he is all the time. But I really can't say one way or the other . . . We know how this has turned out so many times before." She shrugged her shoulders; while looking up at me. "He did tell Mom though that he might stay there again tonight." Judy sounded hopeful I thought.

"Well, I'm not getting my hopes up. Why should we believe anything that lying bastard says anyway? Fact is, I'd rather he stay like he is than see him drag Mom through the same old shit again. I'm tellin' ya . . . I can't handle it anymore. I ah—" James quickly cleared his throat that I not get carried away.

"Judy, how long is this new romance going to last with Tom? It seems like you're going through about a boy a week now. You know what kind of a reputation that'll get you?" I said with a gently elbowed to her side. Her smile said it all as she rolled her eyes up at mine.

"I guess now you're ahead of me, one to nothing, in the kissing department Arnold." She laughed.

"I'm telling you, Judy, it was so short I don't know how he even remembered it," James butted in.

"Yeah, but it was still longer than mine, I'd bet. But of course, we're both a long way from ever catching you, James," she stabbed a finger in his ribcage making him flex.

Judy wasn't 'just a little girl' anymore and other than a few private conversations we'd talk about everything with her. She'd be fifteen in March but looked and acted way beyond her age I thought. I'd always been fond of her laugh and lately she'd practiced to make it sound sexy if she wanted. I could only imagine how she talked to the boys. She'd come of age now and we'd enjoy her company with laughter and everything else.

"So . . . how do you think Mom feels . . . 'bout all this, James asked.

"Mom's back to praying and as hard as I've ever heard before", Judy said. "A little hope is all she needs, you know. Just like always, after everyone's gone to sleep, she starts crying and pouring her heart out to the Lord. I've been staying awake and going to her bedroom to pray with her for the last week or so." Judy had a "tender heart," which Mom described as those who could cry for other people's troubles. I could picture Judy kneeling in the floor with our mother at her bedside, longing that her prayer be answered.

It wasn't that I didn't have a tender place in my heart for some things. But many years ago, in a way to show my toughness, I'd proclaimed that I was too old to cry, which had come back to haunt me many times. To cry for my mother was one thing and all about the love I felt for her. But to cry because of hatred was another thing. I never wanted to shed another tear over the old man. But unfortunately, it was he that I cried the most over as my anger continually boiled with the constant turmoil of what to do next.

I thought how good it was that Judy prayed with her in the lonely world she lived in. I knew that it wouldn't be the same if it were me, although she'd love for James and me or even both to kneel with her and anytime at that. I could only hope that her prayers would come true and without my help.

It appeared that James and I weren't the only people who'd missed school. Almost all the guys in vo-ag had taken days off to get their harvest of corn and soybean crops in. Whatever it took to beat the rain that was forecast, they'd work days and nights if need be. They grew more acres than I could even imagine, but no one else in class grew tobacco. Eugene said you had to go a fer piece south of Greenfield to grow that stuff; down to where the 'briar people' lived, he said while imitated a spit.

There wasn't as much concern about missing school as Mr. Boyd had showed at Willow Springs. Mr. Conner's compassionate look told that he'd rather you were in school, but he fully understood our situations when passing out permission slips to go to class. To my surprise, he asked James and I how many grades we were pulling; only someone who'd been around baccer would have knowledge of such.

Mr. Bader's assignment was that everyone stand in front of the class and give a report on how our crops had done that year, what the yield was, and if we thought we'd used the right fertilizer to maximize its growth. I couldn't tell them that I hadn't helped with the planting or hoeing this year. So I lied, saying anything to steer clear of the truth that I was nothing more than a pulpwooder, which was looked down on by many. I was lucky my presentation was one of the last, which gave me more time to prepare, taking in how the others went about it.

My tension eased somewhat when almost everyone's speech started to sound the same, and it got to the point of boring when Mr. Bader cut some short, saying he drove past their place every day and had seen what they'd done. The biggest laugh came just before my turn, when Gene went on and on about how he'd put so much tender loving care into his corn crop. Mr. Bader cut him short also, joking that he didn't really want to hear about the family garden, which had everyone roaring with laughter.

I made my way to the front of the class, thinking it would be best while everyone beat and banged on Gene on his way back to his seat. Mr. Bader stood up gathering his paperwork as to ignore that I was even there.

"Richardson, what are you doing up here?" he sized me up. "You couldn't have gotten any more than a bushel or so of taters down there off the side of them hills, could you?" The laughter continued while Gene quietly seated himself.

"We don't grow much corn or beans . . .," I started out. "Except in the family garden although we do end up with lots of taters." I directed the joke to Mr. Bader, who dipped his head with approval, smiling, and held his huge hands into the air to quiet everyone.

"We've got a tobacco base. We raise 'baccer," I said, extending my hands out to where everyone could see the yellowish green stains on my fingers and places I'd scrapped my calluses the best I could.

"Very heavy smoker!" someone observed, which kept everyone laughing with some comparing their own calluses with others.

"Yeah, we know how you got all those calluses, David," someone rattled off. There was laughter as no other when David the shortest guy in the class stood up to take a bow. It was good for me that the class had become so relaxed. I couldn't answer their questions fast enough about what all had to be done to raise tobacco and all the things it took to get it to market. Details that I'd always taken for granted, I now explained to the tee. Not one time did I choke as my hands orchestrated how planting, cutting, and stripping all were done!

A few interrupted, saying things like "Sounds too much like manual labor to me!" That got a short-lived laugh just before Mr. Bader frowned at the fellow. They truly wanted to know all about a crop that required so much labor by hand. Gene was right in questioning why we didn't use certain implements. My explanation was that we couldn't grow such large fields as they did; so there was no need. Tobacco bases were regulated closely with none being very big and all recorded and deeded along with the property. We owned only a small base, so even though we had a large family to share the work, we made little more than just enough to survive with our cash crop and certainly never enough to buy things such as a planter.

They did the math themselves as I explained how much poundage it produced per acre and what grades netted the most worth. I'd found that in their presentations, there were several rivalries among them over who'd produce the highest yields of corn or soybeans. It didn't matter who had the biggest farm—all that mattered was the "per acre." I remembered the look in Mr. Cox's eyes when he too had bragged of bushels per acre.

I felt good after my speech when Mr. Bader clapped along with the rest of the vo-ag boys. I felt comfortable as I looked out over the class of misfits of sorts, thankful how they had helped me like no others to gain the confidence to stand and explain something in fine detail.

Eugene—in one of his "step on your dick" moments, as Smitty had called it—reckoned that a person's lungs would look about like my hands or worse after years of smoking. He stumbled even further, saying he figured the reason we didn't have to put poison on our crop was because it was poisonous enough that it'd kill everything, including humans, in the end. Another outbreak of laughter erupted when several packs of cigarettes bounced off his head and shoulders which he attempted to cover up with his hands.

Mr. Bader was a smoker, and Gene had made the critical mistake of slamming the very thing that he enjoyed so much. He'd leave the classroom several times during the two periods to have a smoke. With a raised brow and eyes that implied a threat, he ordered Gene to have a four-page report by the next day on the effects of the poisons used on corn and soybean crops and on how that might affect your body over the years or even kill a person in the end.

It would have been a tough assignment for anyone in that short time frame, but Gene took it with a smile and a reddened face. The laughter continued once more when Gene, in his joking ways, asked if he could leave early to get started on the report.

I knew what Gene said was the truth about the harmful effects of using baccer. I'd been around enough people to know that the ones who smoked were ill way more than the ones who didn't. Gene could have said plenty anytime Mr. Bader would go through a coughing spell but knew better of it. We all liked Gene because of the kind of person he was. He wasn't afraid to point something out as he'd done to me many times, even putting me on the spot. He simply wanted evidence and challenged whatever one might say.

I couldn't say that I enjoyed baccer as a cash crop for the simple fact that the old man smoked. The truth was I disliked everything that was associated with him. Where I'd tolerate my Uncle Arnold and Glenn when they smoked or Harry when he drank I couldn't stand the thought of the old man doing either. But regardless of how I felt towards baccer it was the cash crop that basically got us away from the stone quarry to a better way of life.

Lots of people would gather in the teacher's parking lot after lunch to talk and mill around with friends. Suddenly loud cheers could be heard everywhere. Smitty quickly grabbed me by the arm, practically dragging me to the site where James and three other guys were relocating a teacher's Volkswagen. After they'd finished it would be impossible to move it now as the bumpers were almost touching between two trees.

Mr. Trinity, a math teacher and devout Ohio State football fan, was the recipient of the prank. He was the swimming coach—not very big in stature, but well liked in the way he played along and handled things. He stood at his VW bug, pulling a five-dollar bill from his wallet, offering it to anyone who'd speak out against the culprits. Connie Stevens stepped forward, ratting the four out and taking the reward, which all seemed in fun with everyone clapping. But strangely enough, it was Olson's own girlfriend who had named him as being one.

"I don't think this damned thing's working right." Mr. Conner's voice cracked over the intercom. It was the loud uproar from all the classes that let him know that he'd came through loud and clear. He'd have announcements first thing in the morning and right after lunch of all school activities.

Now with Mr. Conner's voice more clear than ever after his mishap, he announced,

"The following students will report to the teachers' parking lot immediately: Steve Olson, Steve Conner, Paul Grant, and James Richardson . . . Report to Mr. Trinity, where he waits on you to rearrange his vehicle more to his liking." A loud cheer rang throughout the hallways. It turned out that about once a week, a teacher would post a reward for such little things that would help someone out with gas money. How cool, I thought.

Judy rode the bus home that night and lucky for her.

"My god, this is awful, James. I'll bet everybody's looking at us aren't they," I yelled as we headed out of town. The noise was terribly loud sounding as if our muffler had fallen off.

"I don't think the radio will turn up any more!" James yelled. He pulled over, straddling a small ditch where we crawling up under the car, to find that the muffler was almost rotted in half. "We're going to have to come up with enough money somehow to get another one, and replace all four tires before winter gets here," he said, scratching the top of his head. "There's just a lot of damn stuff we need and at a bad time when we're not making much money," he reckoned. "My buddy Steve told me that they've got plenty of good used parts down at Jim's junkyard. He also said there's a bigger place heading out toward Washington Court House but thinks the guy there is a first-class asshole and doesn't like dealing with him unless he just has to." James sighed, wiping his hands clean.

"Now are we talkin' about the same Steve? The smart guy who combs his hair back like you, buys shit from a junkyard?"

"Yeah! and not only that, he goes after school and works there until he pays it off; pretty cool don't you think?" After his quick glance in the rearview mirror, we were on the road again.

James had started pumping the breaks way before the turn off onto Cliff Run Road and finally coming to a stop halfway through the covered bridge. He quickly shut the motor off to kill the terrible noise coming from the muffler. Suddenly it was as if the weight of the world was on him. Frustrated he slowly placed his forehead against the stirring wheel just before falling back into the seat.

"As if I don't have enough problems already Arnold. We need brakes before anything else. If we don't come up with some money soon we'll just have to start riding the bus for a while."

There was nothing that I could do that might help with getting all the things fixed on the Buick. I'd give James all the money that I made through the week other than the small amount I'd spend on lunches at school. It was hard enough to come up with enough money for gas to get us back and forth from school with James putting the car in neutral and coasting every chance he got. But with all the problems we faced his were way more serious than mine. It was the difference in day and night when he stopped going to Scarlett's. His spirit was at an all-time low without someone to run to and escape the harsh realities for just a little while.

"Let's take a leak Arnold," he said while already half way out his door. There were many cracks between the wooden beams in the bridges floor making it easy to find the right spot to pee through. It was from our first visit that we learned to talk low to avoid the many echoes that went on and on a long time after we'd stop talking. But laughter was a different matter. Without the echoes you'd never have imagined just how goofy your laugh really was until it came back to you several times with each funnier than the last. Then in a final scramble the continuous echoes seemed to be laughing at each other and sounded like something coming from an insane asylum. I thought of the night when me and Rebel had been there and not long ago at that.

"Are you going to Scarlett's tonight, James?" I quietly asked that only a slight echo followed.

"Nope . . . nope . . . nope." His words shot back. We sat down on the mid-rail along the wall that spanned the full length of the bridge. I'd already figured that one reason he'd not talked much of their problem was that he'd never been through anything like this before. Hard to come up with an answer, I guess, when you don't really understand the problem.

"So what are you two doin'? Takin' a little break from all that lovin'?" I asked. "I mean, like did you guys finally get tired of kissin' so much? Did you wear her kisser out, James...?" I'd asked, no more than a loud whisper, while holding an open hand to the side of my mouth.

"Oh no, it's nothing like that! You're not going to wear a kisser out, let me tell ya. But we had a pretty good knock-down, drag-out the last time I was over there, and I told her to write me a letter when she wanted to talk again." He said and sounding dreadful. "I just can't believe we went all this time and never had a fight, I mean, about anything . . . Like I told you before, you'll agree with everything they say. Neither of us had ever disagreed on anything, until now." Whatever was behind the meaning of, 'until now', it drew a heavy frown as he reached through the cars window and turned the radio on. Any conversation was best with music where it would fill the quiet voids. It led me to believe that he was going to tell all now as he adjusted the volume low that it not raise an echo.

"Wait! Turn it up, James!" I shouted, while jumping to my feet and landing in front of the Buick, where I skidding to a stop and almost went down in the loose gravel. "Devil with the Blue Dress" rang throughout the bridge with James laughing at me while cranking the volume up. I'd remarked a few times that sad songs weren't my favorite and whereas I did like love songs I hadn't been put in the spot that I fully understand their meaning.

I liked songs best that set my ass afire and made me want to act like those black people on TV, snapping my fingers and shaking all over. But I'd only act the part around family members while trying to get a laugh out of them. I could certainly do my best stuff, however, when no one was around; and a wonder that I hadn't hurt myself on occasion acting the fool as I had.

I used my "fist-a-phone" to sing while jumping around in front of the car and at times going down on one knee. James seemed to forget what was bothering him momentarily while laughing and pointing at just how goofy I was acting. And it was the way I intended doing my damnedest to stay up with the driving beat, while stirring up so much dust that I started coughing like a heavy smoker, forcing me to give up. James clapped at my performance, after which he turned the radio's volume back down.

I thought that maybe my foolishness might loosen him up somewhat, and he'd talk more of his problem. A sudden gust of wind carried the dust and the songs fading echo out the far end of the bridge. James re-adjusted the volume more to a low quiet pitch. The contest over who could name a song first had been ongoing from our first radio. And to name the artist along with the title was a "double whammy," as we called it.

But there was one song that James would always beat me to. In no more than a split second he'd recognize the chimes in its lead off. All of a sudden he stood motionless with a weak looking posture about him. "Cherish" was he and Scarlett's favorite song, which I heard them sing together several times as I'd chauffeured them around one day. It was through the rear view mirror that I could see the love in their eyes as they sang so sincerely to each other. So, it was in the desperate look he gave me hinting that he desired to be alone for now.

Without a word I turned and ran out the bridge and on around a curve stopping to where he couldn't see me. With the volume turned down so low it was hard to make out much of anything coming from within the bridge. But with what I could hear was a lonely person desperately trying to understand the meaning of what the song meant to them. And there was hardly any rhythm without Scarlett being there.

"Cherish is the . . . word," the song slowly ended as I came back into the bridge when James shut the radio off all together.

Is this what becomes of the brokenhearted? I thought. *No more than a fading echo I considered my situation with Linda?* He seemed even more broken and sad, as I made my way to where he sat; leaning heavy up against the bridges wall.

"I'm glad you're back Arnold. I just needed to be alone for a couple minutes. But I'm better now, well at least for the time being. I've just got something hard to deal with and it can't go on for much longer the way it is."

"Well, it can't be that bad . . . I mean . . . uh . . . uh . . .," I stammered as he crossed his arms while drawing a deep breath.

"Well, here's the truth of it, Arnold. And it's been botherin' me for some time, as I'm sure you already know. I've beaten around the bush long enough" He shook his head over the fact. "Scarlett told me a while back that there was a dance at the high school and that she wanted to go to." As brave as he wanted it to sound in his confession, he still needed a short pause before continuing on. "And of all things, a Sweetheart dance at that." He'd choked somewhat with the word sweetheart. "How would you interpret what a sweetheart dance is all about, Arnold?"

"I would... uh ... uh ... would think it meant a dance for . . . sweethearts." I chuckled. "Ah like. . . you and Scarlett would go to." I quickly finished before I stutter even more. Why had he asked me such a thing when the answer was so obvious, I wondered to myself. But then again who else would he talk to of the matter?

He made no immediate come back to my response but instead stood up and walked to the bridge's opening maybe to gain more courage I thought. Nothing was said until he made himself comfortable once again.

"I told her that I'd be over right after we got finished stripping the tobacco and we'd go to the dance." He squirmed for a better position and maybe to hide that he'd choked up somewhat. "She started crying."

"Crying...?" I pressed that he continue, but I'd have to wait as he slowly drug one shoe and then the other to build a small mound of gravel directly in front of him. After which he flattened the top off, detailing it with the side of his shoe. Whether it was intended or not its features reminded me of Seip Mound down by Bainbridge.

"Yep..., crying, which she's never done before other than from happiness. Remember how she rejoiced the day I bought her the dress? Maybe I've been taking everything for granted, Arnold. Remember what I told you, how we never disagreed with anything *ever*, not even once? And we hadn't up to that point. But her words cut me like a knife, and she couldn't even look at me while telling me that she wanted to go to the dance without me."

I was shocked; dumbfounded as to what he'd just told me, with my mouth gaping open he continued on.

"Now I know just about all of her girlfriends, some have boyfriends and others don't. So by her wanting to go by herself wouldn't it make you wonder who she'd be going out with? No matter how I put it together I tend to think she wanted to go with the ones which didn't have boyfriends."

I couldn't answer his troubling question when bad thoughts quickly flooding my mind. It was a no-brainer. *As I'd heard from others in the same situations, she was either looking for another boyfriend or, already had one.* But now I was torn between two realities, one that I'd always wanted him to break up with Scarlett because she was our cousin blood or not, even though Judy had pretty well convinced me that I hadn't been reasonable about the whole affair. And she was right to point out to me that it was my own self-image that I worried mostly about. But the other reality at hand, and certainly one worse than my no-blood-cousin problem was the nightly image of my brother disappearing down the road, pleading that the love of his life not go away.

He scooped up a handful of the small gravel from the top of the mound and started pitching them one at a time to hit and bounce off the car's front tire.

"Hey, don't worry, James. It's like Judy said, there's lots of girls at Greenfield that would like to go out with you. You do know that, don't ya? Like that Smith girl! Now you talk about a good-looker! Man, she's pretty, and have you . . . noticed her legs?" I laughed, while slapping my own. I wouldn't tell him that I'd wondered how it would be to kiss her myself and bring her to her knees as I had Sharon Garman. But then again, maybe I shouldn't dwell on the most beautiful girls in school. "And have you noticed how smooth her lips look when she smiles?" I tempted further.

"Sharon's made a monster out of you," he chuckled. "Maybe you should ask the Smith girl out yourself," he said, looking all serious at me. "But let's get on to the house I've said enough for now." He stood up and dropped the remainder of the stones, before brushing his hands off.

We drove on to the bus without saying much of anything else. For no other reason the noisy muffler had come in handy since we had so much to think about. We parked under the big maple, where James quickly shut the motor off.

"Man, look at old Harry sittin' down there with his cap pulled over his ears and waving that pipe at us. You know he ain't goin' to be sittin' out there much longer—it's gettin' too damned cold! And to tell the truth, I'm ready to sit by his warm stove and chat for a change."

James nodded, not necessarily to agree with me but maybe to clear his thoughts of Scarlett a little more. So with a notion of my own I'd press him even more.

"Now I've got a serious question to ask James, and I don't want you pissin' around with some shitty off-the-wall answer." My pause was short and intentional, figuring that my crazy but planned question might get him to tell me more. "I hope this don't sound all weird and crazy to you. But would you think it strange if I was to tell you that I'd like a girl who didn't keep her hair combed out so nice and neat all the time?" His look was more James like now with the hint of a smile and less wrinkles above his brow. Suddenly he seemed anxious as if he'd entertained the thought himself with his face showing more color to it. I thought.

"Why no . . . I don't think it's weird at all," he answered and peppy at that. "But you might need to become one of those hippie people; you know flowers in your hair and all that. It looks like a lot of those girls like their hair loose and unkept." He snickered.

"Well, that's exactly who I was talkin' about. But I don't think of their hair as bein' unkept. In fact, I think that's what's really cool about them, that they just let it hang wherever it falls. Natural. Kinda like their spirits, I guess, loose and happy," I laughed.

"Did you come up with all that on your own?" he asked. "I like that 'loose and happy' spirit part." He nodded.

"Yes, I did!" I shot back. "I got the idea from a movie with them all sittin' in a circle and smoking that stuff, laughing, and havin' a good ole time. And it looked real cool how the music fit right in with their hair blowin' in the wind."

"Hello!!" James said as my flashback quickly faded away. "Well, I guess there's got to be some good with anything that makes people so happy. And all because of that mar...i...woney," he drug the word as if it were poison. "Or at least that's what the dumbass calls it," James concluded.

"I like that, James. Maybe I'll start calling him 'the dumbass old man, now. But I'll tell you another thing—you don't see those hippies fighting like a bunch of drunks do. And I guess you're right about well-kept hair not bein' important, like some people I know," I stabbed a quick thumb several times in his direction.

Quickly leaning forward with a panicked look he pulled his comb from a back pocket. He didn't use the mirror, but instead, the 'brail method' as he called it, with a slow and pressing hand he guided the wave of hair to its dedicated place.

"You know it's not that I want to keep it neat all... the time. I'm just addicted to the comb Brub." He laughed. I had a moment thinking back to the day that he got his first comb same as I did also. But whereas he went right into training I'd lost my comb within a few days.

"Well, can you ever see yourself smoking that stuff James? I quizzed. "Maybe just one time to see if it really makes you laugh like all those hippies do?" He leaned forward just enough to slip the comb back into his pants pocket and with a glance into the mirror.

"You know, I heard it's not just college kids, but ones our age smoke it too," I said all sounding dreadful. "But, like I said before it's better than what a bunch of liquored up drunks are doin' with the prime example, bein' the old man. And I can tell ya that if I was forced to do one or the other, I think I'd smoke the marijuana." James laughed removing the keys from the ignition.

"Nobody's forcing anybody to do any of it, Arnold, but you've put yourself in a situation where you can't do either one—smoke or drink." He teased. "You hate alcohol because of the old man, and even the talk of smoking puts you ta cussing," he laughed. "And of course it leads to harder drugs," he said stabbing a finger into the seat. "Or at least that's what they said in a film we all had to watch at school the other day.

"It was more like a comedy on TV and had everyone cracking up in class. Some of the boys didn't agree with the guy who showed the film when they continually challenged him asking, 'Well, how do you know so much about it?' The presentation all led up to that if you smoke marijuana just one time, you'll get hooked on LSD and other hard drugs.

"But I think if it was legal. Some of those boys would have argued the point a little further. Obviously some of them had smoked it, I figured. And do you know of all people, my hair-dueling buddy Steve put the guy on the spot the most and said it was all government propaganda. I think it pissed the guy off that Steve was so well-read up on the matter. Steve told me awhile back how Greenfield was pretty backwards compared to the school he'd left in Dayton. He said this place was behind by a couple time zones." James laughed as I figured he had before from the comment.

I wondered what it would be like to go to school in a place like Dayton when even Greenfield was so much different from what I'd left at Willow Springs. James, more settled in now, eased back in his seat to a more comfortable position. We had several good laughs, and I'd succeeded in distracting him from his current problems with Scarlett. But like a bad dream that wouldn't quite go away, he gazed out his window followed by a slow nod. But he didn't linger for long when he turned to face me.

"What did you call it with Linda, Arnold? A reality check wasn't that it. Maybe I need that wake-up call myself!" he sneered. "At one time, and it hasn't been that long ago I thought I knew a lot about being in love, and had no... reason to question any of it. Head over heels you might say is what I've been. But I guess that in the end maybe I didn't know so much after all.

"You know I used to think that what Anna Fay said about us being too young to be in love was a joke. It was like I wanted to prove her wrong and that would have been easy had Scarlett felt the same way, as me. But now I wonder if Anna Fay wasn't right all along. No matter who you pick to fall in love with and no matter if it's over their hair, legs, or whatever that you might like about them, maybe you shouldn't be in too big of a hurry to fall head over heels." It sounded as he was speaking from his own experience.

"There's no contest that says you've got to have your first kiss at a certain age or have sex before you're eighteen. There's just no reason to hurry into any of it. And maybe people are right that you should play the field before you make that final decision. Heck, maybe that's what's on Scarlett's mind. You can't hurry love. It's a game of give and take," he said, tapping his fingers on the steering wheel. "It's like the song." he said, looking out his side window once more. "But no matter the reason, someone is going to end up with a broken heart." Clearly, in his eyes, it was he that ended up with the broken heart.

I wondered if this wasn't what Calvin meant that someday James would pull his head out of his ass and straighten up. But regardless, it would be another lesson for me to learn from, I figured.

He heaved a long sigh with a slow headshake as if he'd done something regrettably wrong. Gripped the steering wheel, as though it were the only thing standing in the way of he and Scarlett. The very thing that so many times had guided him to where his love waited for him.

"Well, let's go chat with ole Harry for a while," he said, quickly opening his door.

As we walked up, Harry pulled his pipe and with the most serious look on his face.

"Now by God, you boys looked like you were into some serious 'leg talk' up there a few minutes ago. Now, I can take this cold weather a hell of a lot better by God when I'm talking leg!" He laughed while pulling his cap down a little farther over his ears, making an adjustment that it not cover his hearing aid, though.

But we hadn't sat long before he declared it was just too damned cold to sit out there any longer. A few minutes later and without an invitation for us to come inside, he bade us good night, obviously with a hint of shine on his breath and no further talk of 'leg' the weather was enough to send him indoors.

The family was in high spirits when we made it to the house. The old man had informed everyone that it wouldn't be much longer that he'd sell the baccer crop and buy the new color TV as he'd promised. It was the last thing he said that night before hibernating to their bedroom where he'd been going through serious alcohol withdrawals for the last few days. I had my thoughts of the matter but wouldn't waste my time for now.

I felt sorrow for my mother when preparing herself for his recovery as she'd done so many times before. Along with the continual cleaning-up after him, she'd bite her tongue when he'd venture to his car, barely able to walk, and have a beer to calm his shakes somewhat.

"Now, Aunt Ree"—I recalled what my uncle Glenn had told her one time. "I've been through it myself, as you know, and there is no other way—period," he'd warned when Mom had threatened to throw all the beer away after one of his staggering trips.

He'd be bedridden with severe diarrhea and cough until he'd throw up when trying to smoke a cigarette. It all added up to the foulest smell as if something were rotting away in their bedroom. The boys knew the exact second to cover their ears to not hear him when coughing turned to vomiting.

Conversations at the supper table were intended to get loud enough to overcome the noises coming from the bedroom.

But as always before, Mom took sole responsibility in emptying the pee bucket and having a wet facecloth to cover his eyes with. She knew that without her help, he'd never even make an attempt to straighten up.

Judy told me that after one coughing spell in particular, he said that he'd wished he'd gotten out of Ohio and gone to Florida for the winter, where he could always breathe better. I cringed at the thought that he would continue to lay blame on something other than himself for all his personal problems.

James asked everyone to meet him at the Buick one evening, hinting a warning as everyone's patience had worn thin with the old man's recovery.

"Look, you guys are gone to school for the biggest part of the day. You need to stop complaining about when that new color TV is going to be here or when supper will be ready. Mom has a full day taking care of him for right now so you guys need to calm down for her sake." He waved a warning finger at each and every one of them. "Most of you are too young to remember all the times that this has happened before. But me and Arnold have been through it many times, and this may not even be the last. It's important that you help in every way you can." He draped an arm over Judy's shoulder, where she stood beside him, pulling her close to his side. "If Judy asks you to do something, do it without question. Arnold and I can't be here at times, as you all know.

"It means that the only way Mom can get your dad back on his feet is that everyone pitches in and helps do something. And I know it's bad enough just being around him. It's his own fault that he gets like this. But we can't imagine what he's going through and how hard it is for him to sober up. Now does everybody understand what I'm asking you to do?" James's point was well taken, as everyone flocked around Judy, asking what they could do to help.

James's leadership skills as being the eldest came out once again. And he meant every word that with everyone's help the old man might become strong enough to act like their father once again. But I had and always would be the outcast in the way I'd never forgive him. I'd not put a time frame, that if he were to meet I'd reconsider as to how I felt. And more importantly I could never live with myself if I were to fall prey to his ways again.

"He'll never fool me... again."

"He'll never what?" James interrupted. I'd not intended for him to hear my last remark at all.

"Oh nothing, just thinking to myself James." I answered back. It was the sickest of all feelings that lay in the pit of my stomach. Would the day ever come that I could stop thinking of the place where yellow and blue flowers bloomed every spring. Where fresh cold water flowed freely from an opening in the side of the hill where rocks had been stacked but never meant to be a head stone.

I knew all too well that James's positive attitude about the old man's recovery could still fall apart at any time. He'd told me time and again that I stop telling him of my terrible thoughts then as always reminded me that I stop dwelling on it.

More and more I had to face the truth that I couldn't do any of it without the help of my brother. We'd simple done everything together no matter the challenge. I knew that the burning of the house in Pike County was one thing. But to be part of doing away with the old man he'd have no part in it. And maybe for that reason alone I would tell him before I'd go through with any of it. It would give him time to talk some sense into me once again.

So, for now I'd do whatever it took to please our mother and that she not hear my continuous blaspheming of the old man. I watched as Judy directing everyone to something they could do and help with the cause. And so now with a new hope they all worked together happy and content it looked.

A couple of weeks had passed by when the old man started wanting bacon and eggs and, on occasion, three times a day. His health had improved to where he was pacing back and forth from the kitchen to the living room for an hour or so each time. He'd also returned to the normal pack and a half of cigarettes, which could be attested to by how bad the house smelled of them.

The same old pattern, as always, was taking shape each day where he gained more strength. But this was the critical time in his recovery where he could just as easily slip and go back to being a full-fledged drunk.

Another miracle Mom would declare when he'd start talking of church once again. God had won him back from Satan, and it wouldn't be long before he'd be preaching how he'd returned from the pits of hell. He'd go on and on about the devil having power over a person until they'd see the bright lights of heaven shining down on them once again. Satan had no choice but to release the hold he had on them. Never did he refer to himself in his explanations of going off the deep end, but put it in a way that anyone could fall prey to the devil. I thought about the many times he'd preached about reaping what you sow, but he'd never confess that our losses were always from what he'd sown.

And to show why he'd fallen from grace, he'd preach of the devil's powers as being second only to God's. And with that knowledge, he could stand behind the pulpit and tell how the Lord still had things for him to do and how Satan could not stop it. Each and every time he came back to the fold, it was always with a vengeance, in trying to make up for lost time it looked.

With hope, my younger siblings talked of a full return to normalcy. In a funny moment, Duck said there'd be no color TV if the old man didn't become a Christian again. There was continual prayer from Judy, Beth, and Mom. I didn't know if James prayed and wouldn't question him about it. If he did so, it was in private somewhere. But along with concerns of the old man, he also was dealing with the loss of Scarlett, which constantly stayed on his mind day and night. I knew there were nights that he didn't get much sleep, and his walks down the road to the dark place whether the moon was out or not were still frequent. But at least Rebel would be at his side most times now.

And whether I like it or not it was time to start preparing myself for the old man's eventual sobering up and what was to follow. On a good note would be that my mother's prayers had finally been answered. But again how long would it last this time. As always he'd be on the teeter tatter edge for a while as I thought back to a particular time that he'd repented but maybe a little too premature that he start preaching too soon.

After recovering from an episode he'd proclaimed himself a Christian once again. His first sermon would be at the invitation of another preacher. It was one of the few times I really did feel sorry for him that with his Bible opened to the page that he'd speak on, but no words came from his mouth as he lowered an open hand from behind his ear. His proclamation that he'd gotten right with the Lord wasn't quite true when he burst into tears.

Mom and many others went to where he stood all alone behind the pulpit and prayed with him. The scene looked rehearsed, I thought, something that high dollar preachers would have done to get attention. I knew that he'd used the pulpit for his altar that night to get saved. And that was as close to a real Alter as he'd ever be. It was only a few months later, he faltered and backslid once more. My praying for him had ended way before that as I'd predicted he'd fall apart again.

But this time simply had to be the last that he's slip back into darkness. With his improving every day and actually speaking to me in a mild-mannered way, I thought that maybe it was I who needed to seek a stump out in the woods somewhere. *But why pray only to be disappointed even again?* I had intentionally angered myself. I'd heard Mom speak many times of being at her wit's end, only to press onward after pouring her heart out to God and singing "Leaning On The Everlasting Arms."

With my constant battle that I should just forgive him and get on with my life, I truly was at my wit's end. He talked more and more at the supper table, ambitious now that he was much better. I needed an uplifting of my own, something more than the old man's recovery or that of my first kiss. I needed once again to feel a small thread of hope snap across my chest as I beat all others to a finish line. I simply needed more victories and fewer defeats in my life.

James and I would rush through supper and go back to the bus, change into our work clothes, and join the gang up at the laydown yard. They'd be ending their day about the time we'd get there. But any amount of work we could do would help the effort. We'd pick up where they left off, either to finish loading the truck or to saw up more wood and logs in the yard. One way or the other, we'd justify a way to get our five dollars with the need for tires, brakes, and a muffler for the Buick.

Freddy wouldn't have it any other way that he still took Kate and Mr. Bill to the pond after work and then on to the barn to feed them. Where at one time, I'd looked down the road as Calvin would push a small maple limb off to the side in order to stay on the path that led to his shack, Freddy now did so. He'd been going to Camp Creek about every other weekend on Saturday's after work to visit relatives and, on occasion, tell how he'd seen Calvin and Mary.

All excited, I asked if he'd heard the whereabouts of Linda by any chance. I wanted to hear that she was happy and going to school and fulfilling her dreams. But it wasn't the case as he simply said he'd heard nothing. I doubted he'd tell me anyway. He'd hardly spoken a word to Linda when she delivered water but told me on numerous occasions that it'd be easy to fall in love with someone like her; after all she was the prettiest thing he'd ever seen. Freddy was worse than me by a lot when it came to girls, however. I didn't think he'd ever kissed one, by the way it sounded.

And besides, I didn't think Freddy's name fit in right with Linda such as Arnold would. James and Scarlett and Ezell and Anna Fay all worked well together, as did so many others such as our grandparents Sherman and Mollie who fit like two peas in a pod I thought. I got a laugh from Mom when I pointed out that many such names seemed to have originated from Kentucky.

James and I'd associated some with such name's that the old man had married over time. Long romances was seldom heard of with poor people, when it came time to get married. In most cases, marriage would come pretty quickly. And no one made mention that the very young girl was usually pregnant. It was termed a "haft to case" with no way out of it. And it was pretty common to look at the young bride's stomach before she wed.

Lots of these people lived off the road as far as possible. They hardly ventured to find a different name for a newborn as it had already been decided like a hand-me-down. They didn't want to be seen by many other people than their own, such as relatives. Lanes that were lined with old parked cars and half hidden by tall weeds all around them, led to dark places at the end of the road. Trash mounded from as far as it could be thrown from both porches. These people would hide behind curtains and stay there until whoever was knocking would leave.

I thought about the woman and the circumstances that would have made her marry old Mickel. Desperation to feed her family and have enough money for a pack of cigarettes, I thought. The name Wanda worked out pretty well for matching old Mickel I thought.

I knew in Freddy's quest to find a woman that her name was the last thing on his mind. He'd spend the rest of his life working in the woods, and there was nothing wrong with that. But it did put limitations on certain things, such as being around people different than from your kind. He'd not wait for the perfect name when someone would become available as the next one might be years away.

In his joking way, Freddy told me that the closest he'd come to having a woman was when he'd blow smoky figures into the air with his pipe. Mom seemed to think that his different ways were from a birth defect. But he acted as normal as anyone, I thought, other than his speech. He never talked bad about anyone other than Calvin when forced to. Calvin had picked more severely on Freddy than anyone else anytime he was feeling ornery. He called him a freak of nature one time, referring to his bald head and a few long curled black hairs that grew in a couple of spots on his upper lip. They were something James and I never spoke of as Freddy seemed proud of them. He had a great comeback, however, when he advised Calvin to go look in the mirror and see just what a sorry son of a bitch really looked like.

Mom asked him once why he wasn't married yet and had kids of his own. She'd teased with the question, and Freddy answered that he was waiting for the perfect person before he'd get married. Mom laughed, telling him that he might be waiting for a long time if that be the case.

"Honey, nobody's perfect. You just need to find a good Christian woman, and the Lord will work the rest out," she advised.

I knew at some point that he'd marry someone; it just might not be the person of his dreams, such as Linda. She'd made it clear that she wanted more than to be stuck up a dark holler with nothing. Occasionally, I still wondered of her whereabouts, dreaming of reflecting eyes from a moonlit pond.

As the old man's recovery had progressed and he was starting to think a little better, he had Bob stop at the bank and cash a check or two so he could pay him, Mickel, and Freddy for the week. I was glad when everyone started getting their money on a regular basis. With what money we'd set back James set a date that we'd go to Jim's junkyard and buy a used muffler and four recapped tires to put on the Buick. But we'd have to go another week or so before we'd get brake shoes.

The many instances of the old man recovering were never easy, but this one by far seemed to take the longest. Another week had past, and everyone was complaining once again about the new color TV. He kept them at bay, saying the condition of the baccer wasn't quite right yet. But I knew better with all the moisture in the air. He'd had something else on his mind for some time now.

He and Mom took off one Sunday by themselves, and upon their return, he told of a church he'd rented over by Marshall which had been vacant for some time. Uncle Glenn had mentioned it on one of his visits; obvious of his intent. A new congregation would forgive the old man's past; after all, it was written in the Bible that they do so. His reasoning for a new place was always the same—that the Lord had led him there. These were people in need of God's Holy word, he'd state.

Mom went along with his desires once again; after all, it was what she'd prayed for to no end. It was also a time that I couldn't be negative about him while around her. I didn't want to ruin any hope on her part that it might all fall apart again. I'd said to her more than once, "I told you so," upon his backsliding.

Her words were the same as before that she thought he was really trying harder this that. In private, James and I joked as to which Holy stump he'd used for his repentance this time. I wouldn't ease up any by saying that it'd be easy to find it simply by the knee-deep Holy bullshit that surrounded it.

Paul, with his sculptured white marbled hair, had become my best friend at school and commented that I didn't look so stressed out anymore. Jokingly, I'd told him of the old man's ways and once again how he'd returned to a Christian life. Paul was a great listener and joked back with me about all the ways the old man could stay Christian. I thought of the old man as being like a bird when it leaves the nest to go out on its own. His efforts were relentless once again with a new church and congregation.

But the real shock came one night while turning thanks that he asked the Lord to bless the place up at the pond where we'd start building our new house. After "Amen" was said, all talk was about the new place and when we'd start building it. I had to say that I was shocked that he'd kept his word. He had some money to do things with now; and for several days, he'd shut all work down in the woods, concentrating solely on getting the house built.

It turned out but not too surprising that Bob and Freddy were both pretty good carpenters. Mickel did whatever he could but still complained about the pain with everything he worked at. We were amazed at the progress in the evenings when we'd get home from school, most evenings of which we'd work and then eat later in order to get as much daylight as possible. He'd borrowed one of Buck Chynoweth's drilling rigs and drilled a well in one single day.

Bob complained of a headache he'd gotten from all the noise. Laughing, he joked that it wasn't from the steady pounding of the drill, but the loud whistling the old man made to keep pace with it. We'd gotten the house framed in with a roof put on before the old man declared we'd need to go back into the woods and make enough money to finish it.

James told me one evening that he was going to drive over to Scarlett's and confront her as to whether they had a future together or not. A simple yes or no answer was all he wanted. After he'd left with the Buick sounding much quieter with the new used muffler, I sat in the bus's front seat, peering up toward the pond where our unfinished house sat. There was warmness in my stomach with the thought that maybe my mother would have a place to call her own and forever I would hope. I could visualize the best place for her clothesline and the perfect place to plow for a garden in the springtime.

My thoughts were interrupted, though, when James came back shortly after he'd left, quickly exited the car, and started walking down the road to his dark place once again. Maybe he feared there was something at Scarlett's that he just couldn't face. His patience was wearing on him that she'd not sent the letter yet. He'd started taking some of it out on me, complaining that I held the covers up too long to get in the bed and that I should stop talking after the light was turned out. He could be grouchy at times.

The long hot days when it took forever for the sun to set were gone now. Winter had its cold hands on everything and would stay for the months to come. Every piece of wood in the laydown yard would have to be kicked loose or hit with a sledgehammer to break it free of the frozen ground.

The snow was a beautiful sight, peppering down while the Buick's headlights shined a path for us to load the truck by. The slow songs on the radio were more fitting while snow covered everything like a thick icing on a cake, it looked. We'd run the battery dead practically every night, and have to jump-start it with Big Red.

"It's just too damned cold to work any longer, Arnold," James declared, blowing on his fingers. We made one last attempt to put a large piece of wood on the truck, which we failed at. James went into a rage, declaring his finger was too damned cold to get a good grip.

We drove on down to the bus, where I grabbed the milk bucket and, with a lantern, I went to do the milking. James waited in the Buick, idling to charge the battery backup.

The small electric heater didn't do much to keep the bus warm inside. You'd shiver and shake to where it felt as if your teeth were going to rattle out of your head when you first climbed under the covers. Thoughts of how much colder it was outside, though, could warm you up a little quicker. Another thing that seemed to help in my need for warmth was all the cozy places in my mind, such as the hay mound in old Harry's barn. I had a spot where I'd broken a bale loose and made a place to curl up and sleep on cold rainy days and sometimes when the snow came down, when it was too bad to work in the woods.

Snow had come in through the cracks of the bus's back door a few times, which would sure put you on your way to the warm house as soon as the morning milking was done. We eventually stuffed rags around the door to fix that problem. There were nights, however, that were simply too cold to endure with little heat in the place.

We spent those nights at the house with one of us on the davenport and the other on the floor by the stove. James had suggested that we arm-wrestle over the privilege of the davenport anytime my turn came up. To sleep on the rug wasn't really bad, though, where small cracks in the stove's door revealed the intense yellow heat inside. I could not break my stare as my thoughts took me to a warm house that I'd loved so dearly at one time.

Harry hadn't sat on his front porch for some time now; he had settled down in the small back room, where there was a wood burning stove, a cot that he slept on, and a couple of chairs. His house had plenty of room, even an upstairs, but he seemed content with the small room and the kitchen only. He shut the rest of the house off for the winter.

We walked to the back where he kept the door unlocked until he'd go to bed. There was no need to knock; he wouldn't have heard it anyway. He didn't mind the interruption when we or anyone else would barge in on him. He'd quickly stop whatever he was up to for a good ole chat. We momentarily watched from the back window as he wiped his mouth with the sleeve of his shirt, then slid the jug neatly behind his chair. We walked in on him talking loud to each other, making lots of noise so we wouldn't spook him.

He was out of the chair in a flash with a grateful handshake, but with some sway to his walk. It was obvious that the single drink we'd witnessed hadn't been his first that day.

"Se . . . down in . . . 'em chairs over there, boys, and make yerself at home." He laughed with all his words running together, then practically fell into his padded rocker. "Now 'ot brings you boys by tonight?" He fumbled way more than usual with the tight-fitting lid on the Prince Albert can.

"Well, we got a bigger heater for the bus, Harry. And seeing your light was on, we thought we'd visit for a minute." James spoke loud and directly at him. He peered up at us as he tried to withdraw a pinch of baccer from the can, where it fell down between his legs and onto the chair's cushion. He looked somewhat surprised at us when he'd gathered the spilt baccer, holding it between a finger and thumb once again.

"Well, hello, boys, come on in and make yerselves at home, by God." He clumsily leaned off to one side of his chair. My quick glance at James set us both to laughing. He gathered his senses a little more after a couple of good drags from the pipe but hadn't done away with the lit match burning short between his fingers. He hadn't heard my warning in time.

"Ouch, you hot son of a bitch," he said, throwing it to where it landed directly on top of the stove. But drunk or not, the whole thing was funny enough for the three of us as Harry went on about how he'd planned the perfect toss. He slowly settled back into his chair, going into a rhythm that was probably close to what the porch swing would have been like.

"Why, you boys wouldn't believe who in the hell stopped by today to say hello." Even though slurred somewhat, he managed to put a little pep in his voice. Harry wasn't much to leaving you at guessing for very long when he was hitting the jug.

"Why, old Jim looked as close to stepped-on dog shit as anything I've seen in a long time, by God." He took another slow draw on his pipe and now with heavy concentration. "Now I know I'm sure not the pertiest thing after I pull a night of drinking, but ole Jim looked like death walkin'. Hell, he set here and drank about a half a bottle a beer. And if you look out there beside that fence post"—he nodded—"you'll see what he had to go do." Weak in his effort to point to the exact place, Harry's hand fell limply into his lap.

"Why, he even said he'd be buildin' a new house up there by the pond, by God, in a few weeks or so." He leaned forward, giving us a questioning look. "Do you think he'll really do such a thang?" He frowned, while leaning forward that we answer his question.

"Well, that's the rumor, Harry." James looked over at me, ready to laugh. His mind stumbled the more he drank with facts that were weeks to months old, such as the old man building the house. Repeats of events had become more common lately, whether he drank or not, it seemed. Bob told me one evening how, like clockwork every day, old Harry would come to where they were working on the new house when the sun was at its highest and spend an hour or so chatting while everyone worked. And continually declared how well, it seemed, everything was going.

He talked of Freddy, who stopped by on occasion to chat with him; and sometimes Bob would also make an appearance, he'd declare. But he figured old Calvin was just too busy getting ready to move back down to Camp Creek for any kind of visit. Harry was slipping more and more as Calvin had been gone for some time now.

But we had the laugh of the night when James asked if Mickel ever stopped by. Harry reared back, looking side to side like he'd planned for it if the question was ever asked.

"I ain't got nothin' to say to that slouchy-ass son of a bitch," he said with a slap to the leg and a good laugh. He'd drunk enough shine that he could've talked the bigger part of the night, I thought. It would have to be us to call it a night when the time came. He went on and on about how he sincerely appreciated us spending our valuable time to chat with him.

James laid a load of firewood in just before we left. It wouldn't be long after that Harry'd break out his fiddle to play a few slow tunes. Most sounded out of key as I pictured his stumbling fingers sliding up and down his fiddle with a soft foot hitting the floor. You could pretty well figure that old Harry had silenced his hearing aid that it not interfere with him being off beat and more than a little.

It was a rewarding time with the old man coming to his senses. Not only was he paying everyone on time, but had taken Harry to the bank to pay down some of his debt; but how much, we'd never know.

There was some reluctance on James's face when Mom handed him the long-awaited letter from Scarlett one evening. Even though he'd practically stopped talking of her altogether, his eyes still told of a broken heart. He'd prepared himself for better or worse for whatever its contents might read. But what he'd not thought of was the way the whole family waited with bated breath to hear that the news was all good. Halfway through opening it, he suddenly stopped, maybe not wanting anyone to see his reaction. We all watched as he ran across the road and on into the woods, where he'd read it to himself and all alone.

I, more than most others, wondered what the outcome might be. *It is what it is*, his very words came to mind as I climbed into the driver's seat of the Buick. I quickly adjusted the rearview mirror that I not miss his exit from the woods. I'd already figured that it would only take him a minute to read it. I'd watched many times his facial expressions with his eyes dancing across page after page of the Readers Digest as if there were no periods to slow him down. But anything over a couple of minutes I knew he wouldn't come home till after dark.

My mother's explanation of 'a tender heart' rang true that I wanted to share such times with my brother. I'd probably have cried with him had he wanted to share the moment. He'd literally burst from the woods with a fast pace and heading towards the house. He'd not taken the time to fold the letter back up as it blew wildly with every hurried step.

One read hadn't been enough as he re-arranged the pages and read to me as I drove us towards the bus. She'd confessed it was a mistake on her part and that she loved him and no other. The whole letter dealt with how she missed him and all the good times they'd had. But nowhere did she make mention as to why they had their break-up in the first place.

I knew there'd be no stopping him after he read the last of the four P.S's she'd written at the bottom of the page. 'Please, please come over and be with me tonight James. I love you with all my heart and 'cherish' the time I can be with you.' I really thought she was sincere as she'd hyphenated the word cherish when James paused there each and every time.

The smell of perfume she'd dabbed on all corners of the letter was throughout the Buick with a fresh memory of her. It was good to see James back to his normal self as he slowly slid it back and forth in front of his nose for yet another smell of Scarlett.

I'd no sooner gotten out of the car than he was gone in a flash, leaving me standing on the side of the road with my milk bucket in hand. The new used muffler was lots quieter but could still be heard on long stretches as he barreled on down the graveled road. But for whatever Scarlett's reason for their breakup, she'd come to her senses and realized that James was the greatest person on earth.

Once again, loneliness came over me as rain started coming down and a minute later turned to sleet. I ran to the barn, where Red had already come in out of the weather. There was no need to get the milking done so fast tonight. I walked to where the lantern hung from a rusty nail and positioned it on the ground a few feet from Red and I. Its flame flickered as if the cold dampness was weighting it down.

Funny how so many thoughts can run through your mind, primed with the first strings of warm milk hitting the bottom of the bucket. Scarlett's letter had not only made James's day but also put a lot of things to rest on my part. Reminded again how selfish I'd been in wanting their breakup and mostly for my sake alone.

It'd always been Scarlett Portman from day one. Maybe over time, they would break up and go their separate ways but it wouldn't be to satisfy me. I lay the small terry cloth across the bucket to keep the sleet out before heading to the house and with a fast step.

Through sleepy eyes, the clock showed midnight, and James hadn't made it home yet. I could only picture them making up for 'lost time', as he'd called it, any day that they'd been apart. I thought about my one and only kiss and how I wished I could do it all over again with many rehearsals so that it would last much longer. It was with that thought that sleepiness finally overcame me.

"Well, how was everything over at Scarlett's place last night?" I asked loudly with no concern if he was asleep or not. I wanted answers.

"It was great, Arnold. You can't even imagine what . . . well, maybe you can imagine what it was like now. I mean, after all, you did kiss the prettiest girl at Willow Springs," he replied with a long yawn, while stretching his arms into the air.

"Jesus, what time did you get in? Hell, I was up half the night, thinkin' you might've slid off the road somewhere."

"Man, you're awful loud for this early in the morning," he said. It was good to see that his true smile had returned.

The timing couldn't have been any better for them to get back together. Scarlett's birthday was that coming Sunday. Mom told James to bring her over and for them to go to church with her, and afterwards, we'd have a birthday cake for her.

It had been great being with my brother so much during his breakup with Scarlett. But now I sat in bus all alone once again. Rebel sensed my sadness when he made the effort to push his nose up under my hand. After supper in the evenings, I'd hang around the house for a while, listening to everyone's dream of the new color TV especially when the screen with the old black and white would get all snowy with its poor reception. Like few things we'd ever got in our lives the new TV would come in a box that had never been opened before.

I still avoided the old man as much as possible with his willingness to talk with me now. A plate of food for old Harry was fixed on a more regular basis since the old man had returned to a Christian life again. And my early departure was for that very reason, to take the prepared plate to Harry. He laughed, saying he'd eaten so well lately that he thought he'd even picked up a pound or two.

The week passed quickly, then I went with James early Sunday morning to pick up Scarlett, who seemed excited to see me once again also. She laughed and joked as always and as if nothing had ever happened. I thought of the way she'd come back to James as the way the old man acted upon his return to being a Christian.

She and James went with me to milk, after which we went on to the house, where Mom had breakfast ready for all. I looked around the table while the old man turned thanks. With his fresh start as a Christian once again, he'd miss nothing in his thanksgivings. It wasn't just James and Scarlett who looked happy, but everyone did as I surveyed them all. It was after the kitchen had been cleaned up and everyone was loading up in the cars for church that Mom approached me in the living room.

"Now, Ray," she said, holding my hand. "Now I think it'd be good if you come to church with Mom also."

"Mom, you know how I feel about him! I just need a little more time to think about it so you go on to church and don't worry about me." I hugged her, thinking that would be enough.

"Well, Honey, like it says in the Bible, you've got to forgive him." It was hard enough standing in front of my mother with it sounding like an altar call and just for me. But I'd made my mind up that I wouldn't ever listen to him preach again. I was simply tired of being torn down so many times and never had the patience or faith that my mother had. I knew that she'd continue to ask me every week to go with her. She smiled and kissed me on the cheek, telling me I'd be in her prayers.

With her happiness once again, I'd weakened to the point that I'd consider going to church with them again. I'd confess that there were things I missed about church. My mother's smile of being blessed to have all of us there would testify to that fact. I missed her clear voice as she prepared for the glorious chorus in each song of God's glory that she sang about. But most of all, I missed seeing her get all the heartfelt compliments from everyone after the services.

There was really only one thing that stood in the way of me going to church with my mother; after all we'd talked of it many times. Maybe that I was never willing to forgive the old man was the reason he would never ask me to go to church. And now I wondered even if he were to go to a real altar would it be enough to convince me that he'd not hurt our mother ever again?

Finding out that I was staying home, Judy and Bertha decided to ride with James and Scarlett. The three of them had done nothing but talk from the time we had arrived.

I stood out along the fence row where apple trees lined the front yard, all bare of their leaves and waved to all that noticed me when they drove past. A sudden loneliness cut deep into my soul as I stood in the shadows of my own making once again.

Maybe I should have gone with them after all. I could have ridden with James and Scarlett and enjoyed the parts of church that I liked. Then while the old man made his way to the pulpit with Bible in hand, I'd walk out the back door and down the road far enough that I wouldn't have to hear him. "Running away from God's callin'," he'd say of those who left early to avoid the dreaded altar call. But then how could the biggest hypocrite in the world say such things?

I quickly got a grip reminding myself as to why I hadn't gone with them.

I gathered an armload of wood, putting a few more sticks in the stove. Rebel had followed me in and went straight to the rug that was spread out neatly beside the stove. After turning in several circles to find that perfect spot he finally lay down. I'd stay around the house until everyone returned from church and after which we'd sing happy birthday to Scarlett.

Warm and cozy with the fire popping and cracking I leaned back on the davenport a little father. It was in the quietest of times when one might be more serious about forming a confession. A small gap in the stove door revealed the fire inside, leaving me to stare with heavy thought. Why was I always in a state of confusion I'd continually ask myself. All questions with hardly any answers; and more especially since James was back with Scarlett.

Everywhere I turned there seemed to be a dead end. Maybe it was my age that at sixteen I was going through so many changes. I was lonely most of the time and yearned for something that I couldn't seem to find.

It had been no more than a week ago when James declared that I was out of control when I talked about moving away and living in a commune with a bunch of hippies. Something I'd seen on TV how some of their stories for leaving home sounded a lot like mine. James simply called it an identity crises; confused in the way that you weren't doing the things that suited you best.

He was right to point out how quickly I could turn any form of rebellion into anger with the old man condemning the hippie's way of life. Lots of hippies proclaimed themselves as Christian while carrying their Bibles at their sides.

But a pointing finger from reverends who had plaques hanging on their wall was quick to declare that such people were unfit for the kingdom of God. With gnashing teeth they'd proclaim them all to be dirty long-haired hippies.

I gazed deeper into the flames thinking that the son of God himself looked as if he could be one of them. And hadn't that been what it was all about in the first place? The Lords will that no one be looked down upon. It sure seemed easy to look down on others from those who interpreted the Bible to suit themselves I thought.

Not all prayers could be answered with everyone fighting for the same cause as I'd seen at track meets the year before. It was when we lined up for the start of the race that some gave the sign of the cross while others prayed in silence. Some won while others lost their events. God hadn't helped them in any way and wouldn't help me win a race either, I thought. I didn't pray that I not stumble at the finish line and fall short.

There'd been an argument in science class one day when a student said God had created everything when the talk of evolution came up. Two students whose hair tempted the code argued that there was no God and that we were there simply because of evolution.

The word "atheist" suddenly was being thrown around as if it were the meanest word that one could ever direct towards someone. The case of Madalyn O'Hair came up as if she had the plague or maybe something even worse. And those who blaspheme such as her will burn in hell for eternity, the religious TV programs would proclaim on Sundays.

It looked easy the way the minsters prompted their congregation while proclaiming the atheist as the worst kind of sinner—the 'antichrist' they'd say to express themselves in the holiest of ways. And it was atheists of course, who had gotten the Lord's Prayer taken out of school. Many including myself had never been exposed to all the differences between the Bible and Science. Whereas religion was a given there was no room for science which certainly differed with it in many ways. Mr. Toll our Science teacher let everyone express their opinions but warned that they should not get out of control. With both hands waving in the air, he finally ended the debate when Anita Wadsworth stood up and started reciting the Lord's Prayer loud enough that no one could talk over her.

"Now I can't teach the Bible in this class," he said. "I can only teach what we know of science that's been around since the beginning of time. So it's up to you to believe what's best to suit yourself." I'd always thought highly of Mr. Toll. I enjoyed the facts of science more than the stories of the Bible as some seemed hard to believe. I thought his words were well put in the way that we all had a neutral corner to return to in the end. And just another thing that would leave me confused as to which was really right.

I couldn't understand why religion had such strict standards to live by, though. I'd not taken time to remember the Ten Commandments with all its Thou shalt nots. Why was it wrong to look at a girl's legs? Was I afraid she'd catch me, or was it that God was frowning down on me? Surely, it was "temptation," just another evil word to ask forgiveness for.

James wouldn't sway that there was no God but pointed out numerous people who weren't Christians but were good just the same. Most avoided talking of the Bible, saying it just wasn't worth the argument. Mom admitted that there were plenty of good people, but no matter how good they were, they'd not be with the Lord until they were washed clean of their sins. I knew of my mother's dependency on the Lord and would she ever have made it without him to turn to?

I was awakened when they turned into the driveway with Rebel wanting out to greet everyone.

Mom had made a pretty cake for Scarlett's birthday the day before. There was some commotion that morning that someone had dragged their finger a short distance on the side of the cake, where they'd thought the icing must have been a little too thick. At first, the blame went on Duck; but after he'd threatened the other boys, Ronald admitted he'd done it but didn't mean to. It all led to a good laugh when he explained how his fingers accidently scraped it as he'd walked past.

CHAPTER 8

An Early Christmas

"Blood should be red, not black," Duck remarked, looking around at the boys as most agreed. It was true that after every shoot-out, no matter if it was a Western or not, the old black and white didn't show the real color. Mom turned quickly, hearing what he'd said.

"Now, Honey, you don't need to see blood anyway," she remarked as if it were a bad word. Duck winked as she went on about how the world would be a better place with no bloodshed at all. Without making much commotion, James gave Duck a warning wave meaning that he's said enough.

It was good to see James happy again, with Scarlett sitting on his lap while the old man played the guitar with everyone singing "Happy birthday, dear Scarlett." You would've never thought that they'd had a time-out at all, as Scarlett shed tears of happiness. She put a small amount of icing on James's lower lip, then with a quick kiss made it disappear. Judy and Beth cheered with approval. I, on the other hand, wanted nothing between my lips and a girl's when my time would come again. Even after all that I'd been through this day it ended up being a festive one. Church seemed to have done everyone a lot of good with Mom the happiest with the way she went about her business and singing all the while, and the old man acted like he'd never backslidden at all.

James dropped me off on his way to take Scarlett home that evening. Mom gave me a piece of cake to take to Harry, who said it looked too pretty to eat. I sat and chatted, telling him of the day's events while he savored every bite along with a glass of cold milk, saying he'd never tasted anything so good in his life. But he'd say the same no matter what I brought him to eat.

I told him about my day and why I hadn't gone to church. He was happy that James and Scarlett were back together and hoped that it would stay that way. Harry never spoke much on religion but complained that his wife should never had died at such a young age. There could have been a grudge of sorts in his words, I thought.

It was getting late when I got back from delivering the milk and shortly after I went to bed. The new heater made a world of difference with the bus fairly warm at all times. I knew that James would stay at Scarlett's until Anna Fay ran him off just like old times, I shook my head with a smile. I could almost picture him driving home with the radio playing he and Scarlett's favorite songs and how once again he'd sing them loudly while drumming the beat on the steering wheel. He'd simple leave his lonely world behind and drive back into the one he loved; knowing that his sweetheart still waited for him.

"Ree's new home," the old man proclaimed with a date that he figured she could move into it. Maybe he'd exaggerated by saying by the first of the year. But I'd have to admit that it was good seeing him excited about something for a change, reminding me of the way he was when we first got the farm in Pike County.

To see my mother move about with song in her heart and more pep in her step was worth more to me than anything else. And with things going so smoothly it would have been easy to cave in and accept that the old man had come back to his Christian ways and of course, forever once again. I doubted.

It was still dark when Bob pulled into the driveway with Big Red's loud mufflers rumbling. The old man planned this to be the day he'd sell our baccer with the weather conditions as they were. The price had been steadily going up, but he felt it wouldn't be much longer that they'd start dropping.

It was a cold rainy morning as James and I followed them over to the farm, where we'd help load the crop and be back to school at about noon, we figured. James asked and got the privilege of backing the truck into the barn as it would be the last time we'd load our crop.

Farm for Sale. The old man had placed one of three signs up at Lapperell Road and another coming down Dry Bone Holler. But the one that truly tore me apart was the one he hung over the old hand pump. There'd never be words that could describe how cold the sign make me feel. I was thankful the pump wasn't froze up and drank as if I were going to single handedly run the well dry. *It is what it is,* James's words came to mind. I didn't put the sign back up which the old man reminded me that I'd forgot to do. It simple went in one ear and out the other as I walked on past him.

I was shocked at how the old man moved about helping with the loading of the truck. He didn't think that anyone could place the stripped hands the way he wanted them. And we were fine with that while passing stick after stick up to him. He'd carefully pull the stick out from where the stripped hands straddled it. Then one by one he'd place the hands of tobacco in two large circles that would stand several feet high covering the truck's bed. He'd give or take an inch or two sliding them back and forth so that the leafy ends stuck outwards, the way they'd look at the auction barn. I handed the last stick up, and as bad as I hated baccer, I felt sad that it was the end of a cash crop that we'd never raise again.

"Ready to sell...." He coughed while climbing off the side of the truck. James asked if he was ok when suddenly his cough got more severe. He shook his head while walking slowly to the other end of the barn and in no time was back to his normal sounding whistle.

With the baccer loaded and covered with a large tarpaulin pulled snuggly over the trucks bed, Bob and the old man pulled out of the barn and headed for Maysville, Kentucky. I had a feeling that he was trying hard to keep his promise of the earlier Christmas present, that of a new color TV.

I looked at the top of the foggy mountain where I'd planted the 150 white pine trees in a vo-ag program my freshman year, thinking someday I'd see them from the road when I'd drive past.

"Well, if we're going to get to school by noon, we better get rolling." James turned to walk to the car.

"Hey, I got something I want to take with me, James."

"And... what would that be?" He asked all curious like.

"You're gonna think I'm crazy, but I want to take that baccer press door with me. Whoever buys this place ain't gonna know what the meanin' of those letters are all about from that time I smashed the hell out of my thumb. I'll put it down in Harry's barn, for now." James thought it a good idea that we keep something from the old place. I couldn't help but notice his gaze to where a house once held his treasures.

After wrestling the press into the trunk, we headed home.

We were already late for school, so we thought we'd stop by to see if Mom needed anything for us to pick up afterward. Judy came silently into the room to see what all the commotion was about. She looked pale and had had cramps the previous day. She seemed to always have a hard time when it came around. I can remember her staying in bed and crying a few times while Mom got her a cold, wet facecloth for her forehead. She did manage a smile while telling us why she hadn't gone to school. She just didn't feel good.

The gloomy, cold weather hadn't dampened James's spirits any as he went after a leftover biscuit and a little gravy left in the bottom of the skillet, which he sopped up. It was good that he was back with Scarlett, joking of things more loosely now. The wave in his hair was more kept up also. I couldn't remember if I'd ever seen the back of my own head, but if it looked anything like the front, then it all matched. I wondered when and if I ever got a girlfriend that I'd start wanting my hair to look better. With a quiet laugh, I thought of hippie girls who might love my hair.

James swallowed the last of the biscuit and gravy, licked his thumb, and, after checking the time on the clock, announced that he wasn't going to school either.

I'd never thought in a million years that I'd be the one to complain that I really wanted to go. James laughed; tossing me the keys to the Buick.

"You remember how to get there, don't you?" he said. Judy, holding her stomach, managed a painful chuckle. And for the minute, I actual thought of taking the Buick and driving it to school, but with the chance of getting pulled over by the police ended that. I laughed, tossing the keys back to him.

"Well, I don't guess I got a way to get there, so I'll stay home too," I said.

"Well, what did Mom do to deserve this?" She smiled while hugging Judy where she sat next to her on the davenport. We talked about the old man's effort at being a Christian once again. Mom didn't linger on the subject very long, saying that you had to have faith in something in order for it to work. I looked out the window as the cold fog itself seemed to be raining down on everything. It was a day you couldn't touch anything without getting wet. I thought about the old man and Bob slowly winding down the road into Maysville, Kentucky, and crossing over the Ohio River. The old man's life kind of reflected the weather in one way, I thought. Cold and rainy with always the hope that the sun would eventually come out.

We joked and laughed about things that'd happened throughout our lives. Mom said she couldn't remember the last time she'd had so much fun with just the four of us.

She told of a Christmas tree she'd spotted those times she'd gone across the mountain to Granma's house and asked if we could cut it in about a week. James suggested that we cut it today, but Mom didn't think that it was close enough to Christmas yet.

I could picture the nine clothespins hanging on the tree with a five-dollar bill attached to each one. That would mean times were good. No Christmas cards, but a handwritten note, where she and the old man would sign their names. I thought back how the only times he'd ever signed them was when he was a Christian. The Reverend James L. Richardson. I thought the five dollars should be given out even with the new TV.

Judy asked Mom if it would be all right for us to play some cards. She'd not play herself but said it would be okay.

"James, I'm going to take the Buick up to the bus and get the cards," I said, jumping to my feet.

"Okay, but remember we've still got to fix the brakes. So don't be hot-rodding to where you can't stop in time," he warned, tossing me the keys once more.

"Okay, don't worry. You act like I've never driven before," I defended myself as having a perfect driving record. But there was no way I could take off without slinging a little gravel. The accelerator sticking was always my excuse. "Bullshit," had always been his answer back.

But on the way back, I held the accelerator to the floor a little too long and was going way too fast as I turned into the driveway, sliding sideways and not being able to stop. I went on past James, who was screaming at me as I pumped and pumped the brakes, but to no avail. I went over a small hill and through a gate that had been left open, where I did a donut in the field. I'd go no farther as I sank axle-deep into the ground. James had been running behind me all the time, yelling, but there was nothing I could do. I'd done the very thing he'd advised me not to do. He opened the door quickly and was visibly pissed off.

"Man, we've got to get these brakes fixed," I said nervously as I climbed out. "You saw me. I wasn't driving very fast at all."

"Bullshit!" he said, slamming the door behind me then walked to the back of the car where I joined him.

"Well, how are we going to get it out?" I asked. I'll never forget the look when he slowly and calmly looked over at me. "It's not my problem you got it stuck, Arnold, and you'll be the one that'll get it out."

And to make things worse, he'd hinted earlier that since we weren't going to school, he might leave early and surprise Scarlett by picking her up at the Bainbridge High School. I felt bad that I'd messed that up for sure. He turned and started for the house. His body gestures told of his disappointment.

"James!" I yelled. "I'll go up to the laydown yard and get Mr. Bill, and we can pull this thing out right now," I said. I thought it was what he wanted to hear but instead waved me off without looking back. I walked around the car several times to give him time to get all the way to the house. I heard the screen door shut behind him; then I got the cards from the seat and went on to the house myself.

"Well I guess the card playin' is out," I said, laying them on the small table in front of the davenport. I'd ruined James's happy day with my stupidity. He looked up at me. "I hope that you learned something from this, Arnold." Judy shook her head in agreement with him.

"I'm sorry, James. You're right, I done the very thing that you warned against." "So when I go up to milk, I'll get Mr. Bill before Freddy takes his harness off and walk him down here, and we'll pull the car out. Will that work for you?" I asked.

"That'll be fine, Arnold. Now deal the cards." He winked at Judy, who managed a smile.

I guess it was my lucky day as all the right cards came my way. I did enjoy winning at everything that I attempted but thought after how I'd buried the

Buick, I should be losing. I tried to play bad hands, but theirs were even worse. I didn't celebrate as I would normally have, so I thought it might be a good time to quit.

"So you're going to quit while you're ahead," James asked. He seemed more upset about the card game than the Buick being stuck all of a sudden.

"Yeah, we've lost almost every hand, and you don't want to give us a chance to win a single game," Judy joked.

"I just don't want to play anymore. I'm sick of winning all the time," I said, meaning it as a joke. And they did laugh along with me. The gloom from outside darkened everything to where the lights in the house didn't seem very bright at all.

"I think I'll run up to the bus for a little while," I told them. "And I'll take the milk bucket with me being you won't give me a ride."

"Well, if you hadn't been driving like a lunatic, you could have taken the Buick," James reminded once again, but sounding more like a tease.

"Well, I'll go and get Mr. Bill right now if you want me to, and we can pull it out." He never answered as he dealt cards out to Judy.

"Your Dad said he'd be here about five o'clock, Honey," Mom said as she washed her favorite frying pan.

"Well, I'll be back a little later. This just seems to be the perfect day to take a nap." And it wasn't long after I'd climbed under the covers that the rain started hitting the bus roof, cozy and putting me to sleep.

"Wake up, wake up, Piggy Wiggy," Duck said, shaking me slightly.

"Hang on. I . . . uh . . ." I was startled to the fact that I'd slept so soundly.

"Your favorite Dad's home with the new TV and James wants you to get down there and help us put it together." There was excitement in his voice. "He wants to put it up before it gets too dark," Duck finished.

"Okay, Duck, give me a minute to open my eyes." We sat on the edge of the bed, talking about how the old man had really come through with the promise he'd made.

"I've got to milk first and then get Mr. Bill to pull the Buick out," I said.

"Man, that sure was a dumbass thang to do, wasn't it, Piggy Wiggy?" He laughed, bumping me with his shoulder. "But Doodle said to not worry about Bill. He thinks with all of us pushing we can get it out."

I yawned a couple more times.

"I think I could have slept all night, Duck. It sounds like the rain has let up a little, though." I slid the curtain to the side to see a cold wetness outside.

"Yea, It's raining just a little bit." Duck said. "You know Piggy Wiggy... just enough to make it shitty."

"That's the perfect description for this day, Duck. And so how's the old man acting?"

"Well, he's whistling loud if that means anything to you," he said with a sheepish grin. "He said the baccer sold for more than he... even expected."

"Well, that's a good thang. Maybe we can finish the house and get Mom moved in before the first of the year," I said, putting my shoes back on.

"Dad kissed and hugged Mom right in front of everybody a while ago. He sure seems like a different person right now." Duck smiled.

"Are you shitting me, Duck?" The very thought put a tingling in my stomach.

"No, It's the truth, Arnold."

"Well, come on with me, Duck. I'll get the milkin' done, and we'll be on our way," I said, quickly tying my last shoe string.

We ran down the road the best we could, sharing the handle as to not slosh out any more milk than necessary.

"Slow down, Piggy Wiggy. You're sloppin' milk all over me. Da-gone what's the big hurry?" he complained.

"This is the night for *Shindig!*, Duck, and I can't wait to see those go-go girls dancing around in color."

"I think it's their short dresses you want to see, Piggy Wiggy." Duck laughed, while almost coming to a stop.

It looked as if everyone was trying to hand James antenna parts all at one time when Duck and I arrived at the house. I asked Duck to take the milk on inside so I could help James separate the mess strung out everywhere in the yard. I took a few seconds, however, peering through the front window, where I could see Mom sitting on the davenport as the old man lay with his head on her lap. She calmly ran her fingers through his hair. The whole thing looked strange to me as it'd been a long time since I'd seen such contact with them.

"Okay, everybody, stop. Stop right there and put all the parts back on the ground." James said and motioned with leveling hands, which also got my attention. "And when I need your part, I'll tell you." He and I looked over the instructions and had to laugh when we looked at all the boys standing perfectly still with their parts at their feet. We called on each for the part we needed until it was completely assembled.

"Thank God it's finished," Judy said, straightening her scarf.

"Judy, you and Beth don't need to be out here in cold rain," I gesture towards the house.

"Oh, it's not that bad. It's let up a whole lot." Judy laughed. "But it is getting awful dark, almost too dark to see anything." She still looked pale, I thought, in the small gloomy light that shone from the front window.

Without hesitation, we quickly attached the new antenna to a pipe that would be connected to the side of the house after we'd stand it up. James had already made the connections to where it wouldn't be so hard to turn the pole when needed.

He'd also made a locking device that would hold it in place and it not turn when the wind blew. I asked him what the little scratches on the side of the house meant. He pointed to the southwest—Cincinnati followed by Columbus and then Dayton, where the antenna could be pointed for the best reception.

There was movement in the living room that caught my attention. The old man sat up from where he had his head resting on Mom's lap. It was predictable as he went for his comb. Whatever they were talking about, Mom seemed to be in full agreement with a slight headshake. I eased closer to the window, trying to hear any word that would give me a clue as to what their conversation was about.

"Wake up, oh, Arnold. Wake up," James said as everyone laughed at me when I moved away from the window.

"Okay! Just get off my ass!" I said.

"Let's hurry up and get this done. It's getting almost too dark to see now," James said. The talk of the darkness gave me an idea to get a rise out of everyone.

"Well, I think we should wait till tomorrow and put this thang up then," I said with a serious sound in my voice.

James quickly caught on to my prank. "Yeah, you're probably right, Arnold. We better wait till tomorrow." We laid all the tools down and started to walk away.

"We can have it up in five more minutes," Beth declared, waving a flashlight she'd gotten out of the old man's car. "Please, please," she said, almost begging. James was the first to give in, and I couldn't hold back any longer myself.

"Okay," James said. "But I think it might be better if I got on top of the house with a rope and pull while you guys raise it up."

"Nah, it's too dark up there, and you might fall off and get out of doing any of the work," I joked.

"Let's put 'er up," I said while grabbing the pole. Duck placed his foot against the end to hold it in place while we stood it up. James, being the tallest and strongest, reached for the highest spot. I'd be next and then Judy, who just really wanted to help. Everyone was jumping up and down with excitement as James counted to three. The plan was perfect as the pole was almost straight up with not much effort at all.

"Beth, where are those wires?"

A long blue streak jumped from the electric wires and onto the antenna. Suddenly, my hands gripped the pole like a powerful magnet, with no letting go of it. It felt as if my head was being pulled down through my shoulders. What seemed like eternity would only be a billionth of a second followed by the sound of a loud blast.

"God, help me . . . Oh, God, help me." Like a cry in the dark with my mind staggering that I catch my breath before I die. Why couldn't I breathe and what

381

strange thing ran wildly back and forth from my chest to my forehead, tapping fast as if trying to find something?

Panicked that I couldn't breathe and with no idea to what danced freely on my face, I passed out. There was no way to gauge how long I'd been out with everything swirling around when I came to. I saw the small light at the front of the house go past several times but couldn't stop it in place.

I'm dying, and this is death tapping on my face, I thought as things swirled out of control once again. I attempted to grab whatever it was as it made its way back up to my face again. And it was in that battle of entanglements that I locked my fingers together. With such a shock, I realized that it wasn't anything foreign at all, but my own fingers trying to communicate something to me as now I choked, gasping for air.

I'd been in a fetal position all that time, my muscles finally relaxed, allowing me to roll over on my side. Thoughts of what had happened slowly replaced the numbness that'd run throughout me.

Maybe I'd been close enough to death that I'd not heard the screams and crying as they now came from everywhere. I knew in my hurting heart that something very bad had happened. But try as I did to get up, all I could do was lay there with the fact that I could identify everyone's wailing cries except, for James's and Judy's. Reality hit hard as I burst into tears.

"They can't be dead . . . They just can't be . . . I never got to tell them that I loved them." I pushed a shaky hand to where I touched an apple tree, wondering how I'd gotten there. Barely able to smudge the tears away, I could make out someone being carried into the house, with Mom wailing at their side.

It was all coming back now like awakening from a dream as I was regaining my thoughts better. And only now I could feel the coldness of the wet grasses pressed against my face as warm tears flowed from my eyes. There was a smell like something burning. My hands felt as if they were on fire when I touched them together, realizing that some calluses had been burned away.

"Oh . . . no," I choked. "They're okay. They're really okay. They didn't get hurt," I told myself as I straightened out and started crawling toward the pale porch light.

"Oh, my God, help me," I prayed for a miracle. I rolled over on my side, too weak to crawl any longer. I lay in a helpless state once again.

"Junior, Junior, where are you?" I heard the old man's words ring through the gloom and darkness.

"I'm over here," I said, barely getting the words out. No one could've heard me as my jaw tightened to where I could barely open my mouth. I managed to roll over on to my knees and stood up, but after a couple of steps, I fell back into the apple tree and falling hard to the ground. I was right back where I'd started—I hadn't gotten anywhere. But I tried again, pulling myself up and using the tree as a crutch. My strength and being able to think clearly were starting to come back a little at a time.

"Mom needs me," I cried out loud.

"Junior, where are you?" The old man stumbled around in the, yard crying. "Oh my God," he pleaded. "Oh...my God!" He started praying.

Ron and Larry saw me staggering at the tree when they came to help me.

"Arnold Ray, are you okay? Did you get shocked too?" The old man asked as he neared.

"Hey, Doodle's over here!" Duck cried out.

"Oh good, he's all right," I said, freeing myself of the boys' help. The rain started coming down hard as the old man shined the flashlights weak beam on James. I knelt beside him.

"James, can you hear me?" I asked in a pleading way. "Oh Doodle please don't die." I fell apart. I prayed. I begged. I made promises to God that I'd really keep this time if he'd just spare my brother's life.

He was stiff as I'd been earlier, but he wasn't breathing. I didn't know what to do to save him, while shielding his face from the rain with my hands locked tightly together. The old man placed a hand on James's forehead, asking the Lord to spare his son. Only a few seconds later, his body went limp—he'd given in to death. I slid my leg up under his head, squeezing him tightly and now I'd cry as never before.

"Boys, carry him into the house. It's cold out here," the old man said. "We've got to get him to where it's warm, and he'll be all right." The old man hurried toward the front door, shining the light while I stumbled to help Duck carry James into the house.

But no words could ever describe the most horrifying sight I'd ever see with Mom holding Judy's lifeless body, rocking her back and forth in her arms while pleading that the Lord spare her child. Her words were loud and clear that the Lord take her instead of Judy.

I didn't think I could cry any harder seeing my mother's pleading hand waving back and forth in the air that God never put on her more than she could bear. She rolled off to the side, fainting, when we laid James on the floor beside Judy.

The old man held James's lifeless hand and prayed only as a preacher could, it sounded. It was hard to make out what he was saying with everyone wailing so loudly. For the first time, I'd heard him pray that he'd never do wrong again.

Still weak from shock, I fell to the floor, wishing I'd never regained my own breath and knowing what lay beside me.

Beth and the others helped Mom back up, where she crawled to hold each of her dead children's hands.

All hope of a miracle quickly faded with dead expression on their faces and cold eyes that would never blink again, and all the while staring toward the heavens above.

"I'm going for help," I said, staggering to my feet. I'd go use Harry's phone to call for help. I knew that my struggle to save them was in vain, but I knew of nothing else that I could do. I couldn't see very well, stumbling and falling often as I ran for all I was worth to get to Harry's phone. I wasn't far from Harry's big maple tree when I fell once again planting my face in the middle of the muddy road, too weak that I get back up. The rain couldn't wash my tears away fast enough as I realized how suddenly my world had come to an end.

"Wake up, Arnie, wake up!!" Daniel shook me rather hard. "You're having that dream again buddy." All the while I could feel Johnny's hand tapping me on my shoulder from where he sat in the car's backseat.

I was tired and light-headed as I'd driven from Rainsboro, Ohio, to Kansas City, Missouri, before letting Daniel have his turn at the wheel. But I was thankful that he'd waken me before I screamed of that tragic night, December 12, 1966.

"You need to wake up anyway. I think we're running out of gas," Daniel said, looking dreadfully over at me.

"You're shitting me!" I said, pushing my long hair back over my shoulders. "And where in the hell are we at?" I asked, looking out my window.

The Chevy sputtered a couple of times as we pulled over by a road sign with big white lettering: Tulsa, Oklahoma, 200 hundred miles.

"Son of a bitch, Daniel, this is not the way to Colorado Springs. And how in the hell did you run out of gas?" I asked. "I just can't fuckin' believe it." I hit the dash.

"Look, Arnie, I'm sorry. I guess I made a wrong turn in Kansas City, and we haven't seen a gas station for miles now," Daniel said, while raising his squared chin into the air.

"Well, this place doesn't look anything like the Kansas in the movie, you know with the yellow brick road and all." Johnny commented while laughing, from the backseat. Daniel just sat there with no expression on his face with his muscular arms crossed over the steering wheel.

I pulled in a deep breath. There wasn't any reason to flip out. Daniel had just made a mistake, and that was that. And I was truly thankful that he'd woken me up from the same nightmare that I'd had for the past five years. I'd cry again but on a different day, I thought.

"They sure got a lot of wheat fields out here in the middle of nowhere," Daniel commented. And he was right for as far as the eye could see was wheat, looking like an ocean of brown waving in the wind. We cheered when a highway patrolman pulled off to the side of the road and right up behind us. After checking Daniels driver's license he spotted the Army uniform hanging in the back window. "You're never going to make it to Fort Carson at this speed," he laughed.

Without another word he walked back to his car and retrieved a two gallon gas can from his trunk.

"Welcome to Kansas where you better get gas before you get down to a quarter of a tank and I'm not joking about that." After emptying most in the tank we saved a little to prime the carburetor. We thanked the officer for his help and after hand-shakes we were on our way once again.

We got back on I-40 and shortly after found a roadside rest to take a break. The wheat fields that looked to go on forever reminded me of a Van Gogh painting I'd studied in college. I grabbed the blanket from the backseat that my mother had made for me. There was a slight chill in the breeze as I climbed over the fence and walked a short ways out into the wheat field. And so it was there that I'd lay down and let the warm sun take my worries away for a while longer.

THE END

Printed in the USA
CPSIA information can be obtained
at www.ICGtesting.com
LVHW040917231123
764443LV00101B/326/J